Also by Meyer Levin

THE SPELL OF TIME
THE OBSESSION
THE SETTLERS
GORE AND IGOR
THE STRONGHOLD
THE FANATIC
EVA
COMPULSION
IN SEARCH
MY FATHER'S HOUSE
CITIZENS
THE OLD BUNCH
CLASSIC HASSIDIC TALES
THE NEW BRIDGE
YEHUDA
FRANKIE AND JOHNNY
REPORTER

Plays

ANNE FRANK
COMPULSION

General

THE STORY OF ISRAEL
THE RISE OF AMERICAN JEWISH LITERATURE
   (edited with Charles Angoff)
AN ISRAEL HAGGADAH FOR PASSOVER

,50

⋙⋙⋙⋙⋙⋙⋙⋙⋙⋙⋙⋙⋙⋙⋙⋙⋙⋙⋙

THE HARVEST

A NOVEL BY

MEYER LEVIN

SIMON AND SCHUSTER   NEW YORK

Published by Simon and Schuster
A Division of Gulf & Western Corporation
Simon & Schuster Building
Rockefeller Center
1230 Avenue of the Americas
New York, New York 10020
Manufactured in the United States of America

1 2 3 4 5 6 7 8 9 10

Library of Congress Cataloging in Publication Data

Levin, Meyer, date.
   The harvest.
   I. Title.
PZ3.L578Har [PS3523.E7994] 813′.5′2 77-13076
ISBN 0-671-22550-2

The author wishes to thank the T. B. Harms Co. for permission to
reprint lines from the song "Can't Help Lovin' Dat Man" by Jerome
Kern and Oscar Hammerstein II, Copyright © 1927 Renewed.
International Copyright Secured. All Rights Reserved.

In memory of my friend of many years ERIC SCHWAB, *master photographer, daring and compassionate, with whom I entered Buchenwald, Ohrdruf, Dachau, Theresienstadt, Bergen-Belsen.*

About This Book

While independent as a narrative, *The Harvest* forms a novelistic pair with *The Settlers*. Told as the story of the Chaimovitch family, the total work is based in Jewish history from the times of the pogroms in Russia at the beginning of this century, the pogroms that set off the mass flight of the Jewish population from that land where many generations had developed a language, Yiddish, a culture, and a way of life. While the massive migration was to America, a smaller but distinctive segment of the population went to Palestine, then under Turkish rule. Coincidentally with the political upheavals in Czarist Russia and with the abortive 1905 revolution, which was, a dozen years later, to lead to the Soviet regime, there was in the Jewish world a socialist-Zionist movement to settle in Palestine. This socialist-Zionist movement was part of the world Zionist movement organized by Theodor Herzl, but it emphasized the return of Jews to the soil, the ideals of self-reliance and of equality.

The eldest son of Yankel and Feigel Chaimovitch, Reuven, belongs to the labor-Zionist pioneers, and with his sister Leah, the young giantess, departs for Palestine and becomes part of an early kvutsa, or labor cooperative, that is to found the first kibbutz. At Reuven's urging, their parents with all the younger children arrive to take up a settler's holding in Mishkan Yaacov, on the bank of the Jordan, not far from Tiberias.

The Settlers followed the family through World War I, with Reuven conscripted into the Turkish Army, and his brother Gidon joining the Jewish Legion in the British forces that finally freed the land, just after Great Britain issued the Balfour Declaration favoring the establishment of a Jewish Homeland in Palestine. With the Soviet revolution still embattled and the Red Army fighting in the Ukraine, Leah managed to return to the family village, there to bring out a group of young Zionist pioneers. Another daughter, Yaffaleh, fighting in Palestine alongside the heroic founder of the Jewish Legion, Captain Trumpeldor, to repulse an Arab attack on their frontier kibbutz, was killed. And the youngest Chaimovitch,

Mati, born in the new land, was sent from the farm by his brothers and sisters to Tel Aviv to be educated.

The Harvest is based in Jewish history from that point forward.

YANKEL AND FEIGEL CHAIMOVITCH come from Cherezinka in the Ukraine. YANKEL is from a poor family, a Talmud student who married into the wealthy Koslovsky family. After trying various trades, he takes all his young children to Palestine. The family settles in Mishkan Yaacov, on the Jordan River. FEIGEL is the sister of Kalman Koslovsky, town miller. Several of her family have migrated to America. She keeps in closest touch with her sister Hannah Leibowitz, in New Jersey. Their children are:

REUVEN, an idealistic labor-Zionist who migrated a year ahead of the family to Palestine, and persuaded them to come. During World War I, Reuven marries Elisheva Shalmoni, of a Damascus Jewish family, while he is stationed in Syria. They return to live in Kibbutz HaKeren. Their children are Yaffa, Kinnereth, Noam, Tsipora.

LEAH, the "giantess," whose kibbutz lover, Handsome Moshe, returns to Russia and disappears into Siberia. Eventually she marries Natan the Red, who fought in the Jewish Legion. Their children are Ehud, Shalom, Ruthie.

DVORA, whose betrothed, Yechezkiel, a member of the early Shomer, guarding Jewish fields, is shot down on their wedding day. She later marries his close friend Menahem. Their children are Yechezkiel, Yehudit, Giora, Josef, Rachel.

SHULA (Shulamith, first known as Eliza), most beautiful and vain of the daughters. She is tempted, during World War I, by a German aviator stationed in Palestine, but she marries Nahum, son of a hotelkeeper of Tiberias, who changes his family name from Bagelmacher to Artzi and establishes a seashore town called Hof HaSharon. Their children are Uri, Chava, Bathsheva, Zev.

GIDON, who studies to become a veterinarian, is deported by the Turks at the start of World War I to Egypt, where he joins the Jewish fighting unit being organized by Captain Trumpeldor, the one-armed war hero from Russia. Gidon eventually returns to Palestine in the Jewish Legion of the British Army and marries Aviva, daughter of a Hebrew teacher and amateur archeologist in Jerusalem. Their children are Herzl, Nurit, Eytan.

SCHMULIK, the "Little Ox," who takes over the farm as Yankel ages. He marries a daughter of the village, Nussya Roitschuler. Their children are Simha, Ilana, Dani, Gidon, Boaz.

MATI, the "one born in Eretz," who is taken from the farm to study in the Herzl Gymnasia in Tel Aviv. At the outset of *The Harvest*, he is taking ship for the United States, to work his way through the University of Chicago.

THE EMISSARY

BOOK I

1

ON THE old docks of Jaffa, exactly where the Chaimovitch family had arrived twenty years back—the extent of Mati's lifetime, since he was already felt in the womb during the drawn-out voyage from Odessa—they were all gathered at summer's end in 1927 to see the lad off to America.

Mati reached the dock early, crowded on the cart seat between his eldest sister, Leah the Giantess, and her life comrade, Natan the Red; although his departure would surely have warranted a special wagon trip, Mati himself had insisted on combining with the morning delivery of carrots, eggplant, and cucumbers from Leah's training farm for girls, at the far edge of Tel Aviv alongside the river Yarkon, to the Carmel market where they would already be almost in Jaffa. For he wanted to arrive early and have plenty of time in case of unforeseen British regulations and procedures, and also he wanted already to be there in case his brother Gidon arrived on the first train from Herzlia. Gidon had so much to do just now, building his house, and with his busy veterinary work in the new town, that Mati had insisted he ought not even come, so at least Gidon shouldn't be left wasting time waiting for them if he arrived early. Though Natan snorted not to worry for Gidon—even in the Jewish Legion, when they had waited months for the British to send them against the Turks, Gidon had never wasted his time—so now if he had arrived ahead of them at the port, Gidon would probably already have found a lame horse to take care of.

The cable from Mati's sponsor, the American scholar Horace Rappaport, at last verifying his tuition grant, had arrived from Chicago only a week ago, at home in Mishkan Yaacov, where Mati had worked all summer every summer during his years at the Herzl Gymnasia in Tel Aviv. With the cable Mati had hurried off to make arrangements for a passport, visas, passage, staying as during his high school days on his sofa at Leah's.

Last night he had said his farewell to his Zippie of the Long Braids, who refused to follow the hairbob rage from America, not out of conservatism but out of vanity, as she herself put it, with her usual mockery; they had gone strolling on the beach, stopping for kisses, strolling barefoot, in sudden serious talk always punctured by Zippie's humor—ach, after his years in Chicago Mati was certain to return in plus fours chewing a big cigar, married to a Chicago sausage heiress, whom he was bringing for a brief visit to his family, while she herself, having faithfully waited for him, Zippie preposterously proclaimed, would brokenheartedly bow to the will of her Orthodox parents and accept a matchmaker's match with a wealthy Polish land speculator; she would cut off all her hair not for the fashion but for a religious wig, a shaitl, at least a gorgeous high-style one such as you saw on Allenby Road, and she would resign herself to raising a flock of little sons with dangling ear curls! Laughing to tears at the image, Mati suddenly felt sure that Zippie with her humorous mouth was really the One and seized her in their longest, most passionate tongue kiss.

From the Carmel market, Natan turned onto the old road to Jaffa. Ah, where in America would Mati ever see a chain of camels still plodding among the droshkies, or even a droshky among the taxis? And at the bottom of the street Mati had his last look at the Herzl Gymnasia itself, still the most imposing structure of the town, with its castlelike portico where he and his friends had so often lingered, and indeed from which he and his troop of scouts in white Russian blouses had marched to Rothschild Boulevard to the wedding of the visiting American scholar Horace Rappaport, who had carried off their favorite English teacher, Celia, to Chicago, where indeed she and her family had come from in the heyday after the Balfour Declaration.

10

As they clopped toward Jaffa, Leah could not fail to remark how on her arrival in the land with Reuven, a year ahead of the rest of the family, all this had been empty sand. And as the minaret of Jaffa's Hassan Beq mosque came before them, the same thought lay unspoken among all three—of the sniping from up there during the evil May Day massacre of 1921, when Mati, a schoolboy from the Jordan Valley, had run with a cudgel, when Natan and Gidon had dug out their pistols kept from their years in the Brigade, when Leah had helped carry back the wounded and the dead from this in-between area, laying them out in rows on the assembly hall floor of the Gymnasia. But now all was quiet, the cart passed among the produce-laden donkeys, and Leah called out her cheerful Maasalam now and again to Arab standkeepers; everybody knew and grinned back at Big Leah. Indeed, ever since that raging May Day outburst against the "muscob" with their red-flag parade of Jewish workers, there had been quiet in the land. Partly because of this sense of peace, Mati did not feel so bad about going away to study.

With the ship cost from America, the scholar might not be back for four whole years, not even during summers, so to say farewell to the youngest, the yingel, born a whole generation after Reuven, mother Feigel got her one richly married daughter Shula to poke chubby Nahum awake at dawn so as to drive from Tiberias with the huge American automobile that he had bought for carrying guests from his fancy new hotel to the city's celebrated Hot Springs. The season of the Hot Springs had not yet begun, and besides, Nahum often used his hotel taxi as a Private; he could very well drive the family even all the way to Jaffa today, to see Mati off to America.

Though Nahum with his heavy-lidded round eyes was quick enough once awake, early rising he had long ago given up, along with the practice of accompanying his pious father for the dawn prayer; now that Nahum had the new hotel, his own, he took his time rising. But of all Shula's family it was to young Mati that he sparked; this one was no ox like the next-up brother, Schmulik, who worked their meshek in constant bickering with their aging father, Yankel. Nor would Mati be likely to settle in a kvutsa like their dreamy, idealistic Reuven. This Mati had a different head on him; besides, in the back of his own head Nahum had certain ideas regarding a vast coastal orange grove development to be sold in parcels to American Jewry, and it might prove quite useful to have a family contact, a college student in Chicago; Nahum didn't at all mind rising this day at dawn to drive the lot of them to Jaffa, where he had some Arab landowners to talk to as well.

Indeed, it was Nahum who had to poke Shula and hurry her through her decisions on what to wear for Tel Aviv and how to do her hair, reminding her that it was, after all, not to greet the High Commissioner that they were setting forth and that they still had to stop to pick up Reuven and Elisheva in their kibbutz on the way to Mishkan Yaacov.

At least those two were waiting at their kibbutz gate. Then at the farmstead Mama Feigel had to load in her hampers and her gift parcels to her sister in America—twenty-three years since they had laid eyes on each other, Feigel kept repeating. Schmulik had already departed for Jaffa on his own, for that one on any pretext would zoom off on his motorcycle; his Nussya was staying behind her with babies—true, there was hardly room for her even in the big Buick because on the way through the Vale of Esdraelon Nahum still had to halt at Gilboa to pick up the middle sister, Dvora. Her husband, Menahem, they'd meet in Tel Aviv, for Menahem was again delegated there on some pretext of agricultural planning, as though every British CID man didn't know Menahem sat high up in the Haganah. Dvora herself, Nahum respected. In her steadfast, single-minded way she had built up the largest and most modern poultry run in the entire Yishuv, even providing other settlements with her special breed of incubated chicks; indeed, if it was ever imaginable that such a one would leave her kvutsa, Nahum could see himself adding a poultry-raising enterprise to his planned citrus-grove enterprise for investors in the Diaspora.

Dvora was ready, wearing her embroidered Sabbath blouse. Squeezing in between Feigel and Elisheva, she exchanged news about everybody's children—all thriving, Feigel said, thank the Above.

With Natan staying by the cart on the lookout for Gidon, Leah and Mati threaded their way to the harbor edge, where the fishing boats bobbed and the catch was being sorted; from here they saw what was surely Mati's ship, fat and whitish, arriving from her stop in Haifa. Lighters were already being rowed to meet her, but as the steamer dropped anchor, few passengers could be made out descending; these days, because of two years of hard times and unemployment, hardly any immigrants arrived. Still, perhaps some had debarked at Haifa, Leah said hopefully. Gazing at Mati, she joked a bit about last night with his Zippie, trying to get him to tell more. And then Leah sighed about how half of her girls at the training farm had been in love with him; Mati knew what a disappointment it was to Leah that with all the maidens she had put in his way in these years nothing had happened, and he broke into laughter now, and she too, while she admonished, "Aye, Mati! You're just at the age! Be careful there in America; at this age a mistake can ruin whole years of a life!" She was still grinning, but a bit woefully, and Mati knew it was her admission about her ten years lost over her Handsome Moshe, a subject Leah still never touched on and that no one touched on in her presence. This warning was the most intimate she could give him in their parting, and Leah suddenly engulfed him in all her flesh, her baby! Mati flushed as though hearing again her unabashed description of how their mama, Feigel, had given birth to him right into her hands. And they threaded their way back to Natan. Still no sight of Gidon. The train had arrived, as droshkies were now bringing more passengers with their baggage; some were tourists, the last of the season, but also Mati noticed a few families plainly from the Yishuv, a pair with two babies and endless bundles and roped-up valises, all their possessions it seemed, and Leah even believed she recognized them, from Chedera. Leaving the land. In the last year this had become a common sight; more were leaving, it was whispered, than were entering the Yishuv. Going down from Zion. "Yordim."

A fleck of worry even now came to Mati that he might be mistaken for one such, ready, bag and baggage, to desert. And Leah must have sensed this discomfort in him, for she led the way to a café behind the dock area.

Now, with the ship already sitting out there—though there was still nearly two hours to boarding time—Mati became fidgety; of course, the family could not yet have got here all the way from Tiberias, but where was Gidon? It was Gidon who could give Mati the greatest certainty that he was doing the right thing, to go.

Though Mati had said his farewells a few days before when he had departed from the meshek to get his passport, a father still had to make the journey to see off his yingel, and besides, Yankel

knew, Feigel would have inundated him with reproaches or, even
worse, taken to her bitter silences had he perhaps suggested staying
away from that cursed port of Jaffa, where he had not set foot
since their arrival in the land, when the bandit Arab boatmen had
stopped their rowing and demanded extra baksheesh, tearing his
last coins from his hand, threatening to hurl him and his whole
family into the sea, like Jonah before him, only there would be no
whale to spit them up! Where indeed had those Moslem bandits
learned of Jonah!

Perhaps for four long years he would not see his youngest again,
or who even knew when young people went to America whether
they would ever return at all to Eretz! Such thoughts, Feigel
cried, let them burn like raw vinegar in his entrails!—Giving him
one of her looks as for a cockroach. So Yankel had defiantly persisted. And what? In the colleges there in America did not Jewish
boys meet shiksehs and marry them? And finish! And an end!
Wasn't that how it had been with Yehuda Schneirson's son from
Kfar Tabor, who had not needed even to go as far as America, but
only to Paris, never to return?

"What do they believe in, your godless children? What would it
matter to them, a shikseh or not?" Yankel continued to complain
in his usual way. "Unbelievers! Heathens! Apikoirasim!" But inwardly he had long ago lost his bitterness toward their yingel.
Despite Yankel's seizure of violence when the youngest had first
been taken off to study in Tel Aviv, kidnapped by the older
brothers and sisters, Leah and Gidon, the ringleaders of the plot,
these years had not proved out Yankel's misgivings. Each summer,
just as in these last months, Mati had returned and labored in the
meshek like a good settler's son; together with Schmulik, he had
extended the groves; a pleasant sight it had been to Yankel,
though he would never speak of this to them, to watch them as he
wound on his tefillin, while they yoked up the two teams of mules
and made off to the fields, leaving him only the smaller tasks
around the cattle barn. And in the wheat harvest he and his
offspring together, even Gidon coming home to lend a hand, following Reuven sitting high on the huge machine he had brought
from his kibbutz for a modest share of the crop. And much as
Yankel had protested, this did turn out advantageously in the end.
No, nor had his first visceral resistance to the yingel's removal to
the city remained in Yankel: his fear of the citified Diaspora luft-
mensh disease infecting his sons, from the speculators and swin-

14

dlers permeating that unproductive nothingness built on sand, arriving in the new wave of immigrants from Poland and Rumania. Rumanians especially Yankel had always distrusted, though the group in Mishkan Yaacov had turned out not so bad if you kept your distance from them, even if Schmulik had married among them. Perhaps also Mati had been protected from all such because he lived in Leah's meshek, outside the city itself, though soon enough that pullulating Tel Aviv would smother it, the speculators were already sniffing around, he had heard. Yet a wonder—now Yankel smiled to himself in his beard—a wonder his young Mati hadn't got himself attached to one of Leah's girls there; as Leah said, all the young chalutzoth were crazy for the boy. Oh, his yingel, he would have his time with the girls! Of all the sons, Yankel had always secretly felt, though only grunting when his Feigel declared the same, Mati was the most favored. And only deep within himself Yankel admitted there would be now a long-stretching loneliness as there had been every winter without the boy; the house was empty now, only himself and his old woman, even if Schmulik and Nussya lived close by.

A whole swarm of porters and beggars and vendors had to be dispersed as Nahum's glossy Private, still shining through the dust of the traversed land, came to a halt at the port entrance.

Amid the greeting clamors of the assembling family all of Feigel's parcels and hampers were handed out, even a specially oilcloth-wrapped huge round raisin kugel, Mati's favorite delicacy, while he laughed. "Ima, it's heavy enough to sink the whole ship!"

Saved up for her mother, Leah had a wonderful tidbit of family news that she herself had only a few days ago received from her chaverah Rahel, the very first person who had greeted her here on the docks of Jaffa the day she and Reuven had arrived, young pioneers of the movement. In those early days it had been the habit of Rahel with her chaver, Yitzhak, or Avner as he was called by his underground name, to come to the Jaffa docks to meet every ship from Odessa on the chance that a few chalutzim might be landing. Today, of course, Leah's friends Rahel and Yitzhak Ben-Zvi were leaders of the Yishuv. Feigel always saw their names in *Davar*, heads of the workers this and the women workers that, of the Jewish Council and of the Histadrut Labor Federation and of the Socialist Party, with their chaver David Ben-Gurion, also a close chaver of Leah's from those early days, a pity he was such a

15

tiny fellow and Leah a giantess, or something might really have happened between them! In any case, as Leah now related, just a few months ago despite the fact that Zionism was already outlawed by the Soviets—might they all freeze into icebergs in their own Siberia where they were sending good Jews—only a few months ago, despite this ban on Zionism, a delegation from the Yishuv had been admitted to the World Agricultural Conference in Moscow, and from there Rahel as a women's delegate had brought back a piece of family news for the Chaimovitches! For around the edges of the conference, Leah related, here and there a Jew, hanging about, had managed to have a bit of conversation with one from Eretz, and thus a longtime Zionist from their own town of Cherezinka, a certain Zalman the Shoemaker—did Feigel remember him? Indeed, Feigel remembered, for her brother Kalman the Rich, the beet-sugar mill owner, used to have Zalman make boots for the entire family; with Zalman's boots there were none to compare! Also, Leah reminded her mother, it was in the rear of Zalman's shop that the Young Pioneers of Zion used to meet. And Leah herself had seen this Zalman when she had gone back eight years ago on her mission to find the remnants of the Zionist Youth and bring them to Eretz. Still faithful Zalman was, a wonder not arrested, except that the commissars too coveted his boots. Thus, during the recent conference he had come to Moscow and approached Rahel and asked for news of Leah and the other Chaimovitches and sent greetings and even given news of their relatives still remaining in Cherezinka. Of Feigel's own family, the Koslovskys, there remained only her sister-in-law, the widow of Kalman, the rich Kalman having been shot, as they already knew, in the Revolution. But still alive was his son Tolya, a revolutionist from boyhood despite his father's riches, the same Tolya who used to have such arguments with Reuven about Marxism and Zionism. This very same Tolya was to this day the commissar of Cherezinka, as he had already been at the time of Leah's visit, and only this year, after two sons, a little girl had been born to him. That was the family news. A girl—wait, even her name Rahel had brought back from Zalman—the little girl's name was Tanya.

Indeed, as Leah had sensed it would, this news momentarily lifted Feigel's heaviness over her yingel's departure for so long a time; this family news was indeed something for Mati to carry to America, to bring to Feigel's sister in America, in New Jersey, to his aunt Hannah. A sign of new life in the family, even from the old land now closed off.

16

And so Mati was admonished by his mother: You hear? Not to forget the baby's name—Tanya. Born to their brother Kalman's son, Tolya. With so many messages, Mati had best write it down, Tanya.

Then Menahem was among them. He often had that way of appearing without being noticed, though Mati was sure that Menahem himself always noticed everyone and everything, yet without the piercing eyes or the tense manner that you saw in some of those onetime Shomers. He looked somewhat like a certain math teacher at the Gymnasia, smallish, preoccupied; he even looked something like Eliahu, who everybody knew was the secret head of the Organization—a bit of an office type, a pakid. Menahem exchanged a few words with Dvora, and now with his small smile that always quickly dissolved he took Mati aside: Had he had any further ideas on what he wanted to study? In what to specialize? No special bent had come to Mati; indeed, he did not feel himself exactly a scholar. Maybe that was not a bad thing, said Menahem, the bit of a smile reappearing and vanishing. Nor, however, did Mati feel a practical call, for engineering or for agricultural studies, such as Reuven had tried to awaken in him. Not in history either, at least not the kind where you had to remember all sorts of dates. Social studies, how things came to change, how governments worked, not so much formal politics, but social ideas, socialism itself, this he had been good at in school. Menahem approved, yes, perhaps politics, he said, political science; the University of Chicago was said to be good for such studies. He even knew a name there, a famous economist, Veblen; Mati must remember. You could trust Menahem to have found out such things. Horace Rappaport might try to direct Mati into theories of education, Menahem said; this was valuable and also highly needed here in the Yishuv, but he didn't believe this was exactly Mati's bent; he grinned, showing a golden tooth. Well, Menahem had no fear but that Mati would find the best field for himself. Perhaps also, an odd thought, but Menahem had picked up the information that in the same University of Chicago there was not only the renowned Professor Breasted, who had carried out the great excavations here in Eretz at Megiddo—wait, he knew Mati was not one to bury himself in the past, even if this meant unburying the past! Mati laughed at this typical touch of Menahem's wittiness, which he showed not in general meetings and such but only to those to whom he was quite close. At this same university there was an outstanding Arabist, Menahem said, and it wouldn't hurt for Mati to study a bit of their history and literature.

Then, as they circled back, for Mati saw a few passengers already handing over their baggage to Arab boatmen, Menahem slipped him a bit of paper containing a name and address in New York. In case. And to let this chaver in New York always know where he could be reached.

There was Gidon arriving, Menahem said. Where? Everyone had expected Gidon to come hurrying from the station, but it had to be Menahem who caught sight of him on his wagon, his little Herzeleh gripping the reins with him, and Aviva with Nurit on her lap—the whole kaboodle had come! The touch of anxiety lifted from Mati; indeed, Gidon was still in good time.

They had come by wagon, Gidon said, so as to pick up some Arab floor tiles, the old-style ones with all the colors, that Aviva preferred for the house. And as Aviva hopped down, Mati flushed at the touch of her fresh lips; she looked and felt so young, as though she were still one of Leah's learning girls.

Though Reuven was the eldest, it was Gidon whom Mati had always felt was the big brother. With Reuven living at his kvutsa, it was Gidon who had set Mati the first time on a horse. And then in the big war, though Reuven too was a sort of soldier, conscripted to labor by the Turks, it was Gidon who had got away to join the British in Egypt, and who had sent letters from the battles in Gallipoli and then from London, and who had been among the first to enroll in the Jewish Brigade, and who had returned with the conquering troops of General Allenby in the very days of the Balfour Declaration for the Jewish homeland!

Though Reuven, the book lover, had also declared that Mati must leave the meshek and study, it was Gidon who had set the wheels back on the wagon after Abba hid them to prevent the boy's departure, and it was Gidon who had brought Mati to the Gymnasia.

Yes, Gidon was telling his Herzeleh, right here on this dock the Turkish police had flung him onto a boat. In the great war. Right here the Turkish police of those days, oh, much fiercer-looking than the British police of today—with bayonets and lashes the Turks had rounded up the Jews of Jaffa and put them on boats and expelled them from the land because, having originally arrived from Russia, they were Russkis, and in the Great War Russkis were the enemies of the Turks. And that had been the beginning of Gidon's wanderings until he returned a victor in the First Jewish Brigade!

And this old tale too gave Mati more heart for his departure; like Gidon who had gone out to the world from here, he would be sure to return.

The hugs, the last admonitions from Ima, Leah, everyone, even Abba embracing him awkwardly with pats on the shoulder and under his breath—as for himself alone—muttering the blessing for the voyage. And Schmulik hitting his back and slipping an extra ten-pound note into his hand, never mind from where, extra money, he had been working outside the farm on the Rutenberg electrification dam on the Jordan. "Take it! Special for some good times!" Schmulik leered. "Girls!" And a last extra hug from Dvora, who was crying. And Mati was climbing into the bobbing vessel, the Arab boatmen this time in great good humor, chanting and laughing, Yallah! Farewell Yahud!

2

THE EARLY mist lifted, and the backdrop of skyscrapers stood revealed to Mati, just like painted scenery, reminding him of the stage backdrop of the Ohel Theater for a show called *America Gonif* that he and the whole bunch from the Gymnasia had gone to see for their graduation party. So now as the liner glided closer to the dock, Mati half expected to behold, just as at the Ohel, a row of chorus girls dancing out, kicking up their legs in a real U.S.A. welcome!

Idiocies. Owing to his excitement. Closer now, he knew the skyline exactly, from American movies. Still the sight was exciting and made him smile anew over the jokes in the show—what was New York, compared to Tel Aviv!

All at once this morning everybody on the ship had a different face; the friendships of the voyage were changing into quick parting smiles as though here was America and things were real. But the chubby pink-faced American girl, Alicia, who had been on a tour with her family seeing Christian places in the Holy Land, came looking for Mati to give him a watercolor she had made, his portrait. It was good, too; his skin glowed not so much with darkness as with strength, she had made him look like a real pioneer, a chalutz; Alicia knew the word, for their visit had included a kibbutz along the Sea of Galilee, it turned out to be Reuven's, and she had inscribed the picture "To Mati, the Chalutz."

He gave her a healthy, clean parting hug, n
her bosom; it had not even been a shipboard r
noble-minded, four years older and a college
now in the friendly parting her body was rigid.
heard about American girls. Indeed, though
fellows had recited tales of wild adventures t
liners, the voyage had been disappointingly pu
to be initiated at last.

take hold,
hand,
her

The three Greeks from his cabin passed, with a quick goodbye,
they intended to make money and go back to plant vineyards. The
Chedera couple, too, had told him how they would save their
money and come back to buy an orange grove. And inevitably
there was the long-bearded envoy, the money gatherer with his
gabardine coat, exactly like the shaliach his sister Dvora always
described in telling of their terrible voyage from Odessa, the
shnorrer weighed down with his girdle of gold coins collected from
pious Jews in Russia, to support the prayer sayers of Jerusalem.
Still wearing their black coats and round hats like from the Middle Ages! Before strangers Mati always had an impulse to yell out,
"They're not us!" and here on the boat he had been at pains to
explain this to Alicia and her father, the professor, but even after
touring the Holy Land, they could not understand about the
different kinds of Jews. How could you expect a goy to understand
when even Jewish tourists from America were confused? And awe-
somely in this moment of arrival Mati was recalled to a sense of his
own mission. Some of the Gymnasia teachers and also his own
comrades in the club called The Just Society had admonished him:
He was not only going to America for a college education for his
own sake, but as a representative of the Yishuv. He too was a
shaliach, an envoy, just like that bushy-beard with his fur hat and
long gabardine coat! At this thought, Mati had to laugh out loud.
"What are you laughing at?" Alicia asked him.

"Me!" and glancing toward the emissary, he added softly,
"Him."

Alicia's mouth widened in an uncertain smile.

His passport stamped, his valises reroped, Mati, approaching the
exit, heard his name shrieked and saw a fat elderly woman propel-
ling herself through the crowd as though by force of her over-
powering joy. From a snapshot he recognized his aunt Hannah,
and now he was engulfed, aunt, uncle, the grayish uncle trying to

21

of his suitcase and the aunt pulling away her husband's crying, "You want another operation!" and calling behind 'Wally!"

Lurking behind was their son, Wally, Mati's cousin, a few years older than himself. A real American sport, with a toothbrush mustache, a hearty handshake. Wally reached for the bag, they lugged it together, but as they kept bumping everybody, Mati insisted, "Please, I am used to it," and swung it up on his head. First they were all half embarrassed; then his aunt exclaimed, "A real Arab! Your mother always said!" and to her husband, and even to the crowd emerging from the pier his aunt cried, "Look what a sample from Eretz Yisroel! So tall! So strong! Oh, will the girls go crazy about him!"

Wally shifted as though he were not with her. The cousin wore gold cufflinks, Mati had noticed when they shared the bag handle, and also a heavy ring with a stone. Of course, in America everyone wore a pressed suit, a white shirt, a silk tie, and shined shoes, but this Wally didn't seem to belong with his aunt and uncle even if they were dressed up. He had a fixed, affable expression and had already complimented Mati: "Say, that's a classy British accent!" His eyes gazed openly, directly at you but didn't meet your own.

Already Mati was glad he had not decided—as his aunt had urged—to stay with the family and go to college here in New York. With unstopping questions from Aunt Hannah about everyone in the family, they moved on; she knew each event as though she had been living with them. This faraway sister, Mati suddenly realized, was what his mother had closest in her life, and his Ima, the whole family, seemed the closest for Aunt Hannah in America. She knew even about the eye trouble of Gidon's Nurit—completely cured now, thank the Above! She smacked her lips joyously for Leah, three children already! And Shula, the beauty, was her husband really a millionaire? Even in Eretz Yisroel there were millionaires? And Reuven? And Schmulik, the Little Bull, with his Nussya—something more on the way?

Before they reached the sidewalk, Mati's aunt had recounted the news of her own children, four—he had made it a point to memorize their names. He would soon see them; besides Wally here, they were all waiting at the house, daughters, grandchildren, the Above be praised, all would be there except for Morris, the son who had moved to California, Los Angeles, and was doing very well owning his own radio store, all the movie stars were his customers, Douglas Fairbanks, did Mati know Douglas Fairbanks was Jewish? His real name was Feinberg!

And at this, Mati suddenly recalled the message he must impart from Russia. The new baby there. The name came to him: Tanya! "A blessing!" his aunt cried, hugging him as if it was his doing. To her husband she shouted, "You heard! The family still in Russia, in Cherezinka! A new baby. Tanya!"

"Nu," her husband said wryly, "a good thing it is a girl. A boy, they don't even allow to be circumcised."

They had threaded their way to an automobile—Wally's own! his mother said, Wally used it in his business. A dark blue Chevrolet sedan; like his clothes, it seemed freshly pressed, freshly polished like his shoes. Wally was already doing well, Aunt Hannah proclaimed, he worked for a big corporation, his position was Credit Rating, did Mati know what that was? Even factory owners trembled, Wally should decide they were good for a loan. Wally was a business college graduate; that was what he had always wanted, not a doctor, not a lawyer, but business! First thing, his own car! Did people have their own cars in Palestine?

Only very few, Mati said. But Nahum, the rich husband of Shula, had bought the first taxi in Tiberias.

"He's a taxi driver?" Wally asked, and Aunt Hannah cried indignantly, "Wally, they own a big hotel, I told you a million times!" while Mati explained that in Palestine every automobile was called a taxi.

Things were quiet now with the Arabs? his uncle asked, and when Mati said in the last years all had been quiet, a sigh came from Aunt Hannah for his murdered sister Yaffaleh, she had held Yaffaleh in Russia a baby in her arms, oh, how she had begged his father and mother for them all to come to America, too!

The British High Commissioner had quieted things, her husband commented, Lord Samuel, a Jew, a lord, and he had done very much for the Arabs, too.

Why trouble them over the well-meaning blunders of Lord Samuel, Mati reflected. What would they understand about his leaning over backward, giving the vast Beisan lands to some Bedouin goatherds, who proceeded to sell piece by piece to the Jews? Or worse, putting in Haj Amin el Husseini, the riot fomenter, as Mufti of Jerusalem! Responsibility would make him behave!

Lord Samuel had finished his tour of duty, Mati told them, and now there was an English Englishman as High Commissioner.

Good for the Jews? asked his uncle.

They were riding in the streets of New York; his cousin was showing him the skyscrapers, Wall Street. Wally intended to be there, a millionaire before he was thirty! Aunt Hannah exclaimed. The area seemed strangely deserted as though the enormous buildings were monuments to a civilization that had departed from the earth. But of course, this was Sunday. While Wally named each skyscraper and the number of floors, Aunt Hannah told of the rest of the family here in America; someone had a big Ford automobile agency in Omaha, Nebraska, and his son was in Princeton, for a Jewish boy to get into Princeton that was already something! He really had to have a head on his shoulders! Or a hatful of money, Wally put in.

Presently the car entered a tunnel, it went under the river to the New Jersey side, where they lived, Mati's uncle explained, in the city of Newark.

The tunnel, that was really colossal! The skyscrapers, Mati had expected, but the tunnel! Nothing he had seen in American movies had prepared him for the stream of cars and trucks and motorbuses that rolled without a stop. What if a car got a puncture? It was all systematized, Wally said, though it had better happen to someone else's car, not yours!

The ship must have passed right over this. For the first time Mati felt the sense of immeasurable, yet subterranean power; this was America in the world, and somehow from this he must draw an energy, a strength, in whatever way it would come to him, for his own small place, the world of the Jews in Eretz, that, even though tied onto the strength of the British, suddenly seemed so insignificant.

Finally arrived in Newark, the car halted before a two-story red-brick house in a row of such houses; this was a good Jewish neighborhood, the aunt explained, and they owned the house, the upstairs was a tenant, though if ever one of the children wanted, they could have it, nothing would make her happier than to have grandchildren running up and down the stairs. Or if ever the family wanted to come from Eretz, this was theirs!

Around the corner his uncle Feivel—"Dad's name is Philip!" Wally interjected—had his business. "Some business." The uncle shrugged. A cigar store, a soda stand, candy and newspapers.

"Never mind, from this you sent four children to college," Aunt Hannah repeated, one a high school teacher married to a high school teacher, another girl a college graduate married to a lawyer, and the son in California, and Wally here.

Over their name on the mailbox, Leibowitz, Mati's eye caught a business card, Mr. Wallace Lee.

The apartment had velour-covered furniture, like homes on Rothschild Boulevard. Mati began unpacking gifts, embroidered Yemenite blouses, silver filigree cigarette holders from Bezalel, Star of David brooches. His mother had made a list of everyone in the family in America, including the grandchildren, for whom there were strings of wooden camels. And already the apartment was filling up with cousins and second cousins and nieces and nephews, how could he remember who was whose, and there was a niece of fourteen who kept staring at him and flushing when he caught her gaze; she had rolled stockings just below the knees. "I told you he would knock them dead!" his aunt Hannah was crowing, and they all sat down to a feast, potted beef with potato pancakes, even a raisin kugel—just from the cooking you could have known his aunt and mother were sisters.

"You want butter?" his aunt offered. "A glass of milk maybe?"

"Ma still keeps a kind of kosher, no milk with meat unless you ask for it," said the schoolteacher married to a schoolteacher.

So even in America some kosherness clung. "At home, if you asked for it from my mother, you wouldn't get it," Mati said. "The old folks are still very religious."

"Kosher," his aunt said. "I go to the kosher butcher, and I never have pork in my house, but real kosher the children long ago made me give it up. For myself I do it, it's a habit, but my children—" She laughed, though a bit apologetically. "My children are real Americans. Oysters, they eat."

It was the same with the generations at home, Mati said, though oysters they didn't have in Eretz. But pork, once his brother Gidon had gone hunting with his Arab friend Fawzi, the two of them had killed a wild boar in the Huleh swamp and even tasted it—the Moslems were also forbidden to eat pork, did they know? The Arab boy's father had found out and beaten him. Abba didn't say a word to Gidon; for a whole month he didn't say a word to him! All day in the fields Abba and Gidon would work in silence, and if the old man wanted to tell Gidon something, he would tell Mati what to say to his big brother, the big hunter of swineflesh.

25

"But I thought in Jerusalem everyone had to be kosher," ventured the niece with the rolled stockings. She meant Palestine; all of them, Mati had noticed, said Jerusalem when they meant Palestine. Didn't these American Jews know the first things about the land? Even in Jerusalem itself, he explained, there was a modern part where people were not so religious.

"Just like the old East Side ghetto and the West Side of New York," his cousin Shirley, the high school teacher, said to her children.

Shirley's husband, Milton, showing he was well read, gave the youngsters a little lecture explaining about Russian pogroms and their own family coming here and Theodor Herzl in Europe starting the Zionist movement to bring persecuted Jews back to Jerusalem—to Palestine, he corrected himself. And many of those pioneers were not religious Jews but even socialists. Like Mati's older brother who had started the first kibbutz in Palestine—a kibbutz meant a commune.

"You mean they're communists?" Wally put in.

"Socialists, communists"—Uncle Feival-Philip waved his son down—"but in Palestine, Jerusalem, it would always be something religious. If not, what is it all for?"

What about the Arabs, Wally demanded; wasn't it as though the Jews were pushing themselves in and the Arabs didn't want them there?

Already. "First of all, who are they not to want us?" Mati blurted. "We have as much right there as they do, even more!" And then he told them about the country being empty, the poor fellaheen being like serfs, the rich effendis worrying that the Jews would bring their serfs ideas. Yet all the while, even with this cousin Wally's stupidity, certain words kept reverberating in Mati, echoing—"they don't want us here." Wasn't it from way back in his childhood, the fight in the field after some Arabs from Dja'adi let their goats graze in the early wheat? And the same words, one of the frightened Rumanian settlers had said, "They don't want us here"? Idiocies. The whole quarrel had been patched up, a sulha that still held to this day. Yet the scar was still on his back, and still throbbed sometimes, from the cut that Fawzi's little brother Abdul had given him when they were rolling over each other in the melee.

Now the lawyer married to his cousin Gertie was explaining to the cute flapper about the Balfour Declaration to make Palestine the Jewish National Home, and about the League of Nations

26

decision for it, and about the United States too being all for it, and also how the rights of the Arabs, there, were fully protected.

Like when the Americans first came to this country and there were Indians, his aunt said. Wild Indians.

No, it wasn't really similar, the high school teacher put in. But the British had given the Arabs a country, too, on the other side of the Jordan River.

"Divide and rule!" Wally put in knowingly. "That is always the British system."

One of the younger girls leaned to her mother, Gertie, whispering, and Gertie broke out into a ringing laugh. "She wants to know if all the Jews there are as black as you!" Everyone laughed, and the little girl got angry and punched her mother on the arm.

"Even in the old country, in Bessarabia," his aunt Hannah said, "our family was all very dark from the sun. And in Jerusalem—in Palestine—it is even hotter. So, Gloria, when you want a good suntan, you will go on a trip and visit the family in Palestine—better than Miami!"

A shame that it was only for one night, his aunt repeated after the mass of the family had left; in such a short time he wouldn't even get to know his relatives, in Chicago he would have nobody. Here in New Jersey there were plenty of fine colleges, Wally was on the road much of the time so it would be like his own room, and she would be only too happy to have him.

But he already had his scholarship in Chicago, Mati said as though with regret.

In Wally's room there was a pennant on the wall, Yale. Had he gone to Yale University? Mati asked, and Wally laughed; anybody could buy a pennant. He showed Mati a wonderful book he was reading, a best-seller, a Frenchman wrote it—Coué. You had to say, "Every day in every way I am getting better and better." It really worked, Wally said, maybe it sounded like bushwah, bunk, well, that meant baloney, but Mati would be surprised how it gave you confidence.

Go out, go out and have a good time, his aunt insisted; Mati shouldn't waste his one night here without seeing something. "Wally will show you a good time!" His cousin made a call to fix him up with a date, but Mati would have to put on a necktie, he said. Mati didn't have a tie; in Eretz nobody wore a tie, it was called a dagma luach—a herring! So Wally pulled out a silk tie, very dressy, with yellow and white stripes, insisting, "Keep it. In America you'll need it."

Listen, his cousin instructed him when they got into the car, these were Irish girls; the Irish were really hot stuff. But one thing, Wally's girl didn't know he was Jewish, in his job, too, he was Wally Lee, why should he have a crazy Russki name like Leibowitz, so he made it Lee.

That was understandable, Mati said; in Palestine, too, people changed from their Russian names, they took Hebrew names, one day he would probably change from Chaimowitz to Chaim, in Hebrew that meant Life.

Yah? Wally said. Hey! He had a great idea. Because Mati was so dark, if the girls asked what he was: "Hey, you'll be an Arab! The Sheik of Araby! A Valentino!" That would be the bee's knees. Mati would say he was the son of a sheikh, his name was Ali, he had just come over to go to Yale, and Wally would say the sheikh was an important business contact and his boss had asked him to show the visitor a good time. The girls were sure to fall for it!

Waiting at a street corner were two pretty girls with cupid mouths and bangs; his was named Mickey, and she kept asking was he really the son of a sheikh and would he say something in Arabic? Mati said certain words about his desires which would have got his throat cut for him in Dja'adi, and when Mickey asked the meaning, he couldn't help bursting out into laughter. Hey, what was the big joke? she demanded, and Wally said, "He asked if you would go all the way," which got Mati a soft slap on the wrist.

The car stopped at a place called the Crazy Cat Club, with a peephole slot in the door; inside, a Negro band played, and on a small dance floor the couples circled, pressed against each other; when his Mickey asked where had he learned to dance so good, Mati laughed. "Tel Aviv!" and she said, puzzled, "Huh? Where's that?"

"In the Arabian desert!" snapped Wally, who had caught it. When the girls went to the ladies', Mati said, enough already, why not tell them who he really was? His cousin seized his arm. "No!" Then his own girl might catch on that he was Jewish, too!

Along a dark road there were cars parked in almost a continuous line; Wally stopped and turned out the lights. At once Mati's girl glued herself to him, and there was wet tongue kissing. From the front seat, giggles. Mati's Mickey guided his hand beneath her chemise but suddenly pulled it out and again gave him a little slap.

After dropping the girls, Wally asked was it true that those girls in the communes belonged to everybody? And hey, what about Arab girls?

Should he even try to explain? Suddenly Wally said, "Hey, Mickey liked you, she told Grace she liked you." A couple more dates, and he bet she would even come across. Then he gave a big guffaw. "They fell for it! They fell for the whole line! Hey, Ali! The Sheikh! You were a riot!"

The next day, for the train, his aunt had prepared a little package of chicken sandwiches, dining cars were expensive.

>>>

3

THUS, JUST in time for the fall term of 1927, Mati Chaimovitch arrived in Chicago, a large, chunky lad, no hat, thick, curly black hair; he was large all over like a young bear, his clothes filled to bursting, the pants tight on his muscular thighs, the chest stretching the belted jacket, his huge paws sticking out of too-short sleeves. In his face was a triumphant excitement, as one who would cry out, "I got here!"

A taxi all the way to the university would cost several dollars, but right outside the station a policeman showed him the iron stairway to the elevated.

From the window he saw back porches above littered small yards; for a long stretch there seemed only Negroes living there; then the houses looked newer, red-brick apartment buildings with white people. What an endless city was this Chicago! And this train on raised-up tracks—he had only had a glimpse of such an elevated in New York—would Tel Aviv ever boast such a thing?

At last came the right station. On the street were young people with books, he was nearing the university, girls, but different from Wally's "gash," bright-faced, coeds they were called, and Mati suddenly felt good; America would be good.

A wide grassy parkway opened before him, and across it, English-like churchlike buildings such as you saw in pictures of Oxford. Here in this Chicago!

Still lugging his suitcase, Mati crossed the campus and came to streets of apartment houses, finding the Rappaport address. Celia Rappaport had stayed home waiting for him. She gave him a hug. "Why didn't you let us know what train! Or telephone from the station!" In Eretz, who had telephones? She laughed and gazed at him, what a giant he had grown, nearly as tall as his sister Leah! They fell into Hebrew; he had news of all her former students— when was she coming back! Oh, as soon as Horace finished his doctorate, he was already in correspondence with Dr. Magnes at the Hebrew University about starting a School of Education. Just then Mati noticed she was pregnant; he was slow about such things.

In 1925, in the excitement when so many visitors had come for the opening of the Hebrew University, there had arrived the lanky Judaica scholar Horace Rappaport, already from his high school days an admirer of New York's outspoken Rabbi Judah Magnes, in those days a pacifist in the war. During the university celebrations the swift romance between Horace Rappaport and Celia had been followed by all her pupils, and among the four favored scouts who were given the glory of holding aloft the poles of the wedding canopy was Mati Chaimovitch.

Horace had not forgotten Mati, that wild lad from the Jordan Valley who had pulled even the rabbi into the enormous hora that blocked the whole of Rothschild Boulevard—Mati must come to study in America. The Hebrew University was not yet ready for undergraduates; once in Chicago, Mati could easily earn his way by giving Hebrew lessons.

Hurrying home right after his early seminar, Rappaport unfolded a list he had prepared for Mati, a rooming house, a faculty adviser, and the address of the temple where Mati must see Rabbi Mike Kramer about teaching a Hebrew class. Also a teaching contact at the Jewish People's Institute on the West Side. That was where the big Jewish population lived, Rappaport explained, while here on the South Side was the citadel of the German Jewish community, older and somewhat exclusive, though in fairness it had to be explained that since the coming of a young rabbi, the same Mike Kramer, to the temple, a number of Russian Jews were being admitted to membership. Russian Jews, German Jews, Mati was a little bewildered; in Eretz there were few from Germany, and they were not a separate community; but he would soon get it

31

all straight, Horace said. Now, in what did Mati intend to major? The School of Education here was first class.

Rappaport was lecturing him about new learning methods, something called behaviorism, and rattling off important-sounding names, John Dewey, William James. The special field of Jewish education was wide open as few American Jewish kids even gave it a thought; the whole field desperately needed revision; on the West Side boys were still being sent to the old-fashioned cheder just like in Mea Shearim in Jerusalem. Once they had their Bar Mitzvah they were through with Judaism forever. "We lose them, we lose them entirely. I don't blame the kids." New methods, new learning material had to be introduced. For that matter the Yishuv itself was in dire need of modern educators.

But was this what he had come for, Mati wondered—to start teaching American kids to remain Jews? Though after his cousin Wally he could see the point. Or even to prepare to become a professor at the Hebrew University? He? Since Rappaport was himself scholarly, he perhaps took everyone to have the same desire, but Mati felt almost like an impostor. Oh, he could be studious, but what he was looking for, he tried to explain, was something—of course, he couldn't say more useful—but something, so that when he got back to the Yishuv—

In what field then? Perhaps philosophy? The University of Chicago was a citadel of pragmatism.

What was pragmatism? Mati asked, and Rappaport, smiling a bit, said it was the truly American philosophy. It meant: What works is right. That wasn't exactly in the Jewish tradition, Rappaport said, yet maybe—a speculative look came over his face— maybe there was more than a trace of pragmatism at the present time in the building of the Yishuv. Maybe it was even necessary.

At this, Mati could join his smile. If it would be useful when he got home, perhaps he should take a course in this pragmatism. For what he really wanted was what would be most useful when he got home.

Celia came back into the room. With her Mati felt easier, as though even though a real American girl American-born, she really belonged to the Yishuv. "You sound like in the old days in the Gymnasia, the Just Society," Celia said. "Is it still operating?"

Well, in a way, but even in the two years since she left, the school had grown bigger and the society was more like a discussion club—how to build the Just Society. In the early days, the first graduating class before the war, that everyone talked about, the days of Moshe Shertok, of Dov Hos, of Eliahu Golomb, when they had formed the Just Society, each member had been assigned his life task for the Yishuv: this one must go to Constantinople to study Turkish law, that one must go to California and study citrus cultivation, another must learn life in a kibbutz; thus, they would serve to build a Just Society in this land. Mati with a few of the boys had even talked of reviving such a secret society.

Rappaport shifted around toward Celia. "What do you think? Polycon for a start?" It meant political economy, Mati already knew. Something like what Menahem had talked about. And what those brilliant ones of the early days, Moshe Shertok, David Ha-Cohen, had gone to study in London.

The valise carried on his head up three flights of stairs, Mati had his room, a cubbyhole at the end of a long corridor. The straight-backed landlady, Mrs. Kelleher, a professor's widow she had already let him know, explained the cleanliness rules about the bathroom and also that visits by young ladies were forbidden. With a good look at him she said, after all, she had to maintain her university listing.

And by the end of the afternoon he had all his courses lined up. Everyone was all smiles. Really born in Palestine! And his accent? Not exactly British? "My English teacher was American." "Is that so?" Americans went there to teach? Ah, Jewish. Well! But still quite unusual, wasn't it? Ah.

Polysci I, and a survey of modern civilization, and also Shakespeare and English composition. For building the Yishuv!

Next, Mati found the temple, a square corner edifice with new apartment buildings pushing against it. Over the high oaken doors, shaped with rounded tops like tablets of the Law, there was a stained-glass Star of David set in a circle, somehow churchlike.

So this was a Reform temple. They had not yet come to Eretz; the rabbonim had a tight grip and would not allow such heathenish Jewish congregations in the Holy Land. In Eretz a shul was a shul; to please his abba, Mati used to go on High Holidays to the little shul in Mishkan Yaacov, but from his grown-up brothers and sisters he had even as a child known that the services were all rigmarole. At the Gymnasia a daring teacher had, with all due respect for the practices which had preserved the Jewish people up to modern times, explained that the kosher laws were hygienic tribal taboos and that some people might even call the tallis and tefillin totemistic. There had been a big scandal, even bigger when the same teacher, vilified in the press of the Religious Party, had then given a lecture on the Reform movement, explaining that it had originated among German Jews after the emancipation from the ghetto. They had tried, in their synagogues, to behave like German Protestants. For that matter, Mati had never got it straight how Christian Protestants were different from all the varieties such as Anglicans, Episcopalians, and Universalists that you read about, besides Roman Catholics and Greek Orthodox in Jerusalem, and all those odd costumes you saw in the Old City, Franciscans, even Ethiopians. All he could keep straight was that Roman Catholic priests couldn't marry, but Greek Orthodox could, and Protestants. At least with the rabbis, Orthodox, Reform, you had no such problem.

Out of curiosity he and a whole bunch from the Gymnasia had gone for a look inside the big new synagogue on Allenby Street, uttering an oo-wah! at its size and splendor, yet here in a side neighborhood in Chicago was a structure twice as imposing! As he entered, it came to Mati that he was hatless, but in the same instant he recalled that these Protestantish Reform Jews had abolished the yarmulkah; they worshiped bareheaded like goyim.

In the large hall was a platform on which stood ornate chairs and a huge bronze menorah; on the back wall, at least the same as in an ordinary shul, the Torah Ark. This one had intricately carved chrome wooden doors, and an electric eternal light hung before it, in a kind of antique lantern. But what was different? Of course, there was no balcony for women. In the Reform, he recalled the main dispute, men and women sat together. Thus, the Orthodox objected, a man in the middle of his prayers could be distracted by the Evil Impulse.

Maybe something like this Reform would one day come to the Yishuv. Mati in himself had never altogether decried the need for worship. Leah, in her training farm for girls, had already restored the lighting of Shabbat candles.

In the corridor Mati saw a shirt-sleeved youngish man and asked for Rabbi Kramer. "Shalom!" His hand was seized. "You're Mati Chaimovitch! Horace phoned me." Adding the Hebrew welcome,

"Baruch Ha-Ba," the Reform rabbi, beardless, though with a mustache, drew Mati along downstairs to a basement social hall with a stage where, Kramer explained, he was rehearsing the temple's drama club in a play, a satire called *The Dollar*, by the famous Yiddish dramatist David Pinski; did Mati know this play?

Unfortunately he did not, Mati said; was it translated into Hebrew? "Here, we're not so afraid of Yiddish"—the young rabbi laughed—"but don't worry; anyway we're doing it in English." Drama was his hobby, he told Mati, so he directed the temple players himself. There was a dearth of good Jewish material for the stage; after *The Dybbuk* and *The Golem* what did you have? Were there some good new Hebrew plays in Tel Aviv? Perhaps something about the new life that could be translated? Otherwise, all his group wanted to do was Bernard Shaw.

Black, straight eyebrows, with his straight mustache, gave the rabbi an underlined look, a man who knew his mind. On the stage several young people, mostly of high school age they appeared, were moving about among cutouts of trees. They called down for instructions; they called him Rabbi Mike.

Mike Kramer was another of the younger breed, like Horace Rappaport, who had been drawn into the "Jewish field" by Judah Magnes and Stephen Wise. Mike had survived his trial year at the temple by a fairly close margin of board-member votes, though afterward there had been a few resignations. That he had even been given the trial year, in this fashionable congregation, was the result of a social tragedy, a crime that had resounded all over the world, which had taken place in this community a few years before. In Palestine, too, Mati had read of it, and the kids at the Herzl Gymnasia had discussed it with amazement and puzzlement.

For this was the very community in which there had happened the strange, seemingly motiveless murder, the "thrill killing" carried out after meticulous planning by two brilliantly precocious university students, sons of leading German Jewish families. They had kidnapped a neighborhood boy, also a Jewish millionaire child, and, while coolly trying to collect ransom, had slain him as part of their exercise in a perfect crime, so that they could not be identified. When caught, because one had by accident dropped his glasses in the field where the body was found, they had proclaimed a lofty Nietzschean philosophy; they were "supermen," above the codes of mundane human law. These strange philosophical explanations were accompanied, in the press, by hints of sexual depravity between the two prodigies and even of sexual horrors committed on their victim.

In *Davar* the case had been written about as a proof of the decay of American capitalist society, unfortunately including leading Jewish families. Bereft of ideals, such Jews could save themselves only by coming to toil on the soil of Palestine. The thrill killers, Judd Steiner and Artie Straus, were examples of a growing world of decadence and iconoclasm, devotees of such writers as Baudelaire and Oscar Wilde; indeed, they had planned to take a vacation in Paris on their ransom money.

Here in these very streets around the temple it had all taken place: the abduction, the murder in the car, the stalking of the supermen. Not far from the temple were the mansions of the Steiner and Straus families, members of this old and prestigious congregation. For thirty years the distinguished Rabbi Gunther Koenig, never quite losing his German accent, had led the services. On every occasion when a rabbi, a minister, and a priest were quoted in the Chicago newspapers, Dr. Koenig was the rabbi.

The Steiner-Straus tragedy had broken him. Unable to overcome the feeling that everyone believed it was his own failure to instill morality in the youths that had led to the anti-God murders, the rabbi had asked for retirement.

Then a spirit of complete change had come over some of the younger members of the board; their ringleader was Sylvan Straus, head of the law firm that represented the family in its vast merchandising and brokerage activities; something of a dandy, a modernist, a patron of the arts, he was an uncle of Artie Straus, the madcap charmer of the two thrill killers, and indeed had been grooming Artie to enter the law firm. Sylvan Straus was himself a much-talked-of personality; already in the early twenties he had been to Vienna for psychoanalysis with Dr. Freud; he had indeed attempted to bring Sigmund Freud to Chicago to study the thrill killers and testify at their trial. An enthusiast for all that was new—he already collected Hemingway manuscripts—Sylvan Straus advocated a clean sweep, a rejuvenation of the temple, and it was he who dug up Michael Kramer.

The son of a noted criminal lawyer in New York who boasted that he had never lost a murderer and that every law could be got around, Mike had reacted to his father's cynicism with a questing idealism. Swept along, as a youth, in the crusading pacifism of

New York's Rabbi Judah Magnes, Mike had decided to go to the Reform rabbinical college in Cincinnati. Once ordained, he had promptly got himself dismissed from his first pulpit, in Los Angeles, because of a fiery sermon protesting the life imprisonment of the radical labor agitator Tom Mooney, for dynamiting the building of the Los Angeles *Times*.

That sermon, curiously enough, had been one in which Mike Kramer attempted to present the case as it might have been argued in the Talmudic tradition. For such a crime, three direct witnesses were required; there had therefore been insufficient proof, and Tom Mooney, the young rabbi declared, had been railroaded to life imprisonment simply because he was a radical.

With this as the cause of Mike Kramer's dismissal, Sylvan Straus was delighted. For though renewal must, of course, turn to the new, best, he believed, was the new that made use of the old, choosing in tradition that which remained valuable, without being bound to the past. Doubtful members of the temple's board had been swept into agreeing to a trial year. After all, the Straus family were the heaviest contributors, and also they had suffered such a tragedy.

Soon Mike had brought about his first important change, a true rupture with the congregation's prideful past. The temple admitted to membership a few families of Russian Jews. A number of the better-off had made the move from the West Side to Hyde Park, and their contributions offset the depletions resulting from the resignations.

On the stage, Mati at once saw, there were plenty of pretty girls. Though he ought really to be looking over the drama group for future Zionist material, the excitement and expectation was upon him of entering a new life, a new place.

One girl standing in the hall had already given him a long, steady look-over when he came in with the rabbi. But this girl could never be the one, Mati immediately felt. Yet, oddly, he also felt that something might happen with her. There was something in her eyes; the eyes were intense, a deep, glowing darkness, with a quality that disturbed you, as if in furtive questioning they hoped from you some answer to what nobody could answer. They reminded him of the touching, appealing look that his sister Yaffa-leh used to have at times and of the lines in the poem she had left about a window lighting up.

In other ways, too, this girl was unusual; she had a striking nose, long and narrow-arched, like among the Sephardim of Old Jerusalem. It was almost the "Jewish" Jewish nose, except it was also aristocratic and fitted with the rest of her face. She was standing in front of the stage, holding a large drawing pad—for costumes, he saw. The girl had huge breasts but skinny arms and legs; her clothes hung on her askew, but even Mati could tell they were expensive, the kind that the girls from the Herzl Gymnasia used to linger and gawk at in the window of Greenbaum's Paris Shop, when the whole bunch from the graduating class, boys and girls, wandered up Allenby Road. To get the girls moving, Mati would tug at Zippie's braids, and she would turn on him; what did he know about *fashion*, he with his sister Leah, the perennial chalutzah, who wore men's clodhoppers and even men's trousers to work in the fields! Of course, his sister Shula, married to the Tiberias hotel owner Nahum, got all her clothes in Greenbaum's, but since Shula was stuck away in Tiberias, what a waste!

All this had come rushing back on him while the rabbi introduced him to the girl, Myra Roth. A niece of Sylvan Straus, it seemed, for this was almost the first thing she let people know when they met her, so they wouldn't make any faux pas remarks about the Steiner-Straus crime. And indeed, Myra would soon also let them know she had had a terrible adolescent crush on her cousin, yes, *that* one, Artie Straus, the charmer, the madcap murderer who was now put away in prison for life. Had they heard in Palestine about the case? she asked, and Mati said, of course.

The young rabbi turned to the group on the stage, making a general introduction, "Kids, this is Mati Chaimovitch, just arrived from Palestine to study at the U of C." They all grinned down at him. But some of the girls gazed.

"You don't mind, Mati, I'll be with you in a little while," the rabbi said, and proceeded with the play. He was making them leap and posture and dance around the stage in an extravagant manner, reminding them this was a satire, they must make exaggerated, stylized movements like the Habima. As though for corroboration he glanced over at Mati, explaining that the Habima had been to Chicago on tour. Then he asked how many had seen a performance.

A few hands went up. One was from a girl on the stage who had already caught Mati's eye, and when she raised her hand, she looked at him as though her response were to him. Lissome, with black hair like two raven wings embracing her small, pert face. He had watched her skipping about, her pleated skirt whirling above her knees, with flashes of her pale thighs above the stocking tops. It was nothing indecent; after all, in Leah's kvutsa the girls all went about with the shortest bloomers and bare legs, and in sports, too, in high school the girls had bare legs all the way up so sometimes you even caught sight of a few hairs. Still, once there was a whirling skirt, it excited you.

But really it was her face now, cupped in the raven's wings, that held him, making him feel he must brush the hair aside and cup her face in his hands.

And several times as the rehearsal proceeded, Mati caught her eyes on him, too. And he had a feeling that the first one, with the sketchbook, Myra Roth was noticing everything between both of them.

That it would happen on this first day, his day of arrival, may indeed have been an expectancy in Mati, like an echo of the fate of his big sister Leah, falling in love on the first day of her arrival in Eretz, when she saw her Handsome Moshe. Hadn't Mati virtually grown up with poor Leah's story of her fated love, of her faithful years of loneliness and longing, after Moshe had been sent back on a mission to Russia and vanished?

With all the things that had already happened to him in Chicago, after the first sight of the university, and here already he had found a job—all, all had to happen on this same day.

Yet Mati could not let himself accept at once the "this is she" of love at first sight. A pretty girl, so light and graceful, not simply the flash of the thigh but the graceful swirling and leaping—that still did not mean this was she. Yet at one instant the girl seemed about to leap right off the stage into his arms!

At home there was Zipporah, his Zippie bird. When they had strolled away from the farewell graduation beach fire and meandered barefoot in the lapping water and then stopped and kissed, clutching tight, while she let his sex throb against her, she had said, "Mati, I won't ask you to be true, but I'll be true, I'll wait. You see I am not such a foolish girl as to ask you; I know they say it is harder for a man than for a woman. Maybe this is not men's bluffery, but even true; what does a girl know how it feels to be a man? And those girls in America, it's said they do everything."

"That's what the Americans say about us, about our girls in the kibbutzim," he had jested, and suddenly Zippie kissed him furiously with her tongue, and he believed if he bent her backward and she fell on the sand, the whole thing would happen; it would be the first time for him, too. Then what had held him back? A sense, a doubt; perhaps Zippie was not truly his fated one, his bashert. Hence even to possess her might be a betrayal of the one. If he took her in the excitement of parting, he might bind himself and not be free should he meet his truly destined one. And then Zippie had broken away. "You'll wait for me?" each asked at the same time, both knowing themselves to be high school youngsters dazed in their blood, and Zippie had recovered first from the moonishness, a girl does, women can be colder in their view of love. "You know what, Mati? We're both liars." She laughed, and at that moment Mati was almost sure Zippie was indeed she, the one, and he mustn't go off to America, he was making a great life mistake.

On the ship he had written her several letters, but then suddenly the longing had stopped, and he was hungrily following that American gentile girl, Alicia, even though she was older than he.

Nor had Dena Kossoff joined the drama club of the temple in order to find a dark young man from Palestine, a Sheik of Araby as the girls would inevitably dub him, humming the tune whenever he passed. Even if this one was not dreamy-eyed like Valentino, even if he was no desert Arab but a chalutz from Tel Aviv, yet he was from far away, the dark one, the stranger, the male.

That first evening her excitement came perhaps from an habitual competitiveness in Dena—oh, she knew herself and her private game, that a new man should look at her more than at any other girl. There were several other very pretty girls in the group; indeed, Dena hadn't even been chosen as leading lady—a blondie, with a round baby-doll face like Mae Murray, was the star—so it was even stronger in Dena, that urge she knew was silly, to get a new fellow to concentrate only on her.

From her earliest high school days Dena had played the flapper, always with boys trailing her, but last year, when the family had moved from the West Side and she had transferred to Hyde Park High, she had found herself with mostly gentiles. Not that she drew the line. There was a small Jewish crowd at the school, but the kids were already paired off, and though she could easily have done so, Dena wouldn't, on principle, steal another girl's boyfriend. It was important to have girlfriends, too, and that would be the worst way to start off in a new neighborhood; she'd be Poison. Only if a real uncontrollable passion happened could you let yourself steal a boy; only if you couldn't possibly help it. But luckily this had not happened to her. Dena was still in that girlish time of wondering, when would the real passion happen to her, how would it come?

A few of the fellows she had dated on the West Side had tried to keep it up after she moved, but none of them had ever made her feel he was the One, and after all, why had the family moved except, as she arrived at this certain age, to get her away from the ghetto?

The big goyish football players were soon trailing after her in the corridors, and Dena asked herself what if the passion happened with one of them? For the sake of peace at home and even to avoid complications in her life—though she considered herself daring and adventurous in spirit—Dena really hoped it would not happen to her with a shagetz. Yet on principle and with her American-born background she was broad-minded. One thing she told herself—if it happened and she even married a gentile, there could be no question of accepting another religion, like becoming a Catholic or agreeing to raise your children to be Catholics. Or being any kind of Christian. "But if we're not even religious as Jews," some of the girls argued. And suppose it happened with a goy who was also not religious? Then you were just two people. Two people in love. Some girls said even so, it would kill their parents. Dena said of course, her parents would be terribly disappointed, but they were very understanding and not too religious themselves; her mother never even tried to keep kosher. And so in such a case, both persons not religious, love would be the true consideration, but still in her heart she kind of wished she would not be put to such a test; things would be so much simpler if it would happen to her with a Jew.

Thus, knowing their daughter, the family had in a way that was supposedly unpointed, though Dena knew what was on their minds, urged her toward the temple's youth activities where she would encounter a fine class of people.

For after all, what else had the costly move been for to the South Side?

Many practical reasons had fortuitously appeared, just when Bessie Kossoff knew her Dena was entering the critical stage of whom does a girl meet? Some of the West Siders were moving out farther west, invading the goyish suburb of Oak Park and living in houses with lawns, real residences instead of apartments. But there in Oak Park for sure a girl would meet mostly goyim. And besides, Sam Kossoff couldn't stand to live so far away from the store. It had been a whole battle for Bessie to get him to move from the flat above the store, a few years ago, even only twenty minutes on the streetcar to Douglas Park, but by the time Dena had graduated from grammar school there were only five Jewish kids left amid a whole eighth grade of Italians as the wops had taken over the old Jewish neighborhood. With a growing girl how could you live there, how could Dena even ask a friend home from high school to Halsted Street, and it was even dangerous with Prohibition and bootleggers and gangsters and the dagos all around them making wine. Though in a crazy way it was good for Sam's business. The jewelry store on Halsted Street he had built up from a watch repair shop started by his father when they came to America and Sam was ten years old. For many years, while it was still a Jewish neighborhood, the store carried nothing expensive, maybe half-carat engagement rings a garment worker could afford. Then some Jews who had become allrightniks and moved to Douglas Park started coming back to Halsted Street looking for bargains, and Sam began to carry gold watches and more expensive stones. And when Prohibition came, the Italian bootleggers became big customers. Though Bessie finally got Sam to move to Douglas Park and keep a watchman at night in back of the store, he never really slept as well as when they lived upstairs and he knew if anything happened he could hear the alarm. Phil, their eldest, got a special telephone to the watchman. He had big, modern ideas. One day to have a store in the Loop, on State Street downtown, and also a chain of neighborhood stores selling on installments, especially flashy jewelry in the black neighborhood on Twenty-second Street on the old South Side.

Finished with two years of commercial college, Phil suddenly got engaged to the daughter of Morris Goldenson, the real estater. Sherrill was beautiful, too, with auburn hair and a milk-white skin that Dena envied. Sherrill knew how to dress and bought only at Field's. Goldenson had just acquired, in a whole long-story combination of trading upward that only Phil could explain, a half-million-dollar corner property in the good part of the South Side, Fifty-fifth Street; he had big mortgages it was true, but thirty-six apartments and four stores, and Goldenson wanted to set up the young couple with a brand-new apartment and also a store. This would be the first Kossoff jewelry branch, high-tone.

The bride refused. Sherrill wasn't going to live over a store! Good for her! Dena declared in the family discussions. Her sister-in-law-to-be intended to live in her own house in the suburbs; that was where to raise children. No, not even for a start before there were any children would Sherrill live over a store, even if the flat was not directly upstairs but around the corner and university professors lived in the building! Sherrill wanted the best; not even the South Side was good enough, she wanted a house on the North Shore, in Wilmette.

"If that's what my future wife wants, that's what she gets," said Phil, and drove out with Sherrill to look around and then, excited, drove out with Goldenson, and what did they come back with but a lease on a newly built Old English-style shoppe next to the station in Wilmette, where Phil would go into high-class jewelry. Also, Goldenson as a wedding gift had stretched himself to the limit, as he said, and put down a payment on the lawn-surrounded house his daughter had set her heart on, so that combined with a second mortgage and a personal loan and twistings and turnings without number, it was all a deal! Part of the combination deal was for Sam Kossoff himself to take the vacant Fifty-fifth Street store and the around-the-corner apartment. Very nice, a sun parlor, a tiled bathroom, and he could have the burglar alarm wired right into his bedroom, and Dena would be living in a tony neighborhood right on the edge of the millionaire homes of Kenwood and Hyde Park. Besides, the youngest child, Victor, could already have his Bar Mitzvah at the temple. And so the big move for the Kossoff family was made.

Membership cost high. And Sam Kossoff soon grumbled that the new store on Fifty-fifth Street wasn't getting many customers from the South Side's German Jews who had to have a Tiffany label on the jewelry box. Still, Bessie pointed out that at the temple her daughter would meet the best. She even urged Dena to join the newly formed Junior Hadassah, as the chapter met in some of the best old Hyde Park mansions, but instead, Dena started with the drama club. Not that she was stagestruck—she had her head on her shoulders, she said—nor did she imagine a movie scout would come to see her on the social hall platform in the temple basement. No, she was not infantile. Yah, her smart kid brother teased, she was going there to find a Valentino, a real sheikh, among those amateur actors!

"The joke is on me, here he is!" Dena told herself, for this dark fellow's eyes never left her. She well knew by now that sensation of a boy fastening his eyes on you; when she was younger, this used to make her blush all over; she would feel herself blushing under her undies. But now she could be cool and even aloof; she had already gone out with college boys. One way to handle the situation was to stare back and even laugh—that broke the ice, and you could chatter.

But instead, with this boy from Palestine she found herself as though peeping out from inside the playlet, now and again, to get a real idea of him. What if she would seriously fall in love and he would want her to go back with him and live in Palestine and be a pioneer! That would be a good one on the family! Instead of marrying a Rosenwald or a Straus! At least even marrying a goy, she would be near home and Pa and Ma could get joy out of their grandchildren. Instead, off to a strange land, and they couldn't even object because what could be more Jewish!

Poor guy, she was marrying him already! And anyway, over there in Palestine wasn't it all free love? Of course, one Friday when Pa wanted to put in an appearance and dragged them to the services, Rabbi Mike had lectured that it was simply foolish propaganda that in the Palestine settlements the girls belonged to everybody, but still, everyone said in those kibbutzes they were communists and free and easy in their ways, and she had seen pictures of those pioneer girls in the fields, bare-legged in bloomers shorter than the most daring bathing suit. They had the most beautiful suntans. But this fellow was almost black! Well, you wouldn't really take him for a Negro, but he could be from India or someplace. And his curly black hair, curly, not kinky—she could feel her fingers roving in his locks! Was there really such a thing as one man, one woman for a whole lifetime? And if so, then why, when still on the West Side and Alvin was her steady, had she felt something akin to these same sexy reactions? Of course, with Phil and Sherrill they were crazy in love, and with her own mother and father you could never imagine anything with someone else happening to either of them; they were settled together for life even if it was hard to imagine when it had been romantic. All they ever thought about was: everything for the children. And with a chalutz, everything would be for Palestine, for their Zionism! No! Why should she let her imagination run so far ahead? Even if it was just for fun.

Thus, a whole discussion was going on between Mati and the girl on the stage; half-formed fantasies flew in and out. He had caught her glancing at him, and Dena even missed a cue, waking up when she heard a titter breaking the silence around her. "Do you want the cue again, Dena?" Rabbi Mike called up to the platform.

So her name was Dena.

During the break the rabbi excused himself, telling the cast to run over their lines, he had to have a word with Mati, and the two of them went into the hallway to discuss possibilities. A beginner's course in Hebrew for the seven- to eight-year-olds, that would be definite, Wednesday after school and Sunday mornings, but maybe also a young people's study group?

So at least there would be several hours a week to start with, enough to pay his rent and food. Elated, all set, as they said here, on his very first day, Mati wanted to rush to his room and write a letter to Leah, or should he go back with the rabbi to that rehearsal? He had not come here for fooling around with girls, and anyway, he knew her name, Dena, and he could always find out when there was another rehearsal.

Going back to the rooming house, he found the streets were lively; there was a city smell, energizing. In spite of the whole night on the train, Mati wasn't sleepy; instead of going upstairs, he even had an impulse to hurry back to the temple and perhaps the rehearsal would just be over and he would meet her coming out. But surely such a pretty girl had friends in the group, probably a fellow who took her home in his own car. Climbing the four flights, he groped in the corridor and, as he switched on the light, saw a typed notice underneath, "Please turn off at end of corridor." He would write to Leah, all about the American Jews and their Reform temple with a rabbi who directed plays.

Their performance would be right after the Friday service during Succoth and was to be followed by a dance, and this would be a good occasion, Rabbi Mike suggested, for Mati to get to know some of the young people and explore the possibilities for a study group. And he invited Mati for the Sabbath Eve meal.

At home the meal always came after sundown, when Abba returned from the services of welcoming the Sabbath Queen in the shul, but here in the Reform it seemed Jews had their dinner first and then went to the temple. Mati put on his white shirt and his cousin Wally's tie, but left the collar button open until he got in front of their house, and then he choked himself up.

Since the rabbi emeritus of the temple still occupied the residence, Mike Kramer lived in one of the new apartment buildings on the fringe of the mansion area. He had married—before he got thrown out of his Los Angeles pulpit—into a branch of the Guggenheims out there. "Which didn't help; he got kicked out anyway," his wife, Sue, would say right off. Sue had that scrubbed Ivory Soap Smith College look; she was a reader of books by Lytton Strachey, rather flat-chested and a bit gaunt like a real New Englander, but careful not to be unfeminine in attire. They had a boy of four named Joshua and a baby girl named Naomi.

The apartment was bright with reproductions of modern Cubist paintings, and Sue smiled when Mati complimented her on the wonderful reproductions; his sister-in-law in the kibbutz, a gifted pianist who had studied music in the conservatory in Paris, had reproductions just like these, he said. The Rappaports arrived, and just after them came hurrying the girl with the big bosom and disturbing eyes, Myra Roth, tugging up her awry shoulder straps, pushing up the bangles that kept slipping over her wrists; she had a good excuse for being late, she had been finishing the costumes, Myra said. She was here for him, Mati supposed, but also she seemed a close chum of Sue Kramer and rushed at once to a bright small picture, a machine-like nude, congratulating Sue on her latest. So he had made a boner, Mati realized; these were real original paintings. Rabbi Mike said his one concession to the use of Sue's private income was allowing her to buy her own art, but he was afraid his personal taste was conventional, and while the girls wore smiles, he opened the door of his study to show Mati a long-bearded prophet painted by Professor Boris Schatz of the Bezalel Museum in Jerusalem, and Mati told how when his family had first arrived in Eretz his sister Leah and his brother Reuven had labored on the masonry of that very museum.

Mati must take off his tie! Sue declared, he looked as if he would choke, and Myra said she thought in Palestine ties were taboo. He told how at home it was called a herring, he'd never had

46

one, but got this from his cousin in New Jersey, describing the date to great laughter. Mike showed the succah that he and little Joshua had constructed out of fronds on the side balcony. "You can see the sky, that's what's important," the kid piped.

During his days at Teachers College in Columbia, Horace Rappaport said, he and some of his friends used to go down to the old East Side during the holidays, you could see the most fantastic succoth made on the fire escapes of the tenements, with colored electric-light bulbs strung out from the flats.

At home in Palestine, Sue said to Mati, they must have the real thing?

Oh, sure, Mati said; his father was religious, and for every Succoth the whole family would come back to the farm, the succah was built in the front yard by the carob tree that his brother Reuven had planted in their first year there, and last year, when they had all crowded around the table, with all the grandchildren there were over thirty souls already!

For a moment he felt a pang of homesickness even for the old man and his religious ways. This Myra kept her eyes fastened on him as though she were seeing it.

Because of the schedule of the services at the temple they would have to sit down for dinner right away, Sue said. On the table stood an antique-looking pair of silver candlesticks, heirlooms from her side of the family, from Germany, seventeenth century, Mike said to Mati.

So how were things different in Reform? Sue Kramer was making the ancient gesture of the hands over the candles. Yet perhaps because she said the prayer in English, the moment somehow was not like when his mother magically drew the spirit of Shabbes into herself. Still, Rabbi Mike chanted a real kiddush over the wine in Hebrew, also the bread blessing, handing a twist of store-bought challeh to each; then in English he recited the Esheth Chayil, the Woman of Valor, to his wife. A large black woman served portions of gefulte fish and glowed as she was complimented on her Jewish cooking.

The meal moved on a smooth time schedule toward the eight-thirty service at the temple. Everything was like a real Sabbath Eve, yet it somehow felt like an imitation. Perhaps because they even sang the song of welcome to the Sabbath Queen in English. Mati told how as a little kid he would half imagine, with the words "Come, oh, Bride," seeing the Sabbath Queen floating in white gauze garments from over the waters of the Kinneret, having followed his abba as he returned from the shul. "In Reform," Mike jested, "the Sabbath Queen makes an earlier entrance."

"And what about the Succoth holiday in a kibbutz?" Sue Kramer asked Mati. Though the chaverim were supposed to be antireligious, she had heard that they observed the festival with dancing in the fields.

Their idea, Rappaport explained, was to connect religious observances with ancient agricultural ceremonies, probably their true origin.

Mati told how his sister Leah had invented such a dance, with a water-pouring ceremony, like she had heard the Jews had in ancient times.

A libation to bring on the rainy season, said Rappaport.

And Leah had a dancing procession, with her girls carrying water jars on their shoulders.

It must have looked like a painting on a Grecian urn! Beautiful! Myra's eyes with their disconcerting glow remained fixed on Mati. Were the Kramers perhaps pushing this girl on him, an heiress, good for the movement? Mati joked to himself.

At least such holiday observances showed that the kibbutzniks were not entirely antireligious, Rabbi Mike said. Perhaps they would develop their own form of Reform! He still had a good many hidebound anti-Zionists in the congregation, and such religio-cultural developments might be a way of moving them gradually to overcome their prejudices.

"Also their ignorance," Celia Rappaport put in.

And so they got onto the perennial discussion. Mati had already heard it, about the fears of these Jews about being regarded as disloyal Americans if they got involved with Zionism. Being Jewish was only a matter of religion, they insisted, so maybe those Palestine settlers weren't even actually Jews! "I'll tell you the truth!" he suddenly blurted, having twice had his wine cup unobtrusively refilled. "Let them help us, fine! They don't want to help us—to hell with them! They want to stay American Jews, okay with us, religious Jews, Reform Jews, unreligious Jews—"

"Reform Jews are also religious," Mike broke in, laughing.

"—or like the ones, I already heard them on campus," Mati said, "the ones that keep announcing they are not ashamed of being a Jew. We, we want to build the land and live our life, the hell with the Jewish question!"

"Hear hear!" Sue Kramer cried, and Mike burst out in Yiddish, "Gut gezogt!" Well said!

He raised his glass. "L'chayim!"

Walking to the temple, Mati could feel the girl's fingers not so much holding as clawing into his arm. All sorts of things, Myra Roth told him in that short walk, almost embarrassingly intimate, arousing in him a compounded reaction of sympathy and wariness, yet a sense that she really wasn't trying to attract him. It was that family tragedy; she never let you or herself forget it. Artie Straus, the thrill killer, her cousin. This time she got to it through Oscar Wilde; the next play the group wanted to put on was Oscar Wilde's *Salome*. Was Oscar Wilde translated into Hebrew? He didn't know, but about Herod and Salome he knew. Artie had been crazy about Oscar Wilde, and her uncle Sylvan Straus even had a theory that Artie had to do something to put himself in prison because of Oscar Wilde having been in prison. They had nothing better than such things to worry their heads with? Mati thought, and she went on. Maybe reading Oscar Wilde was what got Artie started on those homosexual things; when all those strange things came out after the crime, she hardly knew what they meant; why, Artie had had all the cuties, every flapper on campus had a crush on him, and she herself, a real adolescent love, and that was what had made it so incomprehensible when all that homosexual stuff about Artie and Judd Steiner—

This Myra had a throaty, cawing laugh, and suddenly she switched the subject, demanding, well, had he seen the girl? Did he have a date yet? "Who?" But Mati knew who. Myra had at once noticed, she said, how he couldn't take his eyes off that little girl, Dena. Dena Kossoff. So he hadn't even got her phone number? Very cute, very bright, one of those new families coming to the South Side, the Russian Jewish families. Myra was all for it. Then suddenly she said she wanted Mati to know he could turn to her, a friend—her fingers dug—no boy and girl things, a friend. Oh, he needn't worry; he wasn't her type, but if he wanted to be friends—yes?

The rows were almost full; a choir with organ welcomed the Bride of the Sabbath in Hebrew and English, and Mike appeared in a black robe, followed by a procession of three temple dignitaries and a robed cantor.

Tonight's service would be brief because of the program in the social hall, Mike announced. A young matron, called up to kindle the Sabbath candles, carefully read the blessing in alliterated Hebrew and then in English. The cantor chanted the kiddush very professionally with only a hint of a quaver. As Mike announced page numbers, prayers were read in English, all in a kind of dullish, dutiful murmur. Well, was it so different from the Jews in his father's shul racing through the words? Though at least they didn't have to be told page numbers. And these were the same prayers, our King, our Master, our Almighty, interrupted with Mike's "Please rise" and "Be seated" and, in this Reform, interspersed with organ and choir music.

Then Mike delivered a brief sermon, recalling that Succoth was really founded on an ancient harvest festival, perhaps derived from pagan times. And in Palestine today, even in the collective farms, the kibbutzim that were imagined to be so irreligious, these ancient agricultural customs were being revived, almost literally dug up—he smiled—through the passion of the settlers for archaeology. Thus renewed, for instance, was a Succoth ceremonial procession of maidens pouring out water from jars, libations, an invitation for the rainy season to begin.

"Mike had his sermon written out, but he likes to pick up things at the last minute," Sue Kramer whispered to Mati.

The immigrant generation here in America used to festoon their tenement fire escapes with green branches, Mike said, and today their descendants, like himself, put fronds above an apartment balcony. Yet what did this holiday of dwelling in booths further signify? It was a leveling, a restoration of the entire Jewish people to a kind of simplicity and equality, not only recalling the poor shelters of the Exodus from Egypt, but reminding the people of the humble life, of closeness to nature and of produce provided by the Almighty. This was the festival's added importance for the Jews in today's industrial, commercial, citified society, where they desperately needed equalitarian reminders. And fortunately this closeness to the soil, coupled with equalitarianism, was being revived in the most natural way in the cooperative villages and kibbutzim, with the return to the soil in Palestine!

Mike had them rise again as he faced the Ark; one of the dignitaries—this was an honor just as in a shul—pulled open the carved panels, revealing the array of four or five Torahs with their dazzling silver breastplates and crowns. Another dignitary now lifted out the foremost scroll and held it while the first undid the covering and drew it off; the rabbi took hold of the bared parchment Torah by the lower handles and with his two arms raised it aloft.

"This is the Torah," Mike Kramer pronounced, first in Hebrew, then in English, "given by God to Moses on Mount Sinai."

It was all at once another place, another gathering of a multitude. A puzzling, wavelike feeling came over Mati. Moses holding aloft the stone tablets as he came down from the mountain. A moment somehow still existing on this platform in Hyde Park in Chicago. Why, this Mike Kramer was sincerely religious! A religious Jew. Mati kept gazing intently, half-comprehending.

And he himself? And his brothers and sisters, socialist freethinkers, were they, after all, still the same?

After the Torah was dressed again and returned to the Ark, the president of the congregation read a few announcements and invited everyone to the Succoth festival arranged by the young people's group in the social hall downstairs.

It was decorated like a barn dance, with colored electric-bulb lanterns on streamers across the hall, and dangling corncobs, and branches with autumn-red leaves festooning the walls. First came the one-act play of the drama club.

On the stage stood a crazy angular "tree" or signpost, constructed of sections of pipe covered with tinfoil, with rags in a hodgepodge of colors, representing leaves. Sticking out in all directions, including upward, were signs: TOKYO, 3,247 VERSTS, JOE'S DINER, 42 LEAGUES, VLADIVOSTOK, 12 LIGHT-YEARS, TEL AVIV, the infinity sign, TIMBUKTOO. And also MOSCOW—crossed out with a slash of red paint—and MAXWELL STREET, a real street sign swiped from the West Side. The setting was greeted with applause, and Myra, on the folding chair next to Mati, scrunched down, her fingers in his forearm, but a few enthusiasts kept calling out her name. Finally, to stop it all, she bobbed up and took a half bow.

Then there wandered onto the stage a straggling troop of itinerant players: the Tragedian, the Clown, the Heroine, the Ingenue —that was Dena, Mati saw. The costumes were again a triumph for Myra, made of newspapers, cardboard window posters as for Bayer's aspirin, and patchwork. The motley actors crowded around the signpost—alas, too far in every direction. Turned-out pockets, macabre gestures of hunger. Suddenly the Comedian snatched up something from the ground. A dollar! Disbelief! He showed it all around. Worship! The Comedian had the Almighty Dollar! The Leading Lady loved him. The Ingenue offered herself.

There she was, swirling in a patchwork skirt, half chanting her lines, and this time Mati noticed her voice, clear, yet warm, and just as her face had appeared to him as awaited, recognized, so was her voice. The playlet went on, there were pleadings of comradeship, claims for equal sharing, but the dollar finder became the boss, appointing porters for his tattered baggage roll and taking to himself both of the women—when suddenly there appeared a bandit with a gun, who seized the dollar and went off!

Everyone applauded Mike Kramer's clever choice of play, everyone helped fold and remove the chairs, a four-piece jazz combo took the stage, the actors came out, dressed, and Mati was watching for her. He'd first see if she went to some fellow, but Myra brought Dena over to him at once. "Ah, the sheikh from Tel Aviv," Dena repeated disappointingly, but he asked her to dance.

The instant his hand touched the small of her back Mati told himself he knew for certain. Why, what, how these things happened, who could tell? But everything you read, every movie you saw, told of the sudden, fated love. Her sheikh remark was forgotten; everybody at times made silly remarks. So airily, so conjoinedly her body moved with his, and she looked up into his face with an odd, questioning smile, as though questioning what was happening in herself, too.

The warmth of the large, spread hand came right through her crepe de chine; Dena felt as though her entire being lay within his grip. A Jewish word—Yiddish, but one called it Jewish—came to her: gedderim—her mother still sometimes used such expressions. All her gedderim, her inside organs, lay in that hand; it was a feeling such as you read about in the stories of D. H. Lawrence, which Myra Roth had lent her.

The Sheikh of Tel Aviv, as the kids had been calling him since that day he appeared here, did not press her to his belly the way Chicago Romeos did, then thrusting against you, so you had to pretend not to notice, while arching away your hips. Nor was his grip like their grabbing. Still, Dena felt all kinds of perturbing sensations. Then Mati's dancing was really like carrying her off, and she let go, unresisting. His feet were so fast he put in two steps for every one, and his energy was making her fly. Kids all around were noticing. Wow, what a dancer! Jack Sloan, who was in the play and had taken the habit of seeing her home, gave Dena a questioning, protective glance, and she gave him back a smile.

After Jack's turn it was Mati again, and now his exuberance broke into upkicks, it must be a step from over there in Palestine, she caught it, joined, then he and she were the center of attention, several girls were trying the kick, and then suddenly Mati swung free sidewards, keeping one arm around her waist while he caught onto Myra Roth, who was dancing with Jack Sloan, and before you knew it, a whole line was formed, a circle doing the upkicking step, with Mati whooping out some kind of Hebrew chant.

The band picked up the beat, the Rappaports, then Rabbi Mike and Sue were swept into the circle, and thus Mati Chaimovitch brought the hora to Chicago.

Mati was perhaps the first such ambassador, the predecessor of Israeli youth envoys who two decades later were to be found in every Jewish community. From the first day he was embarked on his mission, and soon it was as though he were living four lives in one. At the university itself he not only had his studies but the sense that he was on display, a Jew from Palestine; his accent, his dark complexion made his classmates curious, and some lingered on the walks to pick up conversations with him. Already from names called out in class, from the way certain ones bunched together, he had an idea maybe a fourth of the students were Jewish. Some, you couldn't tell, except certain ones who avoided his eyes, he kind of suspected. In his economics course the professor, after a witty lecture on Veblen's theory of conspicuous consumption, smilingly asked Mati how such a theory would hold in a Palestine collective, and Mati explained that you didn't even own your own clothes. This started quite a discussion, and after class two fellows asked him to drop in at their frat.

Only with the introductions did Mati realize that the fellows here were all Jewish. So it must be that the frats were segregated. Why hadn't they told him? The talk didn't go too well, especially since in explaining about Zionism, he told them the story of Theodor Herzl and his exclusive fraternity—first having to explain for most of them who Herzl was. He told of the time Herzl resigned from his honor fraternity in Vienna because it sponsored a public meeting where a speaker made an anti-Semitic speech. Most of the fellows seemed ill at ease, and only one of them turned up at the study group he had started at the temple.

There things were going better. He told the kids how almost the first person he met in America, his own cousin, turned out to be hiding the fact that he was a Jew. Mati gave them an hilarious account of the date with the two Irish broads and how when his cousin told him they were going to a speakeasy, he thought it meant a place where you had to whisper, only when he got inside, there was so much noise you had to shout. This brought a big laugh, and he had them eating out of his hand. They decided that for each meeting a different member would make a report on some subject of Jewish culture or history, and that fraternity member took on the subject of Theodor Herzl.

Outside of the classes at the temple Mati had those on the West Side, with the long el ride twice a week, but at least out there he had an actual Zionist youth group studying Hebrew. A couple of the girls gave him inviting hints, but Mati had made up his mind, nothing doing; if he started fooling around in his group, all kinds of complications and even jealousies would begin, and besides, he already knew the one he really wanted; he couldn't get her out of his mind.

❦ ❦ ❦

Sometimes Dena felt she had all this Jew stuff up to her ears. Still, she went to his study group, maybe just to keep off the other girls. The report on Theodor Herzl by the Zeta Beta Tau boy with thick glasses was surprisingly interesting. Herzl, it turned out, wasn't just a Jew with a black beard, but a star reporter for a big Vienna newspaper, a playwright and a part of the literati, somethink like Ben Hecht on the Chicago *Daily News*.

To her folks, Dena at first let on, about Mati, that it was just another fellow dating her—the fellow from Palestine, imagine! When he came to pick her up to take her to a movie, her mother gave Mati a good looking over. So black! she said to her husband, when Kossoff came upstairs from his evening hours in the store.

In the southern Ukraine where this boy's family comes from, Sam informed her, it was hot there, and people were very dark-complected. Also in Palestine this boy's family settled in the Jordan Valley, where it was very hot, Sam said. How did he already know so much about the young man? Never mind, Sam said. Around the temple. This Mati had been born and raised there in the Jordan Valley, and doubtless that was why he was so dark. After all, people spent fortunes to go to Florida and didn't get such a tan.

Bessie stared at her husband, set his coffee on the table, and sat down with him. So this was why Sam was going regularly to Friday services all of a sudden?

Sam shrugged. The rabbi had told him a few things. An interesting boy, all alone from Palestine, working his way through the university.

In Palestine, in those communes, those chalutzim were used to free-and-easy ways, Bessie said. Free love. And here the young people were going wild, too. A girl Dena's age could be carried away; the girls went so far now, it was dangerous. Even good Jewish girls. The things they read. Bessie flushed before her own husband.

Sam shrugged. At least Dena wasn't going with a shagetz. They were lucky she hadn't got stuck on some football player at Hyde Park High.

Dena had such a good chance with a fellow like Jack Sloan that she met at the play at the temple, Bessie sighed. The Sloans, an old Kenwood family, the best. What was the use of the whole thing, moving here, paying a fortune to join their temple, if Dena was going to throw her chances away for some farmer from Palestine?

Wait, wait, she is only a high school kid, Sam admonished. "She only went with him to the movies to see Constance Talmadge."

His wife snorted. "A lot you know."

It went rapidly, an established thing that she was his Saturday night date, that they were going steady. Soon enough they came to the limits. The cuddling in the movies, the slow, long kisses in the hallway before Dena made herself stop and ran upstairs, then came halfway down for a last one, just sweet, not hot. Or the necking on the couch after her parents had retired but with her kid brother, Vic, not yet home and her ear open for his key in the door; Mati's hand, the large, warm hand cupping her breast and then even going so far as slipping inside her chemise, the strange dangerous trance, and she must make herself lift the hand away.

The dates, intimate enough now for her to discuss the little money he had and for Mati to accept that she had two tickets for the symphony anyway already paid for.

Even if they got engaged, what was his intention in life? What was her intention? To go back with him there and live in Palestine? Mati's life absolutely was there, and what would she be? Dena did not feel herself such a Jewish patriot, such a pioneer.

There life means something, Mati tried to convince her, and true, she admired all that his family had done when he told her those heroic stories; she was intellectually by conviction, Dena said, in favor of Palestine, of a Jewish homeland, but the urge to go there and be part of it, spend her life there, simply did not arise in her. "I guess I'm not the pioneer type, I'm a city girl."

But Tel Aviv was a city, she'd see! Already in Tel Aviv there were schoolchildren who had never seen a cow and were brought in groups to visit his sister Leah's farmyard. Already paved streets reached as far as Leah's place which had once been a sand dune! Already, Dena twitted him, Tel Aviv has plans for a subway! But seriously, Mati said, why had a famous, important man like Dr. Judah Magnes left America to head the university in Jerusalem? Mati didn't himself yet know exactly what he wanted to do, but where else was there a whole new world with everything yet to be built—"and our own!"

The entire first year went by.

To go home for the summer would take too long and cost too much; Mati decided to get summer credits so as to finish college faster. Dena was graduated from high school and next fall would be at the university. She went to the summer place her brother Phil had rented in Charlevoix, right there among the Loebs and the Rosenwalds and the Strauses.

Maybe after the summer separation it would all be over; things happened like that.

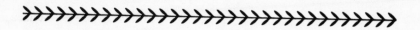

4

IN FALL they rushed together again with such longing that Dena almost, almost on their first reunion cried, "Oh, take me to your room!" And really now that she too was on campus, if he asked her, one afternoon, would she go?

And at the university, although Myra was a year ahead of Dena, they became veritable girl chums. Maybe she was really a climber and a snob, Dena asked herself, but one thing that really drew them together was Dena's awakening passion for modern art. Myra was like a teacher for her in that and in other sophisticated things. There were moments as in the Moderns Room at the Art Institute when they stood wordless before Seurat's "Un Dimanche à la Grand Jatte" and shared the same awe. "Imagine it hanging here in Chicago," Dena said, and Myra told her that one of the first great modern art collections was made by a Chicago steel king, a friend of her uncle Sylvan Straus; they never bid against each other.

On a Saturday afternoon Dena got Mati to come with them, and they stopped in front of the big Chagall. The painting faced you right at the top of the main stairway, a real Jew in full regalia, tallis and tefillin, and at first Mati didn't care for it; the picture reminded him too much of the Jews of Mea Shearim, and if this was great art, what was so different in it from Mike Kramer's painting by Boris Schatz that they all sneered at, the bearded prophet with the arm outstretched? Ah, but it wasn't because of the Jewish subject, Myra explained to him; even Rembrandt had painted rabbis. Now just look at Chagall's wonderful design, the way the stripes of the tallis were used!

※ ※ ※

For several years after that awful tragedy of her cousin Artie, Myra Roth couldn't face anybody. During that time she had even changed her name. Her father was a Straus, but as her parents were divorced and he was remarried to some waitress in San Francisco, Myra had taken her mother's name, Roth, and gone downstate to the University of Illinois. Only even there it didn't stop, the case was so notorious, and kids kept getting her mixed up with another Myra, Myra Seligman, the one Artie had dated and who had been a witness in the trial. So she had a nervous breakdown. Her mother had remarried and lived in Philadelphia, and anyway Myra couldn't bear her stepfather, another philistine who couldn't tell a Leonardo from a Picasso, her mother really could pick them. So now she stayed here with her uncle, who had the penthouse of the Del Prado and gave Myra her own little apartment on a lower floor. She had a crush on her uncle Sylvan, of course, she would say to Dena with her blurt-laugh, but it was normal, he was her father substitute, and as he knew all about Freudianism, he would joke with her; according to Freud, her crush was a natural transfer of her Oedipus complex, which meant girls secretly wanted to sleep with their fathers just as boys wanted to do it with their mothers. Last summer Myra had gone to Mexico with Sylvan and his wife, Jocelyn, his third, a McCormick, who had insisted on being converted when they married. This kind of thing ran in the family— Artie's mother had been a converted gentile, too. In Mexico her uncle had bought exquisite pre-Columbian sculptures, and the three of them had spent a weekend at Diego Rivera's. Sylvan Straus had bought a great revolutionary painting for his collection, a peasant being lashed by an overlord on a rearing horse. And then Myra had confided something else to Dena. Everybody knew the great painter was a collector in his own way—of young girls. And that was when Myra had decided to take the jump. He was awfully fat but really fascinating, and also she had done it hoping to get over the whole thing about Artie Straus. Oh, it had been kind of messy, but at least her virginity was over with. And she stared at Dena with those melancholy eyes.

She had Dena bring Mati to the apartment. What a place with its stunning high view of the lake, it must cost a fortune, Mati said to Dena while Myra prepared them highballs with real scotch whiskey that her uncle had slipped in from a trip abroad. She showed them her own start of a collection, small things, a drawing by Matisse, at least this name Mati already knew, and pinkish watercolors Dena knew—Marie Laurencin! she cried. And wait! She too had brought back a pre-Columbian sculpture, Myra said with her blurt-laugh as she brought out from beside her bed table a small clay figure with a huge phallus standing erect as high as his head. Dena couldn't control her blush; Mati saw it and loved her. Then Myra played them jazz records by a Negro singer from Twenty-second Street, Bessie Smith, she said, as though they would surely know, "Empty Bed Blues." The words of the song had all kinds of double meanings, like grease my griddle, which Myra explained to Mati with gestures.

But despite all her sexy showing off, Dena later told Mati, Myra was really very sensitive and troubled, and in fact, Dena wasn't even sure if she should believe the story about Diego Rivera. One of Myra's worst troubles was a terrible complex about her nose, didn't he notice she was always making jokes about her schnozz, like Jimmy Durante, a famous nightclub comedian with a big nose? Poor kid, Mati had to laugh, it was a real hook nose, poor kid.

Then—imagine—someone loved her nose! Or claimed he did. A young sculptor Myra had met during that year at the University of Illinois—now she ran into him, Joe Freedman. He wanted to do her head. What he claimed to be crazy about, Myra told Dena, was the classic curve of her schnozz, but then this Joe had some bug about being Jewish, he ought to meet Mati, and she showed Dena a magazine, *The Menorah Journal*, with photos of some West Side types Joe Freedman had done; it was a highbrow Jewish magazine started by some group in Harvard. Naturally, when she came to pose, Myra related, it turned out what Joe really wanted was not only the head but the bust, and so she was sitting bare-bosomed for him. But still Joe kept on about the aristocratic El Greco curve of her proboscis, the bastard; she was sure he was playing her along so her uncle would buy the damn sculpture.

Still, Dena could see it was good for Myra; she was falling for this fellow. Myra herself said she was one of those women who would always be attracted to artists. Joe's studio was in that little row of old wooden stores facing Jackson Park built at the turn of the century for the Chicago World's Fair. There was even a novel about that art colony, very risqué, by Floyd Dell; she gave it to

Dena to read. The moral was the only way to find out if it was really love was to go to bed.

She hadn't done it yet with Joe, Myra said, he was carrying a torch for some little West Side virgin; Joe couldn't get over her just as Myra couldn't get over Artie Straus. Anyway, the bastard had too many girls; right now he had a poetess-painter, very handy as she lived in the studio row, just a few doors away, a notorious slut named Andrea, who was still on campus and had slept with the whole English Department.

But a few days later Myra confided to Dena it was already on with Joe. After the sitting he had simply walked into the alcove when she was getting dressed and shed his overalls. Joe was the fastest undresser you could imagine. And now Myra knew that what had happened in Mexico was nothing, not the real thing at all.

When the bust was done, her uncle Sylvan agreed Joe Freedman was genuinely talented, even if he had not yet settled on a style of his own. Sylvan Straus bought the sculpture and had it cast in stainless steel as Joe wanted.

Dena and Mati had to come to Joe's Saturday night studio party—it would be the real thing, Myra promised, with jugs of dago red.

The main thing that happened at the wild studio party was a big discussion about Jewish art, was there or wasn't there? He'd never get away from the Jewish question, Mati joked to Dena, until he went home to Eretz!

The bust, highly polished, sleek and pure, was on a stand in the center, the head poised birdlike on a long, slightly arched neck— Joe Freedman had caught a characteristic way Myra had of tilting her face. And in this uptilt the arch of her nose somehow flowed into the throat curve so that the nosetip she so hated was only part of the line. "Something of Brancusi, something of Modigliani"— the knowing words floated around. There were no shoulders; the throat rose from pure half spheres, just above the nipples.

"The Jewish Nefertiti," a sophisticate punned, and the party was a success.

All the year, Mati realized, outside of the grind at the university he had been enclosed in a fully organized Jewish world, the classes at the temple, the Zionist youth group on the West Side. But this party was a mixed crowd. From the names he couldn't always tell if someone was Jewish or not; he guessed more than half were. The talk was a jumble of art gossip and half-highbrow gab. There were university people, a few writers, and neighbor artists from the colony, including a poetess-painter, a girl who had already been pointed out to him on campus, very lush, with a full red mouth that didn't look like lipstick; she was said to be the mistress of a professor. She too had a studio along the row here, her name was Andrea, and from her easy way in the place, coming around with the wine jug, it was almost as though this were her place, too, but of course it was a kind of art colony, free and easy, he supposed. There was even a tall beautiful Negro girl who had just come back from a Rosenwald Foundation fellowship in Haiti and was writing a thesis on voodoo dances.

Around the studio were things Joe Freedman had done, a whole set of football players, like an American Parthenon, Myra said. Also there were the West Side figurines that had been in *The Menorah Journal*, a delicatessen man behind his counter, a socialist street-corner orator on a soapbox. Joe Freedman himself looked unexpectedly mild; he had one eye cocked as though always inquiring. Right away—what about Palestine art? He fished out the latest *Menorah Journal*, with photos of work by new artists there. The painter Reuven Rubin Mati knew of; a sculptress named Hannah Orlov he didn't know about. She was very good, Joe said; she had had an exhibition in Paris. And there was another sculptor—he showed Mati a full-page photo, a block of marble, cleft in the middle as though struck by a great force. "Proposed Memorial for Tel Hai. Local marble," it said. Why, it was by Yosi the Sculptor, Leah's friend in Jerusalem. And before he knew it Mati was telling about his sister Leah's crazy adventure in the war when she had to get a secret relief shipment of British gold out of a sealed safe in Jerusalem before the Turks identified it, and how Yosi had duplicated the seal; the gold had been smuggled in by the Nili spies—and he had to explain who *they* were— these people had no idea what heroic things went on during the war in Palestine! More and more of a group was forming around him, fascinated, and he could feel Dena's pride as he held all these bright, sophisticated people with his tales. He got back to Yosi the Sculptor and told how Yosi started the idea of abstract monuments in Eretz because especially in Jerusalem with the Orthodox, regular human monuments wouldn't be allowed. So then he had to explain about the monument for Tel Hai, the battle to hold the hill, otherwise that entire upper Galilee area might not be part of the Yishuv today—and all this led to the story of Captain Trumpeldor, the first Jewish fighting hero, who came to Palestine from the Russian army where he had fought on, after he lost an arm at Port Arthur, and then how Trumpeldor organized the Zion Mule Corps that fought at Gallipoli, the first fighting Jewish unit since Bar Kochba. Almost, Mati had to explain who Bar Kochba was. They kept asking questions, especially that poetess, Andrea, and also the beautiful Negress, the dancer. He told how his older brother, Gidon, had been in the Zion Mule Corps and the Jewish Legion, and right after the war his younger sister Yaffaleh had fought and died with Trumpeldor to hold Tel Hai, and therefore the monument.

"Local marble," Joe Freedman repeated. Was there marble in Palestine then?

Sure, right there on the mountain behind Tel Hai, in the kibbutz of Kfar Giladi, they were quarrying marble.

"Hey!" Joe said. He'd have to come over and have a look.

"Sure, come on over," Mati said. "All the marble you want."

But the people had drifted to another cluster. He caught a whole psychological conversation. It was low-voiced, about Myra's cousin in that famous murder case. The psychologist, a gnomish, half-bald fellow named Weiss, had done some of the mental tests for the trial. A classic case of Jewish self-hatred, he expounded. What was that? It was the syndrome long ago analyzed by old master Freud himself, Weiss said: A Jew hates himself for hating being a Jew because of the trouble it brings him. And plunging glibly into his exposition of the case, he declared that the victim, the little Jewish boy, really represented the killers themselves. And what they had done, the mutilation of the organ, was like a super-circumcision, a castration, a violent rejection of being Jewish. Several of the crowd again drifted on, they'd heard it before, but Weiss persisted with Mati. Since Mati was from Palestine, was the self-hatred syndrome noticeable there? "Exactly the opposite!" Mati laughed and felt Dena squeeze his hand.

Myra was approaching with the wine jug, and they changed the subject, art again, names flew, Chagall, Soutine, Modigliani, Pascin. Ah, they were all Jewish artists, but was there a Jewish art?

And they were at it again. Art was a function of religion, a pipe smoker said. Look at Russia—after the icons, nothing!

What about African sculpture? the beautiful Negro dancer injected. All the moderns were influenced by it!

Since Moses had pronounced a taboo, the pipe smoker said, the Jews had no art tradition. It was significant—he turned on Mati—that the archaeological digs in Palestine turned up Roman and Greek statues, even Canaanite household images, but nothing of the Hebrews.

All this art art art stuff sometimes annoyed Mati, as though it were more important to produce art than to build the land. Look at Abraham, he cried; his father was a sculptor, he made idols, and Abraham smashed them all! Maybe he was the first art critic!

Dena squeezed his hand again; she'd never known he could be so clever.

During the laughter a different-looking couple had entered the studio, older, distinguished, the man with that carefully barbered look, a silver mustache, the woman with an English-style aristocratic nonsnobbery. Myra's uncle Sylvan Straus with his wife. Straus had the nose, Dena whispered, but in a man it looked aristocratic.

Myra started to introduce them, but her uncle waved his hand lightly with a smile that said he didn't want to interrupt the discussion. It went on for a bit, and then Sylvan Straus spoke. The whole Jewish movement, he declared, was coming too late in world history. All the folk cultures, African art—with a smile to the beautiful Negro dancer-sociologist—Chinese art, Italian art, iconography, all this, usually connected with religion, had completed itself, just as religion had exhausted itself though hundreds of millions of adherents weren't aware of it. The entire trend of modernity was toward the international form, in art as in politics. An international style, abstraction, would prepare the way for a shedding of national and even of religious differences. This was what was wanted, rather than a return to parochialism and nationalism, the source of wars.

He was still smiling; somehow, not only because he was Sylvan Straus the millionaire collector, but because of his personality itself, with the certainty and finality presented in that tolerant smile, the issue was over.

Mati had heard so much about this powerful Jew. What was he? A pillar of the temple, oddly enough, and yet a sophisticate, always avant-garde. These words on antinationalism had seemed to

Mati smilingly pointed at himself. Thus, Straus was probably anti-Zionist, yet you felt also that he was like some kind of experimenter who out of sheer curiosity touches everything, every substance, every form of growth, to see what will come out.

The art patron wasn't at all patronizing; he and his wife couldn't have been more democratic and charming. Yet the party now seemed a bit subdued.

※ ※ ※

In his West Side group there were some real good ones, several already planning for a training group on a farm, next summer, and among them was at least one girl who showed she was gone on him, a pretty kid with a moonlike Russian face and long braids reminding him of Zippie. The girl had already changed her name from Clara to Chava, and somehow in her eyes, in an intimacy in her voice when the group discussed the freedom of women in the chalutz movement, there was a personal message to him, a readiness. Why didn't he take up with her and put an end to his unending tormenting physical need?

Chava had a way of bringing him special bits of Jewish news as though this were something personal between them; she brought him every tale of an anti-Semitic incident, of a medical school that had kept out an all-A student named Rabinowitz and accepted a B-minus applicant from the same high school, named Kelly. Also, she brought every item of Jewish triumph, every Jew who won an award somewhere, even Barney Ross, the prizefighter, as though all this made a special, an almost secret bond between them. Why didn't he fall for someone like her instead of Dena?

A few times, walking home after a date with Dena, trying to walk off his bursting urge, yet not blaming her, telling himself for a girl it was really different, holding down an impulse to phone Chava, Mati circled out of the way to his room and passed the storefront studios, glancing at a certain one. Once through the half-curtained store window he saw a dim light; the poetess was moving about—and was there someone else there?

Another time, in winter—it was a Saturday night, when for perhaps a whole hour after a movie they had lain locked in caresses on the living-room couch until at last Dena had shaken herself out of the sensual daze and cried, no, no, she mustn't torture him like this, he must go home—Mati had walked in the snow directly to the store studio, made out a flicker of light far in back and crazily pulled a little latch that made a cowbell jingle inside. He had just started away when he heard her at the door. Who was it? Suddenly overwhelmed by the absurdity of himself—she must have someone there with her, Saturday night, a girl like Andrea—Mati didn't answer, but she had switched on a lamp, her face peered against the frosted pane, and she opened the door. "Why, hello."

"I was just passing by," Mati mumbled.

"Why, come on in out of the snow!" There was a flicker perhaps of mockery in her half whisper.

Nor would Andrea have imagined it would be a first time, a male virgin. She, too, had heard all the tales about free love in those Jewish communes in Palestine, as in the Soviet Union. Yet here the boy was, awkwardly making a bit of conversation—he hoped he hadn't waked her, no, some friends had just gone—then suddenly seizing her, kissing blindly. Like a newborn babe blindly groping for the breast.

She let it happen in all his awkward impetuosity, there on her afghan before the glowing iron stove, curling her fingers tight in his hair, almost saying a new poem to herself as it happened.

Andrea's eyes were wide open to his. How should he have known of this transfiguration that took place, of this ineffable beauty on a woman's face in the act of love, altogether different, even in a woman who was beautiful anyway.

Then a whole tumult of doubts and sensations of betrayal came upon him; this that he had so needed, had he spoiled himself for the destined one? Like a ghost image beyond the edge of his perception, Dena seemed there, turning away in hurt, in sorrow. And Zippie was suddenly present, furious.

And then as she, as Andrea stroked his back, with one finger tracing his spine, uttering a throaty delight at his little shivers of response, her fingertip came on the rough line of skin, the cicatrix from his childhood.

"What's that?"

Mati shrugged. "A fight I had when I was a kid. An Arab kid cut me with his shabria."

"Shabria?"

"A little dagger they have."

On her knees, straddled over him, Andrea studied the old

wound mark. "Why, I wonder it didn't kill you." Then the mischief came back into her voice. "Or paralyze you down there!"

Did a girl know when it was the first time? She put her soft, wide lips to the scar. Mati had never felt anything there, the skin was thick and hard, but first her finger touch had brought a faint throb, pleasurable, with far inside a slight echo of hurt, and now her mouth made the whole wound pulse. Like his organ, swollen hard again.

She had him tell her the whole story. The fight in the field— Mati belittled it, "That's how a lot of those Arab things get started." Squabbles. Or testing how far they could encroach; you had to stand firm.

He had never known, even from fellows who bragged, that it came back so quickly. This time the sensation of unfaithfulness, of a betrayal, wasn't there. Then from the joy, the gratitude, a word kept pressing for utterance; he had never said it even to Dena. Mati said, "I love you." Andrea hushed it with her mouth on his lips almost as though saying it was bad magic.

Watching her from the bed in the rear of the store as she moved about preparing his breakfast—theirs, but really his, a woman for a man—Mati brushed away a wild self-accusation: Adam and Eve hiding from the face of God. He ought to laugh at his crazy guiltiness. Even if Dena sensed, saw this on him. How long could she expect a man to— And a sly, unwanted thought: this might even make Dena want to. Oh, the hell. Maybe Reuven and Leah could hold themselves back all their young years, but the hell. Here he was. This girl, this young woman moving about only in her slip, cheerful, humming, with the streak of pale winter light coming through—

When Andrea brought the glasses of orange juice and sat with him, Mati talked of the oranges at home; then presently he was telling her about his sister Yaffaleh, who had written poems, about poor Yaffaleh's worry that she was ugly, and to himself Mati wondered whether in those last days up in Tel Hai with so few girls there, someone had perhaps loved Yaffaleh, and whether if the thing happened, whether even Yaffaleh's heavy face had in some way become transfigured and beautiful. There returned to his mind the last little poem, found after her death, about a squat, dark hut seen in the distance, and then suddenly a lamp was lit inside and all was changed. Andrea made him repeat the meaning of each Hebrew word, and then she wrote down a translation. For a moment Mati wondered if there was indeed some mysterious cosmic determinant through the sexual pull itself that drew the destined ones together from far places and had brought him here. But then why did he still feel guilty about Dena?

And also he saw his big sister Leah's glowing face, as she must have been during love with her Moshe, and Mati thought of how Leah had gone back to Russia into the Revolution itself to find him. And only then Leah had sadly discovered that sex had not been the true sign after all and that Moshe was a different man from the one she had carried all these years within herself. Maybe if you got past the sex need, you could judge better. Would this release—at last—of his physical need even help him know, understand, whether he was truly in love with Dena?

Or was this joy in this back room, this delight in watching Andrea as she moved about so womanly, was this other than merely sex? And also, with her, there was this peculiar feeling of being free, this feeling that he was not bound to her. Was that perhaps not only because she had had other men, but because Andrea wasn't Jewish? Did some absolute, some ancient understanding still hold fast in him? Suppose he had tumbled into bed last night with a Jewish girl, with Chava—oh, God, no! he'd never have got out of it!

And anyway, for Andrea, wasn't he just one more lay? A poetess, a bohemian, with a campus reputation for being easy.

He was just a yokel from Palestine, taking too seriously the favor of a good-natured, free-loving modern girl.

But how was it that on a Saturday night he had found Andrea all alone?

Maybe she wasn't so easy and promiscuous; maybe those stories were only gossip.

Now, back in bed, Andrea said that certain things about her she wanted him to know, as though this were his due. Yes, she knew all kinds of stories were around. It was true she had had an affair with Professor Haber; with a tender little laugh she said it was really a fact that he picked a girl from his class each semester, but she could brag that her affair had lasted over three whole terms!

Andrea came from a small town in Kansas; her father worked for the county office, a clerk. Her first time—she laughed—naturally had to have been with the high school football star. "But honest, I'm not a slut, Mati." There had been only that boy at home, and here, the professor. And lately for a few months Joe Freedman. Then, after a pause, well, to be strictly honest, maybe one or two one-night affairs when she had been drinking. And a young Mexican artist, but he was like Pan. Like—sheer nature. And her large gray eyes looked into Mati's. "Oh, I'm awful, I guess." They wallowed.

A sense of eons ago came over Mati. Samson and his shiksehs. The Philistine girls. Another kind of people altogether. Fornicators. Could a Jew really take it so lightly?

In the quietest, most intimate way, peering into his eyes, Andrea said, "Last night I was the first for you, wasn't I? . . . Oh, I only wish I too—" And he saw she was crying, just a little, a tear that she rubbed out against his shoulder.

Those first weeks were a ceaseless wallow, as though he must catch up for all his young years of repression, erase all those nasty times with his hand. Mati sat through his classes in a state of sexual satiety that did not actually dull or lull him, but somehow evened everything out so that he was less likely to jump up with arguments.

Mornings he went circuitously on campus, avoiding the buildings and the paths where he might encounter Dena. As though he must reek of sex and she would instantly smell it on him. And partly out of fear that when he set eyes on her, he himself would have changed and would no longer feel that instant wondrous gladdening.

Yet, over several dates she did not seem to know what had happened, and how was it that in his kisses with her, nothing was changed in him? The moment he was with her he was lost again in that powerful, almost doomed sense of the One, the fated, the bashert. And when he petted with her now, it was with a man's real knowledge, so that the limit was more than ever unbearable. Perhaps if once he made love with Dena, the whole thing with Andrea would vanish. Yet Mati would go from the drawn-out petting with Dena to Andrea, and he was puzzled, even ashamed, at how the changeover in him could take place at once, so that it was simply as though he had come home to his woman.

※ ※ ※

"Jewish princess," but we must see her in those early years as she began to emerge from the flat above her father's jewelry store; she walked on every campus with her small dark head held erect, the wing points of her glossy hair against each cheek; all the world could see that a Jewish girl held her value high. That Jewish girls didn't.

The prettiest, the smartest, Dena had always been. All A's.

It was Myra who must bring her the campus gossip about her sheikh and the poetess.

In the numbness one need pervaded Dena, to have a good look at him with his paramour. That slut. And so she loitered once, where he would come out of an anthropology class that she knew the poetess too attended. And as the pair of them walked on a path together, Dena strolled by and said, "Hello, Mati," and gave Andrea a good look.

Hardly adroit at such things, Mati mumbled an introduction. But they had already met at Joe Freedman's studio party, Dena said; she added some trivial remark and walked on like a queen.

Sometimes she felt like just getting herself devirginized by the next fellow that made a pass at her. Some big blond dope from Nebraska. Or like Myra, she'd flit from one to another. Or even like Andrea. Maybe with that Mexican Alfredo.

No, she wouldn't give way. And how miserable Myra was.

When Mati had the gall to phone about Saturday night, she said she would be busy; then when he even phoned a second time and asked—could she detect a quaver—what was wrong? Dena calmly said, "You know what's wrong." When occasionally their paths crossed on campus, she smiled, aloof, her head held high, especially if girls she knew were nearby.

One more thing Dena did. She had to see where it happened, and so once in the noon hour she took a walk to Jackson Park and went slowly past that row of storefront studios. As though looking at the art on display, she paused at each window and thus came to one with Andrea's name scrawled under streaks of abstract color. The painting was really bad, Dena told herself, honestly. Over the frame she could get an idea of the interior, a Mexican rug with throw pillows, very bohemian; maybe they did it right there on the rug. The usual partition to the rear, that must be where they slept together when he stayed over. She steeled her heart, as she told herself, and really felt nothing, not even the impulse to give herself to the first fellow who tried, or maybe drop in on Joe Freedman as Myra had split up with him. Dena continued walking, looking with interest at the paintings and wood carvings in the remaining storefronts in the opposite direction from Joe's.

Once, at the temple, Mati looked in on a rehearsal of the theater group; they were doing a play by Noel Coward. Dena wasn't there. He found himself listening for a dropped word of her, just the sound of her name.

In a big snow early Sunday he and Andrea ran into the deserted park and tumbled in the drifts, stuffed snow into each other's mouths, and suddenly she opened her raccoon coat and was naked inside. Under white-branched bushes they tumbled; luckily no one followed their foot marks in the snow! In her studio they toweled each other and lay on the mat before the stove and she read him poems by Carl Sandburg and Edna St. Vincent Millay, and then a verse of her own that had been printed in *Poetry* magazine: "Who is he/Who am I/We come together/Why/Of all the myriads/Earth and sky/Why he and I?"

Then Mati translated a famous song by the poetess Rahel, about her life alongside the Kinneret, "Perhaps I only dreamed a dream," and Andrea insisted on learning the words in Hebrew.

One evening Andrea had a poetry-reading circle in her place, mostly friends from the U, and when people were leaving, Mati was about to put on his overcoat; of course, after he went out, he would slip back, but Andrea put her hand on his shoulder, and one by one the visitors said "So long" to them as to an established couple.

Surely Dena must know it was already like this.

One wallowing night when Andrea cried out, "Oh! You're the best!" a snicker slipped out of him, "You ought to know!" and astonished, Mati felt his face slapped. Then Andrea was sitting on the edge of the bed crying. "All right, I'm a bitch." Then: "Why the hell doesn't she go to bed with you? Jewish girls don't! Jewish girls don't! We're your whores for them! Well, I can tell you a few who do, so you can go get a Jewish broad for your lay!" She jumped off the bed and got a drink. That was another thing about the goyim. Even the women.

For his twenty-first birthday there was a cable from Leah and the whole family; imagine their spending the money. Andrea made a candlelit dinner for the two of them, and on his plate lay her gift, with his name on the wrapping in Hebrew letters she herself had drawn. Inside was a beautiful edition of the Song of Songs printed in Hebrew in Jerusalem, with tinted engravings by the Bezalel artist Lilien, and she had inscribed it, "My beloved is mine, and I am his, he feedeth among the lilies."

And that night in the sweet trough of exhaustion her voice crept in. "Oh, Mati, take me there with you. Marry me and take me there."

It had broken out of her, but in the morning they didn't speak of it, letting it pass as a sort of love cry, no more. But it came back to Mati through the day. He put it off, far off; after all, he was only a college student, with at least two years to go, and who could tell how many girls he would have and break up with during that time? But suppose this didn't break up, suppose he stayed with Andrea? Did he believe in marrying only a Jew? Here in the Diaspora he could see how by intermarriage Jews could get assimilated, lost, but of course in the Yishuv it was the other way around. Look at the Book of Ruth.

Yet the question kept on working in him so that in an odd way he felt ashamed toward Andrea. Wasn't he really only using her for his lay, while in his heart something altogether resisted, banned the idea that he could marry her and bring her there? Wasn't it reactionary, atavistic to feel such laws of blood? No, he argued to himself, it was the thought of her, how would she fit in, wouldn't she feel like a stranger all her life, especially in the one place where Jews were trying to become entirely themselves?

In his temple group they had to have the old intermarriage question. Rabbi Mike dropped in for it, and brought Myra, too. For himself, Mike said, as they knew, he performed marriages for mixed couples only if the non-Jewish partner converted. It didn't have to be a ritual conversion in the full Orthodox manner, mikveh and all if it was the girl, and as for circumcision for the man, luckily in these times most gentile boys were circumcised anyway—"We seem to have convinced them it's good for the health." The listeners released themselves in mirth. But, Mike resumed, he required that the conversion be more than a token. Even though—he grinned—he often wondered if the religion he preached was more than a mere token altogether. Nevertheless, the Christians could afford to lose part of their community; with Jews it was more serious. If you looked at such things in a statistical way, which he tried to avoid. But perhaps it would help to look at it through tradition; as with many complex questions, Jews provided examples on both sides.

"Moses had a gentile wife, the daughter of the priest of Midian," promptly put in a wavy-haired lad named Harris.

"Also a Kushite woman," Mati said, "from the earlier days when he was a prince of Egypt and went to war against the Ethiopians."

"The land of Kush, that means she was black," Harris proclaimed.

"Solomon and the Queen of Sheba," said one of the girls.

Suddenly Mati thought of his sister Shula and how she had nearly fallen for the German aviator. And all the tales of Jewish girls—was it something in women that yearned for the stranger, the unknown? But what about Andrea and himself?

"After all, with Solomon the many outside marriages were simply the usual form of diplomacy," Mike said. "And Moses had not been brought up as a Jew." But there were two very human stories included in the Bible that dealt with the subject of mixed alliances.

"Ruth," said one of the girls.

Indeed. The story of an Israelite who married a foreigner in her own land. When he died, still young, Ruth might have remained in Moab with her own family, but instead, she had uttered those beautiful words to her mother-in-law, "Thy God shall be my God," and followed her back to the Hebrew land and married again among the Jews. Why was this story in the Bible? Wasn't it to emphasize that outside women could be admitted into the Hebrew tribe?

Maybe it was to show the attraction of Jewish men! quipped the irrepressible Harris. Once she had had a Jew, Ruth couldn't imagine having any other kind! Joining the laughter, Rabbi Mike said, of course, Jewish men were supposed to be hot stuff, maybe they fostered the legend themselves, for obvious reasons, but—seriously —just as there were anti-Semites, Judeophobes, there were Judeophiles. "There are gentile girls who seem always to be drawn to Jewish men."

What about vice versa?

Of course, that, too, but—he laughed again with them—it was the Jewish men who seemed to have the big reputation.

"Oh, I don't know about that," drawled one of the girls, and it took some time for the guffaws to die down.

In his mind, Mati found himself casting over Andrea's past. The Kansas football player? And the professor? Well, the latest had been Joe Freedman.

Meanwhile, Mike was presenting the other side of the issue, equally Biblical, the story of Samson, as though placed there in counterpoise. In the same period, he pointed out, the time of the Judges, when tribal mores were becoming solidified. Just as the story of Ruth gave permission for intermarriage, the tale of Samson warned against going outside the tribe. Long before the Delilah part, the story told of Samson's infatuation for a Philistine village girl and how he pestered his parents until they consented to the marriage. And then the girl had betrayed him by giving away his secret riddle to her Philistine boyfriend, exactly as Delilah had later done, by giving away the secret of his strength. Thus, Samson's troubles and tragedy were put into the Bible as a dire warning against lusting after gentile girls!

Could Rabbi Mike be pointing this at him? Mati wondered. The way Myra had dropped in, too.

Now he himself was summing up: In the Yishuv in Palestine the intermarriage problem was scarcely a problem the way it was here, for Jews who came there were already strongly conscious of re-creating, of continuing the Jewish people. To the inevitable question about marriage with Arabs, he said it hardly ever happened, nobody he knew, oh, there was the odd case in the cities, some of the old Sephardi families in upper business circles, maybe in partnerships with Arabs, the Jewish girl would usually be absorbed then into the closed Arab world. The two kinds of society did not really mix. In the villages the Arab family clans were kept intact, oh, with marriages arranged between them, of course, even such rivals as the dominant clans of the Husseini and the Nashashibi had a good deal of intermarriage—and he had to stop and explain about the clans. But this had nothing to do with the Jews. Two separate forms of society. This did not mean Arab and Jewish hostility; Arabs and Jews got along quite well together as neighbors, but—particularly with the modern Zionist settlements—intermarriage was too rare to be considered a factor. Even among the most radical elements who on principle might advocate—oh, of course, there was always the rare case—How could he really explain to them? Impossible to explain to them how as a young boy, sometimes in the field the sight of Fawzi's young sister Fatima with her teasing, yet fearful glance, would bring on the impulse to tumble her, and you knew that in their strict rules the girl's

73

brother would be obliged to kill you and her too. The main thing, he said, to the Arabs, we are all Frenji—Franks they call us—Europeans, and to us they are mostly still not far from the desert.

In another month with classes over, he was thinking, the affair would break up of itself, he would be away, teaching at Horace Rappaport's summer camp, and when he came back, Andrea would probably have someone else.

Since it was in the same direction, Mati walked Myra home; she asked him to come up, she'd make coffee. The fingers clutched his arm. Mati still wasn't clear exactly what it meant, a girl late at night asking you to her place, but as they entered the apartment, she declared, "Mati, we're friends; between us there will always be friendship." Her eyes had that dark luster of intensity or pain.

"Yes, sure," he said, and suddenly she was pouring out her misery. Joe Freedman had taken up with that Negro dancer.

It was her nose, her goddamned Jewish nose, Myra was sure, though at the start Joe had said it was beautiful, it was Spanish, so she had even tried to find out if she came from Spanish Jews—oh, that bastard. "I was just a little Miss Richbitch; he only wanted to sell that damn bust to my uncle."

Drinking the highball, she let drop that she'd seen Dena at the symphony with Jack Sloan. Mati said nothing. A touch wickedly, Myra said, "How's the sex life?" and suddenly, sitting close to him: "Mati, you know what Dena told me; she said if I saw you to tell you just for your own sake—she said, tell him whatever he does, not to marry the girl."

Was it a call from Dena to come back? He almost had tears.

"Poor Mati," Myra said.

He didn't go to Andrea's but to his room. Oh, how he longed for home. There things seemed so healthy and simple, clean, without all this Jewish, not Jewish, Jewish.

Before he called Dena, he had to break it up with his goyetta. No matter how free his ideas, he still thought of her that way. In fun, in affection, Andrea even called herself his shikseh to him.

It was late afternoon with the sun coming through the back window, and she was in a loose smock at her easel. The whole sight as he opened the door was a splash of sun, and her face looked that way too, glowing and joyous to see him. Her hair was different; Mati rarely noticed such things, but this time saw she had a new haircut like a golden cap. "Mati! I sold a picture! A couple just walked in off the street, a darling old couple, and they bought a picture, fifty dollars!" She flung her arms around his neck and pulled him to the alcove. "Just fuck me!" She was on the bed, her smock open and her arms outstretched to him, laughing. "Mati! Today no complications! Just fuck me!"

How could he break it up?

5

THE RAPPAPORT camp was on a lakeside in Wisconsin, a new kind of Jewish summer camp. Most summer places were segregated anyway, so theirs, instead of having the usual scouting and Indian campfires, would have chalutz singsongs and be run like a kibbutz!

Right from the start Camp Eden proved a good paying proposition, with enthusiastic parents telling Horace and Celia how this had long been needed in the Chicago area. There was horseback riding with the counselors wearing keffiyehs, like the early watchmen of Palestine, in the Shomer. At the campfire—no, the kumsitz —Mati would tell tales of his brother-in-law Menahem, the Shomer, and how during the World War when the Turks were trying to arrest every member of the Shomer, Menahem had to hide in a cave, and each morning before dawn Mati himself, then just a kid, would bring a basket of food which Menahem would haul up on a rope.

The lake resounded with "Yahalili," and the barn dances with the stomping of "Am Yisroel Chai!" For assistant counselors, several of the members of Mati's West Side group had been hired, and romances were blossoming, especially a serious one between Malka Rabinowitz, daughter of a leader in the Cigar Makers Union, and a young fellow named David Margolies, who was preparing himself for Palestine by studying in the University of Wisconsin School of Agriculture.

Early in August Horace had even organized a weeklong convention of collegiate Menorah societies; there were now several in the Midwest, and the plot was to capture them for Zionism. For big things were going on in the Jewish world. Even some of the richest, most assimilated Jews in Europe and in America were beginning to help the Yishuv. Much of this Mati learned in letters from Menahem, who gave his explanation. It was because of the terrible unemployment among the Polish Jews, starving and desperate in the cities there. Since America had its new immigration laws, they couldn't get in because of the quota, and the settled Jews of England, France and Germany especially didn't want the Polish plague, so why not help them after all to go to Palestine? The worst of the crisis in the Yishuv had passed, and thousands of Polish Jewish workers were coming. And since large funds were needed to help them settle, Chaim Weizmann with his clever diplomacy had hit on a good formula for drawing in some of the big Jewish capitalists who had stayed out of the Zionist movement. Though Menahem was not a Weizmannite, he admitted that after all, Weizmann had succeeded in some of the things Herzl had been unable to do. Herzl had been unable to get a big government to stand behind Jewish settlement in Palestine, and yet Chaim Weizmann had carried it off with the British and their Balfour Declaration. Herzl had been unable to get the big magnates to invest in the Zionist enterprise, and now it looked as if Weizmann were pulling them in by the simple formula of calling them non-Zionists! The Jewish Agency for Palestine was about to be enlarged, divided half and half between official Zionists and official non-Zionists!

And here in the midst of the Menorah conference, while they were still conducting their endless debates on whether the proper thing was to concentrate on Jewish culture and history or to espouse activism, Rabbi Mike Kramer arrived, just back from the big Jewish Agency meeting in Switzerland, with glowing reports of everybody who had been there, Léon Blum, the socialist leader of France, Albert Einstein and the Warburgs, the Schiffs; vast new backing would become available!

Suddenly a youngster who had been listening to the radio—it was *Amos and Andy* time—came running into the hall. Massacres in Palestine!

Everyone rushed to the lounge, but the news flash was over. Other youngsters who had heard it came crowding, some in their pajamas. A slaughter of Jews. In an ancient city near Jerusalem. Hebron. Where the cave of Abraham was.

All crowded around the big radio. Dave Margolies tried various stations and got mostly baseball scores. Waiting through a commercial for a hair wash, they got an astrologer. Celia Rappaport kept trying to phone long distance to the *Chicago Tribune*, but the line was busy. Horace took the phone and tried several leading Chicago Zionists, but in the middle of August everyone was away. Impossible to know what had happened. Hebron had only a tiny Jewish community, Mati told them, from before Zionism; they had lived there for generations among the Arabs. A few storekeepers, and there was a noted yeshiva, because of the burial cave of the Patriarchs, the Machpelah. In fact, Rabbi Mike joined in, he himself only early this summer had visited the place when he had gone to Palestine before the great conference. A mosque stood over the cave, and the Moslems allowed you to go up only as far as the eleventh step. Yes, Mati had been on those stairs, on an excursion with a scout group. Could trouble have perhaps started, a collegian asked, because some Jew tried to mount a few steps higher? A flare-up of fanaticism?

Someone caught a news bulletin. Riots spreading in the Old City of Jerusalem. At the Wailing Wall.

Aha. It was becoming clear. For months, Mati told them, news from home had touched on the troubles at the Wailing Wall. The Mufti had worked up a whole fanatic dispute about a little portable screen brought to the passage in front of the wall, to separate women from men.

The Orthodox custom, Rabbi Mike explained. A mechitza, the separation was called. Yes, he had been to the Wall on this trip. He had heard about the dispute; the Arabs claimed the screen, or even bringing a chair there, was a violation of the status quo. The British had a few soldiers posted at the entrance to the alley before the Wall, where the Jews had prayed unimpeded for centuries.

Someone caught another bit of news. Scores of dead.

Impossible to sit and not know more. Rabbi Mike decided to drive into Chicago. Mati ran behind him to the car.

It was as though he were on the way not to Chicago, but *there*. What was happening at this instant? Dawn there. Was the trouble already as in 1921? To seize a club and run toward Jaffa! The wound in his back was pulsing. Mati's body seemed to be pressing its own energy into the vehicle, faster, as though the car must drive

78

straight through to Leah's place. Natan would know just what was going on, just where he might be needed.

Rabbi Mike speculated. The outbreak clearly was connected to the formation of the enlarged Jewish Agency. But then why hadn't the Arabs attacked new settlements instead of a yeshiva in Hebron?

"That they'd be scared of," Mati said. The image came to him of the bodies spread out in the hall of the Gymnasia, on the floor. Ashamedly he pushed away the thought that if there had to be dead, better a yeshiva bocher than a chalutz.

Two Jews in the middle of the night racing along Wisconsin roads to Chicago because something had happened over there in Palestine. In Hebron, in Jerusalem—with religious fanaticism the Mufti could always get things started.

"One thing never struck me as strongly as when I was there in Hebron," Mike said. "The Machpelah itself, a Jewish holy place, with a mosque built on top of it. And forbidden to us."

"And in Jerusalem?" Mati said. The Mosque of Omar, built over the altarstone of Abraham and Isaac. And also, no Jews allowed.

"Except for baksheesh," Mike said.

Had they made him say he was not a Jew?

"Do you really think I could say it?"

"Tourists—the guides know when not to ask." Mati added, "You know, the Moslems say it wasn't Isaac, but Ishmael on the rock." Mike actually hadn't known this; he was interested. "Sure. They have a special holiday, the Feast of the Sacrifice. The Mufti calls it the Feast of Ishmael."

It was strange to speculate, but sometimes he wondered if all the religious animosity, all of today's troubles, went all the way back to the old story of Ishmael. In their Koran it was as if Mohammed had twisted or badly remembered things from the Bible or changed them in some ways. The name of the son whom Abraham was leading to the sacrifice was not given there. So why not say Ishmael?

Could it even be that there had been a divergence in tradition itself, in tribal tales told in the desert, generations before they were written down?

It was Evanston before they could get an early edition of the *Tribune*. The main headline, RIOTS SPREAD IN PALESTINE. Only a few paragraphs from the Associated Press. The Old City of Jerusalem was said to be under control, with several dead. In Hebron, men, women, and children had been hacked to pieces by a Moslem mob. The day before, the mullahs had preached that Jews were placing bombs in the Mosque of Omar to blow it up. The Arab press declared that all the powerful Jews in the world had met in Zurich and secretly planned to destroy the Mosque of Omar and rebuild the Jewish Temple on the ancient site.

In a side column was a special dispatch. The British High Commissioner was out of Palestine, and even the Jerusalem commander had been out of the city. An unnamed leader of the secret Jewish defense force, the Haganah, claimed that British police had prevented his men from entering the Old City to protect its inhabitants. Arab mobs everywhere were shouting, "The government is with us!"

Like in 1905 in Russia, Rabbi Mike said, when police stood aside while pogromists shouted, "The Czar is with us!"

Staying at Mike's, but sleepless, Mati went out and walked. How terrible to be in the wrong place, as though lifted away from his life. His very muscles were pulling—he must get there at once. Yet it would take weeks, and right now the worst could be happening. Where were his brothers? Gidon in Herzlia—there at least the Haganah was strong. And at home in Mishkan Yaacov, Schmulik must be standing watch. The kibbutzim—Reuven's and Dvora and Menahem's—the Arabs wouldn't dare attack. But what of Tiberias? Shula and Nahum and their kids? True, Tiberias had always been peaceful. But so had Hebron. And Leah's meshek, with only girls and an Arab village just a mile away? Of course, Natan was there; extra men would surely have been sent—the Haganah headquarters was just down the beach.

Circling through Jackson Park, Mati passed the store studios, all dark; Andrea was in Kansas; Joe Freedman had gone to Paris. How alone and useless to be in this far American city. Would Dena be worrying for his family in Palestine?

Mati walked back to the lake, the dark, lapping waters, and though this was an inland sea in America, it was as though linked somehow by the waters of the earth to the seashore of Eretz.

Mike was asleep. Mati lay on the extra studio couch in little Joshua's room; the night air was oppressive, a saturated atmosphere tinged with a sulphurous acridity from the Gary steel mills. Such

80

spells came in summer in Chicago, reminding Mati of the dense furnacelike August atmosphere that lay in the Jordan rift, upon Mishkan Yaacov. Though he was wakeful, within a dream Mati saw himself clawing his way with a basket in one hand persistently up the hillside to the cave; he kept slipping back. His basket, covered with his mother's challeh cloth, was filled with rifle bullets for Gidon, who had taken his position up there that time of the field fire and the raiders from across the Jordan, when they had driven off the entire herd of cattle and killed Alter Pincus and his grandson Shaikeh, Mati's own age. The whole of Mishkan Yaacov had been evacuated by the Turks, but Gidon had stayed behind at the rock-shielded cave. It was the time Gidon had picked off two horsemen, turning back the rest of the pillagers. In the dream Gidon was watching little Mati as he struggled up with the basket of ammunition, but Gidon waved him away, away, no, no, don't come, it's too dangerous, and on Gidon's face was the strangest expression, something of such goodness, something so eternally brotherly. Then he faded back into the cave, into blackness.

Mati sat up, his whole body sweating. From the heat, from the dream. He found his cigarettes. Since he had dreamed, he must have been asleep. But a thread of consciousness insisted he had not slept; it had not been a dream—it had been an apparition.

The early-morning broadcast had little more news, only assurances from a British Palestine official that all was now under control; in Hebron a heroic British police officer had single-handedly driven off the rioters, or scores more might have been killed. A curfew had been established in Jerusalem.

If he still felt he ought to go there, Mike offered to advance Mati the money, but it would take at least three weeks for the journey, and then he could hardly return in time for his classes. Where he could do the most good right now would be with those young people at the camp; after gathering the fullest information, Mati ought to go back to Wisconsin.

A call came; a reporter at the *Tribune* wanted an opinion from Rabbi Kramer on the religious differences between Moslems and Jews that lay behind the riots at the Wailing Wall. Mike began to explain how Jews had from time immemorial prayed at the Wall without incident, then suddenly said, "Listen, I have someone here, a born Palestinian, he's studying here at the U of C, and can give you all the background on the question. Here's Mati Chaimovitch."

"Listen, I'm worried about my family," Mati first asked the reporter. "Is there any news from Tiberias?"

The reporter had him spell it. Mati explained he was worried because like Hebron, Tiberias was an ancient religious center. He had a married sister living there, and his family lived nearby. The reporter was checking. How weird it was that something might be tearing up the center of your life and even a newspaperman, an informed person, had hardly heard of such a place as Tiberias. No, there was nothing on Tiberias, the reporter came back, though stuff was still coming in on the AP wire, but why were these attacks concentrated on religious communities?

"They're the ones with no defense!" Mati cried. Besides, how else could the fellaheen be worked up? Didn't the fellow understand this religious stuff was always used for incitement? He began to explain about the Mufti.

"Wait, hold it." The fellow wasn't even clear about the Balfour Declaration. "Listen, could you come down here?" Stuff was pouring in, names of places he couldn't even find on the map. If Mati came down, he could be a big help, and besides, Mati could then get the latest news as fast as it came off the wire. "Ask for Fred Nichols."

So it happened that Mati sat in the newsroom; copyboys kept sauntering over with lengths of paper torn from the roll on the wireless machine. Fred Nichols kept grumbling; even the wire services had been caught shorthanded over there, a fellow from the American Consulate had been pressed into service and was filing stuff, but this damned amateur never explained who anybody was; who was someone named Luke, Luke what?

Harry Luke, Mati said. Second only to the High Commissioner. What had he done?

Ordered the Jews not to shoot. Now, someone named Ben-Zvi, who was that?

Not hurt? Mati gasped. No. Okay, Ben-Zvi was the head of the Jewish Community Assembly. What about him?

Protesting.

Here was a story. A girls' training farm burned down.

Mati seized the sheet. Not Leah's. The one near Haifa. The girls had all been evacuated before the attack.

Ah. Wait, here was a good story. The Arab neighbors of a place called Ben Shemen had protected all the Jews there.

"It's a school for orphans," Mati said. But he was beginning to see; the attacks must be spreading all over the land, on the settlements, too. Not only the old religious communities.

A place called Motza, Nichols said, and with a knowing grin: Was that a mistake for matzo?

No, no, right outside Jerusalem, a very early settlement, a brick factory.

A whole family had been wiped out.

The Maklefs, surely. Among the earliest settlers, before his own family, even from before the time of Theodor Herzl.

Suddenly Nichols was excited. There had been an American rabbinical student at Hebron. He had escaped the massacre and given a harrowing story of butchery, noses, ears cut off—could this be true?

When they went wild, they did such things, Mati said.

On the outskirts of Tel Aviv, between Tel Aviv and Jaffa, four dead Jews, several dead Arabs.

Again Mati saw himself in 1921, in the May Day riots, he and the boys from the Gymnasia, running with sticks in their hands to that very place.

The AP said this was worse than 1921, this was the worst ever, the reporter told him.

Why was he sitting here, what was he doing here, he was in the wrong place, the wrong place.

Nichols sent a copyboy for sandwiches and coffee—"Is ham okay for you?"

One hand held the sandwich; the rewrite man's other hand held the latest dispatch. A place called Hulda. Know it?

But that was where Reuven and Leah on their arrival in Eretz had planted trees for the Herzl forest.

A heroic story—the forest was on fire, a handful of defenders had held out against mounted hordes of Arabs, finally British armored cars had arrived and driven off the attackers, but in the heroic stand of the Jews their commander had fallen.

Suddenly Nichols set down his sandwich; he gazed at Mati, oddly, somewhat evasively. Mati reached for the piece of paper. The name of the fallen commander was Gidon Chaimovitch.

He was sorry the shock had come this way, Nichols said, but if Mati wanted to tell him something about his brother—

83

"Twice in our family." His sister Yaffaleh. And now Gidon.

He told. Of Gidon when hardly more than a boy, taking the whole farm on his shoulders. Of how good he was with horses, with mules, how for Gidon even a mule would obey. He told of Gidon when the raiding tribe from across the Jordan had attacked Mishkan Yaacov—Mati spelled it—and set fire to the fields and run off with the village's entire herd of cattle, and then Gidon—and there Mati fell silent. Gidon at the cave.

Then last night it had not been a dream; it had been Gidon in his moment of death.

Mati did not believe in such things, psychic things like his mother's superstitious tales, but it had been Gidon in his moment of death. Gidon had thought of him, Mati, in America. Mati let his head go down on the desk; after an interval the reporter said, "You all right? I just talked to Rabbi Kramer, I told him."

"I'm all right," Mati said.

Could the reporter find out more? Could he find out just when it happened, just how it happened; could he perhaps send a message to the family?

Nichols took down Leah's address and the message. Could Mati tell some more about his brother? Mati told about the Jewish Brigade, about Gallipoli, with Trumpeldor.

The reporter kept glancing at the big clock on the front wall. "And this Captain Trumpeldor?" Mati told how he had died defending Tel Hai at the border, and with him Yaffaleh had fallen—

"Say!"

It came out a whole column in the paper, FALLEN PALESTINE HERO HAS BROTHER HERE. "The family name, Chaimovitch, means life, yet Gidon Chaimovitch was the second of his family to die." The story even brought tears to Mati. Somewhere Dena would be reading it.

Taking him to the train, Mike Kramer kept Mati talking on about Gidon, about the good part of his life, his wedding, his children, the house in Herzlia he had built. And again it came to Mati, what had Gidon been doing away from home, in Hulda, where he had fallen?

And somehow then Mati spoke to Mike about the apparition. Yes, Rabbi Mike said. Again and again in times of a family death people came to him with such experiences. Still, it would only be natural that last night Mati would have been thinking of Gidon.

Mati mounted the train. There were good Jews here in Chicago, but why should he ever come back? Hadn't Gidon, last night, meant for him to return home and remain in Eretz?

❇ ❇ ❇

In the night on the train he had slipped off his shoes and then realized this was like sitting shiva. Mati tried to say Kaddish in his mind. Maybe right now they were burying the body. The brother who had hoisted him on a horse and slapped the flanks, ride, ride! Who had shown him, without palaver, that a man did, always, the thing that came before him to do, and did it honorably and well. Mati could see the attack, swarms of Arabs on their horses circling wildly, shooting off their pistols, their rifles, screaming, "Aleihum! At them! Thah el Yahud! Death to the Jews!" Walad al mawt, they cursed all Jews as doomed, as the spawn of death itself.

At the New York address Menahem had given him, in a small Histadrut office, the Histadrut emissary, Erza, told Mati bitter stories, already in the Yiddish papers. The Arabs everywhere had been yelling "The government is with us!" On purpose the British commander, a notorious anti-Semite—yes, Mati knew—had absented himself from Jerusalem. In Ekron, after the village was looted, the houses burned, the British had at last arrived, and a dazed farmer had asked where to put his remaining cattle for safety. "Put them in your synagogue," the Britisher had coolly told him.

Big protest meetings were being organized here in New York; Mati must stay and speak at the meetings, of his brother, of his sister, of his heroic family, he must help raise money. With lowered voice as though the CID were even here, the chaver reminded him the first necessity was arms; arms must be bought and smuggled in, never again should the Yishuv have to depend on the British. Mati ought to stay; he would be a great drawing card.

At the dock his aunt engulfed him, "Mati, it is enough for one family, enough already, tell your mama they should all come here to America, for one family it is enough blood." And his uncle stood shrunken and solemn, muttering, "Oh those banditten." And his cousin Wally said in a knowing whisper, "You going back to kill yourself some A-rabs?" The idiot. The idiot. . . . How could people ever understand? It was hopeless to try to make the world understand.

On the sea one could reflect.

The old echo—they don't want us there.

But of what he knew in his own life was that true? Leave out all the political wrangling about what the Emir Abdullah said and what Chaim Weizmann had said. And even about the Mandate itself. In the land where he had been born did he truly feel hated, unwanted? A village fight now and again, such as the Arabs had among themselves, over grazing.

Still, not to be blind. With the Jewish population rising from seven percent and now above fifteen? "They don't want us here." Suppose he turned it around and said, "We don't want them here." And what of those big plans for developing Trans-Jordan for them? Instead, Hauranis kept crossing into Palestine.

Did he himself ever dream of going up to Dja'adi and taking their land?

Mati simply could not visualize the country that way; he saw it with their hill villages, he saw it with the souk in Jerusalem, with their produce market in lower Haifa while Jewish Haifa extended itself up the slope to the top of the Carmel.

Would it, as some said, inevitably have to come to a contest for the whole land, either to the Jews or to the Arabs? Was humanity so made that this had to happen? Or was there some kind of process, a moiling of civilizations, and was Jerusalem still the meeting point, the center of the world as ancients believed? Was there some unfathomable intention concerning the Jews? Were they really some sort of catalytic element, a people selected by history, even by a godhead, for testing the creature man? Testing the element of human will? Even as Herzl had said: if you will it. Or was it all a brutal hoax on the Jews, Mati wondered, doomed to be always thrown back, the way in his dream or his vision he had slipped back, always slipped back while he climbed, reached toward Gidon?

At night on the deck, cigarette after cigarette, with the cradling movement of the ocean liner, the pulse and throb of the engines,

Mati found himself at times choked up and almost in tears, not simply with grief for his brother but with this profound pain of being held away from perceiving, like a small child begging, "Tell me, let me see."

6

ON THE Haifa dock Leah and Natan engulfed him. It was three weeks since all had happened, but Leah still seemed dazed; even out of the great hulk of her there came a kind of small-girl look of uncertainty. If only, she kept saying, if only Gidon had stayed on guard in his house in Herzlia. If only he had gone to guard Mishkan Yaacov. But with the first news of trouble, since Herzlia itself was well defended, Gidon had rushed to Tel Aviv for orders.

Natan's eyes kept measuring him, as though to read what America might have done to Mati, two whole years. But at last on the train home Natan spoke of everything. Gidon had come first to them, to make sure, with all the girls at the meshek, that things were safe; after setting up a doubled guard, Natan and Gidon had hurried down HaYarkon to the headquarters. A dozen of their old comrades from the Brigade were among those milling around the street; Gidon had tried to get news of Tiberias, of Mishkan Yaacov. Still, Schmulik was home, the boys were capable there—and then, as a truck was leaving to reinforce Jerusalem, Gidon had almost jumped on—"If only!" Leah interjected. But just then the commander himself had come out on the steps and spotted them. "Gidon! wait!" Natan paused over the fatal call. Mati could feel all that was unsaid, how Natan would have wanted to stay with Gidon on whatever mission—just as they always had in the Brigade—but after all, Natan had Leah's meshek to watch over.

The train rolled across the Emek—how the valley glowed, one continuous tractor-worked grain bed—and now, striding across the valley, were the towering legs for Rutenberg's power lines, which stretched from the dam on the Jordan, just near home. All this Mati saw, done in the few years of his absence.

Natan resumed. The commander had seized on Gidon, just the man to take charge at Hulda. The settlement was isolated; a tender with a dozen fellows was leaving at once; Gidon must take command.

Afterward, from one of the lads in that vehicle—Naftali Sturman—the Sturmans were always in everything—

"Naftali!" Mati cried. A younger boy at the Gymnasia. And his own guilt mounted: Where was I? Where was I?

Naftali had related all. As the tender circumvented Jaffa, the land lay quiet, but not an Arab was seen in the fields. Then at Azur—an ugly spot it had always been—there was a roadblock of stones, with a howling crowd brandishing nabouts, daggers too; a few also had pistols. Since no British were in sight, Gidon had the boys unwrap two rifles concealed in a potato sack. "Go through!" he ordered the driver; the vehicle plunged, swerving among café stools. Arabs leaped in all directions, an attacker jumped on the running board and slashed with his shabria at the driver, but Gidon leaned across, hitting the Arab's arm with his revolver butt, and the fellow fell away.

Again all was eerily still; they passed through Rehovot and onto the dirt road to Hulda. Only six chaverim were in the old stone house; the women and children had been evacuated. Stacks of grain encircled the threshing floor. Taking two of the exhausted chaverim as guards, the truck returned to Tel Aviv.

Gidon had at once stationed his reinforcements at outposts dug beyond the yard. In the yard itself they made a fallback trench. Then he had the boys fill grain sacks with earth and sandbag the windows.

In the morning fellaheen were seen laboring in their fields; it seemed the wave of excitement had passed, as such things did with the Arabs; they must have been feverishly worked up in their mosques on Friday, and then the fever had faded.

The chaverim resumed their threshing. But early on Monday, Naftali, riding guard, noticed a large taxi driving into the Arab village. Presently several horsemen galloped away. After Naftali reported this to Gidon, both had ridden out and watched. For several hours that taxi had remained there.

It was a brazen day. Riding back, they caught sight of several horsemen on a ridge; then from the opposite direction three riders galloped toward them, firing. Both escaped, but on the dirt road from Rehovot they saw a mob gathering. The settlement was cut off.

Gidon himself took the outpost facing the road. From all sides now, Arabs were gathering: mounted Bedouin from a bordering encampment. The attackers circled just out of range; then they were thundering in; the strongpoints would be overrun.

"Into the yard!" Gidon ordered, keeping up covering fire as the defenders leaped for the trench. Behind the horsemen a mob came on, with their bloodcurdling ululations, "Aelihum! At them! Death to the Yahud, the spawn of death!" Into the house then! Some fifteen yards to crawl. A chaver began scuttling on all fours. "Elbows!" Gidon cursed at him. Under covering fire they snaked their way, to be pulled in at the side door. Naftali. Then Gidon, the last. Reaching the doorway, he rose up for an instant to take stock of the attack. In that moment he was struck, his head snapping back, Naftali had related, like a boxer's after a stunning blow. By the time they could pull him inside Gidon was dead.

Mati calculated the hours. In Chicago, it would have been just before he had awakened.

An urge was in him to tell Leah of the vision. Yet he felt impeded; it was as though he must first know still more; everything.

How was it with Aviva?

She was staying in the house in Herzlia, but with three children to bring up, she would perhaps have to go back to her parents in Jerusalem. Leah's large round face bore the recognition of the immutable. Where Gidon fell, she reminded Mati, was close to where, in the Great War, Aviva had first seen him as she galloped alongside the open train that brought the Jewish Brigade from their training base. Then Leah said, "A soldier's death, as he would have wanted." And then that half-pleading, half-puzzled question of the unbeliever in Almighty. "Why us? Why always one of us?" The Chaimovitches, a heroic family, people said, but doomed.

Natan told the rest. Dryly, like a soldier's report. From Natan the Red, who had come to blows with Gidon over Zionism the first time they had met, in a Jewish restaurant in wartime London.

With Gidon fallen, the defenders had held off the attacking swarm; pillars of fire rose from the grain around the threshing floor. Surely the flames could be seen at the British post, only a few miles away. Why didn't they come?

In the yard, dead Arabs could be counted, more than thirty. A rim of fire was extending itself along the edge of the Herzl forest.

Finally, with dusk, headlights appeared. A British army vehicle with a mounted machine gun. The attackers vanished.

A commander bellowed, "Everybody out!"

Two comrades carried Gidon's body toward the British car. "Leave it!"

"Sir, our commander. We cannot abandon here his body." To mutilation. To hyenas.

"Blast it, the lot of you are getting out of here right now. Leave it!" The machine gun swiveled on them.

Dazed, exhausted, the defenders laid the body on the ground, near their riddled water tank. Running back into the house, Naftali brought a sheet for a shroud.

Though appeals were made day after day, Natan said, no approach to Hulda to recover the body was permitted. Leah had gone to the British and begged. Her friend Rahel had got Ben-Zvi to call the High Commissioner himself. No army escort was as yet available.

After another week, Naftali Sturman, in Rehovot, sent word to Tel Aviv that the British roadblocks were withdrawn.

Nahum came with his car, bringing Abba, everyone, but not their mother. Ima was too feeble for the voyage and the shock. Indeed, up to now no one had told her. "Mati, be careful with her." Already last year Leah had written him that Ima's mind wandered.

The last stretch, the wagon road to Hulda, Natan related, had the look one saw in wartime, torn branches fallen across the lane, sand sifted into the wheel ruts. The gate lay broken alongside the road.

In the yard, fragments of torn clothing, a sandal sole, a broken jarra. From the windows of the house, shutters askew, ripped sandbags collapsed over the sills like gutted bodies.

The threshing floor was a heap of cinders, and stark charred trees marked the edge of the memorial forest. Hurrying toward the water tank, they could make out no shrouded form. Then crusts of burned cloth, and earth-dark the shriveled body. Aviva stood. Leah quickly undid her kerchief and covered Gidon's skull.

Abba bent over the corpse, his swollen lips barely moving in the Kaddish. They joined.

Schmulik vowed it must be here that Gidon should remain. He himself would stay and rebuild this place.

To find a spade, a mattock, for the burial, the brothers and sisters searched the burned sheds, the gutted house; nothing, not even a stick. In rage, Schmulik fell to clawing at the cindered ground; with his bare hands he was tearing a hollow. Leah knelt down beside him, Reuven, too, all of them in a circle tearing a grave out of the earth.

The men's shirts shrouded the form. And thus, Gidon was laid in the ground.

A few steps away in the yard his widow saw green leaves still remaining on an olive tree. Breaking off several twigs, Aviva placed them across the grave.

Thus, from Natan, Mati learned all that had happened. On the very day when he himself, costumed like a Shomer, had been riding the Arab fantasia for the camp kids on the shore of Lake Michigan.

Only when he saw the wagons with the mule teams waiting by the old Samekh station did Mati feel his homecoming: Schmulik's same prize mules, the high-legged pair called Gog and Magog, and Schmulik himself the small ox with his boy Simha, five now, leaping off to meet the train.

Almost at once Schmulik burst out, "We'll go there, the two of us. We'll find out who it was." Exactly who had come there to the Arab village in the car, to organize the attack. Schmulik had indeed already once gone into that Arab village near Hulda, but their mukhtar declared he had tried to restrain his people—only what would you, when the shooting began—But who had come in that car, the bastard would not say. "Strangers from Jerusalem," he pretended.

At the entrance to Mishkan Yaacov, Mati saw a trench; Schmulik shrugged. "Nothing. We took turns for a few days, with cookpots on our heads."

The Zbeh hadn't come across the river; they knew from the past what they would get, Schmulik said. Remember when Gidon himself had given them their lesson? And with Rutenberg's electrical works just down the river, there was British money being invested, so Mati could imagine this area hadn't been left abandoned. Even in Tiberias, Nahum had got together with the Arab Mukhtar; the city lived off Christian pilgrims, and besides, half the Arabs worked around the mineral baths, so there had been no spark of trouble in Tiberias.

As for Dja'adi—the old sulha held fast. The ancient Sheikh Ibrim had died, it was said he was a hundred and nine years old. His grandson Mansur-the-One-Eye had even come down to express sorrow over the death of Gidon. Mansur's grandson Abdul, who had given Mati that scar on his back, had become the schoolteacher; yes, the British had started a school. Fawzi, the one who used to go hunting with Gidon in the Huleh, was still an interpreter in Jerusalem, for the Mandate. Schmulik spit. He wouldn't trust any of them, sulha or not. Things had been quiet here because those devils damn well knew the defense was strong.

Like the house itself in the first glimpse as they approached, his mother seemed to have shrunken. The image Mati had carried of her was from his childhood—not even the aging mother figure of two years ago, when he had left for America. Always Mati had seen her as the stout Ima with the voluminous broad-sweeping skirts. But now the aged woman with the sunken mouth and the dry, slack flesh of her arms seemed tiny as she raised herself to embrace her youngest son. Her face had the baby-soft cheeks of a very old woman, but was she so old? When Reuven was born she must have been perhaps seventeen. So she must be a few years over sixty. How was it they never had known their parents' birthdates?

Behind stood his abba, more alone among them all than ever, his beard straggly, like the always-tangled fringes of his ritual undervest. Abba laid his hands on Mati's shoulders: "My son, the student from America." Mati felt the fingers, still powerful, gripping, almost digging into his flesh. "So it is, so it is with us," his father said.

Then Mati heard his mother confuse his name. "Avramchik," Feigel was saying to her husband, with a growing glow. "Avramchik has come back." The little brother he had never known, between himself and Schmulik, the one who had died of malaria during the first winter in this place. No one corrected the mother, but at every opportunity Mati's name was spoken, so she would know. Then, when they crowded into the house, Feigel gazed slowly and carefully around the room filled with her sons and daughters and their wives and husbands and children, so many souls, so much life! Still, "One more is missing," she said at last, looking at Leah with the uncertain smile of a child aware that some adult game is being played.

With Schmulik's Nussya and a few more of the women helping, she began to serve the table. Feigel herself brought the raisin kugel she had made for her returning son; even in her haze she had known to bake Mati's favorite dish.

All had arrived—Reuven and Elisheva from their nearby kibbutz, and with them their eldest, Kinneret, already ten, with a lovely, sensitive face like her mother's, except that Mati recognized Elisheva more in the girl than in herself, for her delicate white skin had taken on a sun-dried look, and her mouth seemed pinched—not bitter, but with that look of persons who have conquered themselves. All at once Mati found himself trying to visualize Dena in her place, for hadn't Elisheva left a bourgeois life, given up her piano studies in Paris for Reuven's kvutsa?

Reuven had patches of gray in his hair and looked somehow like a scholar, though he walked with the wide-planted gait of the fieldworker. Mati had brought him the latest book by Luther Burbank, and at once he was the same old Reuven, distractedly reaching a hand out for his food without lifting his eyes from the pages.

Suddenly Leah remembered something she had to tell Mati, that had slipped her mind on the train ride. A friend of his, a sculptor from Chicago, had been in Eretz.

Joe Freedman?

Yes, through all the troubles. He had been in Tel Hai. Up there nothing serious had happened—this artist had heard about Gidon and had come down to Tel Aviv. He had wanted to wait for Mati, but a telegram had come, about an exhibition of his work, and he had had to leave for Paris. But he had given her a small carving from the marble of Tel Hai, a chalutzah. Mati would see it. The figure even looked a little like Yaffaleh.

So the fellow had come. It seemed to mean something—the first person he had got to come here—and yet all those crazy people,

Myra, Joe, with their art world, could they really be part of this? Even if one day he got Joe to come and make a monument in Hulda. Coming to see, to make monuments, wasn't it only like an extra kind of tourism? Later Mati found himself telling of America, of Aunt Hannah and her son who called himself by the name of Wally Lee and pretended not to be Jewish. And of the separate Jewish and gentile fraternities at the university. But no, he couldn't say it was anti-Semitism the way they thought of it from old Russia or like this crazy Hitler movement in Germany, no. And the Jews were not all so hopeless as this cousin Wally Lee. Indeed, in Chicago he had even succeeded in forming a group that was preparing to come on settlement. Yes, real Americans, American born. And he told of the summer camp, American Jews paid hundreds of dollars for each kid to live like in a kibbutz! He dressed them up as shomrim instead of cowboys—Mati laughed bitterly—and taught them to ride.

Here was Nahum arriving with Shula and their four kids, in still a fancier limousine, a brand-new Ford Lincoln! Didn't he know that Henry Ford was an anti-Semite? Natan eyed the new vehicle ironically and demanded of Mati, wasn't it true that American Jews were boycotting Henry Ford? For printing the *Protocols of the Elders of Zion?* Some of the youngsters didn't even know what that was, and Menahem explained—an old made-up document that a Russian priest had provided for the Czar, about a plot of the Jews to rule the world. So now Hitler and his Nazi Party were spreading the *Protocols* in Germany. And here, too, parts out of these *Protocols* had even been printed in Arabic in *El Carmel* to stir up the troubles.

But Ford had apologized and stopped, Nahum said; the apology had even been printed in *Davar.* There was a short silence as though Nahum nevertheless by owning a Ford was desecrating Gidon. As they all went inside, Nahum explained to Mati, he had already bought the car months ago, he had all the time to go to Hof HaSharon, which he was developing on the seacoast. Oh, sales were growing in America, he had even picked up a new tract, a minor Arab sheikh had died, the eldest son was crazy about driving a British sports car, the kind with the shining pipe outside, so Nahum had bought him one, he had got an excellent deal on the car together with this limousine, and just before Gidon had died—Nahum sighed—he and Gidon had galloped together over the whole new tract on the dunes. Ah, he had wanted Gidon to take charge of it all—

Talking of cars, Schmulik suddenly demanded of Menahem, what of that Arab car that day in Hulda? Had anything more been found out? Who sent it?

That the Mufti sent the cars, did Schmulik have to be told? Menahem repeated. But as to who was in each car in each place— what use? The attacks had to be fought as a movement, not as a personal vendetta, a ghoum.

Schmulik's voice grew louder, for all to hear. "I want to know who was there, who started it in Hulda. For me it is a question of the murderer of my brother." Nussya gave him a nudge, motioning with her head toward Feigel. But the old mother was in back of the room at the stove, the way Mati remembered always seeing her. Pushing off his wife's hand, Schmulik cried, "No!" to Menahem's analysis. "No! I have to find out."

"Long ago the Organization decided that's not the way," Menahem said quietly to Schmulik.

"And right here in Mishkan Yaacov in the old troubles, didn't you yourself settle the score with the two bandit brothers? Didn't Gidon himself do it with the Zbeh? That's the only way the Arabs understand."

"Then and now are different times," Menahem said. "Today we have a government that is pledged before the nations to keep order here, and we must make them do it. This is not the time of the Turks."

Schmulik made a lip fart. Among the others, as they settled around the table, Mati felt—as in himself—a bitter uncertainty. "Obviously," Menahem continued, "we must first of all be strong enough to protect ourselves when our protectors look the other way. But we must not fall back into the ghoum; this is exactly what the Mufti wants."

Now Natan put in his Marxism. "Our task is to work with the fellaheen; that is where we have failed. Each time, in 1920, in 1921, and this time again, their religious fanaticism is aroused." Religion was not only the opiate of the people; it was their hate serum, he declared. "We have to show them they are serfs, being exploited by the effendis."

"You want the fellaheen to understand Karl Marx?" Nahum said.

96

A silence fell. Then a young voice was heard, Menahem's son, Yechezkiel. "What has been shown is that we were unprepared. We simply did not have enough weapons. We relied on the British. We have to rely only on ourselves." He looked at his father, as though even Menahem hadn't understood this enough.

The silence returned, but now as over something that could not be too openly discussed, even at a family gathering. Mati felt Menahem's gaze as though assessing him. All right. What was the use of learning about Adam Smith, while here everything was still on the level of Isaac and Ishmael?

They all departed early so as to reach their homes in daylight, and Mati rode out alongside Schmulik to look at the fields. Everything that Schmulik had done he admired, the enlarged pardess, the banana grove, the tomatoes now trucked over the new road, earliest on the market. Yet Mishkan Yaacov itself had not grown, Schmulik grumbled, because it was the kibbutzim that were favored with the new tracts of land bought by the Keren Kayemeth. The kibbutzim were spreading, three new ones along here with the new wave of Polish chalutzim, though too damn many of the Polish immigrants were opening gazoz stands in Tel Aviv. Reuven's kibbutz was unrecognizable, he'd see—a huge new cow barn with milking machines and also a fruit canning factory!

Then, as they rode a bit in silence, Schmulik burst out, "I saw Fuad!" The sheikh's son near Tel Hai who had thrown the grenade that killed Yaffaleh. While working a steam shovel up north there for Rutenberg's pylon sites, Schmulik had seen Fuad come riding by to gaze at the machines. "He passed as close to me as you are now. Mati, if I'd had a pistol, I could have put an end to that one's riding around on the earth."

And yours, too, Mati thought, but he repeated, "Schmulik, we have to leave it. Yaffaleh died in battle. It was ten years ago. And Gidon, too, has died in battle."

Schmulik leaned from his mount and spit. "What's happening to you, there in America? And Hebron, you call that a battle, too? Mati, you grew up with it—all the Arabs understand is when they are answered in their own way. And if we don't, they despise us."

They reached the edge of the fields, just where the fight with Dja'adi had taken place in the old days. "You think these jackals didn't want to try something here too? Early Friday, a taxi came.

97

We saw it. Husseini's gang from Jerusalem, to talk to the mukhtar. But One-Eye refused. He knows we are strong and on guard."

Turning their horses, they started back. Schmulik was brooding. "In Hebron," he burst out, "the day before the massacre, you know who came to preach in the mosque? Aref el Aref."

This Mati had not yet heard. In the very first pogrom, in the Old City of Jerusalem in 1920, Aref el Aref and Haj Amin el Husseini had been the instigators, convicted by the British army administration. Then, when the civil administration started and Lord Samuel came as High Commissioner, all had been amnestied and Aref had even been given a position. "But isn't he a district officer in Beersheba?" Mati asked.

"And so? He came to Hebron."

Mati rode up to Dja'adi. At the edge of the village was a threshing floor; an Arab boy circled on an old mule, dragging the threshing board in the drowsy ancient manner, while on the rim of the circle a few girls and women squatted with sieves. All at once Mati felt a different kind of sorrow, something embedded in timeless fate, a defeat as at some irreconcilable error in an equation, some buried miscalculation that incessantly and eternally compounded itself—as perhaps a mathematician, even an Einstein, must feel in reviewing over and over his complex approaches to a balance of the universe, while yet unable to uncover the origin of an expanding error. Dismally, within himself, something said, "It won't change." All that he was studying, all theory, all logic vanished before this hill village. The Arab way was immutable; everything here was balanced off; it was a total way of life, a kind of ritual.

On a black steed, an absolute beauty, a rider came flashing out toward him. Mati was hailed by a voice from the old days—Abdul. They dismounted, embraced, jestingly insulted each other, and then Abdul's voice dropped to solemnity as he expressed grief over the death of Gidon. It was sorrow, unfeigned. "What would you?" Mati responded in Arabic. "It is the will of the Above."

"He was a true man," Abdul said, "a fighter and a man of honor. . . . Ah, what a great lover of horses."

Mati deprecated his own mount, a simple farm animal. Long ago his brother Schmulik had sold the blooded mare to buy a motorcycle.

"A motorcycle goes faster," Abdul said, "but is it your friend?"

Schmulik was a great one for machines, Mati explained. He

operated an enormous machine for the Rutenberg works; soon there would be electricity for the whole land.

Abdul shrugged, smiling. "The sun gives light, and we do not have to pay for it."

Mati admired Abdul's mount, stroked the white star on the nose. Yes, Abdul said, his smile now joyous, she was from the pure line of Ayesha, which Gidon had presented to Fawzi. In the years since Fawzi had gone to Jerusalem, Abdul himself had taken over their breeding stock. Thanks to Allah, their strain was prized; from as far as Gaza there came sheikhs and high effendis; every foal was bespoken. He had two stud horses—ah! Abdul chortled and made the upward gesture with his forearm. If only he himself could be paid such a good price for taking his pleasure with a female! Alas, Mati laughed, with people it was the other way around; it was the females who were paid for having the pleasure!

Abdul gave him a look of manly complicity. In America, it was said, girls were easy. No one had to pay or get married either. Did Mati have many girls in America?

Oh, Mati said, he was not starved.

But he was not married?

No. Both laughed.

But that did not keep him from having married women! Abdul was wise to the ways of American wives! Bebe Daniels! Gilda Gray! In Tiberias was a cinema. "It" girls! He gave Mati an elbow jab. "Oh, yes, she's my baby!" Did Mati have many girls? How many?

Oh, not so many, Mati said.

He himself was married, Abdul said; he already had two children—boys! Mati would see. And he demanded of Mati, "You, when you marry, would you accept to marry a girl that is not a virgin?"

Oddly it seemed to Mati that Abdul had picked up the conversation exactly from when they were kids. Abdul was even gazing down toward the kibbutzim; he probably still imagined all the women there were communal property and could not resist asking, "Your sister, the big one—" with a broad smile.

"Leah?"

"Somebody married her?"

"Oh, they have two fine boys and a little girl. Leah married a good man, a friend of Gidon's, who was in the British army with him, the Brigada."

"Ah. Your Brigada."

They had entered the village, and Abdul showed Mati his corral, his older little boy dogging their steps. When each steed had been admired they went to the house, Mati recognizing the courtyard—surely it had been old Ibrim's house? yes, a room was added on; Abdul called to his wife, who emerged from the rear quarters with the second little boy clinging to her dress. She was a Dja'adi girl, and remembered Mati, adding a shy little laugh to her every remark. Then she went to prepare the coffee.

The room had the usual wall bench on three sides, but the coffee table, instead of being of inlaid Damascus work, looked modernistic, even factory made, with a high varnish. A copy of *El Carmel* lay there. Wasn't it *El Carmel*, Mati tried to recall, that Natan had said had printed tales of Jewish plans to blow up the Mosque of Omar?

All those tales about Jews plotting to buy the whole of Palestine and blow up the Mosque of Omar—had Abdul read those tales? Did he believe them?

Abdul smiled. "Are you not buying land?"

"Where one buys, another is selling," Mati quoted.

Abdul's smile subsided. "Still," he replied to the first question, "you cannot deny there are certain Jews among you who want to build your Temple again on the place of our holy mosque. That is Zionism! Even our old grandfather Ibrim knew it; he told it to my father when your people first came here; he told us the Jews want to make a nation here."

"No one denies we want to be our own rulers," Mati said. "Are not the Arabs making nations? Across the river you have a new nation. But, habub, Do you think that *I* want your mosque? Well you know that I and my brothers and all of us—we are not religious. And those old Jews who might dream of the Temple of Solomon, their dream is of the Temple rebuilt in heaven, not on this earth. Why should Arab and Jew allow people to set us against each other with such stupid lies?"

Abdul said, "Only Allah knows what is true."

"Oil will not burn by itself; it takes a spark to light it." Mati offered an American cigarette. "Tell me," he said as between boyhood friends, "you are truly a believer?"

Abdul looked a trifle sly. "Even unbelievers believe," he said. "You too believe." He laughed, as at catching Mati out. "That is why your oldest brother Reuven came back to this land. . . . Look at the Christians. They believe Jesus is the messenger, but you Jews did not know it. We say Mohammed is the messenger after Jesus, but the Christians did not know it, and the Jews did not know it. But Mohammed is the last, and that is the right one."

"Until there comes another?" said Mati.

"There can be no other, habub," said Abdul, with a touch of hardening. Yet then, with a knowing smile, he added, making a chin movement toward the kibbutz below, "Your Moscob believe one came. Do you believe it?"

Ah, but in Moscow God was forbidden, Mati pointed out. The one Moscow believed in had declared there is no Allah, no Yeshu, no Elohim. "They say all is kif." Both laughed, a bit uncertainly as to whether they were in agreement, and watched a smoke ring rising from Abdul's American Camel.

Abdul returned to the argument. "But your brothers"—again indicating Reuven's kibbutz—"they believe in the Moscob." He chuckled; he had caught Mati out.

Mati shook his head. "It is not the same. Reuven and his chaverim believe in sharing equally, that is all. They have been here many years, and you have seen how they live. But the real Moscobs in Russia—they send our people to prison. To the icy land of Siberia."

Abdul sighed as one dismissing a world that is too puzzling.

Just then Yasmin brought the coffee. She had changed to a frock, though she still wore her ankle-length pantalets below it. Mati caught a glint of subdued mischief in Yasmin's glance at her husband; for an instant Abdul seemed undecided. "Your wife has excellent taste," Mati said, "to match her natural beauty."

"You like my dress? Abdul bought it for me in Nazareth," Yasmin said.

Abdul smiled, condoning feminine vanity, but Mati had a feeling that later Yasmin would get it, for exhibiting herself.

"It is well that here there was peace between us," Mati said. "In Tiberias also there was peace. It should be an example for all the land."

"Where there is wisdom there is peace," Abdul quoted, and filled their coffee cups again.

Was not Abdul now the teacher here? Mati remarked. Something between a smile and a scowl appeared. "Since there is no one else, it has fallen to me. What can I teach them? We do not have a college to train teachers!" Like Fawzi, he had learned reading and writing, and that was what he taught. He taught the boys from the Koran. "Our beautiful Koran. Do you not teach from your taanach?" Mati's smile acknowledged they were even. The British had indeed apportioned a small sum, and a schoolroom had been made here. Did Mati want to see it? It was just there by the mosque.

A barren square room. Even if they learned to read, Mati reflected, what would they read but *El Carmel* and its tales of Jewish plotting. Outside the hut, Mati said his farewell, and Abdul repeated his deep sorrow over the death of Gidon. No Arab was a better man with a steed. Many times after Gidon had returned from the Great War and was still living at home, he had come up here to give help to sick animals. Making an injection gesture, Abdul said, "In the time of the big sickness he saved all our cattle." The very steed Abdul rode had been pulled into life by Gidon after several hours when only one hoof protruded and the mare lay panting. "Even in that old fight we had when we were children"—Abdul's eyes met Mati's with a curious nostalgia—"my great-grandfather praised Gidon. As old Ibrim said, a true man is he who is respected by everyone, friend and adversary alike." They embraced in farewell.

In the morning, with Mati clutching onto Schmulik on his huge Harley-Davidson, the two set off for Hulda. Schmulik took the new road passing the hydroelectric works, pointing, shouting. And down there in the enormous basin with the cranes and scoops Mati saw clumps of workers, chalutzim in khaki shorts and also Arabs with tucked-up galabias. Over his shoulder Schmulik complained about Hauranis pouring into the land. "Arab immigrants, nobody stops! And Rutenberg pays them good wages."

By midday, amazingly, they had crossed the whole land from east to west and southward as far as Herzlia. Just behind the souk, Gidon's veterinary station, with its animal shed, stood deserted. Across the lane was the finished house, with a double row of young pines to the door, and in the yard, Mati saw, one of Reuven's saplings, a cedar of Lebanon. There was a porch with two fluted pillars, and the door had panels of colored glass. Gidon had done it all nicely. The bright-patterned tiles, it suddenly came to Mati, must be the ones Gidon and Aviva had bought in Jaffa on the day they saw him off to America.

102

Having heard the approaching motorcycle, the kids rushed out, Herzl and Nurit, home from school for lunch; Aviva appeared, carrying the baby, Eytan.

In the golden sunlight she looked unchanged, and only on nearing did Mati see the tight edges of her mouth. He experienced an upwelling of tenderness, even some vestigial urge, though so much younger as he was, to take care of her, the brother's widow. In their big Jerusalem wedding in the Old City the bride in white had appeared to him as the hero's reward that had awaited the soldier Gidon!

Their boy Herzl at first was silent with him; could it be a reproach that he had not been here in the troubles? Mati was impelled to say how useless, how dreadful it had felt to be away.

Soon the children edged close. Already, Aviva said, they felt the need of a man's presence. And automatically Mati thought, with so many men in the land, how long would it be? And there seemed a wrongness that one day Gidon's children would belong to someone else.

As she brought them glasses of lebeniya and added food on the table, Aviva explained that she was already starting her kindergarten; it was best to be busy. Leah had arranged with the Women's Council to help with part of the fee for working mothers who needed day care for their small ones. Indeed, Leah had a friend in the council, Golda Meyerson, an American chalutzah; her father lived here in Herzlia and was a carpenter; already he was building a seesaw for Aviva's gan—he wouldn't accept any pay, only money for the wood. They had come originally from the Ukraine, where Gidon—she faltered—"where your whole family came from." Also, she hoped soon to sell the veterinary stall; this should tide her over. But Schmulik broke in with vehemence, she mustn't sell in haste, this place would become valuable, and after all, Gidon had a section of orange grove in the Veterans Cooperative working with Nahum.

The boy Herzl burst out, "Nahum is trying to cheat us out of Abba's pardess!"

No, no, his mother admonished, it was not clear that there was anything like cheating! Herzeleh mustn't jump to conclusions, especially against his uncle!

"What about the mare?" the boy sputtered. "Nahum just took her and gave her to that Britisher without even asking Abba! She was Abba's own favorite, and now she would have been for me!"

In the last, a hint of quaver in his voice was overcome by flatness, an intonation exactly like Gidon's—a statement of fact. The boy even stood the way his father had, with his legs slightly apart, solidly planted. And though he had his mother's features, now in this moment the cast of his face was his father's. Was it only the more painful, Mati wondered, for her to have Gidon's image so constantly about her? And what would this likeness evoke, eventually, for another man? And Nurit, too, in every feature a feminine copy of her father.

All at once, while Schmulik declared that they simply ought to go break every bone in Nahum's body, just then, as not until this moment, Gidon's death came with finality upon Mati. At Herzeleh's age he had been rolling on the ground with Abdul's stab wound in his back, and his big brother Gidon had rushed in and saved him.

As for the mare, Aviva explained that Nahum wasn't entirely in the wrong; he had discovered the riding passion of the district commissioner, a minor son of British aristocracy whose approval was vital for the vast land purchase on the dunes; the Englishman had fallen in love with the horse, which Nahum had offered him to ride while Gidon was away, and Nahum had then and there made the Englishman a gift of the animal, just as he had given a racing car to the son of the sheikh. "Nahum paid Abba for the mare," Aviva reminded her angry son.

"Abba would never have sold her for any price on earth! He had promised her to me!"

"Herzeleh," his mother said, "your abba understood why Nahum gave the horse to the Englishman. It would not have been Abba's way of doing things, but he understood."

"Nahum and his dirty baksheesh!" Herzl growled.

The question of Gidon's orange grove was more complex, for the entire development was in the first stages; parcels had been sold abroad, and the Veterans Cooperative was to do the planting and caretaking, with each veteran receiving a ten-dunam section in addition to his wages. Large enough, when the fruit came in, to keep his family. Gidon had intended to combine this with his veterinary practice. But now Nahum declared he could not apportion Gidon's share to Aviva since Gidon's labor would have been part of the agreement.

All at once Mati· felt that he himself was the answer. Why should he waste more years there in America, in the end to become a white-collar paper shuffler, drawing up statistics, maybe sitting in committees in the Histadrut? Ever since he had come home, the feeling had been growing in him that like his brothers and sisters, like his father, he belonged on the soil, in direct contact with the land. This was his intended way of life.

"Listen! I'll do the work! I'll stay!" he cried.

Aviva gave him a long, sweet look, touched with rue. "No, Mati, dear." She smiled at him with a face so ineffable that he loved her in that moment with the surest human love, the kind that sometimes overwhelmed you even toward an unknown, toward the face of someone in sorrow. "You have your own tasks, your own life, Mati," she said. "We'll manage." She was standing half behind his chair. "Gidon wanted you to study. He saved all your letters; he told everybody about the wonderful work you were doing for the Yishuv, there with the young American Jews." She had placed her hand on Herzeleh to quiet his anger. Her voice had that rising lilt as when she had been one of Leah's young chalutzoth, still just a dreamy girl. "Thank you, Mati." She bent and swiftly kissed the top of his head. Besides, Natan and the other veterans, like Gidon's close friend Araleh, had already assured her they would share out the labor.

Presently Aviva brought Mati a small packet. Inside were not only his letters from Chicago but old letters written to Gidon in England during the war, the letters of a young boy to his brother the soldier. Then she gave him something else of Gidon's. Naturally Gidon's uniform and army things were for his sons, but Aviva brought Mati a needleworked insignia, an extra one she said, on which were stitched the words "Zion Mule Corps." It must have been embroidered by some woman Gidon had known in the Jewish community of Alexandria, she said softly. Mati realized she was flushing; how strange women could be, poor dear Aviva, to be wondering about someone Gidon might have known years before he even met her!

Beyond Rehovot, they were on the dirt road to Hulda.

The gate still lay fallen. Yet a figure detached itself from the house and approached them, the galabia white against the charred trees. An Arab! Schmulik leaped from the motorcycle, raging. "What are you doing here? Get out! Get out!"

The skinny ancient Arab peered through his yellowed eyes. "Schwoya, schwoya, chaver, don't be angry, I am the watchman."

"Watchman! On our place! Get out before I tear you to shreds!" Schmulik was so frenzied, Mati put a restraining hand on him.

"Schwoya, schwoya," the ancient repeated, "that is why I am here, I am watching the meshek for the Jews."

Mati asked, "Who put you here, the British?"

"No, I am put here by the Yahud. I am watchman for the Yahud."

Beside himself, Schmulik roared as though the whole land must hear him. What was there to watch! They had murdered, they had pillaged, they had burned, Hulda was destroyed—what was there here to watch but the grave!

Yes, yes, the Arab caught the word. The grave. And like a guide, he went before them, pointing. Already other Jews had come, and he had shown them the grave.

"It is the grave of our own brother!" Schmulik unleashed a stream of Arab curses. "You soil the air! Get out of here!"

The watchman gazed, as at one demented. "I did not take part," he protested.

"Out! Out! Your mother lay with a hyena! Out before I throw your entrails to the wild dogs of hell!"

The Arab removed himself a distance.

What idiot had done this! Just as in Reuven's time when some idiot from the organizations had sent Arabs to plant the Herzl forest here! No! Schmulik would find out what idiot was responsible! The Keren Kayemeth would hear from him!

Too grieved to feel anger, Mati, standing by the grave hand-torn from the ground as they had told him, made an inner vow. "I will take your place, Gidon. Here on this soil. I will take your place."

Here. Why had it not been himself instead of Gidon, who left a wife and young children? While he himself was wallowing with his shikseh there in Chicago. An urge was in Mati's every fiber, as though to erase time, as though he could with some boundless power reverse time itself and drive off the whole swarm of attackers, as though he could release a withering lightning upon them all, leaving only this stone house, with the defenders untouched.

Like the avenging angels sent upon the Egyptians, leaving untouched the dwellings of the Hebrews.

Methodically Schmulik and Mati paced the entire grounds. Mati had to retrace each step of his brother from the pitiful half-exposed outpost to the scrap of trench. Elbowing along this earth, from the trench to the house, Gidon had made his way, the other defenders before him, as far as this door where he stood up for an instant, lifting his head—

Mati followed that last gaze, seeing the frenzied oncoming mob, those on their steeds, those running behind with raised daggers, pistols, rifles, staves; he heard their screams, "Aleihum! At them! Death to the Yahud! Walad al mawt! Spawn of death!"

Again came that inchoate impulse as though to halt, to reverse the movement of time—wait, wait! an eternal error was taking place! In this instant something had to intervene, to prevent; a hand must reach down from heaven!

Did something within him still believe in God? In the ancient intonations about the mighty outstretched arm? Or was his mind infested from Wild West movies of cavalrymen galloping at the crucial moment to drive off the savages? Had not the defenders here with burning eyes stared out for British cars with mounted machine guns that would sweep away the attackers? Gidon's death —a fault, a flaw in time itself? Mati repulsed a phrase, "God—or the British—came too late." Only it spun on in him. If God or some entity "heard," and in that universal unraveling the British were to have been used, to arrive in time, then was it mankind that faltered, a Jew-hating officer—"Don't be in too much of a hurry, give the Arabs time to finish off a few"? An eternal dialectic between God's will and man's? Oh, how could he stand in this place and pursue this sophistry!

Yet even so as Mati stood there, some other impulse, some image, was pressing, trying to rise in his mind. Some other way. It could have been stopped. Not Yahweh. Not the British. Ourselves. Always ourselves was the answer. What had young Yechezkiel cried out, Dvora and Menahem's grown son, named after Dvora's first sweetheart, Yechezkiel, the Shomer, ambushed, shot down on their wedding day? "We, we ourselves."

Suddenly, literally, the image thundered across Mati's mind. No hand of God's, breaking out of the sky, but man himself!

As a child he was standing on the dirt road of Mishkan Yaacov, his head tilted upward, his eyes magnetized to the thundering airplane! That way! Shula's aviator! Mati saw himself in a plane, in one swooping dive, here, over this yard! In wild panic the attackers fled—

He touched his brother. "Schmulik, with an airplane they could have been driven off."

"So the British would send an airplane." Schmulik spat.

"Not a British plane," Mati said. "Ours."

Schmulik's body turned; he seemed in the dusk to be assessing his young brother, carefully following all his meaning. Then with lowered voices, as though even between the two of them, here by themselves, in such an important thing caution was needed, Schmulik and Mati were discussing deeply into the possibilities. The entire plan, from this moment to its realization, appeared to Mati. A small airplane hidden in an orange grove packing house. A secret weapon to be used only in an emergency, such as here. By the time the British rose to explore, the work would have been done. Afterward let them search. To have weapons when you need them. To rely on no one but yourself.

And who would fly?

Gidon was still down here in this trench. He sent up a flare. Mati saw himself in the airplane. From a clearing in a Rehovot grove, he was instantly in the air, quickly overhead, he spotted the circle of horsemen, he hurled down a bomb—Gidon was saved, Gidon was alive! Gidon would still be standing here, whole.

Why impossible?

Surely it was for this that he had now come here. The thought, the impulse, had been waiting for him here. Perhaps some desperate last hope of Gidon's on this very spot, in that upward glance as he raised his head before the bullet struck.

Inside the stone house, a stale latrine smell; on the kitchen floor was the Arab watchman's bedraggled straw mat, his water jarra, a spread kerchief with a dry pitta and a piece of goat cheese.

A few scattered, ripped books left by the looters—Mati picked up a beginner's Hebrew grammar and a copy of a German war novel, *All Quiet on the Western Front*; he had read it in English. Spent shells lay below the windows; a few sandbags were still in place, with the dents of elbows dug into them. A good last job Gidon had done; after he fell, the fortress held.

From his motorcycle bag Schmulik brought food, a canteen, a flashlight, and finally his hidden pistol. The airplane plan didn't leave their minds. Probings, ideas. How could you smuggle in and hide an entire thing like that? Perhaps flown in on a dark night, hidden in a kibbutz? Or—Schmulik had a spark of excitement— why couldn't they put one together? A motor could be smuggled in as, say, a replacement engine for a truck. He was already talking of horsepower capacity, cylinder bore; of such things Schmulik knew, while Mati was ignorant, and perhaps because of this, things became more easy between them, Schmulik wasn't constantly addressing him with irony as the scholar and the educated one. Not until now had their youth-time brotherliness totally returned.

Suddenly Schmulik recalled that this place, Hulda itself, had been the site of a big German truck repair installation in the war. It was a German truck driver who had given Leah a ride from here on her crazy mission to Jerusalem that time, to bring gold out from under the noses of the Turks. And hadn't Leah said—yes! That truck had been carrying an airplane wing! Repaired here! Perhaps some of the chevreh had even had a hand in it and learned about such work! First of all they must gather up the chaverim and get the meshek started again. Perhaps, most fittingly, the whole plan could be carried out right here!

As night fell, Schmulik went to bring in his motorcycle: "They know we're still here, or they'd have heard the machine passing their village." Mati helped him drag it inside; they put the door back in place and barred it with the heavy machine. It would have seemed somehow a disrespect to Gidon if they left the place to sleep in Rehovot or Tel Aviv.

When they lay down side by side on the shred of mat, one or the other kept bringing up a thought about their plan. Before they broached the plan to Eliahu, they must have answers to every problem. Schmulik more and more believed the fuselage could be built right here; still, it would be best to have an alternative plan, how to smuggle in a whole plane. Menahem would have ideas. The wings might be concealed in some large piece of farm equipment —maybe even one of those long incubators that Dvoraleh brought for her poultry house?

But then it all seemed foolish. Eliahu in Tel Aviv would tear the plan apart. An airplane was far too costly; he would insist that basic weapons came first, rifles, machine guns. A plane—you could use it only one time and the British would know.

Yes, Mati said, but suppose that one time had been right here?

Then they talked of Aviva and of Gidon's children. Schmulik was not in favor of her struggling on alone in Herzlia. Gidon's family should live here! Hulda must be rebuilt, he himself would stay and see to it.

No, Mati argued, the task was not for Schmulik but for himself, to see this place rebuilt. All those romantic ideas about the air-plane, perhaps something would come of them and perhaps not, but in any case there would have to be much talk and preparation and meanwhile, he could be working here.

Then Schmulik reminded him it was Gidon himself who had insisted he must go and study. That night in Mishkan Yaacov when the old man had pulled the wheels off the wagon, it was only because of Gidon, in respect for the returned soldier, that Abba had unlocked the shed and let them take the wheels to put back on. Mati must return to his university in America. There was an added reason now; America would be the place to carry out their plan.

Then, sometime far in the night, Mati found himself telling Schmulik of the dream, the apparition. He would not have imagined it would be Schmulik to whom he would confide this—why had he held back with Leah? He told how he had dreamed or imagined Gidon at the cave, alone, on guard over Mishkan Yaa-cov, and how he himself had been climbing up to reach Gidon. The apparition must have been—Mati had counted the time difference to Chicago—it must have been in the very moment of Gidon's death.

Mati's words made Schmulik uneasy. He considered himself a plain man of the earth, of reality, without superstitions. True, their mother believed in such things, she believed in the soul of Avramchik hovering over Reuven that time when the bandit horse thieves believed they saw an angel hovering over him and ran off, even leaving him his horse! Ima still told the story, certain it had been the spirit of little Avramchik. Women's tales. His wife too was superstitious. Still, Schmulik could not altogether turn aside Mati's dream. The hour worked out exactly. Yet if there was indeed such a thing, a spirit, a soul—and who could entirely gain-say this?—then how was it that Gidon had in the last instant appeared to Mati? Not to Aviva. Not to himself? Yet just after Gidon had returned from the war and had worked with Schmulik on the meshek again, the two of them together, that had been a time of real brotherhood, Gidon had begun to teach him English, first a few words off cigarette packs, because now English would be needed with the new rulers of the land. It was Gidon who saw how everyone took Schmulik for an ox, a mere beast of the field, and insisted, "It is your turn now to go and learn something," getting him to go to Haifa to a British school to learn mechanics and pick up English as well.

The Little Ox, Schmulik knew everyone still called him, and as a lad it had even pleased him; then in grown years he took it with a shrug—they meant nothing bad by it. But still, an ox, a stupid, unfeeling ox that pulled the plow, that chomped his feed, drank, pissed, shit, and pulled again.

Coming to Eretz a boy of ten, he had happily discovered there was as yet no teacher in the new settlement and gone straight to the fields, helping his father and Gidon, who was already past his Bar Mitzvah. Schmulik hated to sit and study. But then the whole group of settlers from Rumania arrived, bringing a melamed with them. He took girls in the school; even Schmulik's little sister Yaffaleh was quicker than he, so Schmulik had revolted, running off to swim in the Kinneret or to trail after Gidon and Abba in the fields until they gave him a task.

From time to time Leah would take hold of him in the evening and make him read with her or do sums. Luckily numbers came easily to Schmulik, there at least he was quicker than Yaffaleh, so the family was satisfied that he was not altogether a donkey, a chamor.

Though never to be tall, he was full grown, the year of that village battle when the Zbeh ran off the entire cattle herd. Gidon, known for picking off two of the marauders, had to disappear, so when he went to Jaffa and became apprenticed to a veterinary, it was the young ox, Schmulik, who took over the main burden of the meshek. The old ox, tateh, Abba, still was strong, and they labored sometimes as though yoked together, Schmulik and Yankel like a badly matched pair pulling in opposite directions. Thus, they had worked the farm throughout the years of the war, with Gidon out of the country fighting for the British. Nor had the hero returned to the farm after the war; Gidon, marrying, had set up as a veterinary in Herzlia. Thereby Schmulik knew the meshek one day would be his, for young Mati was destined for higher things.

Already Yankel's bones seemed unequal to the heavier tasks, and Schmulik more and more would go out by himself, leaving Yankel still wrapped in his tallis, muttering the morning prayer. And when Yankel arrived, Schmulik would wave him off the field, don't bother, Abba, I'm already finishing!

111

After Big Leah took Mati off to Tel Aviv to study in the Gymnasia, there were times when a chalutz would have to be hired. Luckily there were plenty coming into the land just then from Poland, and even from the Soviet Union until the Russians, just as in the days of the Czar, again began arresting Zionists.

On the High Holidays, when the whole family would gather, and over the table the big readers like Reuven and Leah's chaver Natan and Dvora's chaver Menahem would start discussing the merits and faults of the new Hebrew translation of Shakespeare, then Schmulik would silently eat and take himself off. An ignoramus. A clod.

When he began to walk with Nussya, he felt better. The granddaughter of Reb Meir Roitschuler loved to relate the plots of stories she had read, just as when still in the schoolroom, she and Yaffaleh used to make up whole tales of their own. Poor Yaffaleh had always thought herself ugly and kept apart from the town beauties; only Nussya did not make her uncomfortable. Quite early Nussya had developed large breasts, and this was the time when all the girls tried to look like the fashion magazines from France, flat boards. Even in Mishkan Yaacov the young girls went about with stretched necks, just the way the prophet Jeremiah had described the women of Jerusalem. Nussya's neck was short. But she had the longest hair in Mishkan Yaacov, hair like a pouring of honey. It was indeed poor Yaffaleh's death, when she went up with the young volunteers to help Trumpeldor guard Tel Hai, that had brought Nussya and Schmulik together, for Nussya came often during the six days of mourning and once talked to him of how she blamed herself for not having gone with Yaffaleh. And only to her Schmulik revealed how he too blamed himself, but Nussya had taken his hand and reminded him that he could not have gone off and left the meshek.

Then, when Schmulik began to walk with Nussya, he suddenly felt approval all about him. A village match! Everyone knew that Schmulik kept the best meshek in Mishkan Yaacov; older men came to him for decisions, when to plant, how much water to give. And the Roitschulers were a substantive family. Nussya's father, who in Rumania had owned a leather shop, had taken to buying sheepskins brought to him by Arabs from Dja'adi and other villages; he set up a tannery in his barn and sold wagonloads of leather to bootmakers in Tel Aviv.

Then the whole thing went wrong with Nussya. She brooded; she suddenly avoided Schmulik. He was not long to understand;

Nussya was smitten. It was with one of the new chalutzim from Poland, a lively one with an accordion who sang songs he made up in his own head. Every night you could hear his accordion in the village square as the young strollers gathered around. Schmulik gathered with the others, but once when he tried to walk Nussya away, she twisted off and cried at him, "Oh! You're nothing but a dumb ox!"

A terrible restlessness then came over him. It was Succoth; Gidon, home for the holiday, had a talk with Schmulik—even about women. After the festival Schmulik took his hoarded home earnings and went to Haifa, where the British had a school for mechanics. Let the old man hire a chalutz to get through the winter. In a few months Schmulik came storming back astride a huge motorcycle, the first in Mishkan Yaacov.

Thereafter he was often absent from home. The devil only knew where he went on that devilish machine, and what for. Some of the lads claimed to have seen Schmulik's iron steed standing for hours before a house of shame in Nazareth, and Schmulik only returned their gibes, saying that a she-goat such as they used might be cheaper, but a French girl smelled better.

Alongside the lake he raced against the swiftest steeds ridden by lads of Dja'adi, giving them a long lead and sometimes letting them win so they would still make wagers with him. Once, when a tire went flat, the Arab riders had their jest for a whole season.

In Mishkan Yaacov the schoolboys ran out of their houses when they heard Schmulik's machine blasting into the village, and he gave them turns riding pillion. Even a giggling daughter or two. And as he roared past Nussya's house, he knew she watched from behind the curtain.

The accordion player was long gone, now working in the Nesher cement factory near Haifa.

Then at last one twilight when Schmulik took the lakeside road, it was Nussya's hands that were clasped over his stomach. Schmulik did not ask himself why this sensation was so different from when he had any other girl behind him; he felt the large breasts cushioned against his back, and peace returned to his soul.

Sometime after the marriage it was his Ima, Feigel herself, who declared that no kitchen was large enough for two women. The Roitschulers gave land for a small house near their own, and Nussya, truly a home creature, kept adding embroidered pillows and getting Schmulik to build trellises and seats in the garden.

After their first child, Simha, came into the world, Nussya's belly never receded; one could hardly tell when she was pregnant with the second. Her face was always placid, her upper lip was always dewy, and some of the village girls said if Schmulik was a bull, he had indeed found his cow.

He was again becoming restless. This was the time when the engineer Pinhas Rutenberg received the concession for the hydro-electric works; the site was where the Yarmuk River joined the Jordan, only a few kilometers from Mishkan Yaacov. Suddenly the area was aswarm with workers and machinery, and there, with his Haifa training, Schmulik came into his element. Enormous earth-moving machines arrived. Huge boulders, embedded since the convulsions of the Ice Age that had formed this great geological rift, could not hold their place before the new mechanical monsters. Like a head-down bull, the earthmover jarred the rocks, forced its path. The machine was called a bulldozer, and of this Schmulik became master.

The work was not far away, so he could still supervise the meshek, even while helping shape the vast excavations for the power station.

On the straw mat the two brothers lay intermittently wakeful, each at times feeling the other asleep and then perhaps uttering a thought out of his half dreams, his self-searching, his memories of Gidon. In Mati there persisted that sudden image of the airplane, the image of himself back in Chicago learning to fly, doubling on his jobs so as to pay for his lessons, living austere and alone in his back room as though to atone for last year's pleasure.

Or was not this plan an escape? He should remain here and rebuild.

With earth machines, Schmulik saw himself clearing a flying field; then he would set up the iron framework of a hangar disguised as a barn, and in a year Mati would come with the airplane.

"How long would it take you to learn to fly?"

"I'm staying here."

"Idiocy!" Schmulik cried. And something came to him. "Even in your dream, Gidon was telling you to go back."

Startled at his brother's perception, Mati took this into himself, and half slept.

Then a vision—he had learned to fly and was bringing Dena here in the plane! Then he felt ashamed, here where Gidon had died, of his sexual arousal. At last Mati slept.

At dawn Schmulik had taken a tallis and tefillin from his pack and begun the Kaddish. Mati joined in the words, recalling how Schmulik used to go on Sabbath Eve with Abba to the shul, the only son to do so.

Then Schmulik started putting the door back on its hinges. Where were the damned chaverim from here, why hadn't any of them yet returned? Suddenly Mati declared he had decided after all to remain and build. Schmulik seized him. "No!" The other plan was more important. They decided to talk of it with their brother-in-law Menahem who was in Tel Aviv these days in the sittings of the inner circle of the Haganah, reviewing all that had gone wrong and planning for the future.

Menahem at once saw, and saw all the difficulties as well, and took them to Dov Hos. Dov's perpetual smile grew and grew. But when Dov took them to the chief himself, Eliahu, the flaws loomed large. The cost. And if the plane could be used only one time before detection, better with the same money to find machine guns for each settlement. Money was urgent; several chevreh had to be sent to Europe, never again should the Yishuv be caught so un-prepared.

As for the cost, Schmulik declared he would take on extra jobs, work day and night. Ah, smiling Dov reminded him, an airplane cost more than a motorcycle. And flying lessons abroad—

The lessons, Mati broke in, he'd manage on his own part. And as for the cost of the machine, in America, in Chicago, he knew a modern rabbi, their Reform kind, a good Zionist with a wealthy congregation. Only, to raise such money, a few people would have to be let in on the secret.

"A few always becomes many." Eliahu worried. Still, he would take up the plan as soon as the way was clear—As they knew, the British Inquiry Commission was coming.

"Sure. To blame the Jews for being massacred," Schmulik said.

He would stay on awhile, Mati said; he was too late for this term anyway. He would stay and help rebuild Hulda.

A half dozen of the chaverim drifted back. Schmulik too lingered on, even getting hold of a broken-down tractor from a Rehovot farmer, promising its repair in exchange for use.

On the Thirtieth Day there appeared surprising numbers for the Remembrance. Scores of Gidon's comrades from the Zion Mule Corps and from the Jewish Legion. Natan the Red tried to speak but choked in sobs. "The best of us all," he blurted. Every leader was there, Ben-Gurion as always with Ben-Zvi, Eliahu, Dov. Wherever in the Yishuv there was danger, there a Chaimovitch was to be found, declared Ben-Gurion. Alongside Trumpeldor in Tel Hai, and again, in command here in Hulda, to each place a Chaimovitch had arrived in the face of attack.

Later Ben-Gurion came over to Mati. Dov Hos had already spoken to him of the airplane idea. "You will do it, Mati. I know your family, you will carry this through. This will perhaps one day prove the most important part of our defense in this land." He reached up his hand to Mati's shoulder—never before had Mati noticed how small he was. "Return to your studies, Mati. I too once had to leave chalutzioth to go and study. In the time of the Turks I went to study law in Kushta. It was necessary."

Still, he waited.

Mati was tree planting when an open car flying the fender flag came up the dirt lane—the district officer. The Britisher looked young, with that sporty-keen all-is-a-game expression of theirs, but it was his driver who gave Mati a start. Fawzi! From Dja'adi!

After leaping from the car, Fawzi embraced him, exchanged fond insults, and then suddenly Fawzi's mien became solemn. He asked to see the grave.

With Schmulik they walked to the mound; Fawzi stood over Gidon's grave, and tears were on his face.

Now the Britisher approached. "He was my brother. We swore blood brotherhood," Fawzi told him. "In Jerusalem I danced with Gidon's bride at his wedding. When he built his new house in Herzlia, he invited me. I was his guest." But what had Gidon been doing here in this place, away from his home? "It was not meant to be!" Fawzi cried out to Mati. "By Allah, this was not meant to be!"

In that moment Mati recalled the tale of the car that had remained long hours in the Arab village here. Persistently, perversely, his eye saw Fawzi at the wheel. Wasn't his family in the

Husseini clan? It could probably be found out if on that day Fawzi had been away from his government job. No. Mati put down the thought.

As they went inside for mugs of tea, the Englishman, named Randolph Longworth, kept studying everyone with that keen expression. He had only just come out to Palestine from Srinagar. He could understand about religious frenzy in Hebron and Old Jerusalem, but then what had happened out here? Had Hulda perhaps been Arab land?

The tract had been bought more than twenty-five years before, from an absentee owner in Beirut; it was unsown land as could still be seen all around, Mati said. The forest had been planted in memory of Theodor Herzl; their own brother and sister had worked in the planting.

And until the attack, Jews and Arabs had been on good terms?

For years the kvutsa had bought its water from the Arab mukhtar, hauling it in barrels. Had Longworth visited the Arab village?

He had just come from there, the new district officer said. The mukhtar declared his people had taken no part in the raid.

Schmulik was getting red-faced. "An auto from Jerusalem came there and stayed all day. They sent horsemen around, even to the Bedouin encampment."

The Englishman turned to Fawzi. Was it known just who had attacked?

Doubtless mostly Bedouin, Fawzi said. For spoils. Horses and cattle. Also southward was a mud-hut village, from the days of Mohemmed Ali.

Oh, yes, the Englishman had read up. Mohemmed Ali, the Albanian who had conquered Palestine in 1840, wasn't it? From Egypt.

"He brought in Egyptian fellaheen to live here," Fawzi said.

More than thirty Arab dead, Longworth understood, had been counted in the yard. "Your fellows did well. Thirty to one."

"The one was our brother," Schmulik said.

"He certainly was an excellent commander."

"Sure, he was trained in the British army," Fawzi put in. And again as though ruminating on fate: "Why did it have to be Gidon? Who sent him here? The Haganah?"

"Who sent that car to the Arab village?" Schmulik replied.

117

The Englishman turned to others at the kibbutz table. He made notes of Naftali's request for added rifles; there could still be a tribal attempt at reprisal for all those Arab dead.

Before leaving, Fawzi again spoke to Schmulik and Mati with deep sorrow for Gidon's widow, for the children. Oh, he too was married and had three little ones—all girls, with a shrug—a trick Allah had played on him. A Dajani, it seemed, he had married. A good connection, Mati realized. Fawzi must be considered a rising young man.

On any pretext Schmulik went into the Arab village. There were greens, cheeses to be bought until the kvutsa was again producing its own. He even found the old watchman he had driven away; he carried back his water jug, gave him a package of cigarettes, excused himself for his momentary anger that had come because of the grief over his brother. No, no, la, la, the Arab said, he had not held bitterness in his stomach. He was an old man and had seen much suffering. Thus, Schmulik led to the recent visit of the new English official; his driver was a boyhood friend, Fawzi, Schmulik remarked. Indeed. Hadn't the same driver visited this village before, in a taxi from Jerusalem? Just before the troubles?

A taxi was no longer so rare a sight in the land, the Arab said. Who came, who went, why trouble? On that fateful day the mukhtar had given advice for everyone to stay in his house. And this was what he and his sons had done.

Long hours of the day Schmulik was out in the far fields, making use of the repaired Fordson. Bedouin shepherds came to gaze at the machine, and with them too he struck up conversation. If not for those who came to arouse enmity, their fallen brothers might not have died. Wasn't it better to live in peace and one day also to possess such machines as this?

Though they climbed on behind him and rode a bit, with great curiosity and laughter, of what he burned to know Schmulik could get no answer.

To finish the field he worked the tractor into nightfall. And just then, an incident led to a degree of illumination.

From beyond the field there came a terrified shriek. Naftali, riding guard, found himself nearly thrown as his horse reared; an

Arab boy had flung himself against the mount, clutching and clinging to Naftali's leg, crying "Save me! A dib!"

The boy trembled in every muscle. "A demon! A dib! Yellow eyes! Pursuing me! Out there!" The dib had come rushing on him, and he had barely escaped!

Taking the boy up on his horse, Naftali delivered him to the tents.

"An old superstition having to do with the nearby caves," Naftali related to Schmulik, over tea in the kitchen. The Bedouin believed in an enormous werewolf that dragged victims back to its lair, drank their blood, and left the bodies to be devoured by hyenas; only the bones were ever found.

"Yellow eyes—but that must have been my lights!" Schmulik said. In the mist the tractor lights must have wavered up and down.

The following morning a small procession approached, led by the Bedouin sheikh on his betasseled stallion. Behind him rode four notables, and then came the young lad, leading a ram and a ewe. More tribesmen, in their finest abayas, completed the parade.

Naftali, as mukhtar, went out to welcome them. Last night, declared the sheikh, a good neighbor from this settlement had rescued his own son, the son of his aging years, this boy Mussa, from the most horrible of deaths, wrenching him from the claws of a dib. In token of gratitude and friendship, Mussa came forward with the pair of sheep.

Nudging Schmulik, Mati was for showing them the "dib" in the implement shed, but Schmulik shook his head. Not to make light of their beliefs. And also, he had thought of certain possibilities.

A modest sort of sulha took place, coffee was prepared, everyone crowded into the dining hall, and there was general talk of prospects for the barley crop and a careful avoidance of the subject of the recent troubles here, the horses and cattle that had vanished.

The following day Naftali Sturman and Schmulik returned the visit. In the guest tent the sheikh put aside his narghile to accept their cigarettes, passing the pack on to his notables. During the second coffee Schmulik edged toward the subject. For many years Abu Hassan's tribe had come in the grazing season and dwelt in friendship with their neighbors here. Heads nodded. Alas, recently there had been needless bloodshed, provoked by strangers. He himself, Schmulik said, had lost his elder brother, and among their own people, too, brave sons and brothers had been lost.

Solemnly nodding, Abu Hassan said, "I will not hide the truth from you. Better a bitter truth than a lie smeared with honey." Good men had died.

But how had this needless strife been fomented? Schmulik asked.

Abu Hassan reflected, then seemed to reach a decision. He rose and opened a small coffer, taking out a sheet of paper. This he handed to Schmulik. It was bare except for an elaborate letter-head, in Hebrew, with a picture of a golden-domed temple, somewhat resembling the Mosque of Omar. Atop flew the flag of Zion.

"We were brought this as proof," the sheikh said.

Schmulik became livid. The sheikh raised his hand. "I know it is not the truth," he said. "I have myself journeyed and seen the great mosque with these eyes."

Now Naftali began to explain. The picture was only a dream of the Temple of Solomon, in ancient days. He read aloud the name of the orphanage, "The House of Benevolence of the Sons of Lublin."

The sheikh nodded and repeated. "A dream of ancient days. A picture of a dream." He offered them more coffee. Schmulik ventured, Surely this unfortunate paper, if brought in the name of a high personage, could have been taken as a call to a jihad.

A slight rigidity came in their host and was immediately echoed in the bearing of each notable.

Neighbors who dwelt alongside each other, Naftali said, should strive to know each other well, so that no deceptions or errors could come between them, to arouse enmity and cause bloodshed.

Surely they would drink one more cup of coffee?

They had learned something, but not yet all, Schmulik brooded as he and Naftali rode back. He would somehow learn the rest.

☙ ☙ ☙

The fall term was half over; Mati must soon decide. They were building a granary, large, with thick walls and a high roof. Mati mixed concrete for the hidden underground vault, the arms slick.

Working his hours, eating the meals of cucumbers and tomatoes and an occasional egg, half asleep through the endless meetings, Mati told himself it would be easy to continue this life, debating with the chevreh whether first to build the children's house or, since there were as yet only three infants, to start with a poultry installation? Was it best, instead of planting orange groves, to use more land for vegetables for the Tel Aviv market and thus reduce the city's dependence on Arabs? But wasn't it important also to have the Arab economy linked to the Jews?

Then perhaps here was his place. Still, at night, despite physical exhaustion and then weariness from prolonged repetitious discussions, there came a longing and a lust. Sometimes the image of Andrea came, even appealing to him like that time she had cried out, "Oh, marry me and take me there!"

From Mishkan Yaacov, Schmulik brought Mati a letter. Was this the one? Schmulik grinned. It was from Dena. Only a few lines. "Dear Mati, Believe me, I know, I know what your brother Gidon was to you, and I know your grief, and I only wish I could have been near you. Ever, Dena."

Was it, after their estrangement, a forgiving about Andrea? What did she mean, "ever"? Why didn't all those things in Chicago recede in the face of real life here?

His letter became a long one; he told about how the place had been named Beit Gidon, about how he felt good when he worked all day with the chaverim building the settlement. But still, there was a very special reason why he should come back to Chicago; he couldn't write about it but when he saw her—He had an impulse to put, "I long for you all the time."

Had he decided then?

Mati pondered a long while how to sign his letter. "Ever yours"? "Faithfully"? In the end he signed "With love."

7

ON THE very first day of classes Dena had found herself in the same medieval art course as Myra Roth. "Why didn't you call?" each cried to the other as they emerged, and Myra gushed out the most amazing story of her summer in Europe; she had gone to Vienna and almost got herself psychoanalyzed by Sigmund Freud himself, at least he had seen her for several hours, her uncle had given her a letter, her uncle, of course, had wanted to bring Freud to Chicago for the trial—Myra bit her lip and burst onward, showing she could now talk freely about it all. Dr. Freud had remembered the offer and chuckled—he could be such a wonderful dear human being—he chuckled, he told her, because of another offer, from a newspaper—imagine Freud writing for the Hearst papers! They offered to charter an entire ocean liner to bring him over! After he had made an excuse about disliking to travel in public!

Suddenly Myra demanded, what about Mati? Had Dena heard from Mati, was he coming back? She had written him, Dena said, but hadn't yet heard, and of course, he couldn't get back for this semester. Those awful Arab killings! Myra said, and Dena wouldn't believe this, but "I could have been there myself!" And told about a crazy night in Paris when she had almost decided to go to Palestine with Joe Freedman! It was after Myra had left Vienna because Sigmund Freud simply could not find more time for her, but in three hours with him she had gained more insight into her problems than in her whole life, and he had advised her to have her analysis here in Chicago; he had given her a name. Her problem was that deep down she couldn't believe in anyone; after Artie she couldn't trust what any man showed of himself to be the truth, for when Artie, whom she had known all her life—not only she but every girl had had a crush on him—then when all those unimaginable things came out about him, a killer, a homosexual, not that she blamed him for that part, it was a condition, but that it could have been so hidden, after that how could you believe what any man showed you of himself? The ghastly and also the disgusting things that came out that he had done with that little worm, that Judd Steiner. So this had caused a trauma, and she had to learn all over again to trust. To trust someone. And only her trauma had stopped her in Paris from going to Palestine; imagine, she might have been there all through the shootings and even got herself killed at the Wailing Wall in Jerusalem! For in Paris by a crazy coincidence whom should she have run into in front of the Dome on Montparnasse but Joe Freedman; she had heard he was in Paris, and maybe subconsciously she had been looking for him, but they had a crazy night, Dena could never imagine what had happened. No, not just what she thought, sex. Myra sucked in her lip. Imagine, Joe had asked her to go to Palestine with him! Yes, out of the blue! Maybe she should have taken him up on it. Joe was in a terrible depressed mood, his work was going badly, he kept saying he was wasting his big chance, his Guggenheim, here he was in the center of the art world, everything was here, and he couldn't connect with anything that was going on, he couldn't find himself. They kept drinking, he was guzzling Pernods like lemonade, she was drinking *fine*—cognac, hadn't Dena read Ernest Hemingway?—they moved from the Dome to the Select to the Rotonde with Joe still maundering; she had offered to take him to meet Gertrude Stein, Picasso, but all he did was sneer, and then suddenly he had decided to get out of it all, to go seek his soul in Palestine! And Joe had asked her to come with him.

Myra clutched Dena's arm, gazing into her face as for the absolute truth. "I should have gone, shouldn't I? Would you have gone with your Mati? If he asked you, just like that?"

"But he didn't ask me, and you know we had drifted apart." Yet this was like an intimacy between them, a bond; imagine, they both had someone over there in that fateful land.

It was the Jewish thing with Joe Freedman, Myra said. Imagine, he had gone all the way to some village in Poland to see where his family came from! And those Polish Jews, no, thank you. Myra wasn't prejudiced, and of course, she knew their poverty, their misery, but in Vienna they swarmed—sorry, but like lice. She had never seen such slums, such filth, oh, much worse even than the Negro district here in Chicago. Anyway if it was Jewish art he wanted, as she had told Joe, Paris was full; around Montparnasse all you heard was French with a Yiddish accent or plain Yiddish; around the Select they swarmed with their drawing pads; they sniffed you out—though with her nose it was no problem—an American Jew! The minute you sat down at a café they came peddling their drawings; fiddlers were all the rage, green fiddlers, yellow fiddlers; one little Jew named Katz, Mane Katz, even talented, painted fiddlers by the yard. So after Poland, for Joe, it was Palestine. He had to see for himself. Myra hadn't even said no, about going with him, by this time he was full of Pernod and she of *fine*, but when they had got to his studio, first of all, one of his floozies had left her underwear all over the place, and then—

Myra wouldn't tell exactly what it was that happened. Little Dena was probably still a virgin. Myra was fond of Joe, and he was really g.i.b., she said, but he was a sonofabitch; he always managed to spoil it with her. She might even have gone along to Palestine.

But what she wouldn't tell still burned. She had been Frenching him, even joking about "when in Rome," when suddenly the slob cried she was great at it, this must run in her family!

Only after a second Myra had realized he meant Artie, with Judd.

So she had come back to be analyzed in Chicago. She had missed it again with Joe Freedman, her West Side Jewish genius.

※ ※ ※

Summoned to Tel Aviv to see Dov, Mati went early and met his old flame Zippie at the Yarkon café. She arrived looking like just out of a beauty shop and with a "mature" air recalled their sweet, youthful high school kisses, for she now knew what love was, she was about to marry Ronnie Levinson. The Levinsons he didn't have to be told about; they were big orange growers in Rishon el Zion. Ronnie he recalled, a graduate of the Gymnasia a year ahead of their class, a decent fellow who took himself very seriously. She would be a real bourganit, Mati teased.

Counterteasing him about his doings with shiksehs in Chicago—oh, in the Yishuv who had secrets?—Zippie suddenly became solemn. "Be careful you don't get trapped, Mati, you're so good-hearted, I know you." And took his hand, uttering a little sigh at what might perhaps have been between them had he not gone away at the wrong moment.

Among the many suborganizations of the Histadrut, Dov, known as the Smiling One, had for his official task the importation of agricultural machinery. As Mati entered the tiny office, Dov rose from behind his desk and gave him a snappy mock British salute. First Flier of the Future Air Force!

Decided then? At last!

Naturally, no funds. But the command agreed that the air possibility could not be neglected. The first step, even before the acquisition of an airplane, was the training of a flier, naturally with a view to his training others. Mati should return to the States; among his contacts in Chicago he could probably easily raise the money for lessons.

"Never mind, I'll find a way! Who needs to eat!"

And more. He should begin inquiries about the best type of airplane.

If absolutely necessary, could he divulge the purpose to a few persons who absolutely could be trusted? In each case, Dov said Mati would have to consult the contact in New York.

And then what of the main problem? How to bring in the airplane? "When the time comes, we'll find a way." The British might not be as stupid as the Turks, but sometimes they could be just as blind.

❊ ❊ ❊

In Feigel's spells of illness, there were times now when she fell into ghastly hallucinations. One Friday night in front of Schmulik and Nussya there had come a heartrending outburst just as poor Abba arrived home from shul. As he kissed the mezuza and closed the door behind him, Feigel screamed, pointing her finger, "That one! It is he! The demon sent by the Evil One! He dragged me to this wilderness and imprisoned me so as to slaughter my children! He is the slaughterer! He has come to slaughter me! Save me! Drive him away!"

Nussya had managed to quiet Feigel and put her to bed, giving her pills left on the last visit by the doctor from Reuven's kibbutz. Then at the table Abba had nevertheless recited the Woman of Valor. His dim eyes were always watery now, so it could not be known if his heart wept. And Nussya, in tears, had served the Sabbath meal that Feigel had prepared.

Nussya and the children, Schmulik knew, were the only warmth of life that remained to his mother. Many times Feigel had declared that only through him had a true daughter-in-law been brought to her. And when Nussya was with his old mother, the glow of Nussya's earlier self came through to him, and he forgot her fits of sourness and scoldings over his absences.

She talked so understandingly of his mother, with a woman's understanding. When had Feigel begun to lose her hold on life, to wander in her mind? Hadn't he noticed? It was after Leah got married, when the long long strain of worry for her eldest daughter was ended, that Feigel's strength had given way. She must all her life have felt so alone here, Nussya said. To the other women of the village Feigel had never come close, not only that they were Rumanians and had all arrived in a group, but that most of them were younger than she. When Leah had returned from her mission to Russia in the midst of the Revolution and told how little was left of the family on her mother's side—the powerful Kalman Koslovsky shot by the Bolsheviks—Feigel's life had begun to dim. Now, when Mati had arrived from America, she had made him talk over and over of her sister Hannah's family there, and this had warmed her a bit. Oh, it was sometimes heartrending to see what life made of us.

Suddenly Schmulik said, "Why are we talking of her as if she were already dead?" Nussya began to weep, and he came and stroked her hair, still so long and beautiful.

※ ※ ※

It could even be said, the doctor pronounced, that Feigel had died of a broken heart. He was a youngish man, recently from Poland, and his lips folded in academic certitude as he explained that there must have been a massive refraction within the aorta itself, meaning a broken heart.

The whole village said it was the death of Gidon. Yaffaleh's death the old mother had borne, but Gidon's had at last broken

126

Feigel's weary heart. Indeed, it was in fear of this that none had named him, but in the month since Mati's return from America it had been as though Feigel were puzzling, puzzling.

Sobbing, Nussya related how Feigel's death had come, though all said she must not blame herself. In the morning she had brought the children there to brighten the day for Feigel. Moving about in the kitchen, fetching them her famous raisin cookies, Feigel had suddenly halted, standing still in the middle of the room. Her face wore a tender smile, touched with a childish triumph at having caught on to a secret, a riddle. Then she began telling little Eliza how her uncle Gidon, a soldier in the great war, had once surprised the whole family. There in the yard, after being away for four long years, he had suddenly come riding home, with a Star of David on his soldier's cap. To Nussya, Feigel again described every dish she had cooked for Gidon's wedding, filling the whole wagon with great baskets to take to Jerusalem. Each recipe, she had explained, so joyfully, with such satisfaction! And then all at once Feigel fell silent. Where then was Gidon? She turned to Nussya, questioning. Mati, her youngest, the yingel who had been sent away to study in America—Mati had come home, yes, the whole family had come to the house to welcome him, wasn't it so? Indeed, it was, Nussya reassured her, the whole family had come! Feigel nodded. Mati had come home, but not Gidon. Where was Gidon?

Feigel had stared at Nussya, as though asking, Why should everyone deceive an old woman, an old mother?

Unable to bear this, Nussya had run out of the kitchen. An instant later she heard the fall. "She must have seen it in my eyes. It was my fault! Mine!"

"No, no." Elisheva stroked her hair.

And Nussya's own mother comforted her. "No, no, it was not your fault, don't blame yourself. Feigel knew. Something inside her knew, the whole time. She knew. A mother knows."

They buried Feigel then, beside little Avramchik who had died that dismal first winter in this place.

More remote than ever from his sons, Yankel sat wrapped in his tallis through the days of mourning that seemed this year to follow each other so closely. For hours on end, swaying, Yankel said psalms, in unbroken davening. It was a way of being isolated from them, his sons and daughters and all the visitors understood, yet they knew also that Yankel's ears heard all that was talked about, even while letting the talk go by as though it were not a part of his life.

※ ※ ※

The Commission of Inquiry had already arrived from England to investigate the "disorders," high Britishers with polite faces, to sit in judgment it seemed, more on the Jews than on the marauders. *Davar* each day was filled with what had been testified before the commission. It was hardly the massacres that were being discussed; why talk of those severed heads and dismembered bodies of Hebron; all those unfortunate excesses had already been described. Let the causes be found. Why had the Arabs risen in revolt?

Revolt! the Jewish leaders cried. It had been a massacre worked up by sheer lies! A call to religious fanaticism, to kill, to loot, to pillage! A false picture of a Jewish flag flying over the Mosque of Omar had been distributed. With such devilish tricks the fellaheen had been misled. Agitators had visited every Arab village, in a carefully coordinated plot, giving the signal for attacks.

And yet, the questioners inquired, was there not a real fear among the Arabs that the Jews were coming to drive them out of their land?

Why? cried the Jews. They had settled on deserts, on swamps.

No more Jews should be permitted to enter, cried the Arabs. No more land should be permitted to be sold to the Jews.

But Arabs had been leaving this land before the advent of Zionism, repeated the Jews, and since then they had been coming into Palestine unhindered and unchecked; their population had doubled in the ten years of the Mandate.

And who was selling Jews land? Schmulik sputtered. Who except the Arabs themselves, at continually rising prices? The rich effendis, the Nashashibis, the Dajanis, even the Mufti's Husseinis, the very ones who piously protested their fears for the poor fellaheen!

Reuven, Mati, Menahem managed to discuss it all with some degree of calm, but Schmulik was beside himself. He would find out, Schmulik swore, just who spread that false picture! That the Mufti was behind it all, everyone knew, but who, exactly, had singled out Hulda for attack? Who had sent the automobile there that day, and who had been in it? It was they who not only had killed Gidon, but through his death had killed Ima, too.

Had a single fellah been driven out of this pestilential valley, which had lain a wilderness and a waste? Here, where everyone in the family had contracted malaria and the baby Avramchik had died of it? Had even one Arab lived on the sands on which the whole city of Tel Aviv was built? And even the sands had been paid for!

And the Jews of Hebron—families that had lived there for generations—had they driven out any Arabs? Indeed, in the house where the worst slaughter had taken place, the grain and seed shop of Reb Meisel, in the dried blood on the floor half-burned ledgers and torn-up promissory notes had been found. Exactly as in Russian pogroms. And what of the Hasidim of Safed, the last to be massacred, a full week after the British had declared the area under control and had prevented the Haganah from coming there to protect the pious old Jews? Had a single Arab ever left Safed because of the coming of Zionism? Arabs driven out!

It was the question of the country's economic capacity for population absorption that was now being raised before the committee. What of Rutenberg's power plant, Schmulik cried out, where he himself had labored? The whole of Palestine could be irrigated, industrialized—

The older brothers turned to Mati, the student of political economy. Oh, the British were being well answered by the Jewish experts, Mati said.

Then why were the British experts declaring the country was full and no more immigrants could be absorbed?

Any expert could decide as he wanted. One expert could declare an Arab family needed a hundred dunam of land for subsistence, another could say that ten dunam sufficed. Hadn't Reuven increased the yield of the land tenfold, with crop rotation and irrigation? Four fodder crops a year! And selected wheat strains, giving double yield! Here came government experts who said only five percent of Palestine was arable, and Jewish experts declaring that eventually sixty percent could be reclaimed. Look at the vast stretches of long-abandoned terraced hills, all through Judea and Samaria. In the days of King Solomon, even without modern agricultural techniques, this country had supported five times as many inhabitants as now.

Old Yankel lifted his head. At least his offspring, the unbelievers, still spoke of Solomon.

While the men's discussion circled over the fate of the land, the women, sometimes suddenly putting in their words, showing they didn't miss what was being said, nevertheless among themselves spoke of Feigel. From the old trunk that had been hauled from Cherezinka, Leah unpacked, even after these years, unused embroidered and crocheted household things, a Ukrainian tea caddy, and finery, a hand-stitched camisole that Shula coveted, a toddler's things that Dvora recognized—she had dressed little Avramchik in them.

But they talked of her good days, too; oddly, in the time of war Ima had been at her liveliest, didn't everyone remember when the Turks came hunting men of the Shomer, and Zev the Hotblood had to be hidden? Feigel had pushed him into the big Russian oven—oh, she had no liking for Zev, always hanging after Leah—and she had given him a good roasting before letting him out after the Turks were gone! Poor Zev, they had caught him in the end and hanged him in Damascus. And it could not be said that Feigel had no joy of the land; long, quiet hours she would sit gazing at the changing colors of the Kinneret.

Yet it seemed sometimes as though they were sitting shiva here not only for their mother but for Zionism itself. For now there were the pious and sanctimonious words of the Mufti, addressed to the British inquirers and to the world. Again his litany against the kinds of Jews who were invading the Holy Land—unbelievers and radicals, with their women going about brazen and bare.

Ah, what a gentle and almost saintly impression the Grand Mufti made on them, with his soft voice and great dignity. Mufti! Schmulik howled. Everyone knew even his appointment had been a swindle! The Husseinis had tricked Lord Samuel into passing by a Nashashibi who was next in line!

Ah, even more, Menahem had said. According to a cadi at their university in Cairo, Haj Amin had hardly finished a year of studies and was unqualified. And as for the title of Grand Mufti he had assumed, no such post existed! Each mufti was the religious leader only in his own place. But there, Menahem declared, was the clue to what Haj Amin was after. Power. To be the great power in the Arab and the Moslem world. By rousing Jew hatred, just like Hitler with his growing Nazi Party in Germany. Palestine was only a corner of the Moslem world, Menahem lectured, but just now the power over hundreds of millions of Moslems lay open; there was no caliphate, no central authority, and the Mufti was out to grasp that power. For this he had in the last few years made his journeys to all the great Moslem centers, even outside the Arab world. The Turkish Sultan had claimed the caliphate, but with the defeat of the Turks and the breakup of the Turkish Empire, that was gone. The Sherif of Mecca, as a descendant of the Prophet, had claimed the power, and the British adventurer Lawrence of Arabia had bought him with gold to their side in the war and later made his sons rulers in Arabia. But England's Sherif himself had long ago been chased out of Mecca by Ibn Saud, of the sect of the Wahabis; the very name of that land was now Saudi Arabia. Thus, both in Mecca and in Istanbul the seat of the Caliph was empty. And into this emptiness the Mufti was reaching.

Mati had never heard the idea propounded in this form. It seemed too neat. Still, why shouldn't a clever and ambitious man be arousing the Moslem world as a whole, stimulating strife in Palestine to gain himself notice and leadership? Calling himself the Grand Mufti. Collecting vast funds for repairing the Mosque of Omar and using them for arms purchases for the recent attacks.

Nahum had listened with an air of respect, even admiration for all that Menahem brought into his argument, yet skepticism. "The only point is," he said, "the Mufti doesn't have all that much power. Even here in Palestine the Arabs are divided. In Tiberias nobody followed him in his jihad. They could have slaughtered us all; they outnumber us five to one. The plain truth is the Arab notables know what is good for them; they have never done so well as since we came. Our job is to build up the opposition to him."

But Natan pointed out something more that was ominous. For the British, he said, their whole strategy of Empire was changing. So they were changing their mind altogether about backing up the Jews in Palestine. For why had they issued the Balfour Declaration? Out of simple love for the Jews? True, everyone knew that Balfour and Lloyd George were Bible lovers, but still, the real importance was the Suez Canal. The British had wanted a reliable, European people, especially a people who would be beholden to them, to protect this side of the Canal. Who better than the Jews? Only now, unfortunately for the Jews, things were shifting. More and more oil was being found in the Arab lands, oil pipelines were being laid from Iraq, and quite simply the Arabs were more important for the British than a small powerless people like the Jews. And so they were trying to use the troubles here—which their own administrators had allowed to develop—as an excuse to declare their obligation to the Jews was finished, the Jewish National Home was already in existence, they had never meant a Jewish nation in all Palestine, or a Jewish nation at all. And they would use the Mufti and his revolt as an excuse and close down immigration.

Menahem added more high politics. The British wanted to curry favor with the entire Moslem world—beyond the Arab Moslems—in order to set off any future inroads by the Soviet Union.

"Good, fine—high politics explains it all!" Dvora broke in, gazing at her husband as one who had long listened and who did not deny his broad thinking. But wasn't it really a plain and simple thing? "From the beginning they attacked and killed." And everyone knew Dvora meant the death of her betrothed, Yechezkiel. "Maybe many of them are only looking for plunder; they see all we have built and they want it. But also in their religion they really hate us. What more do we need to explain of the Mufti than that he hates the Jews? Among our fine British, too, there are plain Christian anti-Semites, and we have to defend ourselves, and high politics will never change it."

Because Dvora rarely took part in discussions, her outburst had a kind of authority. In her kibbutz, too, whenever Dvora spoke, her words seemed final. "The Mufti spreads his hate, and that is all the explanation we need."

Yankel lifted his head. "Edom," he said. "The sons of Cain, of Esau, and of Ishmael."

Yet after a moment Shula remarked, "We shouldn't assume that everyone is against us. There are plenty of British who are really for us with all their hearts. Even because they are Christians. As Christians they really believe the Jews belong in the Holy Land. Not everyone is evil." Shula smiled to her Nahum, as though to remind everyone that her husband well knew why she made friendships with highly placed Britishers. She was smoothing over her knees a black silk corset cover with lace inlets, which Ima had worn in the old days beneath her Sabbath gown. For a sleeveless blouse in summer it would be beautiful, she said to Nussya.

❊❊❊

In the midst of the mourning week came a message for Menahem, and he was off. Surely to Europe for weapons. One last word to Mati—next time Menahem expected to see him come flying out of the air!

And before the Inquiry Commission the testimony went on. Chaim Weizmann himself, again telling how the Arab leader from Mecca, Lawrence's friend Feisal, had declared to him that they would welcome the Jews to Palestine. And Ben-Gurion describing his planning with Feisal's brother, the Emir Abdullah, to develop Trans-Jordan. And in contradiction came Jabotinsky's Revisionists claiming Trans-Jordan for Jews as part of the Jewish homeland.

Why not? said Nahum. The best way to bargain was to demand double!

But why start that territorial argument again when it had all been settled? said Reuven. Already in 1921, after the May Day troubles in Jaffa, the British Colonial Secretary, Winston Churchill, had come and divided Palestine at the Jordan, giving the Arabs the other side, much bigger than this side. He had put Abdullah in as the ruler. No Jews were to settle there. Though the fiery Jabotinsky and his dissidents cried out that the British had no right to divide the Mandate, still, Reuven believed the division was a natural one; even in Biblical times it was only at intervals that Edom and Moab had been part of the Jewish kingdom. The division seemed a fair solution to Reuven, and hadn't the Arabs accepted it and been quiet these eight years?

Before the commission there also came Jews who spoke of long, friendly relations with Arab neighbors. There came the planter and author Moshe Smilansky, an early chalutz, whose life had nearly been burned out of him in the fever swamps of Chedera. Now a wealthy orange grower of Rehovot, Smilansky spoke of the two people dwelling together in peace. "Ach, he himself exploits Arab labor; he pays them less than Jews!" Natan spurted out. The only solution was to organize Arab labor! But Reuven, who once had worked for Smilansky, in the old days, right alongside Arabs, declared him a fair and understanding man.

Dvora read on in *Davar*'s account of the hearing. Wasn't it true that he had written much about Arab life? the English asked Smilansky. Indeed, he was a great lover of their folklore. Oh, Nussya broke in, her favorite was Smilansky's beautiful Arab tale about the lovely sea, the Kinneret, locked in by the stone hills around, like a woman carefully guarded. Even Ima Feigel used to sit and watch the sea and tell that tale. And so again the mourners' thoughts returned to the mother. Though only a young boy, Mati had at times caught a touch of melancholy in his mother, as though she were imprisoned here like the Kinneret. And now, sitting shiva over her life, he wondered, had she been deeply unhappy? Not more than others. Her spirit had been strong.

Indeed, Dvora read on from Smilansky's testimony, he was a great admirer of Arab character. He believed Jews and Arabs had much in common in their lore and their wisdom. Jews and Arabs could live side by side if they were not deliberately set against each other.

But, the Englishmen asked, did he believe the Arabs here as a whole did not resent the idea of Palestine as a Jewish homeland?

Why should they? They had all Arabia. They had never had a nation in this land. Only the Jews, in all history, had created a nation here. Already, under the Mandate, the Jews had created their own elected council. "We Jews want to govern our own affairs, not theirs."

Then how, a commissioner asked, could a government be formed here, when the Mandate was over?

Ah, the difficult and dangerous ground had been reached. Now came the ideas of the B'rith Shalom, and of a binational state. Leaving the Jews in a perpetual minority! Schmulik exploded. Oh, all this came from Professor Judah Magnes at the university. Schmulik glared at Mati. Oh, yes, when the professors came to handing over the Yishuv, even the Mufti would join their B'rith Shalom! Peace! As in every other ghetto! All big brains, fine people, too!

Wait, Reuven interceded. Nobody was handing over the Yishuv. The B'rith Shalom too insisted on continued Jewish immigration. Even Chaim Weizmann shared some of their ideas.

Chaim Weizmann! Schmulik shrugged. A leader who did nothing but beg, plead, and offer compromises! It was time to demand! What kind of B'rith Shalom was it—did it have a single Arab member!

"Even if only one side talks of peace, a movement for peace exists," Reuven declared.

And his Elisheva joined in. "One side has to keep the way open. That at least makes it possible that one day those Arabs not heard from will have the courage to appear."

Schmulik held himself in silence. He burned to say, "No use arguing with vegetarians." And a pacifist, too. But still, Reuven had come here first, with Leah, and faced everything.

134

Mati's mind was in tumult. It was the eternal equation that wouldn't come out right; the end concept couldn't be reached by the given components. He hated what Arabs had done, but did he hate the Arabs? Yet he burned to procure the most powerful of weapons, to fly above their horsemen, next time, and destroy them. But still, that would simply be defense. He had no hatred or spirit of vengeance, he told himself, surely no impulse to drive them from the land.

※ ※ ※

What would happen now to Abba, that was the worry. Even with Nussya and Schmulik nearby, could he live on alone in the old meshek? Reuven's kibbutz had a special kosher kitchen for the aged parents of chaverim; Abba could perhaps find cronies there. But of no kibbutz would Yankel trust the kashrut—all, all, were heathen, apikoirasim! In the end Yankel insisted he would stay in the house alone. Nussya could look in every few days; she would send a woman to clean and do his washing.

As the week of mourning was ending, Yankel brought out and handed to Leah an old silver sugar box in which Feigel had kept her few womanish things, her ornaments. Among the daughters and daughters-in-law Leah apportioned the gold brooches, the earrings.

But one small item Abba held in his own keep. Now, when Mati was about to leave again for Chicago, his father took him aside. "Long ago, when she was already sick she told me, 'This will be for Mati's bride.'" A half-yellowed twist of handkerchief was cupped in Abba's hand. Mati waited while slowly the stiff fingers undid the knot. There lay a gold ring, topped by a small diamond.

Vaguely from far back, from earliest childhood, Mati recalled family discussions over the diamondl. Once when they had all gone to Damascus for Reuven's marriage to a daughter of the elegant Shalmonis, Shula had persuaded her mother to have the jewel taken out of her old-fashioned brooch and set in a ring. In the hardest of years, during the virtual famine that followed the plague of locusts in the war, the decision had almost been taken to sell the diamondl, but Abba had borrowed money on it instead from Nahum's father. Even before—this Mati knew had happened before he was born—when the family arrived in Jaffa port, his mother had hidden the diamondl in the secret recesses of a woman's garments, saving it from the clutching hands of the fierce Arab

135

boatmen. Still more remote was the tale of great care in its purchase, Abba seeking out in Odessa on the eve of their voyage a jeweler who was a cousin by marriage of a cousin; only within the family could there be trust that the stone should be flawless and at an honest price for a Jew making the journey with his whole family to live in Eretz.

"Take it, take it," his father said to Mati. "She told me this would be for your bride. Her youngest."

And then, as years before, only this time who knew if he would live to see his yingel again, Yankel said, "Go, my son, go and study; whatever it is that you study there in America, our Torah I am sure it is not. But go. Go with my blessing."

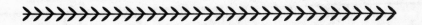

8

TO HIS aunt Hannah with her sighing and eye dabbing the two deaths were one, Feigel and Gidon. Feigel had had such a hard life, not coming to America, and in the end because of the Arabs, she too had died.

Only now with his aunt, it came to Mati that in some Jewish way Russia and even Palestine were the same: the hostile world. It was only the family that existed. Over these long years the letters that had gone between his mother and her sister in America were their real lives.

At least this time he was spared the presence of his cousin Wally, who had moved out and was rarely heard from, though "doing well." The teacher couple and the lawyer had kept up with the reports of what was said before the Royal Commission of Inquiry, but no matter what the British decided, the lawyer was dubious; wouldn't the Arabs always be resorting to violence? Mati had to keep telling of the amazing changes just in these two years, over there, the new places, everywhere new buildings, factories, and how Hulda was rebuilt and now named after Gidon. He even told them the comical story of the Bedouin boy and the dib. They laughed but also were puzzled; was it really so primitive? How could the whole thing ever work? Only the daughter of the teaching pair, Lilly, now seventeen, with bangs over her eyes, seemed to catch something of the real spirit, and Mati made a mental note that here was possible material.

Luckily Mrs. Kelleher still had one little back room. When Mati told her he had been delayed because his mother had died, she gasped. "Oh, the poor woman, was it because of what happened to your brother?" Those awful heathen Moslems, when she had read the descriptions of those beastly massacres—The Holy Land belonged to the Jews; why, the whole world knew it from the Bible, every town, every city, Jerusalem, Bethlehem, Nazareth. Oh, she hoped things were under control now, she had listened to the church bells of Jerusalem on a Christmas broadcast, and she prayed there would be peace, she had thought of Mati over there and even mentioned his family in her prayers, she hoped he didn't mind—a Christian! Peace on earth, all religions believed in peace, though with the imperfections of mankind it was, sadly, in the name of religion that people usually started their hideous wars.

The room was so tiny that the study table was a tight squeeze between the cot and the wall; the narrow window looked onto a three-foot areaway. "But I don't suppose you'll be staying here much?" she remarked knowingly. Let her imagine. In a sense this cell seemed right for him; he intended to be locked into one purpose alone: to get the airplane, to finish the university somehow sooner, and to go home.

Rabbi Mike was at the Rappaports' to hear at first hand. One thing Mati could tell them, never again would the Yishuv trust to the British for protection. First, weapons. In the strictest confidence, the Haganah already had certain chevreh busy in Europe. By the same token, since he would need their help, Mati divulged his own special task. Excited, Mike offered all help. Only—Mati must have heard—the stock market crash just after he left had brought the country to the verge of panic. Things were still getting worse. Demands on Jewish philanthropy were on the increase, with unemployment spreading, while donations declined.

Still, wealthy people could always find money for causes that seized their imagination, Mike had noticed, and for such a project —When the time was ripe, he would make the approach. . . . And had Mati seen Judah Magnes?

Shortly before sailing, Mati had indeed gone to Jerusalem, and the university president had given him a whole hour, there up the ladder steps to the famous rooftop office with its wondrous view of all Jerusalem and the surrounding hills. Enthusiastically he had shown Mati plans for the great expansion he envisioned and spoken of the day when Palestine-born scholars—perhaps like Mati himself!—would be numerous on the faculty.

Indeed, Mati could tell them that the B'rith Shalom views of Magnes, especially when supported by people like Ruppin and Smilansky from among the earliest leaders, were widely discussed in the Yishuv and had certainly impressed the leader of the Royal Commission, Sir Walter Shaw. Mati's own eldest brother, Reuven, believed in the B'rith Shalom. The problem was—Mati described the discussion in his own family as they sat shiva for their mother —people always asked who among the Arabs were the B'rith Shalomers, and you couldn't answer. Mike nodded ponderously.

Well, Horace Rappaport said, so perhaps Mati would one day join him on the university faculty in Jerusalem!

"Teaching flying!" Mati jested.

He was back, Dena knew. Just in time for the winter quarter. The temple bulletin said Mati Chaimovitch would present a direct personal report from Palestine after the services on Friday, in the social hall.

He hadn't called. Dena did want to see him, just to look at him; she wasn't sure she wanted to meet him, though that poetess bitch was no longer around. But this way, sitting in an audience, she would know.

The minute he stood up Myra gripped Dena's hand as though expressing her own feelings for her. He looked more than ever like some Mediterranean god.

Dena had a moment almost of weeping, as from a sweep of music, she told herself. And when he described his nephew with a whole crew of sabras leaping off a truck to rebuild the place where his brother had fallen, Dena had the choked feeling that comes at the sight of a proudly marching band.

Afterward he was surrounded with question askers, some perplexed, worried, some excited. Mati's face glowed with energy. She felt he had seen her, but she slipped away.

He called, and Saturday afternoon they had a long walk in the park in freshly fallen snow. Dena was softly muffled in a gray squirrel coat and matching bonnet so that her face peered out, piquant, yet fragile, like a cotton-nested birdling. In bursts of vitality Mati leaped and shook down snow from branches over her head.

They had snow kisses, all watery.

Then by the lakeside, gazing at icicle formations on the pier, Mati talked about things like how rare it was in Eretz to hold snow in your hand—although from his family's place in the Jordan Valley you could even in summer see the white cap of Mount Hermon, not so very far away. And in Jerusalem every few years there came a good snowfall, but Mati had never been there at such a time. He had never been in real snow until he came here to Chicago.

They stood in musing silence. Only then Mati spoke about his brother and his mother. Dena took his hand. Finally, Mati told her of his secret plan. The airplane. It was as though in troth.

Strictly to a very few, to those who needed to know so he could carry it out, had he divulged his mission. Telling it to Dena was something else; it was, he suddenly realized, the need of a man to reveal himself entirely, his innermost aspirations, to—well, to the woman he told everything to.

Her hand tightened on his, and for a long moment Dena was silent. She was trying to feel what Mati felt, what this plan meant to him. And to herself?

In Palestine would there always be attacks then? There came to her the image of a lone flier and a whole country full of guns pointed into the sky to shoot him down.

"It would be terribly dangerous, Mati." His other hand covered hers; his blood was so warm that her hand between his palms felt as if it were in a heater. "But, Mati," she asked, "would you be the only one?"

Suddenly just by his being with her, his thoughts were leaping, expanding. Ben-Gurion himself had said, "You will be the first." But to have one tiny airplane hidden away? He must learn so as to teach others. And then why not even open an airline? To carry passengers, tourists, all over Eretz? No need to hide! And thus have several planes ready for use in an emergency! Why not planes to fly even to Beirut and Cairo? Right now was the time when flying companies were being started all over the world. Lindbergh was flying around the world to map out airline routes. A real airline, and why shouldn't it belong to the Histadrut! To Labor! And if Haj Amin tried to start anything again, a whole flotilla of planes in the air!

Being with Dena had made this come to him.

And in this exhilaration Mati felt he now understood how it should be for a man and a woman. A woman should bring out for a man all he could do. He did not see his destined woman as a strong chalutzah who wanted to go on guard, like Leah when she first arrived with Reuven in Eretz. Or when the first chalutzoth insisted on learning to plow. Those days were over. Even in the kvutsoth, women had gone back to those natural roles that you saw all through history, the men to the tasks of building, of defending, the women holding the inner life, the child care, the teaching, and taking care of the greens and—like his sister Dvora —the poultry. . . . Why had he suddenly gone off into these reflections? His own life was not likely, after all, to be in a kibbutz. An airline manager, he joked to himself, in Tel Aviv! But look how Dena first of all had feared for him, for his safety.

Her hand had become so warm, hot; Mati lifted it and kissed her palm.

Then suddenly he undid her fur coat, and they squeezed together and were crazy for each other. The thought came of his mother's diamondl, the ring, and Mati wanted then and there to give it to his girl, but he didn't have it with him, and besides, that might be too much too fast for this first time they were together again. Or was he a bit afraid, still uncertain of this final step?

Dena told her mother she had asked Mati to their Sunday family dinner.

For a long time they had not seen him, even before those terrible events that had taken him back to Palestine, and indeed, Bessie Kossoff had understood, with some relief, that her Dena had broken it off with that Palestine fellow because of his having an affair with a shikseh—well, with another girl. To Dena's generation it didn't matter so much if it was a shikseh. But everyone had known that Mati stayed with her in her studio practically every night. In a way the breakup had been a relief because things had already been getting serious between Dena and Mati, and what if she took it into her head to marry him and go back with him and live there among those murderous Arabs? Bessie and Sam had not said anything one way or the other to Dena; with a modern girl you had to be very careful not to push her into something by opposite advice, but fortunately the critical question had not arrived.

Now he had returned, and after the tragedy that had happened there to his brother—and his mother too had died from it, poor woman, imagine what kind of life she had had, two of her children killed—so it was only natural that Dena would invite Mati to the house.

Right away Bessie Kossoff saw how things were; indeed, from the first moment Mati entered she was saying in her heart almost weepingly, goodbye, Jack Sloan, of the Sloan family, such a wonderful prospect. And maybe even farewell to her own daughter, her only daughter, who would go off to that strange dangerous land. The Jewish homeland Bessie was for; she was proud how much Jews had built there, and she donated to Hadassah, but after all, look how good America was for the Jews!

Still, maybe the troubles were finished over there, and things would be all right; people said the sunshine was like Florida over there, and maybe she and Sam would spend their old age playing with their grandchildren on the golden beach of Tel Aviv.

Something had certainly changed in this Mati, and the way her Dena looked at him Bessie Kossoff saw it was no longer only a thing like dates between two young people. Almost as though her own body were her daughter's, Bessie Kossoff could feel the difference in her very womb.

This young Mati from Palestine had become thinner, his face and mouth were firm-looking, and his skin, which had always been so dark, was no longer only dark—a glow of purpose came from him as though in answer, she told herself, to the things that life could do to people, that he had now come up against. Sam himself might not understand the way a woman understood the way the brutal things a man went through in his life could reach right into a woman, a girl, their own daughter, reach and tug at the innermost womanly part of her.

Bessie Kossoff spoke tenderly to Mati about his mother, about all that his mother must have gone through. And Phil and Sherrill, Bessie noticed, while also giving him condolences, were examining the young man in this different way and glancing between themselves.

Phil Kossoff spoke as one who had kept up with the situation over there, spoke about the policy of the British to divide and rule, and Sam Kossoff said to hell with them all, the English, the Arabs; in spite of everything, Sam understood Tel Aviv was booming! In fact, the real estate business in Tel Aviv sounded better than here in Chicago! Indeed, before they went to the table, Sam got Mati aside and asked about orange groves over there—an ex-Florida booster had come to see him with a prospectus from Palestine, they planted your personal grove and tended it for you, and then in five years it bore fruit—

Mati had to laugh. It was Nahum's company! His own brother-in-law, he told Sam Kossoff, had started this plan, and it was his own brother Gidon, yes, the one who was killed, who had laid out the whole irrigation system. Indeed, Mati added judiciously, they should become excellent groves.

Too bad the salesman hadn't shown up a year ago, Sam Kossoff said, but today with the crash— His son Phil's father-in-law Goldenson had lost a fortune in Florida orange plantations, and though Goldenson still owned this building, real estate was crashing all around, and Jewish businessmen were hard hit. Still, to own a little something over there in the Jewish homeland—it could even be a place for retirement in old age. . . . There was a glance at Dena. "Of course, I have never been so much of a Jew myself—" He offered Mati a cigar, but Mati declined, lighting a cigarette. "A cigar is healthier, they say," Mr. Kossoff repeated, and then suddenly as if recalling being an American: "Maybe you would like a drink? I got some real stuff from Canada." From his old wop customers on Halsted Street who were now top gangsters.

But Mati said, "We're not much of drinkers."

"That's a Jewish trait," Mr. Kossoff said. "Jews don't drink, and now I see it is true even in Palestine. But they make wine there; I understand they do a good export business over there in kosher wine."

"We have good wines from the old settlements," Mati told them, from the wine cellars started by Baron de Rothschild.

"Oh, a Rothschild!" Bessie Kossoff put in. "They are Zionists?" You could almost see her respect going up as on an elevator indicator.

"I don't know so much about Jewish history," Dena's mother said with an expression of regret, and Sam Kossoff said, "Oh we joined the temple and go for the High Holidays and we observe Pesach with a Seder, though it is really not the same as when the old folks used to do it."

143

"That's right, we're the old folks ourselves now, but we really don't know how to do it right," Mrs. Kossoff said.

"It's just a fancy meal," Dena observed. "Imagine Victor asking the Four Questions!"

Well—Mrs. Kossoff gave Phil and Sherrill a look—as soon as there were some grandchildren. . . . She understood in the suburbs Jewish was even getting kind of fashionable.

Now Sam Kossoff came back to the orange grove. "You say it's your brother-in-law's company? Is your brother-in-law a promoter?"

"Maybe Mati put you on his prospect list!" jested Dena's snippy young brother, Victor.

"But you have promoters over there?" Dena's father repeated, as though such a thing belonged only here in America.

Mrs. Kossoff joined in. "You know the Jews over there, all we hear about is the kalutzim." She smiled, pleased at having got the real word, but Sam Kossoff pronounced it correctly, "Chalutzim."

"I can never get that Jewish tcha." His wife gave a little laugh.

Several of them tried the sound, Sherrill, Dena, down in their throats, with Dena getting hers almost right, while Mati coached, Chuh, chuh.

"Like chazer?" Mrs. Kossoff said suddenly, quite correctly. Everybody roared.

Sam Kossoff resumed with Mati. "Well, your brother-in-law, the promoter, from his salesman it sounded like that was a good-sized operation over there."

"Oh, Nahum comes from a well-to-do family," Mati said. "They have a hotel in Tiberias for three generations." All the Kossoffs were gazing at him with new interest; he could see them struggling with the changed idea—hotel owners, promoters.

"Three generations," Sam Kossoff rolled it over.

"He is like a real American go-getter," Mati said of Nahum. "He's starting a whole city there on the seashore; he wants to build it bigger than Tel Aviv!"

"Oh?" Phil Kossoff had heard talk of the wild prices already being paid for building lots in Tel Aviv.

Now the father felt his way a bit further. "Then a man, say, studying like you, a professional career as a political economist, there is room for such a profession there? I thought it was all farming and building work."

"Well, we have the Hebrew University," Mati said. "You know the president is an American, Rabbi Judah Magnes. Your rabbi,

Mike Kramer, is a great admirer of his. I brought him regards."

"Mati could become a professor there!" It had come to Bessie Kossoff—why not! With such a high contact already established! That terrible worry—what would it be, what could it be, her daughter's life if she went over there—the whole idea now seemed not so disastrous as she had been imagining.

Mati said he had not thought of a university career. "I'm afraid that's not my kind of life."

"Mati is too active!" Dena put in. "Can you imagine him shut up in a classroom all the time?"

And the way he looked, with his powerful chest and arms and thighs, Sherrill uttered an appreciative laugh.

"But we need people in every field, isn't that the main idea of a Jewish homeland, to have everything our own?" Mr. Kossoff said.

"In Tel Aviv even the policemen are all Jewish, imagine that, no Irish cops," Bessie said.

"We have a whole field of economy to build up there," Phil said. "There will be plenty for an expert economist to do."

Mrs. Kossoff asked them to the table.

Phil started an economic discussion, and soon Mati gathered that the crash need not be such a terrible disaster if a man was clever. He had never put his money into the stock market, Phil said. He believed a man should keep his capital in his own business, which he knew something about; if he was going to gamble, that was where he should take his chances, and just now an opportunity had arisen, an excellent jewelry store in the heart of the Loop at Monroe and State—this goy had been a big gambler in the stock market, so for practically nothing Phil had acquired the lease and a fine stock of stones, as the fellow had gone stone broke.

Victor let out a laugh, and for an instant nobody else got the pun, until Dena added, "I bet he said you had a heart of stone!"

Bessie Kossoff glowed. Her smart kids!

Of course, the jewelry business was hit hard; right now the value of even the best blue diamonds was down, jewels were flooding the market as people tried to scrape up all their assets, big men, families whose names would surprise you, were selling their wives' jewelry, Phil said.

Sam Kossoff concurred; they were even coming to his Fifty-fifth Street store, every day, people from the best Kenwood families, who didn't want their situations to be known downtown.

He himself was still holding back from overbuying, Phil said; he

145

was holding his cash reserves because in his estimate prices would drop still lower. Meanwhile, he intended to change that downtown store to a cheaper line, semiprecious; people still had to give presents, and semiprecious stones and glitter stuff were all they could afford. That would pay the rent. So now, Kossoff and Sons at last had a branch in the Loop!

In a pause Mrs. Kossoff said to Mati, "So when you get your diploma, you are going back to live there?"

Naturally that was his plan.

She supposed, Bessie Kossoff began to hint, that a bright young man with an economy degree could really choose in what country he wanted his career—

Dena stopped her. "Oh, Mother! Mati's whole life is over there!"

"He is an idealist," Sam Kossoff stated. And then: "I can understand this. Being a Jew, I'll tell you the truth, here it isn't a very big thing to me, though naturally I support the temple and the Jewish charities because it is a principle with us—Jews have always supported their own; we don't want the anti-Semites to have anything to talk about us. I happen not to be especially religious, so outside of such things, why not just be an American? But over there, I understand. If you are a Zionist and want to build up a Jewish country, it's an ideal, a great ideal." He gazed at his daughter, a man who had shown he did not have a closed mind.

Victor, the snip, not even out of high school, piped up to Mati, "Well, is idealism itself the highest justification? Communism is an ideal, and even Hitlerism in Germany is an ideal to those who believe in it."

There was a kind of suppressed gasp, though you had to admit the kid was clever.

"With us, it is not an idealism that we want to force onto others," Mati said. "This ideal is our own natural life."

Dena felt wonderful, as though Mati had just ducked the kid's conceited head underwater!

Bessie produced her surprise, fresh strawberries from Florida for dessert!

In their bedroom, Sam and Bessie held an anxious discussion.

"He is certainly a fine intelligent boy," Mr. Kossoff remarked, to be fair.

"Did you see his physique? I don't blame Dena! If I could have grandchildren like that, I'd go to Palestine myself!"

"Already she's a grandmother! From what I understand, if Dena doesn't watch her step, with this fellow you may have your grandchildren before you know it, right here."

Intuitively in her own body Bessie felt her daughter hadn't.

"He knocks them over, all over the university there. He's practically living with a shikseh."

"From who do you know all this? You hired a detective?"

"Philly mentioned a few things to me," Sam said.

What did men ever really know? "Sam, that whole thing was before his brother died and he went back. It was a shikseh that does it with everybody there at the university, from the professors to all the boys. A poetess. So he had a little affair, can you blame him, a boy is hot-blooded. Especially from a hot country there. You just have to read the Bible; they weren't so pure in those old days, even King David! And if you really want to know, that was why Dena stopped going with him last year. But you can see he came back different; now he is more serious. A man."

To put on his pajamas, Sam went to the bathroom, a kind of nice, respectful habit he had from when they first got married. Mrs. Kossoff took off her rings and put them in her hiding place that even Sam didn't know about, in a drawer under her unmentionables, where a burglar would never look. A young man so virile. Who knew even what her own Sam had done before they married? Who knew even what her own Philly had done? And maybe even Victor already. These days with cars the boys started early. She saw no more yellowish blots on the sheets. Ugh. Well, a young man had to get it out of his system somehow. A fellow like Mati with all that energy, but Dena could bind him to her; Mrs. Kossoff just felt it in her own self, how that powerful young man's body could be bound to a beautiful girl like her Dena. Of course, it would be marriage first; Dena was modern, but Bessie had a feeling her daughter just by some kind of natural instinct of purity wouldn't do it until she was married. Still, you had to understand that to modern sophisticated girls the ceremony itself was only a formality; they did you a favor to let you spend a fortune on a wedding for them. Maybe even a few Jewish girls nowadays— and Bess wondered if that Myra was such a good influence on Dena even though she was related to the best families. Even some Jewish girls nowadays started before. If they were engaged, Bessie could see it. That is, a formal engagement, not just a pretense, an excuse so they could go and do it. Bessie tried to keep up with her daughter and read modern books; there was that judge in Kansas City or someplace who wrote a book, *Trial Marriage*, he let his own daughter do it. Moving over, Bessie made room for Sam in the bed. "That shikseh I'm not worried about. Or other girls. Dena can hold her own," she said. "But the main trouble is, if she married him—"

Neither would say it.

Finally, Bessie said, "After all, for his Zionist movement, there are lots of important things that they do over here. Good positions."

"You think a fellow like Mati is going to be a salesman for his brother-in-law's orange groves? American salesmen there are plenty."

Her husband had always thought she was not so clever, Bessie knew, but—like moving here to the South Side—she had always found ways to get him to do what she wanted, and in the end Sam always saw she was right. And maybe Dena too would understood how to handle a man.

There were certain things a man had to do with his life, Sam reflected. Could a woman ever really understand? True, maybe because women had the instinct of preserving the race, women had to do what was safe. But certain women— Sam saw like in the movie *The Covered Wagon* the faces of resolute women in their sunbonnets, with shotguns on their knees. . . . Nu, a kind of anguish denied that he in some way even considered this for his Dena, yet a flicker of pride was underneath the denial. If it should come to it, if his daughter was really the kind who would go with her man wherever she believed he had to go. Because in life even if you are scared, you can't let that stop you. How many years had he himself lived scared, down there on Halsted Street with the holdups and the gangsters all around, everyone saying how can you stay there! And he had to hand it to Bessie—even if she was scared for her daughter now, she had moved right in there with him when they were married; it was a bad neighborhood even then, all the Jews were moving out to Douglas Park, but she had stood it for years. Another thing when you lived right inside danger, it wasn't the way people outside imagined. And Sam supposed in Palestine this was the same way. You lived.

"You don't understand. With those Jews there, the real ones"— Sam meant the real pioneers, the chalutzim—"with them, living somewhere else doesn't even enter the question."

148

Bessie Kossoff didn't say anything. It was not the time to argue yet, there were still years of college, but as far as living somewhere else, Bessie knew a butcher, a real kosher Jew but a patriotic Zionist, too, who had gone from Russia to Palestine. And then because he couldn't make a living there, with a wife and two children, he had moved to America. But he had a blue Keren Kayemeth box, the Jewish National Fund, on his counter and was always kidding all the women to put their change in there and he would put in the same amount.

Sam too was thinking—ten, no, it was already over a dozen years ago, during the war, there were a number of young fellows, garment workers, shneiders, customers of his who had suddenly come and bought engagement rings, a rush of business because they were enlisting in the Jewish battalion that was supposed to go fight in Palestine, the same outfit Mati's brother had been in. They were all excited about the Balfour Declaration—well, what Jew didn't get excited? Those volunteers had even made a parade with a Jewish flag on Twelfth Street, and he had even put a Jewish flag in his own store window. He was a family man with three kids already, so he was in no danger of being drafted by Uncle Sam, but these shneiders, mostly recent immigrants, they would have been drafted anyway in the American army, so they wanted to join the Jewish army. There were mass meetings, and there was even a Yiddish speech maker from Palestine, a radical with bushy hair— what was his name? Mati had mentioned a name, a big shot now, and it even seemed to Sam it was the same fellow, Ben something. Most of those who joined were greenhorns who had escaped from Russia just when the war started so as not to have to go fight for the Czar. He remembered a few who came back from that Jewish Brigade; they never even had a chance to fight, they said; all they fought over there in Palestine were armies of flies. They were kept marching in terrible heat from one camp to another, and the British officers were mostly anti-Semites. Still, a number had stayed there in Palestine to settle.

Those who want to have a Jewish country, I don't blame them, Sam said to himself. Maybe if he had been brought up in Russia, he would have been more of a Jew himself. But after coming here to America, even his father didn't act as if being a Jew were the most important thing in your life; he began to keep the watch repair shop open on Saturday. And if the religion wasn't all that important, then what else was so important about being a Jew?

149

Oh, Sam knew the answers—honesty, pride, helping each other—but he was also a patriotic American, and he had been too busy from the age of fifteen helping take care of the family to have the time maybe to go more deeply into things Jewish, the way every Jew used to study the Bible and the Talmud. Already when he was fifteen, his father's eyes were getting bad, and Sam had to stay more and more in the store and take over; his ideas of going to dental college were forgotten. In the last years his old man had been blind.

A lot of Italians had moved into the neighborhood; they always had made wine for themselves, a barrel in the basement, and when Prohibition came, pretty soon some of them had all kinds of money and liked to buy big flashy diamonds for themselves and their wives and their outside girls, and gold watches, and Sam had more Italians than Jews for customers. Oh, yes, some of those famous gangsters were his customers from before they got so famous. But one thing he hated was when dagos came into the store and talked about Jewing you down, even if it was half kidding. They didn't mean to be insulting; it was like on his side jokingly calling them dagos. And it was true you always bargained a little, it was a kind of game, an act, you came down a bit, but he couldn't stand the way some of those wops started dirty names, kike and sheeny, when he wouldn't go down to their price, and finally, one day after a wop even showed a knife, Sam put a sign in the window: ONE-PRICE STORE—WE MEAN IT. And he stuck to it. "Yah, well, sure I'm a Hebe all right, but this is not a Jew-down store," he would tell them. And when they paid the price, he'd give them a little present, a bauble rhinestone barrette for the wife or outside girl or especially daughters; he even got in some ivory-looking crosses to give them. And pretty soon his one-price policy even proved excellent for the business.

After making the big move here to the South Side, he was accepted and became a member of the Merchants Association, which had both Jews and gentiles. Sam didn't want to make anything of being a Jew one way or another. He had never tried to join the downtown Standard Club even when Jake Nussbaum, who owned the next-door haberdashery here, wanted to take him in. If a gentile club wouldn't have him, Sam declared, he wasn't going to agree to the situation that existed even here in America by joining a Jewish club. That only made the anti-Semites seem right. In time, maybe for his sons' sons, all this lousy discrimination would disappear. He was a man who minded his own business. Exactly. The whole thing. Business. Yes, he gave to the Jewish charities when Nussbaum put the bee on him, but he also gave almost the same to the non-Jewish, and the Boy Scouts and Red Cross, even Christmas turkey campaigns, and even Catholic Charities; maybe one day some of those people would stop telling their kids that all the Jews were Christ killers. He would never try to pass, a Jew had the right to be a Jew, not to be ashamed, but the trouble was he was not interested in the religious side, so what did that make him? Bessie too had been brought over from Europe as a little kid; her father was one of those sweatshop immigrants who lived on bread and tea for five years before he could save up enough money to send a boat ticket for his wife and kids. But Bess had gone to American schools right from first grade. He and Bess had raised their own kids real American; they didn't believe in throwing in Yiddish words and expressions in their conversations, though lately this seemed to be becoming fashionable; sometimes one of the kids would bring home a Yiddish word that was now a joke, like kibbitzer. Or on the radio Fanny Brice with her jokes. He and Bessie would react slowly, as though they had to remember way back for the meaning.

The templegoing on High Holidays, even sometimes on Friday night, was different from a shul. This young rabbi Mike Kramer was a hotshot; he talked about everything, not only Jewish. At least in Reform the High Holiday seats were paid for in your annual membership, no auctioning off the best seats. And socially for the children the temple had proved the way Bess claimed it would, you had to hand it to her—the right center for Dena to meet the right people, like in her dramatic club. But with Victor, the boy absolutely refused to go to temple or even to have a Bar Mitzvah. He said since none of them was religious, it was all hypocrisy. At least he had been circumcised before he could refuse; Sam chuckled to himself. Maybe that was why wise old Moses had done it so early.

Those pioneer families in Palestine were not religious either, so it wasn't as if going back there meant going back to being religious Jews with beards and the whole works. No; mainly in his heart Sam Kossoff felt it was a case of losing their daughter, not even allowing yourself to think of the danger part. Dena would go away and live in a foreign land and—a thing a man mentioned less than a woman, but still it was your grandchildren you wanted

151

to enjoy. When you were getting older and even thinking of retirement, the pleasure in life you looked forward to was grandchildren, where you no longer had the responsibility but only the pleasure, like taking a little child by the hand and walking to the park, tossing him a big rubber ball to catch.

But if Dena would live far away, almost on the other side of the world? And on top of it all, the place was dangerous.

His wife, as generally happened with them, came out of her reflections at the same point as Sam. "That Mati laughs when you say it is dangerous, but he already lost a brother and a sister killed by those Arabs. It's like a family with a curse on it."

They turned in bed from back to back to on their backs, while each stared upward in the dark, brooding on Bessie's words. "Maybe—" she speculated. "After all, he still has nearly two years to his graduation."

"You think with Dena it might be only an infatuation?"

"She's gone on him. Really gone on him," Bessie said. She felt this within her and placed a hand on Sam's thigh. He turned to her.

During the whole thing Bessie was her daughter, with that big virile Hebrew boy, a shepherd with bare legs and sandals, his young wife brought him a jug of water in the field, and sandwiches and apples, and they had a feast and rolled in the grass.

"Maybe," Bessie said afterward, "you should even buy some of those orange tree lots from his brother-in-law. Who knows, if we ever wanted to retire there—"

"If it only would become a land of peace," Sam said, and both sighed.

9

ALREADY Mati had started his flying lessons. The field was way at the end of the Sixty-third Street car line, and even from there it was quite a walk, but he tried to do his studying on the hourlong ride. Lining the edge of the field were stands or cabins with signs for going up, THE THRILL OF YOUR LIFE, $5. And also LEARN TO FLY. Some had things like EARN BIG MONEY, BECOME AN AIRLINE PILOT, with names of the instructors, World War aces with rows of black crosses for German pilots knocked down. If he got one of those aces, could he let on he wanted fighter training? Farther along were some tin-roofed hangars and planes parked off the runway; he even saw a single-wing job, a monoplane like the one Lindbergh was supposed to be trying out, but the training airships were biplanes like the box kites the Germans and English had used in the war in Palestine when he was a kid—the same as the one Shula's German airman had flown over the house.

Another monoplane, shiny white, came swooping down, a beautiful, easy landing, and the flier came climbing out, talking to a friend who approached, also a fellow in flying togs, both of them with that special air that airmen had of belonging only to their own world. These fellows must be exchanging information; they kept putting their hands on different parts of the fuselage the way two men might around a fine horse.

The place he chose had a display announcing it was run by a captain from Rickenbacker's Aces. You had to sign that they would not be responsible in case of accident or death. Whom to notify? He thought of Dena but put Rabbi Mike Kramer. Mati paid for his trial lesson, and sure, why not take it right away, that was what he was there for, he said to the registry girl. She had plucked eyebrows and cupid lips, and her special ready-for-anything look, you felt, was the look of girls around airmen. Turning her head to a cubbyhole where a couple of men in flying suits were playing cards, she called "Kenny," and one of them put down his hand and unfolded himself, a slatlike guy getting taller and taller like an extension ladder. Mati was not in the habit of examining people meticulously, feeling open and warm to people, but this was a portentous moment. His instructor had a seamy face like some cowboy actor, Harry Carey, and as they walked out, Kenny said, "You cherry?" Here it meant had he ever been up. Well, Mati said, he had always wanted to learn to fly.

"Okay, just don't upchuck on me," the guy said, and got him a helmet with goggles. The name was Kenny Patterson, and before they reached the airship, Mati had been told he'd learned to fly in the war but didn't believe in bullshitting people about all the Heinies he'd knocked down; he'd never seen combat, nor had most of these heroes with German crosses on their cockpits.

Also, if Mati—say, that was a peculiar accent, where was he from?

For a second Mati thought he ought to give some other place; this flying business must be a small world, and if it got around that a Jew from Palestine was learning to pilot a plane— Stupidities. If he gave a phony background and they checked up, they'd really get suspicious. He had been brought up in Palestine but was now living here, he said. "Yeh, I guess it gets pretty hot over there with those wild Arabs," the flier said with a kind of snort, as though you couldn't blame anyone for moving the hell away. Mati let it rest at that and, as they strolled onto the field, learned that if he had any ambitions of getting into aviation, well, there was a great future in it especially if you could still find yourself an ocean to hop over and a millionaire's daughter to marry. Oh, hell, Slim was a great guy and a natural flier and deserved it, Patterson rattled on, mentioning how he and Slim Lindbergh had flown the same airmail run from St. Louis right to this field.

The biplane was a Curtiss, and not one of those rebuilt army junk heaps that you saw around here, held together with baling wire, Patterson said; he would work only for a responsible outfit. Now the basic idea of flying was you were riding the air. Once you got the feel of it, piloting a plane was simpler than driving a car; the main thing, you just had to feel the air was your element. "Now naturally it isn't," the instructor declared, getting a little bit excited the way a man does when he touches on his personal philosophy and feels that his listener is coming along with him. "The air is not man's element, but neither is water," he lectured. "You can drown in the sea, and you can fall out of the sky. You can panic and get a cramp in the water, and you can panic and freeze on the stick in the sky. So, after a couple of times up, if you can't get the feeling you're in your element, maybe you're not cut out to be an airman. That's the whole deal. Sometimes in the water, you know, you get a kind of feeling of evolution, of ages back you came from a fish, and sometimes in the air you get that same way-back feeling, of ages back you were a bird, and it's still there someplace inside you." Patterson gave Mati a testing glance, a man who has given you a chance to see his inner truth and wonders if you got it, if you even deserved his telling you. Then they climbed into their places.

From the first zoom upward it was good. Yes, the fellow was right; yes, Mati felt he was in his element! The instructor turned his head, had one look into his face, and gave him a grin—there was something brotherly and also almost lewd in it, like the look, Mati suddenly recalled, that Joe Freedman had given him when Joe ran into him coming out of Andrea's after the first night he had spent with her.

Though, of course, this did not in any way especially mean anything about themselves, Dena told Mati, she had broken it off with Jack Sloan; she had realized it could never be the real thing with Jack, and so it was unfair for them to go on, and though there had never been a definite understanding between them, it was better now to have things clear.

So Wednesdays and Saturdays again became their date nights, but also there were all kinds of moments when they could arrange to cross paths on campus—just to touch hands. All other evenings Mati worked, earning money now for his flying lessons, too; on their dates Dena wouldn't go anywhere expensive, and often Myra had them come to her Del Prado apartment to listen to records. She had a new favorite, a trumpeter named Louis Armstrong who shouted and growled out bits of songs, they were supposed to be songs, even sexier than Bessie Smith, and Dena tried to explain the naturalness and primitiveness to Mati, just as on Sunday when the three of them went to the Art Institute she explained the jungle painting of an artist named Rousseau.

Myra was having a big love affair, naturally again an artist, a young Jamaican named José, no, she wasn't becoming a tramp, she hadn't had anyone since that awful thing with Joe Freedman last summer, but she had worked that through with her analyst, though he was the silent type who just listened, never commented, he guided you to see things by yourself, and she now saw it had been Joe's problem, not hers, Myra told Dena. And oddly, this young Jamaican by sheer coincidence had rented Joe's studio, but that was not how it had started, it was not revenge on Joe; in fact, José had called her up, he had an introduction, and Myra had asked him for tea. The stupid desk clerk, a real Southern jerk, had tried to make him use the service elevator, so after straightening that out on the house phone, by the time José arrived at her door she felt so outraged they practically fell right on the bed! The truth was it was not even revenge on that jerk of a clerk but one look at José—he was a faun, the face, the mouth of a faun, you just tumbled, sheer joy!

When Myra went to see José's work at the studio, there still in a corner was Joe's bust of her, in plaster, the long neck and poised head, oh, the bastard was talented, but he was a sadist, emphasizing that drip on her nose, it was Joe's own Jewish complex. With her faun Myra was free, free, free of Artie, free of Joe, so she had just picked up a pincers and snipped off the plaster overhang! José had a great laugh, and the story even got a rise out of her analyst; she could swear she heard him snicker behind the couch.

Suddenly Joe Freedman was back. The instant he saw that chipped-down nose he exploded, roared at José; even if José hadn't done it, how could he have let the goddamn cunt deface a piece of sculpture; good or lousy, that had been the way he wanted it. Out! Out! He kicked out José, he needed his place back anyway, and next thing Joe called Myra and gave her hell, she could slice her whole damn nose off her face if she wanted, but not a particle from his goddamn sculpture!

And, Myra told Dena, after all, he was right. She had gone straight over to apologize. The plaster bust was shattered on the floor. At least her uncle had the stainless steel—sitting right next to a Brancusi, too. But Joe wasn't mollified. He was in one of his rotten black moods, he'd had enough anti-Semitism in Europe, the whole thing boiled out of him; right after the Arabs in Palestine, when he nearly got his ass shot off up there in the marble quarry at Tel Hai, he had come back to Paris and participated in some kind of all-Jewish exhibition, damn good people, too, got together by Enrico Glicenstein—Marc Chagall, Mane Katz, Rubin, Lipchitz—and did she know what the stinking French critics called it? Chauvinistic, xenophobic, ultranationalistic racism! Here, look, they had to pick him out—Joe threw a handful of clippings at her; one had a big photograph of a statue he had made of the Tel Hai hero, Trumpeldor. "Zionist Art." And another clipping was a long screed about Jewish artists infesting the Paris scene!

But it was from *L'Aurore*, the notorious anti-Semitic paper. Myra tried to calm him down. And that "Zionist Art" heading was from the communist paper *Humanité*. That was politics. What did he expect?

Expect! This was in France! Joe roared. The whole rotten world was out to finish the Jews.

Was Mati Chaimovitch back? He wanted to know. They'd missed connections there in Palestine.

When the four of them got together, Joe and Mati went into endless discussions. The report of the Royal Commission on Palestine was out; granted the Arabs had caused the bloodshed, declared the chairman, Sir Walter Shaw. They were simply afraid of further Jewish immigration. There wasn't room enough in Palestine to swing a cat; there was no more absorptive capacity in the land. A new commission was to go out to decide what to do, and meanwhile, immigration and land sales were halted. Betrayals, lies! Mati raged. They were throwing out the Balfour Declaration! The League of Nations Mandate! In one breath Joe would be with him; Joe had seen for himself the empty wastes, he had seen what the Jews were doing there, for two cents he'd throw up everything and go and live in a kibbutz, who needed sculpture! Then he'd declare it was all hopeless; the thing wasn't even between the Arabs and the Jews; some foreign correspondent Joe had met right after the riots had explained to him how between communist internationalism and rising Nazism and expanding Islam, the Jews were finally doomed.

Mati let Joe in on the secret of the airplane. Great, Joe said, he'd do a monument of him as soon as he was shot down. Why not come back with him and build a monument to Gidon, Mati said, and Joe declared the whole country was a monument, every rock was a sculpture; still, what the hell, one day he might do it—when he knew how. Meanwhile, there was a depression, he had come back dead broke, and he was making miniature doll heads of movie stars, Mae West, Greta Garbo, John Gilbert, Norma Shearer, used in the latest craze for floppy decorative boudoir dolls.

José had gone back to Jamaica, leaving Myra a lovely little drawing of himself with tiny goat horns on his head. So now the damn thing happened the way it always did—with Joe. Of course, she felt like a slut, a whore, but also with Joe it wasn't just fun with a faun—this was a man.

For a time it was really nice. The four of them went to art shows together—at least art exhibits were for free, Joe would crack. There seemed to be hardly anything he really liked, he would tear everything apart, but Dena had to admit he had an instant way of seeing the tricks, especially in the ultramoderns. Brancusi was real, Archipenko was phony. Sometimes Dena thought the fellow was just nasty and bad-tempered but—Myra would give her that certain look—you really got to know a man only when you went to bed.

Dena and Mati could always have her key, Myra kept hinting, and once she went off with Joe Freedman to her uncle's for dinner, leaving the two of them in the apartment. Oh, she did want him so, Dena admitted but then pulled herself from the sofa because it wasn't fair to either of them. All right, not until she really decided, Mati said, even if she wanted to wait until they got married. "Is this a proposal!" Dena exclaimed. And look how he took it all for granted! She pulled his head to her bosom. But then she cried, no, no, she didn't want to torture him, and she didn't know what made her hold back. Maybe even because of the way Myra was. And they left Myra's place and walked in the windy air in the park.

Myra's mood began to go down. She was sure Joe was back to his old ways, having other girls, a little Irish bitch. With her analyst Myra was deep into Jewish self-hatred and certain that Joe with all his Jew stuff protested too much. She was sure that in reality Joe had always hated her nose. She herself was now free of all that. She even understood Artie was a real psychopathic case, that was all. If not for the trauma of his crime and all the sensationalism, she probably would have just normally one day found out he was a fairy and got over her crush on him, leaving him to Ronald Firbank and Carl Van Vechten. The Jewish part had nothing to do with it. In fact, she was even thinking of getting a nose job. No, not one of those silly Irish turnups. Just a simple aesthetic correction. Her goddamn analyst wouldn't give the slightest indication one way or another. But when she mentioned the idea just lightly to Dena in Joe's presence, he shouted that if she did, he would never see her again.

Then one day Joe Freedman cleared out his place and left for New York. He was having some sort of crisis in his work, Myra said. They remained friends.

※ ※ ※

On Mati's big day Dena skipped her classes and took the family car to get him to the airfield, slipping over from the wheel so that the man should drive. All the way out on Sixty-third, though he had to dodge streetcars and trucks and elevated posts, he had his arm around her; he had learned driving the American way, they joked; Dena pressed to his side and kept her hand on his thigh, feeling the subtle muscle movement as his foot moved in and out for the gas pedal. Today was the big day—his solo!

There was a real man's-world atmosphere around the hangar; all the fellows in their coveralls gave her the eye, and Mati emerged looking like Wally Reid in his helmet with the dangling strap. For good luck he allowed her to buckle it. Then Mati introduced her to the instructor, a lanky type, the kind whose eyes undress a girl, and as they walked to the airplane, the reality of Mati's whole crazy plan suddenly came over her. She really saw Mati walking in a small open space in the middle of some Palestine orange grove; behind was a fruit-packing barn, the way he had described it to her, and the airplane was being pulled into the clearing, and then he was actually climbing into the cockpit. He would really do it. She had seen all those movies of dogfights in the war, with airplanes just like this. But also, Dena assured herself, Lindy had flown over the ocean in nothing bigger, and Lindy's bride was flying with him now; they were in a new model with only one set of wings, it looked even riskier, but Mati was crazy to get one like that, he had drawn diagrams for her, and here on the field she could spot a few of them, monoplanes they were called. He was considering which kind would be better for the Haganah; his latest plan was that maybe he wouldn't try to ship the plane from America but would get it in Europe. He would still have to raise the money here, but maybe from Italy or someplace it could even be flown and somehow smuggled in at night. It sounded terribly dangerous. But she had even sat over maps with Mati while he drew tentative air routes, telling her probably this was only a mishugass, probably they would still have to take the machine apart and ship in the pieces in some secret way and put them together again in Eretz; his brother Schmulik was a natural mechanic. But imagine if he would try to fly. Mati would be alone all the way, alone in the air.

Then suddenly, as he and his instructor climbed in, Dena saw herself in a cute fitted tailored flying suit and helmet; she was flying with Mati together: a Jewish Anne and Lindy! But no—seriously. Two beings, flying into an unknown life. Like a modern Adam and Eve.

And as a mechanic spun the propeller and Mati, grave and yet with a try at a grin, gave her a last wave and she saw the plane rolling away, Dena felt she was gaining one more glimmer of the irrevocable; it was as though her fate were drawing her on, and one day she would really be going away with Mati, away to where she wouldn't know a soul, where she couldn't at any moment of need or impulse pick up a phone and call Myra, where everyone she knew and saw would be through this boy who had walked into her life from another world, her whole world would be his world, everything would be decided according to things that her man had to do. Would she really be going into it? Someday fairly soon?

Then he was in the air.

While Mati was in the air, she wasn't at all frightened; she didn't even assure herself that if anything went wrong the instructor could take over the controls; she simply wasn't frightened because all this was only a preliminary. Once for a long while the airplane went out of sight, and she didn't worry but let his absence be as a last free interlude in which she could think and wonder to herself would she really do it, was it really possible she would one day leave everything here, the complete world around her, Chicago with Marshall Field's and Michigan Avenue and IC trains that got you downtown in twelve minutes, and lakeshore elevator apartments, and art seminars—walk out of all this and go there? And something dreadful in her didn't exactly wish—oh,

160

God, no!—but let itself imagine, suppose he would fly on and on and never turn back, fly away already now to his mission in life. That was crazy, cowardly! Dena guessed it must be like the panic that every girl must feel in her bridal gown just before she walked down the aisle. Her sister-in-law, Sherrill, had confessed it to her only lately in a heart-to-heart.

Then at last Dena saw the tiny plane again overhead—how did she know it was his? It swooped and whirled. Oh, that idiot, he was showing off for her! Or maybe it was really part of the test. Dena told herself she'd get even by not even mentioning she saw the tricks, after he came down. But now it was worse! The airplane was diving straight down at the field; he'd crash! Quick, the instructor must grab the controls! Directly over her head the little airship lifted up its nose, and Mati leaned his head out and waved, she could kill him, he'd pay for it, and the plane swooped once more, oh, men were infants, infantile. Dena had a good mind to get into the auto and drive away, let him go home in the streetcar.

But if he passed the test, they were supposed to celebrate at Myra's.

He came nicely down, and even without knowing the fine points, she could see it was a smooth, perfect landing. Mati ran to her. "Buba!" He squashed his face into hers. "Kenny never touched the controls! I flew solo the whole time! Did you see that barrel roll? He gave me an extra ten minutes for free, I was so good!"

Patterson was grinning, but so as not to butt in, he didn't come near.

Riding back under the el, Dena hummed,

Fish got to swim, birds got to fly,
I got to love one man till I die.

The desk clerk said Miss Roth wasn't home but had left word for them to go right up; he handed Mati the key.

In front of the couch was a rolling service table with all sorts of delicatessen, fruit, and champagne in a bucket. A note said, "Congratulations! A toast! Mazel tov! Don't wait for me!"

Oh, Myra the witch! A dizzy elation flew up in Dena; this was like a kid dare that you didn't dare refuse. Or else you were a ninny. Also, whatever happened, you couldn't blame yourself because it was a dare and you had to do it. And Mati, dear, honest

Mati with his straight, uncomplicated ways from over there, he hadn't even caught on. "Yallah!" he cried as he made the cork pop.

They stood eye to eye, and crooked elbows, and they drank from each other's glass. It was a movie of a daring romance, John Gilbert with Greta Garbo. With some extra money from translating Hebrew business letters, Mati had taken her downtown to the Chicago Theater to see it.

Suddenly, even shyly, Mati said he had something for her, for celebration; he even said, "Close your eyes." His voice was tight, almost down to a squeak.

They sat on the sofa, close, and Dena shut her eyes.

Unwrapping his mother's ring with the diamondl, which he carried still in the original knotted handkerchief, Mati said, "Open."

Gazing at it, delicate, antique, and hearing Mati explain what the ring was, from his mother, Dena now really felt the tightening and flutter in her insides; she was gone.

And so it happened there on the day of Mati's first flight.

Perhaps Mati might still have held back because he expected that Myra might come in at any moment, but the phone rang, Dena answered, and it was Myra herself.

"How was it, kiddo?" she asked, her voice throaty, excited.

"It was beautiful!" Dena said. "Mati flew!"

"Why don't you fly, too?" Myra said with growly insinuation like Bessie Smith. "I won't be coming home. I'm at Sinai."

The hospital? "Myra, you haven't gone and done it!"

She had. The nose job was already over! It hadn't hurt at all! Of course, how it looked she wouldn't know until the bandages came off.

Ever after, the three of them would joke—if it hadn't been for Myra's nose job, the whole thing might never have happened.

It went well with them, even miraculously. Dena felt so ready and just a bit drunk she let herself swoon back, let it all continue past the usual limits. She wasn't even sure of the crucial moment, but it must have been when his mouth crushed down and remained long and tender on her lips, and then his head drew back to look at her, and Mati's face was so beautiful, radiant, God! God! the word Myra had cried out the first time they saw him, a bumpkin from Palestine in the basement of the temple, God!

Dena cried it out, and in the same instant she recognized the true meaning of a word in anthropology, "Baal." "Baal" meant god. It was really a Hebrew word, Mati once had told her; they had been right in this room, looking through a large book Myra had bought with stunning photographs of ancient Hittite statuettes, gods, a fertility one, a Baal with a huge man's thing, enormous, like the one Myra had brought from Mexico that had once made her blush, but this time, looking at the pictures, Mati had explained that in Hebrew the word "Baal" meant not only a god but lord, husband, owner, possessor; perhaps the wandering Abraham had brought the word from pagan lands, the word for pagan gods, because in Hebrew they gave God other names, and even said none could know his name, but they kept "Baal" anyway. "Baal," she now whispered, and "Baali," hers, her own.

Now he carried her into the bedroom to Myra's bed, and this time, as he thrust into her, Dena had a shiver of pain and a mischievous thought of perhaps drops of blood on the sheet, her virgin blood to show Myra, and later, in a long daze of lovemaking, there came fleetingly more anthropological things about customs where the sheet was displayed from the window to the whole family, all the relatives on both sides, the whole town, yes! Let everybody know Dena loved Mati, she was his, he was her Baal. And more mischievously came the image of a display from Myra's fourteenth-floor window to all of Hyde Park Boulevard!

But this Mati of hers was insatiable! Could other men be like that? He thrust into her so deeply to wherever it was, the nexus as in D. H. Lawrence, the innermost place that must be the body-soul, the self of herself. She had read and Myra had told her of things that you really couldn't fully comprehend until you had the experience, but a woman was also supposed to have a high point, like an overflow, a shuddering point, yes, like bursting through the skies it must be, like—but not the same as—what happened to a man when he reached his apex, how did they say it, she had heard it from Sherrill—when the man came. In a woman it would not be like the thrills a girl brought on herself—now that she had the real thing Dena was no longer even ashamed of those poor little thrills —but the ultimate thing must be like the innermost self being reached, and there something shuddered like a hand gripping inside you and then letting go. Whatever it was, she was so far gone, only clutching at fleeting thoughts, holding onto one encompassing sensation that said, yes, yes, with him, whatever he wanted, to carry her wherever he wanted, whither thou goest, it was the truth, cleave to, it was true, one flesh, oh, yes, one flesh, one flesh, it was so, inside her they were one flesh, and she felt all she had read and guessed she would feel, his great tensing now, to throw far inside of her, the seed, then slowly to let his weight down on her and immolate. . . . It was not crushing weight; it was good. He stayed there within her, one flesh. Dena wasn't quite sure—was it over? She hardly felt him inside there now. And after it was over, the man withdrew. Why now did a practical thought intrude? But Myra had once weeks ago pointedly, casually shown her the douche bag. How immediately did a girl have to use it? But his mouth was in her neck, and then he was strong inside her again; oh, yes, from Myra's talk and also maybe from dates when fellows tried sex information to excite you, she had gathered virile ones did it even several times a night. But without a pause between? She couldn't ask now and break the spell. A still different kind of incessant throb seemed to be arriving in her flesh down there, and then her mind stopped recording. She shuddered, shuddered inside, yet she floated, it was like being in ethereal space, gliding; her mind came back and said this was what was meant. Her insides still kept on shuddering, they clutched and shuddered, again like an inside hand, but maybe—milking? She had never milked, but she had watched it done on a farm near Charlevoix. And this must be why the milkwoman seemed so at peace, so pleased.

Her eyes were teary. Their mouths were altogether together. Oh, this was, would always be her marriage.

They were bodily perfect for each other. Everything would be all right. Life would be good, whatever came.

Mati had drawn back his head and was gazing at her as though it were a long exposure to imprint the picture in himself.

Again the thought came to him in amazement: How was it, in making love a woman's face became utterly transfigured? What you had seen before as lovely, even as beautiful, became . . . ineffable. With Andrea he had seen it happen—Mati crossed that out. Only now with Dena. The radiance was joined with his; it glowed right inside him.

As a child by the Kinneret when the Sabbath Eve approached and the water glowed, he had sometimes felt almost truly religious, feeling upwelling within himself the melody of the prayer of the coming of the Sabbath Bride. Arrive, oh, bride, come, approach, oh, bride, and the bride was the glow of eternity, the emanation, the one, the Shechina. She.

※ ※ ※

There was even a touch of blood on Myra's sheet, and Dena laughed and said should she leave it for proof, and he asked had it hurt, and she said, no, she hadn't even known when it happened, and it must have been out there on the couch; they laughed together, but she wanted to ask, virgins aren't supposed to be good, that's what she had always read, so, well was I good? Was it different from— No, not to spoil anything, she canceled the thought, and instead, they sat on the side of the bed holding hands, and then Dena got a damp washcloth and rubbed away the little stain, why should anyone make remarks, even a maid, this was theirs, theirs alone.

※ ※ ※

And Dena's father that night lay half awake. Sam Kossoff saw his Dena, his girl child, in one of those settlements over there. Arabs came, like Wild West Indians on horses, shooting. That boy, Mati, was at a window with a rifle, holding them off. The same way Mati's brother had done. And Dena, Sam's own Dena, stood there behind her young husband, loading another rifle, handing it to Mati. Oh, what had he let his daughter get into!

It must be late, very late already. Sam saw on his radium watch, it was three.

Bessie awoke and asked what time it was.

"Two."

"She hasn't come home yet?"

When at last they heard their daughter slip in at the front door and slip past their bedroom, they didn't say a word to her; you didn't dare say a word to a modern girl.

First, Dena showed the ring to her mother.

"But, Dena, you are engaged to him?" Unsure whether to express joy.

Dena couldn't yet bring the family, even her mother, into what was so intimate, so private, but at least part of the situation they had to know. "It was a celebration—he flew solo!"

"Like a graduation? Mati flew the airplane by himself?"

"He even did tricks. I saw it!"

"He wants to become an airplane pilot?" Her mother studied her for what was really meant; Dena suddenly felt it was like a guessing game; she felt gay, impish. She was really fond of Ma, the dear simple soul, besides, of course, loving her. Bessie was undoubtedly even wondering how much could an airplane pilot earn? And the danger of widowhood. "Dena, something hasn't happened?"

Could it really be true that it showed? Of course, that had been a silly high school girl speculation, but maybe someone close to you, a mother, could psychologically feel the difference? "Oh, Mother, we just decided to have a kind of understanding."

When her daughter said "Ma," Bessie knew you could even talk to her, but when she said "Mother," it was supposed to be things about which the older generation was old-fashioned. So this meant they really did have a private kind of semiengagement. And also maybe the thing had happened.

For how could one measure their "understandings"? First, a girl went steady; then she and her fellow had an understanding; then, if the family was lucky, it became a half-official engagement, sort of only for the family. The way Bessie understood, in an understanding a girl wasn't exactly supposed to do anything yet, but it could happen. When it became an engagement, even if only in the family, many young couples nowadays didn't wait. Bessie even suspected that her daughter-in-law Sherrill hadn't waited, but as Phil and Sherrill's engagement had been very short, maybe they had waited after all.

Yet a diamond—however small—wasn't that an engagement? And the setting—if the stone was small, the old-fashioned setting, real antique, was something special. Beautiful! From the shop Bessie knew what was good jewelry. This was from the old country, maybe Bukharan. "It is an heirloom?" she asked.

"His mother left it to him."

"And from his mother's legacy Mati gave this to you?" Bessie looked into her daughter's eyes. Dena's changed. Even a little scared. The eyes seemed even to be asking her back as a mother.

"Dena, this is something, this is serious. He is serious about you. Dena, are you serious about him?"

"Oh, Ma—"

Dena felt tears coming, couldn't stand for her mother to see, and hurried out, saying she had a class.

※ ※ ※

There was in Mati a wild urge to crow like a rooster, to tell someone, but of the two wonders he had touched in that single day what could he reveal, to whom? Just a single word he would send to Leah by cable, "Flew." It almost seemed that with Leah she would guess both! He had been writing her that he was seeing Dena again.

But for the price of the cable he could have a whole hour in the air, and even in his sleep he was debating, which? But how could he worry about spending a few dollars on a cable? How many times in his life would he succeed so beautifully, two wonders in a single day! He'd send the cable and take the lesson; he'd eat rolls and milk for a few days, for a real meal someone would be sure to invite him, anyway there would be Dena's on Friday. Would Dena say anything to her mother? Her brother? Would her family maybe guess? And Myra, when she came back from the hospital with her new nose, she would probably smell it!

In his dream a white dove came down into Leah's hands and was a pair of doves. Mati awakened happy. Myra was always interpreting her Freudian dreams; well, those were the two beautiful things that had happened that he wanted to tell Leah, he could be a psychoanalyst, too! Then more! This dream was also a wish. Myra had explained that our dreams were secret wishes, and yesterday in the midst of their lovemaking weren't he and Dena flying together as in one of her favorite paintings by Chagall? And now half continuing the dream, he saw the two of them coming down to land in Eretz, with Leah and the whole family running to meet them!

Mati smiled at how Myra would right away say, naturally everyone knew that in a dream flying meant making love.

After sending the cable, Mati wrote a long, detailed letter, describing different kinds of airplanes and their cost and range and speed. Leah would know this was meant for Dov, but still, just in case the British should open the letter and get curious, he made it all sound as if he were going into the flying business in America.

Then he wondered, should he write, "I gave Dena the diamond!" Leah would tell the whole family even if he told her not

167

to, she'd be too excited, and everyone in the Yishuv would be saying Mati Chaimovitch got himself engaged to an Amerikankeh. So what? What held him back? Did he have any doubt? It would always be Dena! Only there was a feeling, still to seal the joy between themselves. And so when mentioning Dena being there he wrote, "my chaverah." Leah would know. But not yet about the diamondl.

What she hadn't understood or anticipated, Dena told herself, was that when it was no longer a wrestling match with a boy trying to get you or pet you into going the limit with him, then the whole thing changed. You no longer talked in persiflage or even to show him by your sophistication that he wasn't going to conquer you through your curiosity; you no longer had to be all the time on guard against yourself and against him about not going too far and swooning into it through your own sex desire; and you didn't have to go out places in order to avoid extra-long petting sessions. Also, she hadn't understood how a man would suddenly want to tell you and ask you about all his problems and his plans, really bring everything to you, with the fears included. Before, with Jack Sloan and even Mati, they had left out the fears.

After they were relaxed in Myra's bed—she still was in the hospital—and even in the little talks in the campus coffee shop, Mati would discuss with her all kinds of things about airplanes. It was really kind of interesting; he would bring magazines and brochures and prospectuses to the coffee shop and make calculations about the overhead of an airline with ticket offices and insurance; at last he was really learning economics, he joked. And then the delicate problem arose about how to find out what the British attitude would be to a commercial Palestine airline? Probably the best thing would be for someone in London to make inquiries, Dena suggested, but then she noticed that Mati didn't like to share his project; he wanted to do everything himself. Maybe he was a little vain, maybe it was ambition; it was interesting to see his character unfolding to her, not in the way of "before," when a man showed you only what would make him attractive.

This Dov from Tel Aviv took a long time answering, and Mati was worried about what to do next; should he already begin to try to raise money to buy the first plane? But then what kind? A two-seater, as he had originally planned, just for training other fliers, or a larger airplane that could carry a few passengers? And all the while Dena was really in herself wondering had she already decided to marry Mati and go to live in Palestine? It was kind of scary, but still, she would be doing something really different! Everybody talked about being "different," but this would really be something! All the kids on campus would be amazed at her daring! But did she really want to go there to live? Was that her intended life? How was it, those West Side kids in his group knew that was what they wanted to do? They wanted nothing else but to go and be settlers in Palestine, and while she could intellectually understand their idealism, the movement never took hold of her. She just simply wanted to be with Mati. Her man.

And in fairness to him, should she do it? Unless it meant to her as much as it meant to him? Wouldn't it really have been better for Mati to have fallen in love with one of those Zionist Youth girls? But merely at the speculation, something unfelt before came and gripped her—a fierce visceral jealousy, in her very gedderim!

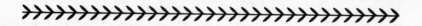

SO IT had happened in America, Leah wrote, and she was happy that he had found his chaverah, yet his big sister could not help asking, would this daughter of Chicago one day think of coming to Eretz? And also, would Eretz be a life for his chaverah, Dena?

Then immediately came another letter from Leah, with a real surprise. She herself was coming right away to America on a mission! She would come to Chicago, too, she was crazy to see his Dena, and also she would be bringing Mati the answers from Dov to all his questions.

Her official mission, Leah wrote, was to help in a campaign of the Pioneer Women. Her friend Rahel Ben-Zvi had been in America a few years ago and had organized Jewish workingwomen to help the workingwomen of the Yishuv, and now the Pioneer Women were raising money. But another part of her mission Leah would explain to Mati when she saw him.

At the station they held each other, laughing, and then Leah engulfed Dena. Instantly, Mati could see, Dena was hers, just the way every new girl who came to Leah's meshek was at once hers.

Already in New York, Leah comically explained to Dena while Mati took the valise, the Pioneer ladies had Americanized her with these ladylike shoes! To ten different stores they had to drag her before anything could be found that was wide enough for her feet!

Look! Indeed it was a laugh to see the cramped Charlie Chaplin way Leah walked. But her whole being glowed, and Mati was sure he could still smell the cucumbers on her hands.

When Leah showed the address where she was to be put up—a Mrs. Charlotte Feld—Dena cried, "Am I impressed! Let me touch you!" It was *the* Mrs. Feld.

"Are they so important?" Mati's sister said innocently as they got into the car.

"Only about the biggest millionaires in Chicago," Dena said. "Don't tell me Charlotte Feld is one of your Pioneer Women!" And hadn't Mati always complained that those hoity-toity German Jewish families were anti-Zionist?

The connection with the Felds, Leah explained, went way back to the war, to that fantastic spy story that Mati liked to tell, about a Palestine family even more heroic than their own, the Aaronsons. The eldest son, Aaron Aaronson, studying agronomy, had discovered ancient wild wheat on the slopes of Mount Hermon and became world-famous; he had lectured right here in Chicago, and the Felds and the Rosenwalds had financed a research station for him in Palestine. That didn't mean they were Zionists; it was for science. Then in the war Aaronson had made the place a spy center for England, behind the Turkish lines, and the Turks had caught his sister Sara, and she had killed herself. Leah was a friend of that Sara Aaronson and her young sister Rifka, who at the start of the war had been smuggled away right here to Chicago; the Felds had taken her in. So when Leah had mentioned to Rifka Aaronson that she was going to Chicago, Rifka had at once written to Charlotte Feld.

As Dena drew up under the portico, a Japanese servant opened the car door. Mrs. Feld, a distinguished woman with short-cut white hair in a sculptured permanent, welcomed Leah warmly. With the Japanese butler carrying the cardboard suitcase—Dena couldn't wait to describe all this to Myra—the hostess escorted them up a curving stairway like in movies about a British manse, and left them in the guest suite, declaring with a gracious smile that they doubtless wanted to catch up on family news.

At once Leah opened her dilapidated briefcase, the tik Mati always described, in which Yishuv officials carried their lunch, producing a list of Pioneer Women, and as Dena began to look up telephone numbers, Leah asked, could Dena, could Mati, get her some Jews with money? Really big money?

"Where do you think you are!" Dena laughed. The Felds by themselves could support training for every chalutzah arriving in Palestine!

"I know, I know, for agricultural work they'll give." But now she explained the secret part of her mission: gathering funds for arms for the Haganah. These fine people, when they learned that their research station had been used for spying, had been highly upset, so it was best to look elsewhere.

Rabbi Mike Kramer would know whom to approach, Mati said. And meanwhile, what was Dov's answer for the airplane?

"Wait, wait, not so fast," Leah told him.

"Well?"

That was the answer. From Eliahu himself. First things first, rifles, machine guns. Menahem had found good sources in Europe. As for Mati's having learned to fly, Dov sent him a well-done! A yashir koach! Increase in strength! And if Mati could find money for the airplane, well and good, but it must not interfere with what was more urgent.

"Leah, I'll take you up in the air! You'll see!"

"Me?" Leah laughed to Dena. "Me, I'll sink the airplane!"

The living room being used for Leah's first meeting was an entire side of the Feld mansion, with at the end a fireplace high enough to roast a camel and, above it, an ancestor portrait of a stern, yet kindly-looking man with a thick gold watch chain across his vest. Along the walls were old masters, even a real Rembrandt! "A million-dollar collection at least," Dena whispered to Mati, who whispered back, "They should give us one painting, and I could buy a whole airline." She responded with an almost wifely look, of you and your one-track mind.

Just then Myra arrived; she was, of course, some sort of cousin of the Felds, and while Dena had already seen the perfect nose job, this was its first public appearance. "Beautiful!" the hostess exclaimed in a hoarse whisper, giving Myra a hug. "You were absolutely right to have it done!" As she drew them into her little sitting room, Dena saw Charlotte Feld's own collection, moderns. "The other stuff I inherited," Mrs. Feld said, as though here she could really breathe. They marveled over her latest acquisition, a huge Fernand Léger of women who looked as if they were made of parts of metal cylinders.

Of Leah, Dena heard Myra whisper to Charlotte Feld, "Picasso's Giantess!" But in admiration.

Rows of folding chairs had been set up in the huge room, and now the ladies were assembling. They were clearly of two different breeds; you could instantly sort them out by their clothing, from Saks to Goldblatt's. Charlotte Feld had invited a "few friends" to meet the Pioneer Woman from Palestine, but where had Leah dredged up these others? Earnest, heavy, gold-toothed, and with accents, not charming accents like Leah's and Mati's, but the Maxwell Street Yiddish accent that Dena all too well remembered. They were introduced, chairladies of the Arbeitsverein and sisterhoods, the International Ladies Garment Workers and the Amalgamated, and after the gracious handshake of Charlotte Feld they gravitated to one side of the room, monopolizing Leah, who should have been making important connections.

For going to the Felds, Bessie Kossoff had got herself an elegant little shantung from Marshall Field's, but the main thing, this was her first chance to meet Mati's sister, and at once Bessie saw this woman was, as the old folks used to say, a real mensh. Suppose even Dena should one day marry the boy and even try to go there to live, here was a real person; with Leah, Bessie felt, you could discuss honestly, and she was no longer so afraid.

The ladies came to order. Charlotte Feld spoke of the heroic tradition of Jewish women, from Deborah the Prophetess to modern times, when this house had been honored by having as a guest during the World War a daughter of a great heroic family of Palestine, the Aaronsons, and today the honor was repeated by the presence of a true Pioneer Woman from another heroic *Mayflower* family of Palestine, Leah Chaimovitch. And, Mrs. Feld added with a smile, Chicago was fortunate in having a young brother of Leah's, Palestine born, studying at the university.

Heads turned. Mati felt his face going red. He was the only male in the room, and all these women, mostly in their middle years, smiled at him with that peculiar woman's expression of approval as though for a future son-in-law. He even felt in Dena's mother a sitting up, as though she were announcing, "Hands off! We've got him!"

Dena too felt her mama suddenly aglow with nachas. At last the pride of it all had come over her—a heroic family!

"And now, ladies, the Pioneer Woman in person, our dear Leah!"

Leah arose. She had made great efforts with her English, mostly picked up from British soldiers who came sniffing around watching the girls in their briefest bloomers bending over the cucumber patch. It didn't hurt to have some British soldiers on your side, but two or three serious romances had developed, with the stricken Britishers ready to convert to Judaism circumcision and all—and suddenly finding themselves transferred out of Palestine. But they had been good for her English.

How effective she was! Dena caught herself feeling proud as though already part of the family. The big woman's goodness, her simplicity, beamed from her even in this formal vast room. "Sisters," she called them, and they were at once all her sisters, even the uppity friends of Mrs. Feld's. As Leah described the plain daily tasks of her life, the ladies solidified on their chairs like hens settling in. "Ours is not an experimental agricultural farm, like the Aaronsons, which made so many important discoveries," she said, "and that was helped by the generous contributions from here, but ours is the other side, which makes use of the discoveries, using every inch of soil, every drop of water, so there should be plenty of room in the land for everybody. We are teaching our chaveroth—"

"It means comrades," someone whispered loudly, and Leah said, "It means good wives, too, it means women equal with men, free women, but not"—she got them laughing—"the kind of free they say of us! We teach our girls the tasks of the woman of the soil, and you would be surprised how it all comes back into our hands after the generations in Russia that a Jew didn't even know how to grow a radish!"

Also trees. "Maybe this is something especially a task for women because when you see a hill covered with green trees—and now we have already lived to see it—it is like on the earth itself a beautiful head of hair!"

They laughed again, as though to help her move their hearts in this language foreign to her, to reassure her, yes, she was doing it fine! "And flowers," Leah said. "In Tel Aviv for Shabbat we send our girls into the city, and they sell bunches of flowers, our own grown flowers."

174

In the recent troubles one of the training farms had been burned down; fortunately every girl had already been evacuated. Now they were rebuilding, in cement, not wood. All this needed funds—

Not only did Bessie Kossoff become a member of Leah's Chicago committee and tell everyone that Dena was going out with a boy from a *Mayflower* family of Palestine, but what surprised Mati was the sudden change in Sam and Phil Kossoff when they learned of Leah's second mission, the secret one. When Leah came to supper, she asked them if they could help out in something confidential. As soon as Phil heard what was wanted, he was a different man. First off, he would get together a little committee of Jewish dealers in the jewelry field, wholesalers as well as retailers, people he knew and could vouch for; every man could be trusted. In spite of the bad times, for certain things people could find money.

Sam told Mati how he himself, had he not been already married and with family responsibilities, had thought of joining the Jewish Brigade, back there in the World War, when a contingent marched with a Jewish flag up Twelfth Street! Phil listened, puffing his cigar; this seemed the first time he heard such a thing from his father.

Later, taking Mati aside, Phil said Dena had confided in him the real reason why Mati had learned to fly. "Founder and Chief of the Haganah Air Force!" he whispered, raising the cigar in a kind of salute. "Okay, fella, count me in."

To start with, Phil said, he wanted some of the fellows downtown to meet with Leah and Mati, to get a personal picture of what kind of people the Jews were over there. He had in mind a bunch of young professionals, boys of his crowd whom he had known in McKinley High School, doctors were doing okay—especially with heart attacks! he jested—and lawyers, too, with bankruptcies right and left. Also there was a certain special kind of depression business—the repossess, on car loans, furniture. He himself had a certain amount of it on installment jewelry, though he tried to work things out with people. But not everybody in business, Mati could see, was jumping out of windows.

The lunch was at Manny's Kosher Style on Wabash Avenue, and all the men in the place, Leah said to Mati as they entered, seemed somehow like Dena's brother Phil. It was true—they all had dark circles under their eyes and talked fast at each other.

Phil jumped to welcome them and called joking greetings to each table they passed, introducing Leah, adding with a wink, "Very important. I'll give you a buzz." Or, "Stop at the store, I've got something good I put aside for your anniversary, a steal, a repossess!" Or, "This lady will come to see you, she's going to twist your arm, and you better watch out, she's got some muscles!" And to Leah on the side; "I'll give you a figure for each of them, and don't settle for less!"

At their table, everyone ordered corned beef or pastrami sandwiches with sour tomatoes and pickles. No, there was no corned beef like this in Palestine! Leah had to admit. Well, if nothing else, Phil joked, Mati could start a real Jewish delicatessen in Tel Aviv and make a fortune.

Then down to business. Phil had assembled half a dozen men— one of them he joshed was his worst competitor, "he sells glass diamonds to the shvartzer." Then he touched on Leah's mission. The organization he didn't have to name; this was all on the QT. But every man over there was in it, risking his life. And so the people over there shouldn't get caught short again, the real supply job was up to people like themselves sitting right here.

Leah spoke as they ate. A rifle bought from the Arabs cost as much as a camel! Oh, sure, you could buy from the Arabs, also from British soldiers, grenades, even light machine guns. But for the quantity needed, the cost was much lower abroad, and the boys had ways to bring it in.

For each man, Phil had set a sum in his mind. Starting with his "competitor"—Aw, come on, Dave, you know I know what you take in, even on a lousy Monday. Then some of the others started giving figures for fellows in their own line of business. "Listen, Nat grosses at least eight grand a week." "Yah, but he has a terrible rent—and big alimony, two kids." "Never mind, he got out of the market just before the crash." By the time the applecake was being eaten Phil had added up a total of nineteen thousand dollars in pledges, and Leah was beaming; such a fortune she hadn't even dared dream of, from one lunch! But wait, Phil wasn't through. He divided up among the men the duty to call on this one and put the bee on that one; only, as the whole operation had to be done in the strictest secrecy, everyone had to be reliable.

"I didn't forget your special deal, don't worry," he told Mati in the men's room. But even with these handpicked fellows, he hadn't wanted to mention the airplane thing at the table. He'd talked to a few in private. Also, he had made a few inquiries about picking up a bargain, but airplanes seemed strictly a goy business. Still, a friend of his who bought up fancy cars, Rolls and Caddies, might run into a repossess—big shots were selling their private planes. He was keeping his eyes open. Phil was putting the whole thing to his friends as an investment, an airline, tourists in the Holy Land, and the need to buy a trainer so the Jews would have their own pilots. Sure, they caught on. A wink, even a slap on the back!

On the el with Mati, Leah puzzled. This brother of Dena's and all his business friends downtown, they weren't Zionists. Some of them hardly knew there had been a Balfour Declaration. She didn't suppose any of them were religious. Then what kept them Jews? What kind of Jews were they?

"They are corned-beef-sandwich Jews," Mati said.

At home in Eretz you spent hours at meetings discussing what could be expected of American Jews. They moved to goyish suburbs. They thought it a triumph to get into a goyish golf club. And yet— And something at this lunch had struck her. The way Dena's brother, in his jewelry business, knew how much each man could afford to give. Clothing stores, shoes—what else were the Jews in?

Junk business, Mati said. And real estate. And movie theaters.

Suppose in each big city where there were a lot of Jews, Leah pondered, suppose you could get someone like Phil Kossoff to do the same thing? Tell you how much each Jew in his line of business could afford?

It was an idea.

After all—Leah grinned—in the old country, the long-bearded envoys used to come shnorring from Jerusalem, they had their lists of each wealthy Jew and what he could afford to give. . . . As their mother, alev-ha-sholem, used to say, every Jew knew what was cooking in another Jew's pot. Leah herself could remember as a child in Cherezinka, the shul at Rosh Hashanah, and each Jew announced before the whole town the amount of his donation. If a Jew didn't give as much as everyone calculated he could give, he couldn't look into the eyes of his neighbors. He had lost his—how did you say in English, derech eretz?

"Community status," Mati said. And as she seemed a bit puzzled: "That's what you learn in a university—big words for what everybody anyway knows."

Still, university knowledge was necessary, Leah said. She had talked before leaving to her old friend Dovidl—and Ben-Gurion had advised that Mati should study even for a higher degree because such people would be needed in the Yishuv. Look at Reuven —every plant that grew in Eretz Yisroel he had unearthed, but to teach this even in a high school in his own kibbutz, he had to break his head and learn the names in Latin.

And this reminded Leah; she had promised to bring back to Reuven from Chicago the seeds for a certain new kind of corn. Fishing in the handbag that Dena had bought her to replace the old tik—here, Reuven had written it down, even in Latin!

And now, fixing her eyes on him, Leah asked, "Well?"

"Well, what?"

Very pretty the girl was, yes. "Naturally I would have felt better if you had chosen one from home. Hundreds of girls in my meshek I kept pushing your way, wonderful girls!" They laughed. But Leah couldn't blame him for being captivated. His Dena seemed really a very fine girl, too. But to come and live in Eretz? Her family were good people, but surely Zionists they were not.

"Why does everybody who comes to Eretz.have to be a flaming Zionist! Maybe it would already be better if we had a few ordinary normal people!"

Leah seized his head between her hands, and right there in the el car she kissed him with a big smacking kiss on the brow. Across the aisle a huge black woman, as big as Leah herself, let out a great friendly laugh.

A small dinner, Charlotte Feld told Leah, mostly family.

There came Raphael Feld, the distinguished corporation lawyer, with very red lips and an air of triumph every time he put a question. Raphael Feld had certain doubts about the entire wisdom of the Palestine venture, as he called it. In his own opinion, being a Jew was entirely and strictly a matter of one's religious confession, even for those who were not strictly religious! And from then on Leah heard the usual points, with the man's wife smilingly nodding to each declaration. In America, for example, there was true freedom of religion, and anti-Semitism was rapidly disappearing. True, in Germany there was a species of crude anti-

Semitism being pumped up by that guttersnipe Hitler; one error was to call attention to this madman's rantings by open protests. The quiet way was the only way to deal with Hitlerism.

The host, Bertram Feld, also believed in the quiet way—through influence in high places. Now Zionism, for instance, was a noisy movement, pushing, and unfortunately certain gentile elements even in this country reacted by saying if the Jews wanted a country of their own, let them all go there! And with a witty smile toward Leah, he added, "I'll bet you couldn't agree more!" But considering the world question as a whole, and indeed, as a member of the American Jewish Committee he could well attest that in some countries there was such a question, was it worth endangering all the gains that had been made through long, careful work and even endangering the unity and stability of the American Jewish community, because of—

To respond would be pointless, Leah knew, and fortunately Charlotte Feld with a hostess smile declared that Leah had told her some fascinating things about folk dances in Palestine—the famous Gertrude Kraus from Germany was now teaching in Jerusalem! Out of all misfortune some good must come! And—again turning to Leah—weren't there other great talents from Germany arriving? The violinist Huberman?

He was doubtful that any important Jews would leave Germany, Bertram Feld stated, as that Austrian housepainter had already shot his bolt; the last election proved he could never win a majority.

Raphael Feld, besides, had information from a highly placed relative in Mainz, a banker, that on the matter of anti-Semitic agitation an ironclad promise had been made by Goebbels that if the Nazis attained power, all this would fade away. Surely it would be better to have National Socialism than for Germany to go communist!

Later, sitting with Leah before the men came to join the ladies —such were actually the customs in this house—Charlotte Feld smiled away her brother-in-law's opinions. Indeed, before dinner he had handed her a thousand-dollar check for Leah's work—strictly the agricultural part, of course.

For her final week in Chicago, so as to spare streetcar travel for the workingwomen from the West Side, Leah explained to Charlotte Feld, who fully understood, the organization was putting her up at a central hotel, not too expensive, the Atlantic.

She could breathe.

Before Leah's departure Mati wanted her at least to buy things for herself for once! He gave Dena a whole twenty dollars scraped together by skipping a few flying lessons—and more than a few meals, Dena bet. Without telling him, she added twenty-five more, from her mother.

Going shopping would be a chance for her to talk with Leah, really to talk. Until now at each encounter there had been Leah's engulfing hug, like actually, physically taking you to heart as Mati's girl. Yet at one moment, last Friday after dinner, Dena had caught Leah's eyes on her with that wondering, almost worried look that asked, What is she like, this American girl of our Mati's? Will she be able to live our way?

Though so far only Myra was supposed to know their secret, Dena felt sure Leah was aware, just as she was sure her mother knew. Without a word between them her mother had suddenly bought her the most expensive and luscious step-ins. As a knowing modern girl Dena had to ask herself, could their physical passion carry them through their lives? If she had to go and live over there? Suppose it all proved too strange, too difficult—could that even spoil their passion?

Almost, almost, a few times she had sensed Leah ready to tell her things, the real things of a woman's life.

Victor dropped her off, not without a certain expression, at the old Ashland Avenue building with office plaques in Jewish, where the Pioneer Women had their headquarters. In the crowded little upstairs rooms everybody seemed to be named Goldie. That brooding enlarged photo of Theodor Herzl hung in the hallway, together with a Keren Kayemeth poster—a rather charming brown-tone engraving of pioneers and trees. "Just one more minute, Denatchka." Leah settled whose name should be above whose on a letterhead and gave a flood of instructions to a chaverah named Mollie, who walked them down the hall. How these women loved her! They didn't want to lose a minute of her! But at last Dena had Leah on the street.

A taxi? No, no, Leah loved streetcars.

And riding downtown, her huge bulk crowding them close together on the seat, Leah came out with so many intimate things in her life and also about Mati. Men were so squirmy if you tried to talk about when they were babies. Dena began to feel really sure and happy in her love. And Leah showed photos of her own children, the bigger one, Ehud, she said looked exactly like Mati at the same age—yes, Dena could see—the round face with the heavy eyebrows straight across. And felt within her an odd choicelessness —a child of hers would look exactly like this, too!

Oh, how Leah wanted to be home already. "But I confess to you, Dena, when Golda Meyerson asked me to come here, I really wanted to travel, to go out awhile and be in the big world!" She gazed at Dena. "In Eretz you sometimes feel yourself locked up. I don't want to frighten you, if someday you will decide and come to us. Your life there would already be different from ours. But you see, Denatchka—" Her huge body moved even closer on the seat, and Dena felt that now, now, what she really needed would come. And suddenly Mati's sister went on with something that at first seemed altogether outside what she needed, though still an intimacy. A whole secret part of Leah's life that Mati had never mentioned. "Once before, Dena, I came away from Eretz. I was in Vienna. Nearly ten years ago already." After the death of her little sister Yaffaleh in the famous Battle of Tel Hai. "You know, Dena, maybe Mati never told you, something happened to me then; I couldn't go on anymore. Maybe also because of when I went back to Russia." That was when after her ten years of waiting, poor Leah had found her Handsome Moshe married, with a child. "So you see, Denatchka, all this together, and then when Yaffaleh was killed, something broke in me." The streetcar rattled over the bridge across the dirty sluggish Chicago River and then the stretches of railway yards. This large, powerful Leah, it was difficult to imagine her as a girl making love. Only now Dena sensed how it must have been in Palestine before Moshe left on his mission and disappeared. Leah so young, and in the harvest, oh, the two of them must have been like Michelangelo's huge angels tumbling in the sky!

"So after I saw him in Russia, and then when Yaffaleh was killed, I couldn't go on. And then my chaver"—she meant her husband now, Natan—"he was there in the battle when our Yaffaleh was killed, with Trumpeldor, and it was he who brought us the news of her last moments. When Natan saw what had come over me, such a nervous breakdown you call it, he took all his pay that he saved from all the years of the war—you know Natan was in the Jewish Brigade with our Gidon—he took all his money, I wasn't even his chaverah yet, and Natan sent me to Europe, to Vienna." Listening to Leah, Dena felt as though she were passing through some ritual, some initiation by a more mature soul. Here in this streetcar she was being told. Leah's face was again the broad, glowing countenance beaming to the world. "Ah, such a beautiful city! Such beauty I had never seen! I lived there in a tiny room in a pension, and with every pfennig I could save I went to the standing place in back in the opera. The ballet. Ah, Denatchka. I went also in the afternoons to a psychologue, not the famous Dr. Freud that Natan had read in books, but also around Dr. Freud there were others; you know most of them are Jews. And from the same Vienna there came our Theodor Herzl, even the same street of Sigmund Freud—they showed me the house! To tell you the truth, I only talked my heart out, and this was good for me. But even better for me—it was the city. In those few months, Dena, I tried to drink in a whole life. In my life I really never went to school. In Vienna everything was beautiful; maybe even what was bad looked good to me, I knew some was good, some bad, but to me all was beautiful." She smiled her broad, half-abashed smile.

"And so the music, the beautiful city, the ballet, and then I was better and I went home and Gidon's friend Natan became my chaver. And we had children. My whole life. I only wanted to tell you I am glad of my life—you understand, Denatchka?"

She had not fully understood but felt the full meaning would come to her later on, just as in some lectures at which you want to ask questions but don't want to seem dense. In the intimacy, she felt, Leah was accepting her; perhaps Mati's big sister simply wanted to instill in her a woman's strength—to dare. How modern they had already been, Leah and her generation, back there!

Leah gazed out the streetcar window. How grim and black this city of iron and the lifeless water. Her heart overflowed with longing for the willowy banks of the Yarkon. It was time to go home.

In Mati's girl, beside her, she sensed a remaining puzzlement. "You are wondering maybe how after such a crazy passion, keeping myself for a man for ten years—what was it?" Impulsively she added, "You see when I went there to Russia and found him again, what happened, Dena?" She took Dena's hand. "This I have not told. Only to the psychologue. Only to my chaver, to whom it was due. Dena, even though Moshe was married, I went back to him. The passion at once came back over me. What one feels so strongly a person must do." This was what she meant then? "Only this time," Leah continued, "I came to understand another thing between men and women. That—how can I say, I don't know if you can be ready to understand it—that because of the manhood, of what happens inside our body, he mastered me. Even from the beginning—to make me always do what he wanted." Instantly in Dena there was a cry, no! Not Mati! He was not, thank heaven, like that! And Leah too declared, "Not always, not all men. I am only telling you about what came to me, Dena, about a time when I understood that this thing in us, this need to have a man, a certain kind of man uses this over a woman. And a woman can also use this over herself—the need even like to be enslaved. You understand, Denatchka?" She turned her head so their eyes met, and she had her wonderfully engulfing smile. "But in truth she can choose her own life."

Dena took her future sister-in-law, as she found herself thinking, not to Mandel's but to Marshall Field's. Whole floors of delicate women's things Leah saw. Pausing now at a perfume display, Dena whiffed a flask, another, but how could any scent ever match the fresh apple odor that was exuded by Mati's sister?

And then nightgowns, an Italian silk—Leah let the fabric flow over her hands like milk. Finally, admitting a lifelong secret desire, she let Dena persuade her to get a voluminous pale blue crepe de chine, and even when she placed the package in Leah's hands, Dena knew she would never wear the nightgown but perhaps keep it folded in a drawer, to pass her hands over it a few times a year.

They still had time before Leah's next appointment, and Dena knew where they would go—she wanted to show Leah the blue Picasso at the Art Institute.

"Honestly, this is what I look like?" Leah stood awestruck before the Giantess. So this was why, she caught on, Dena had bought the gown. They laughed, still more intimate.

Then, standing before the huge Seurat masterwork of Sunday by the river—the picture was like a moment in a ballet, a Shabbat along the banks of the Yarkon, Leah said. Such masterpieces they had here in Chicago! And Chicago was supposed to be a city of gangsters!

Dena laughed. Then, looking closely at her, Leah said, "People have wrong ideas about Eretz, too. Don't worry. We are not all the time shooting like maybe they made you think."

Sitting on the stone bench facing the Chagall wasn't like being with Myra talking of the pattern of the stripes, but as though this real Jew of their past again brought them closer. "You know, Denatchka, when I fell in love with my Handsome Moshe and he was my first man, I knew already he had lain with other women." Something was crisping in Dena, but she would not let it show. "So I understand, Denatchka, Mati too was with a girl here last year. You now know—with you he is in love." Leah struggled as with something eternally baffling. "We try to understand what brings two people together to stay together in this world. And it is the same mystery—what brings Jews to Eretz?" Her broad smile returned. "All my girls from the kvutsa, the ones I thought would be just right for Mati—" She laughed softly. "And he found you. And you are not even a Zionist. Oh, I know, I know you don't feel against it. But it doesn't pull you. And maybe you are afraid of how it will be to live over there. . . . But who do you live among here in Chicago, Dena?" She gazed up at Chagall's rabbi. "Your family and your friends' families, even the fancy Strauses and the Felds, they also come from this one. Besides, anyway, a city like this Chicago, yes, some of it is very nice to live in, and some of it is very ugly. All where the Negroes live, and the Italians, and still some of our Jews, not better than Mea Shearim. In Tel Aviv it already feels like a city, and in Jerusalem live people from all over the world; it is a cosmos." She took Dena's hand. "And our family, too, came from this one."

Just before Leah's departure Myra's uncle Sylvan Straus returned from Europe. Mike and Sue Kramer at once got him for dinner, so Leah could meet him.

Though Myra had been worried that he might not take to Leah, Dena saw that it went fine from the start. A real aristocrat always knew what was genuine. Sylvan Straus had just spent considerable time in Germany; he had never been a Zionist, and he was far from becoming one, he said with his charming warm smile to Leah, but the original premise of Theodor Herzl, with this much he agreed. The Jews had to have a place of refuge. Because of what he had seen of the Nazis in Germany, the Jews might need that refuge very soon. The Nazis were not on the way down at all; if they could not reach an absolute majority in an election, they might resort to a putsch. The unemployed had been organized into Hitler's private army, given lodging and food. Thus, his brownshirts were even more numerous than the small German army allowed by the Allies! And industrialists footed the bill, rather than have communism. A master stroke. Straus smiled; he was half a Marxist himself, he said. "I'm half of everything! I'm pulled from one side to the other! I suppose that makes me a dialectician!" He let out a laugh. Seeing Dena's puzzlement, he smiled at her. "I sway from capitalism to communism, back and forth!" And to Mati: "What does that make me?" "A parlor socialist?" said Mati daringly, and Sylvan Straus cried, "Touché!"

So the paid Nazi lumpenproletariat were picking street fights with the communists. And the Jews, of course, got it both ways: to the Nazis the communists were Jews, also the capitalists holding Germany by the throat were Jews. Anti-Semitism was no mere slogan with the Hitlerites, as unfortunately some of the Jewish leaders both there and here still wanted to believe.

After dinner Straus seemed, without interrupting the general talk, to have his quiet little conference with each in turn. From Mati he wanted to know what was really thought about Judah Magnes and his peace ideas; yes, he agreed that a serious effort at rapprochement had to take place with the Arabs, but also—drawing Leah into the conversation—he agreed it was vital for the Jewish community to be able to rely on itself for defense. And not only did he make it clear that a substantial donation would be forthcoming from him, but he would "talk to some of his friends." With Myra he discussed some exciting paintings he was bringing back from Germany—Emil Nolde, Kandinsky, and Paul Klee, the Bauhaus was greater than ever, all arts unified as one, architecture, design, painting, photography; he had picked up a few pieces of furniture and as soon as the shipment arrived—

From her uncle Myra brought Dena a check for Leah—the largest single donation in all her mission. Five thousand dollars! Maybe rich people were of some use after all, Leah laughed. And maybe Hitler was bringing even the German Jews to their senses.

At least, Mati joked half in earnest, she ought to give him a commission for the introduction; he'd use it for the airplane. She must tell Dov he was ready, he was awaiting instructions.

11

AFTER Leah departed, Dena began earnestly to study Hebrew, copying down the alphabet from a primer Mati brought her. Even the word "alphabet" came from *aleph bet*, he pointed out—this was a little trick he used on all his pupils—and when this intrigued her, as it did all the others, he had an odd feeling, as though his own girl should react differently from other people; he had to laugh at himself.

As soon as she could read a little, they tried his huge Hebrew-English Bible. How was it she had never even read the Bible? What ignorance! Goyish kids knew the Old Testament better than Jews!

All Dena knew were the tales everybody knew, like Moses in the bulrushes and Samson and Delilah from Cecil B. De Mille, she mocked, doing a Theda Bara wiggle.

Still using Myra's apartment, Dena became self-conscious that every time they did it Myra knew. At first Mati didn't want to take her to his lousy little room, but Dena said they'd simply tell his landlady they were engaged and that he was giving her Hebrew lessons—the truth! And she would wear the ring. Her sister-in-law Sherrill had told her that certain girls used to go to hotels with their boyfriends before they were married, and the trick was to turn your engagement ring around so only the gold band showed.

Mrs. Kelleher gave Dena a long, measuring look, and then a

smile with perhaps a hint of lewdness could be seen at the edge of her mouth as she said, well, all right, it was against university rules, and she might lose her listing, but since they were engaged and only studying here in the afternoons—

The moment they were inside Dena let out her giggle. Why did grown, mature people, even like her own mother, accept the pretense that you couldn't do it in the middle of the day, but only deep in the night! If a girl came home before two A.M., she wasn't supposed to have done anything!

What a tiny, monklike cell it was. She wouldn't let herself ask him or even imagine that he had had any other girl up here. No, she wouldn't bring that Andrea up to him; anyway, it had been at her studio. Even after they got married—if they really did get married—would she always resent Andrea? Or was it better that your husband should have had it before with another female. And for girls? Would she always wonder? She somehow didn't want to ask Myra if each time with a different man— When they were doing it and she got kind of wild and felt really lascivious and tried all kinds of positions, she would almost ask Mati, had he done this one before? She wanted to discover, to think up something he could never have done with that Andrea! Oh, she was really lascivious, Dena told herself.

But also in this tiny room Mati made her study. Each time he sternly made her do her lesson first. So once, just to prove her power to herself, Dena teased up her skirt and did a few other little tricks a man doesn't catch onto, until Mati seized and virtually raped her in the middle of the Hebrew future tense.

But after that it was she who insisted on duties first. The funny thing, she was really getting sort of fascinated. They had started, the way he said schoolkids did in the Yishuv, right from the first line of the Bible, "in the beginning," and Mati got her fascinated with a bit of philology. The Hebrew beginning was *b'rashit*, and the exact translation, Mati said, would be "in the heading." The root word was *rosh*, "head," just as in English you might say "heading off." All those old Talmudists had woven ideas around every single word in the Bible, so that you could even speculate, Mati said, that the whole of creation was "in the head"—the way certain modern philosophers, as she was learning in Philosophy II, had theories that nothing was real, that the whole world around us was only an idea that existed in our imagination. So—who was it?—had kicked the wall and yelled "ouch" and proved the world was really there! Mati gave her a kiss-bite to prove the same thing: reality. And they got past the first word of creation.

When they came to the patriarchs and the family stories, Dena got so involved that her eyes kept jumping to the parallel column in English and Mati had to cover that side with his hand, forbidding her to cheat. The peculiar thing was she felt she was getting to know about Mati's own family. The story of Jacob and his sons was sort of like Mati's own father, except sons and daughters. But the early part about Jacob when he was going away from home, and he put a stone under his head and slept and dreamed of angels—that sounded more like Mati's brother Reuven. This dream, Mati said, was supposed to have happened right where they lived; that was why the village was called Mishkan Yaacov, the place where Jacob lay down. And Dena could just see it, his dreamy brother Reuven lying on the ground with his head on a stone, gazing up at the stars. The stars were so bright there, Mati always said, and indeed, she had heard this from Celia Rappaport and everyone who had been to Palestine. This even kind of called to her—the brightness and nearness of the stars over there.

And then the mysterious, weird story about the time Jacob was wrestling with an angel—this, too, had happened in their valley, Mati said, right where a certain river, the Yarmuk, joined the Jordan, right where the big electricity dam had been built. That wrestling match had happened when Jacob was coming back to Eretz after having served his father-in-law for his two wives, Rachel and Leah. Even today among the Yemenites it was okay to have two. "You just try it!" She rubbed his thigh, but Mati slapped her hand to make her pay attention. So anyway, before Jacob had left home, his twin brother, Esau, claimed he had been cheated out of his inheritance because the Hebrew tribes had primogeniture and he had come out first; even Jacob's name proved this, Mati said, as Jacob came out holding onto his brother's heel. "A real heel!" Dena cried, because of that trick when he fooled his old father by putting goat's hair on his arm. So then Jacob was scared that Esau would kill him and left home. And here years afterward the twin brothers were about to meet, and that was the night of Jacob's dream about wrestling with the angel, which you didn't have to be Sigmund Freud to know was wrestling with his conscience. So the next morning Jacob went out and gave Esau all kinds of gifts, sheep and cattle, to pacify him.

But wasn't that the same locality where Mati had told her the

Arabs had come across the Jordan and stolen their cattle?

Yes, but also, Mati said, didn't she notice it was not only Jacob and Esau but repeatedly there were opposite natures, Cain and Abel, Isaac and Ishmael, rival brothers like the conflicting elements of human nature, duality?

And all at once, Dena perceived. For Mati and all of them being born and brought up in the ancient land, and also for the Arabs living around them—as Mati explained it, the Moslems also had tales from the Bible and believed they were the descendants of Ishmael—for all of them the centuries in between had virtually been skipped! All modern history, of Europe, of America, didn't exist! What you read here in the tales of the patriarchs was so strong, so real, it was your family story, the story of your ur-antecedents, and here, still, was the old family quarrel. Could this even be the real source of the trouble today between the Arabs and the Jews? Instead of all those things said before the Royal Commission of Inquiry? It seemed impossible, and yet— If the Arabs to this day really did call themselves sons of Ishmael—the descendants of Abraham's dark servant girl from Egypt—didn't that maybe give them a kind of racial inferiority complex?

In the excitedness of this thinking, understanding together, before they knew it they were on the bed, and Dena couldn't help laughing. "I hope your landlady was listening at the door, so she could hear we were really studying the Bible!"

Another day—Mrs. Kelleher now didn't mind when she slipped into Mati's room to wait for him—Dena saw two letters on the bed. They had Palestine stamps, and a premonition came that they contained her future. One return address was Leah's, and the other was the Histadrut in Tel Aviv, she could make it out in Hebrew, and even the name written above, Dov Hos, the one Mati was always talking about, "If Dov wants me to, if Dov okays—"

What if because of this letter, Mati should have to go back now, would she go there with him?

What would it be like if Mati went out of her life? Could she stand it? Whither thou goest—but that, she now realized, was really a mother-in-law story, a young widow with her husband's family. But wasn't it also what everybody thought it meant, the role of woman, taken for granted, whither thou goest, you followed your husband's career, his plan of life. Even now she felt lost without him; sometimes even in the middle of the day when he wasn't here, she came to sit in his room to feel his nearness, feel engulfed in him.

Why was it she never really imagined herself to be someone on her own? Not the famous-actress dream, but really doing something, maybe being an art connoisseur? She believed in being a modern woman, of course, in freedom and equality, but for example, even when she used to go with Jack Sloan and used to imagine her future, it was as the wife of a distinguished attorney entertaining in a fashionable Lake Shore Drive apartment to which world-famous artists came when they visited Chicago for their Vernissage.

Well, the wife of the founder of the Palestine Air Lines, with an apartment on the Tel Aviv seashore, entertaining Jascha Heifetz and Marc Chagall when they visited the homeland!

And there was another thing about being a woman, even if you felt no drive of your own to "be somebody." It was also by whom she married that a girl could show her daring. All the girls would say, "Look at Dena! she passed up a wonderful chance for a match in one of the fanciest South Side families, to marry a student from Palestine and go and live there. Of course, he was from a heroic pioneer family and a brilliant boy—she recognized what was in him! Dena is really something!"

Seizing the letters, Mati let out a whoop. It was on! His airline! Dov said Mati had to go to England. The whole idea of the airline was complicated, Dov had written, there would be questions of franchise and permits for routes and incorporation and capitalization, all this would have to be worked out with the English, and the sooner Mati got started, the better. He could finish his studies over there and, meanwhile, get the idea planned out in detail and get it moving; Dov himself expected to be in London and would help.

And Leah's letter—Mati glowed; she had told Ben-Gurion all he was doing in Chicago, and B-G had said one day it would be the ones born in the land, chevreh like Mati, who would take over the leadership!

Mati was sitting with his arm around her, but all he was thinking of was his Yishuv and now going to England.

If she didn't go with him? Dena saw her Mati in some tiny bedroom like this, but in London. She wouldn't let herself see, but soon enough, some Andrea—

There, too, Mati said, he could give Hebrew lessons, to get

along. It was as though all over the world Jews were sitting waiting for young men from Palestine to arrive and give Hebrew lessons. Probably he'd find some Jewish Viscount so-and-so's daughter.

All at once, as though emerging from some trance, Mati looked
at her with his let's-get-to-work expression. "You could finish college there, buba."

Living in sin? Or was it again a crazy, maybe even bashful
backsided proposal? Would he ever do it properly?

A British university degree. Very classy. If they got married—
they'd really have to, because being that broad-minded would be
too much for her family. Besides, they were sure to insist on supporting her through college.

And also, with the wedding checks, she and Mati could start out
in a cute little London flat—

They even seemed relieved. Phil said if things really got going
with Mati's airline, he might have to stay on in London; a London
headquarters was not at all unlikely. Living in London—Sherrill
said she envied Dena already! But Dena's father puzzled, if she
married Mati, then would she lose her American citizenship?

For Sam's parents, and also for himself, to become an American
had been the highest thing in the world. It still was. When he was a
boy and his father used to talk over the kitchen table about getting his citizner papers, Sam had been terrified that his father
might not pass the examination. And when papa became a citizner
the flat was crowded with relatives, landsleit, there was a feast like
for a wedding. And now his own daughter, with the highest en-
dowment you could give a child, to be a born American—how
could she just let it go? What would she be? A British? Of course,
British was pretty fine, too, at least the same language—and war
allies. But if she went with Mati and lived in Palestine—even
though with the orange groves you could have a good life as in
Florida or California—what would she be then? Would she have
to give up her American passport?

Oddly, kid Victor, the future lawyer, had gone and looked it up.
"To begin with, Pop," he explained, "even after marriage Dena
can keep her American citizenship and passport if she wants—"

"Oh?"

Yes, a married woman could retain her separate nationality.

That was already better. But then grandchildren? Sam was a
little bashful to ask. Dena might feel embarrassed. But he got
Victor aside.

191

Victor gave his pop that glance of tolerance that from Victor's childhood had made Sam want to call him a snotnose. If she lived abroad, Victor explained, Dena could retain the choice of American citizenship for her children by registering them at birth at the American Consulate, and when they reached maturity, they could choose. Or maybe even have both.

Oho! Sam said. Some combination. To be both British and American! His snotnose would become an expert in international law, the highest type of attorney!

Well, if they should reside in Palestine, the British part was not exactly British, Victor said. They'd be Palestinians, like Mati, under the Mandate; Palestinians had British passports, but if the Mandate ended—and by the time Dena's kids grew up maybe it would—then the people there would have their own government.

Oh? That would be what?

Mati had been listening. "A Jewish medina!" he cried joyfully. A Hebrew nation! That was the whole idea. The Mandate would end when the Jewish National Home was complete and Palestine no longer needed British supervision.

At this moment Victor gave Mati an odd look as though to say he didn't want to interfere with anybody's pipe dreams.

Then it was all for real? Sam pondered. Those Jews over there really believed the thing would come to pass? A Jewish state with a Jewish passport? But despite a sudden inner glow, something also within him asked, how good would such a passport be in the outside world? An American passport, a British passport, anywhere in the world the whole power of the great nation was behind it. A Jewish passport? All alone by itself?

Sam didn't say any more, but the nag of doubt remained. Certain fears he had to sweep away. To fear was almost like treason for being a Jew. He had a kind of plan in mind and would not allow fear to damage his right to such a dream. In retirement, instead of Florida, with this marriage coming off, he and Bessie would be sitting in the Palestine sun under an orange tree with their grandchildren climbing all over them, sturdy brown kids in shorts and bare to the waist.

And if anything terrible happened, he himself, being always an American citizen, could bring the whole family safely back here.

In spite of Dena's plea that a big expensive wedding would be wasteful and that she and Mati could use the money better over there, despite even her hint to Sherrill that in these Depression days such ostentation would be in bad taste, she had to give in. An only daughter, how could she deprive her mother of the joy? And Phil said, considering the family's business position, far from being in bad taste, a substantial wedding would show that the Kossoff stores were doing okay. So the compromise was for a reception, not a full dinner, at the Shoreland.

On the Friday before, the entire family, including Phil and Sherrill but except Victor, went to services, and during "announcements" Rabbi Mike Kramer with a special beam all over his face said this was one that gave him the greatest pleasure, a union between the two great Jewish communities, in Eretz and in America! And moreover, the couple had first met right here in the temple! "Stand up! Stand up!" Mike kept insisting, and Dena and Mati had to stand up like actors taking a bow.

For the wedding, Mati even had to buy a tux since he understood how Dena would feel about a rented or borrowed one. Phil had him come downtown to get it at cost from a friend who ran a State Street men's shop. Phil even insisted it was an advance wedding gift, and the friend, who was taking part in the secret contributions for the airplane, whispered to Mati with a wink, "In this tux you can even fly!"

On his bed was another letter from Palestine.

"My Son in Chicago," Abba had written, "it rejoices me to learn that you are taking a bride." There followed the blessing for taking a bride, and then, "although these eyes may not behold her beauty." For his eyes were growing weak, Abba complained, adding, though, that he was not complaining since his eyes had beheld much in his days, much that was good, if also much that was evil. Of evil on this occasion he would not speak, his eyes had beheld the fruits of his labor and of his loins, but still, as it is said in the Wisdom of the Fathers, what is man? In his old age he was alone, his sons and daughters were gone from the house, even Schmulik was away to operate a big machine and earn money in the port of Haifa, he had quarreled with Nussya's brothers and rented out the fields to a newcomer named Feitelson, a ganef who was surely cheating them, and as for the High Holidays that were approaching, Abba recalled the good years with Feigel, the mother of them all, and the feasts she would prepare with the whole family assembled in the house for Rosh Hashanah, a pearl she had been, Mati should only find such a pearl in his own bride, whom Abba blessed. . . . He hoped at least his son and the bride would be married under a chupa! Until now, despite their godlessness, this had been the case with all of Mati's brothers and sisters, but in America, Abba had heard, and in those Reform temples of American Jewry, not even a chupa was used! Nevertheless, he repeated his blessings, might G-d grant that his dimming eyes would still behold the bride that his youngest son had chosen, who would be a light into those eyes, and might the pair be blessed with children and children's children. . . .

The girls from the temple players had thrown a shower for Dena, in Myra's apartment at the Del Prado, and even though the idea was conventional, Dena had to admit to Mati that she had had a lot of fun. He should only know what went on when girls were among themselves, the smutty jokes they could tell! Myra had told one, but Dena was saving it for their wedding night!

Myra had played her dirtiest records and got the girls stewed on tequila. Anita Holzman—the kewpie doll with false lashes who played Salomé—came all slinky like a Gloria Swanson and confessed to Dena that she herself had had a crush on Mati. "But, Deen, I'll say this for you, I never imagined you'd be so brave."

"Brave?"

"Well, you know, to marry him and go over there to live."

"Oh."

When they were all gone and Dena and Myra were checking over the haul, Myra came out with that wonderful "feelthy" story for Dena to save for her wedding night. It was about a Yiddishe mama and her daughter's *nuit des noces*.

It seemed that Pearl Katz and Gordon Moss (from Moskowitz) got married in a big wedding in the Katz family mansion on the North Shore in Winnetka, where Pearl's parents had moved from the West Side, and Gordon was a young accountant just starting out. All the relatives from as far as California were invited, and if they didn't come, they of course sent checks, and after the whole thing was over, the young couple went upstairs, as they were spending the first night in Pearl's room. The moment they closed the door Gordon whipped out his notebook, and Pearl took the guest list, and they began adding up the gifts. "My Uncle Morris?"

194

"Two hundred." Not bad. "Your Uncle Alexander?" . . . until they got to her mother's brother in the oil business, who had come all the way from Tulsa. Pearl, Myra related, couldn't find the check! "I myself saw your uncle give it to you just before he kissed you!" Gordon cried, and Pearl remembered that during the kiss she had folded the check and slipped it into her glove.

Where was the glove? They hunted. At last Pearl recalled pulling off the long white wedding gloves while still downstairs. She had put them on the piano. "So go down and get the check!"

Whereupon Pearl, already in her wedding nightgown, slipped out of the bedroom and ran down the stairway. There at the bottom of the stairs was her mother, waiting, listening anxiously. "Pearl! What are you doing here!"

"Oh," the bride explained, "I forgot my gloves."

At this, Myra cawed, Mama fixed her eyes on her Pearlie, smiling with prideful tenderness at her daughter's bridal-night innocence. "My baby! You don't need gloves for it! Nehm doss in dayn handt arayn!" Myra's Germano-Yiddish was excruciating. Just take it in your hand! Dena and Myra laughed till they cried.

And that was why Dena burst out laughing the minute she and Mati got into the bridal suite and she began pulling off her formal gloves. During the ceremony she had caught Myra's eye, the joke had come back to her, and she had barely swallowed the giggles in time not to choke on the sip of wine.

The wedding had gone off just perfectly. Even her brother Victor had behaved, consenting to hold up one pole of the chupa, while Phil held another; a third was held by a cousin of Mati's named Wally, who had driven all the way from New Jersey with Mati's aunt and uncle and another cousin who was a high school teacher and her husband just made a principal. They weren't bad at all, though Cousin Wally was a bit flashy; he had a Clark Gable mustache and tried to make business contacts. The fourth corner of the canopy was upheld by Professor Horace Rappaport, who kept repeating how he was claiming this return honor because Mati himself in Tel Aviv had been one of the four scouts selected to hold the chupa up at his own wedding! "May there be many more such exchanges between Tel Aviv and Chicago!"

Mati had never seen Dena so sparkling, her hair cut in a new way, pageboy they called it (she said it was done downtown at Marco's, where you had to make an appointment two weeks in advance, but when he asked how much, she stuck out her tongue). She wore a lacy cap of sparkles and a tiny half veil that didn't have to be lifted when Rabbi Mike handed her the wine cup.

At the reception there was honest-to-God French champagne, a gift from one of her daddy's old Halsted Street customers who had survived all the bootlegger gang wars. There was a three-dollar-a-head buffet for two hundred. Mati had wanted to invite his West Side group of Young Zionists who were training to go to Eretz but, finally, had cut it down to only two, the group leader, a really nice fellow named Dave Margolies, and his girl, Malka. Then they had dancing in the Mayflower Room with a five-piece band.

Mati said it was all conspicuous consumption, and in the Depression, too! He could have bought half the Haganah airplane with the money!

After the toasts and the speeches came the reading of congratulatory telegrams and cables from Mati's family in Palestine, even a cable that Horace Rappaport said was from London, from the World Zionist Federation, with one word—"L'chayim!"—and signed "Chaim." You couldn't tell if this was a fake or really from Chaim Weizmann, the World Zionist president! Everyone kept saying how wonderfully it was all going off! This seemed to Mati to be a trait of American Jews, to observe themselves in surprise when things were going fine, so that everyone remarked to everyone else, "Isn't this a beautiful affair!" And even the younger, real Americans added, "Mazel tov!"

Dena's papa tapped the glass and, with a touch of humor such as Dena rarely heard from her pop, announced he was already endowing the couple for their old age! He had here in his hand a deed to an orange-tree grove planted for them in the booming town of Sharon Shore in Palestine! The deed—for which Sam had secretly taken out a loan on his life insurance—looked something like a combination stock certificate and an old-fashioned scroll. Then Sam read a congratulatory cable from the founder and mayor of Sharon Shore, Nahum Artzi, of the old Tiberias hotel family, and Nahum's wife, Shulamith, a sister of the groom! "So you see it is all in the family!"

"Each man under his own vine—or oranges and grapefruit trees!" Sam Kossoff quoted, and the scroll was thrust into Mati's hand.

So now as Mati put aside the deed, and checks, and a hundred-dollar bill that his New Jersey uncle had slipped into his tuxedo pocket, Dena told him Myra's dirty story. "I swore I'd save it for us on our wedding night!" And after the punch line, as she drew off her long white gloves, they acted it out with hoots of delight.

Though they had for months now been such shamelessly wicked lovemakers, on this night after their joking Dena was startled to find the act becoming strangely different. It was as though this were the real first time. The other first time, she told herself, had been devirginization, but this was possession. That was the only word. Not simply joyous lovemaking, although that too was in it, but something now appeared in Mati, her just-become husband, that she had never anticipated: possession. As though on this night he were stamping himself into her, all through her. His. And then she got the same crazy thing, as though she would incorporate him into her body, the whole of him inside herself.

So this was what it was.

>>

THE
BRIDE

BOOK II

12

WHILE Dena started making a list of all the places the people on the ship had told her they must see in London, Mati started out for Great Russell Street. Within walking distance, the hotel clerk told him, giving directions minutely and adding it was such a nice day. The British at home were really the way people said.

Approaching the building, Mati experienced something other than the adventurous curiosity of that day he took the Chicago el to the university. Here he was not only entering on a new part of his life; here on Great Russell Street was the source and the center of the movement in which he had his being. Here in the Zionist headquarters, during the years of the World War, the little group around Chaim Weizmann had labored and urged and planned and sought influence and brought into being Great Britain's declaration supporting as a war aim a Jewish National Home in Palestine, once the land was freed from the Turks. The Balfour Declaration. And here right now the whole movement, the whole achievement, was again in question, was even threatened with extinction. And what could be his own place in this?

A collection of rambling corridors and dim stairways, small offices with the usual photographs of Herzl, Weizmann, Balfour, desks crowded in everywhere, and everyone with a tight air of keeping calm. Already in the corridor Mati ran into a schoolmate from Tel Aviv, Dani Hirsh, now connected with the Citrus Marketing Board, who was getting the latest from a thin-shouldered young English Jew called Reggie. The signs were bad, the second investigating committee had returned and was writing its report, the chief, Simpson, again declared that there wasn't room enough in Palestine to swing a cat, and the rumor was that he was giving in totally to the Arabs, recommending a virtual closing off of Jewish immigration and a ban on land sales. Moreover, in the Colonial Office the atmosphere was nasty. The best friends were proving the worst enemies, this Reggie said. There was a story going about the Colonial Secretary himself, Lord Passfield, or rather, about his wife; they were the former Sidney and Beatrice Webb, virtually the founders of British socialism, and now, well, the story was that the other day at tea, in the presence of all kinds of high muckamucks, where Chaim Weizmann had been trying to cultivate support, Lady Beatrice Webb had burst out, "Why do the Jews make such a fuss about a few people killed in Palestine! As many are killed every week in London traffic accidents, and nobody pays any attention!"

There was the situation for you. And it was Lord Passfield, always strongly influenced by his wife, who would be making the decision on Palestine.

And what was Mati doing here? He'd be studying, Mati said. "Aha," said Dani, as though obviously that meant something else, especially since Mati asked where was the office of Dov Hos. He'd heard that Mati had got married to an American heiress, Dani said, grinning and imparting big news from home: Mati's girlfriend Zippie, who had married into the rich Levinsons of Rehovot, had already increased the population of the Yishuv—twins! "No regrets!" Mati laughed. "Wait till you see Dena."

Dov the Smiler always made you feel that the sight of you gladdened his day; you were just the person he had been waiting for. Nor was it the pasted-on smile Mati had got used to in America. After all, Dov Hos was an old family friend, of Leah's generation. In the war, while serving as an officer in the Turkish army, Dov had smuggled out rifles in his paymaster's cart to Leah and her friend Rahel, for the settlement defense. He was the son of an early Shomer who used to ride the rounds with Menahem.

In London, as in Tel Aviv, Dov had a desk tucked away in the agriculture department; at once he told Mati he had great expectations for the air scheme, Rutenberg himself, the electrification pioneer, was in London and was interested. But first of all, Mati and his bride—a beauty, Dov had heard—must get settled,

and by sheer good chance Dov had just the place for them! One of
the boys who had been studying here was going home—one of the
Sturman family, Mati knew them? Of course, a Sturman had been
with Gidon at Hulda. This was a cousin. In any case, Mati could
take over the flat; it was quite a famous flat, Dov said with a
twinkle; it had been passed on for years, the same flat that Moshe
Shertok had occupied when he came to London, newly married, to
study, and Moshe and Zipporah had even had a roomer, David
HaCohen, now head of the Histadrut's building enterprise in
Haifa; it had been a never-ending joke, how with his long legs
David had fitted himself into the apartment's tiny alcove. Both
Moshe and David had studied at the London School of Economics
and, Dov supposed, Mati would be going there, too. As Mati
doubtless knew, the London School had been founded by Sidney
and Beatrice Webb—Lord and Lady Passfield of today—

Mati began to tell the nasty story about Lady Passfield, but Dov,
of course, had already heard it. From Chaim Weizmann himself.
Never before had he seen Chaim Weizmann in a rage. Livid.
Never mind! It wasn't the end! Decisions had not yet been made.
Balfour, Churchill—Chaim Weizmann was seeing everybody.

Yet Dov's smile was gone; for a moment he looked directly into
Mati's eyes, an older chaver accepting you and letting you see the
desperate reality.

☙ ☙ ☙

The flat was in a little street just behind the British Museum; it
had a cozy sitting room, plus the famous sleeping alcove, and a
closet-kitchen. The bath was directly across the hall, shared only
by one other resident on the floor, a typical half-bald English
eccentric who spent his life at the British Museum, so the bathroom, said the landlady, was almost private. With her prim but
knowing lips, she even reminded Dena a little of Mati's Mrs. Kelleher in Chicago, so Dena felt right at home.

In addition to the flat, Zev Sturman turned over to Mati several
well-paying pupils for private Hebrew lessons, including a
marchioness. "Don't worry, she's over fifty!" he said with a laugh
to Dena, who retorted, "That's the most dangerous! They'll pay
any price!"

The feeling of coziness and hominess enveloping them from the
start was so unexpected that Dena couldn't stop marveling. Not

only the famous courtesy of the British, saying, "Thank you," when they opened a door for you, but even people in the street noticing you were a stranger and offering directions before you asked them. And from the start she and Mati found themselves part of a warm little circle of their own age, a few from Palestine, a few "real English." Some were fellow students. But the quickest and closest friendship, which clicked from the first cup of tea, as Dena liked to say, was with another newly married couple, Reggie and Maureen Brody. Reggie was the one Mati had run into that first day in the corridor on Great Russell Street. They, too, planned to move to Palestine as soon as he could be transferred from his work here, and Dena felt this was the beginning of having real friends over there.

A born Londoner, with a trace of a Cockney accent, Reggie was in on everything. When he and Maureen came to the flat, Reggie and Mati would go sit in the alcove and lower their voices. The result would be that Mati would squeeze in a few hours the next day digging up statistics for Reggie to use, on land productivity; American statistics were better than British, Reggie insisted.

Maureen offered to steer Dena about the shops and to tell her who and what was "rilly" worthwhile in London. The two young wives even dutifully set aside an hour each afternoon to study Hebrew together. When anyone new from the Yishuv appeared in their circle, before he could ask, Maureen would declare herself a shikseh. She could hardly wait for the day when she would "go home" with her husband, though in fact, Reggie himself had not yet been to Palestine. He didn't even come from a British Zionist family, and Dena was rapidly picking up the names of some of the august British Zionist aristocracy, the Melchetts, Lord Reading, the Sachers, and there were the big money families, department store owners from Manchester, where Chaim Weizmann had come as a bright young chemist from Russia, to do research at the university in dyestuffs. Only now Dena was getting it straight. Already a leader of the activists in the Zionist movement, Weizmann had, on the death of Theodor Herzl, intuitively felt the new base should be in London, and there he had begun to meet persons of influence. Then, during the war, when the Germans had cut off the British supply of acetone, which was needed by the navy for explosives, Weizmann had found a new method to make it, and this had opened doors to the highest government circles. So, from Reggie's explanations Dena was beginning to understand how things worked.

Reggie himself was from a simple Jewish family that turned out to be pretty much like her own, only a generation from the old country; in fact, that was where their name came from, a town called Brody. In the big immigration wave headed for America, they had got no farther than England, where Reggie had been born. His father had done well in war uniforms; Reggie had gone through law school and quite by chance landed as a clerk in a firm whose leading member had had a good deal to do with the behind-the-scenes manipulations for Rutenberg's Palestine electric concession. Before he knew it, Reggie found himself drafting contracts on all sorts of Zionist projects. Lord Melchett had taken a shine to him, and even Chaim Weizmann himself had insisted that Reggie Brody be called in for the wording of the crucial reply to the first investigating commission's report after the 1929 "disorders." The bastards claimed the immigration in the mid-twenties had exceeded the country's economic absorptive capacity and brought on the Arab riots! The answer was in facts, facts, industrial projects like Rutenberg's electrification, like the Dead Sea potash works, statistics, and at last Mati felt that his studies were going to be of some use.

As for Maureen, she was of all things a tennis coach. Indeed, that was how she and Reggie had met—on the tennis courts where some friends had got them into doubles. Reggie proved to be a corker, Maureen said; he'd been a member of his college team. "Smashing serve, corkscrew Jewish style," she laughed. "I fell in love with it!" Next, she had discovered Reggie was keen on dancing, and great at the latest, the Lindy hop! Did Dena and Mati know any new turns? More seriously, both Reggie and Maureen were balletomanes. Dena, too? Smashing! The Diaghilev was just due, they'd all go!

Maureen was the daughter of an army career man, a real Colonel Blimp, she would declare, again with that clear-bell British ladylike laughter. The colonel was just retired to his cottage in Wales; oh, yes, he even spoke the Welsh language, so Maureen could well understand the Jews and their craze for Hebrew. And for her marriage, Maureen had actually gone and done a complete conversion—much to Reggie's disgust! She hadn't told Reggie but had found a rabbi for instructions and gone through the whole thing, except, of course, the cutting off of her hair, but here in England she related expertly, even quite Orthodox Jewish women didn't practice that anymore. But she had taken the ritual bath, the mikveh, on the afternoon of the wedding and had come to Reg with her hair all damp and ratty. "What have you done to your hair!" Reggie howled, and only then had Maureen confessed the Orthodox conversion. "He was hopping mad! He's an atheist!" But she had done it because of Reggie's parents, who were such sweet regular Jews, observant, and besides, Maureen's idea was if you do something, do it right. She rather enjoyed the Sabbath Eve—she said Erev Shabbas—with his family, and when she and Reggie finally would get to have their own home in Jerusalem, she intended to keep the custom of blessing the candles, gefulte fish, and all the rest. Just now they were still living in rather makeshift fashion in Reggie's old digs. Made her feel real wicked—like a sneaked-in mistress!

At this, Dena told Maureen the "take it in your hand" story, and they hooted and hugged each other in female bawdiness. As soon as she got home, Maureen swore, she'd tell it to Reggie, but first she'd put on her gloves!

As for Mati's airline scheme, Reggie's had some warnings about going to Rutenberg. He'd watched him gobble things up! The main idea was to keep this in the hands of the Histadrut, for the original purpose.

Dov was sure some kind of combination could be worked out. The Smiler was a master of the combinatzia, part visible, part invisible.

First, Mati could surely see that the British would never consent to hand over an airline charter to the Jewish labor federation. But right now the British themselves had a Labour government! Mati pointed out. Ah, but control of air routes was a major strategic matter. Besides, the Histadrut simply was not in a position to finance so big a venture as an airline. For example, could the Histadrut have obtained the electrification franchise? Or the rights for refining the enormous potash deposits of the Dead Sea? Who had got those franchises? Capitalists. Yes, one day if there were a Jewish nation in Eretz, it might be a real socialist nation, with all the natural resources exploited by the government of workers and peasants, Dov said with a twinkle, but meanwhile, the British Empire was still run on capitalist lines, even when there was a Labour government.

"All power to the socialist lordships!" mocked Reggie. So here they were all three of them radicals, and they had best go see Pinhas Rutenberg.

But Rutenberg himself was a revolutionist! An engineering student, he had been a leader in the great 1905 upheaval in St. Petersburg, marching along with Father Gapon at the head of the demonstration, when the petitioners were cut down by a volley of fire at the gates of the Winter Palace. Legend had it that later when Father Gapon had turned out to be an agent provocateur, it was Pinhas Rutenberg with his own two hands who had carried out the verdict of the revolutionary tribunal and strangled the czarist stool pigeon.

There he sat, rocklike, a large head on a broad body, with the famous powerful hands on his desk. The socialist-capitalist received them with a warm brotherly smile, and even repeated the name Chaimovitch with a special smile. Wasn't it a Chaimovitch in the Jordan Valley who had raised such a row because in cutting the spillway for his power dam, a little island had been swept under?

"That was my brother Schmulik!" Mati joined the laugh, while thinking there were better reasons for knowing the Chaimovitch name.

"Well, a real temper! He came to shout at me personally! But what could I do, change the course of the spillway?" The big man even remembered that he had employed Schmulik to run a steam shovel—a natural mechanic!

Yet, with smiles all around, Mati felt uneasy. There lay his prospectus, under Rutenberg's fist. Beaming, the revolutionist industrialist went on talking about Mati's family, now at least showing he knew about Yaffaleh's death with Trumpeldor, and about Gidon's heroic stand at Hulda, and even about Gidon's part in the Jewish Legion. Was Mati aware that Rutenberg himself, early in the Great War, had been the originator of the idea of the Jewish Army? He had met with Jabotinsky in Italy and set up the whole plan!

At last the big man held up Mati's prospectus. No need to dwell on the importance of the subject. He himself had long been interested in aviation; in planning the big dam, he had procured aerial photographs of the whole length of the Jordan Valley, with the aid of the Royal Air Force. He understood Mati had already learned to fly? Wonderful! The first pilot of Eretz Yisroel! Ah, if that were but all one needed to establish an airline. To begin with—Mati's basic concept here was certainly full of youthful enthusiasm, and in the right direction as far as it went, but it didn't go far enough. Instead of capitalization at five thousand pounds—

"Only as a beginning. To acquire the first planes right away. You notice I provide—"

Vision was needed! Fifty, a hundred thousand minimum! The age of aviation was in its infancy. . . . And Mati had to sit and listen to all his own ideas being expounded to him, sometimes in phrases right out of his own prospectus.

Now, turning to Reggie, the big man swept into the area of corporate structure, franchises, investments, preliminary surveys. Lord this and Viscount that, the chairman of Rolls, a good friend, and doubtless, if routes over the whole of the Levant were contemplated, as they should be, then this must be an international consortium, the French should be brought in or else they would start a competing line, certainly the Rothschilds, both here and in Paris, should be interested— And then, had Mati taken into account, in any civilian franchise there would have to be certain understandings, particularly in areas of unrest—

But exactly! Mati cried. That was why, at least for the time being, he had envisioned something on a smaller scale, a nucleus, perhaps only tourist flights within the land, even run by the Histadrut itself, so there would be more freedom of action, without getting entangled with too many outside controls.

Rutenberg studied him. Did the chaver imagine perchance that the British wouldn't at once see through the whole scheme? And also the Arabs?

"What of it?" Mati said. "We'd be there." From long ago, from childhood, he had even heard the slogan among the leaders of the Shomer. "Do it. Create the fact. Then it exists." "*Fait accompli*, as we British say," said Reggie.

Dov intervened to help out. "Tourist flights would be natural and legitimate."

Rutenberg pondered. He saw the project in a much bigger way. A small venture would soon be swamped. Still, he would think about the plan.

Mati and Reggie repaired to a Lyons for tea. Reggie thought it had gone off well; something would come of it.

"In five years!" Mati said. What was needed was one airplane right off, just in case trouble broke out again.

"About certain points he was right, old sport," Reggie began, and halted with the word on his tongue. He snapped his fingers. Sports! A sports plane!

That was it! Sports the British would understand! So why not separate the two goals? Keep with Rutenberg for the airline project and, meanwhile, acquire a little sports plane! You didn't even have to pose as a rich amateur. Many of the flying bugs were mechanics, war vets, even clerks who were just cuckoo on air sports. Hadn't Mati mentioned that his brother-in-law in Chicago had promised money for the first plane from some good Jewish businessmen?

Through tennis club friends of Maureen's, Mati was soon out visiting a flying club, soon explaining to Dena the comparative merits in speed, climb, and carrying capacity of a British Moth, an American Curtiss, soon being invited to "take her up for a spin, mate," by British equivalents of the fellows out at Chicago's Midway Field.

Dena, Maureen, and Reggie would stand shading their eyes, watching him sideslip, spin, and show off his whole repertoire of Chicago tricks. Getting more and more chummy with the mechanics and hobby fliers, Mati soon was taking up slightly used and rebuilt jobs to try out. He wanted something really solid, he passed the word, and with a good bit of room behind. One fellow had a trainer from a batch sold off by the RAF; it even still carried a machine-gun mount. No matter, Mati said straight-faced. Dragging Dov out for a look, he took him up for a test, diving so low as to catch a good scolding from the controller when he landed.

But with the gun mount Dena got scared. It was for real.

And Dov was becoming a superenthusiast. Mati must teach him to fly as soon as the political crisis was over!

"If you wait for that, you'll be overage," Reggie promised.

Indeed, things were black. With the Inquiry Commission report came a White Paper issued by Lord Passfield that would put a virtual end to the Zionist effort. The Balfour Declaration and the Mandatory obligation to help establish a Jewish homeland had been fulfilled, the Colonial Office declared. And there came the usual litany: the Hebrew language restored, the schools, the press, the Jewish population's elected assembly to deal with their own affairs, all amounting to the envisaged "national home."

To which the doors were about to be closed.

"My God!" Even Dena was outraged. "There are more Jews in Chicago than in all Palestine! Some national home!"

Mati was in the depths. Even when she tried to lift his spirits with lovemaking, he seemed almost ashamed to let go of his gloom for a while.

But then somehow the pendulum began to swing back. Parliament was in an uproar; the White Paper was being torn to pieces. Britain had accepted a great trust from the nations of the world! And besides, what of the Mediterranean, with Mussolini rapidly extending his naval power? If England backed down every time a few scheming Arabs started a terrorist riot, it would end by losing control of the whole Empire!

In protest the heads of the Jewish Agency were resigning, Chaim Weizmann for once declaring noncooperation with the British. Even indignation. Jabotinsky and his dissidents were screaming that this was what Weizmann's conciliatory policy had come to! Let them take over, and things would change! Bitter jokes were spreading. Dov repeated a suggestion going the rounds: As the Inquiry Commission claimed there was no room in Palestine to swing a cat, His Majesty's Loyal Opposition was requesting that a new commission be sent out, carrying with it a cat. If a place could be found to swing it, the area thus encompassed should be designated for Jewish immigration. But the Mufti raised objections about the length of a cat's tail, so Lord Passfield had decided that a bob-tailed Manx cat should be used.

Leaders arrived from the Yishuv, to fight back. Ben-Gurion himself would tackle the chiefs of the British Labour Party, fellow members of the Socialist International. Every day Reggie had stories. Prime Minister Ramsay MacDonald, himself a labor leader risen from the ranks, was said to be furious with Lord Passfield. True, the Balfour Declaration was two-sided, even-handed; it had promised a Jewish National Home but also protection of the rights of the Arabs in Palestine. But it had not been designed to foster an Arab National Home! And even on that score, Winston Churchill had settled any doubts after the May Day troubles in 1921, by slicing off Trans-Jordan and making it an Arab kingdom.

No, the situation was far from lost. It seemed the worldwide protests were having an effect. And there was a way out. The White Paper could be "interpreted" with a superseding document, a letter from the Prime Minister. Already Weizmann had Reggie and other experts at Great Russell Street working on formulations. "Economic absorptive capacity" could be insisted on, in the broadest sense, thus alleviating the restrictions of the Passfield White Paper. And in talks with Chaim Weizmann, the Prime Minister had suggested that a new High Commissioner would be appointed who understood the spirit of the Mandate. Quite simply, the White Paper could in effect be reversed. Weizmann still had his magic; perhaps it was not yet time to stop cooperating with the British. What other course was there?

And within all this turmoil Mati was, after all, still a student; he sat up nights knuckling his head over the new Keynesian theories, and then he would try to formulate for Reggie how these could be applied to expand the possibilities in Palestine's economic absorptive capacity—that would go down well, Reggie thought, with the British liberals.

And as things let up a bit, one Sunday in the greatest excitement Mati told Dena they were driving out to the club and taking Ben-Gurion aloft!

This was the man, she already knew, to whom Mati looked, more than to anyone else, to guide his life. Dena had not expected him to be so small—he was even smaller sitting in a car than walking, because when he was walking, you felt his dynamism. And he seemed to her a strange man; she didn't feel natural with him. All the way to the airfield he would suddenly in the midst of other things pop out with family questions to Mati—and how was it with Gidon's widow? Then he would turn to Dov Hos, on his other side, and rattle off a dozen political points to be remembered in the next session on Great Russell Street. For aside from the whole struggle with the British, an inner struggle was taking place for control of the movement, this was the time for labor at last to push aside the "gentlemen," the compromisers. Otherwise, Jabotinsky and his wild activists would gain in power.

Another thing Dena noticed—not that she demanded attention of men, but ordinarily men at least recognized the existence of a pretty woman when sitting next to her. This was no ordinary man. There were all those tales about his Paula, a real character. Anyway, everyone was talking Hebrew so fast she could barely keep up with the drift.

They jumped onto the field; Mati ran into the club to get a helmet for Ben-Gurion; there was a good deal of kidding as his shock of hair was squashed down and his face disappeared behind

211

the goggles. Then he marched around the plane with Dov and Mati, like an air marshal inspecting his armada. His legs were too short to climb in so that Dov had to give him a boost.

No tricks! everyone had warned Mati. It was Ben-Gurion's first time in the air! So the most Mati did was to buzz the clubhouse, swooping fairly low; to those in the know it was a demonstration for his passenger of someday maybe having to toss down a hand grenade.

The leader hopped out, tugging at his chin strap so he could start talking. Dena undid it for him, and suddenly he gave her a real personal smile. Congratulations! You have the First Flier of the Yishuv for a husband! And so she was the American girl that Mati was bringing to Eretz! He himself had brought an American wife to Eretz, did she know? Paula was from New York; they had met on Second Avenue. To all the boys he cried enthusiasms in Hebrew. To Mati, an all-praise "Kol ha Kavod!" And again to Dena: "I know him from a baby!"

Then just as abruptly his personal side seemed closed off again. Back in the car, he put his head together with Dov and Mati, while Reggie, driving, kept twisting around to take part, until Dena was sure the car would get into a crash. This was going to be a big thing, a big future. The Histadrut must have an important share. From now on he was flying in the air whenever possible; he would take the British plane to Paris; no one needed to convince him anymore! But—Mati reminded him—for the original purpose? Even in the car the voices were lowered. As a sporting plane? Ben-Gurion chuckled. Good, good, the best joke on the sporting British! But all must be done carefully. Mati was sure he could raise the money?

Right now, Phil wrote, some of the boys were in a tight spot, the Depression was worse than ever, but give him time. And he enclosed a bank order for five hundred dollars of his own in case they needed to put down a deposit.

The Depression was worldwide, and for the first time Dena was carefully adding up how much things cost, even cakes for friends in the evening. With his lesson giving and with little gift checks that her mother sent and that she didn't mention to Mati but used for theater and ballet and symphony tickets, it was getting to be a really agreeable life in London; their cozy little flat was becoming the gathering place for a warm, lively circle, new arrivals from

Palestine would sometimes sleep in the famous alcove and even on the floor for a few nights, and Dena never seemed to have enough raisins and almonds in the little dishes for them to gobble while they discussed What Constitutes the Just Society? After the questions of where to buy things cheapest to take back home, they would ponder, how best to build the Just Society in the Yishuv?

There even came an Arab into their circle, and it was Myra who brought him.

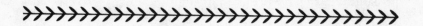

13

ONE DAY from a bus stop Dena saw a news boarding, THRILL KILLER KILLED! CHICAGO THRILL KILLER MURDERED IN PRISON. Excited, she got off and bought a paper. It was Artie Straus. Poor Myra! In the prison shower a fellow inmate had cut Artie to pieces with a razor blade. Homosexual rivalry, it was said. And the whole horrible story again, Artie Straus and Judd Steiner, the brilliant Chicago thrill killers, "supermen," Oscar Wilde, Nietzsche. . . .

In her letter to Myra, Dena kept from saying maybe he was better off dead, maybe Myra would now be freed of that whole thing. Why didn't Myra come abroad, she said, to get away from all this new horror?

And all at once Myra was there. When Dena came from her classes, she hardly had put in her key when the door was pulled open from inside, and there stood Myra with a quirk of a surprise smile. "The landlady let me in," she said, those chocolate eyes of hers gleaming, her face the latest pancake white makeup, and wearing a slinky Paris number that as usual hung awry.

Left Chicago on the spur of the moment without even calling her analyst, the whole thing all over again was too much, every day new filth, that foul little Judd Steiner had offered his blood, Artie just bled, bled, and the transfusions didn't help. She clutched Dena. Judd Steiner had babbled to all the reporters about Artie, his Dorian. "You know, Oscar Wilde's Dorian Gray," he would always love his Dorian. "Dena, it was to puke." Yes, they had called her, all those newspaper vultures, was she still in love with Artie? And letters—"You don't know what crawls on this earth, just because I tried to say a few decent words about Artie, all slashed up, the blood running out. . . . 'So you still love him, that cocksucker,' that's what they wrote. Anonymous." Myra halted. "How's marriage? How's London?" And before Dena could say "wonderful," Myra was ranting on; it wasn't even true of Artie, it was that little worm Judd Steiner who was the fairy, not that it mattered, not that anything mattered, she had simply had a childhood crush, and now she really intended to get over it.

Her eyes caught Dena's in such despair, such loneliness. Oddly, it came to Dena that their relationship had turned around; she had been the one who followed, tagging onto Myra for sophistication and knowing everybody, but here was Myra coming to her. Or no, her letter had just touched off a need; Myra had needed to escape.

By the time Mati got home Myra was under control and wanting to rush around and see all the latest exhibits; they'd go tomorrow to the big Italian futurist show, Martinetti, she had already looked up what was on, Dada was finished, old hat, the new wave was Futurism from Italy, didn't Dena know his work?

At the gallery there was this beautiful man. What Dena saw first was his mouth, and Myra too had got the vision, there came her quick arm clutch. His mouth was full-formed and as though outlined in a Persian miniature. The skin was golden; he could indeed have been Persian, or Hawaiian, or anything exotic—Dena didn't at first think of an Arab; he wasn't as dark even as Mati.

He was lean, not particularly in the face, but in his bearing, and he was dressed the way she could never get Mati to dress, with careless elegance, uncreased gray flannels, a cashmere pullover, an Oxford Street sports jacket of just the right degree of sloppiness.

"Give me five minutes," Myra cawed under her breath, and Dena went to the ladies'.

It was sometimes a game with Myra. Of course, it was no trick for a girl to get herself picked up, the trick was more often to get rid of the man, but the game was to make your own selection. Obviously an art gallery was prime; you had only to move on ahead, stand in front of a work, wait for him to come alongside, and let him drop a remark. First, to know if he'd be a bore.

When Dena returned, she was introduced, Khalid Nashashibi, from Haifa, and himself a painter.

So Myra was sunk again. Just give her an artist.

Khalid's English was beautiful, each word emerging meticulously formed by those delineated lips and with a slightly different throatiness from Mati's. When Dena mentioned that she was married to a Palestinian from an old settler family, he said that in his own family there was no animosity to the Jews. Khalid had been abroad several years, first at Oxford and now a year at the Royal Academy, and before they got to his studio, they already knew that he considered himself a Marxist, though with him art came before politics. Naturally Myra agreed.

The studio was in a mews, and by then Dena had recalled the Arab family name, Nashashibi, it came up in Mati's discussions, one of the important effendi families, and indeed, Khalid had already offhandedly remarked on his father's being a bloody feudal exploiter who owned miles of olive groves. With that amused smile, the exact way an English radical declares that the family fortune started with the slave trade.

The moment they entered the studio—a proper one with a skylight—Myra let out an excited cry: Calligraphy!

The compositions were in radiant enamel colors, with flowing lines and scattered dots as in Arabic writing, intertwined with arabesques. Enormously pleased with Myra's excitement, Khalid explained that though, of course, he was not religious, the calligraphic tradition in Koranic inscriptions fitted in perfectly with modern art, hence he was experimenting in this area.

Khalid's lips as he completed his statement closed into so perfect an oval that a girl must surely wonder how they would feel printed against her own, and Dena saw that poor Myra was already on the rack.

At least the Nashashibis were on the whole the more reasonable ones, Mati said, nothing like the Mufti and his murderous Husseinis. The evening passed off perfectly, with genuine decency and warmth engulfing all, and even a heady sense of their generation soon solving the problems not only of Jews and Arabs, but of the entire world! Though if you thought about it afterward, you wondered how.

While at the bottom among the younger crowd from the Yishuv everyone understood that Mati by upbringing was a devoted laborite, in the gatherings in the flat Dena tried to create an atmosphere—and she saw that Mati liked it—of open, explorative discussions conducted with civilized British calm instead of wild Jewish fervor. Even older people would turn up; once even Moshe Shertok dropped in, joking about visiting his old digs. Everyone had a favorite idea, binationalism, cantonization, federation with the Emir Abdullah, a communal state— If the communists were on principle opposed to Jewish nationalism as in Palestine, why were they setting up a Jewish autonomous region in Birobidjan? Way off on the Chinese border! But communist internationalism was in itself not contradictory to peaceful nationalist expression; after all, the Soviet Union was a compound of various national republics! Ah, but nationalism also gave rise to fascism, xenophobia, wars. . . . Not nationalism, but religion had been the greatest cause of wars! Religion was not only the opiate of the people but their TNT! Was the pan-Islamic movement part of Pan-Arabism or vice versa?

And now it was all familiar, back and forth, feudalism, syndicalism, colonialism. What about the Egyptians; they didn't even consider themselves Arabs, but descendants of the Pharaonic people; an Egyptian felt insulted if you called him an Arab! Khalid quoted a great Arabic Islamic poet, Ibn al-Farid, and Mati completed the quotation. Ah, sheer music, untranslatable! Many Arabs understood the Jewish need, Khalid said, and did they know that a Nashashibi, an uncle of his, had been among the twenty-two Arab leaders belonging to a secret patriotic society, hanged in public in Damascus by the despotic Turks during the World War. So the Zionist movement was not the only one—

And all with a kind of rising mutual tolerance, an overall idealism, of yes, someday, a great federation perhaps through the working people, better understanding of common needs in the entire area—

In the warm but cautious, wonderful feeling of reason-can-find-a-way, Dena served real American hot dogs, and the talk spattered in various directions. Maureen was talking tennis; a Britisher remarked to Mati, "I understand you're quite a bug on flying," Dena began to describe his gifts as a pilot, and Mati had to get her aside and caution her, not a word about the plane, he trusted Khalid all right, maybe even more than this English fellow, but a word carelessly dropped might carelessly be passed on.

Khalid was trying to explain to the Englishman how his own family clan, ah, yes, it was all still rather feudal, separated itself from the Husseini clan's intransigence, and the Englishman seemed mixed up between the Mufti's Husseinis and the Emir Abdullah, who was a Hussein; ah, but Dena had at last got them straight, they were not of the same family, Abdullah belonged to the Lawrence-of-Arabia ones headed by the Sherif of Mecca, but a sherif was not a sheriff, he was kind of the head of the Moslem shrines. Exactly, Khalid beamed at her, and he resumed. "Now the Arab position—" and at this phrase Myra broke out into a hoot! She pulled Dena into the tiny kitchen. "The Arab position"—and she told Dena in her ear just what it was.

It was a kind of nice session, Mati said. At least you learned something about the other fellow's position.

And this set Dena off into her wild giggle. Yes! She had learned the Arab position, as Khalid had revealed it to Myra! And since at times Mati was not too quick on the uptake, she had to show it to him. Oh, they were crazier than ever for each other! Imagine, a married couple! Tonight had really been nice.

❊ ❊ ❊

It was a slow year, with Mati getting impatient about his airline. Endless planning; he even thought maybe Dov and Rutenberg were carrying on meetings without him. And suddenly there was news of an Egyptian line being organized! Well, of course, the British would control it, but the Misr line was planning operations to Palestine and all along the Levant. With British crews, of course. So now a franchise might be even more difficult, but a beginning was even more imperative. The rebuilt war plane with the machine-gun emplacement, Dov decided, would be too much of a giveaway. But a little De Havilland turned up, a beauty.

There were some machines, when you flew them, you felt the mechanism of the craft, of each wire as it pulled each flap, the machine obeyed you nicely and that was good enough. But there were other craft that gave you a different feeling; such a machine became one with you. You never thought of the mechanism; the whole machine was an extension of yourself. This little De Havilland had such an effect on Mati. He never thought: it climbs, it banks, it accelerates, but thought: I climb, I wing over, I dive. And there was the latest in radio equipment; the owner was a flight bug who had borrowed on his salary and now had lost his job. As

Phil would say, this was a repossess. Mati had the aircraft tested by half the mechanics at the field; everyone said it was a steal.

Phil sent the rest of the money.

What would they name her? You'd think this was your firstborn, Maureen twitted, as they wrote down and crossed out lists of names. Something with a bird? An eagle, Nesher? Or a dove, Yona? Or Aliyah, which meant going up, as well as immigration.

Sunday was their wedding anniversary, and Reggie drove them out to the club in his Morris. Maureen brought a bottle of champagne; Mati carried a small can of blue paint and a brush.

Dena did the painting. A Star of David. And in the center, in Hebrew and in English: GIDON.

After Maureen did the christening—by a proper Jewess! Reggie jested—Mati took Dena aloft. At least, kissing in the air was not as dangerous as in a car where you might crash into somebody! And someday, though it might take a bit of acrobatics, Mati suggested in high spirits, they might even—"Mati, you sex fiend!"

Only, he still had his thesis to do, on the comparative economic systems of a kibbutz, a moshav, and an Arab village; the great Harold Laski himself, at the London School, was keenly interested. But then even once Mati got his master's, what was he going to do? In some months, in half a year, the big test would come. Oh, they'd find a place for him. After Chaim Weizmann's defeat at the last Zionist Congress, the labor crowd had finally captured control; even political work was being shifted to be based in the Yishuv rather than in London. The new High Commissioner, Sir Arthur Wauchope, was proving to be really interested in carrying out the Mandate, the immigration quota kept going up, and—a military man—he took no nonsense from the Arabs.

Reggie was among those being moved. Because of his intimate knowledge of British maneuverings, Ben-Gurion believed he was needed as adviser in Jerusalem. Maureen was excitedly worried— would the Jews really accept her? She fretted, making Mati laugh. "It's they who'll be afraid you won't accept them!"

But here their circle was shrinking. Myra had gone off with Khalid to Germany—he must study with Paul Klee! Dov Hos had again returned to Tel Aviv. Mati was getting to be a chain-smoker.

Once more Ben-Gurion had come to London, and suddenly Mati was summoned.

It was to the already-famous hotel room. "Have you been to three twenty-three?" had become a catchword among the lads from Palestine.

There was a tiny antechamber with one chair; an elderly Englishman, derby, furled umbrella, and all, sat there, but just as Mati arrived, the inner door opened, a Jew with payess backed out while uttering a farewell blessing in Yiddish, the Englishman went in, and Mati took the chair.

Something within him told him a life decision was coming. It would be some task first of all good for the movement, and that was as it should be. But also it would not be wrong for himself; with Ben-Gurion you knew you would be properly utilized. And wasn't this a man's main desire, the main gratification in his life? In this little interval of waiting, Mati saw clearly, not even a man's marriage, no, it was not gratification of love that truly eased you, but the feeling that you were being utilized for the best that was in you. An artist, a scientist—they could do it by themselves. But what was he? Simply one of the people, that was it, and through the people he had to be used.

His turn came.

"Nu, Mati? You bought the airplane? A present from your wife's rich brother?" Ben-Gurion had a line on everything.

"He's not so rich, but he got some more good Jews in Chicago to help with the money. I bought it in my name, but it belongs to the Organization. I named it the *Gidon*."

Ben-Gurion nodded. For an instant the memory of Gidon sat with them. Then the chief made a quick-handed movement: to work. Mati was finished with his studies?

Well, he still had his thesis to write, but—

In economics? Ben-Gurion verified. Good. That was why he had called Mati in. Now to work. What was needed—the new High Commissioner was open to more Jews in the administration. Well, Mati didn't have to be told, Arabs there had been aplenty, even if they still used an abacus. But now a few posts, not maybe on the high level but posts of significance would be available for Jews. Particularly what was needed was someone with training in economics—

Already an upwelling of discomfort, even dismay, had begun. To be working for the British— No, of course, it would also be for the Yishuv, but still—

Now, as Mati knew, the question of economic absorptive capacity was of the greatest importance. The whole matter was one of interpretation. The very life of the Yishuv. And an economic adviser, even on a lower level—

But he had somehow seen himself working perhaps under the eye of Moshe Shertok or in the Histadrut. And with the British, how much influence could a Jew hope to have?

With the British was where he would be most useful, Ben-Gurion assured him. Even with complete loyalty to the Mandate administration, as Mati could see, there would be a thousand ways in which a man could be of important use.

Economic absorptive capacity—but he'd find himself overruled on every suggestion.

Still, as a job this could be counted a good opportunity. It would pay better than anything he might expect in the Histadrut, the Keren Kayemeth, or any of the other organizations. He and Dena could set up house properly in Jerusalem. It might even be easier for her to adjust. And if this was what was really wanted of him, why not? Really, why not?

Besides, a private sports plane would fit! A British administrator, a sports flier. Only, suppose trouble started, and the plane had to be used? First thing, he'd have to train a few lads.

In Ben-Gurion's mind, Mati could feel there was not even a question about the proposal. He was being called on to accept a basic decision about his own life from—well, in a way from the Yishuv itself. A term came to Mati's mind that Dena had brought home from some kind of anthropology course: *rite de passage*. That was what they called it when you went through a turning point, like initiation into manhood. Maybe this was such a time for him.

He would hear from the Agency office, Ben-Gurion said; probably Moshe would want him to meet a Britisher named Welby, who had just been appointed to the economic section of the Palestine secretariat.

It was Dena with her Chicago gangster tales who so charmed the Welbys that there could be no question but that Mati and his delightful young American wife had passed the test; the appointment was a sure thing, and also they had made a start to "getting on" over there. At tea in their Kensington house the British couple seemed more interested in Dena's upbringing in Chicago than in Mati's childhood in Palestine. Had Dena indeed seen Mr. Al

221

Capone in person when he came to buy diamond rings in her father's shop? Wasn't she a bit frightened? Did he come alone or surrounded by his bodyguards? What was that word for them? Like—hats? "Hoods," Dena supplied. And when she assured them that it was nevertheless quite safe for an ordinary citizen to walk in the streets of Chicago, as safe as in London, they pretended amused disbelief. But wasn't it true that these . . . hoods—they weren't hooded, were they? Oh, no, it meant hoodlums. Well, didn't they drive about in open motorcars with machine guns going brr-r-rp and knocking off people—was that the phrase?— knocking off people right on a downtown sidewalk? Did that mean knocking them into the gutter? Why, no, it meant killing them, but, she assured them, the gangsters only shot at each other, even if the shooting was on a downtown street. They would have a finger man—that is, someone who put the enemy on the spot; well, that meant this finger man was perhaps acquainted with the victim and pointed his finger at him, or lured him to the place, or knew of his habit of walking daily at a certain place at a certain hour. Then the finger man would step back while the gangster car sped by with the sawed-off machine gun doing its work. Well, she couldn't explain precisely why the machine-gun barrel was sawed off, maybe because it was lighter and easier to hide. But these gunners were quite accurate, and the public was never hit. Oh, perhaps once or twice by accident, but that didn't really make you afraid to go shopping downtown; after all, a person could be hit in an ordinary automobile accident. And most often, really, the shootings were not on downtown streets but inside the gang's own territory. Territory? Then she had to explain that a territory was the part of the city that a certain gang controlled for its bootlegging; the gangs had the city sort of divided up.

Oh, a business compact. Zones of influence.

Like the wartime Sykes-Picot Agreement dividing up the Middle East, Mati ventured, between France and England. Welby guffawed. Very good! Very good!

Yes, Dena said, and then if one side tried to sell alky—alcohol— in the territory of the other side—

Muscling in, that was called, Mati explained.

—that was when the shooting started!

It was indeed quite fascinating, said the Welbys; they had been stationed in Rhodesia, where occasionally there were outbursts of violence in feuds among the native tribes, and there, too, the tribes harmed only each other while outsiders were left quite safe.

And in Palestine, also, Mati explained, when he was a child, much of the violence in the nearby Arab villages had been of this kind, local feuds between various clans, but in recent years unfortunately the Mufti had tried to organize violence on a country-wide scale.

Yes, of course, Welby said; still, he supposed it was at least as safe for an ordinary person to walk in the streets of Jerusalem as in the streets of Chicago!

"Especially if he's English!" Mati said.

"In any case," Mrs. Welby smiled at Dena—"if shooting does break out, you'll feel quite at home!"

His future chief had heard that Mati made a hobby of flying, whereupon Mati in his enthusiasm started describing the De Havilland.

He had his own airplane then?

Oh, it was only a little sports plane, Mati said. Actually it had been a wedding gift from his wife's family.

Their glance at Dena carried a new evaluation. Though she wore only Mati's heirloom diamond ring, Dena recognized from the look in Mrs. Welby's eyes that she was now the daughter of a rich Chicago jeweler, a girl who might have covered herself with diamonds but was actually discreet! And oddly, the look was like the way some men's eyes seem to pierce right through your clothes to see you naked.

Was Mati perhaps intending to fly his airplane to Palestine then? asked the host.

Why, Mati said, as the whole plan burst on him, yes, in small hops, that was what he had been thinking.

"And you'll fly with him? Just like the Lindberghs!" cried Mrs. Welby to Dena. "My dear! What an adventure!"

Though it was really a very light plane, Mati said, giving Dena a quick don't-show-anything glance, he was sure they could do it. A perfect idea, he was congratulating himself, and he had been breaking his head how to take it apart and ship it! They'd even save money! And he'd arrive, right in the open, a British official, legitimate as could be! But then afterward? The hell with them, he'd figure something out.

He had been using a good deal of his home leave to read up on Palestine, said Welby, and though it had its problems, he really looked forward to going out to the Holy Land, a most fascinating country.

She, too, had been reading up, his wife said, and would they believe it, she was quite sure that one of her ancestors had been a Crusader with Richard the Lion-Hearted.

A bit dubious, Dov, once again back in his cubbyhole on Great Russell Street, allowed himself to be won over by the boldness of the idea. A government official's hobby plane! It reminded him of his days in the Turkish army, smuggling out rifles, right in his army wagon. Ah, he envied them, hopping all over Europe and the Greek isles! What a trip!

Already Mati and Dena were poring over maps. Air maps were so different from ordinary maps it took her awhile to catch on; she would have to be able to pinch-hit as navigator. After all, Dena wrote Myra, if Anne Lindbergh could do it, she could do it! First stop, meet us in Paris! Watch out, the Jewish Lindys will be dropping in on you from the sky!

Wireless, too, she had to learn, and every night for practice she and Mati tapped messages to each other; Dena even invented a private sex code. Though she was kind of scared of the part where they would have to fly over water—the Lindys, after all, had it safer in a seaplane—Dena wouldn't let this cramp her style. She and Mati were the talk of Great Russell Street! And from Chicago, Sherrill wrote her, "Why doesn't my stick-in-the-mud husband think up such ideas!" And slipped in was a check, from Sherrill's house money, for Dena's flying outfit, plus a newspaper photo of Anne Lindbergh in tailored jodhpurs with a matching jacket with all kinds of cutely placed pockets. This almost brought on a spat. Mati had enough of being a poor relation from Palestine with his wife always getting handouts from her family to buy clothes. After all, he would soon enough be a British official—"Bourgeois!" she demolished him. And she disappeared into the alcove, emerging waddling à la Charlie Chaplin, wearing his enormous flying breeches. . . . So when her hand-tailored outfit was ready, Mati had to admit it was a knockout. They sent back a snapshot of the two of them in their flying togs, standing alongside the *Gidon*.

At the Aero Club Mati ran into a couple of chaps who had hop-stopped all across Europe and around the Mediterranean. Don was an ex-barnstormer; he'd been part of an air circus but after a nasty crash was confined to taking gawkers aloft on Sundays. Last summer, he and Peewee had flown the entire Mediterranean circle, and they were full of tall tales, advice, and warnings,

Especially about Italy. Mati had better make double sure he had every damn bit of paper and document, plus an extra bushel of identity photos; those Mussolini carabinieri liked to eat foreigners for breakfast. But the Greek islands! Ah, those were people! Peewee marked so many don't-miss spots that the voyage could take as long as the *Odyssey*. And indeed, that was just what the chaps had done, followed the *Odyssey* from the air. Again they were off on tales of the adventure, while Mati copied down useful items from their flight log, ham radio operators on remote islands, cheap places to stay.

The older fellow, Peewee, now mentioned that he'd been in the war, flying in Palestine itself. He could recall chasing some Heinies all the way from Sinai, ending in a dogfight over the Sea of Galilee, and Mati cried out, "I saw it! When I was a kid! That's when I got the flying bug!"

Peewee was in some sort of job at Imperial Airways, but ah, he was really fond of Palestine. He was a great Bible reader, and to him it was plain the Holy Land belonged to the Jews.

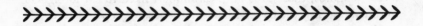

14

AFTER the stock-market crash in America, tourists were scarce, and the new hotel that Mati's brother-in-law Nahum had built in Tiberias was in difficulty. Another difficulty for Nahum was that a growing number of buyers in his seashore orange-grove development had stopped paying the upkeep. He could barely manage the irrigation costs and was behind on wages to the veterans' cooperative that did the labor. Meeting after meeting Nahum held with them, and the most difficult to deal with was Natan, Leah's husband, even though Natan the Red was not himself a participant in the scheme but only a member of the Veterans Committee. But he represented Gidon's widow. On top of everything, as Nahum complained to his Shula, Natan was the worst kind of Red—not even a member of the Communist Party, so you could never throw up their sins to him! If you showed the mess they had made in Russia, he was the first to agree; they had betrayed the Revolution!

To cover the wages he owed, Nahum even offered the veterans a share of the defaulted groves. Useless. Araleh, another of Gidon's wartime friends, demanded cash payment.

A clever man should always be able to find a way out. That, Shula knew, was what ate Nahum most of all; it was as though his picture of himself were spoiled. He had to find some combination that would not only save the groves but even prove advantageous to himself. Most of the American investors didn't take the affair seriously; to them the purchase was a way of helping out Zionism, a donation, and so they let their investment drop. Surely there was a way to gain from this. Every curse contains a blessing, Nahum repeated, from some Talmudic proverb learned in childhood.

To take Nahum's mind off his own troubles, Shula showed him another headline, with a picture, a Munich shopwindow with a Jewish star and JUDE smeared in white paint over the glass. In front of the shop stood a pair of storm troopers. They were tall and blond, and suddenly one of them looked to Nahum exactly like the wartime German airman who had turned Shula's head and nearly got Nahum himself killed by having the Turks seize him for a labor camp. But out of that he had lost so much weight that when he returned, Shula had stopped laughing at him as a fatty and had even come to love him. Now he was fat again, and occasionally at their lawn parties Shula flirted with some ladder-legged Britisher, but no, Nahum knew it was even considered the thing for a hostess to do that, it helped. She was really irreproachable. She kept up with French fashions, so the British ladies always looked out of date, and she reigned in queenly style over the magnificent seashore villa he had built, renowned as the costliest mansion in the land. Shula's figure was opulent, but at the slightest danger sign, as when a skirt refused to snap, she promptly went on a diet; often she would tease him into joining her, but after two days at most Nahum gobbled chocolates in his office.

Still, Shula's wartime Gottfried and his whole circle of fliers, Nahum told himself, were doubtless today drinking brudershaft with Hermann Goering.

"Maybe the German Jews will finally get some sense in their heads and come to Eretz," Shula commented on the photo. And suddenly Nahum had a thought.

When a man thinks cleverly, things combine. On the roof of his villa Nahum had built himself a study overlooking the sea, and there each morning he sat alone for half an hour of contemplation.

In Tiberias, his father, coming home from the early-morning prayers in the shul, had had a habit of sitting alone in his little accounting office in the hotel; he kept a Talmud there and sometimes turned a page. Perhaps, Nahum reflected, his own way was similar. Contemplation of the sea, the sky—a look at the newspaper—and suddenly solutions came to him as from Above.

Primo, German Jews still had money and property. They would be eligible for immigration here under the British nonquota category for capitalists, which required only a show of a thousand pounds. *Secundo,* by investing in repossessed second- or third-year groves, they wouldn't have to wait five years for income. Only a few years, and the golden fruit would weigh down their trees! Two years in which they could build homes and accommodate themselves to the land. Or they could even wait in Germany, and should Hitler be defeated in the next election, Nahum could point out to them, they would in any case have made a good investment!

As for himself, he could buy up the defaulted groves at a pittance and sell them in Germany at full price! Thus, he'd be rescuing the cooperative, with a nice profit for his effort. A delicious maneuver.

He'd have to borrow turn-around capital from one of the Polish loan sharks infesting Tel Aviv; they squeezed you for as high as twenty percent, but with that he could buy out the defaulters, and besides, to impress the German Jews, he'd have to stay only in first class hotels.

The sight of a pair of them, booted, wearing their swastika armbands, marching down the corridor—even in a train they could march—at once raised the terror that remained in Nahum the whole time he was in Germany. They, not the official passport inspector, seemed the authority. However, his papers were stamped with hardly a glance at his name.

And in Cologne, as Nahum emerged from the station and got into a taxi, he looked for shopwindows with the dread markings but saw none. This must be a lull. Over one elegant shoe store, however, there was a new-looking sign, HEILBRUNNER, and in small letters, FORMERLY KOHN.

Pictures of Hitler were on every wall, in every shopwindow. Still, the streets seemed peaceful, normal. People moved about, in his hotel the service was irreproachable.

Nahum had chosen Cologne to start with because in a smaller city the Jewish community would perhaps be more closely knit than in Berlin. Cologne had always been considered a good Zionist city, and he'd got himself a membership list.

They were not frightened, they insisted with tight smiles, in the dining room of the dentist who had assembled a dozen friends. Na, nein, Hitler's anti-Semitism was eighty percent a propaganda

228

show. *Der Stürmer* with its obscene caricatures—had not France during the Dreyfus case seen even worse? And Hitler with his hoodlums could never achieve a majority. That had been proved. The latest election showed a decline. Slight, but a decline. They had reached their peak and were finished. Yes, they had won control of a province or two. Local concentrations. As for their trying a putsch, Von Hindenburg would never stand for it! He hated that upstart Corporal Hitler, everyone knew this, and the old Field Marshal was still the idol of the nation.

Good! Nahum said. What he had to put before them need not even be thought of as insurance. Before any other consideration, this was an excellent business opportunity. He fixed his eyes on the host; the dentist nodded at each of Nahum's points, his double chin folding into a kind of underlining. It was always best, Nahum had learned, to talk as though directly to one person, but occasionally to look around, including them all.

He unrolled the town plan of Sharon Shore, embodying the latest in urban conception. He mentioned the names of well-known personages who already owned groves. First, there was the rector of the Hebrew University, Dr. Judah Magnes. (Nahum had donated a grove to the university in his honor.) By luck, the dentist recalled that in the early days of the great war, before the United States entered, this same Rabbi Judah Magnes had come on a relief mission for German Jewry. A wonderful man!

Nahum spread before them the rendering of the Seashore Plaza. And in the residential district, a householder could virtually reach out his back window to pick his morning grapefruit!

Moreover, the town was also planned as a resort area, for its beaches were unsurpassed! With this he showed them a large photograph of the truly breathtaking beach vista and a sketch by the great German architect Erich Mendelsohn for an esplanade, with resort hotels. On the master plan Nahum pointed to circles for expansion, up to a metropolis of a hundred thousand! The Mandate authority had already approved the entire concept!

And the Arabs? What was the relationship with the Arabs in this area?

That was the beauty of it, Nahum told them. Since all this land was reclaimed from sandy wastes, no Arab had to be displaced. The nearest Arab village was several miles inland, and he was on excellent terms with its inhabitants. He had paid their sheikh well for these unused sands, over which, in actual fact, they had no proper claim. But it was better to pay and have good relations. He himself had been born and brought up in Tiberias, a mixed city of Arabs and Jews, and as they would recall, during the disorders in 1929 there had been no trouble whatever in Tiberias. The Jewish and Arab mukhtars had met and made a peace pact. And the same Dr. Judah Magnes, one of the founding spirits of Hof HaSharon, was the leader of B'rith Shalom, for peace and cooperation between Arabs and Jews.

In any case Nahum could assure them that the troubles of 1929 would not recur. As they probably knew, the troubles had been instigated to raise the price of land. But London had made drastic changes in the Palestine administration, and the new High Commissioner was an excellent man, fair to both Arabs and Jews. Also the district commissioner of the Sharon, fond of galloping on the beach, was a frequent guest at Nahum's villa. And of course, the Yishuv itself would never again be caught off guard. The veterans of the Jewish Legion—partners in Hof HaSharon—were, naturally, at the very core of the Haganah.

Sales were excellent.

From Cologne, Nahum went to Mannheim, to Dortmund, with growing prospect lists, for each buyer wanted to show his friends how shrewd he was. At each gathering the good German Jews assured him that the mass of the German people would never accept the Nazi program. They showed him newspaper advertisements taken by the German Jewish community reminding the good Germans that the German Jews were loyal, heart and soul, to their fatherland and would always remain so. But many bought fully planted citrus groves and building plots in Sharon Shore.

The German Jews—unbeknownst to themselves—had rescued Hof HaSharon, and Hof HaSharon, Nahum was certain, would one day rescue them. He felt wise and virtuous for in saving others, he had benefited himself.

Nor had his voyage been without danger. At every moment when in the open Nahum had felt a blow might strike him from behind. He read of attacks on Jew-communists in the streets of Rotterdam and knew this meant some Nazis had killed some Jews, but fortunately this never happened in his presence. In each hotel he was certain his luggage had been thoroughly searched; he made little tests—a loose pin—and there was no doubt.

230

Now he owed himself a bit of relaxation. He would return through Paris. There Nahum bought a lovely filmy black nightgown for Shula and a flagon of Chanel Five. He treated himself and a potential client to a dinner at the Tour d'Argent, and the client knew a place that had a most unusual *spectacle*, done by a real hermaphrodite.

15

DOV drove them out to the airfield, with life belts in case they dropped into the sea, sleeping bags in case they got marooned on land, and when they were stowing everything in the tail area, he pulled out a small flask of Chanel Five for his wife in Tel Aviv; since this had to be handed over personally, it was insurance for their safe arrival! "One last word," he whispered to Mati. Greetings to Mati's uncle Menahem in Marseilles.

In Marseilles? Mati was surprised. Menahem had been shipping certain things, he knew, from Antwerp.

Dov nodded. "He'll meet you in Marseilles."

And as they taxied, the Smiler ran alongside, waving a schoolkid Jewish flag and howling up to Mati, "If you crash and get killed and wreck our airplane, I'll personally break your neck!"

After all, Dena kept telling herself, this was not such a big deal; airbugs like Peewee flew the same trip just for a vacation. Yet she felt gulpy—like before the wedding. For the takeoff Mati sat solemn, like the time she had watched him solo. Then, just as the plane became airborne, she felt a streak of joy, a cry escaped from her, thank God nobody could hear it! "Whoopee!" Dena cried.

Mati heard it. He turned his head for an instant, scowling, which only made her giggle, and then Mati himself broke out: "Yallah! Ha-bayta!" Which Dena knew meant "Home!"

Suddenly Dena thought of girls who sat on the jump seats of

motorcycles with their arms clasped around their boys. She had always wondered if that really felt sexy. And of course, Dena told herself, she was aware of the Freudian meaning of an airplane rising up—pointed into the sky.

But also she knew now after over two years of "experience" that there were certain unpredictable times when the lovemaking was as though entirely new, times when for no particular reason the two of them simply went wild for each other, and so in flying, though she had by now been many, many times in the air with Mati, there were rides when the pleasure suddenly became sheer elation.

Sometimes when elation came, it was because of a particular sky. Breaking through the clouds to an utter serenity of space—that would do it, too. Or else sometimes the elation came because of an exquisite view, a golden shoreline, like the first time Mati flew her over the dunes south of Chicago, moving from steel mill smoke out into the clean. And now, now there was a sense of coming out from a long waiting into something very great in their lives, something that was about to be revealed on this journey; maybe a woman felt like this when she was going to give birth.

Hardly being able to talk because of the motor noise had one advantage: it left you with your sheer experience, yet knowing it was a shared experience. There was even the sense that you were prevented from breaking the spell as you might if you said the wrong thing. As in making love, you sometimes felt yes, cries could come out, but you mustn't speak words. It was a shared peak of life, only different for each. In making love, you wondered— maybe your whole life you would wonder—if a man could ever really feel what a woman felt or if you could ever feel what a man felt. She was a modern woman who believed in the equality of the sexes, yet Dena couldn't imagine that she would be the one flying the plane and Mati would be sitting behind. Some things were perhaps really different in the psyche itself, as they were in your physiology. It was the man who had to carry you off. Even in a car a girl felt a little awkward, driving, with the man sitting beside her, unless, of course, it was an old married relationship. Like— and she could now unblushingly picture it—like when she sometimes in lovemaking got on top. You did it more as a game. Or like wearing a man's shirt. It was in fun, it was in play, the real thing was for the man to be the man.

Somehow, though with their heads evening after evening bent

together over the maps they had marked out for every stage of the journey, this still was Mati carrying her off, carrying her to his own lair, yes, and this was the mounting ecstasy in her. It would mount and mount, all through this peregrination, Dena felt certain; the joy would increase with each stop on the way and with each rising into the sky.

Already they were over the Channel, but being over the water was not as scary as she had feared, for you could see ships underneath as though stationed stock-still ready to catch you if you fell. And you could almost at once see the other shore. Perhaps the Mediterranean also would be unexpectedly easy, with the short sea hops Mati had planned. Anyway she wasn't at all tense. The airplane took a few little air-current bumps, and Mati turned to her and made a finger kiss, partly for her, for their doing this together, but really for the ship, this ship was a beauty, a beauty!

Then low over the fields of Normandy. How drowsy, how peaceful. And the thought came to Dena of fliers in war. How was it possible? In this utter unbounded peacefulness in the sky, men in planes like this one in the World War had flown over these fields, these villages, each sculptured to a church spire, and the fliers had dropped bombs and seen their explosions. And wasn't this also why Mati had so crazily had to have this airship, wasn't this why he and she were now in this vast serenity and wedded joy nevertheless flying the machine to perhaps some future moment of dropping bombs on people? Yes, but that would be in defense. To save the lives and homes of their own people. Yet there came to Dena a kind of forbidden and staved-off foreshadowing. Somehow the prescience was connected to the Lindberghs. In what joy and good purpose they had flown like this all over the world, and then the tragedy of their kidnapped and murdered baby. Did God have some malevolent equivalence in his design? Mati's family—were they among those upon whom there was some doom, and was she herself now flying into that doom?

Mati had turned his head, beaming; it was time to signal the landing field. Her job! To signal and receive clearance for their landing in Paris!

※ ※ ※

No, it wasn't over with Khalid, oh, no, Myra said; only she had been unable to stand another day in that atmosphere in Germany, but at this crucial time both she and Khalid had felt he ought to stay on with Paul Klee, it had been a real inspiration of hers to bring him to Paul Klee at the Bauhaus; they had a real affinity; Klee had been strongly influenced by Arab motifs on his trip to Egypt, but the Bauhaus was finished, the Nazis were forcing it to close, didn't they know? Myra eyed them with the astonishment of someone who finds the most important event in her world unknown outside. The Nazis had captured the Dessau district in the last election and closed the Bauhaus! To those degenerates the only creative art center in their land was degenerate! Klee was starting to teach in Düsseldorf, and Khalid was following him there. Myra would go back and join Khalid as soon as things got quieter; right now the Nazis and the communists were killing each other all over the place, didn't they know? Yes, this they knew; after all, they read the papers. At least Khalid was keeping out of it, he was not really political, though his sympathies were with the left; oh, she was a coward to have come away and left him there, Myra cried, but she was trying to save the Bauhaus. She had a wonderful idea—to bring it to Chicago—she had been cabling her uncle every day, that's why she had come to Paris; she couldn't possibly work on it from Germany. Maybe only a Jew got that vomity feeling from the moment you crossed the border going in until you crossed it going out. Somehow Khalid was able to work there, the atmosphere didn't affect him the way it affected her; naturally as he was not Jewish, not that he had a spark of anti-Semitism in him. If only Klee would come to America! Dena couldn't know, they couldn't imagine, what the atmosphere was like. Just a few nights ago with Khalid in Berlin she had seen the insanity. They had gone to the big Hitler rally at the Greenwald stadium just really to see what it was; the place was packed with a hundred thousand of those raving maniacs and a hundred thousand more outside all around the stadium listening to loudspeakers. When you heard the *Sieg Heil*, it was like a shout to sweep you off the face of the earth. When the enormous spotlight swept the stands, Myra suddenly had felt as though it were converging on her, a Jew, sitting among them. And when that little monster man spoke, you had to hang onto your sanity with your claws— and at that instant Myra looked as though she were doing it, though she tried to laugh.

Right off Myra had taken them to the Ritz Bar, joking maybe they would see Hemingway, and in the midst of her tension and excitement Myra still kept turning her head, Dena noticed, to check on celebrities. Or maybe not. Maybe it was that other thing that in utmost secrecy in one of her worst despondent moods Myra had once confided—her sickness. Her fear. The sudden terror that struck her at times that her sickness could be *seen*.

But what was there to see? In a Hitler mob had she been terrified that someone would see she was Jewish? It must be something deeper, Dena puzzled, maybe like the feeling anyone had at times that in your very depths, if people could see, there were awful, shameful things—

Myra pulled herself out of her jitters and now related how in the midst of that mass hysteria she had tried a trick; she had looked at them as if she were her analyst analyzing. At every shout from the little superman she had pronounced to herself, "Paranoia, paranoia." And for the crowd, too, "Mass paranoia," yet—

Suddenly Myra halted again, her eyes with that dark glaze.

And the other scene, the one she would not tell, relived itself in Myra while she was hanging on, discussing with them where she would take them for dinner, oh, she wanted to give them the big Paris night, not the Tour d'Argent, of course, only tourists went there, but maybe La Perouse—

It had been an ordinary Bierstube in Düsseldorf, and they had stopped in quite by chance after a movie, Khalid had a liking for such proletarian hangouts, but near them was a whole table of brownshirts in a high mood, and one of them leaned over, asking Khalid—no offense—but a foreigner? Spanish? No, Arab, Khalid said, at which there was a lusty raising of mugs, *Sieg Heil!* And before they knew it, the brownshirt was standing over them, insisting they join the big table. The fellow beamed on Myra. "But you are not also Arab, fräulein?" "American," said Khalid quickly.

Naturally he could not have said "Jew." And one doesn't announce "American Jew." But instead of glancing at her watch to say they had to go, she sat there paralyzed while the brownshirt raised two fingers together, jovially declaring to Khalid, "The Arabs and us like this! Soon Hitler in power! You want to finish the Jews—we come!"

"*Trink! Trink!*" All of them were raising their mugs. Khalid had to raise his. And he would throw his beer in their faces. No, no, she must stop him! Khalid gulped, looked at his watch and said unfortunately—

They had begun to sing. The Horst Wessel: "When Jewish blood spurts from the knife—"

And she saw Artie. Blood in long streaks from the razor slashes. Naked in the shower, falling. And she felt her face—

If she shrieked, Khalid would know her sickness, he would know—

Myra clutched his arm, whispering he had to get her out of there.

Really classic French cuisine, she was telling Mati and Dena, right on the Seine near the Place St. Michel. She had already stopped Mati's gesture of paying, and they were out of the Ritz.

As they were about to get into the cab, Myra suddenly drew back. She made some excuse, looking in her purse for cigarettes; some other people took the taxi. They got into the next one. That driver had given her a funny look, Myra babbled, and for an augenblick she had forgotten she was no longer in Germany.

Could you tell a girl, "Your sickness is showing"? Dena wondered.

The rest of the evening Myra was fine.

❧ ❧ ❧

Chartres, Orléans, dipping down in each delicious place like honeybees dipping, sipping the nectar of human creation, of châteaus and tapestries and delightful inexpensive little hotels and always the easy camaraderie of local landing fields. In Avignon, Mati right off asked the mechanics, had they heard the results of the new German election?

By nightfall the papers had it, the biggest party in the Reichstag, but in the total popular vote not even a one percent gain from Hitler's defeat in the presidential election of only a few months ago. The Nazis would never gain a majority. But Mati was in one of those moods. This was one of those nights when you felt a man's impatience with anything you could say to him, with anything except your body. At least tomorrow in Marseilles, Mati could talk it all out; he was meeting someone there, he had told her mysteriously.

Even in the French port Menahem felt the CID had an eye on him, yet when he got word from Dov in England about Mati's flight, with the landing hour cleverly coded in a Hebrew word, he knew he had to lay eyes on that airplane. Though he had the same queasy feeling that had made him leave Antwerp just after the last shipment, he decided the airfield would not be too much of a risk if he simply loitered in the little crowd that could always be found, watching planes land and take off. He could get a good look at the ship without attracting attention and go back to town to meet them at the rendezvous he had written to Mati.

The small white ship came swooping down to the minute. Menahem could even make out the name on the nose—*Gidon!* In Hebrew, too. Well done!

He watched them clamber out. He had already seen snapshots of the bride, but how lightly she walked, how slender her waist looked above the wide-blown jodhpurs. Just then Dena pulled off the helmet, shaking loose her hair, and Menahem approved, approved of the sight altogether! He slipped away.

As agreed, he waited for them at one of the fish restaurants facing the sign for the Château d'If. Menahem rose, taking her hand and kissing it in the continental manner. This was a surprise for Dena; tales about Menahem, Mati had told her aplenty, even the hush-hush ones of his early days as a Shomer when a certain pair of killers, released by the Turks, had had to be "taken care of." But this Menahem had the face of a Jewish scholar, a musing philosopher.

He spoke English, a bit more from books than from habit, and with a half-British intonation, like Leah's. Menahem had to be told every detail of the flight, the speed, the gasoline consumption, length of field for takeoff, and a few times Mati laughingly said to her, "You see, I told you Menahem knows about everything." To which Menahem shrugged and said, "A little. The most dangerous is to know a little about everything and everything about nothing." Yet he ordered the meal with expert little questions to the waiter about the kind of fish, the kind of wine, and even imitated a Marseilles accent, making the waiter laugh. Then quickly Menahem plunged with Mati into interpreting the German election results. Much as their old Field Marshal von Hindenburg hated the upstart corporal for even having had the effrontry to run against him—and twice!—for the presidency, Menahem believed he would now have to swallow his distaste and call Hitler in as Chancellor. And with Von Hindenburg eighty-four years old, this would certainly mean full power for the Nazis within a short time. He fell silent.

Of course, Dena was displeased like any Jew. But with Mati

and Menahem, as with all the Palestinians in London, the Hitler news was always as though it were happening to them personally.

Well, to look at the other side, Mati said, this would mean a flood of German Jewish immigration. True, Menahem agreed. Just a few days ago he had met with Nahum, who had been there in Germany and was sailing home. According to Nahum, those Deutsche Juden were at last realizing what was happening. Many important professors had already been dismissed from their posts, simply kicked out. And now— But also, Mati pointed out, with a sudden large increase in immigration—provided the British would allow it—the Mufti would certainly start trouble again. The little plane might be coming just in time.

Now they switched to Hebrew too rapid for her to follow, Haganah stuff, Dena supposed, and Menahem slanted her a little smile of apology. He had a half smile; only one side of his mouth parted, and you saw a glint of gold tooth. He hoped he was being too pessimistic, Menahem said. So Dena repeated how in London an American foreign correspondent had told them once Hitler took power, he would no longer need his mob-rousing anti-Semitism so much and would let up.

The look Menahem gave her was like one from a doctor who believes the family should know the truth. "My dear, have you read *Mein Kampf?*" he asked softly.

Dena was about to say she had tried to read it, but the book was such a bore. Except that Menahem was continuing, his voice now quite low, and his tone was no longer that of a man of some sophistication, but—where had she heard it?—this was more like the low rhythmic repetitions in an old shul: "In the Torah it is written"; "In the words of Jeremiah it is said."

"If he comes to power, he means to kill all the Jews," Menahem stated.

"What?" This was in *Mein Kampf?*

"He uses different words, double language, but again and again, if you read carefully, he speaks of the elimination of the Jews, the destruction of the Jews. He means this. Literally."

But such a thing, such a thing—why, if he even began to try to do such a thing the whole world, the Germans themselves— Why, it was plain insane!

Menahem sighed as one who is used to hearing such answers.

Yet within himself it was known, settled. One had only to catch the open clues. There was the remark about the World War—how the mass gassing of perhaps some twenty-five thousand Jews could have prevented the death of millions of Germans. And it was to be remembered that Hitler had been gassed in the war and for a time had lain blind in a hospital. For a long period now Menahem had felt a prescience of doom; he recognized within himself the mystical voice of foreknowledge that he had years and years ago thought to have banished but that remained deeply buried, only now and again over the years sending forth its signals: I am still here, within, and mine is the truth. What form the doom would take he didn't try to imagine, but the foreknowledge was there: This is Haman. He will try to destroy every living Jew, to erase us from existence. And the rest of that Purim myth, an Ahasuerus, an Esther, was but a fairy tale. A Mordecai? Ah, the deep wish for survival. Even within himself Menahem recognized a kind of megalomania of himself as an instrument, just as long ago in his hallucination of a visit from Elijah, calling him forth to save Jews. But could one utterly rule out this insistent sense of prescience?

The waiter came with the fish. Dena saw Menahem's worldly, polite smile; he was back. And the coming elections in America? he asked. What did she think of this Roosevelt?

"You mean, will he be good for the Jews?" she teased.

"Naturally. You know the story of the elephant and the Jewish question." He shrugged a Jewish shrug: That is really how we are.

Then during the meal it was family talk, and afterward Menahem gave them a walking tour of the Canebière and even the red-light district; they actually did have red lights over the doors of certain small hotels! Mati's brother-in-law made amusing expert comments, pointing out a place that had the best *cinéma bleu*. And when Dena asked what blue movies were, Menahem turned to Mati, asking in Hebrew, "I may?"

"Why not, she's a married woman!" Mati laughed and even declared he'd never seen one himself. Oh, stag movies! She got it. In a whorehouse! Some combination! Leave it to the French! And this all-knowing Menahem seemed an expert on this subject, too.

About certain men you felt a sex curiosity—not the same thing, Dena told herself, as sex appeal. About Menahem she found herself speculating. He seemed one of those men in a novel by Wassermann or Dostoevsky, capable of every experience, the whole range of good and evil; no, not actual evil, not any desire to hurt. She supposed with some men, if you knew they had been through

240

whorehouses and places, it made them more intriguing. And if your husband had to be away on far-off missions, it was better he did things like that than got himself involved with mistresses. Wasn't Menahem's wife—Dena had to count over the names of Mati's sisters—Menahem's wife was Dvora, the poultry raiser in their kibbutz. And they had several children.

Now, Menahem was saying, he had something important to show Mati, and if Denatchka didn't mind, they'd leave her at the hotel. "I know, you're taking him straight to the *cinéma bleu!*"

It must be some of their hush-hush stuff; maybe better that she had no idea. A girl could always wash her hair.

Behind the wharf area with its banks of enormous cranes, Menahem led Mati into a junkyard. A footpath meandered among the piles of rusting broken machinery, much of which, particularly in the night, Mati couldn't quite identify—boilers, hoists. Behind was a wooden shed lighted by a few dangling bulbs. Someone yelled, "Shalom, Mati!" It was a redhead named Peleg, whom he hadn't seen since scouting days. Peleg stood balanced on the rim of a huge iron cylinder, working with a welding torch, sealing on a lid. At first sight Mati couldn't make out what that iron thing might be.

Menahem chuckled. Alongside lay a kind of trailer hitch; the cylinder was a road roller, upended. As for what was being sealed inside, Mati didn't have to be told.

At the rear of the shed, unlocking a tin door to a storage space, Menahem showed him the merchandise. A pile of gunnysacks holding grease-covered rifles, World War vintage but in excellent condition. Oh, if you paid cash, you could get any quantity. And also: "I picked up something special for you, tsutsig." Twinkling, Menahem opened a padlocked chest and pulled forth a light machine gun with a swivel mount.

After his last shipment of irrigation pipes stuffed with ammunition had been detected in Antwerp, Menahem had come here to Marseilles, but without a single contact. He had walked the docks, wandered through the back area, and he'd passed this junkyard. First of all, who owns a junkyard? A good chance it's a Yehudi—a Jewish business all over the world. And so it proved. Not only a Jew but a Jew from Czernowitz. And as he poked around the yard, Menahem's eye had fallen on a huge steamroller, the frame wrecked but the cylinders were intact. Somehow this had brought to mind a trick from the early years, under the Turks. A large stone olive-press wheel had been hollowed out, a pair of rifles had been concealed inside, and thus the arms had been transported from Damascus.

A road roller's cylinders could be packed with a veritable arsenal. And the heavier, the more normal it would seem. And in Palestine, who doesn't need road rollers? Every kibbutz for its yard. And Tel Aviv for new streets. And soccer fields. And every moshav has to build its own access road. And the Solel Boneh constantly needed more road-building machines. So steamrollers could be unloaded in Haifa with only cursory inspection. A glance. And then why the whole steamroller? Rollers alone, to be pulled by a horse or a tractor.

The ticklish job was packing. Once the cylinder was upended, someone had to be lowered head first, feet held, carefully to pack the merchandise. Every item must be inserted so nothing would rattle. After fifteen minutes head down, Menahem said, you could black out from the blood in your skull.

Mati tried it, while Menahem held his feet. Soon enough he was dizzy; deep in the iron barrel, his own howl echoed around him making him dizzier. At last they hauled him out. Never mind, the merchandise was getting through. Menahem laughed. The only trouble was on this end; the supply of used road rollers was running out, and with new ones there could be shipment problems, questions asked. Then Menahem in turn, with Mati holding his legs, personally packed in the swivel gun for the *Gidon*.

"You can turn on the light, I'm not sleeping," Dena said when Mati softly closed the door to their room. "How was the *cinéma bleu?*"

The experience that she felt must still come, the one unknown thing more, came at the last stage, when they had left Greece and were over the islands. This night they were to stop in Cyprus, but halfway Dena looked down and saw a place that called to her. It was almost perfectly round and sat on the purplish sea like the times in the Halsted Street store Papa would place a sapphire on dark velvet. A little girl then, she would on tiptoes reach her chin above the counter to gaze. She pointed, now, excitedly.

So Mati dipped down. Fringed with sand, the island had a cluster of white houses that caught the sunlight just now and sparkled.

She tapped his shoulder. Mati nodded, sharing the sight, but then Dena motioned for landing. He lifted his shoulder, questioning. Quickly Dena searched on the chart, and there it was, and it was listed in the directory; it had a landing strip and even a call number. Dena checked the special list that the airclub fellow, Peewee, had given them in London, the *Odyssey* flight. He had it: "Paradise!"

Mati circled. There was no answer to her tapping, but why should that matter? There lay the landing strip, its earth like a red carpet. Mati touched down.

Usually someone would be running out of a hut by the time they landed, but here the field was completely deserted. Still, not far off was a small stone house with a high aerial. Dena took the overnight satchel, and they followed a trodden path that led among haphazard olive trees to the dwelling. Partway a woman appeared, coming unhurriedly toward them. She wore an ankle-length black dress, Dena saw, like all peasant women in Italy and Greece. Just then a small boy came running to catch up with her; he was bare to the waist, with clinging sea-washed knee pants—he must have rushed up from the beach. The kid ran onward past them to the plane. Mati called "Hey!" and made a warning don't-touch sign; the boy nodded vigorously, while his mother reassured them. "Okay, okay," she said. "Welcome!" She pointed to the aerial and to her ear, nodding her head, she had heard; then, pointing again to herself and making a gesture of writing, she shook her head with an apologetic laugh. "Me, no." She pointed to the village. "Husband."

The house nested in a stone-paved courtyard with a well; there was even a tethered goat. Dena could have gone silly with joy, but she only exchanged looks of wondrous delight with Mati. A step-down terrace faced the sea, and almost directly below was a cove holding a few small fishing boats, a fat barge with a sail, and even a modest-looking yacht.

At the rear of the terrace the woman indicated, half smothered under creepers, a separate stone hut. It was too perfect! In her head Dena was already describing all this to Myra, trying not to sound banal.

Two smaller children, little girls, had come from the courtyard; this hut could almost have been their playhouse. It contained a wide, brass-knobbed bedstead laden with enormous pillows with embroidered covers that Dena already coveted, and even more, a crocheted spread with an embroidered red silk inlet. The walls were whitewashed, the ceiling was beamed; there was a kind of olio icon of the Virgin Mary and a table with a fringe-shaded electric lamp. In a corner the landlady was showing her a sink that emptied into a pail, and above this was a mirror with a green frame painted with daisies.

The woman's smile broadened—but she was young! Maybe not even twenty-five! "Stay here?" And then pointing outward: "Hotel."

"No, no hotel, here!" Dena cried as though this were all about to be snatched away.

"Eat?" making the motion to her mouth. They nodded vigorously. Taking Dena's wrist, she pointed on the watch to six. "Okay?" "Okay, okay!"

It was all like that. They put on bathing suits, and the little boy led them down the zigzag path to the beach. As in a travelogue, a stubble-cheeked ancient Greek was mending a fishnet.

The beach here was pebbly, but a bit farther up, the little boy showed them, was a sandy place, and there they saw a few vacationers from the hotel. Dena was pleased to feel the glances of the men and just as pleased to see a few women give Mati the look-over. Scraps of conversation in French and English floated their way. But Dena didn't want to get acquainted with anybody, anybody, and ran plunging into the water.

By mealtime the husband was there; his name was Stavros, and he had the slightly concentrated brows of the seaman always a bit worried over the weather. His face was bony, somehow suggesting the grayish stone outcroppings of the island. "All okay?" he said, and brought his logbook. His English was usable; he had learned wireless on a ship as a boy, he said. "I always want to learn."

Mati signed in. The previous entry had been three weeks ago, he noticed, and altogether there were perhaps a dozen in the year. Turning back a few pages, he found the signature of the *Odyssey* fellow. "Here's Peewee!" he cried to Dena.

The Greek leaned in to read their name. "He told us this was Paradise," Dena said. "That's why we came." And she repeated, "Paradiso!"

"Ah." The smile was a touch melancholy, wistful. Life was hard. Very hard. Poor place. But then he turned the book a few leaves to another year farther back. His wife stood beaming, watching. Dena followed his pointing finger. "Lindbergh!" she cried. "Anne and Charles Lindbergh!"

The wife was nodding, nodding, joyous in their astonishment.

And what did it mean? Why, nothing of course, yet like trivial crazy things in life, it made you feel something was meant, something marvelous must yet appear!

They had come from America? Stavros asked. Ah, not in this little airplane, no, he laughed with them, but yes from America. He had an uncle in America, San Francisco. When he was a boy, his uncle had written to his family, send Stavros. "But now in America is hard, no?" he asked. Depression. He knew the word. And he glanced toward the children in the yard as if to tell himself maybe he had not made such a mistake, after all, staying here; in America also was hard.

For the meal they had broiled fish, with the woman's home-baked bread. She brought them goat cheese and olives, and Stavros brought a small pitcher of wine, asking, "You like Greek taste?" They had already got used to the resin and reassured him. Husband and wife sat with them for a while, Stavros smoking Mati's cigarettes, and yes, he said, both had been born on this island. The wife kept her eyes on Dena. "New marry?" Oh, already their second anniversary! "No baby?" Dena laughed self-consciously. First they had to settle, make their home.

They were going to Palestine, Mati said.

Ah, Palestine, Stavros repeated. Jews come. He smiled as one who tries to see the possible, amid difficulties. Good. Jews bring money. Get better.

It was a balmy half-moon night with drifting fragile clouds. They took a stroll in the village and then back along the shore, climbing up their private path to their stone hut. It was a long time since they had held hands. In cities Dena felt this was something Mati didn't too much care to do, but along the shore she reached for his fingers, and he took her hand. "Is it something like this?" she asked. "Eretz?"

"Yes," he said. "A lot like this." The air, the soil, the warmth of the sea, he meant. Though naturally not especially the people. Though yet the people too. Soon she would know.

That night in their hut for a moment Dena wavered. She had thought she would leave the question until they arrived. Then it would be because she was really sure.

But just because of that last thought she should do it now. She must not have conditions. Life should be—do it! Do it!

So she left the circlet there in its ivory container, a gift from her sister-in-law Sherrill.

The mattress had that sweet intoxicating scent of freshly stuffed hay.

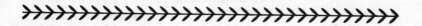

16

WITH the wings and then the entire aircraft shuddering, Mati pushed the *Gidon* almost vertically to circle the peaks of Mount Hermon, laughing happily as Dena shrieked, "Yes, I see it, I see it, snow, are you crazy! Go down!" He made swallow dips; they had a breath-stopping air-pocket drop nearly thirty feet, the worst scare Dena had felt on the entire trip. The drop at least sobered Mati, for he brought the ship level and smooth. Well, Dena told herself, that was supposed to be one way of getting rid of a baby, fall off the roof. But she had to laugh at herself; she didn't even know whether in the very first days it could matter.

Mati was shouting something to her, but this high up the engine roar was louder, and she couldn't understand. He passed a note, "Cedars of Lebanon," and wing-dipped over a copse of wide-spreading dark-leaved trees. She nodded her "interesting" nod, the nut, and then recalled his tale of his oldest brother Reuven at the end of the war dragging back from Damascus a cartful of cedars of Lebanon seedlings and, on top of them, his bride and her piano. Soon now she would meet them all. She would be spending her life with them, it came to her.

And now as they descended, the mountain, silvery-threaded, slanted down into rock slopes, of a blood-orange color reflecting the sun, and farther the slopes stretched into a valley, grass green with patches of pale vegetable green, or newly plowed reddish areas between grayish stony humps, and sometimes a cluster of white cube houses. Was this already the homeland?

A dark uneven line—it must be the Jordan! The line vanished into a mottled wide stain; that was the cross-hatched place on her map, the Huleh swampland, where wild pigs and buffalo were supposed to wallow, where his brother Gidon used to hunt wild boar; Gidon and his Arab pal had killed and tasted one, but Mati's father wasn't supposed to know about this sin even until now! And from the far end of the swamp the Jordan threaded out and led your eye to the flat greenish lake—the Sea of Galilee at last! She must call it Kinneret; it meant a harp, you could see the shape, and in the Hebrew word you could actually hear the music. There was a song Mati loved, a favorite, its melody seemed to rise up now from the water, "Kinneret of mine, perhaps all this life was but a dream," the song said, a poetess named Rahel had written it, a gifted girl from Poland, a chalutzah who tended geese along these shores like Mati's sister Yaffaleh. Only last year in London the chaverim had talked of Rahel's dying from TB—how sad and romantic. "Kinneret of mine"—Dena saw Mati, a chunky, naked little boy, running along the shore, plunging in for a swim. Right now, as though by telepathy, he dived so low, the devil, she could pick out the fishing boats, were those Arabs? Someone even held up a fish! And she could even see a long, underwater streak of a different color, grayish, where, as Mati had explained, the Jordan's current ran deep under the surface of the lake to emerge at the far end. And looking onward Dena indeed saw the stream like a snapped-loose harp string curling on, and along there his family had their farm.

What a place for a lakeside cottage! The sea was so many patches of color, turquoise, purple, spume-green; it was a vision, a music, a beauty unbearable; dotted with sails, it held angelic peace, like that island of last night, and the thought came to Dena that if last night took, then she had made her commitment, even more completely than in marriage.

He circled over the town, Tiberias, black stone walls, and from this low the surrounding sky had colors she had never seen, bronze underclouds, floats of pink and fiery red, while the cliffs on the Trans-Jordan side stood like glowing deep purple walls over the color-patched sea.

In Dena's mind hovered the nearness of Christianity. You could understand a mystical religion coming from here—a brotherliness —and at the beginning it had all been among Jews.

Past the end of the lake Mati pointed down over large rectangular fields, shouting, "Reuven's kibbutz." A cluster of buildings; he dipped, circled; Dena could see children running in the yard, she could see men and women emerging, her crazy Mati nearly took the roof off their biggest building. Everyone was waving. Kids on the ground ran after the airship shadow. He had written Reuven the day and the hour—their first flier in their first airplane! On a rooftop, chaverim waved a Jewish flag. Surely his brother Reuven and his wife, Elisheva, were among them. Waving to their own Mati and his bride from America. She herself! Dena had tears in her eyes. Mati turned his face to her; his eyes too were misted.

He did not alight. Permission was for Jerusalem; the first flight must be correct. Hardly a moment farther over the threading Jordan, and he was dipping and circling anew; this time Dena saw a double row of dwellings, black stone cubes. Mati's own village, Mishkan Yaacov. Her husband pointed the plane at the cube at the end of the lane. Was her father-in-law, the old Yankel, there in the yard watching? On a stone wall connecting the backs of the barns, making a single enclosure of the whole settlement, just the way Mati had described it to her, there were kids climbing up, jumping, waving, each of them her own Mati, a kid from this place grown up to find her in America.

As Mati dropped a note, a boy tumbled off the wall and streaked to catch it. "Shalom, Abba!" Shalom to everybody! He had to land first in Jerusalem but would soon come back.

Once more Mati circled over the settlement. Dena leaned forward and kissed the back of his neck. He turned his head for a quick mouth kiss, to seal the homecoming. They had made it.

※ ※ ※

Turning inland over a broadening valley, Mati showed her now the plain of Esdraelon, the Emek she had heard so much about, the great flat valley—Emek Israel, all sectored into villages and kibbutzim, geometric fields. You could see the tractors like bugs crawling everywhere, and also this was the legendary valley of Armageddon, the place of the final war between good and evil. Maybe?

And the commanding hillock down there must be the famous excavation of Megiddo that had been done by Professor Breasted of the U of C; she had had the course. And now the *Gidon* was rising over the city of Haifa on the point of Mount Carmel, what a view; every house there must have a wonderful panorama of the bay and sea!

Now they flew down the gold-rimmed coast, an endless beach, the entire length of the land! Heaven forbid one day all the Jews of Miami might transfer themselves over here; didn't Mati's brother-in-law—hers too!—already own a whole stretch of this seashore? Sharon Shore. Why, her pop had bought them a grove here! Mati buzzed the town, two white-thread cross streets, a scattering of houses, and there the big white one—that was Nahum and Shula's.

Then the plane was over Tel Aviv. He certainly was giving her the complete tour! Compact, it really looked citified, glistening white. Emerging just like a divided cell from Jaffa. Arabs. One more time Mati circled down, shouting, "Leah!" A few cabins, a barn, at the end of the beach street. So that was Leah's training farm, where Mati should really have found his bride!

Inland for Jerusalem now, rising over the rounded hills and then higher stony hills, you could make out the ancient terracing in long curving denuded shelves. In the crease between hills, a road wound up toward Jerusalem, and its bordering slopes were green. Leah's trees; Dena knew the story.

It was all so quickly traversed, so small, this land of so much fuss and fury.

❊ ❊ ❊

Jerusalem itself Dena was only to come to feel after a time. From above she saw the golden mosque dome with the white court spread around it, for all the world—she'd describe the sight to Myra—like a fried egg sunny side up. The rest of the city was grayish, perhaps pink-tinted in its faint glow. Dena made out a few crooked street lines. It didn't seem this could be a world-important place at all.

So many people had told her of the strange thrill in your first sight of Jerusalem as you made the final turn up the winding canyon road. But who else could tell of first beholding Yerushalayim from the air!

Fairly close in across a valley dip Mati came down onto a neat small landing field; Dena noticed a few RAF planes, a high metal fence—a military field, but after all, wasn't he in the government?

250

Leah with an enormous bouquet rushed ahead of more family, and Reggie and Maureen came waving and grinning, but first a newspaper photographer posed them alongside the *Gidon*, while Mati called out answers to reporters; she could follow the Hebrew. A great future for Palestine in the air, Mati predicted. Yes, an airline was forming; soon there would be an official announcement. No, this was a private plane. And so he had come back a rich American with his own private plane! the reporters joshed. One of them, it seemed, was a schoolmate of Mati's. And when Mati bumblingly explained that the little ship was a wedding gift from his wife's family, there was even broader laughter. So he'd married an American heiress! "If only!" Dena cried, in Hebrew, "alevay!" winning them.

Gazing at the name *Gidon*, one reporter recalled who the ship was named for and the death at Hulda. A glance passed among the newspapermen, Dena saw; they got the real idea behind the plane, and the glance was to remind one another that English officers were present. Mati was again talking about the wonderful future for an airline, especially for tourists, and mentioning how, in London, Pinhas Rutenberg was organizing a company with vast plans and British participation, and also local participation by such elements as the Histadrut; yes, in a few years Mati was certain air travel from Europe would become the regular thing; the route they had traveled was an easy, safe, and beautiful excursion—

"Our own Anne and Charles Lindbergh!" his schoolmate jested, and Dena couldn't help crying out that last night they had come down on a tiny Greek island, just lovely, and discovered the Lindberghs' signature in the registration book! Everyone devoured the story; there was a reporter for the English-language newspaper, a young Canadian, already familiar, he said he'd also put it on the AP wire, and Dena could just see it in the Chicago *Trib*—Our Own Lindys, the Jewish—no, the Hebrew Lindys! They'd be stuck with the tag forever. Oh, hell, why not!

Now the relatives flocked in to embrace her. Another sister of Mati's, Shulamith, the beauty, she was indeed kind of regal like a Queen Esther, and wearing a surely Paris frock. Luscious but on the verge of where a woman had to be careful or she'd get fat. Because of her mother, Dena had always feared this tendency in herself, and now if she really became pregnant, she'd better be supercareful because some women never snapped back—imagine her already thinking such thoughts after one night! The beauteous Shulamith's husband was a butterball with glistening black-button eyes, he was the rich Nahum who was building Sharon Shore, and then there was a brother, Schmulik, chunky, with a thick neck, the real chalutz type in open shirt, shorts, and sandals. And also a young chalutz, quite tall, a bronze statue; his face was a reminder of Menahem, the mystery man of Marseilles: this was the son, Yechezkiel. He hardly looked at her, but his eyes scanned the plane, while there came a small satisfied smile to his mouth. He was the one who had gone to rebuild the kibbutz where Gidon fell.

A British official handed Mati an envelope, "On His Majesty's Service" it said, and inside was a greeting from his chief of section, Richard Welby, the one at whose house they had dined in London; Mrs. Welby joined in welcoming Mati and his delightful American wife, trusting to see them as soon as they had settled in.

Naturally it would not have been protocol for the boss himself to come to the field to greet him.

The collection of uniforms, police wearing high black caracul shakos, Arabs in long white galabias, an RAF officer—the whole show was like movies of the British Empire. Maureen winked and, in her British-accented Hebrew proclaimed, "Baruch Ha-Ba'im," the welcome blessing.

Excitedly squeezing Mati's arm, Schmulik got in a whisper. He was sure he was on the track of who was there that day in the car. For an instant Mati didn't make the connection, but then he knew he was really back. At last, Schmulik said, he had found an Arab boy who had on that fateful day guarded the taxi of the emissaries from Jerusalem. Schmulik had given the boy ten piasters and had at last got a description of the driver of the car. "The same one who always drove for the English." Who could that be but Fawzi, Gidon's sworn blood brother from Dja'adi, who had almost from the start of the Mandate worked as a driver for the British?

The whole story was for Mati too precipitate, yet while talking on all sides on a dozen other things, the questions hung on. Yes, Fawzi was probably mixed up with the Mufti's crowd, the family was in a side branch of the Husseinis, but even if it had been Fawzi, he certainly could not have known that Gidon would be there defending Hulda. And perhaps that Arab boy, for a whole ten piasters, had simply said what he saw Schmulik wanted him to say, the way they were apt to do. But the thing must be heavy on

Schmulik; at this first moment he had needed to impart it. Did anyone else know? Mati asked. He had told it only to Eliahu, Schmulik said. And? "And." Schmulik shrugged. The chief had said it would be investigated. Months. No word.

The RAF officer had Mati sign in the plane. "A beauty!" Schmulik grinned, leaving the dark subject. And glancing toward Dena; "Both of them! Two beauties you brought back!"

In Nahum's car, it was, Dena see this! See that! Look! Approaching the city, the Hebrew University. A view over the whole of Jerusalem, clustered around the core of crenellated walls. Then, driving closer, the ancient walls themselves; though you knew they weren't the ancient, ancient ones, but Turkish, still, the sight brought a shivery feeling as though you were part of some eternal ongoing. And now Dena saw the faint pinkish sheen of the Jerusalem stone that writers were always describing as an inner golden glow. And also the atmosphere had that peculiar lucidity everyone tried to describe; she was getting it, the feeling of the place was coming over her.

᪥ ᪥ ᪥

Reggie and Maureen had luckily lined up for them a three-room flat with a terrace in what was known as the Professor's Quarter, Rehavia, a new section that was the best place to live; a Keren Kayemeth official was leaving on a yearlong mission to South African Jewry.

And so a life began that proved not so much of a jump as Dena had feared. First of all there were friends, a little ready-made circle, Reggie and Maureen, and from Chicago itself the Rappaports—though older, they were familiar, Horace was setting up a department of education at the Hebrew University—and living practically next door was a Canadian couple, Eddie and Ziona Marmor. Eddie was the reporter who had met the plane and written nearly a whole column about "Jerusalem's Lindy" under the photo of the two of them standing alongside the *Gidon*. "First Flier of Palestine." The picture was in the Hebrew papers, too, and Dena could make out the interview in Hebrew, mostly from what she had read in English: all about Mati's plans for a future airline, and also his appointment as assistant in the economic section of the secretariat.

The first days Mati went off tense every morning as though

expecting this time to encounter some until-now concealed power-ful nullifier in his job, but each afternoon he came home more relaxed; so far everything was going all right. He had feared, she knew, being confronted with some kind of bureaucratic opposite number, Arab or English, who would automatically undermine everything he suggested, but there was only his immediate superior, Perce McCleland, who thought of himself as a technocrat and looked at the whole Palestine problem as though it were a matter of graphs and statistics. He was no dummy either; a baldish gnome, he explained to Mati, if you let yourself get involved with passions and people in a madhouse like Palestine, you'd never get anything through; the slide rule was the only way. Yet he gave Mati the feeling that he was kind of slyly sympathetic to the Jews. Above Perce was the section chief, Andrew Hastings, who just wanted things to run smoothly, and in the secretariat itself was Welby. The department had a floor in an old-time pasha's palace on the Street of the Prophets, there were the usual Arab tea bringers and hallway guards, the atmosphere was really not bad, he would have a car to use for fieldwork, and the High Commissioner, Wauchope, was for once, everybody agreed, really opening things up. He was honestly intent on carrying out the Mandate, Reggie declared, including the part about close Jewish settlement on the land. If economic justification could be shown, a large rise in the immigration quota could be expected this year, for the situation in Germany was sure to pop. Hitler was demanding the chancellorship. His storm troopers were encamped all around Berlin, they outnumbered the German army two to one, that was the Allies' own fault, the army limitation. Only old Von Hindenburg was holding Germany together. Eighty-four and gaga. Hitler would be in power in a few months, Eddie Marmor was sure, one way or another. "A movement that has grown so big can't ebb away without a try for power."

Jerusalem itself—would she really be spending her life here?— was already growing on Dena. Where they lived was perhaps like any professional neighborhood; indeed, Celia Rappaport joked that when they went visiting Horace's colleagues, she thought she was in Chicago's Hyde Park except that you drank tea instead of bathtub gin. But the fascinating thing was, Dena wrote home, that this modern area was only a few minutes from the Old City bazaar full of Arabs with donkeys, and monks and tourists in sun helmets, not to mention the open butcher stalls with flies covering the meat. Also in the midst of all this were the religious Jews on their way to the Wailing Wall, in their fur-trimmed hats and black gabardines with knee breeches and white stockings, like medieval Poland! Mati had led her down some narrow urine-smelling stone steps; she had to have the whole tour, he said, and after passing a couple of bored young British soldiers, you made a turn into a stone-paved alley, with hovels on one side and the high wall on the other. That was it. In front of it, a scattering of those gabardine Jews stood swaying. Dena couldn't get over her feeling of foreignness; what did those Jews have to do with her? And the Wall itself—yes, it did give you one of those antiquity shivers, you stood before the everlasting, but what did those strange Jews have to do with her, what contact could she have with their mentality? Especially when she saw the little boys in the same costumes in miniature, their ear curls down to their shoulders, she just couldn't get the slightest inkling of the psychology of these people. For instance, with the modern world, movies, radio, even here in Jerusalem, how could they get their children to keep on in exactly the same medieval way? Even on the old West Side, around Halsted Street in Chicago, the long beards at least wore American clothes and the boys cut off the funny payess. You knew this type of Jew was disappearing, and you felt a kind of tolerance, even sometimes a sympathetic curiosity. Like peeking into an old shul where you saw fine antique hand-embroidery on the velvet curtain that hung before the Torahs. But here the looks they gave you made you feel your kind were the misplaced ones; it was your kind that would one day disappear.

Mati laughed at her. He didn't mind them, he said with a shrug, they were part of the scenery, like the Arabs. He and his generation hardly went to the Old City; it was handy on Shabbat, when Jewish shops were closed and you could get things in the souk. Also, marketing there was really cheaper.

The regular daily life in the newer part somehow didn't fit in with the romantic idea that you were living in Jerusalem. There was the main shopping street, named Ben Yehuda after the writer who had come even before Mati's family, and decided his children should hear nothing but Hebrew, and thus started the revival of Hebrew as the daily language. But to her surprise even now among the Orthodox, on their own streets, the language you heard was Yiddish. Just like Maxwell Street.

In the center of town it was a medley of languages, mostly

Hebrew. Ben Yehuda Street was only a few blocks long, with clothing and shoe stores, a few cafés, souvenir shops, and then you came to Jaffa Road, at Zion Square, with the big movie theater. Along Jaffa Road, there were a few more blocks of shops, and there was Steimatzky's English bookstore with the latest Maurice Samuel and even Thornton Wilder in the window, and there was the Vienna Café where everybody met, and that was it. The downtown.

At night the Jerusalem streets were deserted; from outside appearances there seemed to be no city life at all. But soon you felt differently about life in Jerusalem; it really bubbled. Visiting, talking, tea and cakes, you got the cakes at Kapulsky's, Maureen instructed her from the start, and these after-dinner café coffee klatches were often quite fascinating since Jerusalem was one of those world cities where everyone from everywhere came through. Really cosmopolitan.

Another aspect was the British. Though they didn't mix too much, still they gave the city a certain tone. Some of the higher-ups, like the Welbys, lived in a fancy section called Katamon, built up by rich Arabs. It was just beyond Rehavia and had magnificent residences, modernish but still with a kind of Oriental touch to them, porches with slender carving-topped pillars, and patterns of green and rose glass in their doors and windows. Arab servants in white jackets or Sudanese wearing the long white galabias with red sashes. These she saw at the Welbys, who soon had them to a Sunday garden tea, where they met other government people on the same level or just a step above Mati; Reggie and Maureen were also invited, there were a few Jewish and Arab judges, and there was Edwin Samuel, called Nebi, the son of the first High Commissioner, Sir Herbert Samuel. Nebi had stayed on in Palestine; he had married into a fourth-generation family of Hebrew scholars, among the first settlers of Tel Aviv, and was ramrod straight like a British officer, only more so. There was a very distinguished elderly Arab, a Nashashibi, whose wife, Mati told her, came from one of the aristocratic Sephardi families; oh, yes, it happened, though even more rarely now than in the old days. And there was a flying officer who kept—quite naturally—asking Mati about his plane, but who also kept giving her the eye. Dena got through the afternoon fine, talking about the wonderful adventures of their flight, and of course, she always had her fascinating amusing Chicago gangster stories.

As for inviting back, Maureen coached her, she wasn't supposed to do anything too soon.

To help in the house she had a Yemenite woman, Ada, and keeping house was full of little problems you could write amusing letters home about. You cooked on Primuses, even in a new apartment like this; a Primus was like a camp stove, a kerosene burner that you had to pump up every few minutes, always expecting it to blow up in your face. The kerosene man came by in the street with a horse-drawn barrel cart; he'd tinkle a bell, or some of them sang out, and you or Ada, the Yemenite girl, would run down with the empty can. Shopping was in hole-in-the-wall groceries, each so crowded with piles of stuff that at most two customers at a time could stand inside. Milk was still ladled out of dairy cans into your jug! Of course, by your second visit the grocer or vegetable man and his wife knew your whole life history, a born-in-America girl! And where in Poland did your family originally come from? The vegetable man's wife gave you special recipes for eggplant and had to know what else you were cooking. This old-fashioned Jewish inquisitiveness annoyed Dena a bit at first; then she felt it was kind of homey, but soon it started to annoy her again. If you asked directions in the street, showing an address, the response would be "Who are you going to see there?" or, "They won't be home at this hour," or even, "What do you want to see them for?"

But as for all the imagined dangers, things were really quiet. In the streets of Rehavia, Arab villagers came with their donkeys laden with fresh vegetables, and they even brought goats to milk right at your back door.

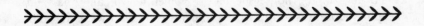

17

THE *Gidon* still sat in the military compound; since there was no
civil aviation director as yet, Mati had to get RAF clearance each
time he took her up. Merely a formality, of course.

He got it for Shabbat. Dena still had to meet the rest of the
family and at last the old man. And besides, at Dvora and Menahem's kibbutz there would be certain people— Yes, she caught on.
Certain people couldn't very well examine the *Gidon* in the RAF
compound in Jerusalem.

This was the very same landing strip that the German fliers had
made, Mati chuckled—the British had had the kibbutz maintain
the strip for emergency use. His sister Shula's golden-haired airman had been stationed here. And as the *Gidon* rolled to a stop,
there was another item that made Mati chuckle: Right there at the
end of the strip stood one of Menahem's road rollers. "What's the
big joke?" Dena demanded.

"Blue movies."

"What?"

"Never mind."

She puzzled. Marseilles, and this was Menahem's kibbutz— To
hell with them with their hush-hush mysteries. A flood of kids was
already around the airplane, with the whole parade of chaverim
approaching, everybody in Sabbath clothes, and Dena was glad she
had worn a cotton frock instead of her flying uniform, so as not to
look too different.

"Don't touch!" Mati admonished the kids, and exchanged happy thumpings with a long-limbed teenager, a nephew named Giora, whom he put in charge of guarding the ship. Then hurrying to them Dena recognized Menahem himself. He'd suddenly come home. The small wrinkle-eyed woman was Dvora. More nephews, nieces, chaverim—she'd never keep them straight. This time he meant to stay put, Menahem said. A fine story, said Dvora. "We're called 'between missions,'" said the first boy, Giora, with a laugh.

All the chaverim were inspecting the airplane, walking slowly around it, in a kind of proprietary way. Some of the kids were trying to climb into the cockpit. "Giora! This is how you watch!" Mati called.

"Then I'm the first you teach to fly!" Giora demanded.

With a shoulder slap, Mati promised.

"He's already built a model," Dvora said. "His whole age-group has gone airplane crazy." Her eyes inspected Dena warmly, but they were the kind of eyes that always had a look of expectant worry.

As they all started back toward the kibbutz, Mati went aside with Menahem. The Marseilles operation had had to be closed up in a hurry, Menahem said. "Don't worry, I got the last shipment onto the boat with me."

On a side lane there stood a dusty Morris; Mati recognized the chief himself getting out; way back in his Herzl Gymnasia days he had run messages for Eliahu. With him was a commander named Gad, one of those types with a perpetually dubious expression. They gave him strong handshakes, a hearty well-done, yet from Eliahu, the perfectionist, Mati felt a touch of reserve. There had been displeasure, Mati already knew, over those arrival pictures in the newspapers. Of course, Eliahu said, Mati was not to blame for the press having been there, and on the whole, it was probably not a bad idea to have the *Gidon* written up as a sports hobby plane, a gift of rich American in-laws. Still, how were they to get hold of it now?

But in the face of the airplane itself even Gad broke into a smile. Giora, left on guard, had climbed up into the cockpit; he grinned a bit guiltily. Keeping the ship on a personal basis, Mati said, there was no reason why he couldn't train a few sports fliers. His own nephew Giora here, for instance. The boy flushed.

Gad grinned. That would be a good one! Even while he worked for the British! Right up their noses!

Eliahu reflected. Naturally Mati could fly here for Shabbat visits. One day a week wasn't much, but it was a start. After all, that was the first objective: to train fliers. Maybe Mati didn't know, but Gad had already got quite a model-building program going in the youth clubs. Yes, Giora was the club leader here.

As Gad and Eliahu took turns climbing up for a look inside, the boy rattled off the names of the instruments for them, altimeter, speedometer, air compass—and this wireless equipment was the latest! He'd studied it in an American magazine!

Eliahu was pleased, as always with eager youngsters.

The situation being comparatively quiet with the Arabs just now, he said, there was no point in exciting them with tales of a Haganah plane at a kibbutz, so it was indeed a good idea to keep the ship for the present in the British compound. . . . And how were things going in Mati's job? Eliahu mentioned a few names in the administration, some useful, some to watch out for. Mati said he always checked with Reggie. Eliahu nodded. Good. Right now, Eliahu said, the Arabs had a real inner struggle going on. The Nashashibis had won most of the town elections, and the Husseinis were out to capture the cities. With immigration from Germany increasing, Haj Amin was sure to start trouble again. One of their preachers in a Haifa mosque was organizing a secret Black Hand society—killers.

Mati offered to take Eliahu up. Why not? But no tricks! The chief had already heard from Dov in London. "You nearly scared the life out of Ben-Gurion!" He gave a dry chuckle.

"What! I flew like carrying eggs!" They climbed in.

Although she had heard endlessly about them and seen all those pamphlets with pictures of earnest kibbutzniks, one question had never left Dena: if Mati would someday decide, could she really live such a life?

Right off she had to admit the kids looked terrific, sturdy, lively, nervy, and who said there was no parental relationship? Of course, this was Shabbat, but in family groups on the lawns, and on porches, parents were with their kids. All right, in America, too, weekends were for the children. As for kids living in age-group houses, it must be like having them in boarding school, only right next door.

The cabins for chaverim had side-by-side rooms, one to a couple, with a communal porch. Even in the newest section, cement instead of wood, the pattern was exactly the same. Toilets and showers outside. Like a summer camp. Sure, she could live simply if she had to, in London they had had the shared toilet, but she guessed she was a city girl. And by now wasn't Mati too a city person? Maybe Mati would always talk about to-hell-with-every-thing and going back to a kibbutz, but she didn't feel much danger of its happening. For a few months at a time, for a vacation, it might be agreeable.

The plane was going up; everyone watched. Whom was Mati taking? Dvora gave her what Dena to herself called "their Haganah look," meaning some things you don't ask about, but Dvora offered, "Someone came especially from Tel Aviv."

The new dwellings were first for the older chaverim, and Dvora and Menahem's room was surprisingly homey: bright hand-woven spreads on the two couches—one of the chaveroth here in the kibbutz loved to weave, Dvora said. There was a wall of books, spaced with bits of ancient pottery. A coffee table with bent-tube chairs—Myra should see this! Bauhaus design, copied right here in the metal shop. A Van Gogh print, the inevitable one of the bridge.

Two doors down, Dvora had borrowed a room for them from a couple away for Shabbat. The same bent-tube chairs and also a Van Gogh print, the self-portrait with the stubbly beard. Didn't any of the couples have double beds? Was this a rule? Dena wondered. But they sure had kids. All at once she recalled Mati's tales of the early hardship times when at kibbutz meetings they would openly debate which couple should be allowed to start a child. Ugh! Like doing it with everybody watching! Suddenly she wondered, had Mati already guessed? Did he keep track of her period? Even in a kibbutz could a woman keep her bit of feminine secrecy? Certain little femininities you wanted to keep to yourself, kind of delicious, and other things you wanted to hide, as with the curse, icky and a little shameful.

The late Saturday breakfast was still going on, and on the way Dvora gestured—over there was her domain, she had to run in for a moment. Dena followed.

The rows of white chickens seemed to stretch to infinity, every year her breed had won first prize, Dvora admitted, and her eyes lighted up as she explained about pounds of feed per pound of meat and the demand for her chicks from all over the Yishuv, moshavim as well as kibbutzim, and the lowest rate of epidemic loss because each bird received Newcastle and other inoculations discovered by a doctor, a veterinarian from Vineland, New Jersey, a good Jew and a Zionist, too, did Dena know about him? Dr. Goldhaft? He was famous all over the world.

Now in the pervading, slightly acrid smell Dena recognized the odor she had noticed coming faintly from Dvora; over the years the good chaverah must have become impregnated with it.

The eating hall too reminded her of a camp or a cafeteria; Dena could see herself taking her Sabbath work turn, her hair in a babushka, pushing the cart with the boiled eggs and the pitchers of milk or cocoa. Dvora apologized for the flies; there were screens, but with the door constantly being opened you couldn't conquer the problem; this new building was better than the old eating hall, but even with a special spring on the screen door still there were chaverim who stood talking holding the door open. The patiently worried look had again come into her eyes, and Dena suddenly wondered about Dvora's whole life.

They heard the plane landing.

The men appeared, Mati looking highly pleased with himself. "He showed Eliahu a few tricks." Menahem laughed as though no secrets need any longer be kept from Dena. "He came down so low over the hayfield I thought he was chopping fodder!"

So that was their hush-hush Eliahu. In London they avoided the name as though the British didn't know who ran the Haganah. Even Dov would speak of him as "the chief." The two of them, Dov and Eliahu, were married to sisters of Moshe Shertok, who, in turn, was married to the sister of another Haganah chief, all one big family, and Dena liked to twit Mati, how come he hadn't become part of it? He was so excited with the big chief's praise, maybe tonight she'd tell him their own secret.

Since Eliahu didn't want the plane to be seen hopping around, to go to Mishkan Yaacov for Dena's already belated meeting with Mati's father, they rode with a truckful of kids being taken to the Kinneret for a swim. The moment the truck started the kids started singing, and they never stopped, from one song to another, all those chalutz songs that Mati had taught his groups in Chicago, and some new clap-hand songs, and there was such a joyousness it got you, it really got you. . . . Hers, too, one day, hers and Mati's—to be happy like this, just naturally happy!

Yankel had been sitting on the bench under the carob tree, and as he heard the truck, he rose slowly on his walking stick. So his godless ones, with their noisy machines tearing the Sabbath to shreds, were doing him the honor of a visit; they'd stop and get off below, arriving on foot so as not to offend an old religious Jew. Never mind that it had taken Mati two weeks to come and show his bride, whom he had married already two years ago in America. Was a father supposed to have beheld her when that flying machine nearly took the chimney off the house? Yet Yankel recalled how this flying passion must have begun with his youngest, his yingel, the little boy standing in this road staring up at the German machine with the flier, the one who had nearly turned Shula's head, thank the Above One she had been saved and had married decently.

Though these days Yankel kept no calves, kept no cattle, not even chickens in the yard since Feigel was laid away, Schmulik's Nussya had prepared a Sabbath feast of tsimmes with calves' meat; at least a good daughter-in-law, better than all his daughters, had been given him. And what would this new one be like? A pretty one, they said, a shaineh; Mati had sent him photographs, and with his enlarging glass Yankel had peered at the Amerikankeh. Nu, perhaps it had all been foreordained, bashert. It had been destined that the older sons should take the boy away and send him to a strange land and there he should rise and one day return like Joseph from Egypt—a British official from London.

So Dena came to the homestead. Compared to what she had imagined from Mati's tales, all seemed shrunken, the house, the village even, and old Abba himself.

The house was more like a hut, a black stone cubicle in an untended, tangled garden, and the old settler stood by the gate like an ancient Jacob, the shrunken old man peering half blind, unable to recognize his sons. No, that blind one in the Bible had been Isaac, she always got them mixed up, but Mati's father thrust his face close to hers, inspecting her with his yellowed eyes, then turning his head to all gathered around. As though making an awaited pronouncement, Mati's father declared, "A shaineh." A beauty.

He was gnarled, and from his Orthodox undervest the fringes, the tsitsit, dangled messily.

Abba wouldn't let anyone help him, he was cantankerous—so said Schmulik's wife, the plump Nussya. She had dolled herself up with her hair primped and too much lipstick and a new-looking dress; Dena complimented her on the dress, and Nussya flushed, saying Schmulik had bought it in Tel Aviv.

Now the old father was trying to make conversation with Mati; it seemed heartbreaking to Dena—out of those shrunken loins all this life had sprung, yet he was lost among his children, what could he talk about to Mati? She had never pictured the progenitor this way, so lost, though Mati had warned her that the old man was a strictly old-style Orthodox Jew. A pretty one, your wife from Chicago, Yankel kept repeating. Then he turned to her. Her own family? From the old country? "Litvaks," Dena said, and he replied, "Ah, we are from the Ukraine." "Galitzianer," she said, to show she was a good Jewish daughter who knew you were either a Litvak or a Galitzianer. And her family in Chicago? Some Jewishness remained? Did her father still go to shul?

To the Reform, she said a bit apologetically, but quickly added, "That's where I met Mati! In the temple!"

"A Reformister," her father-in-law repeated, lowering his beard, but adding, "At least, Jews. Here in Eretz Yisroel we don't have Reformisten temples, a shul is a shul." And with a spark of old cunning, toward Mati: "We have atheisten!" Still, as they had sent him wedding pictures: "At least it was a chupa!" And brightening, he repeated, he confirmed to all, "A shaineh!"

The feast was ready, as in the old days when Ima was alive, the brothers and sisters said, crowding into the dwelling, and Dena saw the old man, with Schmulik's little ones hanging close to his legs, looking proud.

All in these two smallish rooms, here they had all slept. And with the kitchen pump, the great luxury of those early days, still in use! The famous Russian-style oven she had heard about—it made the house an inferno. Nussya was pulling out an enormous iron pot, her cholent. Offering to help, Dena was shooed away with a sweaty smile.

Now at last she met Mati's elder brother, the idealist Reuven, with his wife who had studied piano in Paris, Elisheva. They had just walked over from their kibbutz, bringing their brood, two elfin girls of ten and eight, Kinneret and Yaffaleh, and their twelve-year-old, Noam, solid, round-faced, an image, everyone told her, of Mati right here as a child. Even the baby Zipporah, named after Mati's mother Feigel, had been carried along from the infant house for the occasion.

As Dena had imagined, Reuven had the warmest eyes, dreamy still, a warm brown that gazed into you without intruding. Elisheva wore a yellow cotton dress; her arms were thin, but she didn't look frail, rather New Englandish, with her hair parted and tied in a bun. Oddly she didn't seem like a mother but still virginal. In conversation she had a way of pausing a hardly noticeable instant before each reply. That old piano, Dena asked, that they had brought on a cart all the way from Damascus just after the war? Oh, the piano still existed, though it was quite a wreck! It had been put in a youth house. The kibbutz had bought a new Beckstein; she now was assigned completely to teaching; this year one of her pupils, a very gifted boy, had been sent to the Rubin conservatory in Jerusalem. And in London had they attended the symphony? Had they heard any Sibelius? The longing had momentarily escaped, but her eyes peeped into Dena's with self-humor and discipline. The records Mati had sent them, what perfect selections! She was sure Dena had done the choosing!

At the table the aroma of the tsimmes seemed to bind all of them together and into an older Jewish time, and from this former time Yankel arose to say the blessing over the wine and the challeh and then to add a blessing for the youngest son, who had brought home his bride, and as it was written, might they multiply and increase the House of Israel.

Reuven was already asking Mati about using the airplane for crop dusting; in an American magazine he had read about great progress against certain plant parasites; there were even diagrams of the dusting device, and he was sure the kibbutz mechanics could build one. Still today Mati and Dena must come to the kibbutz; Dena must see his Garden of Eden!

The entire village population kept arriving to behold Mati's bride from America; Schmulik's in-laws, and the mukhtar Brunesco in full suit and cravat, and the girls who once must have had eyes on Mati. Would any of the Arabs come down? Dena wondered. What about that one from the big fight in his boyhood, who had left the knife scar on his back?

They didn't come down much anymore, it seemed, though

Schmulik's father-in-law still dealt in sheepskins with them and had a few working in his tannery. One day Mati would take her up to visit Dja'adi, but today they must go to Reuven's kibbutz.

The rows of cabin dwellings were vine-covered here, though patterned exactly as in Dvora and Menahem's kibbutz. Elisheva and Reuven, however, still had his old upper room in the pumphouse, built when he had started the irrigation system. Now there was a larger pumphouse, so the lower room, with the machinery removed, was the kibbutz music studio. On the walls hung primitive harps they had collected from Bedouin tribes and African drums and masks brought back by a chaver from a mission to South Africa.

Upstairs their whitewashed room gave Dena her first feeling: I could live like this. A few rustic chairs, a tabletop made of colorful Arab tiles, a cruze, a tall black Ali Baba jar. There was quite a good portrait of Elisheva by a chaver, and instead of the usual Van Gogh, a framed reproduction of Lucas Cranach's Adam and Eve, with Eve's curved belly just at the stage where you could believe that pregnant women looked divine.

The Biblical Garden of Eden was between the Tigris and the Euphrates rivers, their girl Kinneret recited, glancing impishly at her abba, and also Adam and Eve had not been Jews. Not yet. But as even the real Garden of Eden was mythological, then perhaps Abba was right, and it could just as well have been here in the Jordan Valley!

And don't forget, her father instructed her, that according to the Arabs, it was near their holy city of Mecca.

But the Bible stories we had already two thousand years before Mohammed and his Koran! Kinneret showed off.

Perhaps they had their myths thousands of years before Mohammed, her abba reasoned.

An enchanting park, everything from a jungle to a laboratory, Reuven had devised. Rivulets from the Jordan had been drawn around an islet, reached by a tiny Japanese-like wooden bridge. Then you entered a density of foliage, broad green fronds, splashes of red oleander, intertwined vines, and miniature clearings cunningly arranged, all vibrating with life. The sounds were as dense around you as the growth: rhythmic chirpings, birdcalls, cooings of turtledoves, a thrumming from beehives, and then chattering—could there be monkeys?

The children laughingly rushed to a broad web of branches; from an interior cagelike arrangement of bentwood, monkey eyes peered. A certain minimal restraint was unavoidable, Reuven regretted the cage, or they'd be all over the meshek.

Enormous lizards, Dena saw, and a pool with swans, and on a flat rock a thick coiled snake. "Don't be afraid," their boy, Noam, assured her, "the big ones are harmless."

A date palm, a species lost to Palestine; Reuven had journeyed all the way to the Euphrates to bring back the seedling. This was the male, he said. Why, she had not even known that palm trees were male and female. Oh yes, Reuven said, and told an ancient rabbinical tale about a female palm, here, close to Tiberias, that when grown had begun to lean toward Jericho, yearning for a certain male tree that was there, and she did not bear fruit until pollinated from that longed-for mate. How sweet and romantic Reuven was, yet not entirely a dreamer, for the kibbutz palm grove was already quite profitable, he said, and indeed one of Elisheva's younger brothers had transferred from Damascus to Eretz and established a branch of the Shalmoni date exporting business in Haifa, because of the excellent fruit growing all down the Jordan Valley, from Reuven's imported stock.

On a knoll stood a pomegranate tree, the first Dena had ever seen. The pomegranate was most likely the tree of Eve and the serpent, Reuven said, since the European apple had not been known.

When they all started back, Dena wanted to stay a bit; the garden was now practically deserted.

Lingering by the pomegranate, she herself was Cranach's rounded Eve, and standing here, Dena experienced the strangest reaching back, like some faint, faint signal from prememory.

Was this the mysterious sense of coming home that she had again and again been told about, the inexplicable feeling people said they had had, usually on their first going up to Jerusalem? An eerie sense of something other than you had ever felt, something in the very air you breathed. But instead of the headiness of Jerusalem's atmosphere, here the air was dense, perfumed; she was utterly at peace. For one instant her hand had a reaching impulse, as though to grasp Mati's, he should be here for this moment with her, but then she was content that all this had happened to herself alone. With his impregnated seed within her.

She would have wanted to stand here as in the Cranach, naturally naked. To slip off her dress, to feel the warm enveloping air and the timelessness enveloping her being, to feel herself in Eden, a pagan, before Jews were Jews. Maybe in a few months she would come and stand here, a woman with her lovely pomegranate-curved belly, under the tree of Eve.

After the evening meal Menahem said to Dena with a twinkle, "You want to see the blue movies? Come."

Across the yard he rolled open a high iron door, and there in the machinery workshop under a dangling bulb stood another roadroller, a huge one, with youngsters working around it. "How's it going?" Menahem called out.

Everything was okay. "Ha-kol b'seder." Two lads were pulling objects out from inside. It took Dena a moment to comprehend; the long dark objects were rifles. A few more boys and a girl squatted on stools, scraping off the grease. With a rhythmic clanking they checked the bolt action of each gun; then they passed the weapons farther back where she saw a pair of arms reaching up from a sump hole. She made out the head of Menahem's boy Giora; the rifles disappeared below. Dena already knew the word, a slick it was called.

There was still a large shipping sticker, Marseilles, on the up-ended roller. Menahem had that clever look in his eye, and she hoped he wouldn't again mention blue movies. He was smiling almost paternally at her, as when adults let you into the secrets of life. So he and Mati, on that night in Marseilles, must have seen to the packing of this stuff; now Mati received a lumpy package into his hands. Unwrapped, there was a machine gun. His. For the *Gidon*.

But since she had known the whole idea of the plane all the time, why did she now feel a shudder?

The kids all gathered, marveling. They had slang Hebrew words, but she caught the drift, the gun's firepower, accuracy—how much these kids knew. Prima! they cried. They worked on, with snatches of song; the camel song she already knew but they had a parody, instead of "Camel, camel mine, you are my pal divine, ziv-ziv!" one boy was singing "Rifle, rifle mine, you are my pal divine, boom boom!"

Once at the university, looking for a boy she knew in the medical school, she had opened a lab door and unexpectedly seen before her a group dissecting a cadaver. And now, as then, Dena had the impulse to babble, "Excuse me," and flee.

But now, as then, she was seeing nothing she had not already known of. Hadn't she married a boy whose one craze was to bring home an airplane to add to their arsenal, and hadn't she flown here with Mati on that plane? All this was simply a part of the life here. Here? Suddenly Dena recalled in childhood, when they had lived over the Halsted Street store, one night the alarm waking her and the whole family and how she stood with Ma by the hall door watching her pop and Phil with revolvers in their hands creeping down the stairs. Thank God it had been a false alarm. Where, at home, had they kept the guns hidden?

Menahem, still gazing at her, had a melancholy touch of a smile: the American girl getting her initiation.

Would all this still be necessary here when her child was grown? And all over the world?

How naïve could she be? Dena told herself and returned Menahem's gaze firmly.

"Tired?" Mati asked.

Well, it was a big day.

A bit hesitantly he began to undress at the other couch. She too undressed. But then he came over to her; Dena drew him down. Mati seemed a bit uncertain. "I kind of thought you?" So he did keep track.

She smiled and said, "I'm late."

"Oh?"

Then she told herself this was the moment. "Darling, on the island I took a chance."

Mati held her, long, tight, in the kind of pure-love kiss of before they had ever done it. "Maybe I'm just late from all the flying, all the excitement," Dena said.

"Oh, no!" Then he seized her, the Mati, the chalutz from Palestine pulling her out of Chicago!

In a pause Mati laughed, raising his head, singing the tune of that Rabbi Hillel song, but instead of the words "If not now, then when?" he sang out, "If not then, then now!"

It was wilder, different from on the island. If there had remained any uncertainty, this was for sure! In between he went and pulled over the other couch, to make one bed. So that was how it was done in a kibbutz.

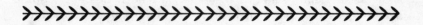

18

IMMEDIATELY after the Reichstag voted absolute power to the new Chancellor there came pictures of Jews, prodded by laughing brownshirts, clawing off communist posters from Berlin walls. The captions mentioned acid poured into the scrubbing water, for their torn hands, a Nazi joke.

Also pictures of smashed shopwindows, the jagged holes right through the smeared-on "Jude" star. And synagogues hooliganized. And tales of street beatings.

Then came edicts eliminating Jewish judges, officials, lawyers, journalists, professors, actors, and musicians from their professions. The press described scenes of Jewish lawyers and judges being herded into garbage trucks and hauled to Gestapo headquarters for hours of insults and beatings. Long queues waited outside the Berlin offices of the Jewish Agency, to apply for Palestine visas.

"Didn't you know, Hitler is really a secret Zionist agent?" became the inescapable jest at the office. Yet Mati could feel a growing tautness among the British—if this Hitler fellow was really going through with his program on the Jews, what about his other bellicose promises? How long before rearmament and war?

Word came of thousands of young German Jews suddenly rushing into the Blau-Weiss Zionist movement; it seemed the Nazis had no objection; indeed, they even permitted training farms to be expanded. Instructors were dispatched to Germany; they were received "correctly."

Deep in paperwork over new projects, chemical plants, pharmaceuticals, subsistence farms for middle-aged professionals, Mati felt at last in his life things were falling into place, his studies had prepared him to put such plans into Colonial Office terms, to prove "economic absorptive capacity" by his own assortment of charts and statistics, and thanks to Ben-Gurion, he had been fitted into this slot where he could feel himself of use at just the right time. Though he occasionally had to play the devil's advocate and question the wild development schemes that Reggie brought over from the Agency for him to push through the secretariat, there came at other times a peculiar satisfaction in putting Yishuv ideas into a kind of quasi-colonialist formulation that slid comfortably into the British mind. Categories. Laborers and capitalists. Here he was, a born and bred laborite, a socialist, yet doing his utmost to slip masses of applications into the capitalist category, which was virtually unlimited. Already the Arab press was demanding that the thousand-pound minimum for a capitalist at least be doubled, and the transfer of funds from Germany became more and more difficult. In Reggie's department at the Agency, a whole plan was evolved for the transference of goods and machinery instead of funds, and all this Mati presented as the equivalent of capital, stimulating commerce and industry, benefiting both Arab and Jewish sectors of the population.

From the Agency, a brilliant young economist, Chaim Arlosoroff, hardly older than Mati but already at the top, went to Germany to negotiate. Now arose a great outcry about trading with the worst enemy of the Jews. Every night the flat resounded with arguments. Reggie was for it. Hadn't Theodor Herzl himself thirty years ago gone to St. Petersburg to see the Czar's "Minister of Pogroms," Plehve, pleading, "We'll get rid of your Jews for you," so as to get czarist support for Zionism? True, the sale of German machinery and goods in Palestine would benefit Hitler's economy, but in a small way, what could it all amount to, the main thing was it would help the Jews. Logically, Mati had to agree, yet the idea stuck in his craw.

One thing was clear: The German Jews were finished; they had to get out, a half million people—but how could the Yishuv with only a quarter of a million Jews ever absorb them? All right, for many, maybe most, the choice was America, but America's quotas were soon filled. And on top of the German Jews, who mostly had some means, there was the crisis of Polish Jewry; in Lodz half the

271

textile workers were unemployed, tens of thousands were actually starving, and these were good socialists, good Zionists, except for their Labor Bund radicals, who had always spit on Zionist "nationalism, chauvinism, and colonialism!"

It was enough to keep a fellow awake all night trying to devise ideas, projects for rapid agricultural and industrial expansion.

Since Reggie was virtually Mati's opposite number in the Agency, the couples were constantly coming over to each other, Dena and Maureen discussing their pregnancies—for Maureen was two months ahead of her—while the boys sat fitting together absorption schemes. How could the Yishuv absorb swarms of middle-aged lawyers who, even if they knew some English, had no knowledge of Hebrew or of the crazy Palestine legal system that was still partly Turkish, mingled with British common law and with Jewish and Moslem religious law?

And professors? Retraining perhaps, as auto mechanics, radio repairmen? While Mati and Reggie explored every possibility, from mink farms—furs in a hot climate?—to strawberries, Maureen and Dena would jest that they too were busy with their own population increase—"interior immigration," as it was called, aliyah pnimit.

On their Shabbats in Gilboa now, once he had finished giving flying lessons, Mati had evening sessions with Dvora about mechanized poultry raising adapted down to family scale. Added to his nephew Giora, who had already soloed, a natural flier, three more kids were learning on the *Gidon*. Luckily Mati could stay over on Sundays, too. For Dena staying idle on Shabbat was okay as everyone was resting, but on Sundays she felt like a parasite. So Dvora took her to the poultry house, where there was a task especially suited for pregnant chaveroth, you could do it sitting down and work as long as you liked.

Surrounding a long tin-topped table, the women sat, candling eggs, sorting, packing. Two more pregnant girls were there, both far more advanced than she; the rest were quite elderly, for a number of the kibbutzniks had brought over their parents from the old country. A beady-eyed chaverah demanded of Dena, did she speak Yiddish?

"A little," Dena said. "But I understand." Alas, here she had planned to practice her Hebrew.

The attack began. An Amerikankeh?

One of the pregnant girls explained, "She's Dvora's brother Mati's wife, from Chicago."

Aha. A fine young man, Mati. And she was really a born Amerikankeh?

True.

Miracles never cease! A born Amerikankeh marries a sabra and comes to live in Eretz! Did she know it was usually the other way around? The American flapperkehs would come here, find themselves husbands, and pitch-patch! They took the boys off to live in America!

"That's the kind of boys you raise here?" Dena retorted.

"Oh, not by our kibbutz!" declared the grandmother. "But it happens, it happens."

"Well, you see with us it happened the other way," said Dena.

The old woman smiled knowingly. "Wait, wait till your time comes. Then arrives a telegram from your mama in America, 'Come quick to an American hospital! The ticket is on the way!' "

Dena joined in the laughter.

Now a second old lady, with bobbed gray hair, using Hebrew, announced that she had read a statistical article: in America all Jewish girls went to college so they could meet shkotzim and marry non-Jewish.

Again Dena laughed. "I went to college, and here I am."

Shaking her head authoritatively, the chaverah, named Bella, replied, "One case like you, it doesn't count. An exception. You met a boy like Mati, you couldn't help yourself, you fell in love." They all glowed. She raised an admonishing hand, holding an egg. "In America Jews have to change their names to get into college. In America there is a numerus clausus from the anti-Semites, just like in the czarist days in Russia!" Why didn't America take in the German Jews from Hitler? They had a quota, Jews unwanted. At least now everything was clear, no more bluffing.

Dena tried to explain. Yes there were anti-Semites in America, too, but—

"You see! She has to admit it! Wait, wait, it can even come there like in Germany—"

"No!" Dena cried. Why, in Washington, President Roosevelt had all kinds of Jewish experts high in the government—

"Roosevelt?" With her knowing eyes, her air of having better information than you, Bella declared, "Yes, Jewish brains, a few Jewish experts Roosevelt has there, but in the American diplomatic service there are Jews? In the Morgan banks you find Jews?" Wait, wait, Dena would see; in America, too, Jews were finished!

"Hold on, don't finish them yet, Bella, we need their money!" the young one, Batya, rescued Dena laughingly.

Now Dena and Batya had to stand up side by side, and the women examined them. Batya's belly swelled lower down—that meant a boy, Bella declared. Dena—a girl.

After supper, while Mati sat on with Dvora over poultry calculations, Dena strolled with Menahem back to their dwelling; he brought out a flask of Courvoisier that he had carried home from Marseilles. And just as in Marseilles, Dena felt from him that peculiar older-man charm, as from a Claude Rains. Then how was it going between her and Mati? he asked.

Wonderfully.

In the souk she had found herself a lovely loose Arab dress, which flowed but nevertheless showed the curve. A fantasy arose, the game every girl had with herself: With him, could I? Not now, of course, but— A strange man, Menahem. So many languages, all self-taught. On his bookshelves, in English, he had Galsworthy, Bernard Shaw. But also she had spotted *Lady Chatterley's Lover*; in German he had Kant and Hegel and Karl Marx, of course, and Freud's analysis of dreams; there were Russian volumes as well, and among the titles of his Hebrew books she read the names of the poets Bialik and Tchernichovsky, there were some Talmudic-looking tomes, and he had a set of Sholem Aleichem in Yiddish. Also in English, Trotsky's *My Life*, and the poems of Rabindranath Tagore. French books too, Voltaire and Anatole France and Rabelais.

He was a man who could kill; he had deliberately carried out an execution; she knew that way-back story from Mati, the ambush of the two Arab murderers. To take aim and kill a specific person— that was different from in a war, firing at the opposite trenches.

He had that way of fixing his eyes in yours, so that even to a routine question like "How are you?" you felt you had to give a real answer. But also Dena had a feeling that if she had trouble, this was the person she would come to. Perhaps because Menahem was more a man of the outside world, a cosmopolitan, with all his missions for the Haganah; he would see things not in the narrowness of the Yishuv, but in all their ramifications. Yet wasn't he too a fanatic of the movement?

274

She was at last, she told him, really getting that Jerusalem feeling; yes, she liked the life. She was becoming involved in the committee for a symphony orchestra. Some of the best German musicians were already being lined up by Bronislaw Huberman. Her main problem, Dena said with a laugh, was that everybody she met in Jerusalem spoke English, so she really was not getting anywhere with her Hebrew. Even with Mati it was a habit from the start; they talked in English.

"Wait, wait!" And his eyes appreciated her Cranach curve. "A little child shall teach you!" They laughed. Then Menahem added, "You don't feel it will be strange, Dena?"

"How do you mean?" Though she knew what he meant.

"That your child shall be a Hebrew child?"

"Oh." How had he sensed that she sometimes wondered about this? More than Jewish, which was natural, but Hebrew. "You know what every girl dreams—that a stranger from a faraway land will come and carry her away. So that's how I got here. I'm very romantic."

"Is it only romance?" Menahem asked. Didn't we all somehow believe in a fated one, a destined one? In every folklore you found this, and it was embedded quite strongly in Jewish belief, the idea of the bashert, the destined one. The Hasidim, for instance, believed literally in souls that were predestined for each other, and had tales of how such souls sought each other out from opposite ends of the earth.

In Chicago Dena had thought that all Orthodox Jews were the same, but since coming to Jerusalem, she knew there were two main factions among the long-coats, the Hasidim and the Opponents. The Hasidim believed in miracles, in reincarnation, they were more mystical, and the old-line scholars were the Opponents. Menahem in his yeshiva days had been in the midst of the great dispute. Still, it was curious, she said to him, that with all their belief in predestined soul mates and marriages made in heaven, the Hasidim, like the Opponents, depended on matchmakers and family arrangements.

"And their rabbi," he said. It was to the sage, the tsadik, that the Hasid went when deciding on a match for his child. For besides the matchmaker with his human wisdom, it was through the sage with his closeness to divine intention that the bashert could be recognized, rather than through the romantic impulse of a young boy or girl.

Their eyes were smiling into each other's, as when something other than what you are saying is being communicated. He would be going away again, Menahem remarked. Fairly soon.

Could she know where?

Poland. Poland was the problem, with six times as many Jews as in Germany. Not professors and merchants; in Poland the masses of Jews were plain impoverished workers, the proletariat.

She knew. And Polish anti-Semitism. Worse than the Nazis, if possible.

With the Poles it was in their blood. They needed no propaganda. It was why he himself had run away.

She had thought he was from Russia?

Poland, Russia—the Jewish heartland, that whole in-between area that kept changing hands between Poland and Russia in the last centuries. The Czars had called it the Pale of Settlement, where Jews were permitted to reside.

Yes, from childhood she recalled hearing of the Pale. Then in a way he would be going back home?

Home? Menahem shrugged.

Did he still have family there?

Long ago he had lost all contact; he guessed perhaps his stepmother was still alive, some half brothers.

In a way it had always been unclear to Dena who Menahem was. A half orphan, he had gone off wandering, from a stepmother's home; after he married Dvora, the Chaimovitch family really became his family, and she thought of him completely as one of them. The same in a way with Leah's Natan. The family drew you in. Was it the family or because all was part of the movement here? Was it happening to her?

There was a crisis in Poland, he told her, because with the endless waiting for immigration certificates, some of the chalutz youth were being attracted either to the dissidents, Jabotinsky's extremists, or else to the Bund.

The Bund she knew was the Jewish Socialist Bund; even when Leah had visited Chicago, there had been "trouble with the Bundists." Old radical union leaders on the West Side, who were against Zionism and who made a big to-do for Yiddish as against Hebrew.

The Bund was very strong in Poland, Menahem explained. And young people were impatient. At the current rate of certificate allocation it would take a hundred years to get all the chalutzim admitted here! So some gave up and decided to become part of the socialist movement in Poland, and others turned to Jabotinsky's Revisionists who were promising illegal immigration, using small boats, forged certificates, any means at all to get here. Fake marriages. Well, the regular Zionists did that, too—boys going back from here to marry girls and bring them back as their wives, and vice versa. Usually they got divorced on arrival. And went back to get remarried, he chuckled. Then also, the illegal ships, with their difficult secret landings. It couldn't be left to the Revisionists alone.

So some of these things he would be doing. It was like that night here at the kibbutz when Menahem had let her see the unpacking of the guns. Like the time once with Myra in a sociology course, their study group went through a Negro slum on the near South Side and you caught a glimpse of the shivery underside of life, the way people really lived, the way things really were. Of course, Mati was in on these secrets, but stationed in a British job, he had to be supercareful and even at home didn't discuss them much. And oddly, with him she didn't get the feeling of it all as with Menahem. Also probably because Mati had never himself been part of that other life, the "real" Jewish life in Eastern Europe.

Now Menahem was philosophizing. Just as in the idea of the fated, the destined one, in love, you also had to wonder, was there a fatedness in all things? It was not uncommon in our lives, Menahem said, to feel ourselves to be instruments. Most of life was routine—the trucking of milk, one chaver could do as well as another—but at other times we could become instruments. Think of this whole movement, Menahem said to her, the return of the Jews. Though it had been attempted again and again in previous centuries, with masses of people following one false Messiah after another, the impulse to return remained like some organic process that now was at last working itself out, "history" working itself out, and certain individuals were seized upon by history itself to serve the process. That was what gave us the sense of fate, of destiny.

His eyes had remained fixed in hers, but all the earlier man-woman atmosphere had dissolved into some pure intensity of human contact. In mystic lore, Menahem said, in the Cabala, and in all speculation about God and the universe, from ancient times until now, there came the same conception—emanations from a godhead. Divine intention, transmuted through mankind.

Was Menahem, the versatile, the practical, after all a mystic? Mati had told her about the time Menahem sat hidden in the cave

277

above Mishkan Yaacov, when the Turks were hunting down the men of the Shomer. But Menahem now was telling her how in endless solitude in that cave he had one day been visited by the prophet Elijah. Menahem's lips took on a tinge of a smile, a rationalist's acknowledgment of just how irrational such a tale must appear. Elijah had come to the cave and declared that Menahem must go forth in the world and bring Jews to Eretz.

Of course, he should attribute his vision to the strain of his fearful isolation. And perhaps to his early years at the yeshiva.

After a silence, but as though between them there was now a special intimacy—as though, Dena suddenly realized, they were a man and woman who had just made love, Menahem said, "You know, Denatchka, this vision of Elijah—I can't explain why, but I never before told it to anyone. Not even Dvora."

She felt shivery.

Then something of pure unphysical love went through her, a sweep of happiness. She rose and quickly kissed his forehead, the kiss of innocence of man and woman before the Fall.

Menahem went on in a quieter way; he told of the mission with Leah during the Russian Revolution, bringing out a shipful of Jews from Odessa. And of his last mission in Europe, for arms. How to smuggle them in? He didn't know what had led him to walk in those back streets of Marseilles where he had stumbled on the junkyard and seen a broken old road roller standing there.

Then he rose and put away the brandy bottle.

Mati and Dvora came back.

❦ ❦ ❦

The joke was that it was indeed an American obstetrician who would deliver her, not in Chicago's Mount Sinai but in Jerusalem's Hadassah Hospital.

Dr. Eppie—Alvin Epstein—was a godsend, Dena told Mati, for not only had he been at the top of his class and interned at the New York Lying-In, but he could explain in English, he had quick small hands, and he didn't paw you! That snuffy Polish professor she had first gone to—he pawed, could you imagine! Every time she came back from him, Dena complained. And Mati only laughed.

Eppie was straight from Brooklyn, and when he finished with his internship, he had discovered that the Depression was not yet over, so, though not a hot Zionist himself, he explained, his sister, president of her Hadassah chapter, had convinced him why not Jerusalem? Why not?

Long before Dena went to the hospital, she and her friends were scheming up matches for him, the joke being, after all, an obstetrician was not so likely to marry one of his patients!

In her last waddly phase she was so big and blotched Dena worried Mati might be disgusted, though there were plenty of other reasons for his sudden temper outbursts, and Mati himself told her here in the East men were supposed to be especially hot for pregnant women; in fact, certain prostitutes made it a specialty and kept themselves perpetually in condition! Besides, Mati certainly wasn't keeping Dena deprived; in fact, as she confided to Maureen, she got a kind of "double kick" out of it herself. And Dr. Eppie discreetly let drop that you could keep on practically to delivery time if you were careful about the position. He even made a crack about did she want to use the latest ambulance he was ordering; it had a double bed.

No, Mati's mood had nothing to do with her. It was the damn office; they had suddenly brought in a statistical specialist, a Scotsman, Dr. Hugh Aylesworth, who double-checked man-hour calculations according to the Taylor efficiency system, as though they were trying to arrive at how few men to employ instead of how many.

On top of this was Mati's old flying itch. Suddenly everybody was starting airlines; a Polish promoter announced grandiose plans and actually flew into a Palestine a two-engine airship with a British crew; they were going to fly to the Red Sea and bring back fresh fish for the Tel Aviv market. Meanwhile, Dov came with news that Rutenberg was actually starting his airline, he was buying the two six-seaters and would connect up with Imperial Airways and was looking around for a manager, even saying Mati had walked out on him in London! What was Mati supposed to have done, waited without a job until Rutenberg was good and ready? Should Mati perhaps leave his government job now and try to go back and get in with the outfit? No, not now, Dov advised against it, Mati had to stay right where he was; the labor quota for this year was the largest ever, and part of it was surely his doing. Besides, it might take another year before Rutenberg's company got started, and as far as the idea of a Haganah plane, Dov doubted the two goals could be combined.

When the Polish fish flight crashed in the Sinai mountains, in spite of sympathy for the dead pilot, Dena told Maureen she secretly yelled hurrah, because Mati's temper improved. All those wild operators with their crazy schemes and their foreign pilots. The first thing to do was still to train boys from the Yishuv.

Another thing that brought tension to the house, Dena said, was the way his brother Schmulik would drop in whenever he took a notion to come to Jerusalem and—the way people did here—would offhand decide to stay overnight, flopping on the couch. Once he arrived right in the middle of a dinner party she was giving for a visiting British lecturer on James Joyce; Schmulik ambled through the living room and parked himself on the cot on the balcony, she could have killed him. But besides Schmulik considering this his Jerusalem home, he always put Mati in a black mood, pushing him to find out more about the death of Gidon. It was all hopeless, Mati had told her. Schmulik had some idea that among the English, in the CID, they really knew who had come in the Arab car that day. Schmulik couldn't wipe the subject off his mind; it kept burning him; he suspected it was this Fawzi they had known as kids and who was with the Mufti's gang. Mati had to keep promising Schmulik that he was going after the information.

At last, now that she was really huge, Mati told Schmulik he would be using the couch himself. Things got easier, and they even went back to the naming game. The whole bunch joined in, and some nights it went from the sublime to the ridiculous. Ziona and Eddie Marmor would come over with Reggie and Maureen, and Eddie would make crazy teasing suggestions like Lancelot for a boy and Guinevere for a girl. Dena offered such names to Maureen, who was due any day now, but Maureen said, no, thank you, she was all set with Solomon or Sheba.

It was amazing how Maureen didn't even waddle. The tennis, Maureen said. Seriously—Ziona resumed—a name was very important psychologically for the child. "Yeah, look at hers!" Eddie said. He had met Ziona in Nahalal when he went there to do a story about the cooperative village contrasted with the kibbutz. Well, sure he liked her name all right, he loved it—something like Britannia, what? Eddie fended off a book she was slamming on his head.

In Hyde Park High, Dena recalled, she and the girls used sometimes to talk about names for their kids; you could always tell what a girl was like by the name she chose, especially for a girl. The favorite was Norma, like Norma Shearer. Beautiful and high-tone. Yah? said Eddie. That was when all the Jewish boys were being named Norman.

And Mortimer!

A name, Reggie said, why shouldn't it be after someone you admire the most in the world?

For a man, Dena said, Franklin D. Roosevelt! For a woman she oddly couldn't think of anyone right off, she certainly wasn't going to say Madame Curie, what was her first name, Marie? Then Sarah Bernhardt came to her mind, but no, not Sarah! As for the man you most admired, Reggie said, maybe Einstein? Albert? It sounded like smoking tobacco, Dena said. Mati came out with Gandhi. What! And not Ben-Gurion? they teased him.

Suddenly Eddie got analytical and declared, as if he were writing an article, there were three factors that influenced people in choosing a name. First was perpetuation—in all cultures, naming the child after a deceased relative. That was of course an old Jewish custom. Thank the Lord, Dena thought, Mati's mother had already been taken care of. Reuven and Elisheva's youngest was called Zipporah, after Feigel. Imagine calling a girl Birdie! And Schmulik had Gidon. Then, secondly, said Eddie, there were very often animal names, like totems, Dov for bear and Tsvi for deer, Aryeh for lion, and so on. But what he had noticed among Hebrew names was how many names had God in them, using both of the God names in the Bible, Yahu—he is God—and Eli—my God. It certainly gave you a picture of a powerfully cultish society. For instance, Eliyahu—that had both names, "my God is God," to play it safe. And look at Mati's name—Matityahu—what Yahu has given. Or Elimelech—God is king. And Jonathan—Ya natan—God gave.

The idea was kind of fascinating, and Dena found herself following it through: Adoniyah—my lord is God. Of course, God was for men. With women? There was Rachel. Soft, compassionate is God. What did her own name mean, Dena? Na-a, pleasant. But what a horrible story, Dena in the Bible! Ugh.

Oh, Lord, Maureen said, why not just pick a name that sounded nice, a flower for a girl, a brave name for a man, and Mati said, why not simply Adam or Eve! Why not! Dena suddenly agreed. But then she said no, if it was a girl, she wanted Lilith, the wicked one!

281

He gave her a look, his old look of right from the start; yes, blotchy and bloated, she was still cute to him!

Maureen had a difficult delivery, seven hours, but kept refusing to take anything, and never screamed—that's the English way, she told Eppie, digging her nails into her palms. A girl—six pounds. And at the last moment she changed her mind about the name, and Reggie agreed—they changed from Sheba to Batsheba. Reggie said he already felt incestuous, he longed to see his naked daughter combing her hair on the roof.

A complete unit of Polish glider experts arrived, including an actual professor of aerodynamics, and Dov even persuaded the British to authorize a glider training center. The *Gidon* could be used to pull gliders into flight; thus, the simplest idea, Dov said, would be for Mati to "sell" the *Gidon* to the school. Then it could be fully and freely utilized.

For two piasters, Mati declared, he would quit his damn job and do the flight training himself! Impossible, they both knew; Ben-Gurion would never allow it! "Economic absorption" had to be doubled this year. So Mati would drop word among the British that with the baby coming he was selling his sports plane to buy a family car.

His nephew, Dvora and Menahem's boy Giora, was taking special instruction in aerodynamics while responsible for mechanical maintenance of the airplane. Thus, the *Gidon* would still be in the family.

Just then, too, Mati's American kibbutz arrived, and this raised his spirits. One thing he had done that couldn't be taken away from him!

They were mostly, Dena saw, that bunch from the West Side in Chicago, real hot young Zionists; oh, she wasn't being a snob; after all, wasn't she living in Eretz and being active on the symphony orchestra committee, and Hadassah's new hospital project, and all the rest! But something about the eager-beaver attitude of those kids had always annoyed her, and especially there was one girl with large thyroid eyes who had always drooled at Mati; once or twice in Chicago Dena had met Mati at their group session and seen this one with her mouth half open actually twitching in her chair. The little bitch had changed her name from Betty to Batya, and it was she who came with a second chaverah to Jerusalem to announce that their bunch—the American kvutsa—had arrived. Just when Dena was looking her most blotchy and horrible. The second girl, a nice serious one named Malka, at least had her own fellow, though even in Chicago Dena had at times wondered whether Malka wasn't really the type for Mati, better than herself. Dena had an aunt named Malka and had always thought it was a Yiddish name until she learned in Hebrew it meant queen. Malka's fellow, Dave Margolies, was head of the kvutsa, mukhtar they already called him, he came hurrying along a few minutes later— red tape at the Jewish Agency, he explained, but since Mati had warned them he had known what to expect. This Dave had a straight face but with a kind of comical eagerness, a bit like Harold Lloyd. He and Malka were now married, chupa and all, they said with an apologetic laugh—you know, the folks, and going away.

Malka and Dave had already adopted the attitude of sneering at all things American. Roosevelt, sure, a great help—to the capitalists! And when she tried to be nice about their coming here, Dave said, "It's better than the WPA!"

As they were leaving, Betty-Batya had to drool, "Congratulations on your aliyah-pnimit!"

But twins! Though because of her bigness they had speculated, it was still a surprise; Eppie hadn't been able to detect a double heartbeat. The first weighed just under six pounds, and the second popped out, Eppie said, like an afterthought, less than five. Two boys! She was fully awake; no twilight sleep unless it got really terrible, Dena had decided—if Maureen could do it, she could do it!

It wasn't so terrible, and she wouldn't have missed this even if it was torture on the rack! Names for two boys they hadn't even thought of! At least no one would want her to call them Cain and Abel or Jacob and Esau or Isaac and Ishmael! And suddenly Dena remembered way back, almost the first time they had met, a discussion, was it Mati with Rabbi Mike? about this curious succession of quarreling brothers in the Bible. Oh, no, not hers; at least nowadays parents knew something about psychology!

Eppie showed them to her like a flash in a movie, with Mati all but crowing cockadoodledo! What was that in Hebrew? Kookara-coo! And why was it that with twins the papa went silly proud, while the mama was looked at more like a cow? Also, why were boy twins the supreme achievement and girl twins just something extra cute? Even here with all their boasted women's equality! And now Dena laughed in herself. Because that old high school flame of Mati's, Zippie, with her rich orange-grove husband, was outdone! She had had twins, but only one was a boy, so Mati was the cock of the walk! Nor could Dena suppress, or even want to suppress, the glee of achievement, just plain primitive, henlike pride, she herself wanted to cackle cockaroocoo!

Mati actually yipped, the moment they let him in, that yip-yip-yippee yell, a hora leader leaping into the air, as he had done in the basement social hall of the temple the first night she saw him, this wild boy from Palestine! Imagine winding up with him here! "Hey," Eppie was joking, "what about calling them Laurel and Hardy?"

They decided on David and Jonathan.

Cables came from Chicago until she felt embarrassed before the nurses. Pop had set up a college fund! And bang! The whole family was coming. Sherrill cabled, WALGREEN'S HAS BIG TWO-FOR-ONE INFANT WEAR SALE! Imagine Sherrill buying at Walgreen's! From Myra came a huge bouquet—flowers by cable to Jerusalem! Aristocrats knew how to do things. But all of Dena's thoughts were really on her breasts. If only they wouldn't droop. Big ones usually did afterward. They were a perfect fit for Mati's hands, and he used to joke, that was why God had made men with two hands! Dr. Eppie told her to nurse for a start, why should women deprive themselves of their greatest sensual pleasure, and that little Brooklyn doc really knew! When she had one at each breast the sensation was like in her imagination in lovemaking when Mati was kissing a nipple and she let herself perversely imagine an unbearable double thrill of both being kissed at the same time.

And at Mati's office, the lady secretaries arched their brows and jested about having him demonstrate his prowess, provided the results were guaranteed. And his family! The son everyone had always said would do big things! Well, it was silly, just a common happening in nature, but it did make a man feel proud.

Maureen had to be the first to cry "The briss!" Though in Chicago it was done at the hospital, Eppie assured her that certain mohels here in Jerusalem were at least as expert as the surgeons. So why not give old Abba Yankel the joy? Nahum drove him up; the entire family crowded the flat; Yankel sat enthroned in their big chair and held each babe for a few moments, uttering the blessing. At least, Dena said, she had had a good look the first moment they were presented to her in the hospital, as she had never before seen an uncircumcised one! Jonathan gave a few yips, more of surprise and indignation than pain; Eppie had assured her the infants couldn't feel it. David uttered not a sound. The boys really had their individual characters, from the start!

Mati in one of his wild bursts of exuberance had invited the entire office, and they came, including the Welbys, also two very nice Arabs, Christians from Abu Ghosh, whom Dena hadn't met before, and smiling Dov Hos arrived, bringing a bright-colored pair of paper airplanes to dangle over the crib. Even Ben-Gurion appeared for a moment with his Paula, who gave Dena innumerable instructions and commands on infant care; after all, she was a trained nurse from New York. Presently Leah had to stand guard at the bedroom door so Dena and the babies could breathe.

There came a letter with Polish stamps from Menahem. The big news had even reached Warsaw, he said, so he was drinking a double l'chayim! To Dena he enclosed a special little note: since young mothers were the most radiant of women, he dreamed of beholding her in her double glory. "He's an old devil, that Menahem of yours," she told Mati, but wouldn't show Mati what he'd written. The letter itself went on with items in that supposedly secret code of theirs that any dumb CID man could surely understand. The sports clubs, Menahem wrote, were looking forward to a boating excursion in the spring. Menahem himself was doing errands for Uncle Eliahu. Mati naturally read this as meaning Eliahu, the Haganah chief, but for herself Dena added the vision that Menahem had confided to her, of Elijah coming to the cave.

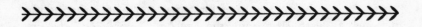

19

IN A popular workers' café on Nevelski, Menahem sat listening to Shimon, who had formed a training kibbutz, named for Tel Hai. The boys were getting impatient, Shimon said. Jabotinsky's orations were drawing huge crowds; he even talked of forming an army to seize the whole of Palestine, including the Trans-Jordan; the Polish government was supplying the Revisionists with instructors and even weapons, so as to rid themselves of Jews. Of course, their tiny ships with only a few dozen illegal immigrants were nothing at all, but for the desperate young Jews even one chance in a thousand was something. Now if the Haganah did it on a bigger scale, three hundred, four hundred on a ship, that would show up the Revisionists.

It would also affect the youngsters who were being pulled to the Socialist Bund. The Jewish Socialist Workers Bund had a fire-brand, Zygleboim. All workers were one, he preached the old line. Polish workers need not be anti-Semitic, Zygleboim insisted; it was all a matter of class solidarity; when they saw Jews devoted to their cause, they lost their anti-Semitism. Zygleboim had got elected to the Warsaw Municipal Council on a united workers' platform. And was this Zygleboim anti-Zionist? Menahem asked. Shimon hesitated. "They leave us alone right now." In any case, if Menahem wanted to meet Zygleboim, there he sat at a corner table.

Serious, narrow-faced, intense. Menahem knew what to expect:

Internationalism above Jewish nationalism. Yiddish, the true folk language, versus Hebrew. Still, they went over. Sitting with Zygleboim were two leatherworkers, nodding their heads when their leader made a point. The arguments were indeed as expected, and yet from the first handshake Menahem experienced that pull of affinity that comes at times with an opponent. Far back in the Bundist's eyes was a dark luster that Menahem knew was matched in his own, perhaps the Jewish sense of doom.

"You over there in Palestine have the fate of less than two hundred thousand Jews to worry about," Zygleboim repeated, "but we here in Poland have to worry about more than three million." Menahem didn't reply. What did slogans matter? Or even ideologies. What was before them was too vast, Zygleboim continued. About Hitler. In a few years the war would come, for certain. Had Menahem carefully read *Mein Kampf*? In regard to the Jews—

"He means total annihilation," Menahem said, and now their eyes fully met.

Then wasn't every way the right way? In the face of that shared sense of doom? At least for Jews not to fight each other.

When they were taking leave, the older of the two leatherworkers got Menahem aside for an instant, giving him a bit of paper with a name on it. "You know how it is, a son often turns the opposite way of his father." His boy had gone off to a Zionist training farm. For a year already the boy awaited an immigration certificate. Perhaps in the next allocation?

At last a message came from another of the lads in Greece. He had found a bargain, a solid freighter that had for twenty years plied the Mediterranean and would not be suspect. By constructing racks of shelf bunks in the hold, he could squeeze in three hundred and fifty.

In groups of ten, Menahem and a pair of the younger emissaries sent them off, students with their rucksacks, going to a summer holiday in Greece. Ah, what chevreh! What material! With one bunch, he even sent along the son of that leatherworker of Zygleboim's.

Headed for Jaffa, the freighter would stop short at a deserted sand cove and discharge her cargo. The Haganah shore unit would be waiting. It was already being trained.

At last came the telegraphed code word. Landed, safely dispersed. Let the British find and count the new immigrants! The *Veloz* was on the way back to Greece for another cargo.

※ ※ ※

Glancing over Mati's monthly summary of labor needs, including specific shortages at the Dead Sea potash works, Welby gave his knowing shrug. The chief secretary would be sure to deduct for illegal immigrants. "I hear you had four hundred more the other night. If the Haganah is going into this business on top of the Revisionists—" He pursed his mouth, eyeing Mati to convey the unspoken words—why make it so difficult when you know how I sympathize? I'm doing my best for you.

It was for Mati to pretend disbelief. The Haganah? Didn't seem like their kind of thing. But with increasing numbers of Arabs coming across the Jordan to fill the labor shortage, even in the Haganah there must be extremists who were gaining support. The way to stop illegal ships was to get London to grant more certificates. And why not put a few checkpoints at the Jordan?

Welby drew a long breath that meant, "You know if it were up to me—"

※ ※ ※

One sunset, Nahum and Shula's eldest boy, Uri, with a dozen classmates went down to the beach for a campfire, a kumsitz. After darkfall, Uri and his ginger-haired Tsila strolled off barefoot on the firm wet sand. Tsila, a bit nervous because of the teasing she might get on their return, thought she heard something. As Uri tried to squeeze her to him, she became rigid and whispered that there were voices farther up the beach. Uri listened hard. Then he too heard something. Other strollers? He caught more sounds. Arabic? Even in the daytime the beach wasn't their habit. Sometimes a few young fellows from Tulkarm would come to sneak a look at the Jewish women in their bathing suits, and they were soon enough made to feel unwelcome. Arabs didn't have a liking for the sea. Except for a few fishermen, they lived inland.

Leading Tsila back to the campfire, Uri said quietly to his friend Boaz that he had heard Arab voices farther up the beach. But Yoram, a hothead from the Revisionist youth group, the Betar, had caught Uri's words; he leaped up. The three boys went, taking the big flashlight.

All at once a counterbeam opened on them. And in their own light the boys saw a pair of young Arabs; one of them they knew at once, Fuad Aziz from the cluster of Arab huts that remained at the back end of Hof HaSharon. Fuad and his partner were a few years older than they were, and behold, they were decked out in some kind of uniform, green shirts with crescent armbands. Both carried stout nabouts and had whistles on braided cords, like police officers. "Oh, it's you!" Uri got out, in Arabic, and tried to make light of things. "What is this getup? What are you up to?"

In a formal tone Fuad recited, "We are on patrol duty."

"Easy, easy," Boaz whispered to Yoram. Though with their whole circle they need have no fear of this pair, who could tell what others might be lurking nearby, in wait for a shriek of the whistle? "Come have a coffee at our fire," Boaz offered, adding casually, "What are you patrolling for? Smugglers?"

Fuad's companion, who was from Tulkarm, stiffly declared that their organization knew all about the illegal ships that landed Jews on the beaches. There would be no more.

"Ah," said Boaz cheerfully, "are you out patrolling for the British? Listen, do you get paid?"

"Our business is our business. You better go back to your kumsitz."

Only Uri's quick arm grip on Yoram prevented the outbreak of a fight. "We've got to report this." As the green-shirted pair made a wide circle past their beach fire, the boys quickly explained to the rest of their group, with injunctions not to spread the tale. Nor, the group decided, should they break up their kumsitz—this was their beach. However, Yoram and Uri must at once report what had happened. Perhaps the girls ought to leave, Yoram suggested, but Tsila derided him. And after all, there were houses on the bluff directly above.

Yoram and Uri climbed the path. Yoram wanted to go straight to Araleh, commander of the Irgun's beach-landing unit, but Uri argued it was better to go to his own house; after all, his father was the mayor, and besides, they had a telephone.

Nahum felt sure there was no immediate danger, but the beach party had better break up fairly soon. It was spoiled anyway, Uri said; only they ought to stay long enough to show they had not been intimidated. But a guard should at once be stationed on the bluff.

"To inform Araleh?" Yoram suggested. Though Nahum contributed to the Revisionists, this was not, he considered, an affair for Araleh and his hotheads. And though there was a British police post in Hof HaSharon, again something told him to hold off. He would first drive over to the local Haganah commander, Pinhas Zussman.

Shula hovered in the hallway. Was anything wrong? Nothing, a few Arabs on the beach; he'd be back in a moment, Nahum told her.

Pinhas, a construction foreman, had already a few days ago heard talk of youthful "storm troopers" parading themselves in Tulkarm; an Arab mason on the job had joked about them. But patrolling the beach! in uniforms, carrying nabouts and probably knives. "May the tide carry them off!" Pinhas swore. As for the youngsters, they had behaved with good sense. He'd go right out to the bluff himself.

It was always best to go to the top, Nahum believed, so in the morning, instead of contacting the district officer he called the area commissioner—he'd drop in at Tulkarm for a coffee. Alfred Macmillan still rode the beautiful mare he'd had the indiscretion to accept from Nahum some years ago when he first came out.

He hadn't imagined, Nahum said, that the British would enroll Arab Hitler youth to patrol the beaches.

What?

The incident was related, uniforms and all.

He'd be double-all-damned! cried Macmillan. Oh, he'd heard of some new scout group in town, but after all, "you fellows have yours, three different kinds, hiking all over the topography." Still, patrolling the beach! Government area! He'd get right onto it! Oh, as for the boat landing the other night, he was sure Nahum had had no knowledge, but that was a lovely party Nahum and Shulamith had given at their house, on the same night, as it happened. Coincidence, that little barge found next day beached near Caesarea, what? He solemnly winked. Shulamith had looked her beautiful best at the party. "Give your lady my highest admiration." A youth militia! Damnall! For quite a while things had been rather quiet.

✹✹✹

On her second voyage the *Veloz* was spotted when only about fifty of her passengers had got ashore; the Haganah lookouts barely had time to signal the approach of British police cars, a truck with the fifty got safely away, the ship pulled off with the remaining chalutzim. Out of provisions, out of water, with one port after another refusing entry, the *Veloz* for more than two months haunted the sea. The British controlled the whole damn Mediterranean all right. Finally, the shipmaster had to agree that the chalutzim aboard would return to where they had come from— Poland. A disaster.

Reggie brought word of all-night sittings in Eliahu's room by the kitchen, in the house on Rothschild Boulevard. The ships were sheer provocation. They gave the Arabs an excuse, the British claimed. "Should Jabotinsky set policy for us?" Why not try for a gentleman's agreement with the British? No more illegal ships and in return maybe a softening on certificates for Poland?

As for the greenshirts, the authorities themselves were seeing to it. Certainly no more beach patrols! But simply as a youth movement, well now, didn't the Jews have their own? Gordonia, Jabotinsky's militant Betar, and all the rest?

20

LINED UP against the rail, the Kossoff family waved.

Mati had special boarding passes—one good thing about being an official British chair warmer. He and Dena went right up the gangplank, and amid the hugging and kissing Phil demanded two cigars, then, grinning, pulled them from his own breast pocket, two shining metal-encased Havanas, like miniature torpedoes, and presented them to Mati. My God! Dena suddenly realized her brother Phil was the perfect American tourist with a big cigar in his teeth.

Only Victor had not come—he had his bar exam, Bessie explained. As Mati took their baggage papers for immediate clearance, Sam Kossoff cried "Wait!" A surprise. Handing Mati an extra bunch of documents, Sam fished from his pocket a set of car keys!

After all the you-shouldn't-t-haves (but this would just fit in with his story of selling the sports plane to buy a car), Mati went to get the vehicle unloaded while Bessie kept introducing her Dena to waves of fellow passengers, this group from Minneapolis and this couple, who had given up Miami this season, and all, all had been dying to meet the American daughter, a real chalutzah, though also her husband was an official in the government. She had married into the most heroic Palestinian family and given birth to twins! Sabras! That's what they were called here; already each of the visitors knew and recited—a sabra is a cactus fruit, prickly outside and sweet inside. Bessie and Sam had really laid it on thick throughout the voyage, gathering nachas all the way across the ocean. With their glittery, devouring eyes the ladies devoured the virile young husband, himself a sabra! A bit dark-complected, but here the sun was very strong! Who could blame a girl for leaving Chicago for that beautiful hunk of man! Just look at this young mother of sabra twins—you'd still take her for a coed! How did Dena like living in Jerusalem? And their voices dropped. Wasn't it dangerous? Danger? After Chicago? she automatically jested. Why, in Jerusalem she never even locked her door.

Phil and Sherrill's kids gazed up at the car being unloaded by a derrick swinging it right down over their heads. "Watch out!" Bessie kept calling, but Sherrill wouldn't order them back. Self-reliance.

Set down on the pier was a brand-new Buick bearing a white streamer with blue lettering in English—and Hebrew! TO DENA AND MATI AND DAVID AND JONATHAN FROM THE FAMILY.

Phil beamed. So it was his money, Dena figured. "Don't worry," Sherrill whispered to her, "he just made his first million."

"With the Depression still on?"

"You don't know Phil?"

And then, inside the car! Packed solid! A superfancy twin bath, and this was crammed with items like an electric bottle warmer— Phil had made sure of the right current for Jerusalem—and baby clothes enough for a whole kibbutz. Gifts not only for Dena and Mati, but for all Mati's sisters and brothers and in-laws. Sherrill had made a complete list; the hardest thing had been to think of something for Mati's father, but on the old West Side she had found him a beaded tefillin bag, which she at once showed to Mati, a bit anxious—would this be okay? As extras they had brought gadgets and toys for all ages, especially model airplane building kits, even with miniature eye-dropper motors—they could actually fly! Maybe Phil had become a millionaire, Dena said with a laugh to Sherrill, but at this rate it wouldn't last long.

Never mind, he got everything wholesale, Sherrill retorted.

Besides, Phil said, he had opened two more stores. Waving an arm expansively over all the gifts, he cried, "Compliments of FDR!"

From the moment they drove out of the harbor, Phil, sitting next to Mati, felt himself possessed with an excitement that almost scared him. The construction! The activity going on here! The port expansion, the hustle! All Jews, all Jews, and there up the side of the mountain a section of new apartment buildings, latest modern! "I'm sold!" he cried.

In spite of his mother-in-law's bursting to get to Jerusalem and see the twins, Mati veered up the Carmel—a shortcut, he told Bessie—and halted for the panoramic view of the bay. While Sherrill raved, better than San Francisco or even Naples—imagine having a house right here!—Mati pointed out to Sam and Phil the huge smokestacks of the new oil refineries, fed by the longest pipeline in the world, all the way from Iran. Hey, this was big stuff, Phil said. "I'm really sold!" he cried again. This was the answer to Hitler's rantings. Look at those high-tension pylons, coming straight across the valley. "Rutenberg electric works," Mati told him. "All the way from the dam over the Jordan." And this long valley itself was the Emek, Emek Yisroel, the breadbasket of the land.

Bessie wanted to get going. The twins.

"One more minute," Phil said. It was sinking into him. It was as if someone had just laid before him a huge flawless diamond.

On the coastal road they marveled at the buses, trucks, at overloaded taxis with swaying valises on top. And taxis full of Arabs, too. So the situation wasn't so bad? Sam Kossoff said. But when the car had to wait for a slowly crossing camel caravan, Bessie cried out. With their camels, couldn't those Arabs at least get out of the way!

Dena pointed out the beautiful monastery of Latrun. At this Christian presence a little silence fell, but, Phil observed, after all, the Christian places must bring a hell of a lot of tourists.

Bessie was the first up the stairs; then the entire family was gathered around the double bassinet; it was afternoon sleeptime, and the twins really looked, you had to admit, like a pair of angels. Presently one yawned. "Look, he yawned!" Bessie whispered. Oh, what darlings! "Which one is he?"

"Jonathan," Dena whispered. "He always wakes first."

Now David yawned. Jonathan opened his eyes at the circle of strange faces and howled. Everyone jumped back guiltily but then laughed—some lungs!

With the babies guzzling their bottles, Sam Kossoff studied the infants seriously and remarked, "Now, as citizens, what are they?"

"Why, like me," Mati said. "Born here. Palestinians."

Yes, but—Hadn't Dena registered them, the way Victor had written, at the American Consulate?

Beneath, in Sam, was that half nightmare that came with every headline of Jew baiting in Germany, of strife in Palestine. Sam could see his Dena fleeing with her babies in her arms, two babies! Fleeing as in an old Lillian Gish movie, running for the American Consulate and just making it—safe!—with a couple of U.S. Marines closing the massive door behind her and standing guard with their bayoneted rifles at the ready.

Dena soothed her father—Dr. Epstein had sent copies of the birth certificates to the consulate. As he understood, Phil said, when the boys grew up, they could choose which nationality they wanted to be.

"Don't worry, whatever they'll be, they'll be Jews," Sherrill remarked, a sudden touch of sharpness in her voice. "Jews with one kind of passport or another."

"Maybe by then we'll have a state of our own with a passport of our own," Phil said, surprising even himself.

"Hey, he's become a real hot Zionist!" Sherrill cried.

"In twenty years"—Mati grinned at his brother-in-law—"everything can happen."

"Look at the Jews in Germany," Phil said. "For centuries they thought they were Germans. Now they're not even allowed to sit in a public park."

Each thought of worse. The pictures of beards pulled out. The story in the papers about an American girl married to a young German Jew, and Hitler's storm troopers had knocked at night, entered the apartment, and shot him dead before her eyes. They said he was a communist.

Sam told of a father and son taken to a Gestapo barracks and forced at gunpoint to whip each other.

And the Arabs? Sam had to bring it up.

It was possible to come to some kind of agreement, Mati said. The world heard only about the disturbances, but there were strong Arab elements that wanted an agreement with the Jews. There were high-level contacts, even certain negotiations going on, but they had to be kept secret.

※ ※ ※

Visiting Leah's training farm, now practically right inside Tel Aviv, they came upon a group of children just arrived the week before from Germany, in the Hadassah's Youth Aliyah program. Many were even blond and blue-eyed, and all had expensive leather luggage, the last their parents could spend on them. Sherrill was shaken. Some were no older than her own Joyce and Billy, and though she tried telling them that the parents of all these kids would soon come, too, Billy had that look kids get of suspecting the whole grown-up world is full of lies.

Over glasses of tea, Leah and her husband, Natan, a radical but not the obnoxious kind, talked to them about psychological problems of the Youth Aliyah children; Natan was surprisingly well read in psychology. One plan was for each new arrival to be paired off with a "brother" or "sister" who was already adjusted. Sherrill took notes with the idea of giving a talk before her Hadassah chapter when she got home. In spite of all you read, until you saw these children, it didn't hit you what was really going on. Children of fine people, judges, professors, who had been kicked out of their careers.

Though Leah insisted she'd find beds, Mati with his pull had got a two-room suite with connecting private bathroom in the Kaete Dan, and there Sherrill had a heart-to-heart with Dena and also gave her some special exercises to keep her breasts perky. But mainly Sherrill couldn't stop talking about those youngsters from Germany, so well brought up and all of a sudden to be sent off to become public charges. Her eyes were still on Dena's breasts, but suddenly they were full of tears, and she hugged her young sister-in-law. "Now I understand, Dena. It really gives meaning to your life, being here."

Phil, too, when he and Sherrill were alone, tried to express something of the same that had come over him. A feeling oddly like when he knew he had to get Sherrill no matter what. Or like when he knew he had to make a million, Depression or not. But today it was not just for a personal purpose of his own. Today it was a feeling that life had a purpose. He was almost scared.

Sherrill caught on to what was inside him, and they made love like not since that first night when they had moved into the gorgeous house that she had so wanted in Wilmette.

To meet still another sister of Mati's, the celebrated beauty whose husband was building a whole new town, they drove down a partly paved street with brand-new stores interspersed with wooden market shacks, reaching the seashore. What a view, better than Tel Aviv! And there along the bluff they came to Nahum's enormous brand-new villa, jutting like a boat's prow above the beach. Sherrill was bewildered—such a mansion, here in needy Palestine?

But Phil argued, why not? Shouldn't the Jews aim high in their own homeland? And soon enough Shula with her gracious hostess manner and the latest French coiffure—oh, yes, right here in Hof HaSharon by a French immigrant whom Nahum had set up in business—completely won her.

The men Nahum drove to the orange groves, now approaching their first season of fruit bearing. Each section had a marker, and here was theirs—Kossoff Grove. Perfectly aligned, evenly spaced trees, you could see they were expertly tended. Indeed, they were just then being watered; the worker, a wry-faced old-timer from Lithuania, showed Phil how with one deft stroke to clear the channel and let the water flow into the saucer hollow around the tree. Phil took the mattock and had a try—watering his own orange tree. Oh, fifteen years in the land, said the Lithuanian with that ironic smile, a kind of smile of moral superiority Phil had already noticed on these chalutzim. So he remarked that his own sister was married to a sabra. "And she is a born American? In this land miracles will never cease!"

On their way back Nahum showed them the residential areas; on several lots there sat huge crates, lifts they were called, in which German Jews had brought their belongings. Some had cut doors and windows into the boxes and were living in them. These immigrants were the lucky ones, Nahum related; they had had the foresight to buy groves from him on his tour of Germany. Each day they congratulated each other!

At the edge of the bluff, chalutzim, bare to the waist, were passing pailfuls of cement—here would rise a hotel. Nahum was building it in partnership with one of the German Jews. One day Sharon Shore would be lined with hotels, just as in Miami Beach, he promised. Instead of going to Florida, American Jews would come here!

On the esplanade would be a fountain spurting thirty feet high, illuminated at night as in Paris! Here, on the right, a concert stadium, and on the left they could see an outdoor cinema was already half finished. A Jew who had operated a cinema in Bialystok. "And you're his partner," Phil jested.

Nahum smiled. "Only a small share, considering the choice location."

This was the beauty of it, Nahum explained, his black eyes luminous. Here no Keren Kayemeth money had been expended to buy the land, no Keren Hayesod money for development! Such institutions were needed, yes, but look at Tel Aviv, who had built it? Private investors! A lot that sold for ten pounds ten years ago was worth four hundred today. And here in Sharon Shore, too, though he would not permit wild speculation, values would rise.

And in America? The way Phil's jewelry business had boomed under President Roosevelt, Nahum half-seriously suggested, the Kossoff family ought to open a Palestine branch right here in Sharon Shore! He'd give Phil a choice location on Chaim Weizmann Circle!

"For a small share," Phil kidded. But then who, he wondered, had money to buy jewelry here?

Who? To begin with, tourists. Yemenite silverwork. And besides, Phil would be surprised—Arabs.

Indeed, there on the shopping street Phil had noticed quite a few Arabs, mostly men, in pairs, often with their hands linked, but this had already been explained as a custom of theirs. They wore that odd combination, a suit jacket over the long white robe. Didn't they have shops in their own towns? Phil wondered. Why did they come here to buy?

Oh, even in a big town like Tulkarm, they had maybe some cheap clocks and other tin stuff, Nahum said. Their wives you never saw, but the better-class wives had a lot to say and wanted fancy things. And these fellows maybe also came here just to get a look at the girls and women in short skirts. Anyway, they had money; many still paid in golden Maria Theresa thalers that their fathers had buried away. Also they had money from selling land they had got free from the government, old Turkish crown lands, and money from the general prosperity brought by the Jews. Naturally you had to know how to deal with the Arabs—he himself had grown up in a mixed town, Tiberias, and so. . . .

All problems seemed to dissolve before this Nahum. Picking up their wives, they drove to a hillock a few miles inland. A clutter of Arab huts, adobe, just like on their trip to Mexico, Sherrill said. Urchins playing, some stark naked, and little girls who looked hardly six years old carrying their baby brothers on their backs. From café stools, a few men greeted Nahum with bits of laughter as at some often-repeated jest. These last ones were waiting around to sell their huts at monstrously high prices, Nahum said. This had been a miserable village, with the fellaheen raising a few patches of melons. Some were employed by the old sheikh on his orange grove. When he had died and his sons sold the grove and the dunes, Nahum had nevertheless bought substitute farmland for the fellaheen, but most of them preferred to come back here and work for wages on construction jobs.

Didn't the new immigrants need those jobs? Phil asked.

Well, they didn't really do the same kind of work. Stonemasons, for example. Also, unskilled labor.

Arabs were cheaper?

The way they lived, a Jew couldn't. And these last were just sitting here in these old huts waiting for the price to go still higher. They had caught on.

After supper, on the apronlike veranda listening to the roll of the waves, smoking Phil's Havanas, while the women were in their own circle talking of women things, Nahum expanded to Phil about relations with the Arabs. The troubles, for example, could be turned on and off. Sometimes they were turned on just to raise the price of the land. Mainly when troubles started, you must not show weakness. He believed in the ways of Jabotinsky, the Revisionist: make every effort toward peace, but answer terror with terror. The Arabs were still close to the ways of the desert, an eye for an eye; that was what they understood.

Well, that was one view of it, Mati said. He had grown up hearing this old stuff on one side and hearing socialism and brotherhood on the other. Phil ought to try to see for himself.

Sherrill could not take her eyes off Shula's pendant, a cluster of rubies, and Phil's eyes, too, she noticed, kept roving there, maybe more because of Shula's Mae West cleft. But as a jeweler he had a great excuse. "Is it Yemenite?" Sherrill asked. Nahum's smile spread, while Phil had his nose virtually in the cleft itself. Graciously, Shula lifted her arms and undid the clasp.

Such rubies! India?

"Afghanistan," Nahum said triumphantly. By caravan. For certain things the Arabs had the best connections. He had a good Arab friend in Nazareth, and would take them.

His old friend Boulos Nashashibi had invited them all to lunch; they would see a real Arab house, a real Arab family, the way most American visitors rarely had an opportunity. In the car Nahum regaled Phil with the tale of a certain antique watch he had once bought from Boulos, a bribe for the Turkish kaimakam of Tiberias, to save old Yankel, Shula and Mati's father, from torture in the Turkish jail, during the war when the Turks were hunting for spies. The watch, when you opened the back— "Stop whispering!" Dena laughed from behind; she knew from Mati—in the works of the watch were tiny male and female figures, the watch's "movement," doing it, in and out.

"Has your Arab friend got any more?" Phil asked Nahum, and Nahm only chuckled.

That gift had freed old Yankel, and Nahum's friendship with Boulos had continued and prospered; indeed, since there wasn't a really good hotel in Nazareth, Boulos had come to Nahum, and they were building one, it would be a boost for Christian tourism, they were discussing the contract with the Histadrut's construction company, Solel Boneh. That was something! Phil cried. A Jewish labor-owned company building a hotel in partnership with an Arab for Christian tourists! That really showed what could be done in this country if you went at it!

After parking and leading them up a narrow lane, Nahum came to a door in a high wall and pulled a bell cord; at once a servant opened the door, and there stood Boulos offering Arab phrases of welcome in nicely accented English. The courtyard! If only Myra could see it! Dena exclaimed to Mati. Cloisterlike pillars on all sides, a stone well, and several cedars carefully placed as in an Italian painting. Oh, you had to admit the Arabs had a kind of natural taste.

Bordering the square were four separate houses—his uncle and brothers', Boulos said; unfortunately today his uncle was in Damascus and could not welcome them. He ushered the visitors through a carved doorway into his own home—marble floors, Persian rugs that made your eyes pop. The furniture was richly inlaid with mother-of-pearl—Damascus work, it was called, Dena told Sherrill. And from the vaulted ceiling hung an enormous Venetian chandelier.

The host's wife and two teenage daughters appeared; the girls were in school uniforms with pleated skirts well below the knee; they were thirteen and fifteen and attended a nun's school. The mother wore a gray silk gown of French cut with long sleeves— from Beirut, Dena imagined. A string of pearls. Elegance. Olive-skinned, with the faintest lip down, gracious, she was somehow a little like Shula.

"Whiskey?" their host offered, with jokes about Americans now being free to drink again. They had mint tea, in lovely palm-fitting glasses, while chatting of the beauty of Galilee, of how surprising it was in this ancient world to find the latest American movies with James Cagney. By then Dena had noticed the icons. From alcoves in the depths of the room they gave forth their aged dark-golden glow. Byzantine? Oh, Boulos smiled, he could not divulge where they came from! Nahum put his arm on his friend's shoulder and hinted about remaining Russian monasteries in the land. Ah, said Boulos, things were brought to him, and at times it was best not to know for certain. They all laughed.

They took formal seats around a long table bearing innumerable little dishes of hors d'oeuvres already laid out. The hostess gave Sherrill the secrets of several of the delicacies, and Sherrill said wait till she served them in Wilmette! She had almost said at a Hadassah luncheon but caught herself.

All went perfectly. The two young daughters asked in quite good English—they also knew French, of course—about American girls; were they really so wild and crazy as Bebe Daniels? And that handsome star who was always driving racing cars— Oh, Wally Reid? Yum-yum! Dena supplied, and the mother teased her fifteen-year-old, declaring, "He is her—how do you say it?—heartbeat!" They got into a brief discussion about Moslems' being allowed more than one wife, Mati pointing out that this was true of the common ancestor of both Arabs and Jews—Abraham. No, Abraham really had only one wife, Sarah, Shula put in, the others were handmaidens. "Handy maidens!" Phil joked, and Sherrill saw he shouldn't have, while the two girls blushed. Dena asked quickly, what were the girls studying? Molière and Racine, since it was a French school, but also Arab poetry was a favorite subject of the older one, and Mati quoted from the classic Rashid, pleasing their hosts. After the meal the hostess took the ladies to freshen up, to her boudoir, which proved to be all-French, a cozy little sitting room, Louis XVI; even the wallpaper was French, and on the back wall Dena caught sight of a stunning gold-on-rose piece of calligraphy. Surely—

It was the work of her cousin, a young artist studying in Europe, the hostess said.

"Is his name Khalid? But we know him!" And Dena explained

how she and Mati had seen much of him in London and how her best girlfriend had gone with him to Germany, to the Bauhaus, where he and she—

Latifa glanced at her daughters, so Dena didn't tell all but asked, where was the artist now? Had Latifa heard from him? Oh, Khalid was the bohemian of the family; he was from another branch, in Acre. When last heard from, he had got into some trouble in Berlin, he was hiding a German artist, a communist, the Nazis were shooting communists, but luckily Khalid had escaped, he was always lucky, and now she believed he was in Paris.

The men, meanwhile, sat in a small office Boulos kept below. For his friend Nahum's pleasure he drew out a few trays of stones. Nahum had mentioned rubies? In Teheran, where Boulos had good friends, see what he had picked up!

Phil controlled his excitement. Already he had given Nahum an idea of what he wanted, for an anniversary gift for Sherrill. In their temple the new young rabbi advocated reviving some of the old customs and in a speech to the brotherhood suggested, why not on Friday, erev Shabbas, recite the Woman of Valor to the wife; they would see how the girls loved it, "precious as rubies." And did Mati know, Phil whispered, that perfect rubies would top even diamonds in price? So his secret surprise gift idea was a single large ruby on a fine golden chain, hanging just low enough down there.

Ah, Boulos said. With a low-cut gown, or even—he permitted himself an elbow poke at Phil—even worn with a nightgown. Phil handed him one of the Havana torpedoes. Boulos brought out a rare arak from a certain village in Lebanon. After the ruby was selected, glowing like red wine, Phil made a knowing remark about rare watches with a certain movement. Alas, he had never found another, Boulos chuckled. But then he unlocked a cabinet and drew out a thin booklet which he handed to Phil. Inside were exquisite miniatures of positions. *Kama Sutra*. Boulos smiled. From India. Phil must keep it. "No, no, really I couldn't, it's too precious." Twice he refused. But Mati had tipped him off, the third time you accepted. What about the price of the stone? he got a chance to whisper to Nahum, but Nahum made a tongue tick. "Don't worry."

In the car Nahum told him the price, not a steal but still a damn good buy. "I thought it was the custom to bargain?" Again

Nahum made the tongue tick. "In the souk." Not in the home. "What a beautiful home!" Dena said. Those icons!

They ought to have seen the main house, belonging to the uncle, one of the wealthiest of the clan, Nahum said. Just then it occurred to Mati that the uncle had perhaps not been away to Damascus. Nor had Boulos invited his brothers to meet his Jewish friends.

Were the Nashashibis all Christians? Phil asked.

No, the clan, the hamoula, Mati explained, was mostly Moslem. On the whole the Nashashibis were probably richer than the Mufti's clan, the Husseinis; the rivalry between the two families went back long before the Mandate. In fact, the Nashashibis considered the Mufti an outsider because his great-grandfather was from the Sudan, named Aswan. He had married a Husseini and taken his wife's name, a thing unheard of. . . . Of the two clans the Nashashibi were the more reasonable. You could deal with them.

"But do you ever feel you could know what an Arab really thinks?" Phil asked. Mati found himself about to say no, yet held back. It was too complex. Nahum chuckled at Phil's acuteness, but answered, yes, he could tell. Only what they said was rarely what they thought.

Now Mati cited a maxim from their Koran, "It is better to please a guest than to offend him by telling the truth." A great deal could be learned about their way of thinking from their Koran; more Jews ought to read it. And he was off on his lecture about Arabs and Jews. Take the main prayer, morning and evening the Jew declared, "Hear O Israel, the Lord God is One." And the Moslem five times a day declared, "Allah is Allah, there is no God but God." The same, no? Their Koran had mostly Bible stories, a bit jumbled up. Abraham was supposed to have been down there in Mecca! And they had Joseph and Moses. Even Jonah. But all jumbled up. Haman mixed up with the Tower of Babel. Since the Koran came many centuries after the Bible and the Talmud, Mohammed must have heard the tales, and in his seizures they came out again. They had some of the Ten Commandments, but not with the story of how God gave them to Moses. Still, just like "Thou shalt have no other God before me," they were told to have no other God before Allah. They had "Thou shalt not commit adultery," and "Thou shalt not bear false witness," and also "Thou shalt not kill," but they added "except for a just cause." They didn't have the Sabbath commandment and "Honor thy father and mother," though, of course, in their way of life, this

303

was seen. They didn't have "Thou shalt not make graven images," but still, just like the Jews, it was a rule with them not to make pictures.

"Only calligraphy," Dena put in knowingly.

Altogether the Koran was a kind of mishmash, Mati said. At the start of his revelations, at least, Mohammed couldn't read and write, though there was a tradition that later on he learned. The way the Koran sounded, he must have sat with Jewish scholars and even known a bit of Christianity.

But didn't Moslems hate and kill Christians?

That was during the Crusades, Mati said. But right now, just over the border in Lebanon, the Moslems and Christians had a government together. Here in Palestine the Christians were, of course, comparatively few among Arabs, though influential, and the first thing the British had done among the Arabs was to organize a Moslem-Christian society so they could work together against the Jews.

No!

Sure. Nahum agreed but shrugged it off. Some of those old-time Arabists from Egypt. They had even provided the money.

But the Mohammedans didn't have real anti-Semitism, like the Christians? Phil asked.

Oh, at least they didn't claim the Jews killed Mohammed!

When he first went to school, Phil told, in that old Italian neighborhood, when he had to pass their church, he went on the other side of the street and made it quick because if the wop kids caught you in front of the church, they'd yell, "Christ killer" and beat you up!

"Look at the Nazis, all good Christians," Sherrill said.

There was, Mati felt, almost a pride in the way they recited about anti-Semitism. No, with Moslems, Jews had for centuries lived in peace, he said, except for occasional outbreaks in one place or another. And against that there was, of course, the great period of Jewish prominence in Moslem Spain. No, they had no Christ-killer type of hatred, but still, you could see how they could be stirred up. Just as in Mohammed's own time he had attacked his neighboring Jewish tribe for not accepting him as the final and greatest of prophets.

It was strange to be discussing it all here, about the religions, as they swerved the car for a pair of monks walking so peacefully down the road from a Galilee monastery.

As for Moslems and Jews, Dena remembered a story they had heard from an expert, a scholar named Billig, the sweetest little man, they had met him at the Rappaports, and for example, he told a cute Talmudist tale about how all the Egyptians came to be drowned in the Dead Sea. First, Pharaoh's stallion hesitated to go into the water, so God sent a mare in heat that ran into the sea, and naturally the stallion chased after the mare, and all the Egyptian chariots followed the Pharaoh's horse, and that was when the waters closed over the Egyptians and they all drowned. Well, Dr. Billig quoted the same exact story from a Moslem commentary on the Koran.

They puzzled. If the beliefs were so close, then why the hatred? Now Mati brought in his own pet theory, the Ishmael complex. Maybe this gave them a kind of national inferiority complex—to know the whole world thought of them as descended from a servant. So they had to prove they were superior. Phil and Sherrill were fascinated. Here on the spot it was all so different from what you read and heard about Arabs and Jews.

"Wait, right here, the view!" Shula cried, so Mati turned at the panorama stop to give them the magic sight of the whole Emek. How the land glowed. Spread out like a cloak in stripes of all colors. Like Joseph's coat, Mati reflected. The vale of Armageddon.

❀ ❀ ❀

The civil aviation man arrived—and it was Peewee, from the London Aero Club! Airmindedness everywhere! Good thing! Right off, he gave permission for a flying school, not only for gliders, but even for motor-driven aircraft. Of course, the *Gidon* could be transferred and used there.

Though he was a confirmed bachelor, Dena was already scheming to find a Jewish girl for Peewee.

The day came to transfer the plane, and Mati decided to take a farewell flight. He'd take Phil along and show him the land from Dan to Beersheba.

He flew from over the Banias, following the Jordan all the way down to Jericho, the land becoming more and more desolate, and then rising over the rock of Masada, how clearly from the air you still saw the traces of the Roman siege camp. Turning inland, Mati dipped over a line of adobe huts. "Beersheba!" he yelled to Phil, and over clusters of black tents, "Abraham!"

These days in the office he was involved in getting approval for a full exploration of the water potential here. Some engineers believed that you could bring up enough water for irrigation. Also, you could pen up the flash floods from the winter rains—ancient cisterns had been found. And there were all the old schemes of channeling water the whole length of the land, from the Kinneret. A population not of today's million and a half, but of six, ten million could be supported in Palestine!

Excitedly he showed Phil the tip of the Red Sea, beckoning, but his gas situation was getting risky, so Mati turned back, flying now over Trans-Jordan, over Edom, where Moses led the tribes. Vast, empty lands—what could be done on this side, too, with irrigation!

An airstrip had been laid out at Afikim, and a tin-roofed hangar built, and all the twelve pupils with his nephew Giora at their head came running, swarming around the plane. "Ours!" Dr. Pfeffer, the professor of aerodynamics, greeted Mati in freshly learned Hebrew.

Mati lingered, explaining every idiosyncrasy of the aircraft. He introduced Phil, the American who had made the purchase possible. "Just one thing," Mati reminded Dr. Pfeffer. The name *Gidon* should remain on the airship.

"But naturally."

Dena and Sherrill had arrived in the Buick to drive them back. Phil gazed over the faces of the class. "Mati, we really started it, didn't we?"

All right. That much Mati could say he had accomplished.

They walked away from his ship. Dena pressed his hand.

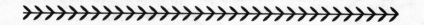

21

AT LEAST things had been fairly quiet during the family visit. Haj Amin was abroad making a big tour of the Moslem lands, calling himself the "Grand Mufti."

Suddenly in Algeria, Moslems rioted and twenty-seven Jews were killed. Bodies of violated girls were found with their heads cut off. And now at home there were signs that Reggie found unsettling. An old-style livestock raid on the Tel Adashim kibbutz of the old Shomer. The raid was beaten off—but still? In the fields of the Dayan family of Nahalal, the young son, Moshe, was shot at while plowing. An Arab claim of ancient grazing rights. Young Dayan made little of it—a skin crease. Still? Worse was a shooting nearby, in Sakneh. A watchman, blinded. The assailant was caught; he claimed a personal grievance and got two years. For two eyes, the Hebrew press commented.

Mati set out alone, using the government car but dismissing his driver. This was frowned on, but what the hell. Riding alone like this was almost like riding in the air, and his mood lifted. From Nablus, for a look at the area, he turned onto a dirt road to Jenin; it wound between hills with long died-out contoured terraces. This once had been the fruitland of Samaria; only occasionally he passed an Arab on a donkey, sometimes a few women with bundles of briarwood on their heads. If he hit a deep pothole here, it would be hours until he could get a mechanic. No cause to feel fear. A bit of uneasiness.

Occasionally you still saw patches of olives. True, it wasn't an easy land, but in the Jerusalem hills the kibbutzniks of Kiryat Anavim had started with nothing better. How different these long curving terraces must have looked with vines. Empty. "No room to swing a cat in," the British investigator had said.

In Jenin, pictures of the Mufti in every shopwindow. He didn't stop for a coffee.

His Chicago chalutzim had at last been allocated a site, in an isolated area on the spine of the Carmel; they were calling their settlement Brandeis. Beyond the Druze village of Ussfiyah there was nothing but a wagon track.

At the top of the hill was an old stone khan, long abandoned, and as Mati's name was yelled out, the whole twenty of them swarmed to their newly erected gate. In the midst of the hugging and babble, one chaver, Maury the Complainer—there was always a chief complainer—demanded, How did you like our main highway? Could Mati do something with the British about a road?

"Wait, at least give him a chance to take in our view!" Dave Margolies propelled Mati up the khan's outside stairway to the roof, with all the chevreh following.

Turning slowly full circle on this ridge of the Carmel, Mati felt what these kids had felt arriving in their place, what Reuven and Leah always said they had felt, standing for the first time on the ridge above the Kinneret. And even the first home builders on the sands of Tel Aviv.

Downward one saw the entire Emek, and across, the Bay of Acre. Turning, you saw Haifa, and closer on the Carmel the green slopes with here and there white dots of sheep. Then full turn to the rear valley, you saw the monastery on the site where Elijah drew fire from Jehovah for his altar, while all his pagan competitors got nothing.

"Beautiful, beautiful," he said.

"You can come and join us anytime."

Atop the "penthouse" their blinker light had already been set up, but alas, Dave remarked, the promised dynamo had not arrived. Before they could hook onto the Rutenberg lines might be a year. From the Haganah, on their day of aliyah, they had got a flare gun and an old horse pistol; one of the boys, Josh Seidenberg, possessed a hunting rifle that he had smuggled in on arrival.

Never mind, their nearest neighbors were Druze. Friends.

"Anyway, in case of attack we just fire off the flare and Mati's Haganah air force will arrive!" Joke.

In the center of the table Malka was placing a vase of wild flowers. How she reminded Mati of Leah!

Already they had put in eggplant, cucumbers, tomatoes; they expected a Polish contingent, and then they'd build the poultry run and also get a flock of goats; they were clearing terraces for apple trees.

"Peaches!" one chaver yelled. "That's a better money crop!"

"Money? What's that?"

At eighteen percent interest he'd soon realize, Dave Margolies said.

All kinds of ideas were popping up, as though for Mati to decide their future activities. A Brooklyner proposed a summer camp for kids—in the U.S. the Jewish camps were gold mines. Why not bring the kids here—with Hebrew lessons on the boat! Get them young! Had they come here to run a kids' camp? Josh Seidenberg objected. Besides, American papas and mamas would be scared stiff.

The Brooklyner, called Skeezix, turned for support to Mati. It did seem like a good idea, but maybe for the future, Mati said; they ought to get advice on running a camp from Horace Rappaport in Jerusalem.

Dave's Malka sat there knitting. Toward the end of every argument she came in with a word, a remark that seemed to be the conclusion. Then she resumed her knitting. Several times their eyes met. If it had happened with someone like Malka—

After the meal everyone was in the yard, a fire got started, a coffeepot was put on, and they were in a kumsitz. Already there were jokes in the land about German immigrants, the Yekkehs; Josh told the favorite one about two Yekkehs passing building blocks to each other, saying with each block, *Bitte schön, Herr Professor! Danke shön, Herr Doktor!*

All right, but why had those yekkehs had to wait for Hitler to light a fire under them? cried Skeezix. And even in the past, what brought immigrants? Pogroms. It had to be said that they, the first kvutsa of American-born, came purely out of conviction.

Yah? Josh Seidenberg cracked. "I came because I figure this is better than the CCC."

Someone began to sing "Brother, Can You Spare a Dime?"

One of the girls said earnestly that Ludwig Lewisohn's book had got her started, *The Island Within*. It made her think about being a Jew. "Sure," commented Dave, but Lewisohn had made his hero —a psychoanalyst already—go back to Orthodox religion instead of having him encounter the new Jewish life here in the Yishuv.

"With all our lunatics, a psychoanalyst would be welcome."

"Wait, wait, Vienna has gone Nazi, we'll be flooded with psychoanalysts."

"No, they're headed for Americhka."

"That's where they're really needed!"

A skinny pipe-sucking type suddenly burst out, No! He was not rejecting America; maybe in a reverse way their own coming here was also a search for the real America, the pioneer American experience, the westering, the confrontation with nature. Born when all that was past, they were repeating the American pioneer experience right here.

Bushwah! cried Josh. America was nothing but an oligarchic capitalist society on the way to fascism! A Protestant hypocrisy.

"You have to admit that under Roosevelt—"

"Roosevelt!" Tilting his chin and drawing aloft an imaginary cigarette holder, Josh imitated, "My frands, we cannot intefeyah in the internah affays of anothah nayshun. The Jamahn policy tahd its citizens of the Hebrew fayth—"

A voice remarked from the darkness, "What this country needs is a Jewish delicatessen. What wouldn't I give for a real pastrami on rye!" A few began to sing the old-time chalutz songs, "Yahalili," then switched to "Yes, We Have No Bananas," and then just as homesickness began to ache, Skeezix, the Brooklynite, broke out his harmonica, "Anu Banu Artza," we came to build and to be built; a few kids were on their feet, Dave and Malka moved into the circle, the pace speeded up, "Hava Nagila" they were chanting now, a couple of hands reached out to Mati—why, it was he, in Chicago, who had taught these kids the hora, and here they were! He swung in.

In the middle of the night Mati woke to a howling, momentarily thinking it was the twins, but it was a jackal. That was a good one, wait till he told Dena!

First thing in the morning Mati set off with Dave Margolies down the Carmel slope; this was where the kvutsa needed a connecting road to the Emek. Scrambling through briar, following a goat track, he leaped after Dave among the rocks, soon puffing. He had become a real chair warmer, a pakid. Pausing, Dave pointed out a large flat-topped rock—could it once have been an altar? Already Dave had the antiquity fever.

They could see right down into Meshek Yagur. It wouldn't take much to bulldoze a road, Dave said, and then in case of an emergency a car could make it in a few minutes. He'd have to figure out a way to present it to the British, Mati said. Maybe he'd say it would benefit the Druze.

✄ ✄ ✄

Perhaps because of the mounting uneasiness, the British were making a big show, a kind of fiesta, for the decoration of a Jewish police officer who had long been stationed in an Arab village on the Gilboa. All season there had not been one single incident in Lieutenant Moshe Rosenfeld's district. And since he was a childhood neighbor from nearby Milhamia and still a close friend of Schmulik, and there would be a real fantasia such as Dena had never yet seen, Mati decided they'd make a day of it, for already in the morning there was the dedication of a model poultry-raising village for immigrants from Germany, to be welcomed by the High Commissioner himself.

The mayor of the new Yekkeh village, in wool suit and vest, high collar, red-faced, started his speech in Hebrew, a new life in an old-new land. All their faces glowed like the sun. Tables laden with chicken, fruit, soda pop, grapefruit juice, and wine. And even the speeches were short! The High Commissioner approached with the Welbys and, as always, complimented Dena on her hat and made an Irish joke for Maureen, forgetting she was Welsh.

Glutted, they drove to the second ceremony.

Ten years before, when Jews had been urged, even selected by the Haganah to join the police, Mati told Dena, Schmulik and Moshe had gone in together, but Moshe Rosenfeld had lasted. Hill and valley, Moshe knew everyone, even to the seasonal Bedouin grazers. He had married a girl in Tel Yosef, the kibbutz adjoining Menahem and Dvora's.

The entire hillside was aswarm with Arabs, Jews, farmers and fellaheen, Bedouin in full regalia, their women wearing all their coins and bracelets, and what stunningly embroidered gowns! Nothing you got in the Jerusalem souk could compare, Dena said.

There were village mukhtars in blazing white abayas, gold-trimmed keffiyehs. The square was packed with British vehicles; mounted Arab policemen, wearing their caracul shakos, threaded their steeds among the parked cars, and the station yard was a weird combination of British garden party and farm feast. Just as Mati had described from his childhood, there was a huge spit with a whole roasting calf.

Schmulik, his cheeks ablaze as though the entire thing were his doing, seized them out of the crowd and led them to Moshe. Despite his spit-and-polish uniform for the occasion, the officer looked totally civilian, an unassuming, smallish fellow with his head slightly cocked—a man who listens. Perhaps this was how he kept the peace.

First, the district chief, Captain Fitzgerald, made witty remarks about sending Moshe to keep the peace in Belfast. Then the commander for the entire north, Major Andrews, a true beaming colonial, pinned a medal on Moshe. The mukhtar of Sha'ata, with a seamed, shrewd face, quoted peace sayings from the Koran, and Moshe's kibbutz secretary brought chuckles from Arabs all around as he too quoted from the Koran and ended with the inevitable Biblical verse, "How good and pleasant it is for brethren to dwell together." Funny, Dena had never realized the words of the hora song were from the Bible; as with so many things, you caught onto the connections belatedly. She still got surprises.

A few days later Mati came home, his eyes ablaze with pain and anger. She hadn't heard it on the radio? Moshe Rosenfeld had been assassinated. An ambush. He had been called to a grove where fruit had been stolen. On entering the grove, Moshe at once had been picked off.

So it was starting again.

Mati drove to the funeral. Of all those Arab mukhtars at the festival, only the one from Sha'ata itself appeared. Allah's will, he said.

The British came, Major Andrews from Nazareth, the full solemn show.

Schmulik seethed. It was no mystery who was responsible—a new Haifa gang. They were bragging all over the souk—especially

a certain banana peddler. The Black Hand, they called them-
selves. The leader was a young schoolteacher, Mouhadeen El
Kassem; he also preached in a mosque down there in the port area.
If the British didn't go after that gang, Schmulik would do it
himself! Mati gripped his brother's arm to quiet him. No!
Schmulik spit on the ground. He was going straight to Eliahu in
Tel Aviv—

"Schmulik, what you know Eliahu knows." Besides, this time
the British couldn't let it go by. One of their own, Jew or not. An
officer.

"One of theirs!" Schmulik cried. "He's one of ours!"

The funeral hymn, "El Maleh Rachamim," God, Filled with
Compassion, had begun. Oddly, Mati thought of the Moslem cry,
"HaRachaman," Allah the Compassionate, the Merciful. Schmulik
stood silently, but his fury radiated.

"Black Hand?" Dena repeated. It echoed. In her childhood on
the West Side, among the Italians, even before the time of Al
Capone and the bootleg gangsters, the terror word had been the
"Black Hand." The Black Hand will get you! She even wondered
if perhaps Mussolini in his broadcasts to the Arabs—Mati laughed
but impatiently. Black Hand, blackshirts, brownshirts, greenshirts
—blood oaths, the whole world was sliding back. Didn't she
remember from courses in social history—primitive societies, no
matter in what part of the world, blood vows and gangs? Here in
the Middle East had it ever been different, with blood feuds and
assassinations? And it was a plague that was infecting the Jews,
too. The Irgun with its retaliations. And now with the Arabs it
was all starting again—

The Carmel slope road project hadn't gone through. McCleland,
the technocrat, dryly declared, "It would really only serve the new
Jewish settlement up there." And as the kibbutz had access
through the Druze village, this road could wait.

Word of the disaster came to Mati in a call from Eddie Marmor
—the *Palestine Post* had received a police report from Haifa saying
that an American up there in the Brandeis kibbutz had been shot.
No, not dead, he was in hospital in Haifa. Dave Margolies. Mati
knew him, didn't he?

"He's their mukhtar. I'm going right to Haifa." Hastily Mati gave Eddie some background.

"Mati, don't drive alone. Don't be a shvitzer."

In any case there were new strict orders against driving alone. The whole way his constable, Saud, complained as always—if your wife poisoned your life what good was it to live? Usually Mati advised him to buy a second wife, but now he concentrated on driving, taking the hairpin turns at high speed. "Wallah!" his protector cried. "You yourself will kill me and my misery will be finished!"

The slug had shattered the knee; two doctors had worked on him for an hour, taking out a zillion splinters, Dave said; they still hoped to save the leg. He was full of dope and groggy, but his mouth tried for the old humorous twist: the docs were from Hitlerland, and that old Yekkeh story was true! As one dug out a splinter and handed it to the other, it was *Danke schön, Herr Doktor, bitte schön, Herr Professor!*

Mati forced a chuckle.

It had been an ambush, Malka said. Dave gave the details. That goat path—it had been widened for going down to lectures and concerts at Yagur, but—

Exactly where Mati had been trying to get them the road.

Two shots, from separate points, Dave said, and what had saved him was that large rock beside the path, remember, like an altar from Elijah's time? Anyway, right there. Just as his leg was hit— oh, the herr doctors couldn't fool him, he knew it would have to come off.

Malka, sitting there knitting, reached for his hand. Dave's eyes were asking her to deny it, while his mouth held onto that humorous twist. And an unwanted, unworthy thought went through Mati; at least it was now finished, his long, lingering yen for Malka. Now he plain honestly loved the two of them together.

Managing somehow to swing behind the rock, Dave had returned the fire. He kept bleeding, and the pain was excruciating. "I can tell you I was getting woozy." But he felt sure the shooting had been heard, and tarum tarum tarum Hi-ho, Silver! A mounted Shomer from Yagur. After the Rosenfeld murder they had doubled their patrols.

That was the last Dave knew until he heard the *Danke schön, bitte schön.* To Malka, Dave quipped, "Hey, woman, you're lucky it didn't hit higher up."

"You mean *you're* lucky," she retorted.

While Malka went for cold juice, Dave added to Mati: Just before he heard the horseman, he had imagined those bastards finishing him. The stories about cutting it off and sticking it in your mouth. Did they do it to you while you were still alive? "Well, anyway, I didn't get a chance to find out."

Dena's family sent clippings. Dave Margolies, his wife, the daughter of a Chicago union leader, had single-handedly fought off a band of Arab marauders. A New York *Times* editorial spoke of the spreading troubles in Palestine, as between Isaac and Ishmael, the one an industrious toiler, the other a wild fighter.

❦ ❦ ❦

What troubled Mati most deeply was the sense that something in a new dimension was developing in the new terror. From talk among the British, from a few bits of inside information passed on by Menahem, who was again back at Gilboa after the disaster with the illegal ships, the picture formed of a movement now differently based than the Mufti's. No longer a simple matter of arousing religious fanaticism. Now it was direct, violent nationalism. El Kessem proclaimed that Haj Amin el Husseini was too inactive. El Kessem sounded almost like Jabotinsky attacking Weizmann! What! El Kessem proclaimed, an uprising in 1921 and nothing again until 1929, and nothing since! Jews must be constantly, relentlessly attacked, on the roads, in the fields, picked off everywhere! "Palestine is ours!" A jihad! And from David HaCohen in Haifa came reports that there were young recruits from merchant families and from the Arab high schools. Now El Kessem was organizing a political formation, the M'oujahadin. And why did you see more and more Arabs with clipped beards like El Kessem's —indeed also like the Mufti's? That short beard was a sign of membership. Maybe the Mufti was behind El Kessem, after all.

"By the beard of the prophet I'll get them!" Captain Fitzgerald's quip was repeated by Peewee. But what was Fitz going to do, haul in every Arab with Mufti whiskers? Still, all the way down from the HC there was now a showdown atmosphere in the government. The British were determined to have it out with Mr. El Kessem, and quickly. Already a few Arab agents had infiltrated their Black Hand; it seemed that El Kessem held initiations in the Carmel woods.

In the first raid that loudmouth banana peddler was killed, but the rest of the gang got away.

At the Brandeis kibbutz, Mati found Dave already stomping around after the amputation. Just above the knee. "They've given us five more rifles; how's that in exchange for only one leg?" But the Chief Complainer, working with a friendly Druze, was exploring certain wooded areas on the Carmel ridge.

A few weeks later came the big raid. A meeting in a grove on the mountaintop had been encircled by scores of police. After four hours of shooting a surrender shout was heard; only a few of the band emerged alive. El Kessem and seven others lay in a morass of blood in the center of the copse.

Schmulik came gloating to Jerusalem. Moshe Rosenfeld, at least, was avenged. Yet Mati was uneasy. Now the fanatics had a martyr.

In the trial of the four Black Hand captured alive, virtually every Arab advocate of note took part. The Arab press—thank God that Dena couldn't read it, Mati told himself. The filth in *El Falastin* could have come straight out of the *Völkischer Beobachter*.

For "conspiracy to murder Police Lieutenant Rosenfeld and other Jews" the sentences were from four to fifteen years. They'd be out in no time.

Just like under the Turks, Menahem said.

Meanwhile, the Mufti was back.

Maybe, as Dena said, it was really only the dark skies and rains that gave him the glooms. Though she herself loved Jerusalem in the winter, declaring that the light-streaked clouds gave the city the look of El Greco's Spain, Mati sometimes found himself wishing he could walk out on everything and go work the farm in the heat of the Jordan Valley.

Or it was the sense of being boxed in at the office, not really among his own. Oh, the British had handled him neatly with a step up, but even the higher-level Jews in the administration acted startled if you raised your voice. And there was the constant

316

squeeze with his statistical Scotsman; Aylesworth was the type who saw the numbers and not the people. And was inflexible. When Mati brought figures showing a shortage of citrus pickers, especially with new groves coming in, Aylesworth insisted to Welby that picking was in the seasonal category—you couldn't issue immigration certificates on that basis, could you? And Welby, with a sympathetic glance to Mati, cut down the allotment. Afterward, he found a chance to remind Mati that the quota was not really up to him. Since the H.C.'s last visit to London, there were new guidelines, and the Chief Secretary watched like a hawk. So now more Hauranis were pouring in; there were fights in Petah Tikva when Irgunists tried to keep them out of the groves. Also in Haifa port, Hauranis were being added on as stevedores, and when David HaCohen came to Jerusalem to demand the hiring of Jews, the Chief Secretary made his famous remark: He couldn't quite imagine a Jew with glasses as a stevedore!

Only, HaCohen could always figure out a plan in that tight knobby head of his, so presently there arrived a crew of husky Jews from Salonika, where it seemed Jews had manned the port since the Dispersion!

More certificates? The Jews were always asking for more, more, no matter what you gave them! At the staff meetings Mati could regularly expect this quaint Oliver Twist allusion. Answered, decently enough it was true, by Welby, "In view of the situation in Germany, can they be blamed?"

Hitler and Mussolini had met in Rome and made their pact, Mussolini was massing troops in Libya to conquer Ethiopia. His Arab-language radio station in Bari incessantly kept broadcasting, "Long live Haj Amin, the Hitler of Palestine!" Even Dena sometimes, turning the dials, could recognize the Arabic outcry by these names.

Maybe his gloom was mostly the feeling of being grounded. With an enormous to-do the Misr airline from Egypt made its first landing; Mati had to attend, all the tarbooshes were there, and with Peewee making the introductions he shook the hand of the British pilot. The Misr had only an eight-seater, and it had arrived an hour late. "The Miserable Airline," Dov Hos at once dubbed the outfit, drawing a big haw out of Peewee, who kept urging, "When are you fellows going to get started?"

Then the Jerusalem municipal elections went bad. The damn thing, Reggie argued, was that though the Jews had for generations been the majority in the city, all those Mea Shearim yeshiva sitters wouldn't vote. The Nashashibi faction was split, and the Mufti's man got in.

Finally came the nasty end of Ben-Gurion's secret negotiations with Arab notables. After months of nudging and pushing from Dr. Magnes' B'rith Shalom people, Ben-Gurion had worked his way up the Arab ladder, from the ever-courtly Mussa Alami, who nevertheless had the ear of the Mufti, to the elder statesman of the Pan-Arabic movement, Sheikh Arslan. Ben-Gurion had journeyed to Geneva for their talk. Unless an agreement was reached, both sides were pledged to absolute secrecy and silence. Yet in the sheikh's own Arab *Journal* there now came the full account, with insult and ridicule. The Jewish leader, "arrogant, foolish, childish, impudent," had revealed the true dastardly aim of the Zionists. No, and forever no!

All right, Ben-Gurion had laid before Sheikh Arslan the same dream he had laid before Mussa Alami and Antonius and the others, that old Herzl-Weizmann dream of Jewish help in unifying the Arab nations and securing Syria independence from the French, that perennial plan for regional economic development— wasn't Pinhas Rutenberg even now offering to electrify the whole of Trans-Jordan for the Emir Abdullah? And Ben-Gurion had again made the proposition of a federation of Arab states, including, eventually, a Jewish state in Palestine. Carried away, he had even hinted to Sheikh Arslan of some future possible exchange of population.

The dastardly Zionist plan revealed! cried their *Journal*.

Distortions! Lies! Ben-Gurion roared from London. Violation of the strictest confidence and trust!

He'd been made a fool of, said the British around the office.

And now Mati's idol turned on the Magnes crowd, the "meddling compromising amateurs," who had led him into this trap. In their own secret talks with Arab leaders, Magnes and Lubin and Smilansky were even agreeing to schemes for a permanent Jewish minority!

Torn between the accusations and rebuttals, Mati hardly knew where he stood. Maybe he too was only a well-meaning, bumbling liberal. But what then was the way? What was the way?

Dena listened, was with him; only she didn't become excited. She just had a kind of what-do-you-expect attitude about arguing

Jews. And to cool Mati off, got him to come along with the Marmors to see Paul Muni in *I Am a Fugitive from a Chain Gang*, which didn't improve his mood. Maybe it was simply that Dena didn't have a sense of politics, just as he didn't have a sense of art. But in the depths of him Mati felt a bleakness.

He was being unfair to her; she was here, she had given up—no! Dena never put it that way, given up America. And yet—

In bed they made it up, as always, even having a great laugh because the twins started their nightly crying spell—luckily only at the exact instant after. Imagine the effect it would have the instant before!

And what was he so gloomy about? Jonathan, even before David, was beginning to walk!

Appropriately it was in David HaCohen's Haifa with its blooming new port and oil refinery that Mati sometimes got the feeling that a way would be found. Even though the Black Hand and the M'oujahadin had sprung up here, nowhere else in Eretz could you see such working together of Arabs and Jews. HaCohen was getting an Arab labor federation under way; who could tell, one day it might amalgamate with the Histadrut. And because this was a labor town, Mati felt his old socialist dreams getting back a breath of life. He even sometimes wondered if he shouldn't quit the administration and pitch in with HaCohen in the Histadrut's paving and building cooperative, an industrial version of the kibbutz. One big operation, a gravel quarry, was in partnership with an Arab who had owned the site on the back side of the Carmel. Renovating the antiquated machinery, HaCohen had got gravel contracts for the new port; with real pleasure Mati had pushed through a big deal for Solel Boneh to build the customshouse. This could be the beginning for many government jobs. What tickled Mati was not only the Arab-Jewish partnership in the quarry, but on the Jewish side, the ownership of the means of production by labor itself. Right inside capitalist society, this was a solution!

In HaCohen's flat, just off the boat from a trip to Germany, was his brother-in-law, the elderly economist Dr. Lubin, the same, Mati was at once reminded, whose office had one day thirty years ago been invaded by the whole Chaimovitch family, father, mother, and eight children, seeking a homestead. "And you the

319

ninth. Your mother of blessed memory was so big I was afraid you were going to pop out at me then and there, and add your first cries, demanding land!"

He too was the son of a large family, Lubin related, and now at last—with a bitter thanks to Hitler—four of his brothers and sisters would be emigrating here.

Soon they were deep in the scandal of Ben-Gurion and the Arab leaders. Dr. Lubin had from the earliest days cried out for attention to the Arab question. Why had Ben-Gurion tried to revive that dream of Arabs moving to other lands!

"They made a fool of him!" HaCohen repeated. "He's never understood Arabs."

Perhaps it was once true, Lubin said, that the simple fellaheen here didn't care if they were moved off a few dozen kilometers to the north or to the east, to similar villages outside the Palestine border; they had never really known it as a border. Indeed, in bad times thousands had wandered to Syria on their own. In those days and for many of them, even today, if you asked a villager what he was, he didn't even say, "Arab," he said, "Muslami fellach." But the Zionist movement itself had changed this. From the Zionists, many young Arabs had learned nationalism; they had learned to say Palestine instead of Syria. No matter if for hundreds of years they had been ruled by the Turks and were now ruled by the British. No matter how many other lands the Arabs had. Perhaps at best, in economic self-interest, they would share with the Jews, but they would surely not give Palestine over to them.

That was true, HaCohen cried. For example even here in Haifa, where his partners were Arabs, where his fellow councillors in the municipality were Arabs, not one Arab he knew would ever agree to a Jewish Palestine! Not one! Not Karamon, the owner of the quarry, for whom they were making a fortune. Not the mayor, who had given every aid to ferreting out the Black Hand. And at the risk of retaliation. No! Not for any inducement would they ever agree to Jewish rule. Not one! The only way was to recognize that two people had to live here. Not per force as a binational state, which Dr. Magnes talked about, but perhaps in parallel states, in full cooperation—side by side. Why not? Basically already Jews and Arabs lived in different areas. Maybe a federation. Both nations moving toward socialism. It could come, it could come!

And yet they all sighed.

Perhaps like himself, Mati speculated, the other men were wondering, with how much blood? And that early slogan, the slogan of their own early secret society of defenders, echoed gruesomely in his mind, no wonder his brother Reuven had refused to accept it: "In blood and fire Judea fell, in blood and fire Judea shall arise."

22

YES? . . . When Jewish blood—?

And again it blurted out of her. ". . . spurts from the knife. . . ." Her trauma of the beer hall, with Khalid.

Had she ever witnessed a circumcision? Dr. Klausner shot at her in that specialty of his, the wild connection. And back to the old favorite, penis envy. And—another wild pitch—her first menstrual flow?

No one had prepared her. She had imagined it was from masturbation. The icky blood—

Yes, yes, but Jewish blood?

Suddenly Myra gave him a hitherto-suppressed detail. From her roommate Dottie Blumberg—at Miss Hagedorn's School they put Jewish girls together—Dottie had been forewarned by her mother not to be frightened when something came there; it was the curse of Eve. And for some crazy reason Myra from this had got the notion that only Jewish girls were cursed with this vile, smelly evil. Gentile girls were always fresh and superclean and never smelled, but no matter how you scrubbed with imported Lady Emerson and used woodsy perfume, the Jewish smell came through.

He pounced on it. They had already gone through Jewish *Selbsthass*, but why had this item been held back?

Myra concentrated, trying to associate it with Artie, Khalid, the Nazis.

Dr. Klausner had come from Berlin even before the Nazis took over, not only because he was certain they'd soon come to power but because in any case he wanted to get away from the orthodox Freudian method, the seat behind the couch. Klausner faced you and entered in, a dynamist, and now he was at it, a dog on the scent—hah! talk of smells! They had started the session over the news of the Nuremberg laws, Jewish blood the contamination, cohabitation with a Jew was a crime, a defilement of the superman, oh, he had led her cleverly, Jewish blood, shame. Untouchables. Vile.

Then her symptom. As if her face were falling away. Loss of face? Shame? Did the trouble go back before Artie? Maybe the symptom had only first appeared with the Artie trouble because of her added fear, shame of what Artie might tell all those examining psychiatrists, her little girlish episodes with him, necking in his car when she was just sixteen and had let him touch her down there and he had her touch his and then even got her to kiss it; many times she had been over this scene and concluded the facial symptom was the fear of being found out, an awful perversion she had imagined it was then. Now she could laugh. Klausner had long ago made her see she enjoyed reviewing her sexual exploits under the permission of analysis. But then why had the perception of the connection not relieved her of the symptom? Maybe this deeper part had been missing—Jewish blood. Maybe it was all *before* the trauma of Artie Straus and his bloody murder— Suddenly Myra bit her lip. The horror image of Artie and Judd and what they were said to have done to that little boy—cut it off—was mingled with the ghastly image from tales related by Mati Chaimovitch of what the Arabs did.

"Yes? Yes, Myra?" She blurted it all out in one streak. She had run away from Khalid there in Germany because— But to imagine someone like Khalid with a knife! She was staring into Klausner's eyes, the way when a child she used to make up stories just to see if they were believed. No, her shock was in the other connection, the Nazi knife. The supermen. Artie and Judd Steiner the Nietzschean supermen. Free to kill. Precursors of the Nazi Nietzscheans. That was why in Berlin it had all come back on her. Klausner was shaking his head with that small, knowing smile. Too easy. Too pat. The patient taking over for the analyst. Oh, she was a clever, intelligent girl, but was this really a case of prevision? Chicago, city of blood, a prevision of a German political movement? No, no, the tormenting brain twisting like a snake's head weaving for the target. Why again? It had happened there in the beer hall because the whole world, because it was rearing up all over the world—the murderous id— He nodded, his smile now a bit malicious, a teacher still knowing better than his glib pupil. And congratulated her on a good day's work.

It went more rapidly then.

She was doing good work with the New Kunstbau project, too, and the school was almost ready to open. Maholy had come over, but there was still some visa difficulty with a few of the others from the Bauhaus because it seemed they had communist records; her uncle Sylvan was doing things in Washington about it. Meanwhile, she again broke off with Joe Freedman; no longer was he going to intimidate her with her Jewish guilt and her nose-job "circumcision." Actually Joe had got jealous of the whole Kunstbau idea, demanding why with Jewish artists outlawed in Germany, she and her whole damn committee with her uncle's millions were setting up this big deal for *German* artists! Good God, Myra swore, they were all anti-Nazis and had to flee for defending their Jewish friends! Bushwah—for being commies, Joe insisted. Somehow he was getting more and more anticommunist; look what they were doing to the Jews in Russia, they had sent Zionists to Siberia, and what about the secret trial of Kamenev and Zinoviev? And on top of it all Joe was getting more and more realistic in his sculpture, old-hat. He was jealous and crabbed about the Kunstbau group really because of their freshness, their innovations. All at once she became Miss Richbitch who fell in with all the fads. Meanwhile, Myra had got him a small show at the Arts Club, but little had sold, and Joe then demeaned himself by doing some monstrous papier-mâché golem for the big Jewish Day pageant at the Chicago World Fair, The Romance of a People; they had even brought over their Chaim Weizmann from London to raise a hundred thousand dollars.

Now Joe was on WPA, and when he showed her his latest, a lifeless figure of Benjamin Franklin for the post office, Myra knew it was over. It finally came to her that maybe Joe Freedman was simply second-rate. Miss Richbitch was no longer intimidated by her West Side Yid. And anyway, that bastard always had other girls on the side.

As if on signal there came word of Khalid.

It came to her by way of Maholy himself, for after her breakdown she had thought it best not even to correspond. Now Maholy brought her an announcement for a one-man show in a Paris

324

gallery on the Rue St. Peres. So the gallery must have standing, even though it was new and she didn't know the name. Maholy said yes, it had standing. And the announcement was superb, silver and turquoise enamel. Khalid had gone over to sheer design, although you could still see the calligraphic forms as roots. On the inside he had scribbled, "Hello kid. Drop in, Your Khalid."

Maybe she would do just that! Drop in for a look. Dr. Klausner was taking a long Christmas vacation, going to London for a conference.

She didn't kid herself that Khalid had been sitting around waiting for her—and in Paris. But perhaps with him, too, something had come full circle. Anyway, Dena had kept at her to come over and see the twins, so she could just make Paris a stop on the way to Palestine.

Dena wrote amusing bits about the place, like how on the Tel Aviv beach she had let the twins toddle naked and some officious geezer had come up and demanded, how old were those naked boys? Imagine! But even funnier, the same geezer carried a tape measure, and honestly, he checked on women's bathing suits! Even tourists! A few had given him what for! It was a crazy country. She and Mati had been all set to go and see Hedy Lamarr in *Ecstasy*, but imagine, the film was banned! The rabbis still had a lot of power, Dena wrote, but then she wrote very touching things about the refugee kids from Germany, at Big Leah's training farm.

Also Sylvan wanted Myra to go over and bring back a personal report. Myra had never seen Sylvan so upset as after the Nuremberg racial laws. The German Jews should have beat Hitler to it and as a mass renounced their German citizenship before they had it taken away from them. And what had that evil cripple Goebbels meant by that strange line in his speech, "We must step up Jewish annihilation"? This was becoming sinister.

It was clear now that every last German Jew had to get out, Sylvan declared. Maybe Palestine was the answer in spite of all the drawbacks. He wanted Myra to bring back her impressions, without Zionist propaganda.

Dr. Klausner said, why not a protracted holiday, she was doing fine, he was just about ready to kick her out, let her take a long Christmas trip abroad. Her own Santa Klausner! She'd stop in Paris; Sylvan even had a task for her there too, some affidavits to get from a few Kunstbau people, I never was a communist, and then she could sail for Palestine from Venice, which was said to be

325

out of the world in winter. Wonderful, Sylvan agreed. He was tempted to take the trip with her as surely she knew he had always felt incestuous!

❅ ❅ ❅

Myra made it for the *vernissage* and walked in. The place was jammed, well, it was quite small, but the crowd was the right mixture, elegance and Montparnasse. And his enamels! Electric!

Before Khalid spotted her, she had a few moments for a rapid reconnoiter. He couldn't have anything going with the gallery owner, an obvious les in a mannish suit. And in the circle around him the women were so meticulously groomed they had to be beyond his age.

Now he spotted her. A passion kiss right on the mouth. Of course, this was Paris, but maybe he really didn't have anyone special right now.

It was on again. Khalid kept her for dinner. The Ile St. Louis apartment of the lesbian from the gallery, a few married couples— backers. Maybe one of these wives? At one moment Myra thought she caught that certain look, a fleeting, comprehending glance from one of the wives to herself and then to him.

Everyone was checking over who had come to the opening—the *Figaro* critic, not the top but the second. Still, very good. And from *Arts and Letters*, their specialist on Oriental painting. And Foujita, and Fernand Léger, and the American Man Ray, Man Ray loved it. She could see that Khalid was on his way.

Afterward he took her to his studio in a courtyard on the Rue d'Assas, and they didn't get out of bed for fourteen hours.

One thing Myra had to say for herself, she was constant. Always back to the same men. The constant nymph, but plural. The music goes round and round and it comes out here.

Khalid couldn't leave Paris until his show was over, but he had promised to go home right after the exposition; his father was not well. . . . That woman at dinner? A minor affair, it was finished. He was—like herself—between engagements.

For the landing in Haifa, Myra suggested they ought to split up; his people would be there to meet him and— Oh, she could simply be a tourist he had met on the boat; they would love her! Anyway, she said, Mati and Dena were coming, and with his family, it might get complicated. Khalid gave in, laughing. It wasn't going to be so complicated as she imagined; his family was quite civilized.

"Hallo, shalom!" the twins chirped together like an act. Darlings. In the arrival crowd, Mati and Dena just had a moment for a hello to Khalid, they'd see him in Jerusalem.

They had a whole house now, Myra could stay with them; they even had a guest room! Unless? Dena was already wise about Khalid. But anyway, Myra had to see the new house; they had just moved in, the owner of their apartment had returned from abroad, and luckily this house had been for sale right down the street, Mati had mortgaged his salary up to old age! It had a garden, a yard for the boys—

Dena was quite a mother; Myra wasn't surprised. She was full of how the twins were at their cutest age and how fascinating it was to watch their different characters developing; though Jonathan was the smaller, he was, of course, the smarter, though David was outstandingly intelligent, too. The house was in the professors' quarter, Rehavia; all Mati would accept from her family had been the Frigidaire, he couldn't very well ship it back; Dena had been holding off her housewarming until everything was in order, at last she could really do some entertaining! And if Myra wanted to be on her own, on the other side of Jerusalem near the Damascus Gate was a wonderful hotel, everybody went to it, all the Palestinian Jews who knew what was good, the American Colony Hotel, journalists and British and distinguished visitors went there, and it would be handy for Khalid.

The place had been built by a pasha for his harem, Dena said as the crimson-sashed Sudanese in his snowy galabia led them across the inner garden and along a rambling hallway; the hotel was run by an American missionary family. Maybe at night Khalid should be careful about going up with her to her room—but look! Myra's room had a little balcony a half story above the rear garden. Something every girl dreams of, a Romeo climbing up! And his secret knock so she opens the french windows, and at dawn he slips away!

The room was absolute perfection, with its arched ceiling, its deep alcove windows, its step-up bathroom with colored-glass panes and intricate multicolored tiles, pure abstraction. Khalid would love them!

The Sudanese brought them mint tea with almond cakes, and Dena settled into a harem-pillowed sofa, saying, "So tell."

In a few days there was more to tell. Khalid's brother Attala, who had the Morris car agency in Jerusalem, had lent him a roadster, and he had taken her up to the old family village in northern Galilee. A tourist friend. Had Dena ever been on that road from Acre where you passed through miles of nothing but olive groves on either side?

Wasn't that the road where there was a tiny village of Jewish inhabitants going all the way back to the Roman conquest? It was on all the Hadassah tours.

Well, maybe, but this wasn't a Hadassah tour, kiddo. A real Arab village. Myra had got herself a long skirt for the trip and worn long sleeves. So she was even equipped to walk in Mea Shearim! Dena joked.

All she had needed was a veil, Myra said. The village was the family estate, the old great-grandfather was the sheikh, and there were still maidens with jars on their shoulders going to the well. Khalid had presented her to the patriarch, you'd swear it was old Abraham himself, at least a hundred and twenty, and of course, the manor house, the one big house of the village, was something to behold. Wall hangings with passages of the Koran in beautiful ancient script; that must have been where as a child Khalid got his love for calligraphy; he used to spend his summers in the village. This old sheikh had told Myra tales of half a century ago, he had sold a tract of land to a noble Jew, the Baron de Rothschild, for the return of Jews. Were not Jews and Arabs cousins, sons of Abraham? He had become lifelong friends with the representative of the Baron, Jacques Samuelson, who lived on that tract, the Jews had named it Rosh Pina, and in the war against the Turks when the Baron could not send gold from France to his friend Samuelson, the sheikh himself had lent the Jews gold.

But Dena knew the story! The gold was to buy a hilltop on the border that became known as Kfar Giladi and also Tel Hai, where Mati's sister had died with the hero Trumpeldor.

Khalid had actually shown Myra the spot in the yard where his great-grandfather had kept hidden his jar of golden coins. And did

328

Dena know that—according to Khalid—the sheikhs up in the villages were once again buying and burying gold? They were convinced from Mussolini's Arabic broadcasts that soon there would be another big war.

After the coffee and the rahat lukoums and the walk with Khalid through the village, feeling all eyes on you, and stops for greetings, suddenly Khalid had whispered he had to get out of there. The fellaheen were still so damn abject! Serfs! He really was very fond of them, but he couldn't stand another minute.

As a kid, he had told her, he would run around barefoot and have a great time; though belonging to the owning family, he was accepted like one of the village boys. He had even got his initiation here! A big payoff had to be made for the honor of the girl; it could have been worse—he might have had to marry her or she could have traditionally had her throat cut by her brothers. That was when he was sent off to school in England, and now, look, he was a stranger, a European. They were devout Moslems here, still sunken in the old ways; after an hour the backwardness gave him the shudders. But what the hell did Myra think had paid for London and Paris?

Of course, he hadn't taken her to visit his parents in Haifa, certainly not yet. With the great-grandfather she could pass as a tourist. Still, they had gone in Nazareth to that very courtyard, it turned out, where Dena with her folks had been taken by Nahum to the house of Boulos Nashashibi. The same! Myra had met his wife, quite modern, really charming. Latifa had one of Khalid's early things, the clan relationship was too complicated to follow, but it seemed they were in the Christian branch of the family, a brother of Khalid's grandfather had been sent to school in Nazareth and fallen in love with a Christian Arab girl, and converted, and so that Nazareth branch was Christian, there were four brothers, four sisters, and they were just like a Jewish family—one son had a shop, the antique shop, another was a doctor, another a teacher, another a journalist. Khalid had even teased Myra, hinting the paper got money from Mussolini. *El Ard*, it was called. Oh, yes, Dena knew from Mati—it was wildly anti-Jewish. That was the one that printed translations about the big Jewish plot to rule the world, the *Protocols of the Elders of Zion*.

But with his family they hadn't discussed politics, Myra said. Only chitchat about art and the beauties of Paris. To his cousins Khalid was the artist in the family. They joked a bit about his wild communism; could anyone imagine Khalid sitting down and actually reading Karl Marx? his cousin the teacher had twitted him. "There is no God, and Karl Marx is his prophet," Khalid had responded. Later, with Latifa, he had picked up a drawing block of her daughters and impishly done a bit of calligraphy looking like one of those Koranic mottoes, but it had made his cousin flush. She snatched it away before her girls could see it. "No, nothing naughty." Khalid laughed to Myra and whispered a translation: "There is no Allah, and Karl Marx is his prophet."

Suddenly Myra became morose. It was true Khalid was really—well, an enthusiast, an artist, boyish and truly sweet as a person. She was truly fond of him, loved him, maybe was really in love with him. Or maybe it was sex; of course, he was g.i.b. and she patted her sex box like a gluttonous little girl patting her tummy. Her Arabian stallion! Sometimes he would make fiery speeches about organizing the fellaheen. But making speeches was to him as if he had gone and done it. Did Dena understand?

That was the Arabs, Dena said, like a knowing old settler.

Did she know when Khalid had been happiest? When they looked up a painter from the Bauhaus. A Jew named Mordecai, originally from Poland. Khalid had known him, even once hidden him in Berlin! Imagine where he now was—in Kiryat Anavim, that hilltop kibbutz right near Jerusalem, a shepherd! Yes, the kibbutz had made him a shepherd, and this Mordecai said he loved it, and Khalid declared he was all set to join him! In his room Mordecai had shown Khalid a slab of stone he had taken from the hills; he was trying to do lithographs on it; he said it was something like the special litho stone quarried in Austria. So suddenly Khalid was all messed up in lithos. The shepherd had given Khalid a sample hunk of stone, and lithography was perfect for calligraphy, as Dena knew, you drew right on the stone, it was based on the principle of oil and water don't mix—Myra gave her laugh: "Like Arabs and Jews!"—but together on the same stone they made a beautiful print. Hah! That would make a perfect slogan for—what was it called, that peace group?—"B'rith Shalom."

One trouble for Khalid, there was really no Arab artist crowd. For her party Dena invited Reuven Rubin, the leading painter of Palestine, with his American wife, Esther; it was going to be a mixed crowd; she picked them carefully, Mati's chief at the office,

Welby, alas, the Welbys were soon going home to England, and Mati was worried about who would come next. The High Commissioner himself had accepted another tour of duty but had come back from London in somehow a different mood, Mati said; that too was worrisome; anyway, Dena couldn't invite the High Commissioner—yet. A new young Oxford Arab from the office, and Eddie Marmor was bringing an Arab journalist who worked on the *Post*, so Khalid wouldn't feel isolated. Also, Gershon Agronsky, the editor, was coming, he was an excellent contact for Myra for her report to her uncle. And Dena had invited Dov Joseph, the Canadian lawyer who was quite high up in Jewish Agency circles, besides her regulars like Reggie and Maureen, and from Mati's family she invited Nahum and Shula and also Leah and her Natan the Red. Khalid should hit it off with Natan! Then by luck, Dena captured Professor Nelson Glueck, the rabbi archaeologist who had just returned with some fabulous discoveries from the Sinai Desert—he had discovered King Solomon's Mines!

In her plum-colored flowing hostess pajamas that Sherrill had sent her from Saks, Mati told her, kiddo, she was a dreamboat. She'd really show them style! And the party went off without a hitch, though once or twice Dena had to slip in fast to sidetrack a political argument.

Esther Rubin had given Dena a special punch bowl recipe, for this happened to be Christmas week, and everybody kept marveling at the spicy taste. Elinor Welby was sure Dena had used a fancy French wine; even after their whole tour of duty here she still couldn't recognize the taste of good old Rishon!

Meanwhile, Dena had failed to stop an argument: there was Professor Zalman Bamberger, a staunch supporter of Dr. Magnes and binationalism, coming straight at Moshe Shertok like a head-down bull with blood in his eye, even though Shertok was just about as liberal as you could be on the Arab question without turning over the government to them! Mati had warned her, but she had had to ask the Bambergers so as to get Nelson Glueck, who was staying with them. Only a few days ago Ben-Gurion had come out with a terrible blast at the whole Magnes crowd, calling them meddlers, because they had been conducting some kind of unauthorized negotiations with high-up Arabs, even saying, it seemed, that the Jews would accept a ten-year limitation on immigration! This meant an agreement to minority status! "Do you really expect to become a majority in ten years?" Bamberger sneered at Shertok, and a couple of Britishers with their ears pricked up were already moving into the circle. Shertok said something smooth; after all, he couldn't speak for Ben-Gurion. But Bamberger charged on; this was almost the last chance to reach agreement with the Arabs, if Shertok couldn't speak for Ben-Gurion, why didn't he speak out for himself? It was everyone's responsibility.

Dena glided in, taking the moment to introduce Myra to Moshe Shertok, who was known for his eye for the ladies, and meanwhile changing the subject, why didn't someone speak out about *Ecstasy* being banned! Everybody laughed.

At least Khalid hadn't been dragged into the argument; he was charming Esther Rubin with that Persian-prince smile of his; Reuven Rubin said he was crazy about calligraphy and knew a great collector, a Sephardi in Jerusalem; he would take Khalid to see the collection. Not only ancient illuminated texts from the Koran, but also fantastic Persian miniatures.

And Professor Nelson Glueck had a circle around him; he was absolutely fascinating with his modest little way of telling about his discovery of King Solomon's copper smelters. Oh, the area had long been known to that breed of desert rats that wandered around the Sinai, lone explorers, not really prospectors, but curious fellows stricken with a love of that desolate area. And near the tip of the Red Sea was a plateau where, because of the conformation of the surrounding hills, you had a natural wind tunnel that made possible the intense flames needed to purify the copper ore. Greenish chunks of ore were still lying about right on the surface, and there he had found traces of primitive smelters! He had brought back a few samples of ore and given them to Dr. Magnes, who was having university mineralogists determine the proportion of copper content. Who could tell? One day King Solomon's mines might be reopened!

Dena served tea and blinis; she had a really good feeling, the house, the gathering—a success. Mati had moved up a notch.

Several people who were at the party invited Myra and her friend Khalid together. In B'rith Shalom circles they were almost an exhibit. And when meeting a Youth Aliyah group, Myra received hand pattings from Henrietta Szold herself, a supporter of binationalism.

Khalid's brother Attala had cleared a workshop for him on the top floor of his auto agency building, facing the Old City walls, and there Myra often dropped in. Sometimes Attala took them to lunch in the half-hidden restaurant behind the Jaffa Gate that specialized in stuffed roast pigeon. Fifteen years older than the kid brother, Attala had been the first of the family to be educated in England. He still told Colonel Blimp jokes. Unfortunately Attala's wife was from a very traditional family—Myra understood. It was not her being Jewish but her being a wicked woman, a mistress. And of course, that was also why Khalid couldn't introduce her to his father and mother either any more than Wally Simpson could be invited to dinner at Buckingham Palace. The father was recovering from a coronary attack, and Khalid would go off home for a few days at a time. If he should present her as his fiancée? Both skirted away from the subject.

With little Dena she could talk. Naturally, by now all Jerusalem knew; this really was a small town! Well, there was the money thing, too. Khalid depended on his family; a few collectors had bought; that Jewish collector, the Sephardi, what an unbelievable house tucked behind a walled garden in the Jewish quarter of the Old City, and Khalid had gone wild over an ancient Persian illuminated manuscript with drawings of two tightrope walkers, spidery, scribbly lines, an absolute Paul Klee in the fourteenth century! And a few days later this old Sephardi banker had climbed up to Khalid's studio, and what taste, he had gone straight for Khalid's best things, particularly one large watercolor he still had from London; maybe Dena remembered it. But Khalid couldn't live on a few odd sales. Myra had thought, maybe once his father got better, of saying the hell with all this, the Arabs, the Jews, and taking Khalid back to Paris. Maybe there would still be a few more good years before the world blew up. But no, he wasn't the kind of man who could live on a woman, and she couldn't stay with a man who could. Then she had another idea: why not get him a teaching job in the New Kunstbau House in Chicago? Perfect, Dena said. And for a moment Myra got a light in her eye; oh, would Joe Freedman be furious! Then she grew melancholy. Oh, the hell, she said, tamping out a just-started cigarette, a moment later lighting another.

They all went to see Ravi Shankar's dances. They went to see the Purim festival parade in Tel Aviv, this year with more elaborate floats than ever; on one truck a huge papier-mâché figure in flowing robes, labeled HAMAN, but with the face of Hitler, swung high from a gibbet.

Hitler entered the Rhineland, a parade of flower-bedecked tanks, delirious joy. Mati raged. Now, now was the time to stop him.

In the old German Templars' colony of Sarona, near Leah's training farm, men of military age, still German citizens though in the fourth generation here, received notice to register for military service.

In England, the fascist leader Mosley declared that since there was free speech, he was free to proclaim his anti-Semitism.

A farmer driving his wagon on a road in Galilee was murdered.

In Rehavia a block away from their house a police car was shot at.

Before Mati left for work, the phone rang. It was Eddie Marmor. Riots had broken out in Jaffa, the worst since 1929. Mati had better not drive alone to the Arab side of town.

Mati had hardly put down the phone when the office called; a car was on the way.

They'd chosen their time again, Mati cried. As in 1929, the High Commissioner was out of the country and the British forces had lately been thinned out. But this time the Jews were not empty-handed. After the Black Hand killings a year ago, Golda Meyerson had made a quiet trip to America, with lists of special contacts. Mati had given her the name of Phil Kossoff, and Phil had raised thirty thousand dollars in Chicago to add to the Haganah arms fund. In Europe, Yehuda Arazi, Menahem, and the rest of the boys had used the money well. Arazi had a whole factory going in Warsaw making road rollers and boilers. On Sundays, Arazi and Menahem did the special packing.

Dena had the radio on. Several Arabs and Jews had been killed, but Jaffa was being brought under control, the government spokesman announced in his dispassionate monotone. The Arab Executive Committee had ordered all Arab shops to close; the Jaffa port was closed; Arab taxis and buses would not operate. Arab leaders demanded a total halt of Jewish immigration and stoppage of all land sales to Jews. The old demands.

Now, now, Mati swore, was surely the moment when he should quit the damn service, get hold of Dov, get hold of the *Gidon* and load it. Should they try any attacks on the settlements—

But the government car was outside, and he had to leave. "Stay in the house, keep the boys inside," he told Dena. "No, not even in the backyard, until things were clear." At least at the office he'd get the full picture.

But insanely, when he got there, Mati was rushed into a meeting over the Levant Fair; the Levant Fair must open, Arab boycott or not. Incoming shipping bringing industrial exhibits must be diverted from Jaffa to the Haifa port, where Salonika Jews could do the unloading.

Suddenly an idea came to Mati—a port in Tel Aviv! Then let them choke in Jaffa! Tel Aviv was now twice Jaffa's size. The idea must not come from him, not even from the Agency. Best from a shipping company. He'd pass it on through Reggie.

The full outbreak had been in the Jaffa marketplace, with the old shout, "Aleihum!" and attackers pouring from the side lanes, screaming that in Tel Aviv three Arabs riding in a gharry had been shot.

British police arrived quickly but were stoned. The district officer, Azmi Nashashibi, standing up boldly in his car, kept shouting there were no Arabs assaulted in Tel Aviv; it was a fabrication. Slowly the square came under control, though side-street attacks on the few remaining Jewish shops in Jaffa were continuing.

Just outside Jaffa at the Mikve Israel farm school a Canadian Jewish student was cut down in the fields. In the vanguard of the Jaffa mob, news reports said, had been Hauranis from the tin shacks near the school.

By morning, the radio said seven more dead had been counted in Jaffa—two Jews and five Arabs. Eddie Marmor phoned to tell them about Zelig Levinson, the well-known lawyer—he had often been to the house. Gunned down.

A Jewish truck driver going through Nablus had been stoned but had escaped. A train had been stoned. Another truck driver was reported shot on the Nablus-Tulkarm road. Ben-Gurion, Ben-Zvi and Moshe Shertok were visiting hospitals.

Declaring the riots were caused by Jews, Jamal Husseini of the Supreme Moslem Council had issued a call for a general Arab strike. Five thousand refugees from the Jaffa area had flocked into Tel Aviv. Newspapers abroad were reporting Tel Aviv in flames.

Dena had Mati get through a cable to the family, ALL SAFE DANGER EXAGGERATED DONT WORRY LOVE. Still, crossing theirs, a wire came: KNOW YOUR COURAGE BUT IF THINGS WORSEN MAMA BEGS DENA BRING TWINS. Dear idiots.

Myra also received a cable. YOU ARE NOT NEEDED THERE STOP NEEDED HERE FOR KUNSTBAU, her uncle wired. She even asked Khalid—would he come to Chicago to teach? Giving her his lambent gaze, he laughed softly and said he would think it over.

A flood of journalists was arriving, and Khalid sometimes took Myra to the King David bar; there was the famous Vincent Sheean who had covered the revolt of Abd-El-Krim, drinking with a young Husseini whom Khalid had known in London, like himself a radical. Except this Husseini was said to be a real active communist. "Look at the stone-quarry workers at Athlit," Husseini was telling the journalist, "the Arabs get fifteen piasters a day and the Jews get thirty." From along the bar Eddie Marmor joined in. He happened to know all about that situation, he said. The Jewish workers had organized a cooperative, borrowed money to buy jackhammers and hoists, and arranged to work by the ton instead of on a day wage. Arab workers could do the same and earn the same.

Who owned the quarry? the journalist wanted to know.

"Arabs and Jews, partners," said Eddie.

"There's capitalism for you!" Husseini snapped. "Crosses all borders."

Eddie Marmor put in again, "Wait, the Jewish part is owned by organized labor, the Histadrut."

Husseini was even more triumphant. "There's your Jewish socialism! Exploiters!"

In bed Khalid brooded. His whole family was having political disputes. Some of the Nashashibis insisted they ought to join the Arab Higher Committee so there would be a united Arab front, but the elder, a remote sort of uncle of his, was altogether against the strike. It would do the Arabs more harm than the Jews.

Khalid felt he ought to get into things in some way, but hell, he had no head for politics. Even his brother didn't know what to do. Attala was getting along fine, selling Morris cars to Jews, English, Arabs, but it was true that if things went on with fifty thousand Jews a year coming in like last year, the Jews could become a majority. The Turks had ruled here, now the British—but to be ruled by the Jews, Attala said no. Oh, for himself, Khalid didn't give a damn; only by now he was an outsider. Deep down maybe he could understand—Khalid pulled her to him almost despairingly. Myra had never felt him so torn, so unhappy. The lovemaking was his need for assertion, maybe even because she was a Jewess; it was the first time she had felt this. Pathetic. She supposed their affair was over. Surely he wouldn't come to Chicago, at least not now. Yet she lingered on in Jerusalem.

Tel Aviv merchants met and demanded their own port, so as to be rid once and for all of the Jaffa holdups. Judges and lawyers met, demanding courts be established in Tel Aviv, since it was a life risk to have to appear in Jaffa. Two Jewish nurses who continued to work in a Jaffa hospital were killed in the street. A Jewish bus on a Galilee road was shot up, with three dead, and the next day an Arab bus was attacked, with five killed. Everyone knew it was the Irgun.

From the Haganah the order was restraint. The word was Havlagah. Everywhere, every man on guard; if there were attacks, beat them off, but there must be no reprisals. At all-night sessions the policy was fought over, but Eliahu remained firm. What use was a bomb thrown into an Arab marketplace, killing indiscriminately? If the Arab terrorists themselves could be caught and fought, that was the only way. Irgun-style retaliation would only arouse more bloodletting. But beyond that was the old question: Have we come here to revert to the old ghoum or to live by our own rules of justice? Strength, yes. Show the greatest strength. On guard everywhere. Prevent or stop every attack. But no "eye for an eye." Not only would the world soon notice—

"Who gives a damn about the world! Do they give a damn about us?"

Nevertheless.

And in the midst of this Mati had to dash to Haifa to get displays unloaded for the fair. With thousands of troops rushed in from Egypt to assure order in the land, the Levant Fair opened on time. The country was prosperous, the High Commissioner announced; despite some trouble and discontent, schools had been opened in hundreds of Arab villages, and roads built and there was even a growing surplus in the treasury!

Ten Jewish children were injured by a grenade flung through a schoolroom window.

At the fair was a large booth for Rutenberg's Palestine Airways, with huge photographs of the airplanes. Two six-seaters. Alongside the grounds was a runway, and for two pounds a ride passengers could see Tel Aviv and Jaffa from the air. And if there were no clouds, even golden Jerusalem could be glimpsed crowning the inland hills. Had he made a mistake? Mati asked himself. With Rutenberg, he might have become manager. Which task would have been more important? How could a man know? He had done what was wanted of him, perhaps not what he himself had wanted. Perhaps he was that kind of man.

At least his first pupil, Giora, had got a pilot job. Giora took up the whole family, in turns, and when he offered Mati the stick, Dena teased she felt safer with the pupil! But Mati took it and felt good, and damn it to hell with them, the authorities, the Arabs, the whole damn world, he did loop-the-loops over Tel Aviv.

With work going on day and night the pier for the Tel Aviv port was ready, and on that night all of them, Mati, Dena, Leah with all her girls, all Tel Aviv rushed down to the shore, and excited tourists danced the hora in the water. As in the old days.

Despite memories of the bloody May Day of 1921, Haifa's joint May Day celebration by Arab and Jewish workers was on. Khalid and Myra drove down with Mati and Dena. With two thousand mixed workers, though mostly Jewish, listening to Arab and Jewish orators, and almost as many police and soldiers outside, the event was peaceful. Khalid was excited. The young Arab labor leader Sami Taha was the real thing!

All the way back to Jerusalem Khalid talked of getting into the labor movement and living in Haifa—what a view from the top of the Carmel! But of course, he still had not taken Myra to meet his parents. They lived below in the Arab section, having moved from Acre to be near a good hospital, because of his father's illness.

Even in Mati's office, Arab employees were having to pay in ten percent of their salaries to the Higher Committee. The strike was ruining the whole Arab economy; it couldn't go on.

In the Old City an Arab shopkeeper, rolling up his shutters, was shot dead. Others were selling at back doors.

Sami Taha in Haifa was shot at but escaped.

In an open square of Nablus, one of the Nashashibi notables made a speech asking, "Do we want to hurt ourselves or the Jews? The strike hurts us; let us end the strike, and concentrate on those methods that hurt the Jews."

His back was ripped by a dagger. The attacker, seized, proved to be linked to the Husseinis.

A vision haunted Myra—she saw Khalid walking at dusk to the hotel, and from one of the side lanes a figure darted, a knife down his back, blood. A Nashashibi. And always with a Jewess.

His brother's auto agency was closed; in the studio upstairs Khalid talked only in snatches. No, his family would not be drawn into a tribal ghoum. All this was politics. After all, there were intermarriages and many other links between the two clans. Myra recalled how in his grandfather's village he had sensed himself a stranger. Yet somehow he didn't feel he could leave, right now. Even though his work was at a standstill. One composition after another was started and left unfinished.

With his brother's agency closed downstairs, the building, the place had become dismal.

The mayor of Hebron, a leader in the Nashashibis' National Defense Party, was assassinated in the street by a volley from a passing car, Chicago style, the *Post* said.

Myra began to feel spooky, realizing she was perhaps the only Jew left in the American Colony Hotel. With the Arab cabs on strike, she was imprisoned. A Jewish cabdriver who one day took a fare around to the Arab side, at Herod's Gate, was yanked from his wheel by a mob and would have been killed but for a British constable stationed there, who managed to pull the Jew behind him against the wall, shouting to him, "They'll have to kill me before they touch you!" The heroic incident was reported in the *Post*, but now Khalid agreed that Myra ought to move across to the other side of Jerusalem; she took a room in the King David, only a short walk from his studio.

More and more foreign correspondents arrived, and she was always being invited for drinks. A few had just come from Ethiopia, watching Mussolini's tanks and planes against ancient carbines and knives. A fellow named Dick arrived from Chicago, from the *Daily News*, he kept giving her that look—he knew about Artie Straus. And what was she doing here? She said she was making a survey of the refugee children, but she was here privately, if he didn't mind. He'd know soon enough about Khalid, too.

The thing was coming back over her. The old symptom. Not for a long time, not since that time in Germany, had it come over her so strongly. She now knew she had simply to draw out her compact and look in the mirror, a little trick that Santa Klausner had suggested; if she felt the symptom coming on, she had only to look at her face; there was no such disaster as she imagined, was there? She fumbled. The damn bar was so dim, and it was vulgar to primp in public. She had to get out, get to her room; Khalid would call her there if he didn't find her in the bar.

Upstairs Myra stared in the mirror, but by now anyway the symptom had passed. Oh, what was she? Oh, it was real with Khalid, he was so beautiful, his mouth, surely, it would never be like this again, maybe this was love. Oh, why didn't some damn Arab just shoot her dead, and an end? Should she make a try and tell him, tell him tonight—you know why I ran off that time in Germany? It had to be possible to say everything.

They had dinner downstairs, and then in the bar the talk was high; there was a comic story about the philosopher Will Durant, who had arrived on a Holy Land visit, and as there were no taxis at the railway station he got to the hotel riding on a donkey. Dick was there, and she introduced him to Khalid; Dick had already been fixed up by Dena with a girl named Ilana, Haganah, and in the lively atmosphere Myra didn't feel her symptom, and they all went off to Hesse's for dinner.

In the Arab Higher Committee, Fakri Bey Nashashibi pressed for the ruinous strike to be ended. The London appointment of an Inquiry Commission offered an excuse. The mufti's cousin Jamal Husseini stood firmly against. This time the Nashashibis walked out of the Higher Committee.

In Nazareth, as Boulos Nashashibi climbed to his house up the narrow lane between the high monastery walls, one powerful dagger stroke from behind cut his throat and he died in his blood.

Khalid could not take her to the family gathered there. Myra understood. But she kept seeing it—the carefully gowned wife with her two charming nunnery-school daughters, her Louis XVI sitting room, there all the family women must be sitting now; how could she ever be among them? But all at once she saw Khalid in his car gunned down on the road. No, this was hysteria. He had gone with his brother Attala, several cars, the whole clan.

She couldn't sit in the damn hotel room, wouldn't go down and sit on a barstool; all the correspondents would be at her. She was falling apart. Pouring a brandy, Myra talked in a stream in her head as on some days before going to see Dr. Klausner. The knife. The spurting blood. Khalid, Artie.

It was still there in her. All that cleverly constructed analysis, menstrual blood, shame, was it only like the surface meaning of a dream? When Jewish blood spurts from the knife— Not only Jewish. Arab blood. Blood. Oh, this bloody rotten world. But was that it? Was that it? Then why her face? Why did her face go away? Thank God the phone rang, her little Dena, the sane, of those uncomplicated West Side Jews with their strong Russian stock.

Dena hurried right over. Oh, that poor nice Arab woman with her two dutiful daughters. . . . What the Mufti was doing, Mati had explained to Dena, was like when Hitler killed off a whole moderate element in his party, the Night of the Long Knives it had been called. Myra held herself together.

She had heard it all, the knives, the correspondents said four Husseini men had been found shot dead in Nazareth, and Boulos Nashashibi was a retaliation. Oh, she was sick, sick of the knives, the guns, of this crazy Palestine, she cried. Okay, the Jewish thing always she got inside her when she saw another bunch of refugee kids, she had gone with Henrietta Szold again, there was one child whose mother had packed sets of clothing in growing sizes for five years ahead for her little boy. Oh, damned God!

And this Jerusalem! she burst out at Dena, this holy Yerushalayim with its Old City that they clawed and stabbed and shot each other over. It was just one big slum, the Wailing Wall was just an alley, the whole city was just a provincial backwater with filthy pseudoexotic lanes, a stinking second-rate souk, and could the Holy Sepulchre compare to Notre Dame? And the Mosque of Omar, okay, it glowed, the calligraphic tiles were beautiful, but should the land be torn up over whether it was Isaac or Ishmael whom Abraham led to the sacrificial rock? And as for all this frantic construction by the Jews, was there one decent original building? The whole of Tel Aviv—imagine the opportunity of building an entire new city, and it was sleazy German so-called modernism of the twenties, and even the Erich Mendelsohn university buildings were not his best, and he had given up and gone to America. Oh, she had done her duty for Sylvan and inspected one of those new villages where German Jewish jurisprudents had introduced strawberries to Palestine. And what about the German Jewish woman just arrived a month ago, shot dead on the Haifa road?

Crazily—this had never happened before—Myra fell into a crying jag. Dena sat and soothed her, but Myra could see she was desperately trying to think who to call; was there even a psychiatrist in this godforsaken land? Among the Germans surely an analyst had arrived. Dena was trying to reach a Dr. Epstein, somebody from Brooklyn, her obstetrician, but Myra said never mind, she felt better.

Dena cabled Sylvan Straus. There came a reply to Myra, with the name of an analyst from Berlin, now in Jerusalem, recommended by Dr. Klausner, should she wish to consult someone at once before coming home.

Though the same pensive melancholy photograph of Freud hung like a totem behind the desk, Dr. Eigen, as though to certify that he was not sailing under false colors, at once declared himself an eclectic; he knew and respected Dr. Klausner and inquired with faint irony whether his friend was getting rich in Chicago, and in any case said she should not just now change but should go back to her analyst; however, in what seemed an emergency he would be glad to consult with her.

Her panic, her symptom of the face, he listened, the faint smile fading. He had an oversized head that looked as if it would flop off-balance, like the head of a baby; she wondered if behind that desk his feet touched the floor; he must be a gnome. Ah, the blood, the knife—indeed as a student he had been fascinated by the Steiner-Straus case in Chicago, he had procured the psychiatric reports, perhaps one really could look at their "Nietzschean" crime as a token, a precursor of the era. A thought—even Hitler must have followed that world-sensational murder case: Supermen. The right to kill. Above the common law. The Jewish law, from Moses, wasn't it? Ah. And for a moment Myra thought he would use up the whole session on this notion. But suddenly he jumped to personal history: parents divorced while she was still very young. She found herself saying the divorce had come as an utter surprise; she had believed her parents were inseparable. So. And with Artie, she had believed he was a gay, wonderful fellow, her only worry that he chased other girls, and then the sudden crime and the homosexuality. So again, he said—as with her parents. Not? Myra strove for the analogy. Someone she loved and believed she knew as you know people you love. And suddenly— Yes, yes? Suddenly they were altogether different, as though she hadn't known them at all. And she couldn't face it?

Was it as simple as this? She couldn't face reality? A bit of wordplay and whoops, your life is straightened out. No, not that simple. But still—

Why had she altered her nose? Her schnozz, as she called it? He had that ironic smile again.

Her face sliding away as if she didn't have one, like a false face—you didn't know anybody's real face or your own real face— too banal.

She had only one more session with Dr. Eigen, and this time, oddly, they talked little of herself. All her nasty feelings, even anger about certain types of Jews, the long-coats in Mea Shearim with their little boys in long coats and with the ear curls that her friend Dena found so cute—she hated the whole place! Ech!

Dr. Eigen was talking, lecturing about German Jews. Since Nazism, there was an interesting movement to self-study. Had she ever heard of Dr. Franz Rosenzweig? Martin Buber? Well, he doubted they were well known in America. But this movement was helping many German Jews find themselves and face their situation.

The damn little gnome.

Khalid telephoned. He was in Haifa. His father had had a stroke; he must stay at his father's side. Perhaps the best thing—as soon as the trouble was over, they must try to meet again in Paris—

Though you had to go in a bus convoy because of the ambushes, Myra on impulse went to Tel Aviv to say goodbye to Leah. Big Leah had heard much, maybe everything from Dena, she was sure.

Taking Myra into her own room and making tea, Leah suddenly talked of herself, of the time when she had gone back to Russia, found her Handsome Moshe. As though there were a new bond between Myra and herself, Leah talked of the intimate part, how even though she had found him married and with a son, she had gone back to him. She had let her body go back to him. Only then, one night, he had said something.

Leah looked into Myra's eyes. "Who knows what holds a woman to a man?" she said. Even before she went back and found him, she had known that in Siberia he had married and also that Moshe had forgone Zionism and was an active communist. Yet if it had been right with them, could she have dropped her very beliefs and remained in Russia with Moshe? Even given up her Zionist mission? As though looking at her own stupid self and marveling, Leah's big smile came over her face. No, it was not a choice, communism, Zionism, love, Jews, Arabs, such as we imagine people sometimes desperately face in life. What had really taken place was that she suddenly saw the man as he was. A remark he made. Yes, even at the most intimate moment. A remark—as though a woman were "mastered" by a man. Therefore, he was certain she would remain. And in that moment she was free of him.

Still gazing into her face, Leah added, naturally, this was only what had happened to herself.

Did it help her—Leah's experience? Leah's wisdom? Khalid, with that beautiful Persian-prince mouth, so sure of her.

Though they sat side by side, Myra felt Leah was engulfing her, as though Leah's entire being sought to alleviate her pain. Then Leah told her something more. The way someone who has been within the same experience can talk. Big Leah, too, had had a breakdown. This huge, strong, woman who appeared so sure of life. After the time in Russia with her Moshe, then the killing of her young sister in Tel Hai, Leah had been sent to Vienna. No, not the renowned Dr. Freud, but a good doctor, a good friend of the movement, too. Natan had given her all his money saved in his war service, so she could go. When she returned he had become her chaver. He was such a good person, Leah said calmly.

Myra kissed her goodbye.

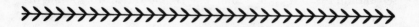

23

ONE could live with it, somehow; it could become a way of life, week after week, month after month, why not year after year if need be? Strangely, sometimes for a few days, a week, you even forgot about it until again all at once it struck someone you knew.

So that Dena would not get the shock from the radio, Mati phoned home. The scholar, the gentle aging bachelor Lewis Billig, among the most erudite of Arabists. In his house not far from the British barracks, an area thought safe, but sitting at his desk with the reading light on, he had been shot dead through the window.

His blood, the papers later said, had spread over an open page of the book, called *Ancient Arabic Literature*.

Early one morning, handsome Max Nurock, Dena's favorite extra man, a member of the Zionist Executive Council, was walking toward a government office on Suleiman Road. A bullet went through his trouser leg. It could just as well have been Mati, whose office was a few doors away. Nurock showed everybody the hole. Dena didn't write this home.

A Haganah boy was alert on the roof, and she brought him up sandwiches and orange juice.

The Iraqi swashbuckler Fawzi el-Kaukji was reported seen entering the Mufti's house in Sheikh Jarrah, on the road to the University. He called himself a colonel. Both Reggie and Mati were dour that night, though Reggie said you could even give it an optimistic interpretation. It meant the Palestinian Arabs themselves didn't want so much to take part, and the Mufti was having to bring in mercenaries from outside Palestine.

In the winding, perilous Bab el Wad ravine a bus convoy from Jerusalem to Tel Aviv was waylaid; she had become almost reluctant to turn on the radio, or to look at the *Post*, Dena said, for fear that one of the dead might be someone they knew. But this time there were twelve dead Arabs found after the convoy battle, and more than half proved to be from Syria.

Ten thousand troops were disembarked at Haifa. British planes scattered leaflets in Arabic calling for peace, promising justice. In Eben Yehuda a watchman was killed. Just outside the Church of the Holy Sepulchre an eminent Nashashibi supporter, Hassan Ali Khalil, was shot dead. There were crop fires in Tel Yosef and Ein Harod. Still, when a fire broke out in the children's village of Ben Shemen, neighboring Arabs rushed over to help put out the flames.

The new immigrant quota was reduced by a third. No, not because of the Arab revolt, the British said. Economic conditions. Two thousand Jews of Zamosc in Poland were left homeless by a pogrom. Mati got into a nasty argument with the chief secretary himself about Houranis filling jobs in the Dead Sea potash works while Polish Jews were refused certificates. Perhaps the Jewish managers down there were pleased since they paid lower wages to the Arabs, the secretary coolly remarked.

And Mati felt a searing stomach twinge, a surge of nausea. He hurried to the washroom, but nothing came up. The pain subsided. He had never had this before; maybe it was because he was putting on so much weight, sitting on his can, eating cakes with his tea every time the server came around.

Reggie brought over an article by Professor Harold Laski, saying quite plainly that Great Britain's policy in Palestine was becoming dependent on its dependence on Arab oilfields.

More foreign correspondents arrived, a bad sign. Eddie Marmor brought over a reporter who had just come from Spain, where that fascist General Franco was for the present halted on his march to Madrid.

Suddenly Mati had an outburst. Ethiopia, now Spain, pogroms in Poland, Hitler, the whole damn world! He shouted so loud that the twins awoke, howling. Then Mati had to rush to the bathroom.

346

Through the door he told Dena he was all right, and Dena went back to the guests with the darling story that she had got, of all people, from Schmulik. His youngest kid, Boaz, when he saw a field burning was told that Arabs had set it on fire. "But why don't we take the matches away from them?" he demanded.

The ulcer specialist, recently from Wiesbaden, said there was no question of an operation; Mati must go on a strict diet, milk, milk, milk, no alcohol. Thank heaven he was anyway not much of a drinker. But could the Herr Doktor Professor put some milk into the daily dish-up of news?

Another convoy in Bab el Wad was attacked; two Egged bus drivers were wounded but got through. The Egged bus drivers were the heroes of the Yishuv, Dena wrote to Phil. Not a single bus, even on isolated roads, had been canceled.

She thought it best not to mention Mati's little ulcer. In spite of the situation, she wrote, the groundbreaking for the Hadassah Medical Center on Mount Scopus was a great success. Henrietta Szold had been inspiring.

Now Mati heard of a new thing at the office, though it was as yet kept out of the press. The oilpipe line from Iraq that fed the Haifa refinery had been sabotaged, where it crossed a wild stretch of the Gilboa. Twice. Covering soil was dug off, and holes were shot in the pipe; the oil burned as far back as the pumping station in Trans-Jordan. The CID was sure this was being carried out by El Kaukji's gangs; they crossed over, stayed a night in some remote Arab village, did their job, and crossed back.

To free more police to guard the pipeline, the British enlisted gaffirs—auxiliary Jewish police to guard roads and settlements. One good thing at least.

When the watchman of a Sharon Shore orange grove was killed and the trees were destroyed, Uri, now seventeen, the eldest child of Shula and Nahum, attended a meeting of the Irgun. It was at Araleh's, in the Brigade veterans' section. To hell with the Haganah's "restraint." The only thing the Arabs understood— All right, maybe not to kill an Arab watchman, but there were Arab groves, Araleh pointed out. To uproot, to kill trees—this, too, though not like killing people, was repulsive to Uri. Afterward he talked with Tsila, "dugri," down to earth. Did he think that she— a woman—well, almost a woman, wasn't shocked to face such things? But how else would it ever stop? And the deep sense of a shared trouble, in the world before them, brought them still closer.

Word of the meeting at Araleh's came to Nahum, and also that his son had been there. Shula insisted he talk to the boy. She wouldn't be able to stand it, having her son hunted by the British.

"But you yourself help the Revisionists!" Uri cried at his father. True, Nahum said, with money to bring in immigrants. But as for the murdered watchman and the trees, there were other ways to retaliate. A Jew must be clever. Why not help those Arabs who were against the Mufti and his gangs?

Help Arabs? How? Why?

Nahum took his son into a secret. Most Arabs were bitter against the Mufti. His strike had ruined them. To oppose him, they needed money to buy arms. Against his terror gangs they would organize peace gangs. So it had been decided to help them with funds for this purpose.

Uri didn't seem enthusiastic. They could simply pocket the money or even turn the arms against Jews, he said.

Nahum smiled. Had Uri read of those four Arabs found dead near Nazareth? Four of the Mufti's men? So the first money had been well used.

※ ※ ※

After his father's disclosure about his way of dealing with the Arabs, an uneasiness came over Uri. Of course there was nothing wrong with it—helping those who helped your side. It was the right thing to do. So Uri couldn't understand his own uneasiness. People admired the clever way his father had of solving every problem. Uri himself didn't have that kind of cleverness, though there was nothing wrong with his own intelligence, he got excellent marks in school, especially in science, and would be sent to Oxford probably, his mother was already getting contacts through her British friends. But still when some of the chevreh, even Tsila, made their little sarcastic remarks about his mother and her British friends he was tempted to make such remarks himself. Instead he hinted that she got plenty of useful information out of the stupid British and of course passed it on. Besides, who didn't know about his mother's side of the family!

When they had still lived in Tiberias, Uri's teacher had once taken the class to visit the famous Garden of Eden at the nearby

Kibbutz HaKeren, and it was Uncle Reuven who had explained all the Biblical plants to the group, indeed the teacher had even reminded the class that this noted horticulturist, Chaver Reuven, was Uri's uncle. Though Uri knew that his father was a man of importance, the richest and most respected in Tiberias, secretly he felt in awe of this uncle who had even brought monkeys to his Garden of Eden. And because of this feeling, when the time came to join a youth group he had chosen Gordonia, named after the idealist A. D. Gordon whom his uncle Reuven always talked about, the thinker who had lived in the kibbutz and inspired everyone with his ideals of laboring with your own hands, and his love of every living creature and everything that grew. Uncle Reuven, like A. D. Gordon, was even a vegetarian, but that far Uri didn't think he could go. In fact even Reuven's and Elisheva's own kids, his cousins in the kibbutz, were not vegetarians!

When the family moved to Hof HaSharon, the new city his father was building on the seacoast, Uri remained a member of Gordonia though most of his new friends were in B'rith Trumpeldor—the Betar. Sometimes Yoram would poke fun at him because of his Gordonianism and even call him a vegetarian though he wasn't, because it meant anyone who was soft. And Tsila too, when she began to like him, kept saying he ought to come over to the Betar. After all, as Uri knew, her father Araleh was a real Jabotinsky man; Araleh had been with Uncle Gidon in the Zion Mule Corps led by Trumpeldor in Gallipoli, so B'rith Trumpeldor was surely where anyone in his family belonged! What was a nephew of Gidon doing in Gordonia, with such pacifists! even Araleh would tease him.

In spite of the teasing, Uri felt himself easier in their house than at home. Though he admired his father he knew there was an undercurrent of remarks in the town, little remarks about the way Nahum Artzi had a finger in everybody's business. And the palace he had built! And even the remarks about his mother's stylishness, her dresses no longer even from Tel Aviv but from Paris. Naturally, Uri realized people were all envious.

Still, as he analyzed himself and Tsila analyzed him, Uri didn't have his father's way of turning everything into money, and Tsila said at least that was good. Nor of buying everything. He liked to make things, he had a passion for radio and constructed a transmitter and receiver so they could exchange messages. Araleh at once wanted him to build one for their illegal ships, and Uri was working on it, but it was pretty much of a job.

When his father explained to him that trick of giving money to a rival Arab clan of the Mufti's, so that Arabs would fight each other, though Uri understood it was a clever and even correct thing to do, he still felt a need to get his mind clear, and as it was a secret thing he didn't bring it up with his friends. But once it somehow came up with Araleh because Araleh himself made a remark about Haganah B, that had dealings with "the other" Arab faction. And so they got into a frank discussion. Well, Araleh said, Nahum, even though born in this land was in some ways a kind of Jew of the Diaspora, a galut Jew as they were called, a twister, a dreher. For centuries their minds had worked that way—they had had to hang onto the coattails of others, to survive. Trumpeldor himself had been one of the first to revolt against this galut psychology and to declare that Jews had to stand on their own feet, do their own fighting. That was the new Jew of this land. But in Tiberias, in the old religious community where Uri's grandfather had started his hotel, it had been natural for Nahum as a boy to take on the old galut mentality. Take the time Nahum had given the Britisher that favorite horse of Gidon's. All this was what was called shtadlanuth. Pulling coattails.

Uri knew the word, the labor leaders were always making speeches against it, and Yoram had even used it against him that time about four years ago when they were just kids having a kumsitz and those Arab boys had come along in their green shirts, playing storm troopers, patrolling the beach against illegal Jewish boats. Instead of beating them up, Yoram reproached Uri, he had run to papa and papa had run to the British.

Once Uri, having missed the last few Gordonia hikes, went along with Yoram and his bunch; Araleh was taking them on a Shabbat campout, a long hike on the coast up to the beach at Athlit, with the high jagged ruins of the Crusader castle there. Of course everyone knew the story of how the heroic Nili spies had used this place for their rendezvous with the disguised British ship, that picked up their behind-the-lines information of Turkish army movements. But while the others were setting up camp, Araleh took Uri around the base of the wall to show him something special, just for him. On a kind of foundation stone, there, you could make out an inscription, hardly more than scratchings, a few Hebrew letters—you almost had to follow them with your fingers. G-D-N. Gidon.

Few knew of this, Araleh told Uri. But once, Araleh and Gidon had galloped along the sands, as far as Athlit, and Gidon had shown this to him. And the story was that after the disastrous Gallipoli campaign, when their Zion Mule Corps had been returned to Alexandria and disbanded, Araleh and Gidon had remained with Trumpeldor, still trying to get the British to start a Jewish fighting unit. Just at that time the British Intelligence needed someone to make contact with the Nili to get information about a Turkish army movement to attack the Suez canal, and it was Gidon, a good swimmer, who had volunteered, he had swum from the British contact boat, left his message for the Nili, and, as a memento for himself, had scratched his name on this rock while waiting for the vessel to pick him up.

Ah, in those days, said Araleh, everybody believed in action, not in restraint; who had ever heard of havlagah!

When a thousand more trees were uprooted, Uri went with Yoram to a meeting. It was a remote hut in a grove; Araleh was there. "The Arabs too have trees." That was still their answer. Yet Uri still could not bring himself, with his old Gordonia ideas, to the thought of destroying trees.

Then Yoram came with an older fellow named Shai, from a group of workers in the tobacco fields at Rosh Pina. That group already had something of a reputation. Yoram brought into the conversation a name whispered in their circles, Yair, as though his taciturn friend, Shai, here, was in Yair's faction.

Shai's friends had heard of Uri's "hobby" with small radio transmitters. His eyes wandered over the workshop as though he understood every detail. For example, for no more than four hundred meters—a transmitter light enough to be easily carried—could Uri do it?

Not long afterward the three of them on horses rode from Rosh Pina to the Jordan, over the several miles of brush, of unused land, along to where the river had already cut down into its gorge, deep below the bridge of the Daughters of Jacob which connected, on the other side, with the road to Damascus. The steep banks were thickly overgrown, excellent for concealment. On the other side, from the bridge, the road wound upward to the control point on the heights of Golan.

Shai had certain information. In the coming week—he knew the day and the approximate hour—the Mufti, now on a visit to Damascus, undoubtedly recruiting more terrorists, would be returning in his car to Jerusalem.

A chaver, carrying Uri's transmitter, could easily slip over to the other side—if he wanted to avoid the bridge he could, some distance upstream, clamber down to the river, the Jordan was hardly five meters wide here, and easily forded. Then clambering up through the growth he could place himself where he could observe the check point, and give word of the passing of the Mufti's automobile. There would be ample time for those hidden at the bridge to light the bomb fuse.

In Uri there was that sense a man gets, at times in his life, of having heard the right answer.

Even his idealistic, pacifist uncle Reuven could approve an action like this. For the thousands of murdered trees. For the murdered watchman.

On the appointed day, they rode out. He carefully checked the batteries, the microphone. And then Uri alone waited, with the fast horses.

He had heard no explosion but it seemed to him that distantly he heard a car pass. Not long after, Shai and the other one arrived. Yes, the transmitter had worked, all had gone as planned, except that the bomb fuse had to be lighted from a cigarette and—perhaps the damned pack had got damp—

Cursing bitterly, they ended by laughing bitterly. A fiasco. The Will of Allah! The murderous bastard had been lucky. This time.

And yet Uri felt one result, a knowledge confirmed in himself. The target. That part had been meaningful. That way, he could understand. Yair was right. Certain meaningful targets.

✳✳✳

The Royal Commission of Inquiry arrived. This one was named the Peel Commission. It fell to Mati to accompany a pair of commissioners on a field tour to Jaffa. The one on his right, named Burney, tubby and energetic, started off with hints of sympathy for the Jewish plight, and the claw squeeze came in Mati's stomach. Why must one endlessly be the subject of sympathy, damn it! The other, a placid-eyed Member of Parliament named Henderson, sat erect and observant, with his umpire air of impartiality.

At the district commissioner's office in Jaffa they were to pick up a local man, and who should emerge, wearing a tarboosh and a London-cut suit, but Fawzi, Gidon's boyhood friend from Dja'adi.

Indeed, on a trip home to Mishkan Yaacov, Mati had heard—bitterly—from Schmulik that Fawzi, sent by the British for a few years of study in England, was returned. The greetings were demonstrative, with the usual hugging, though instantly there had arisen in Mati the old question of the visiting automobile before the attack on Hulda.

Fawzi had heard of the twins and lauded Mati's prowess but then held up five fingers for his own progeny, three boys and two girls. "That's the whole story of Palestine!" he jovially proclaimed to the commissioners. And he hugged Mati again, over the joke.

There were promises of visiting each other and inquiries from Fawzi about all of Mati's brothers and sisters and also the widow of his dear friend Gidon. From childhood, he told the committeemen, Mati's brother Gidon had been as a blood brother to him, and tragically Gidon had been killed in the disorders of 1929. It should never have been, but who can understand the will of Allah? Had Gidon's widow married again?

Yes, Aviva had married three years ago, Mati said. It was better so, said Fawzi; a young woman needed a husband, children needed a father. And the new marriage was well? Yes, the marriage was well, her husband was a builder in Haifa. And they had children between them? Yes, a little girl had been born to them.

The placid Henderson was listening intently: an example of friendship between Arab and Jew! This, too, would go into his notes. Fawzi pointed out a picturesque Arab tomb by the roadside; across the way the Jews were building a flour mill. Now Mati pointed out, in passing, the old wrought-iron gates of the first farm school, Mikve Israel, now more than half a century old. "Ah," Burney said. Such facts were interesting. Everyone imagined that Jewish settlement had started only fifteen years ago with the Mandate. Indeed, many people even seemed to believe it had all started only three years ago because of Hitler!

Just beyond, at Fawzi's indication, the car turned off the road, halting at a cluster of small Arab houses. Behind stretched an accretion of shacks made from beaten-out gasoline tins; a foul, sweetish smell enwrapped the place. Burney took a knowing sniff. "Abattoir?" Mati nodded. "Used to work in one," said the labor man.

Children flocked to the car, ragged, avid, begging baksheesh. Fawzi let it register, then chased them off.

There was a coffeehouse, a tin hut with a few strands of desiccated vine in the guise of an arbor, and on the stools idlers sat over their everlasting shesh-besh. A loudspeaker poured forth a violent Bari broadcast in Arabic, but Fawzi had already caught the eye of the proprietor, who turned the dials and found a singer of love chants.

The domino players were a younger-looking lot than you'd usually find in a village. Stopping at random, Fawzi cheerfully announced that the English effendis had come to learn the truth of Palestine. He turned to a sinewy fellow, in whose speech Mati at once heard the Haurani inflection.

He lived here? Henderson asked Fawzi to ask.

Oh, yes, the Arab understood the question and, pointing to one of the hovels, invited all. Henderson thanked him; there was little time, and they wished to talk with the group, if the man didn't mind. Giving his name, Achmed, the fellow grinned.

He had lived here long?

Three years.

Before that, Fawzi asked in rapid Arabic, before he had lived in his family village nearby?

Achmed at once caught the game. He had been born and brought up nearby, but Jews had bought the land, and the family was dispersed, and he was become a laborer, now without work. He smiled broadly.

"How is it," Mati put in, also smiling, "you have the accent of the tribes of Hauran? Have you not come from there?"

Ah, indeed, Achmed said, grinning to the Englishmen, when his father had lost his land, they had wandered to the Golan, where they had kinsmen, and thus Achmed had been brought up among them, and spoke as they spoke. He looked quickly to Fawzi for approval. Burney exchanged a glance with Mati and chuckled. Achmed's grin broadened, and suddenly all were laughing together. Fawzi shrugged to Mati, as one who had made an understandable try.

And when had he come across into Palestine? Burney asked through Mati.

A year ago.

Ah, not three years, then?

Achmed looked at Fawzi and, as one who is now seriously telling the truth, shook his head.

Alone?

Oh, with a brother, a cousin.

And why had they come?

354

Achmed laughed. Ah, it was livelier here. Cinema. Jaffa.

And Tel Aviv? He went sometimes to Tel Aviv?

Sometimes he walked in the streets. The riches in the Jewish shops! In the windows, everything! And along the sea, you saw like in the cinema—Hollywood—oh, those were the sights! He kissed his fingers and chuckled as a man among men.

He was married?

Achmed ticked his tongue, no.

He had not the bride price? Mati asked.

He intended to save up money.

That was one reason he had come to Palestine? Here a man could work and earn money?

Aywah. Here things had for a time been good. But now there was no work. He looked around his circle, and all the others nodded. Achmed had worked for a Jewish effendi in the orange groves of Rehovot, but lately many Jews had come into the land, and the Jewish effendi took Jews before Arabs. "That is to be expected," he added with a show of reasonableness. "I would take an Arab before a Jew, and a Jew takes his own before an Arab." Then with a wry smile Achmed declared, "If he doesn't, some of his own will come and break his head for him." Irgun.

All chuckled. Several more young Arabs who had joined the circle, now had words to put in, some with bursts of anger; Fawzi held up his hand, easy, easy, schwoiyah. See, had not the English come to hear their grievances?

Henderson wanted to know more precisely how these fellows had entered Palestine. Where had they crossed the Jordan? They shrugged. Above Jericho. At the bridge.

And no one had questioned them? Soldiers? Officials?

They looked one to the other. A few British soldiers were watching the bridges, Achmed said.

And asked for no papers? And did not try to stop them?

"Why, it is all one land," Achmed said.

"Well, after all"—Henderson turned amiably to Mati—"isn't that what one of your own fellows is always shouting, 'It's all one land on both sides of the Jordan!' This fellow Jaby—Jabinsky?"

"Jabotinsky," Fawzi corrected him, smiling at Mati as though to say, we got you on that one, old boy! And to the committeeman Fawzi explained, "Jabotinsky is head of the Zionist extremists. He was outlawed from Palestine, but he has a large following here. They're the ones that threw the bomb killing sixteen Arabs at the Damascus Gate. They bring in Jews in illegal ships."

"Ah."

One of the Hauranis had already shown he understood quite a bit of English. "Sir," he half shouted, "they come from Europe. Ferenji. We are Arab, from here. Sons of Ishmael!"

Writing in his notebook, Henderson nodded sagely to reassure them that all they said would be taken into account.

On the ride back to the district office, Fawzi sat with Mati in front, as thus neither could take advantage to influence the inquirers. Also, they surely had a great deal to say to each other.

Fawzi spoke easily; oh, he had heard that Mati was a regular Lindbergh! And his wife from a very rich millionaire family! Mati tried to reply as lightly, had not Fawzi married well, into the Dajanis? But right inside Mati's head his angry brother Schmulik seemed to be sitting, with all his bitter suspicions about that Arab car, the day of Hulda: "Now find out! You've got Fawzi next to you!" And even if he found out, would he tell Schmulik? Or anyone in the family? It would be a terrible thing to know. Suddenly, grinning, Fawzi said to Mati, "Did Gidon ever tell you about my grandfather, when we were boys and my grandfather said to me if I would learn to read and write like Jews did, he would give me my own horse?" Mati knew the story, but now it seemed there had been a bit more. "Did he tell you what else my old grandfather said to me?"

Oh, he had been a wise and far-seeing man, the old sheikh. "My grandfather told me he had watched your brother, the oldest son, Reuven, in the first days he came to the land. Reuven and your sister the big one, Leah"—Fawzi smiled, as people did, at the image of the huge, strong Leah—"the two of them began right away to carry stones off the field. Day after day they did it. That was when my grandfather said, 'The Jews mean to have a kingdom here.' And therefore, he told me, I must learn to read and write."

He had spoken in English, and loudly enough for those in back to hear.

Quietly Mati asked about London. Fawzi's wife and children had been with him? Fawzi gave him the old knowing masculine smile. No; he had come home a few times. But in England— English ladies! "They like us. They go crazy!" A real Lady, he hinted, his voice now intimate, oh, very high up.

Schmulik turned up in Jerusalem. From an Arab in Dja'adi he'd heard of the encounter. Yes, Mati had met Fawzi; impossible to find anything out. "Schmulik, let it lie." The old excuse—even if Fawzi had been in that car, he couldn't possibly have known Gidon was there. How were things in Mishkan Yaacov?

"They know we are strong," Schmulik said. But in his mind an image kept running. One time, with his big scoop tractor he would be waiting, the scoop raised. At night, at a place where Fawzi came in his car. And just as the car stopped, the heavy scoop shovel would smash down like a giant fist, flattening car, driver, all.

It was a pleasant dinner; politics were avoided. Having always wanted to see the Holy Land, Mrs. Burney had accompanied her husband, and Dena asked her, would Edward really abdicate, giving up his kingdom for love? Mrs. Burney laughed charmingly. "That all depends on what your Mrs. Simpson wants, doesn't it?" Dena laughed, too, saying she had read an interview with Mrs. Simpson, who was on the Riviera and who had declared, "It all depends on what the King wants."

"Ah, do you really believe that what he wants won't be what she wants?" put in Maureen, and they all laughed.

While the men were talking on the porch, Joyce Burney said to Dena that she was quite interested in her reactions to living in Palestine, coming from America, especially as Dena said she hadn't at all been in Zionist circles. Considering what most people meant by Zionism, Dena didn't even know if she should call herself a Zionist now!

Really? How so? What did most people mean?

Oh, making it your whole life. Politics.

What then was it to her? A marriage and whither thou goest, I will go? Was it like an Englishwoman who follows her husband out to the colonies and makes a life, wherever it is? As Dena hesitated, Mrs. Burney turned to Maureen. "Don't look at me." Maureen laughed. "I'm a Zionist!" Now they really had her dizzy, Joyce Burney cried.

Well, Dena said, she certainly didn't think of living here as being a wife in a colony! No, the question had to be, would she by herself have come to live here? Like some of those girls in a pioneer group that Mati had brought from Chicago. Those youngsters were the real thing.

And now that she had lived here several years? There was a further unasked question, Dena felt. What if, heaven forbid! something should happen to her husband? After all, Palestine wasn't very safe. Would she stay on here and bring up her children here, rather than go back to America?

She couldn't honestly answer. If it was just herself? But for the twins?

Maureen said she loved Jerusalem; she could never live anywhere else.

The Mufti decided to appear before the commission after all, but in a closed session. He had solemnly testified, Burney passed on to Mati, that there was a Jewish plot to destroy the Mosque of Omar and then rebuild the Temple on the Holy Mount. He had quoted—wait, Burney had made note of the name, here it was—the Chief Rabbi of Nemirow, of the World Agudah, an international Jewish organization. The Mufti had said—

The quotation proved to be from the daily prayer, "Restore us as of old."

A new Arab leaflet quoted the Koran. "Seek your enemy among the Jews."

❈ ❈ ❈

Toscanini arrived and immediately began rehearsals.

There were still some members of the symphony committee, Dena told Mati, who argued that the first conductor should have been a Jew. Was there a lack of Jewish conductors in the world! And next they argued for Jewish composers—as if you could tell Toscanini what to play! One woman argued back, after all, he was playing Mendelssohn. But Mendelssohn was a converted Jew, a Christian! the Jewish patriot replied. Why shouldn't at least one composer from the Yishuv be included? There was Yehuda Shertok, brother of Moshe Shertok, and even a kibbutznik! Perhaps if Toscanini were to hear his beautiful song of the Kinneret—

"Well, it really is beautiful," Mati said. Why shouldn't Toscanini play it? Dena could have crowned him.

Far in advance the committee had decided who should have Huberman and who should have Toscanini and even who must be invited to whose reception. Dena decided not even to try to entertain; this was strictly for high-ups. But she and Mati were on every important list, even the big reception at the Palatine Hotel with the High Commissioner and Lord Melchett and Lord Reading and Lord Samuel and the Weizmanns. And then the choice list of all because this one wasn't decided by rank or politics but by that certain magic sense that Esther Rubin had of blending together the most famous artists, the rich and distinguished American visitors of taste, the government leaders and university leaders, the whole elite, in their wonderful mansion that was just a few doors from the house of the great Hebrew poet Chaim Bialik. Esther hadn't forgotten Mati and Dena.

In Kibbutz HaRishon, though Elisheva had made no request, the chevreh voted for her and Reuven to go on holiday and attend the concerts. In Haifa they sat with their old friend Yehuda Shertok, and in the intermission he and Elisheva began to plan a kibbutz music festival on the shores of the Kinneret. After the finish, Beethoven's Eroica, Elisheva and Reuven walked for a long time, holding hands, on the Carmel, though it was foolish and dangerous; things that had not been said between them for many years came out naturally: his knowing how much she had missed since he brought her to live in the kibbutz, such great hours as this, that only the big world could provide. Elisheva's eyes teared, but even in the dark Reuven glimpsed that evanescent smile of their long-ago love days in Damascus. She would have wanted no other life, she said, no other life.

To Myra, Dena sent the review from the *Palestine Post*, describing the opening concert, "conducted by an inspired Italian, translating into terms of music by the Jew Mendelssohn to the Shakespeare play, reproduced by a Jewish orchestra in Jerusalem." Also a clipping of an interview with Lady Reading, who said, "Everybody is busy and happy in Palestine, and had I not been told there were troubles, I would never have known it."

24

MATI had sensed it would be partition, and when the advance secret copy of the proposal came in, the chief secretary's secretary, a girlhood friend of Maureen's, left it on her desk open to the map, so when he came by he could have a quick look.

The Jewish part was like a blot, the rest Arab. The British to keep a wide corridor from Jerusalem to Jaffa. Even in that instant glance Mati could not help checking on Mishkan Yaakov; yes, it was included, just barely, along with the Rutenberg works. The rest down the Jordan all the way to the Red Sea, the whole Negev, was Arab.

Tel Hai and Hulda were included. At least the family had done its part.

At his desk, closing his eyes, he could see the map under his eyelids. There was a thudding in his mind. Was it all over? For a postage-stamp state?

But nationhood! Sovereignty!

The outcries began. Zionism without Zion. Even Lloyd George: "A deplorable ending."

From fifty thousand immigration certificates two years ago there now came a four-month allotment: six hundred laborers. The Jewish Agency refused. A thousand young Polish Jews set out to march to Palestine and were arrested; their leader was put on trial in Warsaw.

Phil sent a letter about a huge protest meeting he had helped organize in Chicago, enclosing a clipping of a speech about perfidious Albion by his congressman.

The Arabs refused the plan. Jews said thank heaven.

The troubles increased. In Beisan a German Jewish refugee, a doctor and the only Jew in the place, was shot dead. On Sabbath Eve a Jew was shot while worshiping at the Wailing Wall.

One night when the twins ran to Mati for their good-night wrestle, his face was so bitter and grim that Jonathan burst into tears. After the boys were calmed and asleep, Dena insisted he should see another specialist. What for! Mati thrust the paper at her. *Davar* had a headline about South Africa putting a ban on Jewish immigration. Suddenly she burst out at him, why did he have to scare the kids? The whole trouble here was that every Jew thought he was the Messiah!

To get him out of the Jerusalem atmosphere, Dena talked Mati into a drive to Kibbutz Brandeis for Shabbat. The place always made him feel he had accomplished something. Every time he came there they had built more buildings; Brandeis now looked like every well-established kibbutz; they had prize cows, and Malka Margolies with her poultry production line, as she called it, was even beginning to look a little like Mati's sister Dvora. At Mati's suggestion, they had even started an "industrial branch," a shed where they made automobile batteries.

Dave Margolies was back from the States, where he had been fitted with a fancy artificial foreleg with a knee joint and tricky springs at the heel so he walked with only the slightest lurch.

This Shabbat Mati and Dena fell into a real event. The yard was filled with trucks, gangs of youthful chaverim were loading on sections of boards, and Dena suddenly realized they had arrived in the midst of the latest-style hush-hush operation, a new Haganah stunt called the Tower and Stockade. That was how new settlements were being built, in surprise single-day operations. The wooden sections must be for the watchtower. On other trucks there were huge rolls of barbed wire and piles of folded tents.

"Why didn't you tell me?" Mati caught hold of Dave.

"Listen," Dave responded, "suppose the police come. You think we want a high Jewish chair warmer kicked out of His Majesty's Service?"

"Maybe that would do me a favor."

Well, now he was here, what the hell. The convoy was just

about ready to move out; the police weren't too likely to expect anything on Shabbat since they still imagined Zionism was something religious.

Leaving the twins in the children's house, Mati and Dena piled onto one of the trucks; the site was reached by a jolting, rocky wagon trail along the southern slope of the Carmel, some ten kilometers away. Though the sun blazed, the ride was a joy. At one point Dena took Mati's hand. Half the new kvutsa was on the truck with them, in a tangle of army cots, gasoline tins, farm tools. The chevreh were a conglomeration of German Blau-Weiss and Baltics, whatever that was. The group had already been together for a year as day laborers.

From the Carmel a round-headed spur stood forth; leaping from the trucks, squads were carting sections of the watchtower. A cook tent arose. Mati, bare to the waist—actually he had less of a belly this way—was out there hammering away at the watchtower; Dena partnered off with Malka in the kitchen tent. The British were holding back with settlement permits, but once the structures were up, Malka said, they let them stand. The motto was: "Create facts!" "*Fait accompli,*" Dena said. Just like Mati's family in the days of the Turks. On the outer border of the tract a lemon-haired fellow—must be a Balt—was plowing away with a pair of mules, while at the other end was a chaver on a Fordson.

Trestle tables were in front of the cook tent, and Dena couldn't keep up with the assault. Raising her eyes, she saw Mati on a ladder banging away on a higher section of the tower; he caught her look and waved his hammer. Maybe really she had squeezed him into the wrong life; this was the life for him!

By dusk it was done. They were singing around a large fire when headlights appeared, pale in the twilight. A British command car. "Who's responsible here?" Dave Margolies and the lemon-haired Balt walked to the gate. The Haganah commander touched Mati's shoulder, and they slipped off into the woods.

The British didn't even come inside the compound. They'd report to the district officer, who no doubt would come around in the morning. Dave and the Balt came back grinning. Mati and the commander returned. Triumphant singing broke out. One of the lads climbed to the top of the watchtower, where they had already set up a blinker light, powered by batteries from the Brandeis factory. With the first stars he sent out a signal, and from the nearest kibbutz, in the Emek, came an answering signal. Listening to his tapping, it took Dena a moment to realize the Morse was in Hebrew. "Ha-kol b'seder." Everything okay. And the reply, "Shalom uvracha." Peace and blessings.

They spent the night in the open, on a spread-out bale of hay.

The following Sunday the district commissioner of the Galilee, L. Y. Andrews, was shot to death on the threshold of Christ Church in Nazareth.

This time the British acted drastically. Haj Amin el Husseini was dismissed not only as Mufti but as president of the Supreme Moslem Council and as head of the Wafd with its enormous funds. The Arab Higher Committee and all Arab nationalist associations were declared illegal. Five of the leaders were exiled to the Seychelles Islands. Haj Amin had taken refuge in the Mosque of Omar and one night, some said dressed as a woman, some as a beggar, escaped to Beirut.

Additional Jews in the settlements were enrolled as ghaffirs, armed and even paid, wearing wide Australian campaign hats.

But the land was in chaos. From a villa in Lebanon, the Mufti was sending in killers. Kaukji's gangs took over more and more Arab villages in the mountains, demanding money and refuge. The Nashashibi faction started "peace gangs" to free the villages. Jews were shot on the roads and in the fields. The Haganah continued to impose restraint, the Irgun to carry out retaliations.

There came another attack on an Egged bus in the Galilee, with several wounded. This time there was counter-action. Among the tobacco workers at Rosh Pina a unit of avengers had been formed; some of the boys were Irgunists, but the group staged independent actions too. After a Jewish café right near the British check-post was held up, a nearby Arab café received a bullet-spray from a neighboring rooftop. And now, on the hairpin curve approaching Rosh Pina, an Arab bus was shot at. Unluckily for the boys, a British army car was just then winding up the snake curve. Three were caught, and speedily brought to trial. Though no one on the bus had been hit, an example was made, and the leader, Shlomo Ben Yosef, was sentenced to be hanged. Protests and furor and legal appeals proved futile. Singing "the Jewish song," as he was led to the scaffold, the jailer related, Ben Yosef, the Yishuv leaders cried out, became the first Jew to be hung in Eretz since the rule of the Turks.

In bitterness, young men were leaving the Haganah for the

Irgun. Even Eliahu reacted. Havlagah, restraint against indis-
criminate retaliation, against throwing bombs in the marketplace
or shooting up buses was one thing. Why foster hatred among the
Arab people? But to attack the attackers was another matter.
Picked young men were formed into units under Yitzhak Saadeh,
to lie awake at night alongside the foothill paths approaching the
Emek settlements. Already, a few times, killer gangs were caught
by surprise and driven off, even leaving dead behind. "The night
must belong to us, not them," Saadeh proclaimed. And indeed
there seemed to be a decrease in attacks on the settlements. But
along the oil pipeline, there were more fires.

Late one afternoon a car arrived in the yard of Kibbutz Gilboa,
and from it emerged the familiar, long-legged David HaCohen
from Haifa, together with a smallish fellow, apparently a British
officer; at least he wore the uniform—but with tennis shoes. The
eyes were a cold-burning blue, like what sometimes twists upward
in a campfire. Even aside from the tennis shoes the officer gave the
impression of being someone "different." He pronounced a round
and hearty "Shalom!" to the place in general, gazing intently at
each chaver on the path as HaCohen led him to Aaron, the
secretary-mukhtar.

"This is Captain Orde Wingate, our friend," HaCohen introduced him. A British officer, a friend? HaCohen had used the word
"Yadid" with peculiar emphasis as though to say this one could be
fully trusted.

The officer had been sent to HaCohen by Moshe Shertok; he
had a plan and was authorized by the British government to contact the Haganah. A British officer to be taken into the confidence
of the Haganah?

Nothing less, it turned out. The captain said he wanted first to
look around the area, with someone who knew every footpath,
every stone; later on he would probably want a number of lads as
volunteers.

At supper, his first kibbutz meal, every item evoked enthusiasm.
The bread! Fresh baked bread from their own wheat ground in
the cooperative mill of the local kibbutzim. What bread! Could he
have a loaf to take away with him? Why not—all he could carry!
And the simple, wholesome fare, their lebeniya, their cucumbers,
tomatoes, lettuce. Like one watching a ritual, the Britisher observed each chaver at his table building up his salad, some slicing
a hard-boiled egg on top. Even the table's slop bowl for parings

and leavings, which so many chaverim found unpleasant, was perfect for simplicity and practicality!

In the morning he was impatient to see the springs of Ein Harod; Yosef, the youngest boy of Dvora and Menahem, was given the honor as guide. Wingate knelt on one knee to take the water in his palm. Yosef grinned; all the tourists did it. But as the Britisher straightened up, his eyes fastened on the youngster. "And why did Gideon want only a few, only the ones who were wary?" Why? In second grade you learned it. Gideon was not planning a head-on war but a raid.

And when did he raid?

At night, of course.

As simple, as ancient as that. And when the officer looked at you with his strange eyes like some transparent pale blue stones, you forgot the tennis shoes and the khaki and saw that this Englishman was, in some crazy way, from those Biblical days.

All morning they clambered over the Gilboa. At the site of King Saul's camp, Wingate raged. "The idiot!" To encumber himself with his women, his whole household! And without even leaving an escape line! Wingate leaped down over the rocks. If only Saul had moved his command post down to this point, he might have won the battle!

For several days the captain remained, going off mostly alone with his loaf of bread, his lump of kibbutz cheese, and his canteen of water.

At night he conferred for hours with Yitzhak Saadeh, with veterans of the old Shomer, Menahem, and Hayim Sturman; Sturman knew every mukhtar in the hill villages and could tell Wingate which ones complained most bitterly about being forced to furnish lodging and supplies, even money, to the killer gangs. He was friendly with Bedouin shepherds, too, who had an eye for every footmark.

His idea was now clear to them. Small, picked squads composed of volunteers from the Haganah mixed with British troops, a few ghaffirs added when needed. Special training. Ambushes.

As for locating the gangs, there were several ways. For instance, tracking. Among the Druze, particularly, there were trackers who could from a single footmark tell the weight and height of a man who had passed; the infiltrators could be tracked to villages they had commandeered for shelter. Few villagers really wanted to shelter the raiders. And so there was no lack of informers. Naturally, for a reward. Besides, the police as well had their contacts.

No longer should the Haganah limit itself to standing defense. And as for the Irgun's retaliations by pitching a bomb and killing a bunch of simple Arabs at a vegetable market—madness and evil! Terror breeding terror. Go out and get the raiders, go after them and them only! Like Saadeh he declared—"The night must belong to us!"

When word was passed among the kibbutzim, Reuven and Elisheva's son Noam at once knew he must volunteer. Not since he was ten had Noam felt discomfort about his father's pacifism and vegetarianism, nor was this why he wanted to volunteer. Nor because his friend Avi was going and they were inseparable. No. This was his decision because of his own beliefs.

When he was ten, in the 1929 slaughters of Hebron and Safed, there had been much discussion in his age-group house and even expressions of anger at those yeshiva students in Hebron who let themselves be cut to pieces without making any effort to strike back. "Just like pacifists!" cried Avi, Noam's roommate all the way back to the infant house. Noam flew at Avi and bloodied his nose before the chevreh pulled them apart, and then the whole house had a long intelligent discussion with their youth leader, about the entire subject of pacifism. About pacifists going unarmed onto the battlefield to serve in medical units. About the philosophy of Gandhi. This led to vegetarianism. Sometimes in the kibbutz that word was used with a touch of sarcasm, for the superidealists of the older generation. There were still a handful, including Reuven and Elisheva, who on chicken and meat days received the special dish for vegetarians. Their youth leader reminded the group that the founder of the philosophy of labor, their own A. D. Gordon, had been a strict vegetarian, too. So what was there to joke about regarding vegetarians and pacifists?

Noam and Avi had made it up, especially as Avi was aware of all the heroism in Noam's family; Noam's aunt Yaffaleh was even in the schoolbooks, and then had come news of his heroic uncle Gidon. In the end the two of them grew closer than ever. Their chevreh even had a double name for them, Avinoam.

Both Avi and Noam were among the highest to qualify for the Yadid's special unit, yet the kibbutz secretary-mukhtar, Max Wilner, suggested that instead of just informing their parents, they consult them.

Reuven and Elisheva already knew but felt better when Noam came that evening to their room. He was sturdy and practical, and Elisheva was certain he was far more sensitive than he showed, but somehow his inner personality had not yet declared itself. For Elisheva it was a disappointment, accepted with humor, that Noam had no ear whatever for music, and Reuven had long ago resigned himself to Noam's indifference to horticulture. Though the boy did have good ideas on irrigation. Why, for instance, should water be supplied to the surface, where it evaporated? For more than a year Noam had been tinkering with pipes with pin-holes in them. The trouble was they got stopped up.

Now when he came for—what was it, their approval, their permission; or, perhaps more like in ancient times, a blessing?—their son began awkwardly, the words lurching out of him. "Abba, you know volunteers are being taken for HaYadid, and in our group Avi and I—"

His mother interposed, already with the gently sorrowful tone of a mother who knows her son will go to war. "Noam, if you decide, it should not be because Avi decided."

Reuven said, "Noam, that you decided we can already see, and of course, you yourself should always decide. Even if your decision is sometimes not the same as that of your chaverim." Well, this argument Noam didn't need. But as his abba went on, it became easier, for Reuven to his son's surprise talked of Noam's childhood days when it might have been embarrassing for him that his father was a pacifist and a vegetarian. Oh, Noam said, he understood, everyone understood. With a small smile Reuven continued. True, in the way man had developed on earth, each person, each nation was sometimes faced with the need to fight and kill. But was this first and deepest in the nature of man? was it the intention? In his young days in Russia, Reuven reminded his son, he had studied at first in a yeshiva, and there was a fascinating discussion in the Talmud regarding Adam and Eve—why were they banished from Eden? "Because of carnal knowledge," Noam replied. Naturally young people took to the idea that this meant sex, Reuven said, but the Talmudists, always seeking for a deeper, hidden meaning, considered that as carnal meant the knowledge of the flesh, Adam and Eve had become flesh eaters. And that perhaps to God, carnality had been man's first disappointing choice.

Noam too now smiled, at the ingenuity of those Talmudists.

And so Adam and Eve had been banished, Reuven went on, into the world where beasts of another order roamed and killed and devoured each other.

"But even in your own Garden of Eden that you made here," Noam pointed out, "you showed us that one species feeds on another because that is the order and balance in nature."

"Yes," Reuven said, "but man alone is the creature that kills his own kind."

"A soldier isn't a cannibal!"

"Wait, I am not arguing against the need for soldiers," Reuven said. "And if I myself am a pacifist, it is partly because at all times in every generation there must be some who hold to this idea, holding it before us even in the midst of war."

"Perhaps in the midst of war this is even more important," Elisheva said.

"Being a soldier doesn't mean you want to kill people," Noam maintained.

"I know, I know," his father agreed, troubled. "The tragedy is that in battle some develop such a desire. We hope not ours."

"Don't worry," Noam said. Then, perhaps to ease things, he returned to the earlier discussion. Why, if the banishment from Eden was interpreted to have been because they started to eat meat, why was it a fruit, an apple, that the snake persuaded Eve to bite into and to induce Adam to eat?

Reuven and Elisheva laughed, pleased at Noam's perception. "Well asked!" This was the whole way of Jewish thought, Reuven said; it was filled with contradictions, with opposites that had to be resolved—perhaps even like the dialectics of Hegel and Marx. As he recalled, there were complex discussions on this point: Just what was meant by the apple? He was not enough of a Talmudist to answer, but perhaps Noam's grandfather, who had gone back to the Talmud in his old age, would know.

Somehow the whole first question, of Noam's volunteering, had dissolved away. When he rose to go back to his youth house, his father and mother smiled tenderly, and Reuven, though, of course, without raising his hand to the gesture, but in the casual way a freethinker might say a "Shabbat shalom," said, "Noam, with our blessing."

※ ※ ※

In the last year a change had come over Yankel. Long he had suffered from arthritis, hardly able to move the fingers of his hands, and at times in winter pains seized him in the hip so that he moved from the table to his bed, bent double. Again and again his daughter-in-law Nussya, the good one, urged him to go to the hot mineral baths in Tiberias; after all people came from Jerusalem all through every winter season for the baths, and here, living less than an hour away, he did not make use of them.

Once when the whole lot of them, his own offspring and their wives and husband arrived during Succoth with all their children, to cheer him up he supposed, Shula's Nahum too urged him to go to the baths; soon their season would be starting. "Just give your name at the entrance," Nahum said. "I'll leave word, and it won't cost you." Shula, too, urged him. And Leah scolded him. And even the American wife of Mati, the shaineh, joined in. Nu, so they were really concerned about his health.

So one morning Yankel hitched the remaining horse to the old unused farm wagon. A half-blind, bony animal, old like himself, that Schmulik still kept in the barn eating his head off, always saying the animal should already be taken and killed for his skin.

On the road you hardly saw a wagon anymore, only buses and private taxis. And everyone told Yankel it was madness, a Jew could not drive by himself on the road. Ach!

At the entrance they did not know Yankel's name, his fine rich son-in-law had not done as he said he would, and when they stared and made laughter of his horse and wagon, a fire of his old anger rose in Yankel so that he demanded they use their telephone to call Bagelmacher himself at his hotel and say it was Yankel Chaimovitch here. He was by now holding up several self-important Jerusalemites at the stile; one of them, hearing the name Chaimovitch, looked at him intrigued and told the clerk, why not call? Whereupon the ticket clerk made the inquiry; the phrase "on a farm wagon" could be caught. Suddenly the clerk changed, became polite, and bade Yankel ·nter. ,

For all these many years Yankel had not sat there on the bench in the sweat room, where indeed a man felt the curative salts from the steam of the hot springs penetrating through his crusting, aching bone joints. And here, among the naked bodies in the misted room, one could not tell an old farmer from an important Jerusalemite. To a question from beside him, perhaps the one at the gate who had repeated his name, he replied, yes, he had a son in Jerusalem, his youngest, now married and a father of twins, two boys, for on returning from high studies in the university in America, he had brought with him an American bride, a shaineh. This son had been appointed to an important post in the British government; he was the principal adviser indeed to the ruler, the High Commissioner, as he was called, on all matters of consequence in the land, the crops to be sown, the wastelands to be peopled, the planning for sustenance in years to come. Also, Yankel's daughter was married to the son of Reb Bagelmacher, the hotel owner; indeed, it was Nahum, his son-in-law, now called Artzi instead of Bagelmacher, who had built the splendid new hotel and who was now building an entire city, Hof HaSharon, another Tel Aviv!

Who hadn't heard of Nahum and his ventures? The Jerusalemite brought his head nearer through the haze, to gaze on Yankel with respect and perhaps still a touch of uncertainty, but as it happened, old Bagelmacher himself appeared, Yankel recognized his speckled beard in the steam, and they greeted each other heartily. His mechutan had come only for him, to have a shmooz as in the old days, why had Yankel made himself such a stranger, why did he not make regular use of the baths, and Bagelmacher even insisted that Yankel should be examined by the specialist of the establishment, who would prescribe a course of treatment. Reb Bagelmacher himself was undergoing a treatment, in his case for asthma, and it was a sin on the part of Yankel to have neglected himself, for as was written and decreed, disrespect for the body that the Above One had created was a disregard for the Above One Himself!

Yankel did not recall the ruling, but presently he was driving to Tiberias almost every day for the baths, at times meeting Reb Bagelmacher there.

Now often they slid cozily into a shmooz, as in the very first time when Yankel, one Friday, had driven to Tiberias to prepare at least once for a proper Shabbat and had allowed himself the luxury of entering the baths, and they had fallen into a conversation on this very same bench in the steam room. It was indeed a stout bench, worn silk-smooth, Reb Bagelmacher jested, by generations of polishing from the behinds of Jerusalem notables! Nahum wanted to throw out all these old benches and was only waiting because he intended to build a magnificent new bathhouse entirely.

As they had run out of subjects to talk about, Yankel, after a silence, said that the bench reminded him of the yeshiva benches of his youth, and his mechutan said, exactly. These benches he had bought in the old days from the yeshiva of Rabbi Meir Ba'al HaNess, just up the hill, when the number of pupils there had dwindled.

Perhaps this was what put Yankel in mind of visiting the yeshiva and the grave of Rabbi Meir of the miracles. How was it he had never even journeyed up this hill to the tomb of Rabbi Meir Ba'al HaNess, and even higher up the hill to the cave where the Sage of Sages, Rabbi Akiva, was buried? And this day Yankel drove his wagon up the stony ruts that led to the domed synagogue of the yeshiva. Here, no one glanced twice at the wagon and the nag. On one side of the flagstones a number of women squatted, some with kerchiefs of provisions. They looked mostly to be per-haps Turkish or Syrian Jews, of the poor, and now Yankel re-called: Rabbi Meir of the miracles was said to intercede in the regions above for the barren. Nu, Yankel had never believed in miracles, it was indeed forbidden to believe in them, this sort of thing was a deterioration of the true study of the Law, brought on by the Hasidim, but what then of the wonders performed by Moshe Rabeinu?

Bordering the courtyard was a low wooden house, and as an elderly Jew emerged, Yankel had a look through the doorway—a shtible. There, on benches around a long table, sat a number of Jews, elderly like himself, bowed over their tomes.

Somehow Yankel's whole life slid away. He was again a yeshiva bocher, and there was the same singsong over ancient problems of agricultural law propounded by the exiles in Babylon.

Several days of the week Yankel, returning to the shtible, sat in this warm circle of old men with, in truth, time to make pass, their years to make pass; he had never been a sharp scholar, nor, he saw, were they, one was the proverbial butcher, a katsav who had all the years tended a stall in the Tiberias market; another, who slept overnight on one of the benches, was given to predictions, he was perhaps a bit out of his mind, but who could tell, he might be inspired in his babble. It was homey. With his enlarging glass Yankel would pore over the tomes and then join the discussions. Reb Abtalion said, but in the opinion of Rab it is written—

One or two of them, particularly Reb Zalman the butcher, leaned a little toward Hasidic superstitions. In his old days Yankel felt himself becoming more tolerant, even often recalling with a smile behind his beard the harmless superstitions of his good wife, Feigel, long ago gone to the regions above. The butcher believed in the reincarnation of souls, gilgul, and one day the crazy one, Reb Pinhas, leaped up from his bench with a fiery dissertation, altogether clear and convincing, showing by gematria that the beast Hitler, risen in Germany, was the reincarnation of Haman. And on he continued, his words becoming more tangled, yet with the same fiery certainty, proving with lines from Ezekiel that the days of Gog and Magog were at hand and predicting that the final struggle between good and evil would begin in the Days of Awe in the coming year and continue for seven years, and in the end trumpets would sound from on high and the Temple would be rebuilt on the Mount!

With these words the meshuganer sank down, subsiding into torpor.

Sometimes Wingate gathered them in one of their huts in the back area of Ein Harod, and lectured them. Who were the enemy? Poor illiterate buggers, mercenaries for a few pounds a month, but good shots, taught on antiquated weapons in the barren stretches of half desert across the Jordan. What was the enemy's way? An uncanny way of appearing out of nowhere, murdering and vanishing. Based on desert stamina, so that for long hours they could climb untired over rocky, desolate hills.

To hunt and destroy them, you had to know the ground better than they did, have more stamina than they did. Better weapons you had. Go out and take over the night from them. Small units, appearing from nowhere. Ambush. Kill all you could; the rest would run.

The training marches were night-long, bayonets fixed, behind that inexhaustible, inhuman figure, who would then, in a compassionate glance, become a chaver. Once Noam became so faint before a few gulps from the canteen were allowed, he dizzied, and Avi caught and pulled him along. He was ashamed for the Yadid to know, but when they finally halted, he saw Wingate knew, passing him with a pat on the shoulder.

Again, where the pipeline came down the Gilboa to cross the Emek, it had been cut. When the Yadid arrived at dusk, the boys were certain this time it would be the real thing.

The tender only slowed down so they could drop off one by one at intervals, unnoticed. Just as in practice marches, units made the climb from different sides of the hill. This was a drizzly, chill night, but at least the damp kept their steps soundless. The Yadid had taught them a few tricks—how in the dark to make landmarks for yourself by the feeling of the earth, the rocks under your feet, by shapes, so that even on a starless night you could find your way back. On this same hill they had one night made a practice climb and come down, a perfect exercise without a sound, without a trace, as though they had never been there.

Even in the night drizzle the village was outlined, a clump of dwellings like a large outcropping. They halted well below, before dogs could bark. A poor herders' village, down here a few cultivated snips of soil between boulders, with heaped-stone fences good for cover. He and Avi were in position. On these slippery rocks, if anything should happen, could he carry Avi down? Never leave a comrade.

They waited. It might be hours. It might still be another night of nothing. But not a pebble must roll, or uncannily the Yadid would be upon you.

Tonight, he said, the marauders would be going out to make another attack on the pipe. Maybe his instinct, maybe an informer. They came. Only an hour, and their swagger could be heard. With utter carelessness they came down; even cigarette tips could be seen. The two ambushers above let them pass. Then the Yadid fired his Very gun, and in the ghoulish light you could pick them off just like practice targets, even while their escape was closed off from above. As Noam saw one tumble, a crazy impulse came like running up to see how close to the bull's-eye you had hit. And with this the upwelling satisfaction, a hunter's gratification, as when, still kids, he and Avi had gone out to destroy jackals.

This was what troubled Noam, the gratification, growing stronger in every action. The bitter exultation.

On his home visits Noam became more and more silent, not with the simple silence owing to the secrecy of the Night Squads but with the silence of not being able to talk even about other things, everyday things because of the inner secret that presses you. One day when his father took him out to the fields to show how an experiment with his under-surface irrigation seemed to be succeeding, Noam, half choked, got the words out, "Abba, I am getting a taste for blood. I want only to kill them. It gives me joy when I kill."

Within Reuven's sorrow there was only the slightest glimmer of relief that his son had at last said this to him.

In night awakenings Reuven and Elisheva discussed it. And finally with two of their closest chaverim, from their own time. To try to persuade the boy this was not for him? No boy would leave. To have him dismissed would be worse. Menahem, called back at that time from Poland, said it was a fever he himself had felt in his early days as a Shomer, when his closest friend Yechezkiel had been killed. When soldiers became hardened, at least this horrible joy went out of it. But it had to take its course.

Then Noam and Avi's unit was stationed in the lone outpost, Hanita, the tower-and-stockade kibbutz on the mountainous Lebanese border where the raiders were known to cross. For the fortress itself the Yadid had not much use. To sit and wait to be attacked! Stupidity! Go out, go out after the enemy! But as a base it was all right.

One day a mounted watchman galloped in. On the lower road was a mass slaughter. Four hacked bodies. A car riddled, burned.

Wingate had come up that day; Wingate's rage spilled into anger at the victims—idiots to drive on the border road without giving notice. The unit crowded in, some into his command car, the rest in the tender. He had a strong feeling where that killer gang would be laid up.

The riddled vehicle might even have been left as a decoy ambush, but the Yadid was in the blind fury that dismissed danger. Nevertheless, the tender halted a good distance behind while his command car approached the slaughter site. First, as Noam got out, the stench of disembowelment engulfed him. Then in the narrow hooded gleam of the Yadid's torch held low in the burned wreck, he made out the remains. Like an abattoir. Then he saw what had always been the terror-fear. The two blood-dried flesh lumps over the gouged-out eye sockets. The piece of flesh prodded into the forced open mouth.

Out of Avi Noam heard, as though coming from himself, a wordless animal howl.

From the hilltop village not a glimmer showed, but they were awaited. As Wingate moved forward a distance ahead of them on the donkey path, the first volley came. He fell flat—cut down or for cover? But his Very pistol fired. Hit in the leg, he had squirmed around and was firing; he waved them on. Noam saw gun flashes from a narrow lane, knew he was flinging grenades, darting with Avi from wall to wall. Then he saw minutely an Arab leaping at them with a huge revolver firing point-blank into Avi's face. In reflex Noam's bayonet went through the killer. He was killing, killing, skillfully flinging himself into crevices, firing at fleeing forms, hearing his own screams to the chevreh, kill, kill, kill, kill!

It was finished, the villagers rounded up and insisting that the gang had invaded, forced them to give shelter; twenty-seven rifles found, seventeen dead counted. Some had got away. Avi's body was carried down to the tender. The Yadid, his riddled leg bound, still refused to be taken to a hospital; were all accounted for? An Irish trooper was calling off names; he got to Avi, waited. Dazed, Noam heard himself answer "Here!" He was Avinoam.

※ ※ ※

The whole way down to Tel Aviv for the farewell to Sir Arthur at the Kaete Dan, Mati kept muttering, why couldn't he too resign? Ill health, the High Commissioner had given out, but ever since the quota announcement, that insult, one thousand labor certificates for six months, Wauchope had avoided his Jewish friends. Of course, he knew that no one blamed him for London. London had given in to the Arab terror, everybody said. And Arab oil.

Gallant as ever, Sir Arthur greeted them, complimenting Dena on her lacy hat, turning to Dov the Smiler—wasn't it charming? Now was the moment. Mati got Dov aside. If Dov could find him something useful to do, to hell with his piled-up government seniority; he had heard the port of Tel Aviv might be looking for a new manager. This time Dov didn't even smile. If Mati resigned, his job would almost certainly go to an Englishman. Or even worse, the way London was acting, they might give it to an Arab! Since Hitler's parade into Vienna, he didn't have to tell Mati, Austrian Jews were being picked up and sent to a criminal camp, a place called Dachau. This was not the time to leave, with a tough new High Commissioner coming in.

From crisis to crisis he had to stay on. Suddenly thousands of Polish Jews who had many years before migrated to Germany were rounded up, forced into boxcars, and dumped at the border. Since Poland now refused to repatriate them, the Jews huddled in a marshy no-man's-land. It was a week before the American Joint Distribution Committee could even get soup to them. Desperate appeals for visas went unheeded. Many were small merchants; they might even have qualified as "capitalists," but all funds had been confiscated. In an almost unbroken chain of conferences, Mati and Reggie sought solutions, partial solutions, loopholes, plans for a few thousand, even a few hundred. But if Chaim Weizmann's special appeals in London, if appeals from world humanitarians, if mass meetings in New York could have no effect, what could they hope to accomplish? And soon a catastrophe. Among the deported was an elderly couple named Grynspan who had lived in Germany for twenty-six years. To their son, a student in Paris, came a letter describing their misery. Typhus had broken out. Procuring a revolver, young Grynspan went to the German Embassy and requested to see the ambassador. A functionary named Von Rath appeared to ask what he wanted, and the Jewish student shot the Nazi dead.

Thus came the nationwide pogrom called Kristallnacht, the night of the broken glass. If only it had been no more than shopwindows and looting. Thousands of Jews were beaten on the streets, in their homes, hauled off to concentration camps, and everywhere synagogues were systematically set on fire. Then came the news pictures of Jews forced to lick sidewalks clean. And to the protesters about human rights, Hermann Goering's reply: "Jews have no right but to die."

Why did Mati have to take it as though he personally were responsible? Dena kept telling him. After all, the whole world was shutting them out! She was even ashamed of Roosevelt. A few hundred thousand refugees, and look at that idiotic refugee conference he had set up, getting the whole world to send delegates. There they sit in the fancy resort in Evian—a health spa yet!—and one delegate after another gets up and regrets! Had Mati read what the Australian said? His country had no racial problem and was not desirous of importing one! And America itself! They could take in only the regular annual quota from Germany—which, obviously, could not be confined to Jews!

He had read, Mati had read. Yet what on earth could be done? Broken-down riverboats were heard of, filled with Jews, stranded on the Danube. Jews were paying all they had hiring anything that floated, and now another rotted freighter had gone down with everyone aboard, off the Greek islands, an old hog transport; was it a brutal joke or only an irony of fate?

❋ ❋ ❋

Despite the failure with the second voyage of the *Veloz* a few years ago, Menahem found himself summoned one night to Eliahu's office by the kitchen, where he found the brother-in-law Shaul, his own old chaver from the days of the Shomer, already arrived. When Moshe Shertok came in with Dov Hos, everybody made the usual remarks about the family monopoly—the four in-laws. But tonight even the usual jokes seemed out of place.

The plan was to set up a special Mossad group for immigration, capable lads to spread into Rumania, Austria, Poland, to find escape routes and ships. They went over the names. First, the boys who had already done such work a few years ago—Levi Schwartz, and Braginsky, from Kfar Giladi Moshe Agami must go to Vienna where the zionist organization was still allowed to function, to help "rid Austria of Jews." The Nazis wanted to squeeze out the last possessions from those who had "capitalist" immigration certificates. A special officer for Jewish affairs had taken over the Rothschild House; this Hauptsturmführer Eichmann for extra funds, would allow youth groups to depart through Yugoslavia. Now it was a question of sending someone to Yugoslavia to arrange for a boat. And so they began to weave the underground escape routes and to decide who would go where. At most ten men. To Rumania, Shaul even recommended a young woman, she was burning to do something, yes, she was from the family, yes, she was reliable, and she knew all the languages, Polish, Hungarian, Rumanian, German, too, and this redheaded Ruthie could get sympathy out of a hyena.

Menahem himself must go back to Poland. Also Schlomo Zameret, who had been brought from America to Eretz as a child, and possessed that wondrous document, an American passport. Perhaps in Greece, ships could be obtained even from that same arms runner who a few years ago had supplied the ill-fated *Veloz*. This time things must be done on a much larger scale.

In desperation the young Polish Jews were swarming to the activists. In these few years, Jabotinsky's Betar tripled in number;

they were now over sixty thousand. The struggle over every immigration certificate had become vicious; the Revisionists demanded a higher percentage of the allocation, shouted that Ben-Gurion and his gang through their control of the Jewish Agency were trying to force all opposition into line. Instead, the dissidents were proclaiming that they would march and seize Palestine! It was rumored that the Polish military had actually approved Jabotinsky's plan to embark forty thousand Betarists, a full army, on armed transports. And the youngsters believed this! Didn't they know that Poland had a treaty with England! Menahem recalled the same dream from the World War, when Trumpeldor, leaving Jabotinsky in London to pursue their campaign for a Jewish Legion, had made his way back to Russia at the outbreak of the Kerensky revolution, and tried to raise a Jewish army of a hundred thousand, to march through Turkey and Syria and seize Palestine from the Turks. Alas he had only reached the land after the British victory, coming over the Syrian border alone in a peasant cart. And soon gone back up to the border to command the defense of Kfar Giladi and Tel Hai against Arab marauders. Ironically, Menahem remembered how Jabotinsky had proclaimed this a lost cause and counseled against sending reinforcements. Well, so had most of the Yishuv's leaders; poor Yaffaleh and a dozen others had gone up there by themselves, in answer to Trumpeldor's passionate call for volunteers. But here was Jabotinsky's youth group named after the obstinate hero: B'rith Trumpeldor, the Betar. Repeating his dream.

Hundreds of them were arriving in the city for their big conference, their new commander was to be elected, and Menahem got himself admitted. What youth! What erect, determined youngsters! What material! True, the Gordonia youth were just as determined, as enthusiastic, and the young people of HeChalutz, but here in the packed hall with Jabotinsky on the platform, and their flags everywhere, and posters with their emblem of the rifle uniting both sides of the Jordan, "Only thus!" You could not help being swept by their fervor, even if somewhere deep in your heart it brought a touch of agony. To Jabotinsky's oratory, laced with his satiric wit, Menahem felt as toward the appearance of a great performer: how is he this time? Unfailing were the barbs at the British colonials and their love for the Arabs, and just as unfailing were his jabs at the Haganah's policy of restraint, havlagah, the word brought a shuddery rumble from the crowd, as yes, bare your throats to the knife, brothers, stand fast while your throat is cut! Havlagah!

No! There would be no restraint! No borders! Step by step their movement would advance—

Menahem felt he had caught something different. "Step by step?" At this very time, he knew, Jabotinsky had been in conference, once more with a view to reuniting with the movement. A larger share of certificates was being promised. Could this be a sign of moving back toward the Organization's way? Step by step, instead of armed revolt?

Almost directly across the aisle he had noticed a small group of the dissidents' own dissidents, around the young poet Avraham Stern, known as Yair. Elegantly dressed as always, handsome, self-assured, he had inclined his head to the whisper of one of his followers. He wore a slight, knowing smile. Ah yes, Yair had caught the change of tune, and his smile seemed to say that the betrayal was only as expected.

But with the audience, the analysis "in the light of the situation" was being carried off. The oration mounted to its climax, the ovation came, and the leader at last could take his seat so that the election might proceed.

One more speaker arose, a slight, bespectacled young man, as unmilitary looking as Jabotinsky himself. He had Menahem's own first name: Menahem Begin. A law student, a Betarist leader virtually from childhood, his election was said to be a certainty, and partly for a good look at him, Menahem had come.

Definitely, they had here a young Jabotinsky, but with his own style, dryer, he was a bit of legalist, even with a touch of the Talmudist—he wore a yarmulkah. A speaker who inspected all sides of a question, with a debater's smile of courteous consideration for every point of view. And then a series of arm-chopping demolishments, there was only one way! the way shown long ago by the Almighty! The divine command! He flung forward his arm, like the rifle-holding arm in the poster. "Only thus!" The Jewish nation in the ancient borders of Israel! Both sides of the Jordan! The entire land redeemed! The hurrahs rose after each outcry, each slogan, even higher than for Jabotinsky. As the young Begin was elected commander by acclaim, the Betar song burst out. And in a delirium over their action, the young people surged, carrying him on their shoulders.

Not necessarily to counteract the sweep toward the Betar, Ben-Gurion came to tour the HeChalutz training farms, and when his

379

open car was passing over the bridge in his native city of Plonsk, with cheering crowds lining the street, two youths suddenly leaped onto the running-board, each emptying a large bag of dust onto his head.

They were seized, but in the relief—after all they could easily have killed him but had only thrown dust—the chutzpa, the humor of their act brought spreading laughter, and after a good thrashing the Betarists were let go.

Only, the talks of reuniting broke off. Some said because the Revisionists insisted on retaining a certain autonomy of action. And from then forward, Menahem heard, such hatred could be felt in Ben-Gurion that it was best not even to mention the opposition within earshot.

҉ ҉ ҉

In Mishkan Yaacov, Yankel had already hitched his horse to the cart, to drive in to Tiberias, where he thought to pass some hours in the shtible by the tomb of Rabbi Meir Ba'al HaNess. Nussya came running out to stop him. As he would never listen to the radio, he didn't know. Last night in Tiberias a massacre had taken place; nineteen Jews lay dead. No, not Reb Bagelmacher or any of their in-laws. An Arab gang from the hills had got into the Jewish market section, and set fires, and slaughtered. Nor need Yankel try to go to the shul of Rabbi Meir Ba'al HaNess; it lay burned to the ground.

Presently Reb Roitschuler came to Yankel. He had heard something more. In that shtible where Yankel went, the one who slept there, the crazy one, Reb Pinhas the Prophet, had perished in the flames.

For the raid on Tiberias, Schmulik brought Mati the inside word from the Gilboa hills, there had been a retaliation. The Nashashibi "peace force" had killed the raiding chief and half his band. Now there were sure to be more assassinations, to avenge those. Good! Let them kill each other off! And it was a good thing for Mati's Nashashibi friend the artist that he had got out of the country. The one who had run after Jewish girls. Had Mati heard from him?

He was in Beirut, Mati said; his father had died.

What? They got at him in Beirut?

No, Khalid's father had long been ill. A natural death.

Defiantly, the doughty Fakri Bey Nashashibi, head of the clan, led thousands of Hebronites in a peace march, declaring to the foreign press that seventy-five percent of the Arabs were opposed to the Mufti.

Bringing home the pro-Mufti Arab papers, Mati translated a proclamation to Dena. The traitor, Fakri Bey Nashashibi, was sentenced to be killed like a dog wherever found.

To the last-hope conference of Arabs and Jews in St. James's Palace, Ben-Gurion took Reggie as his assistant. But almost on the next ship Reggie was back. A high-up Britisher had remarked to Ben-Gurion that if the Mandate were being formulated today, they would be giving Palestine to the Arabs. Then, in the wastebasket of Jamal Husseini, one of the Mossad boys had found a letter from the Mufti assuring his cousin he was slated as Prime Minister of an Arab Palestine. In two years at the latest. "Go back," Ben-Gurion had sent Reggie, with word for the Haganah to acquire every gun, every pistol it could get hold of, every weapon at whatever cost.

Dov came from Tel Aviv right to Mati's office. They'd do this the official way, he said. The Histadrut itself was setting up a tourist flight line. And Peewee even suggested, with his best innocent blink, that the RAF ought to be interested in disposing of some out-of-service light planes at a bargain. Easily adaptable for tourism. The three of them went over to the King David bar and toasted the tourist airline.

"So, Mati. At last!" Dov said. Dov would "manage" the tourist airline himself.

After the fruitless London Conference there came the government's own decision on Palestine, a White Paper. Over the coming five years a total of seventy-five thousand immigration certificates would be issued, spaced, still, according to economic absorptive capacity. Thenceforth there would be no more Jewish immigration without Arab approval. Further sale of Arab land was virtually entirely forbidden.

From Phil and Sherrill came outraged letters with quotations from senators, congressmen, non-Jewish, too, and prominent ministers who had denounced Perfidious Albion. Sherrill enclosed a newspaper picture of masses of Chicago Jews marching behind a banner, IF I FORGET THEE O JERUSALEM.

The special night squads were dissolved, and Wingate was ordered home to England. Drawn up for the Yadid's farewell, Avinoam and his comrades heard from his lips the parting message: Always expect betrayal. Rely only on yourselves.

Their chubby Haganah commander, Yitzhak Saadeh, talked of keeping them together, forming a mobile striking force, the Yishuv's first full-time soldiers. They would be placed in groups among the kibbutzim and work half-time in the fields. Noam put down his name—Avinoam.

※ ※ ※

Though the Labor Party had made him a delegate to the World Zionist Congress, Menahem also had, in a sense, a congress of his own to hold, for the meeting in Geneva was an excellent cover for bringing together the Mossad lads scattered over Europe. Now that Hitler had seized Czechoslovakia, different routes out of Poland would have to be prepared.

Shaul himself could not come to Europe; one of those privately hired refugee hulks was in desperate condition, off the Syrian coast. He had sent a rescue team to Beirut and would not risk getting out of communication. Besides, even more important, the red-headed Ruthie in Bucharest had managed to ship off a boatload crowded with seven hundred chalutzim, the pick of the Polish training farms. First, their train had been halted at the Rumanian frontier. Ruthie had in some incredible way got in contact through a Jewish banker with a high churchman who had got her through to King Carol's mistress, Magda Lupescu, and just as the train was about to be sent back to Poland the King himself had given a special order for the chalutzim to be brought to the Port of Constanta. Now at sea on the *Tiger Hill*, these refugees, too, were in great difficulty. Menahem would have to replace Shaul at the Congress.

The atmosphere was somber. There were fewer delegates from abroad than usual—who knew what would happen at any moment in Europe? Indeed, with the Germans now having swallowed all of Czechoslovakia and sitting at the Polish border, Menahem could not help feeling that those seven hundred on the *Tiger Hill* would be the last Polish chalutzim to get out.

The same misgiving came from Yehuda Arazi as they strolled together by the lake. His old friend and colleague, the shipper of road rollers and boilers, had arrived last night from Warsaw with one of his typical Arazi "combinations." But first, a quiet stroll.

The placid lake, Menahem remarked to Yehuda, was like an incredible angel-faced strumpet he had once seen in one of those blue movies in Marseilles. Yehuda had seen it in London. Whipping, whipping, and her expression angelically unchanged. Europe.

Now they had to put their heads together for Yehuda's "combination." There was a Warsaw Jew in the arms trade who had sent a twin-engine fighter on the way to Spain—too late. The plane was in crates, where but in Haifa Harbor itself! It had been unloaded there for transshipment. It could be bought at a bargain, but this Polish Jew wanted immigration certificates; he wanted at once to get his family out of Poland. Menahem thought they had best immediately find Ben-Gurion.

When they reached the hall, he was just going up onto the platform, where Chaim Weizmann was finishing, still pleading for the methods of diplomacy, of influence, surely the British would "adapt" the harsh White Paper as they had done once before, when all had seemed lost, with the White Paper that followed the troubles of 1929.

The response to Weizmann was feeble.

"Buy it, buy it, I'll find him certificates," Ben-Gurion snapped to Yehuda as he mounted the steps. In sober realism, as the man from the Yishuv, he answered Weizmann: No more time for diplomatic niceties. There must be immigration, permitted or not, legal or not. He would even advocate sailing illegal ships openly into the harbor of Tel Aviv. Let the British arrest the entire population!

It was no longer a rivalry between them, Menahem felt, but a desperate searching for the way. Then Berl Katznelson arose, declaring in his slow, grave voice, as though they were all sitting around a table, everyone here, not in a hall, "Chaverim, we are all illegal immigrants."

Yes, Menahem himself had got into Eretz with the usual bribe to the Turks.

"Have not Jews always and everywhere been illegal immigrants?"

What did this mean then—that the Zionist Congress itself was adopting the defiance of the Irgun?

But the debate was never finished. From behind the hall came whispers, murmurs growing stronger; then on the platform an interruption, with the announcement of astounding news. Hitler and Stalin had signed a nonaggression pact.

As the news came over the radio, Natan set down his mug. Exchanging only a few words with Leah, he went out. What was there to say? It struck you like a death. Stalin had opened the way for Hitler to start his war.

There would be things said from all sides, explanations and calculations and accusations, and Natan himself would have to try to make some sort of explanation to the refugee children, and with his own children sitting and taking part, but let him at least first walk out his bitterness.

He went down across HaYarkon Street to the sands, where the houses straggled out to a knoll; atop were a few old Arab tombs, and hardly anybody ever came. There he sat listening to the water.

The war would start soon enough, a month, perhaps even less, that was certain, the same war with the same sides except Russia neutralized, well, Russia hadn't been much use in the other war; again, after millions of torn bodies and a ravaged world, probably America would join at the last moment, and the outcome would be the same; one had to cling to that belief. But deeper, more personal than the sense of the oncoming physical convulsion and suffering for humanity was the death in Natan of the last spark of his belief. Despite all, despite the betrayals, the ghastly show trials, the extinction of millions of kulaks, a spark had persisted: the Revolution was still there, and the Revolution would survive the horrors and chaos of its creation. Today the spark was trampled out.

Oh, he could foretell the cunning rationalizations that would come pouring forth from the still-faithful. The Wise One had in one single brilliant stroke confounded the capitalist and fascist world together, while preserving the motherland of socialism from a brutal, destructive war. Once Hitler and the Western capitalist lands had exhausted each other, the world revolution would sweep away that whole rubbish. Ach, as if humanity were nothing but a chessboard for the cunning, the pipe smokers.

Then what had been the other possible moves? Had Stalin compacted instead with the Allies, Hitler would have been contained. Did Stalin fear the Allies might nevertheless have let Hitler attack and exhaust him? And had he therefore been the first to betray, making his move with the notion he was turning the tables on them? And if Hitler should now make a rapid attack in the west and succeed, would he not turn on the Soviet Union in any case, pact or no pact?

They would say Stalin had done this to gain at least a year's time, so he could prepare against an exhausted Hitler. Ach, all these conjectures were not only fruitless but vile. The plain fact was that Stalin had joined with the fascists, the same ones who had murdered all their own land's communists.

Natan still thought of himself as a communist. Well, a Marxist. He could not work with the party, particularly here, but he had continued along with the left, with the opposition, even while Leah was staunchly Mapai. Socialists they still called themselves. Well, in a way he had lived a socialist life, in his corner of their little kibbutz. But you had only to look around at the city engulfing their meshek—wasn't it a symbol of the Yishuv itself? Already he and Leah were in a battle to preserve their training farm on its present site, just as he had made futile attempts to preserve the Arab village a mile inland. One by one the Arabs had sold out, some getting swindled, a few becoming well-off. In the earlier generation of settlers, at least Arabic had been learned in the daily way of life and in most of the schools. Now, what Jewish child learned Arabic? For this, too—to make Arabic compulsory in the Jewish schools—he had fought in vain. The children of Tel Aviv now grew up without contact with a live Arab any more than with a live Jewish farmer.

National Socialism. In a way those very words had started here! With Ben-Gurion and Ben-Zvi and their comrades, the early socialists, the dreamers of a Jewish nation. The same words—it was too horrible to think. Every ideal seemed to turn into its opposite. All right—dialectics. Natan knew; he had read. He no longer could believe.

In the Congress there had at first come an awed gasp, as at a surprise in a theater. Then those on the platform had with a single impulse drawn together, just as groups began to do in the hall. All murmuring, speculating. How long? And where would he strike first? France? Or perhaps— People glanced at the delegates from France, from Belgium, as though it would be understandable if they rushed from the hall.

Menahem and Arazi were sitting with the Polish delegation.

Almost all of them they had known for years, Jews to whose homes they had been for the Friday meal, and yet already you could feel from them the knowledge that you were more free to move about the world than they. Some were asking each other, should they remain the last few days of the Congress or already start home? And all around, in a dozen languages, discussions had begun— clearly now Hitler was free to attack westward, but perhaps he would first try a surprise move in the north. And Menahem was wondering, wouldn't Hitler first destroy Poland? He saw the same thought in Arazi. "I'd better get back and buy that plane while I can," said Yehuda.

And would he ever come out? Would any of these old friends, these good, faithful Zionists, ever come out?

THE
WHIRLWIND

BOOK III

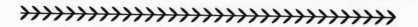

25

THE first shots fired by the British in the war, on the day the Nazis invaded Poland, it was said, were at an illegal ship off the Palestine coast. For after a month of evasive sea wandering, on starvation rations after taking on the Jews from the foundering vessel off the Syrian coast, the *Tiger Hill*, now carrying more than eleven hundred, was attempting to disembark them below Jaffa. The beach had been chosen by the Mossad because it was unpatrolled, but naval boats had spotted the vessel, and now they opened fire. Two of the refugees packed on deck, from that half-sinking ship near Beirut, were killed. Managing to escape beyond the Palestine waters, the *Tiger Hill* was instructed by radio to head the next morning directly for the headquarters house on the Tel Aviv beach.

Among those alerted was Natan. Taking his binoculars and snatching a bundle of clothing, he hurried to the knoll where hardly a week ago he had sat by an old Arab tomb in the bitterness of his last disillusion. He was on the lookout for the *Tiger Hill*'s leaders, Levi Schwartz and Katriel, who had been instructed to leap off and swim, for when the ship was seized, the CID would be searching for them.

Now Natan saw the vessel and strained his eyes for the swimmers.

From the Histadrut house itself people were already running down to the beach, and soon growing streams came pouring down from every side street. Even a band of kids from their own meshek

Natan saw rushing toward the water, and already hundreds of Tel Avivians were dashing into the sea, surrounding refugees who had jumped from the vessel, and absorbing them into the crowd. Natan's own two swimmers had not appeared; they must already have found safety. Now police cars came sirening down HaYarkon Street; from every window came jeers, outcries, screams; the first police to reach the area could hardly get out of their vehicles, pelted with vegetables, with sand. Already military reinforcements, a convoy of battle cars with mounted machine guns, followed by military trucks, came charging down Allenby Street, blocking off the area. At least let there be no slaughter. Natan wished he could pray. Police boats circled the *Tiger Hill*, keeping off the little flock of dinghies, sports vessels, even lifeguard canoes, that had appeared. The remainder on board would doubtless be interned, but perhaps more than half had already been spirited into the city.

Thousands were registering with the Jewish community council for military service. Ben-Gurion had indeed found a slogan: "We will fight the White Paper as if there were no war, and we will fight the war as if there were no White Paper."

Mati tried to get into the RAF.

The cables from Chicago were frantic. If Mati went to war, Dena must come home with the children; there was no point in her staying on alone in Palestine. The dear idiots.

Every night at their house or at Reggie and Maureen's, or the Marmors, the men became military strategists.

Hitler was trying to draw Turkey into the war. Mati was certain there would be air battles again in the skies right over Palestine, dogfights between German and British planes like the ones he had seen as a child. Britain was sure to be short of fighter pilots. He was only in his early thirties, well within the age limit.

Maybe if things did get to look really dangerous, Dena said, they should, after all, send the kids?

As he waited for his physical and his flying test, Mati went on a strenuous diet; at least that was one good thing the war had brought, Dena joked. Also he even took exercises, trotting a kilometer every morning before he went to the office. Of course, he had left out from his application any mention of his ulcerous condition.

Then, on the excuse of surveying Galilee kibbutzim for war production potential, he sneaked a few days away from Jerusalem. At Afikim he took up the old *Gidon*, and it was good; in an hour all his tricks were back; looping the loop over the Kinneret, Mati felt like a kid doing somersaults.

And back in Jerusalem, Peewee for one night got Mati the loan of a Spitfire manual; he broke his head over it. Never mind. If you could fly, you could fly anything.

The Luftwaffe had wiped out Poland in no time. A few weeks. This war would be decided in the air.

His call didn't come. Mati pulled a few strings. At last he was notified of his physical. Though they were damn thorough, he felt sure they hadn't caught on about the ulcer. What worried him most was that he was still twenty pounds overweight, but he kidded with the doctor about how quickly it would melt off in training and how pleased his wife would be.

It was not unusual for their mail to contain an envelope marked "On His Majesty's Service," but this one, Dena sensed, held their fate. Finally, she could no longer resist and steamed it open. Never before had she opened Mati's mail.

In a way she was relieved. Carefully resealing the envelope, she prepared for Mati's disappointment. Would it be depression or fury?

Calling Maureen, Dena told her in greatest confidence. Maybe Reggie and Maureen could come over tonight and help get his mind off it?

For days it was dreadful; he couldn't seem to look anybody in the eye, as though his manhood were gone and everyone knew it. The rejection said for reasons of health. Someone in the office, he was sure, must have tipped them off about the ulcer.

Mati didn't even want to see their friends, as though he had had some personal failure and were ashamed of himself. He began to suspect that that anti-Semitic bastard the chief secretary himself had got him turned down because they were getting short of staff and wanted to keep him at drudgework in the administration. He didn't even laugh when Dena said at least he could stop starving himself and eat all he wanted.

Worse, Mati's nephew Giora called in elation. The kid who had guarded the *Gidon* when they first arrived. He was accepted into the RAF! Well, Dena cheered up Mati, see, his instruction efforts hadn't been wasted! But to hell with them, he said; the British—just as in the First World War—were refusing to allow the formation of a special Jewish unit. It would probably be four years again before they would give in. If it weren't Hitler, he could wish they would lose the war and their whole bloody Empire.

The news was dreadful. Warsaw was aflame. The British aircraft carrier *Courageous* was sunk by a submarine. As though to underline the state of the world, Sigmund Freud died.

A total survey of the Empire's raw materials resources was taking place, and on the list was copper. Ever since Nelson Glueck had brought back those samples from the primitive smelters of the Sinai that he had called King Solomon's Mines, a thought had been in Mati's mind. Though the samples had assayed out too low, that might not be conclusive. Hadn't there been tales of illicit diggings? When Mati mentioned this to Reggie, his friend came back with word that Ben-Gurion was interested. Not for the British, but for the day when this would be a Jewish nation. Somehow—with another person you could have even said "mystically"—Ben-Gurion was convinced that the war would lead to nationhood.

From the air base near Aqaba, with a technical sergeant and a Bedouin driver who knew the region, Mati set out in a Land Rover piled with provisions, a tent, tins of water, gasoline, pick-axes and shovels. Skirting the tip of the Red Sea, they stopped on the Palestine side at a desolate place called Um Rashrash, with a lone adobe fisherman's hut—could this once have been King Solomon's port of Elath? Sergeant Clay bought fish, varieties such as Mati had never seen, all glittering, burnished, jeweled, of every color, the sharp sea life odor still on them. And the sea itself, not red but indigo, with its border of white sand against the multicolored Sinai mountains.

Here at the tip of the sea, Moses and the tribal caravans had passed, the Queen of Sheba had arrived, the copper-loaded vessels of Solomon had sailed, and suddenly, just as they stood there with Sergeant Clay amusedly bargaining with the Bedouin fisherman, a rush of wings was heard, the sky darkened, and at no great distance, Mati saw as a cloud rising from the burned ground, a dense flight of migratory birds. "Quail," the sergeant said. The feast that fell from heaven?

An eye-creased old-timer in the service, Sergeant Cross, regaled Mati with desert lore; besides the flights of partridges you'd see songbirds, too, and sometimes a flight of Egyptian hawks, even squadrons of eagles. They'd get all the quail they wanted in some Bedouin camp in the wadi. This was the smuggling route for kif, from the Lebanon into Egypt; the route passed not far from the Pillars of Solomon where they were headed.

In the quail season these fellows set up nets; just as maybe in the days of Moses, and the masses of birds got tangled in them. All you had to do was pick them off. At the Bedouin camp, also, they could hire a few laborers for their digging.

From the bumpy, stone-littered plain, the twin pillars rose like some gilded entrance, Dena would have said, to a Balaban and Katz movie palace. All about lay chunks of greenish rocks. They set up camp.

Clay was a man who took a few snorts from his bottle and became rather silent and contemplative. The young Arab driver smoked his kif. Mati lay on a blanket spread on the ground, his hand folded under his head, and was entirely well again. He heard the great whirring, the myriad migration of the birds, immutable, eternally the same route, like the movement of a constellation. And of the Tribes of Israel to this day.

No, he did not feel inevitably directed, subject to a force. Yet he did feel himself within it, within an eternal movement. How in place he felt, yet free!

Before sleep, reveries came—of tall mechanical smelters on this plain. And at the tip of the Red Sea, high cranes like in the port of Haifa. He must have soundings made in the water at Um Rashrash, that looked so clear and deep. A deep-water port, and freight ships departing down the Red Sea, filled with potash brought down the Arava, the dried fertilizer from the Dead Sea would be transported from here to Africa, even to Japan; from here the entire east would be open to commerce from the Yishuv, here a city would grow, and also, along these golden beaches— Ah! he was getting to be a regular Nahum!

This was the smelting area, described by Nelson Glueck, and the ore brought here for smelting must have been mined not too far away. Ah, the driver knew where. Others had come searching.

Several miles along the gritty surface, they arrived before the low-curved hills, sand color, and purple, and reddish, with breast-like contours against the blue-black Sinai mountains. The driver churned upward close to the reddish outcropping. Here a few years ago diggers had worked. Up the slope he showed them an opening the size of two men. The tunnel, slanting downward, had first been made, who knew, perhaps by Solomon's Nubian slaves.

For a few days they camped, while Bedouins half-indolently chopped out rock samples from one tunnel and another. Perhaps as they dug deeper, the rocks would be richer in copper? Squeezing his way downward, Mati could not help feeling the sense of retracing himself, returning along the dark narrow course of time. That eerie sense of a personal connection, a continuation, like an excavation of your own distant origin. Who had labored here? African slaves? Egyptians? And he, Solomon's overseer?

His Bedouin chopped out more samples to carry back.

As the chill came with the dark, and they roasted quail at their small fire, a spark in the vast emptiness, Sergeant Clay turned on the radio.

And so in their pinpoint of nowhere the word came in that calm tone of firm equanimity, the BBC voice of omnipotence, if not the thunder of Jehovah. A bomb had gone off in the Munich beer hall where Hitler annually appeared on the date of the founding of the Nazi Party. But the Führer was unharmed.

On the quiet western front it was said that French and German soldiers had arranged a football match between the Maginot and Siegfried lines.

As the Nazis took over their share of Poland, Jews by the hundreds of thousands were fleeing into the Soviet area. Of those who remained caught in the Nazi-occupied land, thousands were being rounded up and dumped in the district of Lublin, in open muddy fields. There were rumors of impending massacres.

Mati only half heard the end of the BBC broadcast and an exclamation from Sergeant Clay, "Well, I say!" Douglas Fairbanks had died, the BBC said, marking the end of an era.

26

CAREFULLY pulling himself along the landing rope through the night-black water was a long-armed fellow, who cried, "Nein!" when Uri swam alongside to relieve him of his rucksack. As soon as he could touch bottom, the fellow swung the pack in front of him. In fragments of Yiddish-German, Uri tried to explain that the bottom here was treacherous; with his free arm he caught the fellow as the refugee stumbled into a trough. But the man's panic was for his precious sack.

Refugees behaved this way, Uri well knew; they clung ferociously to their last belongings. "Gold?" he jested as they got to knee depth. This immigrant had long slatlike legs, a real stork. In the night reflection his teeth shone in a lip-lifted grin. "Not gold. Diamonds," he replied, and Uri took it for a good retort.

Behind the sandbar, Araleh's trucks waited; this time there was an absolutely model operation, no alarms of arriving British, no separated children, no half-drowned hysterical mamas. In awe and admiration over the precise operation, the immigrants were moved on dirt tracks through orange groves to a packing shed, where Araleh's wife Saraleh and their daughter were ready with hot coffee and false identity cards; khaki shirts and shorts were quickly donned, and within minutes the first batch was trucked off for dispersal.

Still hugging his rucksack, the Stork stood a bit apart as though waiting out everyone's exhilaration over the successful landing. Many were repeating names and addresses of relatives they hoped to find. Finally the Stork approached Uri, inquiring, *"Wo ist der Führer?"*

"Führer!" Uri repeated. A real jester, this one. *"Hier kein Führer!"* He laughed. But the Stork made him understand that he had something very important to convey and must speak to a person in authority.

Everyone had something important to convey. But the fellow said, "I have a message from Menahem," and Araleh himself caught the words.

From Menahem? Why should someone on an Irgun boat have a message from the Mossad? But now in the crisis there was a degree of cooperation. "You can tell me," Araleh said.

"Menahem instructed me to get in touch with one Mati Chaimovitch."

Araleh eyed the immigrant. You could never be too careful. This man could even be planted.

"Menahem gave you a note or something?"

"I have something better than a note." Still clutching his rucksack, the immigrant motioned Araleh to a corner. Uri, simply out of curiosity, nosed along. What he had with him, the Stork declared while unlacing the top of his rucksack, would be of utmost importance for Jewish industry here. From the sack he now extracted a kit, tools or instruments of some kind, and then a small lathe— what was so important about that? Araleh gazed at the immigrant, puzzled, a little bit annoyed, but patient. Sometimes they arrived half-crazy.

"Diamonds," said the Stork. This was a special high-speed diamond polishing machine, such as no doubt did not exist in Palestine.

"Good, good." Araleh nodded. Though in the port shops of Haifa you could find any kind of machine. Maybe the fellow had simply pestered Menahem for a contact to find a job? But why had Menahem sent him to Mati—in the government?

"Mati Chaimovitch is in Jerusalem," he began.

"I go. I will go."

Mati, the British—anything to do with the British must be avoided. Suddenly recalling that Uri's father, Nahum, was quite a collector of precious stones, Araleh said to Uri, "Take him to your father in the morning. Find out what it's all about."

The Stork spent the night with four of his shipmates in a remote cabin; in the morning, when he had already begun to pester the farmer about how to get to Jerusalem, young Uri arrived for him, driving a car. When Uri had mentioned the incident, Nahum had become curious.

At the sight of the seashore mansion, the immigrant smiled as one who recognizes that things will now be on the proper level.

As customary, Nahum began, "What language shall we speak?"

"Here is a language we all understand," the immigrant said in German, and producing his leather pouch, the Stork let a flow of diamonds pour out onto Nahum's desk blotter.

After the first effect, Nahum peered closer; with a silver letter opener that Shula had given him, he pieced apart a few of the stones: on the whole they were quite small, less than half a carat, he judged by eye, and of poor quality. The immigrant handed him a jeweler's glass, which Nahum expertly applied. But these were third-rate diamonds, full of flaws. He glanced up to show he was no fool.

Nein, nein! They were not gemstones. *"Industrie."* Industrial diamonds, for cutting steel, for machining, for war production.

So that was why Menahem had sent him to Mati. Yet already something was blossoming in Nahum—luck or fate, this man had first come here.

Though he had heretofore only vaguely known of industrial diamonds, Nahum, in twenty words from the Stork, grasped the entire situation. His mind was already leaping ahead with schemes and projects. In the machine industry, diamonds were irreplaceable. Holland was the world center for preparing these cutting diamonds, using stones unsuitable for jewels. As in the First World War, the Germans would certainly strike through Belgium, isolating the Netherlands; the entire diamond industry would fall into their hands. A shortage, even a total shutoff of industrial diamonds could become a major disaster for the Allies, one of those bottlenecks that could determine a war. Already it was clear that this would be a war of industrial production; factories would be the final determinant. Thus, it would be a vital precaution for the British at once to set up a diamond-cutting center outside German reach—in case of a German success westward. In spite of the quiet front, the soccer games, the Nazi attack was sure to come at most in a few months. And in case of a prolonged war—

Where better, for this emergency center, than Palestine? A hundred master cutters must be brought here at once, quickly, from Amsterdam. And this was a Jewish craft. Amsterdam Jews would be saved. And after the war, Nahum already was thinking, wasn't the jewelry trade virtually a Jewish area in world commerce? Why, Jews were masters in the industry all the way from the mines in South Africa to the processing, to the wholesale dealers, even to the jewelry shops all over the world. Like Mati's in-laws, who had been here from Chicago.

Nahum felt that heady vibration he had experienced the time he took Shula up on the hillside over Tiberias and showed her where he would, one day, build the luxury hotel. And the time he and Gidon bought horses and they had galloped over the shrubby sands here, that were to become Hof HaSharon. Nahum understood, now, he understood why Menahem, while still abroad, had directed this long-leg to Mati. But what would happen? Once Mati took it up with his department chief, the British might simply say thank-you and develop the industry in Canada or New Zealand. No, this needed immediate personal action, decisiveness. From what the Stork said, the necessary machinery was light and fairly simple—electric grinders, special abrasives, small whirling wheels. Why not set up a factory right here in Hof HaSharon? First, it could save the town itself; already with no ships for transport to the European market, the citrus crop was a total disaster. Oranges were being used as cattle feed.

At one stroke, Nahum saw the entire operation. He would round up some Yemenite jewelers; the Stork could train them, even with the little machine and the tools he had brought in his kit. But for a serious industry on a wartime scale, a whole group of master cutters must be brought at once from Amsterdam. Special immigrant visas must be obtained for them with their families—in that, Mati could help. This fellow, Warshawsky, must be kept right here in Hof HaSharon; Nahum would find him a hut, let him get busy setting up his little workshop.

But there was something else that Warshawsky was explaining. They must make sure of a supply, a steady supply of raw stones. From Africa? No, no, all raw stones were sent directly from the African mines to the diamond cartel in London. Warshawsky said this impatiently, as though this basic fact should hardly have to be explained. And from the world diamond monopoly in London, the raw stones were parceled out to the various cutting houses in Amsterdam, Antwerp, and a few other centers.

Intrigued, Nahum realized he had been quite ignorant of this amazing situation. A world cartel existed! Yes, yes, of course, he had known of the vast mining operations in the hands of the Oppenheimers; who hadn't heard the name among such world names as the Rothschilds and the DuPonts and the Guggenheim copper interests, all symbols of immeasurable opulence and power? And weren't the Oppenheimers Jewish? No, something fuzzy there, Nahum wasn't sure. But meanwhile, there was something else forming in Nahum's spirit, like some immeasurably beautiful sight coming into view. Like what Mati's Dena and his own Shula had made him recognize and even feel in the last great harmonious chords of a symphony, rising as a single united utterance under the evocation of a Toscanini. The perfection of the whole, under a single control. The beauty of a world monopoly! Quietly and smoothly operated from London. He must go there at once! He must bring himself, bring Palestine into this wondrous concerted mechanism, this enclosed sphere. He must persuade the monopoly that their structure should include an emergency element out of reach of the coming attack. Just like a spare dynamo. Let them allocate raw stones for this emergency line of production. In London he must also see high officials for the allocation of immigrant certificates for the diamond cutters. After that he must rush to Amsterdam to select the best. All this before the expected Nazi onslaught. In how long? Any week. At most, two months.

All these leaps Nahum's mind had made while Mendel Warshawsky was still methodically explaining why diamond cutting and polishing could become an excellent small industry here in Palestine.

Arriving in Jerusalem, Nahum installed himself at the King David. He indeed had his own government connections but first got Mati to come over because this affair was right in his department. A new industry. More labor. The Yishuv's war effort. Nahum told how through a hapless immigrant trying to find a job, a project of vital importance for the war effort had come to his mind. By that very afternoon Mati had arranged for Nahum to put his plan before the chief secretary. The Englishman listened with that bemused little smile the British had for overenterprising Jews with their harebrained schemes. Then he half closed his eyes, and over his face came a different look, the kind you sometimes saw when they were forgetting you and your schemes and making calculations concerning the Empire.

The following morning a call came assuring Nahum of top priority in a military plane to London. On his own part, a series of cables went off, to Lord Samuel, to Chaim Weizmann himself, to Moshe Shertok.

Nahum had never flown over the sea. Yes, Mati's early airline vision had been correct, but Mati had got stuck in the Haganah idea, which should have been secondary.

In London the military had got him a reservation at the Mayfair but seemed uninformed about contacting the diamond syndicate. On Great Russell Street he was put straight—with the family in question there had generations ago been a conversion. Unfortunately, there was no contact.

People in high places promised to try to gain him entry, but this might take awhile. Nahum sent a most respectful letter. On the third morning a hotel page brought up a vellum envelope bearing his name in flowing script, with the words "By Hand" in a lower corner. In response to his request for an appointment having to do with the war effort, Mr. Reid-Baker would receive him at eleven.

He had time to put through only two calls, and neither yielded any hint to the rank and power of a Mr. Bryan Reid-Baker at the diamond syndicate.

The office exuded the hushed rubbed-velvet atmosphere of an emptiness impregnated with power that Nahum had, on previous voyages to London, encountered in obscurely named governmental bureaus in ancient buildings where the desks and chairs had the glow attained only through generations of hand rubbing by servitors whose posts were passed on in the family.

On the paneled wall hung the portrait of the founder, in fleshless flesh tones. On a small table lay a trade magazine, and having arrived five minutes early, Nahum studied it.

From the subdued half-technical reports there came to him a confirmation of that elated vision he had experienced at a certain moment when the Stork explained the monopoly. Even more clearly here, Nahum beheld the perfection of a seamless closed entity. In his own life he had perhaps sought this in creating Hof HaSharon. In his small way. But all at once Nahum perceived the meaning of totality. Even in the evil genius of a Hitler, this same urge. Totality. The totalitarian state. The closed world! No matter whether for evil or for good, an urge in man. Wasn't this what you heard of about legendary American financiers who "cornered the market"? In steel, in copper, in oil, in worldwide wheat markets. It was a thing Mati had once discoursed on, very interestingly. From his studies in economics. Here Nahum saw. An all that was one. A global syndicate. A sphere, smooth, solid, with no protrusion that could be grasped hold of, no cracks where an opening might be pried. And part of this totality was that it could remain so self-contained that ordinary people could never perceive the inside workings; indeed, like himself, most people had never heard of its existence. There even awakened in Nahum a boyhood imagining of the world being ruled by some secret, invisible, everywhere-connected society of power. Nonsense, of course, like the legends about the Masons (but hadn't he heard somewhere that every American President had belonged to the Masons?). And what of the tales in that crazy made-up book about a mysterious secret organization of Jews that ruled the world, the Elders of Zion? The Nazis printed it in every language, even though in a trial in Switzerland, Nahum had lately read in papers, the book with its "protocols" of "secret meetings" was proved simply to have been made up! Yet people believed it, and they kept on printing it. This must be because people, Nahum grasped, had a wish for this kind of unity, singleness—even like the sense of one God! And imagine the beauty of this monopoly, this world operation. The efficiency. Utter control of the raw diamonds coming out of the depths of the earth. It was said that the black miners lived in guarded compounds and that every opening in their bodies was searched whenever they were allowed to go home to see their families. From the mines the entire flow of stones came here. One organization, perhaps one man, decided where and to whom the packets of rough stones should be allocated for cutting and polishing; which stones should be for ornaments and which for industry; and what would be the world price.

How could a person like himself come here and suggest that they, even they, were threatened? Suppose the Germans captured Amsterdam? The syndicate could hold the raw stones in Africa. Would Hitler try to conquer Africa? He was going way off, Nahum told himself; he must keep his mind on the immediate reality. He was here to gain entry into this closed structure. For the sake of the Yishuv. Within the perfect structure were substructures, components that fitted together to make the whole, and if he were to organize such a substructure in Palestine, then the entire allotment of stones for that area would pass through his hands. Even now, at the very outset it would be for him to decide which

401

master workmen should receive immigration certificates. Their very lives! It would be for him to say who should build workshops. First at Hof HaSharon. Then elsewhere, too, before others would pry their way into this closed circle. In Tel Aviv, Jerusalem, small workshops. And by the end of the war Palestine would be established as a center with skilled labor, cheaper than in Amsterdam. Why should not the syndicate after the war see the wisdom of continuing such a competitive center? Surely they would see the advantage commercially of direct inner lines through the Jewish community in the jewelry trade, as, for instance, Dena's family with their chain of stores in Chicago? No, that would be too trivial; he would not mention it.

And after all, much of the diamond business was in gentile hands, too, also in Holland. Perhaps he should simply confine himself to the immediate question—if the Nazis captured Holland.

Exactly on the hour the inner door opened; Nahum could not prevent in himself the quick image of a cuckoo-clock door springing open, for a long-beaked secretary stood there, ushering him into a sanctum containing a broad, polished desk on which there stood a globe on a polished brass base.

Judging by this inner office, he was before a man of importance. A man who could decide? Or only transmit?

Nor could Nahum tell from the man himself. One of those seriously listening faces wearing an aspect of well-disposed fairness, yet perhaps only the kind of person utilized to put visitors off with the impression that they had received a thorough hearing, at a top level.

Nahum launched into his plan.

Yes, Reid-Baker was, indeed, aware of the menacing situation. While the probabilities of disaster in the Netherlands were not, he judged, as great as might be imagined, it was, of course, always sensible to have alternatives. Indeed several alternative centers did exist and could readily be expanded; however— The dexterity of the Yemenites? Ah, of this he had not been particularly aware. And now many of these people were available in Palestine? Nahum related how thousands of these traditional craftsmen had been brought to Jerusalem from Yemen, beginning thirty years ago; he told how industrious they were in producing their delicate filigree jewelry. Then, as Nahum was speaking of the organizing and business endowments of another immigrant element, arriving in the last years from Germany, he became aware that a side door quite soundlessly and as though motionlessly had opened and that a tall apparition hovered there for a moment, then advanced toward Reid-Baker, impersonally but politely nodding to the visitor while he left a folder on the desk. Then the personage turned back to the door but again hovered. Nahum sensed that he should simply continue with his exposition. The tall person was there a few moments longer and finally disappeared the way he had come.

Nahum summed up. If the syndicate would agree to allocate raw stones, he had assurance that the British Foreign Office at the request of the military would grant special Palestine visas for expert diamond cutters. With these entry permits he would proceed at once to Amsterdam to select the experts.

Reid-Baker arose, extending his hand over the desk. The matter, he could assure Nahum, would receive full examination without delay. "I may say," he added with not even a flicker of personal quality in his voice, but rather as a matter of exactitude, "I may say that it was the brother who happened to come into the office while you spoke. You might consider that rather fortuitous."

Had the intrusion been accidental? Arranged? Though now far removed, did not the Oppenheimers after all originally come from a Jewish family seeking its fortune in South Africa? Should he perhaps still press on, as soon as he got back to the hotel, for a direct contact with the masters of the syndicate?

Nahum hurried to Great Russell Street for advice. "They're a peculiar lot, you know. Be sure not to press them in any way. And don't touch on the Jewish aspect. Especially not the Zionist aspect." Yet there was that momentary speculative gaze into the air, as though wondering what vestige might remain. "You must simply wait for a sign," the expert declared.

The very next morning the sign came, not directly from the diamond syndicate, but from the Foreign Office. A first batch of thirty certificates would be at his disposal for diamond cutters from Amsterdam. Air transportation for him to Amsterdam, although already difficult and perhaps precarious, would be provided on first priority, so that he could proceed to select his technicians. Nahum must stand ready to leave at a moment's notice.

In later years, as Nahum envisioned it, when a twenty-story Diamond House would send rotating blue-white beams from its tower in the city of Sharon Shore, and when Israel vied with Amsterdam itself for the Number One place in diamonds, both jewels and industrials, he might tell of the hazards of this brink-of-war exploit. And even of the incredible nature of a certain last difficulty that he encountered in Amsterdam itself. For there he arrived with certificates in his hand, to snatch thirty Jewish families from the maw of the Nazis, and only with considerable difficulty was he able to find expert diamond cutters to accept them!

Though the outbreak of the German onslaught westward was so imminent that he had been warned in London that his plane might be shot down, the leaders of the Diamond Club in Amsterdam, the Jewish one, seemed unperturbed.

The Stork's former employer, a distinguished-looking, slow-speaking Sephardi with a velvet yarmulkah and a Vandyke, director of a small firm that had been operated for generations by his family, smiled bemusedly over the alarms of that Polish Jew who had fled, paying a fortune for passage on an illegal ship. In any case, an indifferent workman, he commented, a man without a real love for the craft. It seemed that a Zionist Revisionist recruiter had frightened the excitable Warshawsky with terror tales of impending Nazi conquest and taken the fellow's savings for the boat ticket.

As the Sephardi saw the situation—half closing his eyes into wisdom crinkles—the Netherlands would remain neutral. As it had in the last war. Amsterdam was too important to both sides for the city to come under attack. Should Hitler attempt anything so foolish, the dikes would be opened and the land would become impassable to his panzers. And besides, as Nahum surely knew, already in the other war, the great powers had managed to arrange for certain essential war matériel to be available in either direction.

He personally was not a Zionist. His family had for many generations been a part of this land, and surely the tolerance of the Netherlanders, from the time of the Inquisition itself, could make a Jew feel that it was perhaps more necessary to encourage this example before the world, and remain in such a community, rather than to build a separate nation. True, he upheld the Messianic return to Zion. But such tolerance as the Jewish community enjoyed here was not everywhere to be found. Therefore, no Jew should flee.

Neither was he an opponent of Zionism. As a land of refuge for

Jews from intolerant nations, he was even ready to help Palestine with funds, and he regularly did so in support of Jerusalem's religious institutions. But for the creation of a secular Jewish state that gave every evidence of godlessness, he was not in favor. Nevertheless, he would willingly give Nahum the names of some persons in the diamond industry, people who were only a generation from the East and were terrified of what was now happening in Poland, people like Warshawsky, and among those, no doubt, Nahum could find what he sought.

This done, Meinheer Perez leaned back and offered Nahum his interpretation of the possibilities for realizing his scheme. Quite possibly, the diamond syndicate would give some encouragement to this idea for a Palestine branch of the industry. They were clever people, and by their astuteness had built up their world monopoly, and by encouraging his venture, they risked nothing. Only, Nahum must understand, the industry was rooted here, it had existed even before the syndicate, there were important relationships between the Jewish community and the good Netherlanders, and it might not even be wise to let it be bruited about that a Jew from Palestine was spreading panic, predicting the fall of Amsterdam, and talking about creating a rival center in the Middle East, with its cheap labor, for diamond cutting and polishing.

Quite similar was the reaction among Ashkenazi diamond dealers. Caution. Nahum was directed to Rabbi Yitzhak Feitelovitch, the head of a Polish Jewish family that had made a place for itself in the trade. This time he took the precaution to stop and buy himself a yarmulkah.

The rabbi wore a frock coat and welcomed him in Biblical Hebrew, blessings on the visitor from Eretz Hakodesh. At once, Nahum let fall that he had been born in Tiberias, and that his father and father-in-law still studied a page of Gemara every day in the yeshiva of Rabbi Meir Ba'al HaNess. A small diamond industry would provide ideal conditions, he pointed out, for the religiously observant artisan; also, the Orthodox element in Eretz Yisroel would be strengthened, for surely one must not allow the godless socialist chalutzim to dominate the Yishuv. The rabbi nodded and nodded. He must first speak to his family partners. But he feared that few of his own people would want to leave everything here to risk having their throats cut and their wives and daughters violated by Arabs.

The leader of Amsterdam's Zionists was indeed excited by the news of special certificates, but said surely they should go first to those most devoted to the movement, regardless of profession, and they would have to be distributed according to the long-standing code of allocations among the various Zionist factions. Yes, personally he understood Nahum's problem and would even suggest to him a number of good Zionists who worked in the trade. But, perhaps the allocations should be made through this office?

Finally, on that first intensive day, Nahum met with the head of the third largest diamond firm in Amsterdam, a sophisticated, assimilated Jew, intermarried. Presenting the situation entirely in business terms, Nahum hinted at partnership possibilities. He stressed the importance of reassuring the London masters of the syndicate as to the wartime cooperation of their Dutch affiliates, even through establishing branches elsewhere. All the while they consumed many highly spiced dishes in an Indonesian restaurant. He must first, the diamond man said, sound out certain non-Jewish leaders of the industry.

As Nahum entered his hotel, there approached, somewhat furtively, from a corner of the lobby, a youngish man who had been waiting. He had heard, the young man timidly began—and Nahum knew he had his first recruit.

And so one by one they came. But they wanted to be sure of many things. Dwellings, and the transfer of their possessions, even furniture! Now, with all shipping space mobilized! Some even wanted to be assured of a return to Amsterdam if things didn't work out as Nahum presented them.

It took a whole week, and each day he trembled. The war, the real war, might begin. But at last, having secured emergency ship passage for his recruits and their families, Nahum flew back to London to assure the syndicate of his success and to pick up a War Office priority for his flight home.

In three weeks the blitzkrieg pierced Belgium, and then the Netherlands capitulated. Immediately with the entry into Amsterdam, Nazi officers, lists in hands, appeared at the diamond-cutting workshops, demanding the instant surrender of all stocks of raw and polished stones, particularly industrial.

They had special lists of Jewish dealers, with their home addresses as well. SS men tore open house walls, dug up backyards, clubbed and tortured the merchants, the artisans, and had their orifices painfully searched. SS women came to strip wives and daughters, roughly examining their private parts.

Every road, every lane was blocked, to stop those who sought to escape with packets of stones. The Jewish diamond men of Amsterdam, if still alive after the searches, were shipped off with their families to a concentration camp at Westerbork, to await "resettlement" eastward.

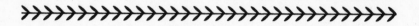

27

EVERYONE at the Rubin opening was saying to everyone, "You wouldn't know there was a war going on!" and the answering quip was, "Well, is there?" After the onslaught in Poland, all was still quiet. Even the Arab situation had died down, so the land was peaceful. After all, what more could the White Paper have given them?

Only Esther Rubin could have arranged the opening so brilliantly. She ought to be put in charge of the world situation, she could bring no matter who together in a civilized atmosphere. Never had she looked more queenly, and Dena frankly told her she was envious.

The British were there from the High Commissioner down, with dress uniforms in abundant display. The entire leadership of the Jewish Agency, the top Sephardic families, Dr. Magnes and the university crowd, and quite a few Arab notables, and there suddenly, in front of Rubin's masterpiece of the Hasidic Jews of Meiron, standing with the rubicund Mordecai no longer a shepherd but pulled out of the kibbutz to teach in the Bezalel school of art, there Dena saw Khalid.

Elegant in a tailored suit, he had come back from Beirut, as had the whole family, he said, just before the fall of France. And with him, a lovely young Arab woman, Dena's own height but very slim, even in her merely standing still you could feel her gracefulness. His wife, Mouna. Khalid glittered. He had known they would be here, so instead of calling up, he had waited to give them a surprise.

Beautiful, warm eyes, you could hardly tell the touch of kohl. Yet in their direct gaze, a personality. Oh, this girl knew exactly what she wanted . . . and she'd got it! But in other things, too, not only marriage, Dena sensed. She took to the girl at once. Real style. Those Lebanese dressmakers must have been trained in haute couture in Paris. Yes, they'd met and married in Beirut, though she was from Haifa. She had been getting her degree at the American University. Social sciences, she said, but not in the tone of an American student who would dismiss this as a catchall, what else does a girl take these days; no, she said it with liveliness, a girl who meant to do something, and indeed, as Mati had joined them and was practically gaping at her—no need to worry Dena told herself with an inner awry laugh, he'd got too fat—indeed, the girl said she wanted to get a job in the Mandate, in the education department. Mouna wanted to be an inspector and to get the villagers to send their girls as well as their boys to school; did Mati know whom she ought to approach?

A few more exchanges, and Dena had the background; she was from Haifa, even somehow related to the mayor—they had come back for his funeral. Imagine, he had died a natural death, after all, though several bombing attempts had been made on his house and two of his brothers-in-law had been assassinated. But the feuds seemed to have stopped. Khalid's brother would be reopening his agency in Jerusalem; they intended to live in Jerusalem, too, and Khalid would take back his studio.

Oh? Dena said. And as soon as she could whisper, told him that with a cute wife like that he had better behave! Ah, all that was finished, he was indeed behaving, Khalid said, he had even been teaching in Beirut, yes, calligraphy, in a high school, he was now a serious family man! Had she news of Myra? Dena said she had not heard for months, but Myra had been very busy with the New Kunstbau School. "How is she? All right?" The note of concern included even a touch of masculine apology, yet self-defense, what could he have done? His liquid eyes were appealing. At the same time it was a man's appeal—for her not to think badly of his behavior toward her friend, since now his life had become quite another thing.

As though by instinctive knowledge, his bride turned her attention back to him, and Dena saw the girl brush slightly closer against his side. "Have you written to Myra about your marriage?" Dena asked Khalid quite openly, she just couldn't suppress her touch of cattiness, but the girl gave her husband a wise, all-knowing look.

"Oh, I made him write to all his old flames!" His Mouna had a delicious accent in English, not the same as the sabra accent, with its throatiness, but softer, mixed with French.

They would surely all get together in Jerusalem, the couples promised each other.

And indeed in those winter months that came to be known as the phony war, they became close, particularly Dena with Mouna. Just as before, in the time of Khalid's affair with Myra, he hardly ever, when he was around their little bunch, talked of the Arab-Jewish thing; it was mostly of movies and art, and was there really a stalemate with the Germans and French soldiers playing soccer in no-man's-land outside the Maginot Line. Mordecai the ex-shepherd even got Khalid a part-time job teaching calligraphy at the Bezalel school, doing Hebrew as well as the Arabic, and once they all had a fascinating discussion about national character as seen in the two scripts, the Hebrew square and sharp-cornered and the Arabic all flowing and rhythmic except for sudden leaps. Well, what about the Hebrew cursive script? Maureen had pointed out; while the printed Hebrew was square and solid, the written Hebrew was more easy and flowing, and in the ancient scripts you saw sometimes there wasn't so much difference between the two. This led to discussions about national character, the kind of conversation Dena loved. Sometimes Mouna would tell delicious little stories about her experiences with women in the Arab villages, for she had got her job and was playing on their curiosity, their vanity, and also the deep sense of feminine unity to get them to send their daughters to school. Occasionally a woman would chase Mouna out—all her daughter had to know she would teach the girl herself—but sometimes the chasing out was only a demonstration, and the mother would find a way to let Mouna know that her words had borne fruit.

It was when Mouna met Dena one day for coffee at the Vienna that an intimacy grew. They slid into a real womanly talk, and Dena sensed that Mouna had a great curiosity about Myra, just as she herself had once wondered over Mati's affair with that poetess before they were married. Was it love, in some way, or only sex?

410

Somehow you didn't want your man to have done it only for sex, yet you didn't want him to have loved, really loved, another woman either. Khalid had had quite a few others, of course, but it was Myra his young wife wondered about since that had lasted the longest and Myra had even openly lived with him here. He talked about the others more easily, even joked about his big affairs, but didn't like to talk so much about Myra and would just say he really didn't understand what it had all been about. It had just broken up, one of those things, not even because she was Jewish, and she had left, and it was over. He had really been fond of her. But she was really neurotic, he guessed.

Then Dena told the girl what even Khalid didn't know, about the symptom. About Myra's deep personal trouble from that old murder scandal in Chicago, that the boy she had been in love with—a cousin—had got caught in. The Steiner-Straus case; imagine, Mouna was so young her generation hadn't even heard of the Steiner-Straus case! It was Myra's personal tragedy and maybe had ruined her life, Dena said. But recently Myra had written that her psychoanalyst was finally helping her get over the thing. Yes, Myra had truly been fond of Khalid, and he of her, but it was a passion that was finished. Dena said anyone could see that now with Mouna he had found the real thing; he was a different man.

And writing to Myra, Dena mentioned, did Myra know that Khalid was married, saying only a little about the girl—quite pretty and intelligent, one of their own. Yes, Myra wrote back, Khalid had written her. She was glad for him. As for herself, she was very busy with the New Kunstbau, and she was making great progress at last in realizing that there was a kind of smallness and selfishness in interpreting the whole world through your own personal problems.

Then the Europe they knew was slashed up so quickly. The blitzkrieg was reaching Paris, the French government had fled to Bordeaux, now it was fleeing to Vichy. The whole British army, plus French units too, had been cut off against the Channel at Dunkirk. All kinds of ships, even tiny sailboats, got most of the British troops away to England; it was a great victory instead of a great defeat because the army was saved to fight again.

Winston Churchill replaced Chamberlain, the British would fight on; wherever you went, the conversation was like a war conference, if Chamberlain hadn't given in at Munich, expecting the

Germans to attack Russia, if Stalin hadn't made the pact with Hitler freeing the Germans to attack France. Enormous air battles were taking place, a hundred and twelve Nazi planes fell in a single battle over England, a French general who had escaped to North. Africa declared France had lost a battle but not the war, France would fight on, Léon Blum was arrested as a traitor by the Vichy government, the Nazis split France into occupied and unoccupied zones, and in the occupied part the anti-Jewish laws were already in force.

Trotsky was assassinated in Mexico; Haifa was bombed, and seven people were injured. In twelve weeks of raging air war, the Luftwaffe was beaten by the Royal Air Force, and England was said to be safe from invasion for the time being. When would the USA get into the war? It would be just like in the First World War, Menahem said—almost too late! Roosevelt couldn't move any faster because of isolationism, the big German population in America was pushing isolationism, and also the totally obedient communists were blindly carrying on a peace mobilization campaign with mass meetings and even strikes to keep important factories from being geared to war work. In the middle of all this, the British still had ships to hunt down the few hundred refugees who came on illegal boats across the Mediterranean; two of these battered leaky vessels were captured and brought to Haifa, and their eighteen hundred souls were to be transferred onto a British ship and exiled to an island in the Indian Ocean. Suddenly the transport, the *Patria*, was blown up, in Haifa Harbor, before the eyes of the whole city, the waters black with thrashing, drowning Jews, the ship vanishing with who knew how many caught inside. From the windows, from the streets, from the whole of the Carmel, a single howl resounded, while thousands ran to the port to help in the rescue. Too late, it proved, for nearly four hundred, most of them caught inside the ship.

Embittered refugees themselves had blown up the *Patria* in protest, it was being said, but from David HaCohen Mati heard also that a Haganah underwater man had affixed a bomb that was only to have blown a small hole, and the plan had miscarried. Everyone went about heartsick.

There was an Italian air raid on Tel Aviv with ninety dead. At last people were taking the blackout seriously. In Haifa, attacking planes were driven off by ack-ack guns. Mati was there, consulting with David HaCohen on a rush project; his Solel Boneh was building a road for the British straight across the desert, intended to reach Baghdad in case of trouble with Iraq. The Nazis were intriguing heavily there, trying to get an army commander named Rashid Ali to stage a revolt. The Mufti, arrived there from Syria, was hand in glove with Rashid Ali against the British.

Mati was working directly with the military, now. It was better, cleaner, he told Dena. Nearly half the Yishuv was now doing war work; the Brandeis kibbutz had expanded its battery factory to ten times the original capacity. Even the Haganah's undercover hand grenade plants now were openly setting up factories for the British. A complete intelligence unit was being infiltrated into Syria, for under the Vichy government, who could tell when Hitler might completely take over, bringing the Nazis right onto Palestine's northern border! To add to that nightmare, the Italians were building up their forces on the Egyptian border. Then in a crazy attack they found the way open and took Sidi Barrani. Of course, they would be thrown back; some ex-Wingate boys, now in a special commando unit, were already with the British there; Reuven and Elisheva had a card from Avinoam hinting. If by some wild mischance the Italians got the Suez, Palestine could be caught in a deathly pincers. King Farouk was untrustworthy, the Egyptians were altogether no good, and if the Nazis succeeded in getting Turkey into the war, then Egypt too might even turn against England. Nazi agents by the hundreds were all over the Middle East, swarms of them in Teheran and Damascus, tourists with briefcases. The Turks and the Germans, just as in the First World War, could try to sweep down through Palestine to attack the Suez Canal, while the Italians, with German support, attacked from the other side.

It wouldn't happen; it was just one of those nightmares that armchair strategists invented, as if there weren't enough real troubles, Mati told Dena. The Turks too well remembered that their partnership with Germany in World War I had ended in total disaster, costing them their Empire.

When the whole outside world seems to be slowly closing in on you, suddenly something can happen in your inside world, and it outweighs the looming catastrophes. At the end of the year Mati was again in Haifa, to meet Dov, triumphantly, with clearance papers that the ever-understanding Peewee had at last got through for the twin-engine plane that Yehuda Arazi had bought

413

in Poland. She was to become part of the Histadrut's "tourist" air fleet. Jubilant, they packed off the crates to Afikim, where the plane would be assembled. From Haifa, the Smiler rushed off to bring Chanukah cheer to the Haganah's unlucky Forty-Three, already a year in prison, caught by the British in a practice drill, carrying arms. With the war getting worse, there they sat, some of the Yishuv's best lads, Moshe Dayan, Yigal Allon, stupidly in jail. The British!

After the visit, with several of his family in the car, Dov headed for Tel Aviv. Always a wild driver, perhaps he imagined he was flying the twin-engine, for the car overturned, and all were killed.

The one who had been the first to help Mati in London, the smiling Dov, who was at ease with everyone, keen, yet light, the way Mati himself would like to be, Dena knew. He could hardly drag himself to the office. He must come away, they'd go to Gilboa; from there Mati would be able to oversee the transformations on the plane that Dov was to have supervised. And she herself, meanwhile, could start a little course in wireless for some of the girls in the kibbutzim, which Menahem had asked her to give. Seeing Menahem was always good for Mati. And for herself.

On top of everything came Menahem's trouble.

Returned from the Congress just before the Nazi attack on Poland, Menahem was working closely with Shaul of Kibbutz Kinneret, smuggling in groups of children from Syria who were brought over the northern frontier to Kfar Giladi. The difficulty was then to get them down past the British checkpoint on the road at Rosh Pina, so they could be placed at a settlement. One method Menahem used was to fill up the tender with children from Gilboa itself: they would be going on a Shabbat outing, to Kfar Giladi to see the famous huge stone lion, the monument over the grave of the hero Trumpeldor. At the Rosh Pina checkpoint the children would be counted—the British were becoming more and more exact. A few kilometers beyond the checkpoint was the kibbutz of Ayeleth HaShachar, where the kids would jump off, to spend the day, and be taken home by the local chaverim. Meanwhile he would go on to Kfar Giladi, load up the same number of youngsters just smuggled across the border, already dressed like kibbutz kids, get them through at Rosh Pina, and bring them home to Gilboa where they would be mixed in until dispersal places were found for them.

Dena sometimes saw them, overquiet children, with lustrous black eyes, small-boned bodies.

At least Menahem's new task seemed better than smuggling in weapons, though maybe in a way it was the same, smuggling in boys who one day would use them. Yet how else, how else, in this world? From bits Menahem dropped, Dena had by now pieced together the route.

In Syria, Jewish children in small groups were sent up to a mountain resort. Those from Damascus went up Mount Hermon maybe even with their parents, and then on the appointed day a guide came, usually a Druze from one of the villages down the slope. Partway they were taken in a wagon or truck, sometimes on donkeys, and at one of the rocky wild stretches of the border, smugglers took them across. At night, and on foot, holding hands. Dena pictured her twins doing it.

On the Palestine side, one of Menahem's unit would take over the children, moving them on to Kfar Giladi, to be mixed in with the children there, to await the pickup. Most of them could already speak a little Hebrew—a least they could sing Hebrew songs.

So it had gone on for some time, with almost no mishaps. Now there was a new influx, children from Baghdad. When the Mufti had transferred himself to Iraq, he had been received, Menahem said, like royalty; he was established in the best hotel, with his henchmen openly coming and going; the Haj was invited to all the diplomatic receptions, he and some military "strong man" there were said to be plotting a putsch to take over Iraq and join the Nazis. That could be the beginning of the end for the British in the entire area. And so the Baghdadi Jews had begun to send out their children. For centuries, ever since the first destruction of the Temple, when Nebuchadnezzar had dragged the Jerusalemites into exile, a Jewish colony had lived in Baghdad. By the waters of Babylon they wept, but not too many joined when they were permitted to return to Eretz. Many had prospered, up to today.

Now Dena saw the little groups of Baghdadi children, their round eyes huge, their skin coffee-colored, more exotic than the Damascus children, and gentler, it seemed. Lonely looking. Though some, Menahem said, had relatives in Jerusalem, where there was a Baghdadi colony in Mea Shearim.

Again Menahem went off in the pickup with its benches filled with Gilboa kids. All went well; after the checkpoint he left them

415

at Ayeleth HaShachar, and went on for the refugees. Loaded up, he got back through the Rosh Pina checkpoint without incident, making a few jokes while the British counted heads. And then, a few miles down on the snaketurn before Tiberias, suddenly there was an improvised roadblock that hadn't been there on his way up. A car parked halfway across the hairpin turn. Two police and an officer who reeked CID. There must surely have been a betrayal. The lieutenant approached, had a look at the cargo of children, and in good Hebrew asked Menahem where they came from? "Gilboa. An outing," Menahem said, but the fellow had already turned to a little boy, demanding in Baghdad dialect, "When did you get to Palestine, habub? Is your family also coming from Baghdad?" The child became confused, started to answer. "Go!" Menahem commanded his driver; the pickup shot around the police car, two wheels churning the road shoulder, the children tumbling and grabbing at each other, shrieking. Gad regained the road. Good boy. He had been with Wingate. The vehicle careened on downward. On a steep stretch the police car reappeared. Menahem leaned out, firing at the tires, saw the command car swerve and overturn into the ditch.

Lower down was the entrance to Kibbutz Ginossar, on the Kinneret. He just had time for Gad and the kids to jump off. "Tell the chevreh to take them across the lake to Ein Gev. The British are sure to search here."

Alone, Menahem took the wheel, racing on. By now the alarm must be out, he'd be stopped in Tiberias. He swerved onto a dirt road up to the old village of Migdal. Could he save the vehicle? The British doubtless had taken down the number. Perhaps by some feat the tender could nevertheless be hidden and the number later changed? Stupidities; the whole immigration route was now in jeopardy. That damned CID linguist. And here he was worrying about the vehicle. He drove it into a copse and jumped out.

The pickup, for whatever eventuality, Menahem left standing, but he took the papers and keys. In back were still a few little bundles, even school knapsacks of the smallest; though it was a rule that baggage be sent separately, they still carried things—snapshots of the family—mother, father. What did the damn world want, for these children to have stayed home to await the Mufti's slaughterers? The British still baffled him: Couldn't they wink at a few hundred children slipped over the border? Now, in the midst of a war for their very existence, and that was going so badly! But there was an insane purity in it. What you did, you did to the hilt, even if the Arabs were with Hitler, you followed your rule to the letter! What was incredible was the inflexibility, the way cruelty could come into their "fair play." And then came "fair game." He himself was fair game, even, he supposed, a big one for them, with his years of work in the underground. What a beautiful still night, you could hear every insect, see every star.

Above him were the massive rocks known as the Horns of Hittim. In this narrow valley centuries ago the great Saladin had slaughtered the Crusaders, caught in their multitude, unable to maneuver or flee in their heavy armor. A turning point in history.

The pickup truck had of course been traced to the kibbutz, but the mukhtar stoutly maintained it had been stolen. Children? The British were welcome to check; every child here was accountable—totseret ha'aretz—our own product. Illegal immigrants? Perhaps that explained the theft of the tender. Maybe the Irgun. As for Chaver Menahem, just now he was away on a war mission. In Persia, it was thought. The mukhtar suspected, he told them, that Menahem was in the British Intelligence, ferreting out followers of the Mufti who had gone to Baghdad to take part in the pro-Nazi revolt of Rashid Ali. Perhaps the police should check with the CID?

Wonderful luck that Rashid Ali had been quickly finished off by that armored column rushed from Jerusalem on the new highway through the desert! But the mukhtar did not mention the leader of the flying column, Raziel, commander of the Irgun whom the British had let out of prison for the task. Killed by an air-bomb. Some said Raziel had gone on the condition that he be given a chance to hunt down and finish off the Mufti.

As for the Jewish children from Baghdad, unfortunately there were none here. Had many of them survived the Baghdad pogrom? What was a pogrom? Why, a massacre of Jews. Seven hundred Jews of Baghdad were known to have been killed in the wild, vengeful pogrom after the Rashid Ali revolt had collapsed.

The CID man looked surprised, even a bit sympathetic.

※ ※ ※

For the visit, Dena borrowed Maureen's ankle-length black skirt, never worn since her London bridal expedition to the

417

mikveh. Then Dena bought a pair of black cotton stockings, a long-sleeved button-up blouse, and found an old babushka. She couldn't resist showing herself fully costumed to Maureen, who was supposed to believe she was only going for a curiosity stroll in Mea Shearim. Even Mati was not supposed to know; in the utmost secrecy Dvora had given Dena the name of a certain orphanage. She must ask for Rabbi Weintraub. The visit would cheer Menahem up. He would soon be going away, for unfortunately the affair on the Rosh Pina road had turned out even more serious than all that went before, his arms smuggling, and the illegal ships. When the police car turned over, the driver had died. Menahem was charged with the death.

Behind a high wall sat the Bialystoker Orphanage, squat and gray as though even the Jerusalem stone had lost its inner life. One of those institutional buildings that abounded in Mea Shearim. Where they found enough orphans and aged Jews to populate all these institutions, Mati always said, was a great mystery. Maybe when there was a visit from American donors, Dena would quip, they suddenly shifted the boys with their dangling payess from one orphanage to another!

The entry hall was barren, but in a side office she found a youngish clerk in a gabardine coat, who instantly averted his eyes, as from a streak of light. Rabbi Weintraub? he repeated, and asked her in Yiddish, what did she want of him? "He'll know. I come from Dvora." With a peevish growl, yet a stolen underbrow glance at the female, the young man left the room.

On the walls were old brown-tone Keren Kayemeth posters. She must collect a few. A painting of a sage, in Boris Schatz style, with glowing eyes and white brows, opposite a huge, gilt-framed photo-enlargement of a donor, with the golden watch chain across his vest. And over the door, that meditative profile of Theodor Herzl. So in Mea Shearim, after all, there were good Zionists.

Rabbi Weintraub came in on small, slippered feet, chunky, with a crinkly black beard that seemed to give off sparks. He looked at her without turning away his eyes, even a bit like a man sizing up a girl and having a few evil thoughts. Why should she be so nasty about them? Dena reflected; after all, here they were taking a pretty big chance. They must even be in the Haganah. "Ah, the Amerikanit," the rabbi said, and he led her down the hallway, down a flight of stairs, along a dim, cool stone-smelling basement corridor; he unlocked a door. They were in a book-walled cubicle with oversized dilapidated tomes, a single blue-paned window up at ground level, and against a side wall, a ceiling-high ornate wardrobe, a real hand-carved rococo beauty, the central panels covered by a pair of velvet curtains with faded embroidered lions. A Torah cabinet, Dena realized, just as the curtains parted, and there, real thriller style, stood an oldish Jew, in a girdled black sateen capote, wearing a blue velvet yarmulkah. He had a straggly gray beard and long gray-streaked payess. Then Menahem's ironic smile appeared.

Handing her the huge iron key, Rabbi Weintraub warned, if a buzzer sounded, Menahem must disappear. She must lock the room and return upstairs. If too late for that, then here was a dust rag; she could be wiping the books. And thank heaven without any innuendo, he left them.

Menahem came forward, gave her a brief uncle-like hug, then gazed at her, still twinkling.

"But it's a prison," she said.

"Better than a British one."

The basement room was the school's genizah, for used-up scriptural works. Torn, worn writings, as she ought to know, by Jewish law were never simply thrown away or destroyed. And so here among the worn books, Menahem said, he fitted very well.

Oh, yes. She laughed.

Already in the time of the Turks, this place had been used for hiding Jews; Menahem showed her how the back wall of the Torah cabinet could be opened; behind was a cubicle barely large enough for a cot, it was there that he slept; during the day he could allow himself this "library," for if the buzzer sounded, he could slip back into the inner dungeon. Once the British had even come as far as the genizah, but like the Turks, they were intimidated by religious objects and had only glanced at the Torah cabinet. Even if they should catch him in this genizah, he had one more chance; he was Reb Elijah, a sage withdrawn from the world, and Menahem possessed the genuine identity papers of a sage who had passed on.

All the while Menahem gazed at her in that intent way, as though a whole other conversation were going on between them, beyond the family news, the war. He had the latest newspapers here and even knew that the Mufti had been received by Hitler in Berlin, and—the latest—that some of the gang that Husseini had left behind in Baghdad had finally carried out the death verdict on Fakri Bey Nashashibi, gunning him down from a passing bicycle.

On all sides the Nazis were conquering. Now in Greece, after Yugoslavia. If only, Menahem hoped, they would stop without attacking Crete, for from Giora's letters, it seemed Crete was where he was stationed. If only America would hurry up and enter the war, Dena said. Menahem smiled. Didn't she know that her hero, Lindbergh, the goyish Mati, was keeping America out? Hadn't she heard of Lindbergh's America First Committee? Yet their eyes smiled at each other as in another conversation.

The Nazis would soon attack Russia, Menahem said. And there, in the end, they would be swallowed.

Did he really think they would do it? Everyone said Hitler would still try to attack England. That the Nazis had already tried to cross the Channel, and only a huge fire of oil over the water had stopped them from landing.

No, it would be Russia, Menahem said, as though here in this cellar he had seen the plans. If Hitler hadn't turned aside to take Yugoslavia and Greece, he would have attacked Russia already. And the massive Jewish population lay right in his path, in the old Polish-Russian Pale of Settlement.

Then Menahem turned from all the bitter news. "I asked for you," he said, "just to gladden my eyes with the sight of a pretty young woman." He gazed at her as though storing up the sight. There was nothing more in it. Even almost nothing personal. On his lips was that melancholy, yet stoic, all-tolerant smile, like that photograph you always saw of Sigmund Freud.

And how was it with Mati? he asked.

"He hates them so!" It came gushing out of her as never before to anybody. "Sometimes I'm afraid for him, it will burst." There had never been a burning hatred in Mati; it wasn't his nature, Menahem agreed, knowing him from childhood. Mati had always been overflowing with good-heartedness, like Leah. Yes, that was why she had fallen in love with him, Dena said, even if he might sometimes seem naïve; it was his decent, good-hearted nature. Of course, the Nazis he really hated, but that was something else, and you didn't have to deal with them, see them every day, you didn't even have to think of them as people, but the British, he had really believed in them for a long time, all these years, admired them, and now, ever since the White Paper it was getting worse. Every new one that came seemed an anti-Semite to him.

Menahem knew. A last thing that had made Mati boil was when he heard from Giora that none of the boys accepted in the RAF was allowed to fly. All were on maintenance crews. And once again the request for a Jewish Brigade had been turned down, even though the British were now accepting Jews into Palestine units without any question of getting the same number of Arabs. Mati believed London's refusal of the Brigade came from the administration right here. His own bosses.

Not exactly, Menahem said. There was a certain Lord Moyne, the chief of Middle Eastern affairs, stationed in Egypt. Moyne was against it.

"But on advice from here, Mati says. It makes him sick."

Still, Mati was doing good, necessary work. Four hundred war factories. Menahem knew that, too.

Yes, that was what kept him going, Dena said. All the war things that the Yishuv was learning. Her voice was a little bitter.

Menahem's hand reached out along the table.

There were men you met in your life with whom you knew, if the right conditions came, it would be natural, you would lie together. Those were the words, no others—a complete, natural, joining. Not just men you speculated about physically, how they would be, or men with whom you had kept up an easy flirtation, like Reggie—oh, why was she thinking all this unworthy stuff? Not that she ever intended or expected to make love with Menahem— like a kind of incest, with a dear uncle. But in what other way of thinking, how else could this tenderness and total sense of acceptance be thought of between a man and a woman? Wherever he was now going—for surely this was a farewell—wherever he would be, she would think of him this way, truly innocently, as though they were blessing each other.

Without knowing what made her think of it, Dena said, "And has Elijah come to you here?"

"I will soon be going on an errand for him." Menahem smiled. As soon as he was fully grown into this disguise and felt he could face close inspection, he would go. Naturally, she didn't ask where. He would go under the guise of a shaliach for this orphanage, Menahem said, and even showed her a paper on the stationery of the institution, already prepared, asking all to help him on his mission. The name, she read out, was Rabbi Eliahu Yerushalmi.

Together they laughed.

"Let me tell you an Elijah story, not the kind for children," Menahem said. After all, what did she know of Elijah except the

Bible story, and that Elijah came to every Seder on Passover—like a Santa Claus but without gifts! You opened the door, and he was supposed to drink up a goblet of wine.

Ah, but also, Menahem told her, Elijah arrived whenever and wherever a Jew in distress cried out, "Elijah, help he!" Especially if it was to save the Jew from committing a sin.

For instance, there was the tale of the Jewish peddler in Poland who traveled about with a suitcase filled with tempting feminine things, perfumes from France, lotions, and finery. Even in the baronial mansions of the high Polish landowners, the paritzim, he was made welcome. One day as Chaim-Yankel was displaying his wares to a baroness in her upstairs boudoir, the scent of a Parisian love potion overcame her. Baring her bosom, the lady would have dragged poor Chaim-Yankel to her bed. "Elijah, save me!" the pious peddler cried, and leaped straight out of the window. Elijah heard, and in a single instant traversed the space between heaven and the mansion of the paritz, getting there just in time to catch Chaim-Yankel before his skull crashed onto the flagstones. There in the courtyard Elijah set the peddler safely on his feet and even put his merchandise case in his hands.

"Delicious!" Dena said. She had never known that pious Jews had risqué stories! Where had he heard it? here? Maybe from Rabbi Weintraub?

"Ah, why not?" Menahem laughed. For actually, it was from ancient times—even written in the Talmud!— But in each land the Jews told it anew. And if Dena wanted to know something odd, this same tale was told by Moslems, except that their peddler, after leaping out the window of a sultan's harem, was saved by the angel Gabriel.

They might not see each other for a long time. Perhaps not until after the war.

Impulsively Dena leaned and kissed him on the mouth.

❊ ❊ ❊

Yom Kippur, Menahem spent in Istanbul's leading synagogue, among the Turkish Sephardis, wearing the floor-length voluminous tallis he had brought with him in his guise of a rabbinical emissary from Jerusalem. Not that he was still maintaining the pose. Once arrived in Turkey, he had clipped his beard and pro-

422

cured identity papers as a grain merchant from Lebanon. Nor was he returning to Orthodox observance; it had long been his habit to observe Yom Kippur in quiet meditation.

But as he was much in contact with the Sephardic community, it was well that at least for the High Holidays, he came here. Nor was this pretense, for the Jew of the tallis and tefillin still lived in him. Shimon Brod, the good, wealthy local Zionist, was well aware that Menahem was no more kosher than the rest of the Palestine band in the Mossad. But the others, except for the chieftain, Shaul from Kibbutz Kinneret, who came and went, were a collection of youngsters. The boys.

To Menahem, one or two of the boys rather abashedly acknowledged that they fasted, though in their brash generation he had also known some who would gather together on Yom Kippur to flaunt their "freedom" in a feast of oysters and other traifa delights.

Never mind, the boys were a fantastic, devoted group, and there was even Ruthie the Redhead, of the families of brothers-married-to-sisters. After getting two shipfuls of refugees out of Rumania at the outset of the war, right under the noses of their Nazi allies, she had escaped and was here. And the flamboyant Yehuda Arazi had arrived in Istanbul after twisting his way out of Warsaw, fleeing southward in a car bearing the flag of the Vatican. Like the old days! Menahem and Yehuda had fallen on each other. All they needed was to start a road-roller factory! But Arazi was soon up to different tricks. Working with the CID, he concocted a plan to ship steam-heat radiators from neutral Turkey to Vienna. But the radiators were filled with gasoline, and when the heat was turned on, they exploded. And there was Teddy Kollek, in secret negotiations with Major Pennfield, with a plan to drop a thousand Jewish parachutists into Poland, Hungary, Yugoslavia—in Eretz you could find lads from any European region you wanted. They would have a mission for the British—organizing escape routes for shot-down RAF pilots—and as a second mission they would be rewarded with the opportunity to organize escape routes for Jews. Within the quota, of course.

Yet so many plans failed, Menahem felt he was useless. Hardly any vessels were coming through—over several weeks only a private sailing boat with thirty people crowded on board, and the only help the Turks would allow to be sent were "religious articles"—so though Passover was far away, Shimon Brod brought them quantities of matzos and wine. Though the boys haunted the port area cafés, ships were impossible to procure, even at astronomic prices.

And when a sturdy freighter was found in Greece and slipped out before the country fell to the enemy, there came a bitter internal dispute that almost destroyed the center in Istanbul. Arazi had devised a brilliant scheme with the British. Since the enemy agents doubtless knew this was a Jewish vessel, the Rumanians would allow it to enter the Danube estuary to take on refugees, for the Jews, after being fleeced, were still allowed to depart. But once inside the estuary the ship would be sunk across the river mouth, blocking it to the oil barges from the Ploesti fields, serving the German war machine! This could practically win the war! Only Ruthie stood wildly against Arazi's clever plan —the *Atrato* was for refugees; she would never give it up! And for what? The crazy scheme would never work! For thirty-six hours the argument raged, and then Ruthie revealed that the vessel had meanwhile taken on eight hundred refugees; if Arazi wanted to sink it, he'd have to sink them, too! In anger, Arazi went back to work for the British Intelligence in Palestine and meanwhile to steal British arms for the Haganah.

Among the few left in the Istanbul apartment, whenever downheartedness showed, someone would be sure to quote the Torah with irony, "To save a single soul is like saving the whole world. But bring us a single soul!"

Some days Menahem and Ehud sat for hours writing postcards to be sent into the dark lands, as into a void. In the archives of the Zionist offices from the old days when a fiery Odessa journalist named Jabotinsky had edited a newspaper and directed propaganda here, there were European membership lists. Though the chance of addresses remaining valid was dubious, still, from neutral Turkey it was possible to send mail into those lands, even indeed into Soviet Russia. And so day after day they wrote postcards, family greetings, signing them "Ezra Moledet," which every Jew would know meant help from the homeland. For a return address, a Turkish Jewess took the risk of letting hers be used.

And out of that dark void a few responses began to come. Even the spark of contact, though it probably could lead to nothing more, warmed the heart. In roundabout ways they asked if Ezra could send certificates for Palestine. What could be answered? The British would not honor any certificates brought from enemy lands. So even if a Jew managed to smuggle himself out, he had to possess a certificate issued before the war.

And yet Menahem sat writing the postcards, sending them out like little balloons adrift into the great void. Once, to his astonishment, he saw a return postcard bearing the name of Dvora's old town in the Ukraine, Cherezinka. The writer asked about the Chaimovitch family, even recalling the visit of Leah, during the great Soviet Revolution, and sending her his greetings.

Then there was a new kind of horror rumor heard. In Istanbul every rumor was heard, and this was said to have been told by a drunken Nazi courier in a café. In the Lublin area, it was said, gassing vans were being used to kill Jews.

Inside Germany for a few years now, in the greatest secrecy, closed passenger vans had been used in a program to finish off the incurably insane. They were placed in the vans to be "transported," and these vans had exhaust pipes turned into the seating area. The transports arrived at some burial place in the woods with a dead cargo. Now such vans had been brought to the Lublin area, where, since the conquest of Poland, trainloads of Jews had been dumped, sometimes in open fields, with the story given out that this area was to become a Jewish state.

More recently the Jews had been rounded up into camps, and at a camp called Chelmno the gas vans were being used.

Some said the vans were only for Jews who were hopelessly insane or infirm. But others said the vans made trips all day long, always returning empty.

And then the Nazis had attacked Russia.

On this Yom Kippur more than for many years Menahem felt the need for an accounting of the soul. His exile seemed endless, for the British charges against him—war or not—remained. True, for some of the tasks here he was better suited than the young lads. From the far-off time of Turkish rule in Palestine he knew the language. Sometimes he was needed to translate confidential documents for the official Jewish Agency representative, Chaim, in his little office in the Pera Palace Hotel. Though he mainly kept to the apartment, Menahem even at times ate with Chaim in a hotel dining room, while the Germans were nearby at their large tables, boasting loudly that the war had already been won. Their legation was directly across the street, and on grim days the chevreh would half-seriously plot to station a sniper at a hotel window and pick off the arrogant Von Papen. Indeed, had not Von Papen in 1932 stepped aside, Hitler would have failed to become Chancellor.

It was a dark Yom Kippur. When there came the haunting reverberation of the Kol Nidre, particularly here in its Sephardic intonation, Menahem thought of the source of the prayer in the Spain of the Inquisition, "Let all our vows not be vows," repeated in secret by Jews who to save themselves had ostensibly undergone conversion.

And when he recited the most wrenching of all the yearly prayers, the Al Chet, for each conceivable and inconceivable sin, Menahem began, out of conformity with the other worshipers and perhaps out of old habit, to strike his breast with every outcry, but presently the movement became true. "For the sin which we have committed before Thee by our own will, or by compulsion. . . . For the sin—"

As he swayed to each cry, Menahem was startled by a touch on his shoulder. Mika had come for him, wearing no tallis, but at least a yarmulkah. On the Turkish radio it was announced that the Germans were about to enter Kiev. From the CID Major Pennfield had called with questions about possible contacts in that area. Perhaps the British were now at last thinking of Teddy Kollek's proposed parachutists? Menahem had better come back to the apartment.

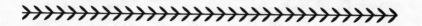

28

WHEN Tolya Koslovsky confided to his wife and their young daughter, Tanya, that he had been accepted into a special unit and would stay on for a time in Kiev, they refused to be evacuated. Hitler's invading fascists, after the greatest betrayal in history, were already at Zhitomir! The treacherous Ukrainian nationalists, led by their archtraitors the priests, were welcoming the murderous fascists as liberators, saviors! Here before Kiev the enemy would be stopped! Just as the enemy had been stopped at Smolensk, where Tanya's two brothers were fighting! Before Kiev, tank traps were being dug. Tanya went out with her Komsomol comrades, digging.

Her mother, Raisa, with other women of their apartment block, built street barricades. Already two families had been evacuated; both husbands were in high posts, though no higher than Tolya. As supervisor of the sugar-beet refinery he had just gone through a sleepless week of intense activity, but had succeeded by patching parts of one broken-down truck to another, and even commandeering peasant wagons, in sending eastward almost the total of the sugar stocks.

To have been accepted for the demolition unit was for Tolya a kind of vindication. Though with two sons at the front—neither Nicolai nor Dmitri had been heard from since the start of the Battle of Smolensk—and with Tolya's own record in the October Revolution, why should he still have need for vindication? Yet

427

even Tanya knew that her papa, though he never spoke of this, had certain doubts that went back into her childhood, to the time Papa had been moved from his important Cherezinka post to Kiev.

It was the time of the traitor trials, every child knew the cursed names, Zinoviev and Kamenev, Radek and all the spies and wreckers who had tried to betray the Revolution, with the arch-traitor Trotsky, who had escaped to the capitalist world to plot the downfall of the Soviet Union. Indeed, the despicable traitor only now had been liquidated there in Mexico, where he had plotted this war. He and the other plotters were Jews. Even as a child Tanya had known this, though the evil truth was not spoken of at home. Papa and Mamushka had had nothing to do with any of the religious cultists who were still permitted, in Soviet freedom, to gather in their synagogue. But it could not be forgotten in Cherezinka that her grandfather, the owner in czarist times of the sugar mill, the Jewish exploiter of the whole area of beet growers, had had to be shot during the triumphant establishment of the People's Republic.

Despite this, Papushka's origin had not been held against him. Papa and Mama had both been in the Movement from the earliest days, when they had been her age now, and as a fighter in the victorious Revolution her papa had been named the party's commissar for Cherezinka. And in this pride Tanya had grown, although from her earliest childhood Papushka had taught her that every true comrade is as worthy as a commissar.

Only there was another side, or perhaps a little corner, in her upbringing. When her grandfather's mansion, the largest house in all Cherezinka, had been taken over for the party administration, a few upstairs rooms had been assigned to the commissar, so the family had returned to live there: even the widow of the exploiter had been permitted to remain with her commissar son.

Tanya's grandmother, Manya, or Minna, was mostly called Bobeh, a Jewish folk word which, by habit, she preferred, and Tanya's father and mother tolerated it. Like all old grandmothers, Bobeh Manya was filled with family tales of other days, and a child heard them with a kind of wonder, just as you learned in school of bygone civilizations and of old superstitions and strange cultish practices that existed in this world. Tanya's Bobeh never discussed political ideas; the aged Manya behaved quite correctly, accepting that the Soviet way was the right way. She sighed sometimes in describing her husband, an exploiter and capitalist, but after the sigh Bobeh would say her Kalman had really been a very kind man, with a wonderful head on his shoulders for the operation of the mill. As between women, she would mention to young Tanya that in certain ways, for instance his stubbornness, Tolya resembled his father, Kalman. Though, of course, Tolya's gifts were in the service of the people.

Among Bobeh's tales were those of the old, old times before even the 1905 Revolution, when there had been a large-spreading family here in Cherezinka. Bobeh herself had had many brothers and sisters. In those days of the Czar there were dreadful attacks on the Jews, called pogroms, beatings, even killings, from drunken muzhiks stirred up by the Czar's agents provocateurs, for this was a way of having the peasants take out their misery on the Zhid instead of turning to revolution. Also, it was taught them in their churches that the Jews had killed their god, Jesus Christ—well, all this was complicated and no longer so important since religions were vanishing and anti-Semitism had long ago been outlawed by the Soviets. Still, superstition did not die simply by being outlawed, as Tanya with her bright little head (Bobeh didn't say Jewish head, but Tanya knew what her old Bobeh meant) could understand. Well, in the aged such lapses could be overlooked. With her bright little head that ran in the family, Bobeh said, Tanya could understand that not all people were equally intelligent, even though all people were equal. And from her first days in school Tanya could agree—while all people were equal, some were brighter, some were stronger, some were meaner than others. These were, however, characteristics of humanity, not of any racial group, as her grandmother perhaps still mistakenly believed.

"And the Ukrainians aren't mean and stupid?" her Bobeh would retort. And sometimes with a peep of the eye Tanya would show that she herself was not entirely free of this particular prejudice.

In any case, Bobeh had somehow kept track of her many brothers and sisters and in-laws and even their children; some had fled the pograms to capitalist America and were rich, owners of their own automobiles; doubtless they were exploiters of the black people. And a whole other branch of the family had gone to Palestine. Misguided Zionists, tools of British colonial imperialism, alas.

In those czarist days in Cherezinka, her Bobeh told her, Zionism was not the horrible thing it had perhaps since become. In those days, even before socialism was achieved here, Tanya's aunts and uncles had gone off to build a Jewish socialist land. Indeed, only a few years before Tanya had been born, one of her cousins from a kolkhoz in Eretz Yisroel had reappeared right in Cherezinka. Right in the middle of the Soviet Revolution, all the way from Palestine, the Big Leah had appeared.

To take part in the Revolution?

She had come to save Jews, because in the revolutionary battles between the Whites and the Reds, again pogroms had broken out and again Jews were being slaughtered. Ah, what a girl was this Leah, Bobeh said, a giantess, yet beautiful, the daughter of Bobeh's own younger sister Feigel, whose husband, Yankel, had at one time been employed by her own husband Kalman alev-ha-shalom. (A superstitious Jewish expression, Tanya knew, for the dead.)

This Yankel, a pious one, had failed in everything he had undertaken, poor Feigel had had a hard life with him, but it seemed from the tales of their daughter, the Big Leah, that in Palestine Yankel had of all things become a man of the soil and that all was well with the whole family there! And this Leah—

Of her, Tanya already knew the legends, but she loved to hear them repeated. In the midst of all the Red Army battles with the Ukrainian gangs led by their General Petlura, a Jew killer, Big Leah had set out to find the remnants of the Socialist Zionist Youth clubs, and through fire and flame Leah had made her way up as far as Vilna, and back again with her young followers to Odessa, where they took ship!

In those days Zionism was not prohibited, Tanya must know, so there had been no disloyalty in following Leah. They were simply Jews who wanted to live in their own land, like Uzbeks or Armenians. Why, then, Tanya asked, hadn't they gone to the autonomous Jewish region in Birobijan? Ah, it didn't exist then, her grandmother said with the faint smile that meant she meant something else, best not to say. And besides, Palestine was the old, old Jewish land. And Bobeh would turn from the subject lest she be accused of influencing her granddaughter to wrong ways of thinking.

But such as Leah! Bobeh related how Leah had been in love with—well, his name was Mischa, but in Palestine he had been called Handsome Moshe. A young revolutionist of 1905, who had fled the Czar's Ochrana, the secret police of those days. In Palestine Leah fell in love with him, but the Handsome Moshe had returned to work for the Revolution and been caught and sent to Siberia. For ten years Leah had longed for him. When the Revolution came at last, Mischa had emerged from Siberia to fight with the Red Army, and could Tanya imagine, the Big Leah, arriving here, had sought and found him! But alas, in Siberia her Handsome Moshe had married—a real Russian girl, a revolutionistka who had followed him into exile, and they had a child. So then, with her young Zionists, Leah had returned to Palestine.

Opening a carved old sewing box in which she kept yellowed photos and letters and a few brooches and rings, Bobeh had drawn out an ancient photograph of this Leah. As Tanya studied the picture, her grandmother remarked, "You know, though you are small, you have her features." With sudden spirit Bobeh began to do over Tanya's hair. She coiled the braids atop the girl's head, as in the photo of Leah, and looking in the mirror, Tanya indeed saw the resemblance. She even tried to assume the eager, warm expression in the photograph.

Bobeh had had news of Leah after her return to Palestine. She was married, with two children! There was still, here in Cherezinka, an old-time comrade of that Zionist group, Zalman the Shoemaker. The Youth of Zion, Zeire Zion, they had called themselves. And even up to a few years ago Zalman, a harmless dreamer to be sure, had in some roundabout way got word of those in Palestine.

In the time of the traitors, after Comrade Stalin revealed how the wreckers were plotting to undermine the Soviet Union, a change had come for Comrade Tolya Koslovsky and his family. Not that he was in any way accused or even suspected! His record was untainted, nor had he ever associated with anyone connected to the suspected or the accused. Still, Tolya Koslovsky was replaced as the commissar of Cherezinka and put in charge of the sugar mill. Naturally it was right for the Soviet Union to utilize the technical knowledge Tolya Koslovsky had gained as a young man in his father's mill. Still, was this a hint that his origin, the son of an exploiter, was still remembered? And the visit, though more than fifteen years ago, of his cousin from Palestine and the departure with her of a whole group of Soviet youth, turned Zionist?

A few years later he was moved to an administrative post in the sugar cartel in Kiev. As this was a move from a rural town to the regional center, it could be seen as a gain in importance. The family was assigned a four-room apartment in the newest block, where administrators, academicians, and even the director of the opera lived. Still, could a trace of doubt have remained? Look what had happened, here in Kiev, to the food commissar, Mischa, once known as the Handsome Moshe. Denounced by his wife for having Zionist connections, he had been sent off to a labor camp, and in the labor camp he had perished.

In Kiev Tolya had plunged into his work, bringing about an enormous rise in productivity at the sugar refinery. In 1939, when Comrade Stalin had made his astute pact with Germany, Tanya's father had explained to her the great wisdom of the arrangement —Stalin had discerned the precise moment to turn the Soviet Union's two evil adversaries against each other! Let the fascists and the capitalists destroy each other and then the Soviet Union's way would be embraced by the workers and peasants of the entire world!

The capitalist nations had proven craven, weak—also the French workers had no reason to defend their master capitalists— and thus, the Nazi beast had rapidly triumphed. Then the treacherous Hitler had broken his pact and turned on the Soviet Union. But like Napoleon before him, he would be entrapped. The Hitler armies, too, as Tanya could see on the huge map at the Komsomol, would be drawn into the vastness of the land, swallowed, and destroyed. Great sacrifices would have to be made: The earth would be scorched in the face of the enemy advance; thus, the Hitlerian beasts would find only emptiness and starvation, and if they lasted until winter, they would perish, starved and exposed, under snow and ice.

Already Tanya had said farewell to half her dearest comrades in her Komsomol Club, whose families were moving inland to continue the battle. But her father would not leave one wheel in the refinery behind for the enemy. And she suspected there was another reason for his staying to the last—something of which she would be extremely proud when she knew.

Already the city was under air attack and shellfire, many buildings smoldered, she had seen actual dead in the streets, and when her group marched out to dig tank traps, they carried gas masks. Only a few days from now their leader, Yuri, would reach military age, and Tanya had formed a decision. Nearly a year ago she and Yuri had discovered that they understood all things in the same way, almost without words; a look of the eye was enough. At her sixteenth birthday party her devilish friend Masha had bought an American jazz disc, and it was also Masha who declared it was customary to turn off the lights when this was played, and in the American way of dancing Yuri had held her very tight so that she felt his entire man's body pressed against her, and her breasts pressing against him, and in the dark they had kissed, with tongues. It was soon understood that one day if feelings did not change between them—and how could this happen?—they would go to the marriage registry.

Yet she sometimes felt Bobeh looking at her with that odd, ironic little expression she wore in her silences. It contained a kind of judgment. Every time Yuri appeared in their flat that expression appeared. Tanya knew what it meant. Her Yuri was not from the Jews. Her papushka and mamushka did not reproach Bobeh, tolerating her backward attitude because of her age.

Today Tanya's friend Masha brought even worse tales of the fascist invaders. What they did to women. Even old grandmothers were seized and violated. Masha said she would kill herself but first kill the attacker. She had a boy's pocketknife, the blade long enough to plunge into the heart. Yuri shouted at Masha to put an end to these demoralizing stupidities. Even if the Red Army strategically fell back, their group would also cross the river and never be taken by the fascists.

It was then that Tanya's own intention became insistent in her. If the worst happened in the coming days. If the fascist beasts should get into the city. And if her papushka remained to what she was certain was a secret heroic task. Then before all this, she decided to have one thing happen. Some way she must arrange it. Perhaps even already tonight. So that no fascist beast could seize and soil her, be the first, leaving a lifelong pollution, should she even want to survive. To put herself beyond the worst possibility was simple. Night after night she had had fantasies of her first lovemaking with Yuri. Even if he would go the next day into the Red Army. Especially so. All at once Tanya recalled Bobeh's tales of that cousin the Big Leah in Palestine, who had given herself to her Handsome Moshe and for years waited for his return. Tanya felt she now understood. Not simply girlishly; she really understood.

Early in the afternoon a messenger came with a special task for them. They were carried back in a truck to the new-built center of the city, the Kratchatchik, and to the party headquarters. Their

433

group had been selected; it was a great trust. Important documents in padlocked filing cases had to be carried to waiting vans. With furious energy they worked as the apparatchiks continued to sort out dossiers. The bombardment intensified; a spectacular air battle was overhead, and they did not even pause to watch through the window. When a plane fell in a streak of fire, Yuri glanced and cried, "Theirs! Theirs!" Before they could carry things to the truck, they had to wait out a nearby shell hit.

Blackout came; the task was almost completed, but a few were needed to stay on, and Yuri picked Tanya.

After they had finished, in a commissar's office upstairs where there was even a sofa, they decided. Gravely, almost ritually, they uncovered themselves. It was as though their bodies were luminous to each other. They lay on the couch and were solemn and beautiful for each other, then even playful—they had played their trick on the world's evil. Whatever happened, they pledged to find each other after the enemy was destroyed, and they would rebuild Kiev and have children. For Yuri, too, it was the first time, but for a man perhaps this was not the same. Suddenly Tanya said she wanted to see. He laughed and went and made sure of the blackout and then put on the desk light. She studied his organ solemnly and laughed in delight as it rose again under her gaze.

When they dressed and slipped downstairs, there was only an elderly citizen guard at the entrance of the building. Startled, he half raised his rifle, but seeing a boy and a girl with Komsomol emblems, he gave a chuckle and said, "Good night, tovarichi."

Through the deserted night streets Yuri walked her home; her mother and father waited. Tanya explained they had been chosen for a special task at party headquarters. Before her parents, Yuri didn't kiss her goodnight, but as their hands stretched out, the lingering touch of their fingers was as though they never could be separated; the current remained even when the very tips had parted.

Three more days their unit was called to work. An enormous battle of increasing intensity was taking place not far off so that the sky was never clear or silent. Often in the daytime Tanya and Yuri found a moment to touch each other, but there was nowhere to meet again; this was not the time for personal gratifications.

Just before blackout Bobeh answered a knock at their door, and a Red Army man stood there, his head stiff on some kind of high

434

metal collar. Wounded. He had hardly repeated their family name when Bobeh made a choked, dreadful sound. She had seen in his avoiding eyes. Then Tanya's mother cried, "Which?"

Both. Both. When Smolensk was obliterated. From the air. Of their entire company, only a dozen survivors.

The Red Army comrade had not much to tell. To Tolya he handed over their army booklets, a few bits of personal effects.

Hardly a word could come out from any of them. Both. If only the boys had not got themselves into the same company.

A few of the neighbors remaining in the building somehow learned and came. What could be said?

A day arrived of almost entire silence over the city. As though the silence in the family had simply spread. Tanya's unit was not called out to work. Occasionally a single shellburst sounded, like a single dog bark after a wild clamorous fight.

In the room of the boys, Tanya and her mother packed away clothing, books. Dmitri's mineralogical collection they put in cotton wadding as though he might yet want it.

The following day the city was entered. Through loudspeaker announcements in the streets, radio proclamations, they remained with their own sorrow.

On the fourth evening her father slipped out. He should be back in an hour, he said. The women knew it was for his special task.

From the launching of the German invasion nearly two months before, the sabotage unit had been formed. The charges had for the last two weeks been in place, some of them in subcellars of hotels that would surely be taken over, and of central buildings. Each stay-behind had only one post to set off, so that whatever happened to him, the work could go on. Thus, Tolya made his way from the subcellar of their own apartment block, darting through other cellars, reaching the coal bin of the Moscow Hotel. There he connected the clockwork already set for the middle of the night, returning safely the way he had come.

Explosions on the Kratchatchik began just before midnight. There came sirens, shooting, more explosions. When they peeked from behind the edges of their blackout, enormous flames could be seen. The flames rose from the Officers Hotel—hundreds of them must be torn apart there, flung into the air, burned, crushed. Tolya's face, from stone, was alive again.

All four climbed to the roof and, lying together with a growing number of neighbors, watched the spreading conflagration. At intervals convulsions spouted new flames; even their own building felt the shock of the blasts and shuddered beneath them. Tolya waited for the moment of his own. Tanya saw her father gazing at his watch. When the blast came, she knew this was his, his! Though her papushka said not a word, only let drop his hand with the wristwatch. His lips were almost smiling.

During several more days the blasts continued, as though the central city were a huge dying beast still at intervals emitting its roar of defiant wrath. All was cordoned off by tanks, troops; not a soul could approach the Kratchatchik, yet sporadically thunders came; then the blasts were echoed in crashes of collapsing walls and shrieking ambulance sirens.

Through their apartment block exultant news spread. A film theater taken over for Nazi soldiers—full, chock-full at the moment of the blast! And the party offices that the fascists had taken over and inspected in every corner and crevice—sky high! With hundreds of commanders, officers, and an entire section of their worst, the SS!

On the air came proclamations. The vicious ring of perpetrators had been caught and executed. The city of Kiev would be saved from its criminal destroyers despite the communists and Jewish plotters who had attempted this subhuman sabotage. Order was being restored, and normal life could soon be resumed. The victorious forces of the Reich had taken over a million prisoners; the criminal enemy warmongers were on the verge of total collapse. All those who cooperated with the liberators had nothing to fear. Heil Hitler.

Then an entire day without an explosion; the job was apparently finished. The entire length of the Kratchatchik was a single smoldering ruin.

The next morning the city was plastered with a new announcement, regarding Jews. On the walls of their apartment building and in the courtyard the pronouncement could be read. All Jews to be resettled. Command: All Jews must report at eight in the morning on Monday at Melnikovsky and Dokhturov streets. They must bring their documents, all money and all valuables, also warm clothing and food for three days. Any Jew failing to carry out this instruction would be shot. Anyone looting their apartments would be shot.

So it was clear they were meant to return, after things got settled again.

Nearly half the families remaining in their block were Jews. All day neighbors came in and out. Some women were hysterical, and Bobeh and Mamushka tried to quiet them. Some who had small children were desperately trying to place them with Russian families, leaving all they possessed. Some consulted Tolya as to whether they should try passing as non-Jews. But how? In their papers, "Jew" was stamped as ineradicably as if it were on their skins. Gradually as each family made its preparations, the visits ceased.

They too prepared. Her mother said it might even be better to be resettled as Jews in a labor camp, harsh and hard as it might be, than for Tolya to be caught as a communist. Party members were being executed in masses. Tolya had been a commissar. Someone was certain to give him away; the Germans had agents everywhere, among the Ukrainians particularly. It needed only one greedy or disgruntled workman from the sugar refinery to point him out. But Tanya, a neighbor had suggested, could say she was only fifteen, a schoolgirl still without papers, thus without the Jew stamp. Now her mother pondered—perhaps one of Tanya's non-Jewish friends would take her in? But Tanya stopped her mamushka at once. She would not separate.

It was the grandmother who behaved most rationally, collecting bread, potatoes, sugar and salt, and even butter in a little sack. Then Mamushka dazedly but with increasing practicality selected clothing. Their valuables—her gold earrings, a few finger rings, lockets, trinkets. The photographs of their sons. And those last mementos brought from Smolensk, a little address book of Dmitri's; she had meant to write to all his friends; perhaps from wherever they were sent she could still do it.

Once, over a year ago, when their company had only been on occupation duty after Poland had been divided, Dmitri, home on leave, had told them something he had not written in his letters. How swarms of Polish Jews had come fleeing across to the Soviet sector to escape the Germans. Of course, it was known that Hitler was anti-Semitic, but these Jews had come fleeing as from death. Allowed to pass into the Soviet Union, they had been sent to labor camps. The Germans, they had said, meant to destroy all Jews.

Tolya had fallen back into his stoniness. There were certain citations for his meritorious achievements that hung on the wall.

These he took down, watching them burn on the kitchen stove. With his party card in his hand, he moved about the apartment seeking a safe place to hide it until the Germans were swallowed in defeat and they all could return. It was difficult to find such a place. Despite the German proclamation against looting, the moment they left here all would be torn apart, cleaned out the way they had already seen in the apartments of those who had evacuated a few weeks ago.

In the early morning Tanya dressed quickly and put water to boil. Each trying to show calm, to be strong for the others, they were soon ready. The rooms were in perfect order, shining clean. Tolya locked the door and on the way out left the key with the block caretaker, who said a quiet dosvidanya. A few other Jewish families were coming out at the same time—a housing planner, slightly older than Tolya, with his wife. Luckily their children were grown and long ago on their own far from Kiev. In the courtyard was a younger woman with three small children and her father; her husband was at the front. Tanya had only known her to smile to and not even thought if she were Jewish.

Walking in families, one little group behind another, they soon formed a lengthening cortege. From other streets, Jews came. Some had bulky valises and rucksacks and last-minute hand parcels, surely far more baggage than would be allowed, according to the posted-up notices. When she saw the first baby carriage, Tanya suddenly felt a shock, as though this could not be meant.

As they approached the appointed crossing, the street was already filled. From the lower part that led to Podol, even a greater swarm kept thronging the avenue. Down there was a workers' area, the old Jewish district from even before the great Soviet Revolution. Tanya had discussed the Podol problem with the housing planner, Ilya Meierovitch, who had come to lecture at her own school, and shown plans for apartment blocks. As the families from Podol crowded in, she heard some of the aged ones speaking the Yiddish language that her grandmother understood; a small circle of bearded old men clung close together, a few even wearing the striped white shawls of the Jewish cult. In Cherezinka she had occasionally peeped into the little synagogue and seen Jewish worshipers. They wore a peculiar little black cube tied with thongs on their forehead! Just now in the crowd an aged Jew's hat fell off and he stooped frantically to find it among all those legs. It was a rule with them that their heads must never be uncovered, and Tanya saw that underneath the hat he wore one of those little skullcaps—to make sure, she supposed.

The entire mass was sluggishly moving forward; passing a side lane, she saw one of those German army cars with a mounted machine gun, but the soldiers in the vehicle seemed lazily relaxed, even amused.

Propelled now into the main, broad street, the crowd was somewhat looser, but more people kept coming, riding on carts atop their luggage, some even in droshkies they had managed to find, though every last vehicle had disappeared across the Dnieper in the evacuation. There were handcarts piled with bundles of bedding, baby carriages piled with pots and dishes, she even saw an artist with a roll of canvas under his arm, his belt stuffed with brushes, clutching a paintbox and a folded easel as though going on a sketching trip. Carpenters with their long toolboxes, children with their school satchels on their backs, filled with food; she saw women padded in three layers of clothing with a fur coat atop, yet one could not laugh.

Already in the crowd movement the neighbors from their house block had been separated away, though at one moment the Meierovitches were again beside them. All this, Meierovitch declared, was a reprisal for the hundreds of German officers and soldiers who had been killed in the Kratchatchik explosions. No, Tolya said—if a reprisal, the enemy would have taken hostages and shot them, even ten for one. And not only Jews. Before Meierovitch could answer, a crowd movement again carried them off. The family held onto each other; the great dread had become to be separated. But what was ahead? Where were they going? To a vast labor camp for Jews? But where? How far? One even saw wheelchairs.

Once again, as after the news of the death of both sons, Tolya's mind seemed to be turning to stone. A relentless process of petrification, as in some early stage of matter, even before the age of ice. Why had he not insisted, even driven the women to leave when they still could have been evacuated? His deed, part of the deed of all his comrades, had needed to be done. It was an action in the war. This that was happening here, this was not part of war. This was something else, from some age of herds of predatory beasts roaming the earth. Tolya could not look at his mother, his wife, his young daughter, his Tanya with her fervid youthfulness, her belief in all he had believed in. This purity penetrated even his petrified self and was such a grieving pain within him that with something akin to an inner prayer Tolya begged that it all be over, that he be already nonexistent.

What should he have done then? Better to have remained, barricaded, and, when they arrived, made a wild resistance at the door, better to have been murdered there. Oh, his sons. If only his sons, still hurling iron and fire, were killing, killing these invaders. Tolya saw unwanted images of the last few days, shaming images of Red Army men in flight, through back lanes, young men glimpsed in loutish clothing they had seized from peasants after casting aside their uniforms, their rifles. Soon afterward, watching the German army entry, he had comprehended, though not condoned, their flight. Such mechanization! Every vehicle with mounted machine guns, even to the endless column of motorcycles. Every monstrous panzer unscarred, with its fresh-shaved commander erect in the open turret, confident that not even a sniper's bullet could come from the conquered Soviets. At least when he ceased to live, Tolya said to himself, there would also be in his brain-turned-to-stone the images of the exploded bodies of those same supermen in the flames of the Kratchatchik.

Slowly the family was pressed onward in the tide of the mass, and now they were alongside the wall of the Jewish cemetery. At each closed gateway was a machine-gun vehicle, with the soldiers sitting back no longer even amused at the spectacle. On the other side of the cemetery wall, only silence. No wailing, no child crying as here in the thronged street. Then even within the throng there came an island of hush, where the crowd pressed back onto itself, leaving a small open circle. It was Mamushka who first recognized, and whispered as in awe to her husband, her mother, her daughter. "Dr. Belnikoff with his whole family." A family like their own. Visits exchanged. A girl older than Tanya. Another who was younger, dressed here in her school uniform. The wife, a laboratory worker. They lay in the opened-up space, each face slightly surprised as at an unexpected taste. The doctor had possessed cyanide pills.

A squad of Ukrainian police in their black uniforms angrily pushed through the fringe of Jews, picked up the four bodies, the baggage, the doctor's medical bag, flinging all onto a street-cleaner cart, which they pushed away.

The crowd, pressed from behind, for a moment still avoided the small area on the pavement; then the space shrank and vanished. A screaming woman with the strength of the insane suddenly came tearing her way back through the crowd, crying, "Let me out! Let me out!" She passed them; her cries were no longer heard; they couldn't know if she had got back out.

Then they were before the inspection point; perhaps here the woman had been seized by her hysteria, for a barbed-wire barrier closed the street, leaving only a gatelike passageway flanked by German soldiers, officers with an odd insignia on their caps, crossed bones and a skull. Also, more of the black-clad Ukrainian police.

As the people slowly funneled through, each had to hold out his identity booklet. At this point the non-Jews who had this far accompanied their Jewish friends, their spouses, had to say farewell. Some even pleaded to be allowed to go as far as the train but were pushed back with horizontally held rifles. Here mixed couples were parted, scenes that tore every heart, husbands from wives, the non-Jewish one crying out, "I'll go too!" A few even managed to throng past the inspectors, only to be caught by a second inspection and made to stand over in a separate group. Just as the Koslovsky family reached the inspection, a woman fell to the ground and embraced the legs of the Ukrainian police officer. With a Jew curse and a violent thrust of his leg he shook her off.

Each person's identification, Tanya saw, was only glanced at for the Jewish nationality stamp, then tossed onto a growing pile. But how would they ever be sorted out? Probably new papers would be issued. That must be it. And yet when her identity booklet was snatched from her hand, Tanya felt startled. Less than a year ago she had received it, and even with the Jew stamp inside she had felt that now she was arrived in her own person as a part of the Soviet population.

A German plane roared down, very low, directly over the street filled with Jews; the plane skimmed so low you could see clearly the black crosses under the wings. Would it drop a bomb, would it machine-gun the mass of Jews? Terror shrieks came from children; near the Koslovskys a mother bent to a little boy who had befouled himself. The plane lifted and was gone.

Beyond the checkpoint there were commands, cries, *schnell, schnell*, though the crowd could hardly move. They were past the cemetery wall; dwellings dwindled away, the city dwindled away into vacant lots, some with patches of vegetable gardens, and now

441

the procession was turned into a crossroad with even a few trees alongside. Again everything stopped and they waited. It was past noon; there was a slight breeze behind them. Someone said wryly, a good place for a picnic. As they stood and stood, people indeed began to take out food from their packs, and Bobeh too untied her kerchief filled with piroshkis she had prepared last night. Tanya opened her water canteen, used on scouting trips. An almost quiet came; there were only echoes of far-off sounds, faint, for the wind went the other way. Perhaps trucks starting into motion. Would they be taken on trucks then?

Tolya listened intently; the sounds to him were oddly like distant bursts of fire. Could there still be a resistance somewhere? Another man of about his age said he knew this area, a bit farther along here was a ravine, Babi Yar; the sounds must come from across the ravine. Perhaps on the other side of Babi Yar a military cleanup action of some sort was in progress.

Once more the mass was moving forward. After an hour they came to an area where something was going on; again, amid confused, pleading outcries, they heard shouted commands, *"Schnell, schnell."* On one side was a long pile of satchels, rucksacks, bundles. Everything people carried, even the food parcels for three days, must be deposited. Soldiers now swarmed among them, pulling things from people. But why? How could their things ever be sorted out again? Many were trying hastily to write their names on their baggage. Some said there would be a footmarch and the belongings would be carried on trucks. "Medicine!" Desperately a woman with a crying child tried to hold onto the provision bag a Ukrainian was pulling away from her; she managed to snatch out a medicine bottle for the child. *Schnell, schnell.* Bewilderingly the entire atmosphere had changed; from the turmoil mixed with sudden bursts of impatient brutality, it had become strangely sinister. As they were pushed, herded before a long table, a solid rank of guards moved in behind them. Valuables. Everything. Money, gold, jewelry, *schnell*, deposit there, everything. Old Jews, the real graybeards from Podol, were being pulled out of line and searched, their coats yanked off, the buttons flying. Cloutings, howls. Tanya's Bobeh and her mother hastily emptied their handbags onto the table. Bobeh perhaps still had something hidden in her clothing—if only they didn't search her. A German soldier seized Papushka's wrist, pulling off the watch, the gift of Mamushka. A strange surprised, half-choked howl came from her

442

father, but they pushed him stumbling on, and he could only reach around as he gained his balance, reaching for his women.

Tanya still could not grasp this. Thieves. Looters that in the Soviet army would be shot. Worse than the worst that had been said of them. *Schnell, schnell*, again thrust into ranks. Perhaps the most awful was now already behind; a few people were whispering to each other what they had managed to save. The forward movement seemed somewhat quicker, and then there was another halt. But the long line before them was no longer there! Emptiness. Only a rank of soldiers, each with a huge vicious dog on leash. Who would even try to escape? Whatever was meant would come. Behind the soldiers, a long, barren field. Nothing. Where had all those people vanished to?

Once more the intermittent sounds were heard. Less distant. Not truck gears.

A squad of soldiers came rapidly down the empty area and counted off some twenty people, *schnell, schnell*, hurrying them at a rapid pace until at a turn the group was lost to sight. Almost at once another squad arrived, and this time their own row was included.

The finality revealed itself. A chalkstone ridge stood before them. Huge trucks and military vehicles formed side walls to a space littered with tatters of clothing, stray shoes. One truck was being piled with garments. "Undress! Sanitaire! Inspection! Naked! All!"

The horror dogs strained on their leashes, growled, snapped. In blind terror, Tanya's hands moved to her clothing. "Now we will die, my darling," she heard her Bobeh say. "Naked as we are born, it is so that we must leave." Bobeh's voice was soothing, as when giving a spoonful of medicine to a frightened child. And blindingly all fell into place. True, death was naked. The reflex of shame, the refusal to uncover, all fell away, but instead, thudding pulsations, as though her life had to escape from her and live, dizzied her, around them bludgeons swung on people already fallen on all fours, streaks of blood spread on half-undressed bodies, there in the middle two dogs had been let loose on a heavy, formless, shrieking woman, Tanya's father with a strange guttural howl flung himself on a soldier. "No, no!" she shrieked and heard a crunch of truncheons on her papushka, saw him under their kicking feet, a Ukrainian pulling off his boots; she and her mother tried frantically to reach him, streaks of blood from his nostrils, the three of them, his mother and Mamushka and Tanya all as one cleaving to help him, the cluster of them together with him on all fours, trying to rise, others like themselves stumbling behind them in an echoing uproar of cries, horror shrieks, all of them thrust now between two lines of kicking, clubbing soldiers, *schnell, schnell*. Then in the midst of this her papa raised his head, his eyes dazed but penetrating into hers, for one instant in such grief, such total eternal grief. Then he looked at her mother and his mother. In the oneness of their bodies it seemed there flowed a last wave of love, of life love, and then they were being pushed, squeezed through a cleft in the ridge, an opening. Facing them across the narrow ravine was a soldier squatting behind a machine gun on a tripod, as though anyone could run away here! And they were having to move along a ledge. Glancing down for one instant, Tanya saw the bottom a surface of bodies with streaks, swatches of red; her ears heard cries, whimpers as from a distance, not from here, as from an antiexistence, in school she had learned a theory, a brilliant professor explained that all, all was dialectic, even existence, life and the nether side of life, matter and antimatter, he said. Then the gun stitched; so this ridge was the execution wall. As her father fell, they were all pulled, her hand in his, she clasping Bobeh's, her mother's, but in the fall their holds broke, their oneness splintered apart, and now the sound from below engulfed them, moaning and pain and grief and screams commingled, the sound of creation and anticreation; she had felt a burn against her side; her mind was acute as under some injected stimulant, she fell on bodies, in warm, half-slippery blood, thudding around her came others falling dead and dying, blood spurted across her face, and her arms of themselves made a movement and rolled away a woman's form, the hair clumped in blood. Another body fell across her legs, she could not move, turning her head, she could not find her father or any of them, her menstrual flow had come, though it was not the time, perhaps it came with death. Underneath her now Tanya felt a sluggish, wavelike movement, a settling of the whole mass of which she was a part.

Above, repeated bursts of fire continued, with cries, children's terrified shrieking, and then within the chasm around her came words, half-whispered or gasped, even names, "Sacha, do you live?" And an old man's voice, a feeble "Yisroel." A few words that Bobeh had once tried to implant in her. Still acute, Tanya's mind recorded another sound that she had never before heard, a death rattle. A body rolled by the sluggish tide movement was crosswise over her shoulders; now she would be stifled. Yet her automatic reactions continued, her arms and torso twisting until her mouth had a breathing space. Then her mind's acuteness lapsed, and in a vague form of consciousness Tanya felt that she, her person, was dissolving into some element, something like before life, the dense primordial chaos before the birth of the world. Out of some massive life-death such as this, the world had anciently been born, and all was now once more subsiding into that massive chaos, which still stirred like a lava and included her.

From this her consciousness again awakened. She did not want it. It persisted like your mind still working on an unfinished school lesson after you have given up and gone to bed. When she had received her identity booklet, she had felt that the nationality mark "Jew" was a needless perpetuation, an error. Her father had declared that only those should be marked Jews who clung to their cult, their ritual superstition. Then what of Bobeh's tales of that Leah from Palestine, a socialist, not religious? But Tanya's mind skipped away from all this, halted its thinking; why let these be her last thoughts as she lay here ending?

Yet what purpose could there be, to amass and slaughter all those who happened to be born of Jews? Her mind gave up the problem and at last left her to die in quiet.

As through chinks among the tangled forms and limbs she could see a few stars in a patch of sky. Her body worked itself upward until her entire head was above the surface. The sky was murky, and the steep side of the ravine loomed black above her. Then, arching her head, Tanya made out the surface of the glutted chasm, an undulating pale surface, they must have dumped sand, but areas of flesh emerged. Once or twice, at a party after she had drunk vodka, everything had swayed; now the entire surface had such a movement. Or else like descriptions of molten lava. And did she not even feel pulled as though the entire mass were slipping slowly downward in the ravine?

Above, behind, there were occasional single shots. Once she even saw a flashlight moving for a long moment over the lava of flesh and sand.

Now her entire naked body had worked itself to the top layer; the crease on her side throbbed faintly; she put her fingers there—a crust had formed. In slow, short movements Tanya began to glide along the surface of bodies. She shifted sidewise as well, toward the other wall of the ravine. After a long time she was where the ravine widened, she was slipping downward, as though on thinning blood, perhaps mingling with water from a joining rivulet. Her hand touched cold water, between bodies. Only a scattering of corpses had been washed this far, they lay among pebbles in the stream bed. On her back, half-immersed, she felt a kind of living-ness quickening in her from the water. Then she turned over and on all fours, still with a halt after each movement, made her way still farther downward. Once, and then again, she thought to venture out on the embankment, but each time drew back; perhaps she had heard some metallic sound.

Forms of trees and bushes appeared; the night was ending. A clump reached into the swamp. With a burst of daring she crawled among the spread branches, then to the top of the embankment, found a thicket, and lay within it. Before her was a field divided into garden patches; in the distance were a few dilapidated tool huts, the doors hanging awry; looters had already passed. Tanya crept to one of these sheds, found in it shreds of sacking, pulled the door shut, and curled on the earth, half covering herself.

A peasant stood over her. For a moment they looked into each other's eyes. Then he closed the door behind him; between the boards came streaks of light. He was squat, whiskered, one of those you saw bringing their carts of produce to the free market. "Ju-dovska?" he said. She remained silent, her eyes still seeking in his.

"The swamp is red." He shook his head as over the unbeliev-able. "They have declared a free Ukraine," he said. "They took my pig."

He let himself down on her. It was her dead body being be-fouled.

Then he arose; as he pushed the door, she could see a few goats nibbling at bushes. "You are as well here as elsewhere." He threw down a piece of bread. She heard him prop something against the door from outside.

After a time the Ukrainian returned and gave her goat's milk from a small crock. He squatted beside her but did not molest her. "I have three daughters," he said. "Two grown and married and one still in the house." Taking the crock, he departed, again bracing the door. This whole day Tanya lay numb, yet with something returning, rising like pain that came long after a blow. Distantly up Babi Yar she could still hear the bursts of shooting. All day long.

Toward dusk, though without a sound in the field, Tanya became certain someone was approaching. This time nausea mounted in her; she was back in existence. But it was not the peasant; a young girl stood there. She wore a school dress, and Tanya saw she carried another on her arm. The girl was younger than herself, perhaps fourteen.

"As soon as Papa brought in the goats, I saw something had happened," the girl said. "Papa can't keep anything from me." Handing Tanya the dress and a shift, she said her father was not a bad man but backward. Then she asked, "Everyone? Your whole family?" Her name was Katerina. She was even a comrade in the Komsomol. When Tanya said she was nearly seventeen, Katerina said she was so small she could pass for fifteen, especially in these clothes. They were old, left by her grown sister. All she could bring. Some old shoes, too. And a whole bread, and a cheese. Tanya could not be hidden here; already the Germans had taken away a villager for hiding a Jewish child.

What she had done was truly a comradely deed, Tanya said, and both found themselves sobbing and embraced. Katya vanished.

Still, that night Tanya lay in the shed. A decision to live had become definite in her; she must take part to destroy the evil in mankind. Surely for this she had been spared. A thought of Yuri came, but already as someone in an existence into which she could not enter again. There kept recurring . . . Cherezinka. It was an instinct, she told herself, the return to her birthplace.

Tanya decided on the story that she was Ukrainian, her village had been destroyed in the bombardment, her entire family had been killed, and she was going to an aunt who lived in Cherezinka. She could use field paths. The German soldiers, Katerina had said, were under orders not to molest Ukrainian girls because the Nazis sought to make an ally of the restored Ukrainian nation.

With daylight Tanya set forth, skirting the village. Later in the morning a peasant wagon on a byroad took her a distance. Other wagons helped her on her way. She slept in the fields. Her worst fright came when a motor lorry appeared on a wagon lane, as from nowhere; a pair of German soldiers, happy, boisterous, tried to persuade her to mount and ride with them. She pointed that she lived close by. At last the older one said, "A child, leave off!" and they drove on.

The best was to approach only women, the women of a family digging in a potato field; if she saw young girls among them, that was easiest. Once, a mother asked about the holy monasteries of Kiev, and Tanya said she had gone with her mother to the grotto, even though in school she had been taught not to believe. The woman said she must return to belief and gave her a small crucifix on a chain to wear around her neck. Once when another old peasant couple took her on their cart, the peasant declared at last the land was rid of the Jews. It was the Jews who had brought the kolkhoz and forced him to deliver his grain there, but now, under Ukrainian independence, each would be given back his land. Half his life he had waited! At last the anti-Christ was being driven out, and the Jew was being destroyed. First, when the war began, the Rumanian army had crossed the Dniester, they had seized Jews in the town, marched them along the roadside here, and shot them like dogs, letting them rot in the ditch. But cunningly, many of the Zhids had hidden or fled. When the German soldiers arrived, they first made the Rumanians clean up all the corpses, burying whatever remained uneaten by wild dogs. Whatever you wanted to say about the Germans, they were clean and everything was organized and orderly. Also, they had special soldiers whose task it was to finish off with the Jews. Now who but the Germans would have thought of such an excellent plan? These special soldiers were like an army in themselves, with their own commanders, and they knew exactly how to find Jews, even those hidden by neighbors of his, for money, in holes in the ground. These special soldiers took Rumanian troops and taught them the proper way to kill Zhids so as not to strew the countryside with Jew bodies that bred disease. When these German specialists arrived in a town, they sealed off each courtyard and examined each person's papers, and with their trained hounds that knew the smell of a Zhid, they ferreted out the hiding Jews, men, women, and their spawn. They marched all the Zhids to their Zhid cemetery, and there in the field behind, they had them dig a long trench, they made them hand over all the gold and the jewels that the Zhids tried even then to hide, they made them undress stark naked. Some of the shameless female Zhids even offered themselves to the German

448

soldiers, but it didn't help, for when the soldiers were finished with them, they shot them like the rest, at the edge of the pit, so they fell on top of the heap.

No longer able to hold back, Tanya doubled over sidewise, retching onto the road. Na, na, the old wife stroked her head and rebuked the peasant, "To a young girl, still an innocent child, you should not tell such foul tales."

The wagon came to their turnoff, the woman asked her to stay, but Tanya muttered she must reach her aunt, and to their "Christ protect you" she responded with the blessing of the saints of the ancient monastery of Kiev.

Keeping to the banks of the Bog River, Tanya knew she was coming close; one night she spent in a half-rotted rowboat tied among thick rushes; her brothers, when the family lived down here near the Bog, had had their own boat and caught fish, and sometimes Nicolai and Dmitri had taken her along with them. She lay now, sleepless, feeling the vessel cradling her on the river flow, and at times the current was as though washing through her, washing away the great animal fear. But when the fear for a moment was gone, an ache of emptiness pervaded, of utter solitude on this earth. No one, no one. And if she tried to reach for an image of someone, even Yuri, he became like a distant tiny figure carried away on the current below her, until she was tempted to roll herself over the side of the boat and lose herself in the water. But the life instinct, Tanya told herself, prevented her from doing this. "They don't intend us to live; not one of us should remain alive." This kept becoming stronger in her. That which had meant the least in her life, the Jewish part, now claimed her. Perhaps because it was linked to death. In creeping her way back to Cherezinka, it was to some link that she was making her way, as though the place itself, where generations of her family had lived and died, was her link to existence. But if in all those villages the destroyer had come, then surely also to Cherezinka. And there she was known to everyone; surely some Ukrainian would point her out as the last living Jew. It was as though having failed in dying in Kiev with her family, she must offer herself again. She thought of her early schoolmate Irina, whose father had been made manager of the sugar mill by Papushka. Irina's family lived in a house that stood by itself near the factory.

There, hanging laundry in the backyard, was Irina's mother,

who did not recognize Tanya but squinted and asked, "What do you want?" And then, at Tanya's expression, stifled an exclamation and hastily drew her into the kitchen.

The story told, the woman wept. Ah, here in Cherezinka, too, a clean sweep had been made—she drew in her lips—no harm had been meant by the expression. But not such a horror massacre as Tanya told of. When the Rumanians had first come, they had killed some, that was true, and had burned down the wooden synagogue where a few old men still used to worship. With many Jews inside, it was said. She herself had not gone near. Then a vast German army with enormous panzers had swept through, everything on wheels, on iron tracks; it was said they were now already at Rostov. Soon after those German panzers went through, all remaining Jews had been rounded up and taken across the Bog into Trans-Dniestria. A few stole back at times. Across the river, they said, they were in special labor camps for only Jews, where life was very hard. Some came, trying to dig up money they had buried away, trying to hide themselves with peasants.

Then, studying Tanya, Irina's mother became silent as one deciding it is best not to say more. She led the girl to Irina's room, where for the day she could remain hidden. Irina was at the mill, where her father had her work in his office, as the Rumanian officers were devils with nothing else on their minds, they had perfumes, silks, already several of Irina's friends had been seen walking with them—and on and on the woman talked of her troubles as though all this were worse than anyone could know, but at last she left the room, and Tanya lay on the covers of the bed.

When Irina came home with her father, it was decided best for Tanya not to come down to eat with them since at all hours workers from the sugar refinery came with their problems. But Irina brought up stuffed cabbage, and later the father also came up; he sat and pondered and at last raised his head as though he had found the rule that applied: It would be best for Tanya to go to her own.

Her own? Irina sounded frightened.

There was one he had thought of. Did Tanya perhaps recall Zalman the Shoemaker?

In that remote life when she had been a child here, there were beautiful boots of three colors in the softest leather, made privately, outside the cartel, for such as Papushka and other high comrades.

Zalman the Shoemaker had been spared. High Rumanian officers had at once demanded boots of him, giving him papers as a worker essential to the war. The best plan would be for Tanya to go to Zalman. Irina would take her early in the morning when few people were yet about; they would be unnoticed, simply two girls going to market.

Before they slept, Irina chattered worriedly. Perhaps it would still be better for Tanya to go to some other town where she was not known and get work as a Ukrainian girl in an officers' mess; they always needed girls—but then she bit her lip. She started to talk of boys and recalled Tanya's handsome brothers. But when Tanya said both had been killed at the front, her friend at last fell silent.

Now Tanya recalled. Her Bobeh had spoken of Zalman the Shoemaker; he had known her cousin Leah.

Examining Tanya closely, Irina's mother even brought from her room her precious rouge compact, so as to give the girl more the Ukrainian red-cheeked appearance. The father pressed five rubles into Tanya's hand.

They set off, Irina's mother watching them fixedly from the yard. On the street a few soldiers made inviting sounds. Without being stopped, they arrived—but Tanya knew this house well! When she was small and went walking with her grandmother, Bobeh had often pointed out to her this courtyard building that had once been a Koslovsky possession. Part of the family had lived here, Bobeh used to say, the ones who had gone to Palestine. The same Big Leah, when she was still a growing girl.

On each side of the courtyard entrance was painted a large yellow star, and atop it the words "Jewish House." Sensing a trepidation in Irina, Tanya said, "No need for you to come further. No. Truly."

"Perhaps, not to attract too much attention—" But if anything seemed amiss, Tanya must simply say that she came for shoes. "And return to us, we'll find another solution." Irina gave her a quick troubled kiss.

The courtyard Tanya well remembered. All around had been workshops. Several were boarded up, but a carpenters' kolkhoz was still there, and also just to the right, the shop with the little display window behind which stood a beautiful pair of boots.

Zalman, the leatherworker, had a rim of white hair, his eyes blinked, but looking down at her feet, he whispered, "I know you." Hastily he led Tanya behind to the kitchen; there his wife, Beileh, peering with the same pinched eyes, also recognized her. But the wife had a bitter mouth. At Tanya's story she kept nodding her head as though every evil were known, expected, and this were but further confirmation.

This house, too, had seen the slaughter; in the first wave of killing the Rumanians had left the yard strewn with corpses. Neighbors whom they had known for years, children who had played at the shop door. But luckily their own sons and daughters had grown and left Cherezinka, two in Moscow, one in Leningrad. Zalman himself told how twice in his life he could have left—he could have gone off with her cousin Reuven and her cousin Leah; he too had been a young Zionist in those days. And again in the Revolution, when Leah had returned to gather young people, he had brought together for her a group of Zeire Zion, but he himself had remained here; it was a family matter.

He could have left! the wife broke in, and Tanya saw it was a lifelong argument. The bootmaker's wife, like Papushka, had been convinced that Jews must be part of the Soviet Revolution. "And if you had gone!" the wife demanded. "You think that now your Zionists will escape, there in Palestine, in their British colony?" Oh, she knew her geography. Although in her day Jewish daughters got no schooling, in the Revolution she had learned. The same Nazis who had swept through here were already in the Caucasus and would sweep on through Turkey and down through Syria, and they would arrive in Palestine, and with them would arrive their special death's-head troops to wipe out the Jews. And at the opposite end of Palestine the same invincible Germans were already sweeping into Egypt, they would cross the famous Suez Canal like a ditch, and then the two Nazi armies, from north and south, would meet in Jerusalem! "And there in your Palestine they won't even spare a bootmaker!" she cried at her husband, her bitterness triumphant.

"There at least the Jews will fight."

She snorted. Then suddenly the wife returned to their own problem of the moment: This girl must have been seen entering the shop.

452

What then? A Ukrainian schoolgirl. For shoes.

They had best go back into the shop then.

Tanya's broken shoes were truly dreadful; at least he would provide her with something for her feet, Zalman said. She must not remain here in Cherezinka. She must go to a larger place, perhaps Kishinev. The safest, his wife put in from behind the door, would be to take service the way other Jewish girls were saving themselves, posing as Ukrainians. If caught as a Jew, she would be shipped across the Bog; tens of thousands were dying there in Trans-Dniestria in guarded camps, without food, without medicine, in raging epidemics.

Perhaps Beileh's plan was best, Zalman said. A life saved must not be wasted. Then, lowering his voice, he began to speak in great haste, while his hands kept molding her feet, then marking her sole on paper. God had sent her! God had spared her and sent her for a task! His voice shrank to a whisper. Though he was not an observant Jew, there was a God! She must find her way into Rumania itself, she must try to reach Constanta, from Constanta it was said there were still ships, there was still an underground, the Jews of Rumania proper had not been deported to Trans-Dniestria, she must find a contact— Wait! He hurried to a corner and quickly returned with a furtively held postcard. Here! Tanya examined it, puzzled. It was postmarked from Turkey, with Turkish stamps, addressed in Russian to Zalman Gurevitz, here in this house in Cherezinka.

"You see how it is signed?" He pointed. *Ezra*. He repeated the postcard's message, a word of greeting from the family Moledet. "We hope this finds you in good health and would be happy to hear from you." "But do you know what this means? In Hebrew, Ezra means help. The family Moledet, it means from there, from the homeland." The postcard had come some time before the invasion; he was certain it was "from them," a contact to Zionists in Istanbul. They must have found his name on an old list of Zeire Zion; perhaps even her cousin Leah had given it to them!

An ordinary open postcard, a family greeting.

She must go, he whispered, she must somehow reach the outer world to reveal what was happening here, for it could not be that the world really knew. What had happened in Kiev had now happened in Odessa; twenty-five thousand Jews had been massacred. And there was more that he would tell her, because for this task, to make all this known to the world, Tanya had been spared. She must do it!

"Hear me. There will come later today a Rumanian medical officer. He has told me much. Everything. Out of his own conscience. Yes, a Rumanian with a conscience, perhaps because he is a doctor. Also some of them hate the Germans. Hear me. Only to those who have a part in it, among them, is this truth revealed about the Jews. It is called the State Secret. He has been troubled in his soul at the things he knows and is forced to see. I don't believe in the Jewish God, but sometimes an event happens that— who knows? Some call it the working out of history. I don't believe in Hegel or Marx either." Swiftly, with a sharp tool he was cutting out the sole. "But what sent you here? It is you who must reach the outer world as rapidly as possible, for every day tens of thousands die. You must tell what is happening. The State Secret is the planned total extermination of the Jews. You hear? All. From you, from one who has crawled out from the mass of dead, the outside world will perhaps believe. For in the State Secret it is calculated also that even if the world hears rumors, it will not believe." He paused, then said. "You were spared for this alone. To bring proof." His eyes, with an intense luster, were fastened on her. Was he insane? But had she not seen?

Even if she reached the outer world, who would believe her, a young girl? And would the world fight any harder against Hitler so as to save the Jews?

But it was not for her to ask, to decide this question. She must impart all he was telling her.

When the Rumanian army entered Cherezinka, Zalman said with his gruesome smile tight over his teeth, what they did was still a pogrom. A bloody pogrom, yes, such as only Rumanian brutality could produce—not simply the drunken beatings and plain hatchet murders of the Ukrainians. Did she know what the Rumanian Iron Guard had done one night in Bucharest? No, of course, how could she know? They had seized hundreds of Jews, among them the most important in the city, dragged them to the cattle slaughterhouse, and when the Iron Guard was finished, those Jews had been found hanging from meat hooks, their heads cut off, their naked bodies stamped "Kosher." The heads were in the iron barrels used for the heads of slaughtered animals; thus, they had been identified.

Then how, Tanya pleaded, could she hope to do something through Rumania?

She must listen. In Rumania there was still a government; after the pogrom the Iron Guardists had been held back so that those Jews who survived could live. But where the Germans took command, the State Secret was being enforced. Not one Jew was to survive. Not one. Not he himself or such as he, for when full use had been made of them, they too would be killed.

With the Rumanians here in Cherezinka even a few months ago, after their troops had finished their first killings, bribes and money began to work. But when the Germans came, quickly they instructed the Rumanians—searches, deportation, labor camps, death. The State Secret. This was what the world must be told. It had all been written and vowed by Hitler. Had she not seen, in Kiev, the ones with their special insignia, a death's-head, a skull? The SS.

On the last field. They.

Leaning in as he fitted the leather, as if the utterance he was now making could release all evil, he whispered, "These death troops are called Einsatzgruppen. A special task. Their task is the death of the Jews."

Into this house had been moved the few temporary exceptions, special craftsmen and others useful to them, a few dozen Jews out of the three thousand who had lived in Cherezinka. Perhaps he had been spared for just this, by fate, to wait for her. His eyes lifted, held hers. The strange luster was gone. They were everyday eyes. Then he darted to the rear of the shop, and from a hiding place below a heap of scraps the shoemaker brought her two gold coins. Working rapidly, he concealed the coins between layers of leather at the instep. "The heels they search." With final insistence Zalman instructed her. For a young girl things were possible. She must do anything, did she understand, anything to live, to make her way to Istanbul. Now she must memorize the Istanbul address on the postcard. She was an intelligent girl; she had been through death itself; this was now her mission. For this, destiny, history, had brought her here.

A change, a softening came in his gaze; he was a silver-haired Jew who understood even the most desolate need of all, the need that kept pulling her powerfully downward to be swallowed in the earth, in the water. "My child, you now have a reason to live,"

455

Zalman said to her. "If you reach Eretz, greet your cousin Leah for me. Chaver Zalman."

Tanya heard an automobile entering the courtyard. "Sit, sit quietly. Take off one shoe." Zalman went to the door; there entered a Rumanian officer of middle age, with a protruding belly; on his cap was a medical insignia. Though the officer already wore fine, highly polished boots, Zalman at once brought him the newly finished pair, even more elegant. While fitting these on, they conversed. Once the officer glanced at her, a long glance; she kept her eyes turned away.

At last the Rumanian stood up in his new boots to leave, Zalman carrying the others behind him. As Tanya heard the automobile drive away, the bootmaker hurried in and told her what she must do. In half an hour she must be standing by the road where it turned toward the provisional bridge. This officer, as he approached in his automobile, would see her and take her in. He could not have taken her from here, the Jewish house, as his driver would then know. But on the road there often stood Ukrainian girls, it would not be unusual.

As she waited by the road, a farm wagon came, behind it a cluster of Jews. The wagon was heaped with bundles; atop, a few haggard ancients lay huddled, hardly distinguishable from the baggage. Two guards herded the procession; this must be a last sweeping of Jews caught hiding. She watched them pass, among them several children with drawn, grayish faces. The cortege went onto the bridge, which was made of boats lashed together, with planks on top.

Then Tanya saw the officer's automobile; it halted just beyond her. She ran to the opened rear door. Surely for the driver to hear, the captain asked where she was going. Tanya said her village had been destroyed, her family had died, and she was on her way to her aunt in Bessarabia.

At the bridge the sentry half glanced into the auto and made a salute like the Germans. In his glance she had been seen, nothing, a girl. And a spark arose in Tanya: The knowledge, the mission she now carried within her, none of them could see.

Beneath the car the lashed boats undulated. The Rumanian placed an arm around her. For his driver.

As the automobile caught up to the Jews on the bridge, the driver pressed the horn unendingly. "Damned vermin!" The people tried to run, bunching forward against the wagon; then came a scream. Tanya saw a figure, a woman; in the panic she had slipped over the edge of the bridge, her skirt caught on something, for a moment she hung there head down, and then the body plunged and was carried away. Amid the outcries, the wailing, the captain's driver kept on pressing his horn.

Approaching the other shore, Tanya saw broken sections of the former bridge and lines of men carrying huge logs on their shoulders. "Two months, and look where they are!" the driver sputtered. "Lousy Zhids, never worked in their lives."

As they reached the embankment, the cortege of Jews jumped aside, their wagon at once got out of the way, and the car sped on. Under a light snow, a twilit beauty prevailed, as of a final desertion of the earth after all human evil had been accomplished. With dark, the car came to an undestroyed village and turned into a yard where a sentinel held a red-dimmed flashlight. An inn for officers. A young one glanced at her, made a remark to her captain in Rumanian, and they laughed a male laugh.

He led her to a room upstairs; Tanya stood until he told her to sit. The driver came with the captain's valise, saluted, with a smirk at her, and left. There was a lighted stove. The captain took off his jacket and necktie, then declared to her in a lowered voice, "Do not mistake me. I have no use for Jews. But I consider myself a humanitarian. I am a Christian. For the murder of our Saviour, the Jews were doomed to wander the earth, a despised people, but they were not doomed to be wiped off the face of the earth."

She said nothing.

He gave her soap and asked if she had lice.

A large Ukrainian woman, motherly, brought in a feast— borscht, cutlets, tea, even cake, and a bottle of wine. He did not urge the wine on her. He talked again about his humanitarian views.

After the meal he said he was going downstairs. She looked extremely tired; she could go to bed if she wished.

Tanya lay atop the feather quilt; she was in the little fishing boat; all transparent, it was rowed by the shadows of her brothers.

When she awoke to the daylight, the officer lay in a drunken sleep, he had not used her. His clothes were strewn; his pistol holder hung on the chair.

In the car, with a leather map case on his knee, the captain told her he would be making some inspections. At first they drove down the main highway, at times standing aside for long convoys passing forward, huge military trucks and panzer tanks such as had entered Kiev, all going onward, onward into the Soviet land. "Do you know how far they are already? To the Volga!" her captain cried out.

Their car turned onto a sideroad, onto ruts of snow-crusted mud, the driver cursing; farther on, men were filling the ruts with stones, they jumped aside for the vehicle. Most were gray-stubbled. A few of them still had tattered jackets; the rest were in shirts; some she saw wore only wretched carpet slippers on bare feet.

Before a barbed-wire gate the car halted, then entered a yard with half-smashed buildings, once a kolkhoz, she saw. From a structure with most of the roof fallen in, a lesser officer appeared, reporting to the captain, who did not get out of the car. Through the broken wall Tanya saw animal stalls; an old woman holding an infant lifted her eyes and met Tanya's. The captain was writing down numbers on a chart paper; she heard the word "typhus." Then, as they drove out, he said typhus was spreading in these camps; it could spread to the troops; these camps must be liquidated. She supposed he meant the people—the Jews—must be moved.

They reached another highway, passed through another undamaged village where people moved about as though nothing had happened in the world. Farther on he made more inspections. In one camp, Tanya saw a pile of corpses, a pit being dug; the captain got out to make sure all was properly sprinkled with lye. A short way farther, behind more barbed wire, she saw a column of smoke laced with flames. Within the enclosure the car halted before something she had not yet seen. Thick, fire-streaked smoke came from layer on layer of logs; figures moved about, tending the fire. An overseer stepped to their car; he was all in a black leather uniform, and this time her captain got out of the car and, giving the Nazi salute, said, "Heil Hitler!" This other officer was a German. The two walked to the pyre, the captain nodding and nodding as the German explained. They halted, and Tanya could see there a trench of yellowish bodies, skin-covered bones, and from the long trench men working in pairs, at the head, at the legs, were pulling out bodies and placing them crosswise on the top layer of logs. Then over the layer of bodies the men again crisscrossed logs, and again bodies, crisscross, crisscross.

The captain and the Nazi returned to the car, the captain once more saluted Heil Hitler and got in. His driver squirmed around, on his face an excitement, a kind of awed appreciation. "The newest method," the captain said, picking up his chart and drawing a line across an item on the list. The entire camp here had had to be liquidated, and this was a new sanitary way. "A demonstration." It left no traces.

Not long afterward they came to another river; again a smashed bridge. The driver turned onto an embankment road that would take them to a ferry crossing, he said. They had not gone far when a cluster of figures rose up from a side ditch, making hesitant signs of appeal, and as one of them stepped forward, a white-haired man with a goatee, Tanya saw that like the others, he was naked, except for a piece of underwear, and barefoot. For a shuddery instant she seemed at Babi Yar. The captain ordered the driver to stop; in a clumsy Ukrainian, while gesturing to the river, the spokesman said they were from the other side, Rumanian Jews from Cernauti, they had been taken across here on a raft. He pointed, and indeed on the opposite side was a raft. They had been too many, he said, and those who could not crowd onto the raft had been shot and pushed into the river. The rest, arriving here, had been stripped of everything, the food they carried, even their clothes, as the officer could see; they had been told that another set of guards would come, and take them to a resettlement camp. But here they had been left for five days now, exposed to the freezing nights. They had tried to beg food, water, shelter, from nearby peasants and been driven off. The spokesman gestured—behind the ditch lay their dead, several naked corpses of aged men and women, and apart, a mother holding a dead infant.

The captain said he would send someone. And indeed some miles farther where the car reached a bridge he gave instructions. As they crossed the Dniester, he said to Tanya with a touch of relieved distaste that they were at last out of Trans-Dniestria. To his driver he said, "I have decided to take our little friend to Bucharest to buy her some clothes." The driver snickered.

It was night when they reached a military compound just inside the city. Here the captain dismissed the driver, who gave her a last smirk, as though one day they would do business, the two of them. The captain himself took the wheel, driving through the looming black city; Tanya saw only red slits of vehicle lights; then the car came to a halt. "Here you will find some of your own," he said, and instructed her: the third landing, to the right, Professor Ianescu, but under no circumstances was she to reveal how or through whom she had reached Bucharest.

An impulse welled in Tanya; after all, he had taken her at his own risk. She wanted to touch the man's hand. As he leaned across opening the door for her, in a ghost of light from the dashboard, she caught on his face a look compounded of a kind of revulsion and yet pity; he pulled away his hand. Tanya whispered, the words coming unprepared, "And yet you are human." The car drove away.

After mounting a dim bluish stairway, she pressed the bell; after a long moment a presence was behind the door, and a thin, oldish voice said a word in Rumanian. The question was repeated, higher, in anxiety, and Tanya spoke a Rumanian word she had learned, "Please."

Another person, she heard, a woman; the two discussed, a bolt was drawn back, and the door opened narrowly on a chain. A man's face peered at her; he had a white goatee like that naked Jew across the Dniester. Behind, Tanya glimpsed a woman, also old, very frail, with pale hair, wearing thick glasses; they seemed to be losing their fear of her. Suddenly it came to Tanya to try her foreign language from high school, and she asked, *"Parlez-vous français?"* with the woman guessing words, helping her, she explained she had escaped from where all Jews were being killed. Someone—she could not reveal, they understood—had brought her to this house and given her the professor's name.

They let her in. The woman seemed feeble and lay down on a couch.

Tanya spoke somehow more understandably; all, all she told. The ravine outside Kiev. The pyres in Trans-Dniestria made of logs and Jews. Her task to the outside world.

He would try to help her, the professor said. After many years of teaching in the medical school he was dismissed; they had been moved from their apartment—only now Tanya saw that the room was crowded with stored furniture. In the morning he would see what might be done. Whoever it was—perhaps one of his former students, but he assured her he was not curious—had brought her—he smiled wanly—to the right address.

In the morning the professor walked with her, it was not far, to an apartment house courtyard. Already he had explained that a boat was being organized, to try to reach Palestine; here she would find a Zionist youth group that was allocated places on the ship. She must understand that few such boats succeeded. The British would not allow more Jews to enter Palestine, and they might seize the vessel and send the refugees to their own concentration camp. But in the British camp at least the Jews would be neither starved nor killed. Many wealthy Jews had bought places on the ship. He himself—as she had seen, because of his wife's condition, such a difficult voyage was out of the question. The Rumanian government did not oppose the departure of these vessels, they were glad to get rid of Jews, and at the least—as she so wanted in order to accomplish her task—she should arrive as far as Istanbul.

He led her up to a kind of office where a young man named Joel was in charge. Escaped from Russia itself! The youth leader spoke Russian, his parents had come from there long ago, in the Revolution, and he kept interrupting her with questions. This bootmaker —even in the Ukraine he had received the postcard from Istanbul? She absolutely had to reach that address! Yes—almost before Tanya had spoken of the State Secret—he was convinced that Hitler planned to annihilate every Jew. But she was the first eye-witness to bring complete information. There was still time to arouse the world! He gazed at her, the warm, enveloping gaze of a comrade who says, "Well done, tovarich!"

Until now the mass killings in Kiev, in Odessa, had been claimed as retaliations. In Odessa Jews were declared to have signaled to Russian war planes. In Kiev Jews were responsible for the vast explosions. After all, in Poland the Jews had simply been resettled for their own protection in walled ghettos. So the Nazis declared, Joel said. But at the start of the war an officer from Berlin was known to have come here to Bucharest, a specialist on the Jews. A Captain Eichmann, the same who was known to the Jews of Vienna as the specialist in Jewish affairs. In Vienna he had only liquidated all their possessions. But here in Bucharest he must have come to set in motion the liquidation of the Jews themselves —what she called the State Secret. Indeed, it was rumored that in Yugoslavia, conquered only a few months before the assault on Russia, the mass shooting of Jews had already taken place. And that the same Eichmann had appeared there.

Tanya followed the young man to a room filled with cots and sleeping sacks; there were a dozen young people, girls, boys, and their clear, unfrightened eyes suddenly brought back her Komsomol. Everything since then—could it have happened?

Joel announced her name, Tanya. "Who among you speaks Russian? Ukrainian? French?" Two girls spoke a little French, they would help her. One of them, Pnina, would teach her Hebrew.

Day after day all of them were constantly repacking their rucksacks, going out and returning with small packages of biscuits, of prunes, a triumph! Or they were studying or holding discussions. Tanya tried to become interested. She had to learn that among Zionists things were complicated; there were factions, just as in the history of the great Soviet Revolution. This group belonged to the socialist labor movement of the Zionists, but the boat was being organized by rivals called Revisionists; no matter, there was co-operation against the British, who tried to stop the boats. Though the British were fighting Hitler, and Palestine Jews fought in their army, the same British fought Jews who tried to reach Palestine. This was because Palestine had been long inhabited by Arabs— sparsely, Joel insisted—and now certain Arab leaders, fanatic Moslems, wanted no more Jews in the land. Yet it was the British who ruled Palestine and had promised the League of Nations they would help Jews come there. Only now they were against this. Not that the Arabs were with the British in the war. On the contrary, the chief Arab leader, called the Mufti, was an ally of Hitler. He wanted to kill Jews.

It seemed to Tanya that she had at times, before the war, read in her Komsomol paper that the Jews wanted to take Palestine away from the Arab people. "No, no, we want to live with them in peace," she was told. A cheerful, energetic girl with reddish hair, called Gingi, instructed her. Gingi was a special friend of Joel— his chaverah they called it.

Though they all had great warmth, Tanya did not as yet feel at one with the group, as in her Komsomol. She took part in the kitchen work and housework and tried to study Hebrew, but sometimes fell into long silent spells. Remembering. Gingi said she ought to write everything down; it would help her, and one could not be sure what would happen to them. For several days Tanya wrote. It seemed all this was not about herself. Gingi took the sheets to Joel who would make sure the record was in safe hands should anything happen to them on their boat.

There came a night of jubilation, bursts of song; in the morning they would be taking a special train to Constanta to board their ship!

All night they were repacking. Tanya had been given a rucksack and clothing from the girls; they insisted they had too much and also pressed on her packets of food.

The voyage to Istanbul would hardly take more than a day, they said. Certificates of immigration to Palestine for all of them were waiting in Istanbul, and from there to the homeland would take only a few more days. The *Struma* had a powerful brand-new engine.

Joel had arranged everything perfectly; a truck came, but they must not sing going through the streets, and by eight o'clock they were at a small railway station outside Bucharest, and there they beheld a long train waiting for the passengers for the *Struma*, fifteen cars they counted, even two sleeping wagons for the richest. Taxis began to arrive, horse-drawn carriages, trucks with other youth groups, here was even a group smuggled from Hungary. Hundreds and hundreds of people; children, even some mothers with baby carriages. Suddenly one of those black instants went through Tanya—this was the gathering crowd of Jews in Kiev in the street that led to Babi Yar. But the black image passed as Gingi pointed out an enormous, somehow comical fat man, a Greek who owned the boat and was charging a fortune to the rich. He was everywhere, talking to police officers, to army officers, to officials, to passengers, reassuring, explaining, laughing.

There were inspections of documents; she had only one, given her by Joel, on the letterhead of a Jewish orphanage, with official-looking stamps and signatures, saying her family had been killed in a bombardment. She needn't worry, everything for their group had been arranged, Joel said, and the Rumanian officials would pay no attention to her.

At last they mounted the train. All day and into darkness it did not move. Officials again and again examined papers. Perhaps they would yet take her off the train? At least Joel had safely hidden away what she had written. Cries and singing awoke her—the train had moved! In the morning, peering behind the edges of the blinds, they saw the port of Constanta. As the train halted, great news burst in: America had just entered the war!

Now Hitler was doomed! What an omen for their voyage!

Hitler's ally, Japan, had suddenly attacked the American navy. The war still would take time. But—America!

Her mission now was even more urgent, Joel said, for there were six million Jews in America. Once the State Secret was known, America would put a stop to Hitler's massacre.

Four whole days they remained still locked on the train, while officials searched everyone, taking hidden money, jewels, watches from wrists, extra clothing, all extra food. Each day that America did not know, thousands more were being slaughtered. But at last they could go to their vessel.

How could it hold all these hundreds of people? And on its sides, painted-over cracks could be seen. Many of the wealthy ones drew back; on the rough sea it would surely sink! They turned on a young man who, Gingi explained, was the Revisionist who had arranged with the Greek for the boat. But never mind, what choice was there? Joel led them down, down ladders; at the bottom of each ladder were people pressing to go up; in the murk one saw tiers of boards, people were squirming into their places, Joel cried out, here was their section, they were near the hatch, not too badly off for air. Looking up, some would even be able to glimpse the sky.

She had only to reach Istanbul, to reveal, to tell the State Secret. America would send giant bombers to destroy Berlin. For this she had been saved in the fusillade; for this she had crawled from Babi Yar.

※ ※ ※

Crowding at the window of their flat that gave onto the Bosporus, taking turns using the binoculars, Menahem and the three chevreh watched the vessel with decks aswarm being towed into the small harbor across the water. Police boats darted around her, but at least she was afloat. Three days and nights they had agonized over the *Struma*. When the call telling them the vessel had finally sailed had come from Bucharest, they had been jubilant. Even if it was a Revisionist ship—seven hundred and sixty-nine souls! After thirty hours with no word, no sign, the worries began. She was an old tub, a riverboat that the Fat One, the Greek, had salvaged from the Danube, and the wintry Black Sea was rough. Even creeping, she should by now have crossed. In each of them, though they did not yet speak of it, was last month's nightmare,

464

the *San Salvador* that had foundered on the rocks near the entrance to the Bosporus, and their ghastly race in taxis to rescue what they could from the raging waters. The freezing hours of plunging, clutching, towing what proved to be corpses. Out of three hundred and sixty aboard, hardly a hundred survivors.

Yesterday Menahem had taken the ferry that plied up the Bosporus and then a bus from the farthest stop. He carried an empty sack, like anyone from town out to buy provender, perhaps fish, and then from the end of the line walked as far as the Black Sea, the closed area. It was a windy, dismal day, and periodically came the mournful call of the lighthouse siren and, like a dismal echo, the warning toll of the minefield floats.

At the fishermen's huts there had been no word of any vessel sighted.

On the *Struma*, too, the minefield warnings could be heard. Her engine again out of order, the vessel was adrift; though the sea had calmed the ship was slowly borne on the tide, irrevocably closer to the warning buoys now becoming visible. Panic, screaming! There were struggles at the ladders, the group monitors strove to restore control, the deck became so crammed there was danger of being pushed overboard. At the single lifeboat men fought until a tight ring of guards from a youth-group was established, keeping the boat for mothers and children. Monitors were trying to control the handing out of lifebelts; there wouldn't be half enough. Louder and louder, as though the terrified people were become a single organism, the screaming coalesced into a unified enormous howl. Perhaps it would be heard on shore.

Tanya tied on the circlet of wooden blocks that Gingi reached out to her; she would not join the scream. At daylight she had mounted with the group for their fresh air turn on deck, and then the tolling began to be heard, and the panic started. Her body was pinned in the crowd; she could only fixedly watch the drift of the vessel.

The question had lain in her all this time, what was meant, what was intended in her being still alive? Or was creation only utterly erratic? From whence her impelling will to creep from among the bodies in Babi Yar? Each further step had to be taken through self-will, but once she boarded the ship she was carried. When the engine had first broken down with the vessel still in

Rumanian waters she had felt violent anger, as though fate was itself the enemy, thwarting her after all she had done; but then a bitter almost impersonal curiosity had come upon her as to the outcome. At last mechanics had arrived on a tugboat; to pay for the engine to be repaired, women had to hand over their wedding rings. Tanya had removed one gold coin from her shoe. When the engine started again she had accepted this as still another reprieve: perhaps an evil fate did not entirely rule. But now she would not take part in the screaming. She would only let herself be carried. She would even let herself be carried by this circlet of wooden blocks, if that was part of the grotesque intention for her. But scream she would not.

A motorboat flying a crescent and star churned toward them. The screams halted.

In the two days since they had watched the Turkish tug pulling the ship into the sealed harbor across the water, no one, not even Istanbul's Shimon Brod, with all his connections, had been able to arrange contact with the vessel. Menahem made the rounds of seamen's bars, but no sailor had come off the *Struma*. The Jewish Agency representative, Chaim, from his little office in the Pera Palace, had used every sympathetic acquaintance among the diplomats, only to be treated with surprise, as though surely he knew more than they about this situation. Calls offering united efforts to the Revisionist leader in Istanbul, Zaccaria, brought his usual style of guarded response: It was best not to confuse matters with too many intercessions.

In the crisscross of the Mossad's operation it was Ruthie who usually approached the British. But this time Major Pennfield jested, What, old girl! *She* was asking *him* for information!

There the ship sat, with her hump of added cabins on the afterdeck, tied between two other impounded vessels, but those were empty. From calls that had got through to Bucharest, Menahem even knew of some who were aboard, wealthy leaders of the community, the president of Rumania's Revisionists, dozens of doctors, engineers, businessmen, and a whole gamut of youth groups, including the Mossad's.

That morning, as he peered through the glasses, he uttered a cry. From the ship they were signaling with flags. Menahem spelled out the letters. E - A - U. Could they even be out of drinking water! The signals continued. Food. Medicine. Save us!

Across the Bosporus, the great city with its minarets faced the ship, and when dark came and the patterns of streetlights appeared, a lighted city at peace, omitted from the war, the vision drew the heart out of you. There before your eyes. Even the bridge dotted with lights, crossing to the city—to you unattainable. But still the sight gave hope. And after the first days food began to arrive. Oranges, perhaps grown in Palestine itself and each wrapped in tissue! In addition to the golden fruit, at last a bit of tissue paper, even if it could hardly help against the slime and stench that pervaded the vessel. And food—twice a day two handfuls of peanuts to each person. And surely now that the world knew of their plight, things were being done! Even half a cup of milk and some crackers for each child, and on another day small portions of bread that the Jews of Istanbul must have contributed out of their own rations.

On the motorboat bringing the provisions stood two policemen, and two more were stationed on their ship, not unfriendly men but silent, with fixed smiles; contact was forbidden to them.

Another day there was a great excitement. A pair of officials came on board. Then a certain family was beheld entering the captain's cabin. An oil magnate. Intercession had been made, this family would be permitted to disembark and continue by rail to Palestine! Surrounded by authorities, they could hardly accept messages to carry, but once they arrived in Eretz—even tomorrow—the plight of the ship would be fully known! Every detail! Even about the twice-collapsed engine that had proved also to have been salvaged from a sunken wreck. Surely help would come!

The fine luggage of the oil magnate's family was passed down by crewmen to the official launch, and then they themselves, one by one, descended the ladder. Contact with the world would be established!

That night two young Betar boys brought out their accordions, and a lively atmosphere developed on deck, first with chalutz songs, then even Rumanian folk songs, and a tiny space was somehow cleared for a hora.

The very next afternoon a launch with a special flag was seen approaching—postal service! The entire population of the vessel surged to that side, and the deck slanted so dangerously that monitors pushed people back. Telegrams were delivered to the captain, one of them already from Palestine, sent by the United Rumanian Jews, addressed to all the people of the *Struma*. Courage! Every effort was being made!

Meanwhile, hundreds of outstretched hands were pressing letters on the postal official, but he was not authorized, he announced, to accept outgoing mail. Nevertheless, afterward, in some mysterious way, a few people obtained Turkish stamps and handed down letters to the boatmen who brought food. On the quiet Gingi told Tanya that the boat leader had agreed with Joel to include a few messages from their group, in a packet they could send out. Thus, Tanya could get in touch with the Istanbul address that had been on that postcard from "Ezra."

Her letter, in a packet smuggled to the Revisionist office, finally reached the Mossad apartment and Menahem. Thanking Ezra for his postcard, Tanya had written that she had recently "been with the family in Kiev and had much to tell of them." Also she wished to send greetings to her cousin Leah and the rest of the Chaimovitch family in Moledet.

Almost, as he held the bit of paper, Menahem could believe what clairvoyants must feel when they held an object in their hands and thus had knowledge of the owner. Too many inexplicable things happened in the world, you finally had to accept some degree, some unknown manner of intervention. At the same time he experienced a peculiar trepidation, as in the times when he had succeeded in sending out an arms shipment but was fearful whether it would arrive. Already the treatment of this vessel was not as with others. The British, of course, knew it was Revisionist-organized, probably even knew of their leaders who were aboard; in London the ship must be labeled as filled with Irgunist terrorists. There were rumors that the *Struma* would be turned back to the slaughterhouse of Europe.

"The family in Kiev." So this Tanya must have witnessed the massacre. Somehow Menahem had to find a way to see her.

Shimon Brod that same morning brought hope. For ten thousand Turkish pounds, two officers of the port would arrange to have the *Struma*'s engines repaired. Then the Turkish authorities might, as in previous instances, simply allow the vessel to continue on its way. Even if the British seized the ship once it reached the Mediterranean, eight hundred Jews would have escaped the Nazis.

Shimon could raise part of the bribe money, but the Jewish Agency would have to authorize the remainder.

Menahem proposed one small condition to the Turkish officers: that he be taken aboard as an additional repairman. He was a welding expert.

In work clothes, along with two mechanics, and escorted by special policemen, he headed for the ship. Though his Turkish was fluent, it was foreign; Menahem spoke little.

Eagerly the passengers made way for them. The captain himself, a Bulgarian, led them down the ladders into the deepening stench, slime, vomit. From the bunk shelves, the eyes even of those who had given themselves over totally to apathy followed their passage. In the bottom depths the ship's engineer, another Bulgarian, with defeated gestures showed a broken valve and places where the engine, from vibration, had come loose from its cement mooring. Alongside this Bulgarian stood a distinguished-looking passenger, his good clothes smeared, a civil engineer who had tried to make the repairs. To him Menahem found an opportunity to whisper, "I am from ours. I must speak to a young girl named Tanya Koslovsky, who came out of Kiev."

The civil engineer went off. Soon he returned, gesturing to the ship's engineer that he wanted to show the welder an oil drip from the tanks. Menahem followed him.

Crouched, cramped in the closed-off fuel compartment, the girl waited.

The straight brows, the round face—it was the Chaimovitch family! Dvora's own! The girl resembled his own children! Yet so as not immediately to overwhelm her with his relationship, Menahem first of all asked her to tell everything, all. And in a controlled factual tone, almost as a schoolgirl might recite a history lesson about Tamerlane's mountains of skulls, she told.

Of the ravine outside Kiev only vague rumors had reached Istanbul. A few months before, with the assault into Russia, there had come ghastly tales of Jews gathered in each village, each town, and slaughtered over mass graves. But in a large city, in tens of thousands!

And from the Rumanian sanitation officer: the State Secret. The planned total extermination. Everything that Menahem had for so long known in his depths. All came pouring from her. Special troops to slaughter Jews. Deportations, death areas, pyres of logs and of corpses; in an unearthly way he had known and awaited the details.

Now as she told of Cherezinka, the shoemaker, the postcard, he could tell her of their amazing coincidence: who he was to her.

For the first time the girl became pale. Menahem reached out, took her head, pressed it to him, stroked her hair, put his lips to her icy forehead. He himself was sobbing.

This one he must bring out. He would somehow bring her out, bring her home. For this child there could be no more cruelty. That could not be.

From the harbormaster, Shimon Brod brought an order: The additional mechanic would not again be permitted. Also, Brod said, the two who had taken the bribe could not be found.

Menahem wrote his report. The pattern could now be put together; the testimony from the Babi Yar survivor made all clear. The transfer of Jews into closed ghettos and concentration camps in Germany and Poland must now be seen as only a first stage; with the advance into Russia the second stage was begun. Mass slaughter. After the girl's escape from Kiev and the massacre of the Jews of Kiev, a Rumanian medical officer had, out of his own horror, told the survivor of the State Secret. The plan for total annihilation had been revealed to certain officers by a Nazi specialist sent to Bucharest to plan the destruction of the Jews. This information must now be combined with the report of a Polish Jew who a few months ago had escaped through Greece, and told of gassing vans being used at the concentration camp of Chelmno. The exhaust pipe was turned into the van loaded up with Jews, so that the van arrived with only corpses at the mass grave. The annihilation program long suspected was now in full process; the world must be aroused; rescue work must be intensified, for it was now clear that each rescued Jew was snatched from certain murder. Now that the United States had entered the war, this information—

Though the repairs were said to be progressing on the engine, for some days the two mechanics did not appear at all; they were waiting for a sack of cement, it was said. Meanwhile, two more passengers were taken from the ship and escorted by Turkish police to a train for Palestine. They possessed prewar immigration certificates.

That same day a woman lost her mind; she screamed incessantly.

Dysentery was spreading; of the thirty doctors and four pharmacists on the ship, none had any more medicine.

Mass meetings were held in Tel Aviv; cables were sent to London, to Washington. Palestine's two chief rabbis, Sephardic and Ashkenazic, appealed in person to the High Commissioner in Jerusalem. Week merged into week. The Mandatory Government declared that the *Struma*'s passengers could not be permitted into Palestine as there might be enemy spies among them. Then it was declared that the entry of nearly eight hundred persons would seriously overtax the country's already-strained food supply situation.

Mati came home sickened from remarks heard around the office. Let them through? You'd just be showing that England could be made to give in to a bunch of Jewish terrorists.

As never before, Dena felt Mati's torment, his held-down anger. Everyone else could at least cry out, organize meetings, Eddie Marmor could write editorials, but Mati had to go every day to the other side, to be among the British. She could even understand the Irgunists, the Stern gang, no wonder they sent letter bombs.

Even if he knew he was accomplishing things with war production, at times like this how could Mati contain his rage? Any day she feared his ulcer would perforate. What an inverted, awful way for a man to fight a war! Until a few months ago, when America got in, something had impeded her own anger toward the British. After all, they were standing alone. But to make such shameful excuses—food for a few hundred people! A strain on Palestine! As if every Jew in the Yishuv wouldn't share all he had! Besides, there was plenty of food! If a few items were short, you could get something else. It was one of those infuriating bland British lies— the way they handled "natives." And that insulting pretense about Nazi spies! As if the refugees weren't all known to one another, to their organizations!

And in the midst of all these insults thrown in the face of the whole Yishuv, Mati was frantically working on the newest danger, the Nazis with Rommel's panzers were barely being held; they were already inside the Egyptian border. Rommel was boasting he

471

would be in Cairo in a week! If they broke through—Farouk would welcome them, too! Correspondents were reporting that the British in Egypt were madly burning tons of documents, and Mati told Dena it was true. But not to get scared. The entire Haganah was secretly being recruited for a last stand here; the boys in a new unit, the Palmach, were getting quick commando training. No need for Dena to panic; in war you had to make plans for even the most unlikely contingency. If worse came to worst, the last stand would be on Mount Carmel—everyone was saying it. Like the story of Musa Dagh. A secret plan had been worked out for the entire Jewish population to be moved to the Carmel. Only who would come to the rescue? The American fleet?

When she and the kids drove with Mati to visit Kibbutz Brandeis, he went off with Dave Margolies for hours. No one spoke of it, but everyone knew. They were picking caves for secret stores of arms, hard rations, bombs, sabotage equipment, wireless senders. Even if the Nazi tanks rolled into Jerusalem—she must not shut her mind, she must recognize the possibility, and saw herself fleeing with the kids down Mamillah Road to the American Consulate— But America, too, was now the Nazis' enemy. Fleeing then, before they reached Jerusalem, to Haifa, to an American warship! Mati would never agree to leave, he'd stay on to the end. And U-boats. That enormous British airplane carrier had been sunk right here in the Mediterranean.

Dena stopped herself. She was a baby. Those hundreds on the *Struma* must be saved, and she was in a panic about herself. She wrote out a cable to Phil, Phil could even get to Roosevelt in person, she'd ask Eddie Marmor to rush out the wire. America must insist to the British; the refugees on the *Struma* must under no circumstances be sent back to Europe!

The High Commissioner's office announced that the children on the *Struma* would be permitted to enter Palestine. Those between eleven and sixteen.

The thought went through Dena, the twins were only nine.

Menahem hurried to Zaccaria. Had the list of children already gone to the British? Why? Zaccaria asked. One name must be added, from the youth group of the general Zionists. An orphan, Tanya Koslovsky. Sixteen.

Zaccaria wasn't sure. The British had specified "to sixteen." That could be interpreted as only up to the sixteenth birthday. "Then say she's fifteen!" There were no papers. Her parents had been killed. Still, Zaccaria hesitated. If one error were caught, surely Menahem knew the British, they were capable of canceling the entire list. In the end Menahem had to make the plea personal. Tanya Koslovsky was the last of his wife's family, escaped miraculously from the slaughter in Kiev.

But now, Mati called Dena in elation, all, all were going to be saved! The six-month certificate quota had just come through. Three thousand. Everyone on the *Struma* could become a legal immigrant!

Refused. No certificates could be allocated to persons from enemy lands.

However, in addition to children between eleven and sixteen, those under eleven would now be accepted as well.

The list of sixty-seven qualifying children had been forwarded to Ankara. All that was needed was for the Turks to authorize the descent of the children from the boat and their transfer to the train for Palestine. Day after day in the little apartment they waited the call from Epstein in Ankara.

Jerusalem got through. The Jewish Agency had just been informed that the *Struma* had been sent back into the Black Sea. Had the children been taken off?

No, no, Menahem replied, the *Struma* was still there before their eyes. The children had not yet been taken off.

The postal launch approached the vessel; a cable was handed up—from America. The boatleader, Yossi, the indomitable Irgunist, read it out, and translated. From the American Jewish leader, Rabbi Stephen Wise, who was the Jewish representative to President Roosevelt! "Don't lose hope. Two thousand certificates available. You will all be admitted to Palestine." They were saved!

Again Ruthie tried the CID. But Major Pennfield had no idea what could be holding things up in Ankara. The British had approved the list of children. Alas, she knew the dilatory ways of the Turks.

"Tell him we also know the ways of the English," Menahem

sputtered. Luckily, Ruthie had put her hand over the mouthpiece. Then she cajoled Pennfield. Perhaps he could call someone in Ankara? Perhaps Von Papen was interfering? "My dear girl, patience, patience."

Early on the twenty-third, all four crowded to the window. A swarm of police launches, a tugboat. With the binoculars, Menahem saw refugees wildly trying to beat off the boarding. A sheet was raised, H-E-L-P! Then the police were on deck, clubbing. Passengers were forced back to the hatchways, swallowed in the hold. The decks were clear. The tug was pulling the *Struma* away, back to the Black Sea.

In the midst of the sea, the tugboat cast off, leaving them. The ship radio for once was working, and the captain's voice came, announcing he would try to reach Burgos. If there was enough fuel. The engine started, all could hear. In an hour it halted, once more broken down. All night the *Struma* drifted.

In the morning the civil engineer and a few crewmen were still trying to repair the engine. The ship's engineer, shrugging, went aloft. Suddenly a rending explosion came and the *Struma* instantly sank.

At first the Turkish radio declared that more than half had been rescued. The vessel had been only six or seven kilometers from the shore.

Menahem, Ruthie, the boys, Shimon Brod, a few more Turkish Jews, in two taxis scoured the shore, the fishing villages, the rocks as far as the vehicles could proceed; then they ran afoot, clambering farther. Nothing.

Some days later it was announced that one young man had been saved, half-frozen, hanging onto a plank. The Turks were holding him under police guard in a coastal hospital.

The survivor said there had been a torpedo.

Some said that the Germans, with the war practically won, had persuaded the Turks, in the interest of good relations with the victors, to have a tug pull the shipful of Jews to a position where a submarine lurked in the Black Sea and abandon her to be torpedoed. Others said the *Struma* had struck a mine. The Revisionists declared it was the British who had sunk the refugee ship, from a secret battery of artillery that the Turks permitted them to maintain on the Black Sea coast. A broadcast from Rome declared that a Russian submarine had sunk the *Struma*; a broadcast from Moscow denied this and accused the Nazis. Rumor had it the Jews themselves had blown up their ship, rather than be delivered back into Nazi territory.

Many years afterward a Soviet submarine commander consulted his wartime logbooks and declared that in the time of the *Struma's* sinking, he had been in those Black Sea waters, under orders to fire on any unidentified vessel. In his entry for the twenty-fifth of February, he found a notation of having, in the morning, torpedoed an unidentified vessel.

And as an historical coincidence, it had by then become known that in those same weeks when the *Struma* had lain under guard opposite Istanbul, a highly secret conference had been in progress in Wahnsee, a suburb of Berlin, to coordinate what was called the Final Solution of the Jewish problem.

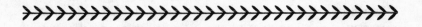

29

YOU HAD to squeeze your way through the corridor, and there was hardly room to stand against the walls of the conference hall; at least seven, eight hundred Jews must be here, Phil estimated; this session was even more crowded than for Chaim Weizmann. Yet though he went along with everything Ben-Gurion was saying, he didn't get from the platform that feeling you had from a world personality like Weizmann, nor was Ben-Gurion even halfway an orator like Rabbi Silver, who really stole the show. Still, in He-brew, B-G was supposed to be terrific. Probably the trouble was the language, because Ben-Gurion's English had a real Yiddish intonation, and even the way he talked made you think of some old-style union agitator from the West Side. So, wasn't that what he was, a union boss? But Mati claimed his vision was far above those early labor struggles, he had grown just as their labor ideas had grown in Palestine—their Histadrut was more than a union, it was a whole system, with complete medical care, with big factories they owned, and the kibbutzim, and even, according to Mati, their own wholesale marketing. Their system could be the future system of the whole world; even here in America the AFL might one day produce a President, and Phil wasn't against it, so long as it didn't become a dictatorship like Russia. But with a Jewish nation, as they were at last outright demanding, as this conference was certainly going to demand, and he, Phil, in the Chicago delegation would certainly add his vote to it, with Jews you didn't have to worry about any kind of dictatorship. Jews would always be split up into so many factions there would be a democracy. Even here at the Biltmore, every Zionist faction, from Mizrachi to the left Poale Zion, whatever that was, had somebody snagging you in the hallway, twisting your arm.

Then his attention was caught back, the shrill voice was strong, the chopping arm hit out each slogan; you forgot the intonation, you didn't see him small, but saw only the head that seemed larger and larger as though you had a loupe in your eye and the stone was shooting off light. Who had suffered more, who had fought harder, who was more in need than the Jews? A homeland, yes, but what was a homeland if you had no right to enter it? If shiploads of Jews, like the *Struma*, fleeing annihilation were ruthlessly sunk? Only full nationhood, only a nation with sovereign rights to bring in its people, with no White Paper restrictions, only a nation and not an appendage at the mercy of a mandatory power, could be a homeland!

And this, once and for all, cried the chief from Eretz, this must be the declaration of this conference, of American Jewry! Of all Jewry!

In the hall, as the meeting broke up, in the corridors, the slogans echoed. Why pussyfoot, why worry about England's reaction, weren't enough Jewish boys dying for England right now, and had America, had Roosevelt ever endorsed their damn British White Paper? Never!

All the insiders were saying Weizmann now had to take a back seat; he was too much of a compromiser with the British, though it seemed to Phil that Chaim Weizmann too was for nationhood. And B-G had taken the thunder from the Revisionist noisemakers who kept putting full page ads in the *Times* and yelling this was what they had been for all the time! Nationhood! Oh, Phil was onto them. What they were for was a nation that would start their own war to take over the other side of the Jordan from the Arabs. God, what a crazy people the Jews were. And the American Jewish Committee crowd still saying, pipe down, pipe down, don't antagonize the gentiles. Okay, let them stay out of this resolution! And all those that said, wait, wait, first win the war. The war was turning. Phil was convinced it was turning right now even if it still looked bad. The winter was gone, and the Nazis still hadn't made a dent in Stalingrad. The Russkis were holding the line, stuff was beginning to pile in for them, all the way from here around the back door through Persia; even though on the map things still looked bad with that Desert Fox Rommel threatening to shoot across Egypt into Palestine itself, no need to panic.

Phil could tell these chicken-hearts a thing or two from his own sister, Dena; she wouldn't budge from there with her kids! And besides, Phil knew plenty of stuff was being delivered there, too, big stuff being delivered to the British to knock out Rommel; it had taken some time, there had been plenty of bottlenecks, but U.S. industry was now churning at over capacity, and that would turn the war. He himself knew there had been a real bottleneck in cutting tools, industrial diamonds, scientists had even tried a crash program to make a synthetic substitute, but that smart little in-law of Mati's, Nahum, had foreseen the whole thing right from the start of the war, setting up industrial diamond cutting with some refugees from Amsterdam, and industrials were being flown all the way here, across the Atlantic. Nor could you beat family connections—Phil was doing fine. Even on this trip to New York he had combined the convention with a few business lunches, it would make Sherrill's eyes pop when she heard who were the giants that had practically come begging to him, but he wasn't making any black-market deals, the war effort was no place for it, he didn't need those call girls with the Vassar voices they had phoning him in his room, and anyway, business was terrific.

Ah, American Jewry had at last proclaimed itself for a Jewish state! And Ben-Gurion had at last boldly pronounced the goal, Menahem reflected somewhat wryly, for even here in Istanbul the Revisionist Zaccaria was fulminating about how Jabotinsky's enemies had only waited for his death, to take over his program! One day, he predicted, even Ben-Gurion's socialists would be demanding Trans-Jordan too, as a part of the State!

Alas, there would be neither Trans-Jordan nor even Palestine, if the Nazi pincers closed. They had opened their new drive into the Caucauses, and in North Africa, Rommel had at last taken Tobruk.

In that deadly summer, Menahem found himself virtually alone; the apartment had become hardly more than a listening post. Even Ruthie had been sent elsewhere—to Egyptian Jewry, he believed, to raise funds, though reports had it that trains from Egypt to Palestine were jammed with people fleeing the advancing Nazis.

Since the end of the *Struma*, no ships came. But the words of that poor girl, Tanya, never left his mind, for the State Secret of which she had spoken was slowly revealing itself. It had come to him again in a strange way. From a Swedish courier whose acquaintance he had cultivated, Menahem heard details, after which he could only lie silent in darkness, in immeasurable, powerless grief. The story was at second remove, yet he did not doubt its truth. The courier had himself heard it from a colleague in his service, who had been cautioned that it was yet in need of proof. On a train to Berlin, that courier had happened to sit next to an SS officer, a Nazi who had begun to talk, to tell of something on his conscience. Yes, a conscience-Nazi; for hours he had given details. He was the son of a pastor. His task was in the sanitation service— epidemic prevention, chemicals. But this young man had found his way there through a special interest in a humane program called euthanasia, administered to the hopelessly insane. He had heard of it a few years before, since an aunt of his, in an institution, had been administered this treatment. A closed ambulance was used, the selected patients "taken for a ride" as the Americans would put it, with carbon monoxide fumes entering the closed ambulance-bus from an upturned exhaust pipe.

Then, some months ago, the conscience-Nazi had heard that such gas vans were in use in the Lublin area, where Jews were being concentrated. And then he had got himself sent on a mission with respect to a certain problem. The carbon monoxide was too slow in its effect, particularly when large numbers of subjects had to be treated. He had been sent to a certain concentration camp, at Belzec. The idea of the gas vans had led to closed installations, chambers into which was piped the exhaust gas from stationary engines. He had witnessed the effect. When the doors were opened after perhaps half an hour, sometimes longer, there in the chamber was a standing mass of dead, many befouled, some women's menstrual blood released, many faces distorted in a last struggle to breathe. Entire families, mother, father, children, all naked, interlocked, a block of flesh, a child held on the shoulders of the father, aloft to gain one more breath of life.

The problem, the sanitation officer had related, was to find a quicker-acting and more humane material. His superior had made inquiries of a well-known company long specialized in vermin extermination, and a cyanide-based formula had been suggested, efficacious for rats. This was now beginning to be used in a vast new camp in Poland, in the town of Auschwitz. The new product worked much faster—fifteen minutes. To Auschwitz came trains with Jews from the conquered lands of Europe, France, Belgium, Holland, Greece. Behind the gas chambers, rows of furnaces had been constructed for incineration of the bodies. The ashes were used as fertilizer.

The conscience-Nazi had tried to send a report to the Vatican, also to Sweden. The world must know. But in Sweden, the courier had related, the report had been held back as unbelievable. Either insane, or the work of an imposter, a horror propagandist.

Menahem had written it all out for Chaim, and also on his own got a copy through to the Mossad. Sorrowfully, though they believed him, they had to wait for more certified evidence. But from Switzerland, and even from secret contacts to Poland, fragments were being assembled.

And meanwhile? Meanwhile it was already known, the Jews of Warsaw were being transported somewhere. Every day, every day, thousands. It seemed to Menahem that all he heard were echoes of death. The destruction of the Jews had entered a total phase, as though no matter what else came in the world struggle, this was the principal aim, and this part Hitler would accomplish.

And then, a balance point seemed to be reached in the war. The Russians were holding the Nazis at Stalingrad, and the British had stopped them at El Alamein. The needle trembled, and even seemed to veer to the other side.

※ ※ ※

Lacing tight his old Wingate tennis shoes, Avinoam was ready. Sneakers. That really was the right word. A black night, just as with HaYadid. Only this time they'd sneak in from the sea. The British must have had a map of the harbor mines—maybe even their own mines that they had laid when they held this place for a time after they first chased the Italians out. But since Rommel had put the Italians back in, there must be newly sown fields. British Naval Intelligence must have got their map; the hell with it, that was their problem, their part of this job. He climbed down after Aaron, his squad leader, and without a whisper was in the assault boat with his own chevreh. Since the Wingate time, only three outsiders had come into their squad in the Palmach, and those were now also of the same flesh. Even here Micha stuck out a foot to trip him, and he sat down hard.

There was only one difference from climbing into a half-track that would carry them over the dunes to blow up a gasoline tanker behind Rommel's lines. There the vehicle waited to carry you back. This boat with oars dipping soundlessly would deposit them and goodbye. It would return to the destroyer. Their only way out would be when the Australians assaulting across the sand linked up with them.

They were two squads of Jews, as usual mixed into some other unit, New Zealanders or wherever. Mostly they sat around waiting. His uncle Gidon might even have waited in the same lousy camp outside Alexandria, and lined up for the mothers of the same whores.

The Death Brigade, the commandos called themselves, death for you or for the enemy, was there a difference? These were the things he used to talk about with Avi, far back in the Night Squad when they were boys. Avi believed there was a kind of area of death that you entered in an action, an arena where death ruled as in the ancient days of gladiators, and who survived was only an accident. That was the only way you could do it and endure it. Avi had had the imagination.

These were his thoughts after they were assembled on the beach and waited for Zvi and Uri, the scouts, to come back. He had never wanted to do scouting. He had never wanted to be even a corporal. Not to tell others what to do. Better to be told. Maybe that was the last thread of his cowardice. It was a matter of psychology Avinoam told himself, for he liked to read psychological books that were not too full of scientific words. With all he had done in the Night Squads and in the special task unit, he could not accuse himself of physical cowardice. But as the books said, and he could see it in himself, soldiers who went into the most dangerous units might do so out of a need to prove to themselves that they were not cowards. Maybe even still because of his father's being a pacifist.

At last the scouts returned and led them to the first silenced guardpost at the edge of the harbor. Zvi motioned not to stumble, three bodies lay there. Good job they had done. The creep up, the leap and headlock from behind, the blade across the throat.

In their Italian uniforms they marched on the road inland, past the town. Predawn came, and truck movements started. If only the sneakers didn't give him away. At last they could make out the series of blockhouses that guarded the desert approaches to the port. Exactly as in the briefing. They cut onto a field path.

Now down, creeping.

Zvi rose, flung open the iron door that those Italian fools had left slightly ajar for air. Noam, he was Avi, too, sprang with his knife onto a form on a cot. Shooting would alert the other blockhouses.

Casting aside the bodies, manning the machine guns. From the desert you could already hear assault cannon. If only this damn blockhouse itself wasn't hit by the Aussies! The Italians were coming rushing from rear barracks to meet the desert assault, and as they ran past the blockhouse, the commandos got them from behind. A slaughter. A perfect operation. Avi in him was laughing, watching the little Italians whirl around dazed as they fell. Kill, kill, kill. Now let Herr Rommel break through to Eretz! Kill!

Getting the BBC a few minutes after the broadcast had started, Menahem, puzzled, recognized the voice, a voice he had last heard in Poland a year before the war, from across the table—Zygleboim, the earnest, unswerving leader of the Jewish Workers Bund, those anti-Zionists who believed with all their faith that their home must remain Poland, that their future was in brotherhood with the Polish proletariat, that their culture must be Yiddish, not Hebrew.

As he was alone in the apartment, the radio voice seemed there with him, speaking in the carefully learned English. Authentic reports passed on through the underground Polish Home Army told of the daily deportation of six thousand Jews from the half million walled in the Warsaw ghetto. They were taken to an installation named Treblinka, where they were all gassed. Faced with supplying lists for the daily deportations, Adam Czernikov, whom the Nazis had placed in the position of head of the Warsaw Jewish Community, had committed suicide. If the world did nothing to halt the systematic extermination of a people, "it will be a shame to live on, a shame to belong to the human race."

The speaker, said the BBC, had been Mr. Schmuel Zygleboim, labor member of the Council of the Polish Government in Exile.

So it was now official. Announced on BBC.

A moment afterward Menahem picked up Berlin. Another voice he knew. Haj Amin el Husseini, the Grand Mufti of Jerusalem, in Arabic, urging all support for Adolf Hitler, the friend of Islam, who was liberating humanity from the diabolic Jewish plot to rule the world.

In September, before a vast ecstatic audience in the Sports Palace, the Führer cried out his defiance to the outer world; those who had laughed at what he said regarding the Jews could now stop laughing.

At long last, the British and American governments jointly proclaimed that reports from Europe "left no doubt that Hitler's oft-repeated intention to exterminate the Jewish people in Europe was being carried out." In London the entire House of Commons rose for two minutes of silent grief.

In Eretz a day of mourning was observed. A stillness, as on Yom Kippur. In New York masses of Jews assembled in Madison Square Garden and on all the surrounding streets, where the solemn, disembodied voice of Rabbi Steven Wise was heard in the Kaddish.

All this Menahem heard in Istanbul, and sometimes it seemed to him that if he could go and fling himself, girdled with dynamite, under a death train, it would at least be one deed done, if only a gesture to show the way.

And now in Istanbul a new horror was heard of—the scattering of German Jews who had early escaped to Turkey on temporary visas, on false papers, were being tracked down by Von Papen's crew; the German embassy demanded that the Turks return these persons to the Reich. Shimon Brod told of a refugee doctor who had been notified he must depart, his wife and children also must return to the Reich. Hiding places must be found.

To help out, two new lads arrived from Eretz: a slight young kibbutznik named Venya, whose family was in Poland—if they still lived—and Ehud, who before the war had negotiated with the devil Eichmann himself in Vienna. When Shimon Brod could find no more hiding places, they found their way even to a priest who was said to be kindhearted, the Vatican's legate to Turkey, one Angelo Roncalli, who helped them spirit away a cellist under order of deportation. The legate even pleaded with Rome for intervention to save Europe's Jews.

Then, from Budapest, came sparks of life. Even though they were Hitler's allies, the Hungarians—by nature, as everyone quipped—had kept an eye open in the other direction, and now—perhaps another sign that the war was turning—their faces too seemed at moments to turn around. Though tens of thousands of Hungarian Jews had perished as army labor conscripts, though the government had rapidly enacted the Nuremberg laws, driven Jews from their professions, confiscated and plundered, still with Hungarians there was always a loophole, and somehow, in Istanbul, contact with Budapest had been maintained. Officially it was through Chaim at the Jewish Agency. While the bulk of relief funds, for food and medical supplies, went through Geneva, special allocations could sometimes be forwarded by Chaim. They were received by a Budapest journalist, Dr. Reszo Kastner, who seemed to have contacts everywhere. Appointed head of the still-functioning Zionist office, he had brought all the Jewish community factions, even the Revisionists, together into a Rescue Committee that worked, as Menahem understood, largely underground. A businessman named Joel Brand was maintaining secret apartments, hiding places for chalutzim and also for children who had escaped by bribery, by chance, by bravery from Poland, fleeing first into Slovakia, and when the deportations started there, across into Hungary. There, despite all the anti-Jewish measures, the activation of the Nazi "State Secret" had been avoided.

For this rescue work, every courier brought appeals for funds, from Kastner. Geneva was too slow, too legalistic. Though some of the couriers were Red Cross emissaries, others were of a shady sort that Chaim could not risk meeting—doubtless they had connections to the Hungarian secret police. And once more Menahem, to relieve the unending death count that added itself day and night in his head, could feel he was of some use. In certain cafés, sometimes even in walking along a street, he met the contacts. Repeatedly he had entrusted sums to a pudgy, always grinning Hungarian known as the King of the Oriental Rug Smugglers, Bandi Gros by name, who hinted of high connections, seemed to know much about Dr. Kastner, and claimed also to have been a schoolmate of the businessman, Joel Brand. Still, the money had always arrived there.

Now, Bandi Gros also brought messages sent to Budapest from Bratislava. In Slovakia there was a Working Group. The leader, a Rabbi Weismandel, wrote in careful allusions—"himmel"—heaven—obviously meant Himmler. By the grace of heaven the rabbi wrote, all of the remaining books—meaning the Jews—in Slovakia could be saved! For fifty thousand sterling the rabbi with himmel's help could buy 25,000 volumes!

Himmler himself could be bribed?

Bandi was grinning at Menahem as though he knew every word in the letter, and had only been waiting to see Menahem's face when he read it. The trains in Slovakia had been rolling, Menahem knew, perhaps fifty thousand Jews were already deported. That corresponded to the rabbi's letter. A third, some 25,000, remained.

Suddenly Bandi offered information. For the last few weeks already, there had been an arrangement, and the trains had not rolled. The Working Group had been paying money, some of it coming in relief funds from Geneva, some of it raised among themselves, about ten thousand dollars for each canceled train, to the Nazi commander for deportations, Baron Wiscizleny. Thus, proof already existed—arrangements could be made.

And now, according to the rabbi's letter, for some $250,000 the deportations could be halted not from week to week, but entirely. Ten dollars a head.

Then why, since Geneva had already supplied money for the weekly bribes, wasn't this also arranged through Geneva?

The King of the Rug Smugglers, with his knowing grin, had perfectly followed Menahem's thoughts. Even this last doubt, he had seen. And he could tell Menahem something that his old schoolfriend Joel Brand had revealed to him. To the Budapest Rescue Committee there had recently come a young woman from Bratislava. From their Working Group. Her name was Giselle Fleischman, it was she who dealt with Baron Wiscizleny and he had even provided her with a visa for the journey. A Baron—"he is as much a Baron as I am a King!" This Wiscizleny was Eichmann's deputy for the Slovakian job, but he was not such an all-out Jew-killer as Adolph Eichmann. To the Baron, the Jew-department was a soft war-berth. More of a cultured person, a lover of ease and luxury, this Wiscisleny really lived like a baron. He had high connections of his own, for he was said to be related by marriage to Himmler himself. And so—Bandi winked—it was not Eichmann who was behind this deal. The SS chief himself might already be looking around for a way out, if the war turned.

This Giselle Fleischman was a woman of nerve, she had found a way to see the Baron. Her husband was a wealthy importer, and she had been the head of the Women's Zionist Organization, the Wizo, in Bratislava. Their own two children she had sent off to Palestine before the war, and it was Gisi Fleischman who had been finding ways to smuggle youngsters to Budapest. Her jewelry, whatever she owned, she had used up in payments to border-crossers, trainmen, peasants with haywagons. And in Budapest, Joel had filled up two apartments with those children. It was she who had arranged the week-to-week delays with the Baron, and now this offer. But, if Menahem wanted to know, for this paltry fifty thousand sterling those fine Jewish officials in Geneva were holding things up. To transfer such a sum they needed a permit from some financial control department in Washington. In desperation, Gisi had come to Budapest—the money must be obtained at once.

Bandi's eyes fixed on Menahem's, with the wide-open earnestness of a man who realizes he is always suspect. He placed his large hand over his heart.

With Chaim, Menahem went over every possibility. Where could they lay hands on such a sum? A diminutive man, even timorous-looking, Chaim had proven himself again and again ready to take risks, to shift funds around, but this was far beyond the resources of his office. He could appeal to Shertok—but for this task, someone must go in person.

Menahem picked Venya, the kibbutznik from Ramat Rahel. His whole family had remained in Poland. Venya was the sort who, given a task, would find some way to carry it out. He must go to Shaul—let every operation of the Mossad be suspended, and the money used for this! If necessary, said Menahem, he could do like the Sternists, and rob a bank! But then Menahem caught himself up, sorry for his jest. Avraham Stern, who had refused to follow the way of the Irgun and the Haganah, and declare a truce with the British for the duration of the war, had only recently been tracked by their police to his hiding place in Tel Aviv, and shot dead.

In a week, Venya was back with the funds. Part, he had even got from his kibbutz—the kibbutzim were doing well in the war, supplying the British, so in a way, Venya said with his little smile, it was British money that would be used.

Not long afterward, through a different courier, came a long letter from Giselle Fleischman. Somehow the letter exuded the young woman's personality—Menahem could almost see her! A shrewd judge of people, with her lively descriptions of the lavish tastes of their baronial friend, a lover of fine old Jewish silver, of heirlooms, of Old Masters. But he was a man of his word. All transports had stopped. In the detainment camps, workshops had been established and artisans could even earn a bit of money. Most important—there were ideas for further transactions. She would soon send details.

In mid-winter, Chaim heard the details in a cautionary letter from his colleague in Switzerland. The Working Group in Bratislava had sent an amazing proposal, called the Europa Plan. For two million dollars, deportation of Jews from all Europe, aside from Germany itself and Poland, would be discontinued. France, Belgium, Holland, Greece, Bulgaria, Rumania, the Scandinavian countries—perhaps a million Jews still alive in those lands would be spared.

Two dollars for a life.

There were enormous difficulties and because of this, no independent actions should be taken should appeals be made to Istanbul. Funds of such magnitude could not be paid to the enemy. It had been suggested that the funds be deposited in Switzerland to be collected by certain individuals after the war. But even for this, Allied clearance had to be obtained. It was doubted if Britain would agree. Nevertheless, the World Jewish Congress was already securing and setting aside the required sum.

Week after week, month after month. The matter was being dealt with. Echoes came to Menahem. Discussions were in progress between Washington and London. It was a most delicate and difficult matter.

From Giselle came frantic messages. Could they in Istanbul give more information than the Working Group was getting from Geneva?

What could he inform her? That a remark had been quoted from a high British official, about their deep concern over managing large numbers of Jews who might be released from enemy territory?

The affair took a turn for the worse. Through an intercepted letter, the Baron learned of the Geneva plan to sequester the funds until after the war. He had Giselle called in. The money must be placed here, in cash, on the table! It could come in installments, $200,000 at a time.

All over Europe, the transports were rolling.

In the most desperate effort, with Shimon Brod taking loans at high rates of interest, and with another trip to Palestine, they were able to raise almost $60,000.

It had been handed over; Giselle's message came through a

courier used by the Nazis. The transports would be "administratively delayed" for fourteen days, while the Baron waited for the remainder of the sum.

The rest of the $200,000 could not be managed.

From Bratislava came word that the Baron had returned the cash deposit.

The Europa Plan was at an end. The transports were rolling again.

A letter arrived, smuggled from Poland. The remnant of a resistance unit. "By the time this reaches you, we will all be dead." Venya recognized several names. Chevreh from his youth group.

On the BBC came word that a resistance unit in the Warsaw Ghetto had appealed through the Polish underground for arms.

By now only some fifty thousand Jews out of over a half million who had been walled in the ghetto remained alive. Only those who labored in the war industries that had been established there. At last, a united command of fighters had been formed, embracing all groups, both the Zionist youth and the Bundists. One member was on the other side of the wall, sending out appeals through the Polish resistance. And it was again Schmuel Zygleboim from London who told of their heartrending appeal for weapons.

One morning, encountering Menahem in the Park Hotel's lobby, Major Pennfield let drop a bit of information received from London. The Polish Home Army in Warsaw had transferred ten pistols to the ghetto.

Yet on Passover the revolt began.

All he could do was sit by the radio, hoping to catch a few words about Warsaw.

It was rumored that with Molotov cocktails and with dynamite the Warsaw fighters had killed scores of Germans, even blown up tanks. But they were being attacked in their bunkers with flame-throwers.

On that very day there also began the meeting of a War Refugee Conference, summoned by the United States, in Bermuda.

On the fifth day of Passover another cry was heard, over the BBC, relayed from the fighters in the Warsaw Ghetto. "Alert the whole world! This is your fight as well as ours! Appeal to the Pope for official intervention and to the Allies to declare German war prisoners to be hostages. Only you can save us! The responsibility will rest with you."

488

The Bermuda refugee conference ended with no action taken.

With Passover's end, Menahem heard the final radio call from the ghetto. Venya and Ehud sat with him, in silence. "The heroic rising, without precedent in history, of the doomed sons of the ghetto should at last awaken the world."

Once more there came information, no longer out of the Warsaw Ghetto. In his London hotel room, Schmuel Zygleboim had turned on the gas. With Shimon Brod, Menahem sat listening to the suicide message.

"I cannot live while the remnants of the Jewish population of Poland, whose representative I am, are perishing. My friends in the Warsaw Ghetto died with weapons in their hands in the last heroic battle. It was not my destiny to die together with them, but I belong to them in their mass grave. By my death I wish to make my final protest against the passivity with which the world is looking on and permitting the extermination of the Jewish People."

A man he had known, sat with, over tea, in discussion. True, not a Zionist but a Bundist, yet not so bitter an anti-Zionist as some of the others. Essentially a labor man—he could as well have risen in the Histadrut. And Menahem saw the man in the London hotel room, alone, his wife and children suffocated in the gas chambers at Treblinka, a man still unfree of his guilt at having left them when he had been selected by the Bund to escape and carry the truth to the world. Menahem knew of Zygleboim's early passionate outcries to the Warsaw Jews to refuse, to resist the order to move into the ghetto. Of the Gestapo search for him. Of his fantastic escape, with the help of a Polish comrade who had valid papers, sitting beside him on a train across the whole of Germany. Even reaching America, to tell, to speak at meeting after meeting, union meetings, Jewish meetings, to write in the press, exhausting himself in trying to arouse people. But that was still the time before the operation of the death camps became known. A year ago there had been only the mass slaughter of Jews in obscure shtetlach as the Einsatzgruppen accompanied the drive into the Soviet Union, only Jews digging their mass graves, and who could confirm, and who could believe? In Kiev, in Odessa, in all the conquered Soviet areas, a slaughter of a million and a half. Unbelieved. And after that, the fantastic tales of a new device, the gassing chamber, improved from the gassing van, so that two thousand at a time could be killed.

Then from America, Zygleboim had been summoned to London to sit as the Jewish labor delegate in the Polish Government in Exile, and there he had received the reports relayed from the Warsaw Ghetto. And he had cried out and cried out. And even such a man, in the center of London, the city of the war command, could find no way to bring anything to bear, to bomb the rails to Auschwitz, the death factories themselves, to send arms to the Warsaw fighters, and finally could only offer his own death. And it would not help, it would not help, his death cry would not change anything.

One last bitter reflection came to Menahem—the suicidal impulses he had had to confront in himself, in the face of this long frustration, were in a pathetic way impeded by Zygleboim's act. For if the last tragic protest of the delegate in London had no effect, what would be the use of the suicide of a hidden Jew in Istanbul? No, it would only be an act in vain, even an act of vanity. And even, paradoxically, in conformity with the plan for total extermination of the Jews.

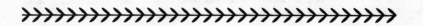

30

IN PALESTINE the atmosphere almost of relaxation prevailed. Both north and south were secure, Syria taken, and Rommel chased far back across the desert, finished.

This year the land hummed with production. Mati's ulcer had been quiet for months; he had lost much of his overweight. Perhaps to catch up with Maureen and Reggie, who now had four, perhaps—Dena even speculated—because of subconscious compensation, as in all wars, for the human slaughter, and this time especially for the slaughter of Jews, but really, she said, because with the twins already nine the gap would be getting too great, she and Mati had decided to have another child. A little girl was born; from Menahem the story of the girl on the *Struma* had come, and they decided to call their daughter Tanya.

Along the coast, rest camps had been built for Allied soldiers. In Tel Aviv, Jerusalem, Haifa, hospitality centers were opened. Indeed, quite a few romances even developed between the Tommies and Jewish girls. And in spite of the bitterness over the refugees, there came one of those examples of British correctness that stirred every heart. This was the odyssey of nearly a thousand waifs who came to be known as the Teheran Children.

Little had been heard of the hundreds of thousands of Polish Jews who at the start of the war had fled into Russia, except that they had been sent to camps in Siberia. Then with the German attack on Russia came an amnesty. Polish Jews were allowed to leave the work camps and were finding their way southward.

Also, an army of Poles who volunteered to fight on the Allied side was being recruited from war prisoners and escapees in the Soviet Union; they were sent by train on a long circuitous journey southward, eventually to join the British. Somehow, whenever such a train was heard of, particularly in Tashkent, Polish Jews would appear with their children, the parents offering whatever they still possessed for these soldiers to smuggle their children into the cars. With the first trains arriving in Teheran a small flood of children disembarked, starved, savage, lice-ridden, fleeing, hiding, wild. Though a few Jewish recruits had been on some of the transports, they had been able to do little to save the children. Hundreds, they said, had died of disease and starvation on the long, slow journey.

The Jews of Teheran tried to round up the wild survivors. From Palestine, monitors arrived, temporary care centers were organized, and then began a struggle to bring the Teheran children to Eretz. At long last, special immigration certificates were granted. But while the Polish recruits had continued their journey directly across Iraq, the Arabs refused transit to the Jewish children.

Then came British correctness. Entire naval units in the Mediterranean might be on watch against tiny ships carrying a few dozen illegal immigrants, but as these children had certificates, several destroyers were assigned to carry them all the way around the Arabian subcontinent and up the Red Sea to Egypt, where they were assigned two special trains for the final stage of their journey to Palestine.

Over the arrival of this remnant of Polish Jewry the entire Yishuv was at fever pitch; a wave of adoption offers, even from America, had to be refused because who knew which parents might survive and come in search of their own. Placements began to be made at various kibbutzim and Youth Aliyah centers, a small number at Leah's meshek. There Dena saw them. How different they were from the first group of children from Germany, now grown and dispersed, some even fighting in the British forces. A whole squadron of psychologists, Natan said, would be needed to deal with their troubles. There were ten-year-olds who still had not recovered their toilet habits. And several, no matter how repeatedly you assured them they could have all the food they wanted, still hid bread from the table.

492

Leah showed her pictures they had drawn, of Siberia, of bomb-ings, of their families as they remembered them. From the daubs of five-year-olds to some remarkable pictures made by a boy of twelve, snow scenes with blue and yellow patterns in the white. Leah called him in; the boy's name was Adam, he was small for his age and solemn-looking, already declaring he wanted to be an artist and running to fetch a new picture he had made since he got here. For a moment Dena thought it was abstract, but then he said, and she saw, that it was a picture of the huge electric power station just across the mouth of the Yarkon; the building had been camouflaged by Khalid, whom Mati had got into the work when the Nazi bombing raids began, and Khalid had laid out large surfaces in earth and sea colors, patterned in squares and oblongs. This the boy had adapted; his picture could almost be a Mon-drian! "I want to buy it!" Dena cried. Khalid would be delighted. The boy didn't know what price to name, so she gave him a whole pound, his first sale. But he must sign it! He would sign it in Hebrew, Adam said proudly; he was already learning. And with a crayon he awkwardly drew the letters. Almost fiercely the artist declared: one day the whole world would know his name!

When she gave the picture to Mouna and Khalid, they were tickled with the story. And studying the boy's painting, Khalid said, "You know, one day it may be true."

❊ ❊ ❊

The American expedition that had landed in North Africa and helped finish off Rommel was now moved across the Mediterra-nean; Italy was invaded, Mussolini was captured, but the Germans seized the north.

After their great victory at Stalingrad the Russians were steadily driving back the enemy; if only the Allies would land in France, still this year, the war could end. It had even begun to seem possible that a portion of Europe's Jews might be saved, for at last President Roosevelt had created a rescue commission and sent a personal envoy to Istanbul. Ehud and Venya sought him out—a third of Rumania's Jews still might be saved, for the Rumanians trembled before the Russian advance. With Menahem, too, the American conferred, listened to all that Tanya had related of the starvation camps in Trans-Dniestria. A true, dynamic American type who, as he said, went right to the top and never took no for

493

an answer, Mr. Hirschmann at once got hold of the Rumanian emissary in Istanbul and promised him immunity from war criminal charges and even American visas for himself and his family if he would arrange for his government to recall to their homes the deported Jews still alive in Trans-Dniestria. And indeed, repatriation began!

That all this had come late, tragically late, Hirschmann was the first to decry; the American told incredible tales of anti-Semitic intrigue in the State Department itself, which had prevented President Roosevelt from knowing the full truth. Cabled reports about the death camps had been kept from him by a third-ranking bureaucrat, the same who had sabotaged the Bermuda conference. No, not necessarily a Nazi sympathizer, but quite simply a normal American Jew hater! At last a member of the Cabinet, named Morgenthau, yes, a Jew, very wealthy and assimilated, still, a Jew, had written a furious personal memorandum to his friend the President, and things had begun to happen! This emissary, an advertising genius from a New York department store, had suddenly been called to Washington and given full presidential authority to save Europe's remaining Jews. In a few weeks he had not only saved the Rumanians but won back Allied prestige, as he pointed out, in Turkey! For—a music lover—he had countered the elaborate receptions given by Von Papen by inviting the entire governmental elite to a symphony concert he had organized, in which Jewish refugee musicians were prominent, including the cellist whom Venya and the papal delegate had rescued from "repatriation."

The rescuing American envoy had then flown back to the United States, just as, it turned out, a Nazi-controlled government seized Hungary, in the face of the Russian advance. At once, Adolph Eichmann and his staff arrived in Budapest, to organize the deportation of the Jews.

Nor did it seem so certain that the war would end before this last million Jews was gassed. In Istanbul, Von Papen was arrogant as ever. Ah, he shrugged, there were strategic fallbacks to shorten the lines of communication, but any day now the decisive secret weapon would be unleashed. Did anyone doubt that the Reich had perfected such a weapon? Already London was crumbling under a lesser invention, the rocket bomb that crossed the Channel. Not the RAF or any antiaircraft weapon could stop the deadly V-2. And this was only the prelude. The secret annihilation bomb, an atomic explosion as everyone had guessed, was virtually ready. Had not the British in frantic, futile commando raids on well-hidden scientific installations tried to hold back its completion? Ah, the Allies were doomed, and they knew it.

Thus in every belly-dance café, in every brightly lit restaurant in Istanbul, the secret was openly discussed. As for the power of the Wehrmacht, look at Hungary. When Hitler decided to strike, he struck, and the entire country fell in a day. The new Nazi-installed government would not waver!

And yet in the Hungarian apparatus in Istanbul one saw many of the same faces. Through one regime after another, there were certain agents and double agents, certain couriers who still appeared. And it was Bandi Gros, the grinning King of the Rug Smugglers, who arrived in the Pera Palace several weeks after the putsch, bringing with him a person long known through messages, Joel Brand of the Rescue Committee.

Telephoning Chaim at the Jewish Agency office, in a voice almost strangled with tension, Brand declared that he was the bearer of a proposal that could save the lives of the Hungarian Jews.

Menaham, Ehud, and Venya hurried to Chaim. At Brand's hotel room door, a Turkish policeman indifferently allowed them to enter. But the first person they saw was Bandi Gros with his big grin as he welcomed them, crying out that he had a big wonderful deal from the top, the very top.

Brand, a chunky youngish man with earnest eyes in a fleshy, round face, now rushed forward, seizing the arm of Menaham, the eldest-looking. "They forced him on me, but never mind, he won't do any harm," he half whispered.

With Bandi sitting back like a proprietor, Joel Brand blurted out the essential. Eichmann himself had called him in. They knew who was Eichmann? They knew. Ehud personally knew, from Vienna. Eichmann had the names of the Rescue Committee, Brand said, and knew that funds came from Switzerland to Brand and his colleague, Reszo Kastner. Funds of the American Joint Distribution Committee. Already in the first weeks Brand had found his way to several of Eichmann's underlings, bribing them with two million pengö to delay roundups in Budapest. Now Eichmann himself offered to halt all deportations, sparing the lives of Hungary's million Jews, in exchange for certain goods and money.

Was it the Europa Plan, revived, after that other million had gone the way of Auschwitz?

What goods did Eichmann want?

That was the problem, but the list must not be taken as final. The main thing was to start discussions, to bargain, to delay—

What goods, then?

The main problem, said Brand, was a request for ten thousand trucks, at once, but—

That seemed to finish it. With ten thousand trucks, an entire panzer division could be moved from one front to another.

Then, half-ashamedly, half-desperately, Brand added: Eichmann was ready to promise that the trucks would be used only on the Russian front. Wait! wait! he cried as he saw their faces. The demands could be negotiated, perhaps limited to medicine, money, certain foods they wanted—coffee, chocólate— Brand glanced back to Bandi, whose grin broadened. Lowering his voice, the envoy pleaded, didn't they see? This was an effort to make contact. To open a channel. Who could tell what it might lead to! The important thing was to show a willingness to negotiate. He had been given two weeks; he must by then be back in Budapest with an answer. His wife was a hostage. Also her mother. Eichmann had agreed to stop all deportations for those weeks, but Brand couldn't be sure. A message should be sent at once, tonight, agreeing that negotiations were possible.

They could not go that far, Chaim declared, without consulting the leaders of the Yishuv. Ben-Gurion himself. Moshe Shertok. Doubtless they in turn would have to consult the British. If only that American representative hadn't gone back— What power could they, here in Istanbul, have to make any—

Brand caught at his hand. The envoy's eyes were frantic. Listen. He, Brand, was not clever, perhaps not the man to have been sent on this mission. Yet certain things had come to him that they must be told. In his opinion this offer was not really from Eichmann. It came from a higher source, Himmler himself! The Reichsführer SS! Eichmann was under Himmler's direct command. The Germans knew the war was lost. It was rumored that Himmler would be the one to take over and seek peace. Therefore, this proposal must be regarded as a feeler. To make contact, first through the Jews. Eichmann would never himself have made an offer to save a single Jew, for he considered himself to be carrying out the most important of Hitler's programs, the annihilation of the Jews, and he would not swerve. Therefore—

This theory, Menahem realized, tied in with the rumors about Himmler already rife in Istanbul, "Should anything happen to

496

Hitler—" Something else that Brand had touched on struck Menahem as plausible. The Nazis actually believed their own propaganda stories about a secret world Jewish power! Thus, Brand said, Eichmann had shouted it was clear he was the agent of worldwide Jewry because it was he who received funds from the American Joint Distribution Committee, the powerful arm of America's multimillionaire Jews. Amazingly, even now, after slaughtering already five million Jews without any interference, the Nazis believed their own tale of a world-powerful Jewish conspiracy! The imaginary "Elders of Zion," now meant the American Joint! Even in beleaguered Budapest, didn't their funds still come through devious channels to Joel Brand and Reszo Kastner? Therefore, Brand said as Bandi lolled, these Nazis thought that without appearing to seek contact with the Allies, a feeler could be extended through the Jews. Thus, Himmler had instructed Eichmann to make this exchange offer to Jews. Goods for blood! But felt certain there could be bargaining so that other goods, more medicines and such, could be substituted for the military trucks. And now he explained why he believed the feeler came from Himmler. Already a most prominent Hungarian Jewish family, that of the magnate Manfred Weiss, had been flown out from Budapest to a neutral land! This had been done not through Eichmann but by a high-ranking Nazi finance officer named Becher, responsible directly to Himmler. In return, Manfred Weiss had handed over to the Germans his entire arms industry, the largest in Hungary. Forty members of the family were flown to Portugal. Reszo Kastner had contacted this Becher, and Kastner was convinced, as was Brand, that Becher had carried out the transaction at Himmler's order. Now, Himmler must also have ordered Eichmann to offer these negotiations. And it was most likely Eichmann himself who had put in the difficult condition of the ten thousand trucks, knowing that it had to be refused. Thus, he could go on killing Jews.

Complex as it all sounded, Menahem felt the envoy's analysis could be correct. Brand had seized his arm, begging hoarsely— every day meant ten thousand lives. They must bargain, discuss, delay, perhaps even send some money, some medicaments. Do everything to hold up the transports.

Yet Menahem had to ask, if the Nazis, as high as Himmler, still believed the Jews had such power, how did they explain to themselves that during three years of the extermination program—

Brand's eyes filled with tears. Who could explain? How could it be explained that after millions of deaths people still let themselves be herded into boxcars and even believed they were going to "resettlement?" Perhaps after the war all this would become clear. "We ourselves in Budapest"—Brand glanced at Bandi and plunged on as one who must give up all caution in a crisis—"we had plans for resistance, to blow up the tracks, the bridges, we had the boys, but to get explosives, weapons, this work would take all the money from Switzerland. We took a vote in the Rescue Committee"—he was half sobbing—"either to use the money for this work or for bribe rescue. We knew that with bribes the last twenty-five thousand Jews in Slovakia were saved from deportation to Auschwitz." Gisi Fleischman—yes, Menahem knew, with her the Baron had kept his bargain.

And now, Brand said, this same Baron Wiscizleny had been brought by Adolf Eichmann, for the big job in Hungary. "Therefore, we began with the Baron." Already Wiscizleny was making promises, taking gold, to save the finest minds, the best artists, the most important Jews. "In the Rescue Committee we voted three to two for the way of bribes and not the way of bombs. We voted to use the money for buying lives. The Revisionists were against. I—I myself would have gone out to put the dynamite under the bridges, but I voted with the policy to save lives, whatever lives we could." He regained control of himself. Please, he must send some kind of word to his colleague Reszo Kastner, word for Eichmann. Even vague. A beginning, he begged. A message of "agreement on principle to negotiate."

What harm could this do? No trains would meanwhile be moving. This promise, Brand believed, would be kept.

Even before this, Chaim insisted, he must get permission from the Agency, from the Yishuv.

The next day, Brand was arrested; he had no visa. Somehow, after frantic inquiries, and many bribes, they got him out of a Turkish lockup.

Still no reply from Jerusalem. To save time, Menahem labored with Chaim and Brand over a possible statement.

Into the third night they worked. It must sound official, yet avoid commitment to terms.

The document declared that the principle of negotiation was accepted. Members of the Jewish Agency Executive would come to Istanbul at once, and German negotiators would be expected to meet with them. Manufacture and delivery of the specific goods demanded would involve certain difficulties, and this would be discussed. Meanwhile, the halt of deportations must be scrupulously observed. A million Swiss francs would be deposited and remain in the Swiss bank as long as there were no deportations.

"How can we promise this?" Chaim demurred.

"Promise! Promise! What does it matter!" Venya cried.

Emigration to Palestine should be permitted, and for each convoy of a thousand persons, four hundred thousand dollars would be paid. Emigration to other lands would be paid for at the rate of a million dollars for each convoy of ten thousand persons. Food, medical supplies, and clothing would be allowed by the Germans into the concentration camps and ghettos; in exchange, they could retain fifty percent of these goods.

It seemed to Menahem insane to be writing these words. Yet who knew, who knew? A headiness overtook them all. The words were lives.

As they argued over each point, over the amount of money to promise per head, the whole situation seemed like an hallucination, like some hanged man on the way to the gallows offering a deal to his executioners. And yet could they dare refrain from trying?

Still no word from Jerusalem. Brand begged, wept.

They signed, Joel Brand of the Central Council of Hungarian Jews and, as authorized representatives of the Jewish Agency, Chaim and Ehud. Brand handed the document to Bandi Gros, who had been sprawled like a man of great patience but now beamed and, as a man who with limited assistance has succeeded in a great achievement, raising his whiskey glass he cried, "L'chayim!"

They must at once cable Reszo Kastner to inform Eichmann that the proposed agreement was on the way. Bandi knew a courier who would take it.

It was during many hours in the hotel room with Joel Brand in the ensuing days, keeping his spirits up, keeping him from drinking too much with Bandi, while no word arrived either from Budapest or from the Jewish Agency in Jerusalem, that Menahem began to understand more clearly the complex rivalries among the factions there, the Hungarians, the various German formations, the rivalries between the Abwehr and the SS, each out to grab the money of the doomed Jews, and to see that within all this something yet might be done even if the big negotiation failed.

The King of the Smugglers was perhaps a buffoon, perhaps the real emissary.

Joel Brand, the son of a well-off engineer, had indeed known Bandi in school, and early in the war had through Bandi been led into the tangled Hungarian political underworld. For Hungary too had suddenly rounded up Jews from Poland who had long been living in Budapest, and put them in a camp. The parents of Joel's wife were among them. Joel, searching the half-world of bars and nightclubs, had found Bandi, who had arranged, for a sum, to have a police car go to the detention area and fetch Hansi's parents back home. In this way had begun an expanding rescue operation. The Brands had hidden people in their apartment, then rented extra apartments. Some of the chalutzim had even gone on the "tiul," the hike with rucksacks on their back, getting across the Rumanian border as far as the Black Sea ports, to try to reach Eretz. Joel Brand, who in his younger days had leaned toward communism, had thus become an active Zionist.

Now, with Dieter Wiscizleny in Budapest, Brand believed negotiations were really possible. In the inside Nazi politics, Brand said, there must be some reason why Adolf Eichmann, technically his superior, had cultivated the Baron, even naming his newborn child Dieter. And in this tangle, Joel Brand insisted, the way could be found to save Hungarian Jewry.

Already, to the Baron, jewelry and gold had been passed for the promised "token train" to be sent out to Switzerland. The rate was a thousand dollars a head. And Reszo Kastner had, of course, hinted to Wiscizleny that with the war ending, those who saved Jews would not be forgotten. It was hoped that this word had been forwarded to Himmler.

Of the two weeks allowed for Joel Brand's return, a week was already gone. Each day he became more despondent. Not he, but Reszo Kastner should have been sent here. Reszo was cleverer and would by now have thought of something. What hadn't they thought of, in the Rescue Committee? Printed hundreds of false baptismal certificates. Played cards at high stakes with Eichmann's lieutenants, always losing. They were roisterers, greedy to seize what they could before the end. Eichmann too. In a country house, his Hungarian fascist friends provided beautiful women, orgies. With his staff, anything could be arranged.

Then word came from Jerusalem. Moshe Shertok was ready to meet with Joel Brand but could not get a visa to Istanbul. There was only one way—for Brand to come to Aleppo, across the Syrian border.

But Shertok had several times in the past year entered Turkey! It must be the British, Menahem felt sure. They had seen to it with the Turks in Ankara for the visa to be refused. For once Brand entered Syria he would be in the area of British control, and could be arrested.

He would go! He would go to Aleppo, Brand insisted. How could he sit here? The two weeks were over; the trains must be rolling; his wife and children, also her mother, might already be dead. No reply had come about the "agreement to negotiate" that had been sent off. Doubtless Eichmann, without assurances from a higher level than their own in Istanbul, had become furious.

Ehud went with Brand, and returned alone. The British had indeed arrested Brand and Bandi Gros as the train arrived in Aleppo; after hours of cross-examination they had allowed Brand to meet with Shertok and then had taken off the two envoys, presumably to Cairo.

And from Reszo Kastner in Budapest, desperate cables. Deportations were under way. Brand must return at once.

They replied with reassurances. Shertok of the Jewish Agency had already flown to London with the offer.

"Deportations continue" was the response from Budapest. In place of Joel Brand, a representative of the Jewish Agency must come there at once.

Chaim offered. The Agency forbade it. Nor Ehud, even though he had known Eichmann in Vienna. No one officially connected could enter enemy territory. The only logical envoy, Menahem pointed out, was himself.

Chaim wavered. And then an enormous event decided them. The Allies had landed in Normandy.

Now, now, something might be done! Even the Eichmanns would be seeking to prove they had saved Jews. He must go, Menahem insisted. Yet within him something asked, would he find them, instead, like enraged dogs, out for the last kill?

Dressed in his good suit, shirt with cuff links, and tie, appearing as a dignitary of some sort, a semidiplomat, with a fine dispatch case and leather bag, Menahem was to be picked up, alone, by a car at a certain street corner. Chaim's hand trembled in farewell.

Only when inside their airplane with the Hakenkreuz on its tail did there come over Menahem the full sense of parturition. Even in the car he had still been on neutral soil. Then he was in the aircraft on an inside seat next to his body's custodian. There came again his sense of process—even as though birth and death must be part of this single process and thus, even birth and death were the same. But he must not take refuge in fatalism. All, all of his power of decision, of will, must be in readiness, at peak.

The guard proved uncommunicative. Ceaselessly Menahem in his mind rehearsed his possible approaches. The first goal, an extension of time, could, with good luck, be achieved with little else than the fact of his arrival, his substitution for Joel Brand. He could even suggest that Brand had simply wanted to escape and had made off to the British. While unfair to the decent man, in the situation it might be necessary.

But what of Brand's family, held in hostage? He must put it differently. He must first ask to consult with the Rescue Committee, with Reszo Kastner.

But suppose, indeed, that he found the enemy so enraged by the Allied landing that the annihilation program was intensified?

Here his mind stood before a glacial impenetrability. As when you approach a border, with false papers. You have tried to prepare for every eventuality, but then comes chance.

Menahem let himself sink into a reverie. Of Giora still in their prisoner-of-war camp, perhaps with the Allied landings soon to be free. If only luck held and they did not, in this last phase, single out Jewish prisoners and destroy them. . . . Or if he himself should be put to torture, his identity discovered, could they even get from him the fact that Giora— Idiocies. He made himself think instead of Nurit married and a mother since he had been away. Of the earliest years with Dvora, a young mother, when he would come riding home to the kvutsa, a Shomer on his horse.

He was taken directly to the headquarters in the Majestic Hotel, and precisely as Ehud and Brand had described, there was the outstretched riding crop pointing for him to halt, to keep his distance, to keep away the Jewish contamination. The head cocked with an ironic knowingness.

502

He had been empowered by the Jewish Agency, Menahem said, and held out a copy of the provisional agreement, as it seemed they had not yet received this. A lieutenant handed the document to Eichmann, who glanced at it and tossed it aside. "We have since received it," he said tonelessly. Then suddenly his voice, his face changed, "Shit Jew!" he cried. He should have known what trust to put in a Jewish pledge of absolute confidence! Ah, perhaps this shit Jew had boarded the plane without hearing today's BBC? At a British press conference in Cairo, Joel Brand had divulged the entire secret proposal. "Blood for money! Money for blood!" The most vile inhuman proposal in all history, made by one Adolf Eichmann! Eichmann's eyes glittered in savage, yet triumphant mockery.

Menahem made an effort. Brand must have been forced—the Jewish Agency itself had fully respected secrecy. Though Brand had fled to the British, here he himself had come, as proof that the Agency would keep its word.

Ah? This office, too, kept its word. Two weeks of delay in deportations had been promised. Now, as further promised, the deportations were resumed.

"Our work of Jewish resettlement has continued steadily during these years with no intervention whatever on the part of your Allies, so presumably they do not oppose this policy, except for some propagandistic speeches," Eichmann said dryly. "Indeed, I am sure they are glad of it. As for your Hungarian coreligionists, you will see that despite all your atrocity tales, they have prepared themselves for resettlement and are ready to depart of their free will. I will send you to see this for yourself. You can report *that* to your Jewish Agency!"

And Menahem found himself escorted by two subofficers and embarked, at a side door of the hotel, in a Mercedes bearing the SS insignia.

The ride took less than an hour. They halted before a train siding, across from what must have been a temporary detention camp, an open brickyard, where some attempts had been made by the deportees to construct provisional shelters out of blankets, out of sheets. Jews in family groups, clusters, were being herded to the train by Hungarian police. The yard was littered with belongings left behind, makeshift bedding, a huge pile of clothing, shoes, and on a guarded trestle table a last confiscation of money and jewelry.

The end cars were being loaded. True, people were climbing into the cars without coercion, the older people turning to lift the children, the family men making sure of their permitted baggage, all moving hurriedly so as to find place inside.

Sitting thus between the two SS officers in the closed limousine, Menahem watched as from within some prolonged nightmare of submersion, all soundless, where no outcry can emerge. Then like a double-vision came a recollection of a time once before in his life when he had seen such a sight as this. In the First World War. A train of animal cars filled with leading Jews from Jerusalem, that the Turks had seized, to be hauled to prisons in Damascus, in their savage reprisals over the Nili, spying for the British. Like a Black Plague believed eradicated, that in its cycle reappeared, a thousand times more virulent.

A conglomeration of cries, commands, anxious calling of a name, came to him in the car like street sounds into a hotel room, but still the train loading was without reality. Now, already in the summer of the third year of death camps, how could these people not know? Even in this satellite land many must have heard the BBC, known of the battle of the Warsaw Ghetto, perhaps even listened to the last desperate outcry of Zygleboim. Could they have discarded all this as atrocity propaganda, as invention? Or did they perhaps believe the end of the war was so near, they would now be safe? Watching them hoisting up their fine leather valises, he could partly see into the boxcar where a family was hurriedly spreading and crowding onto a blanket to establish its space on the floor. And if he himself could possibly be heard, would he shout out, "Flee! Let them kill you here! At least some of you will escape!"

And the whole time the two hulks pressed on him from either side, and he remained soundless.

As the Hungarian police were finishing their task, SS men moved along the train, sliding closed the doors. All at once, the officer on Menahem's right flung open the automobile door, and in a single movement Menahem found himself pulled out, marched between the two, lifted and flung inside the last boxcar, the rumbling door closing behind him even before he could turn around.

Regaining his balance, he moved tentatively so as not to tread on bodies. In the dim, closed space, all the sounds seemed to coalesce, "We should have—" "Do you think—" and children beginning to wail in the dark, amid reassuring, yet terrified voices,

504

and the train did not move, and after a time some began to pound on the walls, on the door, and still later a woman in hysteria had to be held by force, her husband and a brother locking their arms around her.

A sense of having arrived, an almost gratifying horror sense, as when a held-down vomit finally gushes out, came to Menahem. Now he was inside his destiny. This need, this masochism, had for years, had perhaps always lain there in a remote layer of his self; perhaps through some minute gland within the skull it had exerted for a long time now the determining directions for his actions. Surely when he had insisted on the mission to Budapest, he had known he would come to this. Yet at least now all his guilt, all the hallucinating fever of the last years would be ended, he would no longer in his night agonies be trying to explain himself to Zygleboim, to all the dead, to the ghetto fighters, to the Vilna partisans, to little Tanya of the *Struma*. Trying to justify himself: "What more could I have done, what more can I do?" And that last outcry to the whole guilty world, feebly caught on the shortwave in the Istanbul apartment, as flamethrowers seared the Warsaw Ghetto bunkers—perhaps. now this cry would cease resounding accusingly in his soul.

Yet what should he answer to the uncertainties, the fright, to the pathetically repeated reassurances that he heard all around him now? And how in himself should he extinguish the livid streaks of illusory hope that shot through his mind. Inquiries would be made about his whereabouts. Already the people of the Rescue Committee must be making telephone calls, sending cables. The Nazi financial officer through whom Reszo Kastner worked, who had contacts directly with Himmler. Or this was perhaps only a grim joke of Eichmann's, to kidnap him just as the British had kidnapped Joel Brand. Before the train began to move, the door would roll open. Should he then refuse, demanding that the entire train—

Was he losing his mind, with such fantasies? Who in Budapest even knew of his arrival!

The train jolted, began to move, and from its entire cargo came that animallike reverberation between terror and relief.

Now basic questions forced aside all these fantasies. First, the same question that had, for three years, been agonized over, is it better if the deportees know for certain? Just as in normal life when a family member is stricken with an incurable disease.

Should the stricken one be told? And told how much time remains?

And for himself? It seemed virtually impossible to Menahem that he would pass the selection that took place on the platform when the trains were emptied. To the right, to the left. A Dr. Mengele. To the gas chambers, or to slave labor, where the healthy body might endure for a few months, under hunger and exhaustion. He was fifty-six. Impossible that he should pass the selection. Still—and Menahem watched how his own reasoning clung to life—he was never taken for his age; he appeared to people to be in his late forties. Indeed, it had been a mild enjoyment with him—was he already viewing his life as past?—an enjoyment, particularly with women, to startle them by declaring his true age. They would invariably insist he was jesting. Those were some of the warm, amusing times in a man's life. Well, despite the last few years of sitting in Istanbul he was still compact and wiry. But his hair was grizzly; that would be enough. Unless he kept on his hat? A religious Jew? The irony struck him now, of balancing their added antipathy for a Jew-Jew, against the value of covering his graying hair. Ah, why cling, what more could he do in life? Why hang on for a few months of horror and starvation? Yet why give in to death when the war was ending? All those other times when he might have been killed—he had lasted well beyond a man's chances and this time had tumbled on the wrong side.

He had merged into a space, just enough to sit with his knees to his chin, and his eyes were now dark-adjusted; Menahem was even already speculating on the possibility of escape as related by a few survivors, of digging with a pocketknife around the bolts that fastened the iron bar across the high, narrow air opening. And when the train slowed, rolling out. Also, it had been told, floorboards in some boxcars could be removed, and a body could drop down lying flat between the tracks until the whole train passed.

A few candles had been lighted. Menahem looked for faces among the younger men. But not yet was the time. Perhaps he would not even make himself known.

Then came that disturbing sense of mission that had intruded so many times in his life. Hadn't he been placed even here for some purpose? To rescue even a few, even one? Or else at least to prepare groups of young men, several strong ones together, for the moment of arrival on the platform—a fierce suicidal attack, leaping on an SS, wrenching a weapon, killing. . . . Like the doomed

Warsaw revolt, somehow such an act would become known to the world.

In this speculation Menahem heard himself spoken to, at first in Hungarian, and as he could not answer, the man used German. It was the father of a family cramped together on his right, three children from perhaps ten to sixteen, the youngest a boy, all well dressed but now sweating in their woolens, put on for the cold weather to come. The mother even here retained the lustrous gleam of Hungarian women accustomed to being known as beauties. The daughter, perhaps sixteen, already had the look as well. They had opened a rucksack containing food, spread a towel over a suitcase, and the mother was pouring coffee from a vacuum bottle. The father said, "We notice you have nothing with you," and the woman offered him a sandwich and coffee in a paper cup. Menahem accepted. "But you are not from our community and do not speak Hungarian.—How?"

Menahem replied in Yiddish. "I'm not a Hungarian, but they caught me as you see." The man varied his German a bit closer to Yiddish; it was clear that in their world common Yiddish was no longer spoken.

How caught?

He had managed to hide in Budapest but had taken fright, tried to find a better hiding place in the countryside, and been caught, Menahem said, leaving the impression he was Polish. The father said he was the town pharmacist. With lowered voice he declared to Menahem that he and his family did not permit themselves illusions, they knew that conditions would be very hard and that the old people were not likely to survive, but they hoped only for one thing, that the family could stay together. So in Budapest, deportations had begun?

So far as he knew, only one train, Menahem said. Also, a certain special train was said to be in preparation—

Ah, he had heard of it, the pharmacist whispered, but it was believed a Nazi trick. Reszo Kastner's train. The cost was high. And none could say for certain where it would go. He had reasoned, he hoped he had not made a dreadful mistake, that the best was to gain time, the war was surely in its last stages, and he hoped even now that if they could but hold out a few months and stay together— The Russians were advancing.

Then he believed the train was really going to a labor camp?

Why not? Ah, the grisly atrocity stories of gas chambers and crematoria had indeed been heard on the BBC, yes. He also knew of the resistance in the Warsaw Ghetto. But all this phase, with the tragic fate of the Polish Jews—now that the war was turned, he believed this was finished. For example, the Germans were now desperately in need of labor, and with all of Hitler's insane anti-Semitism he was diabolically shrewd and would not destroy capable hands. See how he had been able for four years to manage the war against the greatest powers in the world, and if not for the American industrial power changing the balance of the conflict, he might have won. That was a shrewd, if hateful, man; he would not destroy labor power of which he was in desperate need. But even as the pharmacist spoke about destroying capable hands, his glance for a moment fell on the child, his youngest son, and Menahem felt his inner shudder.

Did Menahem perhaps have more information? Was it true that in these labor camps, as it was rumored, the men were separated from the women and children?

In less than a whisper, so the man alone could hear, Menahem said, "You had best now know that what is called merely atrocity propaganda is absolutely confirmed and true."

"You know these things? Tell me, who are you?" The pharmacist now whispered.

"A Jew. A Jew from Poland."

"And you escaped?"

"Until now I escaped."

Appealingly, begging agreement, confirmation, the pharmacist pleaded, "Every train, every locomotive is now urgent to them for the front. If all they intend is to kill us, they could simply have done it on the spot. The way I heard they did two years ago in Litzmanstadt and other places, on their path into Russia. Why would they waste a train to deport us unless it is for their factories, where it is known they are in desperate need of labor?"

The boxcar had become an oven, saturated with sweat-laden, stagnant air, with urine and excrement stench. In the corner, where someone had even managed to put up a blanket, the toilet pail was filled; a young man, boosted by another, lifted it to the air opening, but as he tried to empty out the content, a train jolt brought much of it dripping down the wall. There was no more water; the single pailful had long been exhausted, and those who had thermos supplies and bottled fluids were now carefully sip-

508

ping in crouched half hiding. At a prolonged stop, voices, vehicle sounds were heard alongside the train, but pounding, entreaties, shrieks, brought no response whatsoever. One desperate mother, her baby howling incessantly, began to scream, "I can't, I can't! Let them kill us now! Let us all die now!" The pharmacist somehow threaded his way to her and gave her a sedative.

The train bumped backward. Cars were being added. More Jews? Perhaps only ordinary freight? Were they at a border? By now they might have reached the Polish frontier. The word raised dread, but an ironic voice commented that there was no more Poland, only the Greater Reich.

The pharmacist's girl, Bella, constantly saying, "Excuse me," got to the circle of her schoolmates, standing closely pressed together, five boys belonging to the soccer team her mother told Menahem. One was Bella's sweetheart. His family had got pushed into another car, for the boys, even in the brickyard, had stayed together.

If he could bring himself back from his profound, undermining sense of failure in his mission, then it was those boys he must talk to, Menahem knew. Now he saw they had already themselves thought of the way. Mounted on the shoulders of a comrade, one of them was prying with a pocketknife around the bolt at one end of the crossbar.

The pharmacist talked on. All in this car were decent Jews, all clients of his pharmacy. The pharmacy had been in his family for three generations. The Jews of the town were not ultrapious; like himself, they were of the modern persuasion, of the Reform. Still, they had taught their children to be loyal Jews. Some families had gone away to small villages in the Carpathians to hide, and he himself had thought of hiding with his family in a subbasement of the pharmacy, stocking it with provisions, for surely soon the war would be finished, but the police had come knocking before anything could be arranged. Menahem nodded, nodded, to reassure the man that he was not at fault. And in their town, were there many Zionists? he asked. Ah, the pharmacist said, not too many, though indeed, the family of Theodor Herzl had originated not fifty kilometers away, Herzl's great-grandfather had been a grain merchant there. As for himself, he made donations, yes, he had had a Keren Kayemeth box on his counter, but after all, what hope was there with the British closing Palestine off and the Arabs as bad as the Nazis?

The night deepened. Some were dozing. An aged Jew was humming into his beard, a Sabbath melody, "Eliyahu Hanavi," oh, come unto us, come in our time, bring Messiah, of David's line. Yes, Jews, call now on Elijah, Menahem told himself, and thought bittersweetly of the comic tale he had told to Mati's Dena, in that hiding place in Jerusalem, in the genizah. Cry out "Elijah, help us!" and perhaps a British plane will swoop down and explode the next railway bridge, and partisans led by a parachutist from Palestine, for hadn't Reuven Shiloah and Teddy Kollek at last persuaded the British to train, if not ten thousand, then ten, maybe even fifty volunteers? Thus, partisans would emerge from the woods and liberate this entire Auschwitz train!

In a drowse he was in the cattle car, that time before everything, even before he had come to Eretz, that year of working on cargo ships and of wandering across America. And his job—the gallows humor of it—suddenly awakened Menahem; his job had been tending a boxcar of cattle, walking in boots through their piss streams, to shovel away their manure clots on the long rail journey to the abattoir in Chicago.

One crossbar had become undone. All through the car, even among those who seemed asleep, it became known. Something had yielded.

Menahem picked his way to the small circle of athletes. In a low, quiet voice he began to speak to them: he knew certain things that might prove useful. What they had begun to do was right; there had been such escapes. "It is by a certain accident that I am on this train, I am from the Jews of Palestine. I came on a mission and was caught. Don't as yet speak to anyone else here, of this. Listen. Which of you is to go first?" It was the slimmest, named Geza. Yellow-haired. "Geza, we are now probably in Slovakia. They have a strong partisan movement, did you know?" The boy shook his head slightly. "You must not be hasty to disclose yourself; try to keep hidden in the woods, to move only at night. The partisans may find you before you find them. Either way, it will be a dangerous moment. You don't speak the language?" The boy shook his head again. His eyes remained fixed on Menahem. "Try first to speak Hungarian, not German. Try to win some contact, some human contact, before you disclose you are a Jew. Say you were in the resistance, got caught by the Nazis, and escaped. Now listen, from Palestine lately were sent a small number of parachutists. One was sent to Slovakia and we believe she reached the partisans. Her name was Haviva. Haviva Reik. From Palestine. Haviva. This is one name. Secondly, there is another name to remember, Gisi Fleischman. She is of our movement, a wealthy woman in Bratislava; should you reach there, seek her. She may know of Haviva. Through this woman many Jews were saved by bribes to the SS. The deportations there were not completed. If in desperation you have to reveal yourself, rather than go to a peasant who may prove a Jew hater, risk yourself with a priest, take refuge at night in a church, in a chapel; you may succeed."

The boys had taken in every word in utter concentration. "Who are you then?" the leader whispered.

"My name is Menahem. If any of you succeed, if you live, then tell that you knew Menahem on this train."

The boys had removed both bars. A body could wiggle through. Now, in the predawn, an attempt would already be somewhat more dangerous than at night—there must be guards atop the train. But to wait for another night might be to lose the chance. Half the car had come awake, discussing in fearful, hushed tones.

Geza was raised on the shoulders of the sturdiest. The train was on an upgrade, moving slowly. The right situation. Now! The boy grasped the edges of the opening and projected his head through. Then farther. His body was balanced to tumble. With one more thrust, his legs were partway out; only his ankles were still held from below. The entire community of the boxcar now watched as though all were one being, suspended.

A gunburst came from the roof. The body pulled loose and tumbled, the feet in hiking shoes yanked out of the hold of his teammates; an astonished cry came back to an anguished echoing in the death car, like a commingled throat rattle.

Perhaps he was not dead, only wounded, and would still manage?

But if only wounded, the boys said, would not the train be halted with SS men leaping off to destroy him? This also was not certain, Menahem told them, as the train was on a difficult climbing pitch; it could not halt; the engine would not be able to start up this incline again. "He may yet have a chance." But now no others could be risked.

Only shallow breathing remained possible.

Where might they be now? For a long time no one even dared

hoist himself to look outward. To Menahem it seemed that the train must have taken the line through Bratislava and farther on waited most of the night on a siding, perhaps at Brno.

The entire journey to Auschwitz could already have been made three times over. If the train moved again at night, perhaps a second attempt could be made. Perhaps himself.

Late in the afternoon came a death. An elderly man suddenly crimped into a tight gasping, his teeth bared with pain, while his wife cradled his head and called his name, Moritz, Moritz, and the pharmacist like a doctor with his little valise tried to reach the stricken one. He lay for a time with upturned eyes, while his wife pleaded—he had had these attacks twice before, he should be taken at once to a hospital—and caught herself up. Then he was dead, and she sat rigidly repeating, Perhaps it was best—if only she too— Their married daughter was in Budapest, God grant that the daughter and her children would be spared; it was said Budapest would be last; the war was nearly over; all that she and Moritz had prayed for, if there was a God in heaven, was for Him to take them instead of the children.

A space, a hand breadth of emptiness was around the corpse. Distractedly, the woman tried to spread her shawl. A square-bearded pious Jew edged close. Did he have a tallis? Yes, yes, Moritz had possessed a tallis, but she had not brought it. "I am afraid I did not bring it."

The pious one turned his head, calling the names of a few men, "Jews, let us say Kaddish." For anyone to move closer to the corpse was difficult, but from all corners, voices joined; Menahem too joined in, and quietly, as though should their voices carry outside the wagon they might be forbidden, the Kaddish was repeated.

Sanctified and glorified and hallowed and exalted—the words rose and then fell, with an uncertain, even puzzled intonation, and Menahem too almost could not bring himself to say them.

Then what should be done if the train halted again, should an effort be made to tell the guards, should the body be removed?

Menahem recalled descriptions already heard in the outer world, of transports arriving from France, from Holland, a week on their way, the doors at last pulled open, with a few surviving wraiths emerging from piled-up dead.

Again the train was halting somewhere in a railyard yard, *Wasser, Wasser, wodo*, people cried out, then came the iron sounds of doors rolled back, at last theirs. Two SS men called for some shit Jew to bring out the filth pail; meanwhile, everyone gasped air. Carefully holding the pail aloft, the lad called Lotzi threaded through, was led to a cesspool and quickly back, the pail hardly rinsed, and filled with water. Meanwhile, the water pail, in charge of the pharmacist, had also been taken to be filled. As it was handed to him, he kept trying to explain—there was a corpse. The door rolled shut. Clanging iron was heard the length of the train, and suddenly the cars jerked into motion as though now there was haste.

From the old days of shipping road rollers from Poland, Menahem thought he had recognized the Katowitz yard; then Auschwitz was not far.

All was flatland. From the observation hole: "It's all gray. Marshes. Nothing. Some factories—I don't know."

Slowing down. People were nervously arranging themselves. "Don't leave my side." "Stay together whatever happens." And children were solemn, obedient.

The train had halted. *"Raus! Schnell!"* A long platform as though known to Menahem from before; SS men supervising, but all along were stationed shaven-headed heftlings, in their striped pajamalike convict clothes, the "welcomers" as he knew from reports, the special platform commando, speaking Yiddish, Hungarian, giving a hand to the aged, to the children. "Nein, nein, have no fear, yes, indeed, it is Auschwitz, but as you see, we ourselves are Jews, here we are alive and working, leave your baggage here, it will be sorted out, you will find it all, later, but be sure your name is on your belongings. First you must be registered, just like in a hotel—not so?"

Menahem glanced behind. The train had passed through an archway and from above, machine guns covered the platform. This must be Birkenau, the adjunct to Auschwitz, this would be the concentrated slaughterhouse, with the newest, the underground gas chambers, already nearly two million dead in this place. The British had still refused bombardment, for technical reasons, they said.

Ahead on the platform the selection line was forming. Already from here, some reports had said, the smoke of the chimneys could be seen. There was a row of trees, but behind them, smoke would be seen, rising. Perhaps just now there was an interval. The smoke will arise from us, Menahem thought.

There was the legend of the Jewish girl, an actress, who, on

513

arriving before the selection officer, had seized a pistol from the holster of an SS and shot two of them dead before she was destroyed. Should he try? And if the four athletes together— It would unloose machine-gunning along the entire line. Even those selected for labor. Did he have the right to make the decision?

And even in this feeder line, five abreast, the people wanted to believe the welcomers: "Don't fear, the men and the young women will be sent to labor; the old and the children and their mothers will go to a separate place. That is the reason for the selection. Don't worry. It is all well organized here."

From up front came the desperate cries of sundering, wives, husbands, the last sundering of hands. One of the athletes, Georg, was trying to find his sister. An SS pushed him back. All were calling out names, seeking, while the welcomers kept reassuring them, "You'll soon be together."

And even here people wanted to believe.

Menahem took his place along with the athletes. Would it be Dr. Mengele himself? Suddenly it came over Menahem that his two-day stubble must show gray. He glanced upward again as though now already he would see the smoke from his own body.

The boys Muntchik and Lotzi pressed themselves close on each side of him. But wouldn't he seem even more aged, between the young lads? The boys kept turning, trying to see into the other line, the women and children, calling out names. Silence! They were menaced. Their line neared the platform. Two officers. The dandy must be Mengele. The finger moved. To the left, to the right. In the line before them, only one to the right. Now Lotzi. To the right. Saved. Menahem held himself erect, head up. The sun was low, his face in shadow. Did something less than a flicker, something direct, pass between Mengele and himself? An irony in those eyes? Lotzi seized him—safe! The three other boys came— their whole row!

Straining to keep sight of the line of women and children, the boys began to mutter against themselves for having got separated at the loading itself, into different cars than their families. Suddenly Menahem saw the large one, Muntchik, go rigid, with a stifled "No!" He had caught sight of them all—his mother, small brothers and sisters, on the other line, to the left. Then Georg cried out, "Magda!" He had seen his sister among the few girls sent to the right!

But now all, all, from both male and female columns were being sent to the fatal side. At the head of that column stood a Red

514

Cross van. One of the reports had mentioned it. The van carried the containers of gas.

Just at the end, in the line of doomed women, Menahem glimpsed the pharmacist's wife with the younger children. But not the girl Bella. Lotzi too had noticed. The female group chosen for labor was already led off. Perhaps. Perhaps.

Now at a run, SS alongside with hounds, all exactly as though he had already done it, *schnell*, run, you damned shits. A turn, and here you saw. From two of the four chimneys. A slight breeze took the smoke rearward. And then as they halted, gasping—the full odor. In the first whiff, before the fullness entered him, there was insanely for Menahem the recollection of his first inhalation on arrival in Palestine of the oversweet orange-blossom aroma blanketing Petah Tikva. Then, from even earlier, the sweetish stench, the abattoir in Chicago.

Into the long, barren shed. Strip naked, clothes here. On a bench, head seized, clipped, the wrist seized for the tattoo needle, number 892641, name, age—he took off twelve years—birthplace, all his identities fallen away. *Fach?* Somewhere in his mind Menahem had considered this—if he should pass the selection. Masonry? "Ironworker, welder," the words came out.

Remnants of clothing flung to each in line, sterilized rags, already with the Jew patch from the dead.

The barracks, all as described, the block chief with the criminal patch, a Pole he looked, a face that was simply meat. "Mine is a clean block, I don't give a damn if you live a few weeks or die right away; only obey rules and keep my block clean." He motioned to vacant bunkers. Quick, try for the highest tier, headroom enough to sit up, places for the four lads and himself, the planks strangely like those on a refugee ship except the spaces were even narrower.

Another approached; greenpatched, smallish, he was a block assistant, a small man with a knowing, intimate look in his half-hooded eyes. "You heard of the attempt?" he half whispered, his eyes peering from one to the other. The attempt? The eyes still peered as though to catch them. His voice was even less than before. "On the Führer." Was it some trap? "We heard nothing," Menahem said. "We were on the train." "It was yesterday. A bomb. All were caught. He escaped unhurt." Menahem glanced quickly at the boys: show nothing. The small eyes had an intimate, malicious gleam. Then the block monitor shrugged and went away.

On their shelf they whispered, Could it be true? And what matter if true since he had escaped? No, but still—a bomb! It showed there was still— And a kind of strength seemed to seep up through remnants of their torn, deadened selves. If it should be true.

The work commandos were returning, shuffling, stumbling in. A few came to their section moving dazedly in their exhaustion. Still, one or two asked, "Where from?"

About the block monitor's tale—"Should we believe him?" "What?" "The attempt?" An uncertain nod. Yet a gleam. Then: "Be careful before him." In the latrine someone had it from a sure source. The bomb was at a high-up meeting. A few had been killed. But the devil had protected the devil. Still—

He could endure. If not too long. What strength the news had given. If it had only happened a few days before, perhaps even Eichmann— He must not allow himself to think in this way. Indeed, this event, like the Allied landing, might lead to even greater fury. But he must endure. As he stood with the four boys an hour and a half through their first appell, Menahem overcame the slow, dragging desire to give way, collapse, be finished.

The other two chimneys were now active, with red streaks in the smoke. The odor was heavier. In the row ahead, someone from their own train retched and was clouted down into his vomit.

Four dead, carried in by their workmates for their final roll call, lay alongside the ranks, like patches of still-articulated bones dug from the ground. Almost all the heftlings were equally skeletal, yet as long as a being stood, he did not seem a corpse. They stood in their muddied tatters that were like rags hanging with only the skull and the hands attached; those with the vacant eyes were the mussulmen, Menahem knew the word, they had reached that state of total absence that could continue for weeks before the body, too, was finished. But still, one saw men whose faces had the mark of having passed beyond all destruction to endurance. And long ago, in the First World War, from the dungeon prisons of Damascus, Menahem had seen wraiths emerge, like these, and Max Wilner still lived, to this day.

Of their own transport, who lived? Already in the admission process and now in their barrack, those from their train tried to put together what each had seen. Georg had seen his sister Magda. Lotzi still hoped for Bella. To another lad who kept asking for a girl named Juli, from their class, Muntchik was able to say yes, he had seen her on the side of the living.

Up to two thousand in a single batch, reports had said. Fifteen minutes, even less. Then the doors on the furnace side were opened. How many furnaces in the row? Menahem didn't recall. But there returned to him the image from the report of the conscience-Nazi, related to him by that Swedish courier in Istanbul. The opening of the giant iron evacuation doors, and there in the death chamber a standing mass of naked dead. A child held on the shoulders of the father, aloft to gain one more breath of life.

The final curiosity persisted in Menahem. Was he yet to see this? It was as though the sight had to come as the completion of what had propelled him from Istanbul, this far. A Medusa sight. Did a soul in death carry away the image of one's death, as some believed?

Only the furnace tenders, the sonderkommando, saw and lived on for a while until, in their turn, they were destroyed. And whoever else of the heftlings might in some way, even by accident, catch sight, he too was destroyed. So that into eternity, except for the destroyers, this sight would be as though it had never been.

He was to see it.

They were marched off, all in the same commando. Nearly an hour's march. Pick and shovel work in mud-clay, some thought it was for drainage. But the channel went too deep. Some said it was the foundation for a factory. The Nazis still meant to build factories! The experienced were indifferent, concentrating only to slow the pace after the SS passed.

The kommando was entirely Jewish; as much as half from their own train, mixed with Jews from Salonika; they were strong, they had been porters; one day he would talk to them of their cousins who worked on the Haifa docks. They had already endured a month, losing only a fourth of their number. At the other end of the ditch were non-Jews, resistants from Holland who had arrived in a transport two weeks before.

Menahem noticed that the channel they were digging was, in width, the length of a man.

In unwatched moments he tried to show each of his four boys

how to hold, how to handle a pick and shovel. Until their hands hardened, the blisters would come, but with a proper hold the worst could be avoided. Suddenly he received a crack on the head from the kapo; the blow hurled him into the mud, his left leg tripping against his pick handle. Regaining his feet, Menahem labored on in a daze of pain; in Muntchik's eyes he saw tears.

Half dozing at last despite the throbbing in his leg, Menahem was wakened by cramps. He had downed the nauseating soup. Now he tried to hold back the diarrhea; he was between two of the boys and would have to climb over Miklos to lower himself to go out. But Miklos had awakened; he too felt it coming and climbed down first.

The night was unutterably serene, starry, as though the whole universe were uncontaminated.

In the excremental ooze in the latrine, two or three other figures were doubled over the trench; almost before Menahem could squat, the diarrhea explosion came. Surely it would recur. Better to wait here? Farther down, a heftling was slumped against the wall, asleep or dead.

They returned to their lager. Again the need was there, but it must be near wake-up time. Menahem held on, so as not to disturb the whole tier. Finally, it became impossible. He climbed over Miklos. In a few days his body must become adjusted.

The third night the diarrhea still woke him. During the day he sometimes had to drop his pants quickly, in the trench, lucky not to be caught by the kapo. The boys shielded him. By now nothing came, hardly a leakage; Menahem had always bragged of a cast-iron stomach; it was true that in Turkey he had eaten well, he had gone soft. But the boys were adjusting better than he, at least in their bodies.

He had not thought he would deteriorate so soon. From those who were longer in the barracks it became clear that many bodies endured only a few weeks, but this was also because of demoralization. He must endure.

The diarrhea stopped, but his strength was going. Each day the boys had to keep closer watch, always one had an eye on the kapo to warn Menahem when to lift his pick.

In the hour before sleep, Menahem would lie and talk quietly with the boys, of Eretz. The presence of the four of them brought back strength, almost as though they were his sons. He told of

Giora, imprisoned since the Nazi conquest of Greece. A flier, though the British had only let him service their machines. He told them how at their own age he had come to Eretz with his close friend Yechezkiel, as close to him as they were to one another, and how Yechezkiel had been shot down from ambush. But, instead of vengefulness, he had felt he must try to understand the Arabs. And he had gone to live with a Bedouin tribe. No, such shootings had been different then, from the Arab revolt of a few years ago in Palestine. Even that, the boys remembered only from headlines in the papers; they had been too busy with schooling. In his early days, Menahem explained, the raids had in them nothing of politics. Often the bandits were from a Bedouin tribe; they had a contempt for the settled Arab villagers and raided them for cattle, for horses. So they raided the new Jewish villages for plunder as well. But once you showed you had courage, it became different. You could make peace. Only twenty years afterward had a political movement started, among the town and city Arabs.

It was strange to be lying here preaching Zionism: Menahem thought fleetingly of Christians in the catacombs preaching their faith before they became martyrs. They had done it to save souls that must soon go to heaven or to hell. But no, it was not for life after death that he talked to his boys, but still for life in life.

Muntchik was the strongest-minded of the four; also, he had a logical mind. With the Arabs, Menahem explained, there was another factor—one had to try to understand. A balanced way of life, centuries unchanged. It had been even enjoyable for him to go out with the flocks and in the evening to hear Bedouin tales by the fire; all had seemed simpler. This had been the life of Abraham. You could still feel the ancient tribal fear that others would come and make use of the scarce water from your well. This fear perhaps still lay even in the Arab who was no longer a Bedouin but a settled villager, a fellah.

The whole of Palestine was perhaps, to the Arabs, like such a well. Indeed, if you thought back, even when Abraham came into the land, down in Beersheba, he had made sure to dig his own well. And he had got on with his neighbors. And the Jews of today also could do so. See how during the war years there had been no trouble between the Jews and the Arabs.

He told the boys the tale of the dib, an experience of his own son, his eldest, Yechezkiel. One evening a Bedouin lad came running, believing he was pursued by a dib, a yellow-eyed werewolf.

The settlement watchman had "saved" him, taking him back to his father's tent. The next day the entire tribe arrived with gifts. But the "dib" with the burning yellow eyes had only been a tractor with headlights, working late in the outlying fields.

Muntchik nodded. The terrible lag between the old and the new. A problem all over the world.

Menahem slept well, but still, the next day he was weaker and at one interval was in a kind of vacancy that he recognized only when he revived from it, a lapse of mind like the lapse of energy in his body. How long had he been "away"? Not long enough for the kapo to catch him or even for the boys to notice. Was he beginning to slip into the condition of the mussulmen? He looked quickly to Muntchik and thought he caught, before it disappeared like a figure around the corner, an expression of frightened concern. After a time, Muntchik slipped into his hand a fragment of bread. "Take it, take it, I am all right."

Menahem swallowed the crust. A weepiness arose in him and was banished. All the way back to the camp, the boys took turns supporting him.

Those same days began the frantic apogee of the action on the Hungarian Jews. Long trains arrived unceasingly; sometimes twelve thousand Jews from Hungary were spilled on the platforms in a single day; the barracks were jammed; Mengele came through them, making selection after selection, all the mussulmen were carted off to make room, and after dark, truckloads passed from the women's area, crowded with victims uttering their last screams, one glimpsed them under the watchtower beams, streaks of whitish nakedness.

Then the platform selections for new arrivals were abandoned altogether; some trains were run on a prolonged track directly to where Menahem's commando had been digging. There the arrivals were mowed down by machine-gun fire; most fell across lengthwise. Gasoline was poured over the human mass, and the long, wide trench was set aflame. The crematoriums were inadequate.

In a frenzy to finish before prevention might come, the final fernichtung must take place; even the old gas chamber, the first one in Auschwitz, which had become an air-raid shelter, was reactivated. From every chimney rose black bursts, almost solid, with streaks of flames in them. On the fields of the death trenches could be seen the scar lines of smoldering flame, and the entire flat morass lay under the solid sweetish stench.

In the second week of this continuous slaughter, their kapo one morning in the appell called out Menahem's number. He had to stand aside. As the rest marched off, the eyes of the boys lingered on him.

Menahem was marched by an SS. It was the lane to Auschwitz proper. Then a turn toward the workshops. Could they after all have plucked his labor classification from their files?

They entered a broad shed filled with iron clamor. Somewhere in the rear he saw welding sparks. The work master seemed to be a Czech, by his patch a political, a tallish, middle-aged man with a glistening dome. Indicating a blowtorch and a toolbox to Menahem, he said, "A bolt has come loose. I am shorthanded."

Menahem followed the SS.

It was all the way back to Birkenau; the toolbox was heavy. His leg still sometimes throbbed from that first-day blow. If now the leg collapsed under him, Menahem saw that he would not have far to be transported, for the SS was conducting him beyond the masking stand of trees. Three chimneys smoked, almost torpidly, as though in afterdigestion.

He was being led down the paved incline toward the entrance doors. It seemed to him the five-abreast column was there with him, herded down this incline between lanes of SS, *schnell, schnell*. By now surely all knew. Didn't there rise in them, engulf them only one desire, to have it over with, quickly done with, no more agony, no more self-deceiving hope, no more existence in a world where this could happen. Even a haste to be finished in themselves with whatever had made them consider there was God, whatever had made them believe in humanity. Hurry! Run! To be done with it! An end, an end to being in such a world! And where had he, Menahem, heard a tale that Jews went into the gas chamber as in a holy procession, chanting "Ani Ma'amin"—already the sanctified legend, I Believe. As of the Spanish Jews solemnly offering themselves to the auto-da-fé, sanctifying the Name, crying "Kiddush HaShem" and the Shma. Legends! Blaspheme and die!

They halted before a broad door. The SS pushed a button.

And what of the tale whispered of a selection last week in the women's camp, half of them in the mussulman state, some from the "hospital" barracks with typhus, some too weak to work. Then, locked in the gas chamber, waiting the whole night. Cries and entreaties eerily heard emerging half audible as stifled whispers. Finish with us already, finish, finish. There had been a temporary shortage of the canisters of chemical pellets. Zyklon B.

The door opened. A large empty chamber with benches, like an undressing room in a gymnasium. Even hooks on the walls with notices to remember your hook number. Then to the side a wide pair of yellow-painted metal doors. Each had three sets of bolted hinges; on the right-hand door the end bolt in the middle hinge was loose. "What the devil are you waiting for, get to work! Soon comes the transport."

To make the repair, Menahem indicated, the door would have to stand ajar. Another SS appeared and unlocked the door. Inside, empty. The size of the undressing room; rows of shower heads in the ceiling. Floors and walls still damp. Then only a real shower such as he had been through in his own reception? Now he saw the vertical pipes with apertures. Mentioned in the reports. For the gas from the dissolving pellets. Did there still linger in the chamber some vestige of acridity? He did not know the odor of prussic acid. The dampness was all the way up the walls; a hosing afterward. In the opposite wall were two huge iron doors on rollers, now closed.

Then quickly Menahem lit his torch and began to braze the hasp. Cracked from the sudden force of a tumultuous terror wave. Their tumult seemed to resound in his ears. A solid mass surging against the locked doors. Then at one moment, as he looked upward along the inner side of the doorframe, Menahem saw on the wall the marks of finger scratchings, clawings, up to the height of raised arms, and then, even higher, he saw a small hand imprint, a child raised up on a father's, a mother's shoulders. One more breath.

Why didn't he turn the acetylene flame on the SS, on himself?

Perhaps as they emerged, he would receive the shot in the back of his neck. And even now in fleeting gallows humor, he wondered if they would drag a single body to remove the gold from his teeth, or fling it directly into an oven.

Returned to the workshop, Menahem set down the toolbox on a zinc table. The work master glanced at him. "You repaired the shower-room door?"

"Yes. The shower-room door."

His SS guard departed.

The Czech opened a drawer of his desk, took a heel of bread the size of a double ration, and handed it to Menahem. There was no communication on his face. But with a chin movement he summoned a heftling, who led Menahem to the rear of the shop, where sections of ventilation pipe were being welded together for the new underground factories.

Some days later, when he felt that the Czech would keep him on in the workshop, and an occasional bit of conversation came between them, Menahem found a moment to ask his question. The first part of the answer he thought he already understood. For the repair of the door, Anton had not wanted to send one of his regular heftling workers, since to see the death chamber meant death. So he had called for an ironworker, and Menahem's card had been pulled out. Only, after the task was finished? True, he had been careful to say he had repaired the door of a shower room. But still, Anton had doubtless in some way protected him. One day the Czech stood alongside him during a truck-axle repair, and remarked, not unkindly, "Well, you have learned here more about this work than you ever knew in your life."

"I wondered why you kept me."

"Your white hair."

Startled, Menahem realized that on his shaved head a white stubble had grown. He gazed at the Czech. The same, though the work master was, at most, in his early forties. "Why should only the young have a chance to survive?" the Czech said, his odd seriousness tinted with irony.

The frenzy seemed to be abating. After several weeks there came gaps in the procession of Hungarian transports. The burning pits for the overflow were less in use, and it even seemed that a slightly larger proportion now survived the selection on the siding. In the barracks, a youngish sports teacher from the latest transport, whose team had even once played against the boys, brought word that the provinces were Judenrein; all except the Jews of Budapest had been deported. It was said that President Roosevelt had threatened the bombing of Hungarian cities if Budapest's Jews were yielded up to the Germans. Paris had fallen, and the Nazis were in full retreat across France.

Yet trains continued to arrive. Not only sweepings of hidden Jews, but resistants and communists from all lands. A sudden wave from a failed revolt in Slovakia. Then came the Jews of

Bratislava, the thousands that Gisi Fleischman had bribed for.

There was a glazier who sometimes made repairs in the women's camp, and from him Menahem tried to find out if the name of Giselle Fleischman had been heard.

In their barracks, despite Mengele's weekly selection rounds, heftlings whose bodies had already adjusted, now even permitted themselves to think of survival, though in the face of liberation the entire mass would probably be destroyed.

A few of the kapos were becoming less brutal. Unhinted, not even by a glance, there yet arose from some of them a certain approachability—what Menahem had wildly dreamed of finding in Eichmann. A sense of afterward.

As from the kapo who singled out Lotzi for the coveted Canada kommando. "Don't forget who brought you here."

Lotzi was the sort who usually got chosen, just as he had right off been chosen to help fetch the soup caldron; though one could not say there remained in his face that boyish readiness, that glint of fun that had made him so popular in school, he still, even here at an odd moment, would produce the clipped voice of a Ronald Colman, the breathy tone of Marlene Dietrich, that gave a laugh. During the Hungarian action, mountains of suitcases had piled up; the warehouse known as Canada needed more heftlings. Soon Lotzi was bringing back under his jacket, bars of chocolate, tins of liver pâté and sardines. The real valuables, of course, he turned over to the kapo; money, gold, jewels, he wouldn't fool with; if he were caught, shooting was instant.

With a gift of liver pâté to the glazier, Lotzi one day received overwhelming news: His Bella was alive. He even managed to send her chocolate, and daily his spirit flourished. Bella was working in the Krupp plant, the glazier said, once even bringing a note for Lotzi on a scrap of the chocolate-bar wrapping. But of the other one they had asked about, Georg's sister Magda, he had no word, nor did Bella say anything of Magda in her note.

For more than a month Georg had been unable to get news of his sister; now the boy fell into depression; they had to drag him out of his bunk space to the appell. If there was no word, it was a good sign they told Georg—his sister must have been sent outside Auschwitz to a factory; in those places conditions were better. He remained dark, even began to shun Lotzi. At the workshop Menahem started inquiries for Magda through a carpenter who went more often to the women's camp. This one found out. A selection, a month ago.

Only to Muntchik did Menahem pass on the truth. It was best to keep silent, Muntchik agreed.

One twilight, as their commando was marching back to the camp, a returning commando of women was seen not far off, and from group to group voices began to call—French? Greek? Hungarian? A woman's voice cried, "Ungar," and Georg suddenly broke from the ranks, crying out his sister's name, Magda, did anyone know Magda of Kaszovar? He was lucky to be brought down by one of the hounds rather than a bullet. The flesh of his thigh was ripped, but he was allowed to stagger under lashes back to the ranks; Muntchik, hastily binding the wound with the ripped trouser cloth, managed to bring him in as he hopped on one leg. Georg would not report to the hospital block; only corpses ever came out of there. At roll call the boys managed to hold him up between them, and after the morning appell—perhaps it was already a sign of things changing—Georg slipped back and hid unmolested the whole day on the upper tier.

The wound festered. The third night the boy burrowed, doubled up against Menahem; Menahem turned and held the body, even trying to cradle it in its fetal bend. Somewhere year after year in a prison camp—his own Giora. But at least not as a Jew. As a prisoner of war. Menahem held the boy closer. Then finally let go of the body.

He lay all hollow, all feeling dissolved away, there remaining only his continuing existence. Then in his vision all, all throbbed, and in the boundless, infinite organism there was iridescent greenish maggot decay, veined blood and an undersea of fathomless harmony. All human solitudes and this boy's death were suffused with some ineffable womanly face, the peace-bringing to the tormented soul, the Shechina.

Could he still continue to live?

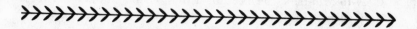

31

AFTER some weeks during which there had been no letter from Menahem, Dvora's disquiet had grown to alarm. He had written steadily during these years, and whenever an emissary returned from Istanbul, Menahem had sent little gifts for the grandchildren.

It was a difficult correspondence, over the years becoming more and more impersonal, and then yet sometimes, in a line or a few words, closer. From her side, Dvora could easily fill in with family news, war doings, news of the children and the sayings of the grandchildren, and even gossip of the kibbutz. Also inner news of the Yishuv, still given in the roundabout code, oranges for grenades, "our guests" for the British, and Dovidl for Ben-Gurion. But from Menahem's side, what could he write? From Istanbul after these several years his information had to be like Giora's guarded letters as a prisoner of war. Menahem's identity was still supposedly unknown to the British, though how could that be? He still, as Mati had managed to find out, must not come home. The charges against him were still "active."

Certain personal things a man couldn't write to his wife; although Dvora did not grudge Menahem what a man needed, she had always felt it better not to know. For herself she had long ago in his absences conquered the longings and desires that still, she was surprised to find as she aged, were not wholly ended. But she would not touch on such things even in letters personally carried to Istanbul by one of the Mossad.

Yet in the three years since the beginning of his exile, Menahem would write more and more of some inner reflections, thoughts such as he had never spoken about, and that made Dvora again feel "my chaver." Speculations, increasingly, from the time the gassing became known, on what meaning there could be in God, in being a Jew. From long, long ago, the time of his hiding in the cave from the Turks, Dvora knew her Menahem was still in some profound way religious. So she would reply, trying to meet him in these thoughts, hoping that her simplicity would not discourage him and diminish his inner words to her.

Then all communication had ceased. Had he been sent somewhere? Was he even alive? No, if he were dead, she would know. Within her she would know.

Menahem's silence, perhaps absence, had begun at the time of the furor over the emissary from Budapest, bringing to Istanbul the cold-blooded Nazi offer to spare a million Jews in exchange for needed lorries. But already that whole affair was no longer heard of. The emissary had been arrested by the British and taken to Egypt, and there it seemed the high British minister Lord Moyne had even said to him, "What would I do with a million Jews?"

And thus the Hungarian Jews were left to the Nazis. Where was the difference, a Hitler or a Lord Moyne?

Menahem must be on some mission, utterly secret. At last Dvora begged Leah to try to find out through her old chaverah Rahel, who could ask directly of Eliahu. The answer came back that Menahem had indeed gone on a special mission, but despite all effort, nothing more was known. And not a word of this was to be mentioned.

Had the British finally in some way got hold of Menahem? Dvora voyaged to Jerusalem. Mati felt sure the British didn't have him, or they would have brought him to Palestine to stand trial. Still, could the British perhaps know what might have happened to him? Mati would have to feel his way.

After Dvora went back to her kibbutz, Dena kept prodding Mati. Somehow she had an intuition Menahem was alive. How strongly she remembered that last meeting when he was here in Jerusalem in hiding. Oh, surely a man like that must remain alive!

Yet with the British, even with a CID man who often tried to pry things out of him about the Haganah, Mati got nowhere. He tried Moshe Shertok—had Joel Brand perhaps mentioned Menahem as among those he talked to in Istanbul? Indeed, Brand had described him warmly, Moshe said. But that seemed all.

Dvora would not rest. If Menahem had been there at the arrival of Joel Brand, then where had he disappeared to? Surely she could be told whether or not he was sent on a mission? And she went to the head of the Mossad himself, to Shaul in Degania. In his deliberate, thoughtful way Shaul spoke of all Menahem had done, as far back as the work in Poland and also here on the Syrian border. Was he speaking as of a chaver who is dead?

"Surely you can tell me if it is known whether he is alive or dead?"

"Dvora, chaverah, if I knew, I would tell you." One thing about Shaul, he would not deceive you. If he could not say, he would simply remain silent.

"Then it is not known if he is dead?" No. "Nor if he is alive?" No. "Can you tell me if it is known where he might be?"

This, he said, he could not answer. He gazed at her and Dvora suddenly felt—he was so warmhearted, how could he bear his task?

At last Leah told Dvora she herself would go to Ben-Gurion. Of late years, though he was still a chaver approachable to everyone, you knew he had so many problems on his mind, a real statesman he had become, that you did not want to trouble him. It was through Paula that Leah arranged the meeting so as not to make it an office affair. "Come to the house, come on Shabbat late in the morning," Paula advised, "you'll sit with him over a glass of tea; it is the only time they don't torment him with their schemes and their intrigues and their party disputes. It is the only time he ever sees the children." And Paula went on about how the weight of the whole Yishuv rested on him—the others only saw that the war would soon be over, but Ben-Gurion foresaw that for the Jews it would only begin.

Still, Leah had to wait out a dozen others who came for a glass of tea. At last he sighed, Leatchkeh, with a push-away motion of his two hands from his ears, to clear his head of all those other problems. Nu, he was aware why she had come. Did she have to prod him about Menahem? How many were left from those old days? He had made every inquiry from those in Istanbul; they were even in touch with that chaver of Brand's in the committee in Budapest—Reszo Kastner.

In Budapest?

528

Then at last that much came out. Not a word must be said; Leah was allowed to tell only Dvora, and under strictest secrecy. At the peak of the Joel Brand affair, Menahem had taken it on himself to go there to Budapest. It was believed he had arrived, though neither Reszo Kastner nor anyone of the committee had seen him. No one. Unlike the three parachutists who had been traced to Hungarian prisons, of Menahem nothing whatever was known. And for this very reason there must be absolute silence. As long as the Jewish population of Budapest itself had not been deported, there could be some hope. He might be hidden and unable to give a sign.

Or, Leah told herself, she had to recognize—Menahem might have been swallowed into the Nazi maw.

As much as she had learned Leah told Dvora, but even from Menahem's children the secret had to be kept.

Within Dvora something changed. Even up to these years there had persisted in her, at times when she still drifted to the early girlish dreams of pure love, the image of young Yechezkiel. The Sabbath Eve when Yechezkiel had come riding over the hill to Mishkan Yaacov, a suitor. The romantic sweet days in Sejera just before their wedding was to have taken place. In her heart, none of this had ever been a denial or a betrayal of Menahem. It had only been the way any woman dreams of an early sweetheart, of her time of innocence. But the dream-memory had gone on sometimes into fantasies of what her life would have been like with Yechezkiel had he not been shot down. Perhaps the very same life here in the kibbutz. She would stop herself from imagining other children.

And now, only now these imaginings of Yechezkiel actually ceased to appear, and instead, she kept seeing the way in which Menahem had come for her after his absence among the Bedouin. And the image of the first night she had lain with him on the ground. Because of this change in her imaginings, an uneasiness developed in Dvora. Could this be a portent that Menahem no longer lived?

※ ※ ※

After Rommel had been chased out of North Africa, Avinoam found himself transferred back into the Palestine Buffs; no more commando operations: it was trucking water to desert outposts. The only difference between this and World War I, he told Gil, who usually rode with him, was that in Trumpeldor's outfit thé British had the Jews driving mules, and now they let them drive six-wheelers.

When he heard of the hush-hush operation, the parachutists to drop behind enemy lines in Europe, he put in, but you had to have been born and raised in someplace like Yugoslavia or Hungary so you knew your way around, and could talk the language to perfection.

Yet dull and useless as it felt, there was a kind of bearableness, even the close comradeliness of the barracks routine, and sometimes the chevreh wondered if they'd ever be able to get used to any other life. Gil, too, had been in it ever since Wingate; though he'd been in a different squad, they'd seen a couple of actions together, and Gil would sometimes even fall back into calling him Noam. Gil had known Avi, too, even before Wingate, as he was from Kibbutz Degania, right down the road.

On the long nights they often talked of the Yadid, trying to figure him out. Gil thought of him as a goy-Jew, but Avinoam said no, he was a true Christian Englishman, the crazy kind the English sometimes had. He was a Zionist the way those crazy Englishmen adopt a cause.

When Wingate's death came in the crash in Burma, the old blind wrath came over Avinoam as though he could go out and mow down the whole damn world. The rotten years the British had given the Yadid after they took him out of Palestine, until he had tried to kill himself, slashing his throat. Then at last they'd given him his kind of job again. On the long desert drive that day with Gil they talked and talked of the Yadid. There was the time the Arabs had ambushed Sturman, the old Shomer, planting a mine for his tender to hit, while he sat in one of their little cafés in Beisan. And when Wingate got the news at Ein Harod, rushing straight to that café, dragging an Arab outside and stuffing dirt into his mouth, forcing him to eat it until he told where the gang was from. The squads had stormed up the Gilboa. "I want no prisoners." The way his eyes were when you couldn't look into them. So they had done it.

For long desert miles the two of them discussed this. Perhaps a Jew would not have given such an order to kill. Sure, there were Jews who would. It was like divine wrath, like the slaughters of the ancient days, falling on the Amalekites. You killed the enemy who killed your own. There came back, in Noam, the time of the death of Avi. And presently a grief, a mourning silenced the two of them, as though they were riding in this limitless desert to their true commander's burial. The Yadid.

Finally that fall, as the end seemed in sight, there came the formation of the Jewish Brigades; the Buffs and scattered Jewish units from every British formation were assembled for training. Paris was already taken and here they were still drilling in the desert wastes. Substitutes to be sent into the game before the whistle blew.

All the chevreh talked about was would they get a chance finally to get into Germany.

Some even imagined themselves sweeping into the death camps, liberating the last Jews. One fellow, Dov Gruner, a Hungarian who had got out of there before the war, said part of his family had stayed behind, and could be in those convoys right now.

Then Gil learned the destination. The Italian front.

All right, as the Italians had already been knocked out of the war, it would still be Germans facing them. They still might get their chance.

A troop ship, and then an Italian mountain town for another month of drill. Oh the British.

The rabbi chaplain held Yom Kippur services, and Moshe Shertok and other bigwigs came to tell them the whole world was excited over them, Jewish fighters at last at the front facing Germans.

And the day came. They filed into the dugouts, replacing an outfit of Ghurkas. There would soon be a push on the whole line, was the story. Before their bunker lay a flatland cut by wide irrigation canals; on the opposite embankment of their canal they could make out the small dark holes of German firing posts, and behind were a few two-story houses where the enemy had heavy machine guns. All between, the Ghurkas said as they left, was heavily mined, watch out, the favorite German footmines, you'd get your balls blown off.

Though the attack order was welcome, Avinoam saw that Gil shared his puzzlement. To attack at noon? in broad daylight? Was this some joke on the Jews? A surprise raid, to straighten out a kink in the line before the big push. Tank support would follow.

The surprise didn't last long. Their squad had managed to sneak across a dead spot where the opposite embankment was cut by a

531

railway; now a couple of sappers were digging out the mines, tossing them back into the canal, there was a footmine at every step. Gil motioned, and crawled ahead, when heavy machine-gun volleys hit them from the upper floors of the houses back there, and from further back came artillery fire, perfectly ranged in. Five men were hit before they could back off in the narrow mine-cleared path, and take cover. No tanks. No counterartillery. They made it to the half-wrecked railway bridge and lay underneath, on chunks of concrete that kept them out of the water. Navo, a medic, went out and managed to pull in a wounded. Bullets trailed him as he rolled his man under the bridge. He went out a second time and was again under fire but made it, and insisted on trying once more. This time Navo didn't come back. Gil screamed in outrage on his walkie-talkie, and Laskov, at their command post, got on the German radio wave and protested about violation of the Geneva convention for medics to pull out wounded. The reply came back, the Geneva convention was honored by the Reich, the voice said with mocking formality, but the Jewish unit had perhaps not been informed by the Command of the British Eighth Army that the medical armband could be honored only after a temporary local ceasefire for removal of wounded had been agreed upon.

In the middle of the night, on watch, Avinoam heard something. As in the Wingate times—nothing more than a rolled pebble. He peered through the firing aperture. A bare sliver of reflection from the canal, a black mirror. Yet he sensed. They had probably done the same thing: waded across under that wrecked bridge. A surprise counterattack to get the Jews. They must have sappers working in the mined approaches, right now.

Laskov himself answered the field telephone. He too had awakened with that eerie feeling. All right—from up there in the command post he might spot them. "Alert the chevreh." They were to keep their heads down so his Vickers could fire close above them. "Listen, I'm coming to help," Avinoam said and snaked back to the command post.

Laskov used Wingate's old stunt, the flaregun, and as he saw the enemy Avinoam had to laugh. They were caught cold in startled half-upright poses just like the Arabs over the oil pipeline. He opened with the Vickers. It was slaughter.

The next morning the tanks appeared. Assault troops moved through their position; the whole line went forward—the big action. But the Germans had evacuated.

In the lull before their unit was to join the forward sweep, Avinoam walked with Gil over to the field of last night's slaughter.

There they lay. The real ones. Real Germans. Walking among them with Gil, Noam found himself saying the usual hating things, the foul bastards, the herrenvolk, served them right. And yet, perhaps in Gil's quietness, some underneath feelings were there too. Maybe a plain brute pity, like he had even felt for those Hauranis that came to get themselves killed for a few pounds a month. Here it hadn't even been for the few pounds, but then why? for some crazy Hitler's idea of ruling the world? There were even middle-aged men, balding, nothing like the blond supermen of their pictures. You walked among them, these sprawled and torn bodies, coated and helmeted and strapped, all kinds of equipment they carried, strapped on, their gas masks, and a trench shovel tied on the belt, even their dinner kits, their ammo belts, trench-knives, and their weapons still clutched, and some with binocular cases which you automatically stooped to examine, were they worth picking up? Even packs on their backs, where did they think they were going? Dead now, with all the bits and pieces of gear, their helmets—some had a couple of holes. Maybe he had done it. This one, with a helmet can-opened from a chunk of a mine, and half of his brain hanging out. And this one with his face gone and only the clean black hollow of his skull still there. And this one with his head dug in his arms, trying to protect himself from what hit him. And this one, curled in a ball. And a kid that looked sixteen with a bazooka in his hands. Next to him lay a fatherly one with iron-gray mustaches and an expression of acceptance as though he had expected his end here. Poor buggery bastards, driven to this field in Italy where their lousy ally Mussolini had fucked up. Still clutching their wooden-handled grenades to hurl, and with their waterflasks on their webbed belts, and here was one with a map case. You even felt a kind of shame for them, for having kept on until this happened to them. Oh they had really caught it here last night.

A few Lugers to pick up. But he couldn't somehow bring himself to pull the binoculars from the hands of the schoolteacher-looking one, who still held them to his eyes. At night, what did he imagine he would see.

Gil too looked down on the man, and shrugged. The two of them stood still. So they had finally come to the real enemy. In the commando raid on Bardia, Avinoam had seen only Italians. And though the war would still continue for a time, and though they

533

might still be killed, Noam supposed that for them it was finished here on this field. He spoke inwardly, "Nu, Avi, here they are. The supermen. That's all there was to them."

✣ ✣ ✣

Rotten luck, the two boys had been caught right off, as they tried to get away on their bicycles. They had been blocked in traffic on the Nile bridge, with shrieking whistles, horns, and howling Egyptians. Why in hell hadn't they planned a better getaway! If Stern was alive, he'd have seen to it. Was this a reprisal for his murder? Lord Moyne himself! Right at the door of the Residence! No, this was surely for the million Jews. "What would I do with a million Jews?" Moyne had said to that Jew bringing the proposition from the Nazis. Well, he had his answer. He was also the one who had held up the formation of the Jewish Brigade from the start of the war; it was Churchill himself who had had to push it through at last. Uri hadn't put in for it. Araleh believed he could do more here. Last home leave, he had taken along the newest compact transmitter, a beauty.

Uri kept his head close to the work table, his eyes down, though even through the headset, in the small tight communications room, he could hear the Britishers, and knew they knew he could hear them: "The cowardly Jew bastards" . . . "all alike, the whole bloody lot . . ." More and more, these war years in Cairo, he had got the feeling that the Sternists had been right, it was the British, more than the Arabs who were the enemy. The new Irgun commander saw it, calling off the truce and declaring war on the British. Tsila said Araleh had met with him, a brilliant mind. His real name was Menahem Begin—the last elected commander of the Betar in Poland. He had escaped to the Russian side in the surrendering Polish army, and when the Nazis attacked Russia, was in those Polish troops that volunteered to join the Allies. They had been brought all the way from Siberia, down through Teheran, many of them to be encamped in Palestine. Luckily for Begin, he had got there, and then slipped out, to be hidden by the Irgun.

If given an order, like these two boys, Uri wondered—could he have carried it off? When he got back home—the war couldn't last much longer—and when he got back he would go on an action. He would insist on going on an action.

534

At home, this thing today would mean a terrible crackdown. They already had half the Stern and a big part of the Irgun in a detention camp in Africa, but now, this would mean a real hunting season. They might even get Araleh. Never Begin, Araleh said.

The insane idiots, Reggie cried, did they imagine the British would open the gates just because of an assassination? Ben-Gurion was so furious no one dared go near him. Once and for all the leadership had to be able to work without being stabbed from behind, each time something was about to be achieved. B-G had enough of the dissidents. The Sternists and Irgunists, both.

But what the British demanded now, couldn't even be whispered. Some said the CID had all the lists anyway. Others dropped bitter enigmatic words about "the season."

That B.-G. hated with a deadly hatred was widely known. There was the tale about the sack of dirt dropped on B.-G., in Poland, in his own city of Plonsk, by Irgunists. But Mati could not bring himself to think of Ben-Gurion as a man who could take personal revenge. It was simply that with all the ghastly problems confronting him, the Old Man didn't need more. The British were threatening even to cancel the Jewish Brigade unless there was "cooperation." A clean sweep. The arrests were all down the line. But dammit the CID had all the lists anyway. This was rubbing Jewish faces in the dirt.

You couldn't look your best friend in the eye. There were even moments such as Mati had never before felt with Reggie. The thing lay between them. Once when the girls were busy with the kids, Reggie suddenly broke it with his way—a flip remark. "You don't want to ask me what I don't want to ask you." They had a bitter laugh over it, and it was almost gone. Mati knew Reggie didn't work with the CID. But Reggie must know who did.

And you couldn't help feeling pity and grief for the two boys, like all the other brave, idealistic boys, what they had done they had carried out because of pure idealism. How could they ever be made to understand that such wild actions set things back to zero. Sometimes you just wished you were free to do something like that yourself.

Like rat-teeth the gnawing went on inside. Sometimes during those few months of "the season" Mati even welcomed the gnawing ulcer.

❧ ❧ ❧

That there was an underground Menahem already for a time had sensed in his bones. Perhaps it did not extend into their barrack, but in the workshop it might exist. One felt it, through bits of war news that at times seemed to circulate of themselves in the very air.

Still, he asked no questions; if they decided to approach him, they would. Probably it was a very tight group, linked by some powerful discipline from when they were still outside. Indeed, if they were communists, even here their rigid attitude toward Zionism might keep them clear of him. Since there were only a few Jews in the metal shop, he deemed it best to make himself small, even sensing from the work master Anton a kind of unspoken advice in this regard.

With the fall rains, the early gray sleet, there was much work, every SS commander demanding new gutters and drainpipes for his dwelling.

The rumble of explosion came from Birkenau at midday. Menahem's first, instant reaction, with others in the shop, was toward the sky—had the Allied bombing come at last? But no planes were heard. The metalworkers had made an involuntary rush toward the shelters and from the doorway got a glimpse of high flames instead of smoke around the Birkenau chimneys. Already SS men shouted, "Back! In your places!" and as Menahem backed into the shop, he thought he saw distantly as one sees a heavenly phenomenon, the curve of the No. 3 chimney sundering into collapse.

With the sirens, the firing from all directions, the speeding armored vehicles, whatever had happened was surely doomed, and in an hour all was quiet. Only a kind of pulsing aftertension remained. Words dropped. One chimney, dynamited. The sonderkommando only was involved. They had even cut the electrified fence and broken out. All but a few mown down in the field. Through the rest of the day one heard occasional faint far-off bursts of shooting. Like afterthrobs in a corpse.

In the barracks, with nightfall, more was whispered. A handful had got as far as a copse, held out for an hour, and, as the SS closed in, set themselves afire. The plan had been to dynamite all four chimneys, but something had gone wrong, and the action had been started too soon. Who knew this? It had been heard. Dynamite and even grenades had long been gathered, the explosives slipped out by a few girls in the Krupp works. Many were being questioned, tortured.

Feverishly Lotzi ran from one whisperer to another. Was it known which girls? Muntchik had to push him up to the bunker; he would bring suspicion on himself, on all of them, even on Bella. He must not worry about Bella. She would never have taken part in such a thing—she knew she had Lotzi still alive; she would certainly not risk her good luck. But the SS were sure to put all the Krupp girls to torture, Lotzi moaned.

Two days later the names of four girls were announced. Jewish.

Of the sonderkommando revolt, all were dead. It had been led by a French Jew, a socialist.

The entire women's camp was assembled to watch the hanging of the still-breathing remnants of the four girls.

Yet, like the attempt on Hitler only a few months ago, the failed revolt left a sense of hidden strength. It was coming; the end was nearing. On some nights thoughts began to surge, beyond the constant hunger craving. A Belgian Jew, from a transport even before their own, declared he had retained the strength to survive because someone had to live, to tell.

"Tell what!" It was Miklos, who even in the unity of the boys had seemed to stay within himself as though inwardly preserving every shred of energy. "The world knows. And they won't care afterward any more than they cared during the years it was happening." As though now, nearing the end, he might risk some strength in revealing his inner thoughts, Miklos declared, "The main reason to survive is to take revenge."

"If we live," Lotzi responded, "it will only be because they are defeated, finished. Then, if I live, I want to go on with my life and not use it only in revenge. To be eaten by the need to revenge, that would be a sickness. It would be like continuing their torture of us."

"No," Miklos declared. "Revenge gives strength. And it is necessary to cleanse the world."

"Revenge, revenge, on whom? Even if you kill the worst, a few kapos, do you think you will be able to get at the leaders?" the Belgian asked.

"First, here. Mengele," Miklos said

"He'll escape. He'll never be found."

Menahem agreed; doubtless all the top ones had made their

plans. Some, like Himmler, in the last moment, would try to win amnesty by replacing Hitler and making peace. There had already been such hints. Still, he said, if it helped a heftling to imagine himself taking revenge, in that way it was of some use; it helped him get through, survive to the end.

"Not just on this one or that one!" Miklos suddenly blurted, as though it were time to bring them all into his full thoughts. Revenge on all the Germans! All of them! They believed in exterminating a people. Then they should be given their turn!

In the thread of light, his skull-face was not fanatic, but elemental, as though eaten down to its final truth. "If the world adopts your way," Muntchik said, "then even if the Nazis are defeated, they win."

"So you want to live with them in the world, after the war?"

The Belgian now gazed on Miklos, not with agreement, but with apprehension. Menahem, too, felt the impossibility of the question. The thing could not be looked at. The thought was more exhausting, more penetrating even than hunger. To imagine living with them in the world was like erasing what had happened. You could only cry to your mind, "Stop asking! Let me only try to live through this, to live beyond this time, this place, this other side of creation into which I have been cast."

"Live with them in the world!" Miklos repeated. "What happens to the world I don't give a shit! It is me, myself! To give them back what they did!"

Now Lotzi said, "To kill Mengele with my bare hands around his throat and watch his face go black, that I can understand."

"I know it is impractical, we can't kill all of them," Miklos appealed now to Lotzi. "But there must be things that could be done." He whispered, "An epidemic. A whole city." He turned to Muntchik. "You! You learned chemistry."

Muntchik said harshly, "Miklos, forget it."

There was no more smoke from the chimneys.

After the revolt of the sonderkommando, only one large transport had arrived for gassing. The platform welcomers reported these Jews were from Theresienstadt, the "show camp" of the Nazis. With this transport it seemed that all was being terminated, that Europe must be Judenrein.

One day, on order of Himmler, it was rumored, the remaining smokestacks were dynamited, coming crashing down, the destruction of a machine that had finished its work. The gas chambers too were demolished. No sign should remain.

Yet on the farther reaches of the compound, the construction work on vast new factories was speeded. Some said the secret fernichtungsweapon that could destroy entire armies with a single rocket was about to be brought here to be launched from these constructions. Already London was half destroyed by the smaller rockets; with this new one the war would yet again be turned.

The SS in their greatcoats and their boots hurried them out to work, shouting, faster, faster, as the heftlings headed into the icy winds that blasted their faces. Sleet covered the mud. Then snow.

Miklos began to weaken. Muntchik rubbed snow into his face, shouted at him, but the unfocused look of the mussulman was coming over his eyes. In the bunker they shouted at him that he stank. In the morning they had to drag him to wash. He must be made to last a few weeks longer; at most it would be a month.

From the shop Menahem brought the news that Budapest was under siege by the Russians. Lotzi and Muntchik kept repeating to Miklos that they would all three go back; they would soon go back home together. Sometimes he nodded, he understood. They would yet again one day run down a field kicking the ball to each other in their old forward pass, Lotzi said. Miklos burst into tears.

The glazier brought word that from the women's camp evacuation was taking place. Lotzi, still in the Canada job, took the risk of holding back a small ruby and gave this to the glazier, who now learned that Bella's entire barrack had been evacuated. Either to a women's camp called Ravensbrück, it was said, or to a large camp near Hamburg, called Bergen-Belsen.

Faint reverberations were heard eastward. Some said air raids; others said heavy artillery. Miklos seemed to shake off the mussulman daze. Laboring on the new constructions, whenever the SS had their heads turned, he stood intently listening for artillery.

One night they saw distant fire flashes. The Belgian said that before the Russians arrived, everyone would be machine-gunned. The next morning the appell was endless. But all around, from the officers' quarters to the SS barracks, there was activity. Trucks piled with belongings moved off. Then groups of heftlings were marched out of the gates into formations on the snow-slushed road. Apparently there would be no slaughter, after all, but evacuation.

Their turn came. SS with their dogs marched alongside. Those in the outer ranks who fell were shot and kicked aside; those who fell within the ranks were trampled on by the ranks that followed. At night the column halted in a farm village; the heftlings were herded into barns. Lotzi found a stall where the four of them huddled, whispering whether it would not be best to make a break during this night, for how many more such marches could be endured? But dogs barked in killing fury. Shots were heard. They would try one more day.

Reaching a railway track, they were herded onto empty coal cars. For days and nights the train moved fitfully; sometimes they made out landmarks where they had already passed; sometimes the train waited for hours, it was said bombed-out tracks were being repaired. Sometimes an SS threw loaves of bread into the open car, and claw-hands tore over them. The bottom of the car became a single frozen surface of corpses, urine, and feces. Miklos lapsed totally into the mussulman state; on the fifth dawn he was part of the underlayer. The train passed through a stark forest and came to a high brick wall with a gateway across which was a banner with the same words as in Auschwitz: ARBEIT MACHT FREI.

The place was called Buchenwald; someone said it was in the heart of the Reich.

❊ ❊ ❊

"Now I have seen it," wrote Dena's brother Vic; he had seen it with his own eyes. There were things you knew to be facts but did not know, could not know until you stood before them. Thus, he had entered Buchenwald.

He need not describe it to her, as she must already have read the descriptions in the press. He had come on the second day after the camp's liberation; only emergency measures had as yet been taken, disinfection squads using the new miracle powder DDT, food trucks. But you saw the skeletal wraiths with the protruding, glazed eyes. One thing he had to tell her, like Dante penetrating the rings of hell, he had reached the end of the compound only to find a second barbed-wire barrier with GIs posted at the gate, for in the lower camp typhus raged.

And only there did Vic finally grasp the whole Jewish story. In the first area were German criminals, plain thieves, murderers, sex offenders, and also political prisoners, including many from France, Belgium, and the rest of once-occupied Europe.

540

In the lower camp were the Jews. As he passed through the gate, creatures swarmed on him, their claws with amazing strength gripping his arms; the stench was like being gassed; they were—you found yourself thinking the ghastly term—subhuman. Hitler had made them into what he said they were. Most were like zombies, living dead, moving in a trance, their eyes unfocused. The still-conscious ones had fierce, unbearable eyes that shredded you. A Jew? Bist a Yid? they croaked at him. And used an odd word: Amcha? He guessed it meant "our people."

What Vic did not describe to Dena was his first moment of visceral revulsion. With a tinge of shame he had mastered himself. Yet even in these depths he must not be limited by his special reaction as a Jew. Though brought to their condition by a psychopathic Jew hater, first of all these were people.

Naturally, Vic wrote, he told them he was a Jew; never in his life had he denied he was Jewish, and this would be the last place to do it! He went on to describe the rows of slave barracks, different from the upper Buchenwald camp, which was comparatively clean and had a bunk for each prisoner, as well as mess halls with tables and benches. But here, as she must already have read in the press, the barracks consisted of three or four layers of shelves on which you couldn't tell dead from dying except for the eyes, those fierce, devouring eyes of the still-alive. There were hundreds, sometimes five hundred Jews like that packed into a single hut. He had seen dead, lying in the lanes where they fell. He also had personally seen, Vic wrote, the lampshades from human skin, the wall against which droves of Russian war prisoners had been massacred, the chambers with the peepholes, the ovens.

Directly out of the University of Chicago law school, Vic had specialized in labor cases before the NLRB, then gone into the Labor Relations Board itself and risen fast. He had married the daughter of a noted libertarian, the constitutional authority John McDermott, one of his professors. Vic naturally had fought anti-Semitism wherever he encountered it, just as he fought every form of prejudice. He and Muriel got a kick at certain gatherings, when a certain type of remark might be made in their presence, by casually letting it be known that Vic had a sister living in Jerusalem, married into a prominent Zionist pioneer family. When the war broke out, Vic volunteered and was commissioned a captain in the Judge Advocate's Section, though later, trying to get near to the front, he had wangled his way into Intelligence.

Vic's position on the Jewish thing had always been that he was simply not personally interested in the happenstance of being a Jew. Hitlerian anti-Semitism had unduly exaggerated the attention the Jewish question should receive in the entire spectrum of human affairs; this overattention created a giant distortion in the play of world forces, but one should not permit it to distort one's thinking. Those who were religiously or emotionally involved with being Jewish were, of course, entitled to be so, just as those who were imbued with Jewish nationalism had a right to be so, so long as they did not infringe on the right of nonnationalistic Jews to abstain, or curtail the rights of other people such as the Arabs. Finally, those persons of Jewish derivation who, like himself, had more universal interests, of course had full moral right to their own pattern of behavior and should not be affronted by nationalistic or cultist Jews as though they were traitors. He was definitely not attracted to that peculiar lokshen kugel world of third-generation American Jews who were suddenly enamored of Yiddish expressions and had an "in" society of their own, even around the university.

Though his confrontation with the slave-camp survivors had jarred him, Vic was soon restored in his own mind to his previous conviction that the best solution was gradual assimilation, absorption, and disappearance. He saw no compelling necessity for the Jews to interbreed and bring forth more violin prodigies and even Nobel prizewinners. Jewish genius could enter the general stream of humanity. That would be the only way to end anti-Semitism. Then there would be one poison less to pollute the world, to break out in horrors such as he saw here.

And yet if viewed objectively, simply on the basis of the human right to self-determination, what one saw here, done to people many of whom like himself were probably not interested in maintaining their Jewishness, what he saw here— No, he couldn't yet fully analyze his position.

At the time of the liberation, Menahem, Muntchik, and Lotzi were no longer in Buchenwald. Shortly after arrival they had made a long day's march to a labor camp called Ohrdruf. An underground airplane hangar had to be completed at once. As the

542

heftlings were needed to push earth-loaded rail carts up from the excavation, their soup was thicker and the bread ration slightly increased. Nor were the barracks overflowing as in Buchenwald; each had his lying space. For Menahem there was a special piece of luck. On the work site he encountered the same Anton who had befriended him in Auschwitz and who at once placed him in a welding crew. The underground hangar, Anton told him, was intended for another of the inventions with which the Germans were still confident of winning the war: a fighter plane with a revolutionary type of engine, operating on air jets and reaching a far greater speed than any British or American aircraft—they would all be knocked out of the sky. With mastery of the air regained would come victory. It was said the air-jet plane had already been tested and would any day appear in combat, invincible. With underground hangers, the new weapon would be safe from bombers.

Even before the hangar was ready, they saw the jet fighter in the air. An entire squadron of American planes appeared, the new fighter easily rose above them and stabbed two down, but suddenly was itself aflame and spiraling to destruction, while a white speck floated down more slowly, the pilot on his parachute.

Then for Lotzi came a stroke of misfortune. Still with that look about him that attracted the eye, he was chosen one morning at appell by the kapo of the sonderkommando, and marched off.

Though there was no crematorium as at Buchenwald, there had been numerous executions here, Menahem learned from Anton, and the sonderkommando had a special task in the mass burial trench. At a distance outside the compound there could be seen a constant small pillar of flame. Menahem recalled the pyre described to him by that poor girl Tanya on the *Struma*. No trace to remain.

The Americans had crossed the Rhine and were on the Autobahn. All knew. It could be a matter of days.

From the appell they were marched out onto the road. When the entire camp had been assembled, they heard behind them, at the entrance, a series of shots. Muntchik and Menahem said not a word to each other.

It had to be the sonderkommando. Lotzi.

The column was marched to the railway. Freight cars waited,

like their first train, from Kaszovar. The door rolled closed on them.

❧ ❧ ❧

All across France, Joe Freedman had followed the front, partaking in that curiously privileged life of the war correspondent, with only your touch of guilt for being always a fairly safe step behind the front of the front, for being always able to leave the scene of battle. Still, a few times by ruse he had managed to go along in a forward patrol, sketching combat.

The sketches went back to *Paradise* magazine: stiff-legged bloated Normandy cattle littering the invasion fields, the dead German in his panzer at the St. Lo breakthrough, his hand still protecting a looted set of silverware. The GI dugout with the pinups from *Paradise* magazine. But there was his own worm in Joe. From the time of the first gaunt, pallid Jew with his eyes still blinking as though he had just now crawled out of his basement hiding place into the Paris liberation. Passing the Dome, the wraith had paused at Joe's table, half whispering, "A Jew?" Then his outpouring.

A place called Drancy where Jews caught in the razzia were assembled for deportation to a place called Auschwitz, uttered with finality. And a bitter Yiddish pun—ausgevished. Wiped out. Joe had given the Jew cigarettes, chocolate, but the Jew kept protesting, no, no, it was not for this that he had sought another Jew. "No matter, take it." But if anywhere farther on the American should encounter live Jews from France— Joe had written down the name. Sketched him. And then in some awful, harrowing way Joe wanted to be free of him, to be off, though knowing that this clawing would be in him all the way to the end.

Thus, for months, all the way to the Rhine, and across, and on the autobahn, with GIs marveling—hell, nowhere in the whole USA was there a superhighway to match this! And suddenly the column came to a special place. It didn't have any of those legendary names, Dachau, Buchenwald, already heard of before the war.

Toward dusk the tank column pulled off the bahn and spread through a cabbage field; there soon came a few thick-legged girls who turned out to be Polish slave labor. And as Joe with his jeepmates were trying to pick a farmhouse and maybe a couple of these girls for the night, an apparition appeared alongside the jeep. The first they had encountered: in bluish prison stripes, shaven-headed, skeletal. Making insistent gestures—he wanted them to come somewhere—"Kommen, wiessen." Joe tried, "Bist a Yid?"

Jude. Ungar. Danke. He seized and gulped the chocolate bar but persisted in his gestures. To come. He would show—

Only one of the jeepmates wanted to go, Eric, the French photographer. The prisoner mounted the fender, his stench unbearable. "Watch out, he's probably got typhus—" The two other correspondents grabbed their stuff and headed for the farmhouse. "Nein, ich kein typhus." The Jew pointed them down a side road. It hadn't been checked out; they risked possible mines. But with his urgency, something still personal, even winning, in his eyes persuaded them.

Not far. Only a kilometer, and they were at a camp entrance. He climbed down. The gates were open. Just inside was a graveled traffic circle, and spaced out around the circle lay a dozen prison-striped dead, each with a bullet hole in back of his head.

"Mein—" His kommando, Lotzi tried to explain to them. "Sonderkommando!" Sonderkommando always killed. The other heftlings evacuated. He himself had hidden the night before; luckily the evacuation had been too rapid for them to hunt for him. Come, he would show—

In almost an unbroken twisting line on his pad, Joe sketched the dead figures. The French photographer rapidly clicked off his Leica shots; by pushing the developer, something would still come out, stark, strong, he told Joe excitedly.

Lotzi kept urging them, come, come, something more important, secret. They climbed back into the jeep, and he guided them now on wagon ruts across a field. Nein, kein minen! The ruts trailed off into a muddy area, and with amazing energy the skeleton led them, half running, the mud sucking on their heavy army shoes. There on a slight rise he halted, pointing. A square of logs, several layers, crisscross. Approaching, Joe saw. It took a moment to comprehend. A kind of pyre. A layer of cadavers, then a cross layer of logs. The yellowed skin-skeletal bodies were ranged with precision, not a limb out of place. The bottom logs rested across two parallel rails, a grate.

"Sonderkommando," Lotzi repeated. Special task unit, Eric explained to Joe.

Then just behind the pyre they saw the pit, the bottom still a tangle of limbs, heads, torsos, twisted as they had been dumped.

Involuntarily, they backed a step. Nein, nein, Lotzi reassured them, disinfection, lye. Then he pantomimed—the bodies dug up from the pit, burned on the pyre. Strict SS orders, even the cinders scattered in the bog.

Not a vestige to remain.

In Joe Freedman's mind came an expression, something picked up years ago, the time he had been in Palestine—a kind of curse, the most drastic curse of all, for it meant to be erased from the book of eternity. Y'mach shemah. As though one had never existed.

Or as though their crime had never existed.

Taking Lotzi back with them, they picked a house. There was even an automatic electric water heater. The Frenchman, Eric, carried disinfectant powder in his knapsack, and after Lotzi's bath only a faint stench still emanated. Joe pulled out clothes for him; the closets were full. Hastily stuck away behind the clothing was a large Hitler portrait. On the living-room wall you could see where it had been taken down. In the master bedroom were two black-draped photographs of sons fallen in the war. On a sideboard in the dining room was a cut-glass bowl filled with printed death announcements. For the glory of the Reich. Next to this stood a souvenir miniature Eiffel Tower with a little hackenkreutz flag at the top.

Where had the Allies reached? Lotzi kept asking. How far?

One place he needed to know about. A camp called Bergen-Belsen. Did they know if it was yet liberated?

Joe Freedman thought he had heard that name mentioned a few days ago in a broadcast. Lotzi said he had to go there. At once. The girls from Auschwitz had been taken there. His girl, his high school sweetheart. Just before the evacuation he had had word she was still alive.

Walking over to battalion headquarters, Joe checked. The British had liberated the place a few days ago, as they closed in on Hamburg.

He would go! Lotzi cried.

He was crazy. It was maybe a hundred miles.

He'd find his way. He had to go.

Suddenly Joe and Eric decided—why not? It was even rumored

the British up there might be the first to make it to Berlin. They'd take Lotzi to try to find his girl.

At the mess they had to hold him back or he would have killed himself eating. He talked and talked. If not for his comrades, he could never have survived. His team. His gymnasium had held the regional championship, and they had been five Jews on the team. And together in the deportation train. And then each death. The first, trying to escape from the train. Shot, he had tumbled from the opening. But perhaps, a slight chance, perhaps he had survived. Then in Auschwitz their best forward runner, Georg. When he discovered his sister was finished. He had let go, and in a week Georg was gone. Then on the transport from Auschwitz, Miklos. Only one other teammate, Muntchik, remained. Up to this place. Evacuated this morning. As soon as Lotzi found his Bella he would start out to seek Muntchik and the old one from Palestine—

From Palestine?

The SS from Budapest had thrown him into their train. He had come to Budapest to negotiate, to save Jews, perhaps they had heard of it—a million Jews for ten thousand trucks.

The whole world had heard of it.

This emissary, Menahem, an absolute miracle he had survived.

Joe Freedman stopped him. "Did you say his name was Menahem?"

Yes, Menahem. A man! What hadn't he been through!

From Palestine? Did this Menahem say if he was from a kibbutz?

That was so. Lotzi even recalled the name: Gilboa.

It must be he, the one Myra had talked about when they were still together, Menahem, an in-law of Dena's, he had been mixed up in everything, smuggling arms, smuggling refugees—

No, Lotzi had no idea where this morning's evacuation train had gone, but as soon as he found his Bella—

In the shrinking thousand-year Reich the train could only have gone southward. What incredible insanity, still dragging off their slaves! Should he try to get a news guy to cable the story? What did he imagine, that Patton would send a task force on a wild-goose chase to stop a slave-labor train and rescue a Palestinian Jew?

547

Still, the Jews-for-trucks proposition had been a sensation. Only a few months ago a pair of Jewish terrorists sent from Palestine to Cairo had gunned down that British minister who had snapped, "What would I do with a million Jews?" When he went to the press camp for passes to Bergen-Belsen, Joe passed on the story about Menahem.

At the Bergen-Belsen gate the guard glanced at Lotzi's arm number, asking the correspondents, "Where'd you pick him up?" Before the British entry here the typhus-ridden inmates had burst loose, swarming over the surrounding farms and villages, pillaging, even murdering. British troops had had to round them up for epidemic control; strays were now coming back on their own; they had ravished the area and were hungry.

Here in Bergen-Belsen also they found the camp divided into two sections; the correspondents could visit the "star" section, the press officer said, with a British twinkle to Joe about those starlet photographs in *Paradise* magazine—alas, nothing like that here! The star section had been for a few hundred Hungarian bigwigs. Special privileges. It seemed the Jews had made a deal with Himmler, a million dollars paid into a Swiss bank. A trainload had even been sent off from here to Switzerland—part of that proposition of a million Jews for ten thousand trucks that had never come off. But the main camp was still closed—pestilential. Typhus. Hundreds were still dropping dead all over the grounds.

It was in fact about the Hungarian Jews that they had come, Joe Freedman said. They were looking for a certain young woman who was known to have been in the transport from Auschwitz. And as he saw the obtuse expression returning, Joe added that this young Hungarian girl was a cousin of his.

But there were no lists of any kind. Utter chaos. It would be weeks before a census could be made.

This survivor in their jeep had known the girl in Hungary.

Well, the press officer didn't mind if they inquired around. Perhaps some of the Hungarians remaining in the star camp might have heard of his cousin.

Captain Albright, the press officer, had given him permission, Joe told the guard, *Paradise* magazine—at which the Tommy grinned—smashing pin-ups! They wouldn't find any models like that in this place! And let them pass into the forbidden main camp.

Lotzi, until now excited, even confident, turned rigid. Directly before them, between rows of barracks, a bulldozer was clearing a lane. Under the shovel blade tumbled a growing pile of human refuse, striped rags mingled with body parts, bone, limbs, skulls with some hair grown out. What must have been young women, girls.

The bulldozer maneuvered the pile to an enormous pit.

They went among the barracks. Outside, creatures hovered, even responded to questions. Inside, on the tiers lay inert forms, the eyes vacuously open.

Among the walking they found a girl who had been on the Auschwitz convoy. But neither she nor others she asked had known Bella. One said perhaps Lotzi's friend had been sent to Ravensbrück, the camp for women.

Ravensbrück proved still in the Nazi-held area; Captain Albright showed them its location on his wall map. Above Berlin.

Lotzi decided not to return with them. He had encountered here a few heftlings he had known in Auschwitz; they had taken over a barracks in the star camp, and he could stay with them. In a few days the way would be open, and he would start for Ravensbrück. He took Joe Freedman's press camp address—he would from time to time inquire, should they perhaps find trace of Menahem and Muntchik. How could he thank them enough? One day perhaps—Lotzi repeated to Joe a Yiddish saying he had often heard his grandfather use: May we meet on better occasions.

Joe Freedman said, "Shalom."

At the press camp, with so much news breaking, only a correspondent for the Jewish Telegraphic Agency had sent out the story of a Palestinian emissary said to be among the last death-camp survivors. And marked it cautionary, as who knew what the Nazis were capable of doing in these last insane days?

Eddie Marmor called Mati to meet him in the little café on Hazolel Street. Best not to print it as yet; they'd get word straight to Eliahu. Some fellows from the Jewish Brigade were already making contact with the liberated camps and could look for him.

At home, Mati and Dena debated long whether to tell Dvora. After all, Menahem was not yet found. If it should turn out that in the last days— No, Dena insisted; she herself in such circumstances would want to be told.

They drove that same night to Gilboa. As they entered the room, smiling so as not to frighten her, Dvora cried out, "Alive!"

But, scanning their faces, she demanded, "Yes? Yes?" As much as they knew, they told her. He was alive, Dvora said firmly. Not once had she thought of Menahem as dead. If a woman's man was dead, she'd know. And Dvora told of a chaverah here in the kibbutz whose chaver had been killed in the battle with Rommel. That very night she had felt it. A week later the official news came.

How lucky the family had been. Their family that had always been so unlucky! Giora already freed from prison. Not one dead in this war.

❊ ❊ ❊

Halted and shunted aside. Hours, motionless. Then a thunder overhead and a shrieking downward, but the explosions were a distance away. The train crawled rearward; the tracks must have been hit. The last sliver of bread, the last water long gone.

Muntchik's voice reached him; he had perhaps lost consciousness, perhaps slept. They were moving again, forward. More had died. It was difficult to know who lay dead, who lived. Light could be felt beginning. Again the train stood. Suddenly doors rolling open. A few began to crawl over bodies, to get out. Halt! Wraiths, heftlings like themselves, clambering in, flung in. Schnell! Somewhere down the siding, a few firebursts. Wasser, wasser. Loaves of bread were thrown in; in the scuffle a heftling died; the loaf had to be pried out of his claws. Muntchik and one of the new ones stood guard over the two pails of water. Mauthausen, the new one said. This had been Mauthausen. The door rolled shut. The train moved.

When daylight was felt again, Menahem was still conscious of himself. But the eyes, the knowing eyes of the bandit, the one of the two brother bandits who had murdered Yechezkiel, and how many others, and whom it had been his and Zeira's lot to execute, the one whose eyes caught his own through the tall rushes as his

550

shot went off, those eyes were on him and for this, after all the enduring, Menahem conceded he was not to see Eretz again; he must no longer hold on; let it end here.

For the last hours of the night the train had been standing, and no sound came from without. Muntchik, with another who still had some strength, lifted up a gaunt heftling to the barred air-hole. Fields of grass, he croaked, trees, mountains. No one.

Some began to strike their fists against the walls, even attempting to shout. Raucous half cries emerged, in separated spurts, as from the jammed radio in Istanbul.

Menahem let himself flicker out. The sounds intermittently broke in, but fading, fading.

And then a clamorous intrusion. Now it was grotesque. Now it was too late. But there came iron sounds, vehicles, shouts. Not German. Iron blows on iron, the door rolled, and sunlight seized him, pulled him back.

He heard an American voice above him, "This one's alive."

The American was shouting, to penetrate into them—"Hitler dead! Kaput! Hey, Hitler finished!"

In the Berlin bunker. Shot himself. The Russians had found two incinerated bodies, Hitler and Eva Braun. These Americans were scouring the area; this mountain area was the last fortress, the redoubt. Here in the Alps the Nazis had prepared strongholds and brought scientists to complete and to launch the secret weapon that would annihilate the Allies. Goering had been caught nearby this morning.

Again opening his eyes, Menahem saw above him carved and painted beams; Muntchik said it was a schloss, a castle. The American captain was shouting at someone. A German nobleman declared he had always opposed the Nazis; here in his remote barony he had managed to keep his hands clean; welcome to the deliverers! All he had was at their disposal! A great day! Schnapps! A toast!

An American soldier came; a medic he called himself, a doctor. A Jew, a young doctor from Brooklyn, Dave, he said, David. From him Menahem asked—a message home to Palestine: Alive!

To Palestine?

Muntchik explained to him.

Dave said he had seen Buchenwald. Though he had never especially taken part in things Jewish, too busy in medical school and then straight into the army, he knew about Palestine.

Another day; Menahem could already stand on his legs, walk a bit. Emerging from the schloss, he sat on a rustic bench watching a bee go from flower to flower.

A jeep drove up. A soldier in British uniform leaped out, started walking toward the schloss, then hesitated and came toward Menahem. Now Menahem saw the insignia—the Star of David, the Palestine Jewish Brigade. "Chaver Menahem? In truth, it's you?" In Hebrew.

Danny, son of his old friend Max Wilner from Kibbutz Ha-Rishon. Since childhood, Danny had known him. And the story of how in the First World War, Menahem had smuggled his father out of the Turkish prison in Damascus. Now, Danny grinned, it was his turn, his unit was smuggling survivors over the Alps— Menahem could even already laugh. News tumbled. Everybody well! Giora released but not yet home. From the American doctor's cable, the Mossad had got in touch with the Brigade, in Treviso; a transport unit was stationed there—just across the Alps. They were already sending trucks through the Brenner on one pretext or another, bringing survivors to a special Mossad camp in Italy, oh, things were starting up again, Yehuda Arazi had arrived, ships would soon be moving. True the British were tougher than ever, but ways would be found— But he didn't want to tire Menahem.

Ah, then, Menahem thought; with all this world of twisting, of subterfuge and resistance also starting again, he must indeed be alive.

Eliahu himself drove from Tel Aviv to Gilboa with Danny Wilner's report and found Dvora in the poultry house. Then how soon would Menahem be coming home? Eliahu took on his patient expression that meant a problem. Despite the atmosphere of shared victory with the British, as she knew, here nothing was changed. Menahem was still on their wanted list. And it seemed that their forces released from the war had no other function now but to block the death-camp survivors from coming to Eretz. But— he lifted his eyes, with that little glitter—a solution. Dvora could be sent to Menahem. In some weeks, as soon as he had recovered—

He was ill?

No, no, only the lingering effects of starvation and exhaustion. She could be sent on a mission. Many emissaries were being gathered to teach, to train the survivors; as she knew, they still sat in the same camps, hundreds of thousands—

To know he was alive, to feel he walked the earth, to be able to send him news of the children and grandchildren— But a panic was forming in Dvora. After these years of separation, after all he had been through—

She could even teach poultry work to kvutsoth of survivors! Training farms were already being established. Did she know—his rare happy smile came—the Mossad had just received word, a group of young survivors had taken over the farming estate of Hermann Goering himself! They had formed a kibbutz there, preparing for life in Eretz.

>>

OUT OF CHAOS

BOOK IV

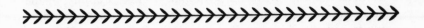

32

JOE FREEDMAN was having a difficult time getting back into things in Chicago. First there was a fight with the owner of *Paradise* over Joe's death-camp portfolio. Too gruesome. A drawing or two might be used as a reminder, but the portfolio should feature Joe's sketches of fräuleins and GIs in forbidden fraternization.

So then he got the idea of a portfolio on Palestine, but the boss (himself a Hebe) had to remind Joe that, after all, *Paradise* was not a Jewish magazine. Nor was *Paradise* interested in a portfolio on Hiroshima after the atom bomb. It had ended the damn war, hadn't it? For crissake, give people a rest!

Yah, Joe knew he had streaks of contrariness. As Myra in one of their times together had pointed out, he must be self-destructive. That was the time long ago in Paris when he had the Guggenheim and one night smashed every piece of work in his fancy studio. Maybe there was something to psychoanalysis, after all; Myra had finally got married to one of her Kunstbau guys, their Jew, an architect, distinguished gray hair, and she even finally seemed okay. They had Joe over to a fancy dinner, and Myra scolded him, why was he wasting his life on magazine stuff, he had to get back to sculpture.

At least he had some money saved from the war years. The art snobs were now on the near North Side, but crazily the old store-front studios facing Jackson Park were still standing, and Joe got one. At a party he ran into Andrea—good God, how far back! Still beautiful, though somewhat spread. As was the thing now, she was married to a Negro communist, even had a little pickaninny. Andrea recalled that gorgeous boy from Palestine she had seduced —Mati. And was his Dena still with him? Twins! Dropping by the studio one day, getting excited over the death-camp portfolio, going to bed with him just for old times' sake, yes, she still wrote poetry, even sometimes got into the *New Yorker*.

Off and on, even just sitting reading, Joe would find himself carving abstracted bone forms. Not stickmen, not Giacometti. Pared smooth elements in ultimate reduction, in ultimate purification, the absolute.

Prize contests were constantly being announced for memorials to what was now being called the Holocaust. The Warsaw Ghetto. The winning pieces were always heroic resistance fighters hurling their last grenade. The whole idea of art as competition, judges, cliques, pull, made him want to puke.

Once on impulse Joe arranged his carved wooden forms in crisscross layers. Like that place—Ohrdruf. The pyre, the altar. The eternal flame should emerge from it, but in wisps. The thing must be unconsumable, irreducible. Stone? Welded iron? Steel. Stainless, pure. One day to stand full-sized on a high place, a barren rock. Overlooking Jerusalem.

❄❄❄

One soft June morning a jeep with American officers drew up to the castle, and the Baron was arrested. As Menahem had by then gathered, he had been a high-ranking Nazi, after all, having to do, from the earliest days, with party finances. As for the vast estate, the property was to be sequestered and operated for the time being by the farm manager.

About this Menahem had some thoughts. The cattle herd was superb. Apple orchards, beekeeping, vast fields of clover, oats, wheat. What could be more perfect as a training farm?

Thirty-seven from his last transport had survived. A few had gone on the road to former homelands; crossing borders was not difficult; you held up your left wrist, the blue numbers were the best passport. Finding no one, they returned. Muntchik knew none was left; he had seen his entire family sent to the other column.

One day in the jeep of a young American rabbi chaplain, Dvora came. A longish embrace, with each stroking the other's shoulder.

A kiss, almost dry. Then simply looking at each other, four years, their faces had not changed so much, not even Menahem's. He was still thin, but he was restored. In his room she told him all the news of the children, the kibbutz, the family; most of it he already knew but didn't say so. No, the war had not been bad at home; only now things were really getting bad between the Sternists, the Irgun, and the British. As for Menahem, with the British being so inflexible, Eliahu said he could not yet safely come home. She would stay here if he wished. An almost-wistful smile came with the words, and an old, seamy-faced couple, they were reunited.

"After all, we have been among the lucky ones," Dvora said.

Shortly afterward—Dvora was already supervising a group of girls in the poultry house—Menahem was summoned by Shaul himself to a gathering of the Mossad in Paris. There much of the old band was assembled, Venya, Ehud, Ruthie—the whole crew from Istanbul! Already Ruthie had enscorcelled an American naval commander, getting him to load an entire warship with survivors and land them in Haifa!

In a small pension-hotel near the Étoile, operated by a French Jew who had been hidden away during the entire occupation in a subcellar, Shaul and Menahem embraced—the two old ones! With eyes that knew everything, all Menahem had been through, Shaul asked if he was ready to go back to work? "What do you mean, you think I haven't been working? We have the best training farm in Europe!"

Shaul meant work with the Bricha, as they were now calling it —the Escape. The main route had already formed itself, with survivors moved along by stages from one DP camp to another, across Europe to Italy. There Yehuda Arazi had arrived, disguised as a Polish airman, for like Menahem, he was wanted by the British. After returning from Istanbul to Eretz, Yehuda had "transferred" tons of arms from British warehouses to the Haganah and, ever since the British caught on, had been hidden behind a false wall in Eliahu's apartment. In Italy, Arazi was already busy getting ships.

Much of the problem before them Menahem already knew from strays who had wandered through the farm. Polish Jews who had fled into Russia and were being repatriated, to find only mass graves. Scattered Jews who had been hidden by gentiles, also some veterans from partisan groups, and remnants from Auschwitz and Mauthausen who had wandered from camp to camp, seeking.

Their movement was turning into a flood; it had to be organized. A few of Shaul's Mossad boys had already slipped into Poland and contacted the last commander of the Vilna Ghetto, a poet named Abba Kovner who with a group of ex-partisans was trying to organize survivors. As more and more Jews returned and sought to reclaim their homes, Kovner said, murders were occurring. New pogroms were to be expected.

So Shaul laid out, before Menahem, the route that was forming. On the Polish-Czech frontier, a prewar chalutz training farm was reopened. And from there at night groups crossed into Czechoslovakia. With the Czechs, an arrangement had been made to ship them by train down to Bratislava. From there they crossed over at night into Austria. Through the Russian-occupied zone, cigarettes, when necessary a wristwatch or two, opened the way to Vienna, where the old Rothschild Hospital was being used as a hospice. And from Vienna, dispersal to various DP camps, mostly in the American occupied zone. Finally, across the Alps to Yehuda Arazi's assembly camps in Italy, to wait for a ship.

Luckily the Jewish Brigade in the British army had a truck unit almost at the Austro-Italian border. Filling in their own movement orders, the drivers were roaming Europe to pick up DPs. As for visas and all the rest, Menahem would be working with the renowned Abbé Glassberg, a French-Jewish Catholic originally from Poland, who even during the war had saved hundreds, thousands with false papers.

Ah, it would be the old life again for Menahem. Group visas for Honduras were just now being prepared, the Abbé Glassberg said, a burly figure in his loose soutane, and as they strolled down the Champs-Élysées he and Menahem fell to talking Polish, also Yiddish, getting into technical discussions over various chemical ink eradicators, different kinds of paper, and whether, on principle, it was better to falsify real passports or to make total duplications so that there was no tampering to detect.

As they walked along, lights began to go on, pale golden blurs through the frosted glass of café terraces. The sky, the grayish stone of the buildings, had something of the luminosity of Jerusalem. Down the Champs-Élysées one's eye was caught by the French girls on their bicycles, their blowy frocks, their legs. And with this, Menahem felt at last fully returned and felt almost painfully: how enjoyable life was! With Dvora, though at first embarrassed—two old fools—they had one night groped their way to each other, each surprised that with the partner there was still desire. They did not speak of the years of interval. He could even have wished for her that in his long absences all through their marriage her life had not been arid.

Now, suddenly, his other life—Paris was still here, the world, the world.

❆ ❆ ❆

When at last Lotzi had managed to make his way to Ravensbrück, he found the immense camp nearly empty. Only the sick remained, under the care of the Swedish Red Cross, which had appeared just before the evacuation. Of the last trainloads reaching here from Auschwitz, who could know?

Touched by the lad with his appealing eyes, a young Swedish woman agreed to walk with him through the row of barracks used now as their hospital. In each barracks Lotzi called out, "Bella?" and "Ungarisch?" In the third a transparent hand was raised. The young Hungarian woman had huge gray eyes that seemed to float unfocused; "Bella," she repeated, and finally shook her head, no. But lowering her voice, she secretly confided, did he know what was done here in Ravensbrück? Operations. It had been done to her. A woman did not remain a woman, did he understand? Perhaps it would even be better if he did not find his sweetheart.

Before one barracks the Swedish woman hesitated; then, firmly raising her head, she took him inside. These were madwomen. After one glance—at least she was not here—unless, still ghastlier, unless he could not even recognize her, Lotzi was backing away when a creature seized his arm. She cried out in Hungarian, "Do you know who I am?" Then, "Horsie, horsie!" she sang out, doubling over and making an ungainly back-kick, like a horse, and neighing.

The administrator detached the woman's grip from Lotzi and took him outside. "In the evacuation," she explained, "four women had to pull a carriage. The camp commandant's wife and her baggage. We found this one on the road."

Lotzi made his way southward then; he would try to cross into Hungary.

❆ ❆ ❆

A few days earlier Bella had come. She had appeared first in her father's pharmacy; the Hungarian who had taken it over indeed welcomed her warmly, sympathetically—no, no one had returned except only a few Jews who had paid farmers to hide them, and they had now gone away. As for the pharmacy, it was about to become state property, under communism, and in any case what could she do here, she was not a pharmacist. Perhaps she should go to Budapest, where many of her people remained.

Still, she passed her family's house, but had a dread of entering. A woman noticed her through the window and hastily opened the door; Bella glimpsed changes and did not want to see the rest, saying she only wished to leave word should someone come looking. There had been a notice in the papers of a registry for returning Jews, the woman said. In Budapest. She ought to register.

And in Budapest Lotzi found her. Adjoining the main synagogue was a search office, and there he was told Bella Kertosz was in a hostel, the old Jewish orphanage building. Lotzi ran there. A kindly-looking woman showed him a small room with three cots; one was Bella's. She must have gone walking but would surely be back for the noonday soup.

He sat on her cot. Presently she did come back, and they kept putting their hands on each other to make sure. Each cried, "You are the same!" Meaning as beautiful, as handsome as, as— They pretended they meant as when they were in high school. A year ago. Only one year. Then their meager bodies began to grip, to coalesce, as though to make certain quickly, hastily to make sure of doing this before anything more might intervene—at once, this must be done! Except that one instant before it was happening Bella held him still. "Lotzi, you know there in Ravensbrück—"

"It doesn't matter," he was saying as she said, "I can never—" and they were one.

☙ ☙ ☙

Then Muntchik found them! Lotzi, whom he had thought destroyed with the sonderkommando in Ohrdruf! And Bella!

Come to search on a wild hope for Geza, who might not have died when he tumbled, shot, from the train opening, here he found Lotzi and Bella! And brought them back to the farm.

Everyone had similar tales, for if not for such miraculous happenings, who would be here? At first, to each, his survival through such a chain of miracles seemed to have an intention, a meaning. He was chosen. But why? For what purpose?

In those few months a fever of discussion took place among the young people, and often they turned to the atomic bomb that the Americans had dropped on Japan, on a city called Hiroshima. Muntchik particularly was obsessed with the subject, brooding over it during the day, asking Menahem, when he went on his trips to Munich, to bring back books on the science of atoms that could be understood by a Gymnasium graduate. Physics and mathematics indeed had been his favorite subjects.

The world was lucky that the Germans hadn't perfected the atom bomb first. That was to have been Hitler's final card. He had already brought the scientists to the schloss high in the mountain here, to finish their job. If Hitler hadn't driven out Einstein and other great Jewish scientists, would Germany have had the bomb first? If Hitler had used the bomb, it would have been inhuman, and if America had used it, killing a whole city of civilians, had it been right? Back and forth the chevreh argued.

But Muntchik pondered in a somewhat different direction. Several of the great physicists in America who had taken part in the work even seemed remorseful, from what was heard. And yet, other powers, soon the Russians, would solve the secret. And only those peoples in the world who possessed it— From what was forming in him Muntchik shrunk back. Nevertheless the obsession grew.

A number of the boys had, like Lotzi, gone searching among the camps and as far as "home," and if they had not been as lucky and found a sweetheart living, a few had found a sister, a cousin, and some simply had brought back girls from other DP camps to this small paradise. Only Muntchik did not seem to find anyone for himself; he worked alone in the evenings on his studies. Menahem even suggested that he could be sent to a university; many survivors were studying in Munich— But not there, no! Besides, just now he was active with Menahem in the Bricha; two large army trucks had been "organized" and painted with false numbers, and often Muntchik and Menahem joined convoys to the DP camps to help transfer immigrants a stage farther along the route. Landsberg, where you could be shown where Hitler at the very start had written *Mein Kampf*, a political prisoner but in his own suite of rooms. Massively crowded now with survivors, a suspended sheet the only separation for a family, smells, short tempers. And Feldafing, and Mauthausen, people had to be moved along on the way to Eretz; they drove their truckfuls at night with the canvas tightly down, along the Innsbruck road and then partway up the mountain to a final gathering place for the march across an Alpine pass—a dilapidated ski hotel once owned by a Jew and now declared a DP camp. Each time the camp filled up, lads of the Bricha would trek the refugees several hours across the snow into Italy, where again Bricha trucks awaited them.

The turn came for Lotzi and Bella. Bella had begun to learn nursing; also in Eretz she and Lotzi intended to adopt a baby.

There was to be a convoy of ten trucks joining together shortly after darkfall on a crossroads near Landsberg. From Paris, Ehud had brought a group visa for Paraguay, a perfect copy, with a new list of three hundred made-up names attached to the document.

Their column would be preceded by a legitimate American jeep assigned to Rabbi Chaplain Lipton, officially delegated to DP work. To pass the military-zone checkpoints, he would show the visa; then the convoy would take a side road to the Bricha's mountain ski resort.

As planned, it was on toward midnight when the column reached the last American checkpoint, for at night the check-up was likely to be merely perfunctory. Holding the documents, the rabbi chaplain jumped out of his jeep. But instead of the barrier's being unquestioningly lifted as was usual with the Americans, Menahem saw the chaplain being led over to the checkpoint headquarters hut. After a quarter of an hour, unease spread. Muntchik went behind to sit with Lotzi and Bella; the worst that could happen was that the convoy would have to go back.

The sergeant emerged, followed by the convoy leaders. Rabbi Chaplain Lipton smiled to Menahem—"A mere technicality." Approaching the rear of the first truck, the sergeant called, "Open up." The canvas was raised, and he moved his flashlight slowly over the faces, then back onto the list in his hand. Menahem caught sight of Muntchik with Lotzi and Bella and gave them a reassuring smile. After again peering at the flashlighted faces, the sergeant shrugged and started back for the house. "Ah, these DPs, what's a goddamn list of names, you can't tell one from another."

"You're right," Chaplain Lipton said. "The Germans just used numbers."

"You wait here," the sergeant instructed; the irony hadn't reached him.

Hastily Lipton explained to Menahem: the British had been through here with furious complaints about Americans letting through illegal convoys of Jews; there was a sticky lieutenant in charge inside who said he had strict stop orders. No DP convoy had been signaled for this night. They all must return to their camp unless he could get a clear order.

From his wallet, Menahem selected a press card that he had arranged for in Paris, official, from a new Yiddish weekly, with the stamp of the French Bureau of Information. The name *New Life* appeared in both French and Yiddish; he had noticed that goyim were often impressed by the sight of Jewish print. Entering the checkpoint house with Lipton, he explained that his journal was carrying a series of articles on the growing refugee problem. American papers were translating the articles, for the problem was of major interest just now with the Anglo-American Commission of Investigation visiting the DP camps. He himself would like, if possible, to speak on the phone with the lieutenant's immediate superior. As there were so many women and children in this transport—

Shrugging—one more headache, the press—the lieutenant picked up the phone and called his regional command center. "Well, Major, there's another little complication here, there's some kind of a newspaperman . . . yah, he has credentials, French . . . he's doing a story on these DPs, and he wants to ask some questions. Yah, he speaks English."

As he was handed the phone, Menahem had no clear idea what to try, except perhaps to say he had seen the group visa which appeared in order, so— "Major Kossoff speaking," he heard. "What's on your mind?"

The name echoed to Menahem. Was this once again one of those coincidences that came in his life, so improbable that you were tempted to imagine— "Excuse me, before anything else, Major, do you happen to come from Chicago?"

The voice came back somewhat tart and wary. "Why, yes."

Then Menahem made the leap. "If you will permit me to ask, Major, do you have a sister named Dena, married to a Palestinian?"

"Well, I do. Who are you, anyway?"

"By sheer coincidence, Major, I happen to be a relative of yours, through Dena's husband, Mati."

"Well, as you say, this is a coincidence indeed. Mati comes from quite a family, but I wasn't aware there was also a journalist. How's Dena? Were you there lately? I haven't heard from her in months. She must think I've been discharged."

The old saying was thrumming in Menahem's mind, "Kol Yisroel mishpacha achat." But even if all Jews were one family, he must be careful not to blunder—what had Dena ever told him about her brother? Surely this was not the millionaire business-man; it must be the lawyer. "Then which of Mati's family are you?" the major was asking.

"My name is Menahem—"

"Good God! You are the one who was in Auschwitz! Dena wrote me the whole thing! Well, I'm glad to hear you're all right again and even busy! Perhaps we can meet? How strange. Tonight I just happened to have my weekly turn on night duty."

"Major, there is a little mixup with this refugee convoy. Can I come to your headquarters right away? Perhaps we can straighten it out and spare these people a very bad night."

It was forty miles. Menahem and Rabbi Lipton sped off in the jeep.

Vic could have obtained his discharge months ago, and been home with Muriel, and practicing law. But wanting to get in on the Nuremberg trials, he had somehow convinced himself he could work it more easily from this side. Why, he had even been in on the arrest of Goering, when his outfit had captured this area! Of course, Telford Taylor and the other big attorneys had their own favorites—but still. He had used every connection of his Chicago partner and had even finally resorted to his father-in-law; the old man pulled a lot of weight in Washington; maybe it would still work out. Then Muriel could come over. Why was he so set on Nuremberg? Naturally, there would be prestige to it. But Vic flattered himself that his deep interest was truly in the basic question of human responsibility. Also, of international conceptions of jurisprudence. Naturally there was the Jewish question, it would be a major question, and he could not help speculating whether there might not have been some scruple about loading up the prosecution with lawyers of Jewish origin?

He put the coffee to perk, real coffee, not the powdered stuff.

They showed up sooner than he expected; they must have burned up the road. This Menahem—Dena had given him an idea of the man, but still the presence affected him. No, no burning, visionary eyes, but maybe the rock-bottom look he had sometimes seen on a strike leader who had really been through the mill. As for the Auschwitz experience—if you didn't know, you wouldn't guess; but if you knew, it fitted.

They exchanged a few family things, and then Menahem said, since all those people were waiting on the road— The rabbi presented the group visa. Though younger, this Lipton reminded Vic a bit of Rabbi Mike Kramer in Chicago. Sure enough, Mike Kramer was his ideal. The visa, anyone could see was a phony, a forgery, or one of those documents the small Latin American diplomats dispensed for a few hundred bucks. Never mind. Who was he to make forgery tests? A document presented by a rabbi chaplain attached to a major relief organization. Anyway, the British were being pretty shabby about the whole thing. Okay, Deen! Vic said inwardly with a private grin. Here's to you and your Jews! He picked up the phone. "Their papers look okay to me, Lieutenant. As soon as these gentlemen get back, let the convoy go through."

Gulping the coffee, neither of them noticing it was the finest mocha, the rabbi and Dena's in-law, the amazing one, practically ran.

"Come, Muntchik, come with us after all!" Lotzi and Bella cried. Not yet, he said. He had decided first to study. "Menahem, tell him he must come with us!" Menahem smiled sorrowfully. He was not yet entirely certain of Muntchik's purpose. Though these two were all that remained to him, such a one as Muntchik could not be persuaded. "He'll find you there," Menahem said. "Make a place ready for him!"

33

AFTER a week—the military trials came swiftly—the whole family could breathe again as Uri was one of the three who got out of the death penalty. It was believed the British would really carry it out on the two boys who had fired. Luckily, Uri had only been driving. Imagine the nerve it took, driving right up to the supply dump in British uniforms. Dena went down to see Shula, thinking Shula would be depressed over the twenty-year sentence, but she found her radiant. "Thank God they will keep him in prison! My one hope is the boys don't try one of their crazy escapes!"

Twenty years—it might really be only one or two, if the British would only leave, and in any case Nahum, while in England to see about the war-end crisis in the diamond business, would contact a few people about Uri's sentence. Oh, it was that damned Araleh who had brought it all on, making Irgunists out of the kids before they knew what they were doing. All right, Nahum had given money, but it was to bring in ships, when even the Haganah wasn't doing it. Not to start a whole war with the British! That crazy embittered Araleh; it was time a man of his age forgot already that the British had once given him a few lashes. A child that never forgot a spanking. What, Mati hadn't told her—the time Araleh and Gidon were in the Zion Mule Corps in Gallipoli? Araleh's wife and baby were in Alexandria, he didn't get any mail for a whole month, so he slipped onto a boat to Alexandria. Saraleh had moved, and something had gone wrong with the mail, that was all, but when Araleh got back to Gallipoli, the British arrested him and gave him ten lashes before the whole assembled army! Forget it already! Not Araleh. Thank heaven she had no idea where he was hiding; she'd be tempted to tip off the British so they'd send him to prison in Eritrea with the rest of the Irgun leaders.

Oh, it was enough to embitter your life, Shula cried out, the poor children, the whole generation, all they knew was blood, poor Uri's wife and kids, Shula had begged Tsila to come live here with them, but the girl was strong. Shula knew how it had been for her every time Uri went out. Before his marriage, when he had still lived here at home, every time he went out, her own life hung suspended. You didn't dare ask even when he might return. Agonies. Shula dabbed at her eyes. Once after three whole days they at last got a message, and she had been led to a cave deep under the walls of Jerusalem where he lay, his eyes covered with a bandage. Could Dena imagine her first fright? Shula dabbed her eyes again and smiled, controlled like a British woman.

She had brought to that cellar the best eye specialist in Jerusalem, dear old Dr. Axelrod, whose daughter, very pretty, had married an American, the correspondent of *Time* magazine, of course Dena knew them, and the doctor had saved Uri's eyesight. Oh God, Shula had hoped Uri would stop then, but no, he went right back and got himself picked up standing guard outside their radio broadcasting place when the British made their big raid. Luckily Uri had thrown away his gun. They broke his teeth, but they got nothing out of Uri. Luckily, that first arrest, a good friend of Shula's for years, a high officer in the British police, let him out. Dena caught Shula's slightly glittering look. "They really had no proof against him," she continued. He had managed to slip his pistol to a young scout, who darted away. The officer? Oh, no, really. No. Well maybe only for a short while, years ago. He had just kept after her and after her with that British bulldog persistence and—the glint turned mischievous—hadn't Dena ever been curious about what it was like with a gentile or even—she pried— with another man?

Dena evaded. The truth was everybody here knew everybody, and besides, she had discovered a trick for herself. Whenever she got hot and bothered, she simply would get Mati aroused.

This last time, Shula said about Uri, with even a flash of pride at his cleverness, he had completely fooled the British guards, in his uniform and with his perfect accent, from the war years in Cairo. Only, with the truck already loaded, one of the boys had got nervous and yelled at a fellow who was trying to take an extra machine gun. The nervous one had yelled in Hebrew, and the British had started shooting.

Dena asked after their youngest daughter, the real beauty, Chava. At last back from the ATS. She had been going out with a British flying officer, a goy. "Just like her mother in the First World War." Shula giggled.

Dena asked, "It's still on, with Chava?"

"More than ever. I'm afraid my little girl isn't a little girl anymore."

"Oh?"

"Today they just do it. He wants to marry her, but she doesn't want to leave Eretz." He was at least from an excellent family, the third son of an earl.

Dena complimented Shula on her new coiffure, it made her look younger, and Shula, though catching the bit of bitchiness, touched her hand to her upsweep and said she had a wonderful hairdresser, a Paris Jew named Emile had opened a shop in Tel Aviv on Allenby, she would introduce Dena as Emile was usually booked for weeks ahead.

President Truman proposed that a hundred thousand DPs be admitted to Palestine.

From the Hassan Beq minaret in Jaffa, using high-powered rifles, snipers killed several Jews in the streets of Tel Aviv. The Irgun retaliated with attacks on the Jaffa outskirts. The British brought in a tough unit that Mati heard was full of London fascists, Mosleyites. All Tel Aviv was put under strict curfew, with machine guns posted along Allenby Road. An hour a day was permitted for shopping. Children broke out of courtyards and taunted the Tommies. Two ten-year-old boys arrived in the hospital with bullet wounds. An American correspondent cabled: THE BRITISH EMPIRE VERSUS THE CHILDREN OF ISRAEL. The British Foreign Minister, Ernest Bevin, declared the reason President Truman wanted a hundred thousand refugees sent to Palestine was that "Americans don't want too many in New York."

Nahum returned from London and triumphantly announced to the press that although the diamond industry was reviving in

Amsterdam and there was strong pressure to discontinue the war-time facilities in Palestine, he had procured an agreement for the permanence of the works here.

Albert Einstein and Rabbi Stephen Wise pleaded the Jewish cause before the Anglo-American Commission of Inquiry.

King Farouk and Emir Ibn Saud issued a joint declaration that "Palestine was an Arab country."

Two more illegal refugee ships were caught by the British; the refugees were interned in the concentration camp at Athlit.

Two Jewish survivors who had returned to Lodz in Poland were found beheaded.

The radar station on the coast at Givat Olga, used for spotting illegal vessels, was attacked and demolished by the Haganah.

Not far from Givat Olga, British troops cordoned off a large kibbutz on the Sharon plain, Givat Haim, for an arms search. The chaverim resisted, and eight were killed.

In the House of Commons a member arose to equate Zionism with Nazism.

A pogrom broke out in the ancient Jewish quarter of Cairo. In Tripoli, where there had been no trouble between Arabs and Jews, Arabs sacked the mellah, leaving thirty dead.

Mati spent much time with the American engineer, Professor Lowdermilk, surveying the Jordan rift, and in growing excitement watched the development of a plan that could be much like the TVA in the States—a construction of dams and aqueducts that would utilize the waters of the Jordan to reclaim vast areas on both sides of the river, for both Arabs and Jews. The Rutenberg dam was only a starter. Day after day, as they went out in their Land Rovers, as they hiked along the ghor in the desolate, burning depression, as they talked in terms of American practical idealism, about the power that could be produced here, the lives that could be changed here, with the glowing, almost innocent face of the good professor seeming to banish all the factors of resistance to change, and incomprehension, and venality and hostility, why, all these things would vanish before a program obviously for the good of the area, for the good of mankind, each day Mati found himself reviving, found himself almost believing that this was the real reality, this zestful confidence in an improved world, and that the war with the British over the immigrants, the three-sided horror among Arabs, Jews, and British, the mutilations and assassinations and brutalities that multiplied every day were some unreality that would one day pass as a fever sometimes passes when a medicine is found. And the Lowdermilk plan could even be that medicine!

The plan was published. It was said that King Abdullah was in favor. That America would grant enormous loans. But complications arose, with Syria, with the British. Technical criticisms were being made. Perhaps a variation—

By sheer bad luck Italian road police on the lookout for a notorious fascist stopped Yehuda Arazi's Maserati alongside a column of trucks heading for the port of La Spezia, and became curious when they found the trucks filled with people. Arazi managed to reach a high local official who intervened and allowed the convoy to proceed, but by the time the refugees boarded the waiting vessel the British had been alerted. A destroyer moved into the port and stationed itself across the bow of the *Fede*.

Arazi, who had mounted on board as just another refugee, declared a mass hunger strike until the vessel was permitted to sail. The world press arrived. On the second day, as people began to collapse, they were laid out on deck next to a large sign listing the hours of the strike. Photographs went out to the world. Now Arazi printed "immigration certificates" with quotations from the prophets, the Balfour Declaration, and the United Nations Charter, issuing them to the illegal immigrants. When the hundredth hunger hour arrived, he announced a new measure to the press. There would be volunteer suicides on deck, before the world. The final protest. He would be the first. Tonight would be Passover Eve. In order not to desecrate the traditional freedom celebration, the suicides would begin the following morning.

In Jerusalem, Ben-Gurion and all the leaders were joining the hunger strike. Rabbis decreed that the command to eat matzo could be fulfilled by the consumption of a symbolic portion the size of an olive. The members of the Jewish Agency would assemble to hold such a Seder.

Mati and Dena had planned to take the children as usual to a big family Seder in Mishkan Yaacov. The twins under no condition would eat more than the sliver of matzo and indeed insisted on remaining in Jerusalem to stand in the crowd outside the Agency building.

It was a mild early evening with a beautiful bluish-washed sky. The broad semicircular courtyard of the Agency was overflowed.

You saw and nodded to so many people you knew, in an atmosphere awed, yet festive. Ben-Gurion, Ben-Zvi, Moshe Shertok, and all the others emerged and took turns reading the main portions of the Haggadah, about the escape from slavery in Egypt. Golda Meyerson had got her doctor to let her out of the hospital.

Dena wondered if this was like ages ago when the crowd stood in the courtyard of their Temple—only a mile or so away it had been—and listened to their priests chanting. It gave you an eerie feeling. Mati had his hands on the shoulders of the twins, on either side of him, and Dena herself lifted up little Tanya so she could see. Then the shivery words came, and she recited with all assembled there: "In every generation each person is bound to see himself as if *he* had gone forth from Egypt."

In the morning the radio announced that Professor Harold Laski had arrived at La Spezia, conferred with Yehuda Arazi, and given the Labor Government's pledge that these refugees would be permitted into Palestine. The hunger strike was ended. The British warships withdrew. A second vessel was permitted to take on part of the refugees from the overcrowded *Fede*. Named the *Eliahu Golomb* and the *Dov Hos*, the ships were authorized to sail. A great Passover feast was held, given by the people of La Spezia for the Jews.

If they could fast with Arazi's survivors, they should also feast with them, declared Eddie and Ziona Marmor, so they invited everybody; they'd have the real thing, matzo ball soup and all! For the "stranger at the feast" they invited Dick Mowrer, the foreign correspondent of the Chicago *Daily News*, whose standing boast at the King David bar was that he could be so pro-Jewish only because he was a goy.

Since Dena and Mati had had a movie date with Mouna and Khalid, instead of calling it off, Dena invited them to join the party and taste some of the Passover delights. Though if they felt . . .

Not at all! Mouna had always wanted to go to a Seder; after all, Moses was a prophet for the Moslems, and when she had been a little girl, Nebi Musa was a great feast; most of her family still held it, though, of course, since college she had kind of dropped religion.

At the party quite a discussion started, for Dick was curious about the festival of Nebi Musa and the Jewish feast of Moses. He even recalled how the first Arab-Jewish troubles, in 1920, had got started with Arabs becoming all worked up during their Nebi Musa march to Jerusalem and then falling on the Jews of the Old City. Was there a rivalry, then, over Moses?

Until she was grown up, Mouna remarked, she hadn't even known that Moses was Jewish!

Suddenly everyone was curious.

But of course, she said. Few Arabs knew anything of the Old Testament, with Abraham and Joseph and Moses and all the rest. They knew about the patriarchs as *their* patriarchs, out of the Koran. So the prophet Moses was their Nebi Musa.

After all, since unfortunately very few of the Moslem population could read, what they knew was what they heard from their cadi, and why should they know about the Jewish belief? Here in Palestine, from the minority who were Christians, they knew something about Jesus and Christian ideas, but while Christians had the Old Testament as part, as the foundation of their holy writings, the Moslems, of course, did not. Mohammed came as the last prophet, she explained, and everything that had been before was subject to his revelations, and if there was a difference, then his was the truth. So to the mass of Moslems, there was nothing else.

Maureen became keenly interested. Take Nebi Musa itself. She had visited the site—most of them had been down there—the hilltop on the way to the Dead Sea, revered as the resting place of Moses, in the Moslem belief. Yet the Bible clearly described his burial place as Mount Nebo, over on the other side of Jordan.

Well, there was more than that. Mati brought up the point that had always fascinated him, that to the Moslems it was Ishmael and not Isaac who was the subject of the story of the sacrifice.

"Of course!" Mouna said. At the Feast of the Sacrifice, even today, her family killed a sheep, in memory of the event, and sent the meat around to friends and to the poor. A sheep—just like Jews in ancient times, with their sheep at Pesach, Eddie remarked.

They could puzzle at these odd resemblances, since all here were basically nonbelievers—each a nonbeliever strictly according to his own belief, Reggie quipped, but far back in the centuries something had become twisted up between the two faiths, and Dick even wondered if it ever could be straightened out, to bring the Arabs and Jews closer together, rather than farther apart. "Yes," said Maureen, "just look at the Christians, Catholic and Protestant, killing each other off in Ireland!"

574

Well, did the Arabs have anything like matzo ball soup? Dena asked Mouna, and Mouna laughed; maybe an exchange of recipes was all that was needed. Dick had heard that Yehuda Arazi had himself taught the Italians how to make matzo balls, for the feast at La Spezia.

Was Arazi's whole struggle worth it? someone wondered. After all, the British were taking off the entire number of these immigrants from the quota.

"It got headlines all over the world," Dick said. Arazi had handled the thing brilliantly. Not only that, everyone felt he would have gone through with his suicide.

"And he would have." Mati knew him.

Dena couldn't help thinking of Menahem. He'd have done the same.

"So the whole world was aroused. Does public opinion really help?" Eddie Marmor was skeptical. Even if it was in a way his profession.

One thing Dick believed. All this resistance was changing the way the world thought about Jews. It was counteracting all that talk that Jews went to their death like sheep to the slaughter. Now they saw a different kind of Jew, a Jew fighting at worst odds, taking on the whole might of the British.

This was important, but Mati still wondered, with Eddie, how much effect public opinion could have.

What did have effect? Maureen asked.

In the end, production. Industrial capacity had decided the war. It could also bring peace to the world. Mati started to give an enthusiastic account of the Lowdermilk plan, but nobody got excited. Dick had just been accorded the regulation secret interview with the terrorist chief Menahem Begin, having been taken blindfolded in a series of cars, and of course, those people believed terror had the deciding effect.

Not terror! Not assassination! About this, Dena felt strongly. Could anyone believe the British would give up Palestine because Lord Moyne had been assassinated? Had it changed their policy one bit? Only for the worse. Look at the British general Barker who told his soldiers to stay out of Jewish shops: "Hit them in the pocketbook, that's what the Jew understands." Plain anti-Semitism.

And Bevin? Maureen quoted, "The Jew is always trying to push himself in at the head of the queue."

"He must have seen an Egged bus queue!" Reggie quipped, and they all laughed, and recalled to the ritual, drank the second cup of wine.

☙☙☙

The Mufti, "detained" in a Paris villa while under investigation as a war criminal, went out for a drive, boarded a plane, arrived in Egypt, and appealed to King Farouk for asylum.

There began a coming and going of emissaries from his cousin Jamal, whom the British had permitted back in Jerusalem.

A Haganah man familiar as a Hebrew teacher in the Athlit detention camp prepared a plan, and during a violin concert by an inmate, hundreds of illegal immigrants broke out of the camp and were led over Mount Carmel to disappear in Yagur and other settlements.

Illegal immigrants would henceforth be held on Cyprus, the British proclaimed. German war prisoners there were constructing a detention camp.

After a mass arrest of Irgunists, five British officers were kidnapped in Tel Aviv and held as hostages.

On the Sabbath—Black Sabbath it was to be called—the entire Jewish leadership—the Agency staff, the heads of the Elected Council, of the Histadrut—a thousand persons altogether were seized and imprisoned in Latrun. Ben-Gurion, just then in Paris, in the Mossad's little hotel, would have to stay out of the country until the crisis was resolved. Meanwhile Golda Meyerson had been left free, perhaps out of British gallantry, perhaps so that there should remain a caretaker to deal with. Reggie, too, was still free. "In my case it proves my unimportance," he said.

But Nahum was proudly among those taken to Latrun; he wondered if he was in the same barracks where his son Uri had been held.

Tanks, armored troop carriers arrived at Gilboa as at a dozen other settlements. Armed resistance had been countermanded as suicidal. Two or three soldiers to each chaver, with the chaveroth screaming insults and beating at the Britons, the Jews were dragged off to detention. Name? Ish Ha-Eretz, man of the land, was all that each would say. Squads with magnetic mine detectors went inch by inch over the grounds and through the buildings,

576

searching for slicks. Under the tile floors of a children's house an emergency cache of grenades was found, placed there in case of an Arab attack. But then the huge slick below the machine shed was discovered; stacks of rifles were hauled out, with everything set on display for the press to justify the "bit of rough handling." In HaRishon, Avinoam, just discharged from the Brigade, had to be subdued with a gun-butt blow to his head. In Yagur, a major Haganah arsenal was uncovered. A disaster.

At a full-scale press conference the British commander declared that the Jewish resistance was now finished.

All Jerusalem heard the enormous blast, saw the pillar of smoke from the King David billowing into a cloud.

From Mati's office in the new PIO building almost diagonally across the street, the southern end of the hotel could be seen bulging out and then melting downward. He thought at once of Reggie, who should be over there seeing a certain colonel with whom he sometimes exchanged intelligence. And Peewee's office was in the King David. He started to run, but jumped back to a phone and luckily managed to get a call through, telling Dena he was all right. He might just have been over there himself.

Bodies, parts of bodies, were on the street. Men in shreds of clothes, of uniforms, wandered dazed. Fire engines, ambulances, troops, the whole awful terror response that had become routine. Only never anything so immense as this. Someone was sputtering the Irgun couldn't have done it alone, it was the Haganah, too, the bloody Jews were all in it together. He saw no one he knew. He was stopped from going in. At last with others he was helping pull away debris, timber, stone. A crushed body—a woman, a secretary, the hair clotted over an unidentifiable face, a Jewish girl he guessed, black hair. Milk cans, an officer was saying. The bastards had brought milk cans filled with explosives, looked like a routine milk delivery. To the basement.

When the explosion came, Dick Mowrer had just emerged with his Jewish girlfriend from the King David bar; he lay in the Hadassah Hospital with a broken leg. In the cordoned area for close relatives Dena remained close to Maureen. Fewer and fewer were still being brought out alive. Though it was by no means impossible. Under the fallen ceilings even a strong desk could give protection. The fire was under control, so if someone had not been crushed at once—

By midnight the group had dwindled. Mostly wives. And parents of office girls. The chief secretary luckily had stepped out of his office a moment before the blast, but his office girl had been inside, a bright, lively young woman whom everybody knew; her parents waited. A warning telephone call had been made, the Irgun had announced, instructing that the building at once be evacuated. The British did not confirm the call. The parents wondered bitterly whether that was why the chief secretary had stepped out of his office.

Already forty were known dead, of the British some of the most decent, and Jews who had dealt with them, and Arabs who had dealt with them, and Jews and Arabs who had worked there, clerks, officials, tea bringers.

After two days, eighty bodies had been removed from under the collapsed floors. Including Reggie's.

During the mourning days Dena could feel the determination growing in Maureen: She would not rest until she found out. All that was possible to know. That the Irgun had called the *Post* with their warning for the King David to be evacuated, Eddie Marmor verified—he had stood beside the operator while she alerted the police. But the exact number of minutes? Until they reached the proper authority?

Half an hour, the Irgun kept declaring, had been allowed from the time of their call to the *Post*. Enough for everyone to get out if the Chief Secretary had passed on the warning. But when you counted the time for the calls, for all the intervening operators, it came down to hardly more than twelve minutes.

And the other part: the hints going around that the Haganah had approved the action. It was true there had lately been a period of high-level coordination, Maureen had known from Reggie himself. But if the Haganah was aware, why hadn't Reggie been warned to stay out of the King David?

And who in the Haganah? With Ben-Gurion in Paris and all the leaders still in Latrun, Maureen reasoned it had to be Saadeh himself, as he had evaded the arrests.

Mati supposed so, too.

Did some of the foreign correspondents know more? If Dick had had any inkling would he have taken his girl with him to the K.D. bar—even though he might have risked it for himself? Because of Black Saturday the correspondents had expected a reprisal, he said, but nothing so unimaginable, and so soon.

And Mati pointed out—among the dead was Jacobs, one of the highest Jews in the administration, but known to have been friendly to the Irgun. Why hadn't Jacobs been warned, or got out of the building on some pretext?

In the hospital, Dick told Maureen that a *Times* man had learned that the Chief Secretary had indeed received the telephone warning. He wasn't taking orders from the goddam Jews, he had been heard to swear as he strode out of his office—probably to give some orders. Rumors were that the instruction he had given was for no one to leave the building.

Those who had saved themselves declared, no, they had heard no such instruction, but they had already run out when there was an exchange of shots in the basement. That proved to be the shots frightening off several Arab workers who had got in the way of the "milk" delivery.

Finally Maureen reached someone who had talked to Saadeh in hiding. In preliminaries with the Irgun, Saadeh had insisted on an hour of warning, instead of half an hour. Saadeh's consent to the action had been put off from day to day.

Then, there came a vagueness as to whether the actual day had been known and approved.

Maureen said to Dena that her thoughts were now clear. The deaths, including Reggie's, were due to human failures. If the Haganah, as seemed the case, had accepted the action, then Reggie would have accepted it. With a faintly bitter smile—still the brave smile of a British woman, Dena could not help thinking, Maureen said Reggie's was a death in war. Reggie had fallen, as sometimes when a soldier is struck by a shell from his own side.

Maureen would not think of leaving Jerusalem. Reggie's children belonged here. She herself would have no other life.

In the town of Kielce in Poland a boy one day didn't come home; a half-witted playmate told a priest he had seen the boy killed and bled by Jews. Forty Jews were murdered. Some had returned from death camps. The missing boy came back home.

This time Mati finally had to have the ulcer cut out; lying in the hospital, he wrote letter after letter to Ben-Gurion, but did not send them. Was this really the time to bother B-G?

To his astonishment, he was scarcely out of the hospital when a call came from Golda, who sat virtually alone at the Agency while all the rest remained at Latrun. Golda had a message from B-G. Mati could leave the British. He was to replace Reggie.

He simply felt cleaner, freer. It was Maureen who remarked that Reggie would have called it a double ulcer removal. Whenever you got together, you still expected to hear these little straight-faced remarks of Reggie's.

Now, in Mati's discussions with the British, he no longer had to twist things so that every project was shown to be in the interest of the entire land when goddammit, everyone knew it was needed by the Jews. No more of that feeling that the Britisher he was talking to was weighing, suspecting, judging him even when—as with pushing the Lowdermilk plan—it was something plainly good for the whole area, regardless of Arabs or Jews.

And with the Jews, no more of that feeling that certain ultimate things were held back from him, not because of any suspicion of his loyalty but because with a man being day in and day out among the British, he might accidentally let something drop.

One day Mati got up before dawn to leave on some mysterious task, and Dena heard him doing something he had not done for years. Mati whistled.

Soon after, Dick called to ask if she wanted to come along to the Negev as some friends of his from Chicago had room in their film truck.

What were they filming?

Didn't she know? Had he perhaps let the cat out of the bag? By now it was out anyway. Eleven tower-and-stockade settlements were going up in one full swoop, spotted all the way to the Egyptian border.

Below Gaza the film truck got lost, then got stuck in the sand, and even Dena helped push. Finally, they sighted a row of over-loaded lorries swaying across the desert like some new type of camel. Joining the parade, they were presently among trucks un-loading cabin sections, even a huge chicken coop full of hens.

It was like the time during the Arab troubles in the thirties, when she and Mati had gone out from Kibbutz Brandeis to a tower and stockade. Ten years! Bare-legged young girls were twisting barbed wire onto fence posts. But where was Mati? Maybe at another of the eleven sites. The cameraman motioned to Dena to get into the scene, why not, no longer might it embarrass Mati on his job with the British! Wait till the folks at home see me! She couldn't think of anything brighter to say, and there she was twisting wires. A couple of cars appeared across the sand, the first had a British flag, and behind in an Agency car was Mati. He rushed around with the British district officer, explaining that all was legal, the land acquired years ago, unused desert, dwellings were already set up.

And suddenly Mati caught sight of her, kind of gasped, and Dena winked.

The British car departed; Mati stayed on. A huge ex-army tent had been set up, sandwiches, bottles of grapefruit juice were distributed, the watchtower was up, and like a switch off, the day was gone.

At the kumsitz, Mati had his arm around her—a long time since— Under the big tent, Bedouin carpets covered the sand; youngsters were bedding down on the carpets, but at the rear were a number of army cots. The kibbutz mukhtar insisted they use cots but Dena wouldn't hear of it. Just far enough away on the rug, to one side of them, lay the film man and his girlfriend, and on the other side a young kibbutz pair, Dena noticed the blue numbers on their arms outside their blanket. The girl, she had worked with during the day—her name was Bella. A real Hungarian beauty.

This was the most heavenly night of her life, Dena declared. With her Sheik of Araby in the desert.

☙ ☙ ☙

The Nuremberg trials dragged to an end. Goering bit on his cyanide pill, but eleven Nazis were hanged.

Theodor Herzl's grandson leaped from the George Washington Bridge to his death; Herzl's sister had died in a concentration camp, and so the family line ended.

In Jaffa, a sheikh was killed, the fifth of the anti-Husseini faction to be assassinated since the Mufti had arrived in Cairo.

Arabs set the Haifa oil refinery aflame.

The American left-wing journalist I. F. Stone arrived on an illegal ship and wrote an impassioned account of the voyage of the survivors and of the British capture of the ship just as the coast of Eretz came into sight.

The British-American Commission of Inquiry made a unanimous report calling for the admission into Palestine of a hundred thousand refugees still waiting in the onetime concentration camps. Though pledged to comply, the British government now refused. The United Nations appointed a new investigating commission on Palestine.

At last the Yishuv leaders were released from Latrun. The whole of Nahum's town of Sharon Shore lined the street for his homecoming, but the trouble in the land was not over. Jailed terrorists got out word that they had been flogged by the British. At once a British officer and three soldiers were captured by Irgunists and flogged.

She could swear it was Araleh who had done the flogging, Shula told Dena. At last he must have revenged himself for the time in Gallipoli when the British whipped him, just because he had gone to visit his Saraleh.

In London a synagogue was set on fire; a placard read YOU WHIP, WE BURN. In Jerusalem, a British captain arrested a young Jewish boy posting a Sternist leaflet and then dumped him out of the car on the Arab side, in front of Damascus Gate, where he was immediately cut to pieces. With the Jewish community enraged, the captain was court-martialed—and acquitted. The Irgun raided the police fortress of Ramat Gan and was repulsed, with a wounded man later found by the British in a ditch. His name was Dov Gruner, he had got out of Hungary in time, and had fought in the Jewish Brigade in Italy. But he was sentenced to be hanged, together with another Irgunist captured at the time. Two British officers were kidnapped as hostages for the doomed pair. Delays came. Gruner's story was attracting world-wide attention and it seemed he might not be hanged after all. As the case went through one crisis after another, there were more kidnappings, escapes, a judge was seized, and released as the hangings were again put off. Gruner's letters, smuggled from the death cell where he wore the red garb of the condemned, were noble and heartbreaking. Avinoam, visiting Mati in Jerusalem to enroll in the Hebrew University, said he was sure he had known Dov in the Brigade, but not well. Dov Gruner's sister arrived from America to plead for his life. And then suddenly it was announced that he and his comrade had been moved to Acre prison and hung.

Two British sergeants, the last hostages, were found hung in an orange grove.

Two more Irgunists, about to be hanged, placed between them a grenade that had been smuggled inside an orange skin, and blew themselves up.

Shula thanked God that their Uri was safe in prison.

☙☙☙

But already the breakout was being planned. Even the blowing up of the King David would be outdone. The entire world would see that the British Empire was powerless before the Irgun! The fortress walls that had withstood Napoleon would be breached!

In the jail, Uri had found his old chaver Yoram in command of the Jewish prisoners; not for years had they seen each other—not since Menahem Begin had issued his declaration of war against the British. Yoram had been among the first to be picked up. Long before the "season," the British had had him on their list.

Both from inside and on the outside, every possibility was being examined. Inside, in conversations during the exercise hour with an Arab thief who had spent half his life here, Yoram had heard of an escape attempt long ago, through a window on the upper floor, but the fellow had broken his legs and been cut to pieces where he lay. What window? The wall was solid, there, unbroken. Ah, the window had been sealed and made part of the wall, it had been in one of the larger cells, in what was now the Arab section.

By coincidence, on the outside, Saadya, one of the best lads in the intelligence section, a Yemenite who passed perfectly for an Arab, had learned of the same former window. He had been frequenting a small, cheap bathhouse, nothing but a hovel built against the lower part of the wall. In the hamam he had got into conversation with the aged attendant, how did the structure come to be built right against the wall? Ah, it was a spot that had been shunned after a prisoner had jumped from a window in the fortress, and been cut to pieces here. Though the window had been filled, you could still see where it had been, by a discoloration in the wall.

Perhaps, then, Saadya speculated in his report, the wall was weaker at that point?

But if the wall were breached there, the prisoners would have to reach the Arab cell to get out. Between the Arab cell wing and the Jewish wing there stood a heavy wrought-iron gate; when there had been only a handful of Jews in Acre, the gate had protected them from assaults and knifings. Now with a few hundred, the Jews ruled the jail. But still, that gate would have to be dynamited. A small charge would take care of it, Yoram said, it could be brought in a jar of jam, one of the boys from Petah Tikvah said his mother would do it.

Messages had got through, in and out. Yoram passed the word: five o'clock; it had to be in daylight or the getaway trucks would be caught in the curfew. Only forty could be taken, as to wait for more to get out would endanger the whole operation.

Uri was on the list.

At exactly five, as all of them had their eyes on him in the yard, Yoram nodded, they thronged to the cell-block, before the guards knew what had happened the blast had gone off and the dividing gate was down. In perfect coordination a thunderous blast came from outside. The Arabs had to be held back—there were scuffles, but two holes gaped in their cell wall. They could jump afterward.

Uri was third in his unit. The drop to the domed roof of the hamam was easy but from there to the street was a jump of four meters. The lane was in pandemonium. He hung an instant by his hands, let go, and landed well. It was working, all was working. At the end of the lane, three lorries waited. Commandeered from the British.

He was pulled aboard the first truck. Then from the driver they heard wild angry curses. The starter whirred but the motor was stalled. It couldn't be. It couldn't be. After such a triumph, a brilliant operation. Uri thought all at once of that first action at the Bridge of the Daughters of Jacob when the cigarette failed to light the fuse. At his crazy laugh the fellows got angry.

On the beach below the ramparts, only a few hundred yards away, at the foot of the picturesque ancient wall that Napoleon had been unable to breach, a few Tommies, taking an after-duty swim, heard the blast, rushed for their gear, and still in swim trunks came shooting toward the trucks. The assault squad, already having to deal with the roof sentries of the fortress, turned to give battle but the British had excellent cover inside stone doorways and arches. The driver, even under fire, had the hood of the first lorry raised and was desperately tinkering with the carburetor; he collapsed with his head inside.

"Everyone to the second truck!" Yoram shouted; Uri leaped

584

down, ducking for cover, everyone was cursing that they had no weapons but he seized a Sten from a fallen man of the assault squad.

The last to jump on the crowded second truck, his feet hanging from the lowered tailgate, Uri spotted a bare-waisted Tommy, the cursed bastard had even slapped on his red beret, and as the truck passed the doorway Uri fired, and then heard, coming out of himself, a startled, almost quiet sound.

Crowded in among the chevreh, his body sat there, and then as those behind him felt the increasing weight, they knew. A hit directly between the eyes.

On that first night Shula with Tsila and Nahum listened to every broadcast. Uri's name was not among the dead or recaptured.

Only on the second day could Yoram get a message through to Nahum. But no one could come where they were, and the dead were already buried.

Meanwhile all Palestine was covered with posters carrying photographs of the hunted, in long rows. Thirty-one had made good their escape. There in the third row was Uri's face, serious and handsome, Uri Ben Artzi.

Everyone talked of the amazing breakout, the greatest feat of the Irgun, the whole world was talking of it. Those Jewish terrorists! They had even broken out of the impregnable fortress where Napoleon had failed! Again they had thumbed their nose at the whole British empire!

As yet the British didn't know that they had succeeded in killing one more. For a long time the posters faced you wherever you went, with Uri's picture among the Wanted. Reward, dead or alive.

☙☙☙

This time Muntchik was to leave; Menahem had persuaded him. He had done more than his share in the Bricha, Menahem said; the movement was well organized now, with plenty of lads familiar with the different mountain crossing points. Perhaps Muntchik should go at the outset to Lotzi and Bella in their kibbutz in the Negev; they were his only friends from before. Their kibbutz had already, as they triumphantly wrote, constructed a huge catch basin for the winter flood waters and achieved early high-priced tomato yields. If he should after a time choose to enter Hebrew University, Menahem told Muntchik, he would certainly be given assistance, and as he knew, the university had an excellent department of theoretical physics.

In the far reaches of the Soviet Union, it was reported, an atomic bomb was tested successfully. Not even to Menahem had Muntchik more than hinted at what he hardly dared contemplate in himself. Why need he be consumed with the feeling that this task was for him? That he must be the one, for the Jews? And how could he take on himself such a responsibility, an awesome decision that some of the world's greatest scientists, in America, now spoke of with doubt and even regret?

34

NEVER before had there been such a convoy; it reached back an entire mile. To augment the Bricha's own transport, since the British had disbanded the Jewish Brigade unit with its roaming trucks, a fleet of German vehicles had been hired. Nor did the convoy take the route to the Alpine pass; the British had made the Italian shores too difficult. Instead, the line of trucks moved across southwestern Germany to France. This departure was to be from a tiny obscure harbor not far from Marseilles that Venya had scouted out.

Again Menahem rode in a U.S. army jeep at the head of the column. Beside him sat a different American chaplain with the emblem of the Tablets on his uniform, and there was again a many-paged list of random names attached to a group visa for Paraguay; with this was a transit visa for France.

The convoy proceeded in broad daylight, this time with the canvases open. Before the pontoon bridge at the French border, where the documents were presented by the chaplain, the refugees were waved on with a smiling bon voyage. The night was spent on the grounds of a secluded villa that Yehuda Arazi had rented on the seacoast. A picnic, an excursion!

Muntchik was in charge of a group of twenty, mostly teenagers from an orphanage just outside Paris, near the estate of Léon Blum. Now came a meeting of monitors for final instructions. This voyage was to be like none other. Nearly five thousand refugees would be taken, on a huge vessel that the Mossad had brought across the Atlantic. The British were already watching the ship; indeed, the entire world would be watching this greatest effort of all to defy the English and bring survivors of the Holocaust to the homeland. There must, therefore, be perfect discipline, for the British were certain to try to seize and board the vessel, and organized resistance would be made. Understood? Understood.

In the morning their convoy entered a pleasant French fishing village, and swelling the tiny harbor like a whale in an aquarium, there sat their ship. Broad and high, she looked almost comical. Had this object really crossed the Atlantic Ocean? Already the youngsters were making affectionate jokes about their Ark. On the side was painted the name *President Garfield*. Who was he? Of President Roosevelt, even of an American President Lincoln some had heard. But who was this Garfield? Never mind! From every direction, more and more convoys kept arriving; overhead a British plane already circled, coming down close. "They're taking pictures!" The young people struck nose-thumbing poses.

They could not yet go aboard; a final inspection was being made by the French authorities; in a cordoned harbor area they waited.

Hour after hour they saw cars arriving and rushing off, harassed Bricha men running across the plaza to a café that had a telephone, French officials arriving, then driving away.

In Paris at the highest government level frantic verbal battles were taking place. Members of the British Cabinet, arrived in France for consultations on high matters of state, had suddenly turned to the subject of the illegal ship brazenly prepared to load and depart from a French harbor. Orders went out for new inspections of her seaworthiness, of her Panama registration, of her engines. Into the night, Ehud and the Abbé Glassberg sped around Paris, rousing highly placed contacts from their sleep to intervene. Venya's secret radio transmitter was seized by the French police; he drove hundreds of miles to a relay transmitter, giving Menahem instructions from Shaul to have the ship sail at all costs at once.

At the small port the world press began to arrive. Meanwhile, with bundles of bribe money, Menahem and the ship's captain, a young American named Ike, scoured the town for a pilot to take the vessel out through the narrow fishermen's channel. Town and port officials were invited to a feast, cases of champagne were dispensed, and at dawn the customs officer went happily to the compound, shrugged, stamped everyone's false papers, and allowed the refugees to board the vessel. Just as the boarding was completed, another stop order arrived from Paris. Menahem rushed to the telephone booth. "Sail! sail!" Shaul shouted. The bribed pilot had failed to appear, even to collect the second half of his fee. Ike tried on his own to guide the vessel through the harbor entrance; she ran aground. There were no tugs. With wild thrashings of the propeller under full-open engine power, the American seaman tried to back her off the sandbar. The ship shuddered. On the outermost edge of the breakwater, fishermen appeared, making incomprehensible gestures with their arms. Menahem, on the quay, closed his eyes. He could not live through the *Struma* again. Then in a sudden lurch the vessel was free. The entire population of the village was by now on the quay, even singing "The Marseillaise" as the Ark churned out to the open sea.

The RAF planes at once appeared overhead. In less than an hour two British destroyers fell in behind the ship. Soon the escort increased to four.

On board, in high spirits, all marveled at their ship, for compared to what they had heard of Bricha vessels, this was a luxury liner. American jazz and chalutz songs resounded everywhere from loudspeakers. Every hour, news in seven languages. The crew were young American volunteers, Jewish boys, ex-soldiers, college boys, and they didn't even speak Yiddish, much less Hebrew. They knew hardly anything about Palestine except, "Hey, those sabras are tough!" Some had been in the army in Europe and seen the concentration camps. There was even a red-cheeked youthful Christian minister, a Protestant named John, abounding with energy, reminding Muntchik of the rabbi chaplains, so eager to be seen as plain fellows, not solemn men of religion at all. And from the Bricha, there was a good handful he knew from different truck convoys and from various camps, Shlomo of the Palmach, who had trained many a squad of DPs with wooden rifles. But in the thousands that packed the strange vessel under her flag of Panama, what a medley of Jewry! From Poland, from Greece, even Finland, even the tiny state of Luxembourg, and the Poles who had survived in Siberia, and there were even a few Warsaw Ghetto fighters who had escaped through the sewers; there were children who had been hidden in monasteries and still clung to their crosses; there were families with babies born in the DP camps, the father and mother each telling you this was their second family, the children of each one's first marriage having perished in the massacres. One woman in ten was pregnant, and all the others seemed frantically bent on increasing this statistic, so that on the sleeping platforms you could hear the quickened breathing, the half-muffled gasps.

Muntchik was drawn; there was one in his Paris orphanage group who drew him strangely, Annette, but she was so young, sixteen, not time yet. Her spirited ways kept him from others, and perhaps altogether, he told himself, he had managed to be drawn to an impossible one so as to keep himself free for the years of the task still ahead of him. If he should finally decide. And beneath all, he was fearful, unsure whether a person should bring children into this world. All this glowing flesh, as clothing was shed in the sun; all the soft teasing and laughter was the cunning trap; all this copulating was perhaps not triumph over fate, but surrender.

Ominous, yet somehow comical, the escort of British destroyers only added to the mounting euphoria, as if the pulsating life on the ship were a perverse dare in the face of the enemy. In the same daring mood the ship's leaders would when the time came make a sudden dash for the coast and everyone would leap into the shallow waters where the warships couldn't possibly pursue. And these excited plannings seemed to stimulate even wilder copulation—in the lifeboats, in corners of the deck, shameless and triumphant.

At the time of his deportation Muntchik, hardly eighteen, had had no sex experience. After the liberation, even before his strength returned, the need had suddenly become ferocious. As though this urge, thwarted by the time of Auschwitz, were a power fearful of being thwarted again. On the farm estate and in the nearby village the German girls were easy enough for the occupying American soldiers, but they had an odd, uncertain look when one of the surviving Jews came near. Some of the boys nevertheless took them, at first vengefully. But for Muntchik this vengeful impulse was counterbalanced by an overwhelming repulsion for the whole German people; he would not even acknowledge desire.

But then on a truck errand with an ex-heftling like himself, in American army fatigues, they had picked up two fräuleins on the road; he could not spoil the atmosphere for his chaver, and halting, they had used the back of the truck. Later Muntchik had simply regarded such incidents as physical relief, nor had he pretended to himself that he didn't enjoy them. Here on the boat he was pleased to find that feelings of idealism had returned, of wanting a real love with a girl.

After he had begun intensive study and made his long-range plans, his love hunger had for a time subsided. Now on the ship in the wondrous warm-breezed evenings and nights, with the universe above exposed, illuminated, equations would all at once stand clear to him; already he comprehended the chain reaction, the physics of heavy water, by which the Germans had thought to be the first to unleash the nuclear secret. Already quite a conversation had started when one of the Americans, the ship's engineer, named Bill, glanced at Muntchik's open book. "Hey, you mean you're studying thermodynamics on your own?" and the talk soon enough got onto the atomic bomb, and a French chaver joined in, he had had two years of theoretical physics at the Sorbonne, and soon there was the question, had Russian spies really stolen the atomic secret in America? And the higher question, shouldn't a true scientist who knew such a secret, give it to the whole world? Also, the peaceful uses of nuclear energy. But mankind being what it was, would the peaceful uses prevail? And the enormous unimaginable cost that would confine atomic power to the great powers. But no, Bill believed, in time, even a small land such as Palestine, with no natural resources to speak of, might benefit from the atom. The discussion was getting so close to his inner secret Muntchik felt himself flushing. The fact was, Bill, the engineer, was saying, there really was no great secret to the scientific part of it anymore, ever since the first nuclear reactor pile had been started in Chicago, at the university under the football stadium, he had been a student there at the time; ever since then it was an open secret. The real secrets were the technical tricks, there must be a thousand such secrets, but in time any group of scientists could figure them out, the United States had merely had a head start, which now was practically gone. One day the cost might not even be so great as to confine the atom to the Great Powers. And then watch out, the French student said, that would be the end of man.

The combat units practiced taking their stations. Altogether some eight hundred men were counted as combatants, the shock troops; there would be strictly no use of firearms, no one aboard was supposed to have any, for one shot could give the British excuse for a slaughter.

Everyone was acquiring some sort of weapon. Clubs were made from balustrades of the stairways of the old excursion ship. As the Americans had brought food far beyond what was needed, hundreds of soup cans were to be hurled as bombs; the younger girls would be passing them to the combatants. But the "secret weapon" was a steampipe with jet holes at set intervals, girdled around the entire ship. There was also a hose that would spurt hot oil.

On the sixth night, as they were off the coast of Egypt, all were told to rest—surely the battle was for tomorrow. From Bill, Muntchik knew the planned strategy. When the vessel entered Palestine waters and the British commanded her to halt, only at that moment, Bill confided, would the engine be opened to full speed, for all through the voyage, to deceive the British, she had been held back. At full speed she could possibly even outrun the destroyers. She would head for a beach, agreed on by wireless, where units of the Palmach waited, and with luck most of the immigrants would get ashore and be dispersed in waiting trucks. More than once, this maneuver, this turning and rushing the few miles to the beach, had been successful.

With the coded message for the landing beach had come the Mossad's name for the ship. She was to be called *Exodus 1947*. Now, immediately Ike had this painted on a board and hung over the old name on the prow.

But suddenly, in the very middle of that night, glaring chalk-white searchlights converged on the vessel; on both sides, destroyers had silently moved nearer, and from a powerful loudspeaker came a dispassionate British command voice announcing they had entered Palestine waters, the ship must surrender, or it would be his regrettable duty, using the overwhelming force at his command, to board her, and take her to Haifa.

They were still far out in international waters, Captain Ike responded, and in any case they would not allow themselves to be boarded.

Tumbling out with the others, Muntchik was already at his post on the foredeck. Like nutcracker jaws, the destroyers closed in. Ranged on their decks were special boarding units that seemed to be from some film of the future. They wore white helmets, black gauntlets, carried large white rubber shields and black truncheons, and were girded with grenade belts and holstered pistols.

From the destroyers came a spurting fluid, a volley of grenades. A veil of tear gas engulfed the *Exodus 1947*. Soaked rags had been prepared for the fighters, but still the acid smoke startled them, and in that moment the assailants thrust boarding planks onto the deck; behind their shields, truncheons raised, came the first wave of Britons.

As he flung himself forward, grappling at a form coming toward him, Muntchik had to overcome an almost laughing realization that this was the first time he was fighting, really fighting! A truncheon blow slid off his shoulder. Why, compared to a kapo's blow it was a tap; he had a fleeting feeling—maybe these fellows didn't have their heart in it. A pair of eyes he caught—puzzled, dismayed, even a bit frightened. But no matter, in the heat of the fight they'd be brutal enough, and he doubled down his head and butted straight into his opponent, so powerfully that the man lost his footing and fell backward into the sea. Simply with his head, his damned precious head full of equations he had done it. In his momentum Muntchik nearly followed, except that another assailant struck him down from behind. Squirming around, he seized the man's legs and brought this one rolling onto the deck. Some of the chevreh jumped on the enemy, and Muntchik, his eyes smarting, rolled away. Several of the English were rushing up the stair to the bridge; going after them, he saw them seize Bill, who was with Ike at the helm, heard a tremendous thud and a ghastly bone-cracking sound. Bill fell, blood came from his mouth. Ike began pulling him into the bunkroom. Behind Muntchik other chevreh swarmed up the stairway, storming into the pilot house; four British were seized. In terror, one pulled his revolver and shot; an Auschwitz survivor fell. The chevreh leaped to kill. Ike managed to push the British into his bunkroom, where he had taken Bill. Prisoners.

For half an hour the first phase of the battle continued. Tiny red light signals gleamed from the sea, where Britishers had been thrust overboard. Twice again pistols were fired; two youngsters were wounded. The engirding steam-spray pipe had been crushed by the destroyers; the deck was black with oil, slushed with water and blood. Muntchik saw one Briton with his face split open from a hurled can. Seventeen more Englishmen were surrounded, their pistols thrown overboard; these were imprisoned in the lounge. Then for an interval the ship seemed cleared of them.

The radio room had been smashed up, even while the Protestant minister was broadcasting an open account of the battle to Tel Aviv. A second, hidden wireless was put into use. In the lull, the Panama flag was hauled down, while huge flags of Zion were unfurled from the mast. Slogans painted on sheets had been prepared. Lit up by the British spotlights, one proclaimed BEVIN = HITLER.

In the salon, in the infirmary, the ship's several doctors were tending wounded. In the salon, Muntchik found Annette being bandaged up, but she was laughing, only a cut over her eye, it wouldn't even mar her beauty she laughed to him, and she had almost bitten off the Britisher's ear! Four transfusions were needed at once the chief doctor said, he had no facilities, Muntchik must report this to Ike. Meanwhile, the second assault had begun.

This time two more destroyers, coming at sharp angles, cut against the bow of the ship, staving in the timber down to water level. With each roll of the sea came an inundation. The older women, the families with children, all who had been placed below for safety, in panic began to scream for an end to the battle. As the water reached knee height, Muntchik formed his youth group into a bucket line. At last the pumps got started, but on the deck a new battle was under way. This time the fight went on for an hour.

The bridge was overwhelmed; the deck swarmed with British; more than half the Jewish fighters had been seized or were beaten out of action. On the wireless, Tel Aviv instructed truce talks.

With surrender and the removal of urgent cases to the medical ward of the British flagship, some of the Tommies, as though trying to separate themselves from what they had had to do, began to offer sweets and chocolate to the children. From the officers, British politeness prevailed. The *Exodus* was escorted to Haifa.

In the salon lay the three dead. Muntchik stood long over Bill with his crushed skull.

At each stage of the remaining two months of the apogee of the *Exodus*, just as at that moment when he saw Bill laid out dead, Muntchik felt his fearsome decision deepening. In Haifa he was dragged, clinging to every railing, every stanchion of the vessel, carried deadweight and flung onto the steel floor of a large prison cage in a British transfer ship.

There were three of these transfer vessels, but in the mass cage of the *Empire Rival*, Muntchik heard Annette call his name. Luckily they found themselves together, almost his entire group on the same vessel. In a few hours, all calculated, they would be in Cyprus.

But a full day passed, and they were still on the open sea.

The infuriated Foreign Minister, Ernest Bevin, as the world already knew, had ordered that the refugees be "taken back where they came from."

But when the ships at last reached Port-de-Bouc, frenzied diplomatic interchanges again took place, the British insisting that the refugees must debark here where they had embarked, while the French declared that none should be delivered by force onto French soil. They would offer asylum to these refugees, for all who wished to accept—indeed, because of the extraordinary ordeal of this group, the French announced, all those who accepted would even be offered eventual French citizenship. But none would be coerced.

It was now that the test must come.

From Paris, Menahem, Venya, the Abbé Glassberg, Ehud, drove all night to the small port. Would the section leaders aboard each ship have understood, and would the people, after the broiling week in the cage ships, still hold fast? There was no way to communicate.

Again the world press had arrived, and Menahem and Venya with their journalist cards boarded a motorboat among the several that sped out toward the British flotilla. Reporters with megaphones were shouting up questions to the commanders. Crowding close under the portholes of each ship in turn, Menahem and Venya howled up in Hebrew, "Lo laredet! Don't come off! Lo laredet!"

But the survivors of their own accord had understood.

Ten days and nights the three vessels lay alongside the French port. In the sweltering cages the refugees had flung off all but a few shreds of clothing. Daily they heard the French loudspeakers proclaim their carefully worded offer.

Tents had been put up to receive them. A row of ambulances

stood waiting. One woman debarked to give birth. Three others gave birth in the steel cages.

Menahem, wearing a white doctor's smock, got himself taken along with a medical team. Not until he reached the last ship did he see Muntchik. They had only a moment—a British officer accompanied the team. "Don't worry." Muntchik winked to Menahem.

Of the forty-five hundred, after the ten days, four thousand remained unbudging. These Jews who had refused French asylum, the British now announced, would be indeed delivered "where they came from": a camp was ready in Germany, near Hamburg.

The Hamburg port was ringed not only with British troops, but also with German police. Muntchik was among the first to be carried off, three Tommies seizing his arms and legs in expert lockholds; wriggling, he saw Annette flying at a trooper, clawing his face, kicking, biting. With a violent slap the man sent her reeling. She was carried, limp. It was at this moment that Muntchik finally made his vow. No matter how long it took, no matter what the difficulty, he would complete the dread task he was setting for himself. Never again should the Jew be without means to control his destiny.

Through the barbed wire of the detention camp the reporters shouted a piece of news to those of the *Exodus*. The United Nations Commission on Palestine had today issued its report. It was for partition into Arab and Jewish states. There remained only the vote in the General Assembly.

Also, Muntchik heard them shout, the British had already declared they would not accept this solution and would evacuate Palestine on May 15.

※ ※ ※

Phil and Sherrill hadn't dared invite anybody in advance to celebrate since Phil, on long distance throughout the crash campaign for UN votes, knew that even now the two-thirds majority wasn't sewn up. He had used every big business contact he had made during the war—and some of them swung weight with obscure uninvolved delegations. Every big Jew he knew was calling contacts, in South America, even in Liberia, but the result was a toss-up. Still—just in case—he had stacked up on champagne. And when he and Sherrill, sitting with the kids before the TV

596

marking their checklist of nations, with the result still uncertain all the way down to Venezuela, heard that "Yes!" his Sherrill screamed, hugged him, hugged the kids, and rushed to the phone. Every phone on the North Shore was busy. But soon the cars began to arrive anyway.

It was an all-night party, scotch pouring like water. To listen to Phil, if it were not for his brother-in-law Mati, working right in B-G's office in Jerusalem, there would only have been half a state, the size of a miniature golf course. No Negev! Naturally, Chaim Weizmann also had had a little to do with getting the Negev, Phil consented laughingly; Weizmann's last-minute plea to Truman—that had clinched it! But who gave Weizmann all the facts on the Negev to present to the President? Who? Naturally, B-G had had a little to do with that phase; Phil happened to know that B-G had driven the Jewish Agency's New York delegation out of their minds, insisting they absolutely had to get Chaim Weizmann in there to Truman to make the last-minute plea. Chaim was the only Jew that Truman would listen to outside of his 1918 war buddy Jacobson, whom he had gone into the haberdashery business with. And in the last minute Jacobson had got the President to open the back door for Chaim. Very good—only, where had B-G got all the potent facts on the Negev, with which Weizmann had blitzed Truman? From none other than Phil's own brother-in-law, Mati Chaimovitch, who had once actually flown Phil over that whole stretch of the Negev to show him its importance.

Even while Mati had still been with the Mandate, he had, Phil explained, talked the British into a full exploration of the resources of the area. Just before the Nazis started the war, Mati had gone down there in the wilderness and explored the old copper mine diggings. Sure he had given the British his report—half of it! Also, he had made soundings in King Solomon's port on the Red Sea; the name was in the Bible—Elath. And just a few weeks ago B-G had called in Mati—this was in a letter Phil had just received from Dena—and Mati had dug out all his Negev facts, and this was the material rushed to New York to brief Chaim Weizmann! Solomon's mines! The port of Elath! Open spaces that could be irrigated from the water sources they had discovered deep down! And after hearing all these facts, President Truman had got right on the phone to the U.S. delegate at the UN and given the order: the Negev absolutely must be included for the Jews!

※ ※ ※

But there still remained a few months before the British would leave, and now came a series of horrors in Jerusalem, hardly more than a week apart. First, the explosion at the *Palestine Post*. It sounded to Dena as though all Zion Square had gone up; a radio flash said it was the *Post*. Casualties unknown. Immediate house curfew.

She ran across backyards to Ziona Marmor; Maureen was already there, the telephone was out. After a time David came running, he had somehow squirmed his way to Mati at the Agency and Abba had word that Eddie Marmor was okay, also Gershon Agronsky and Ted Lurie, but three printers were dead. The explosion had come from a British army vehicle left in front of the building.

Next, an entire block of Ben Yehuda Street. A British army half-track, parked at dawn not far from Zion Square. People blasted from their beds as walls fell away, mangled bodies on the sidewalk. The café where you had met yesterday scattered over the entire street. Forty-four dead.

Even those who had seen the London blitz, seen smashed cities across Europe, kept dazedly repeating, "But in Jerusalem!"

A week later, one morning as Mati sat at his desk, the floor trembled under his feet, pieces of window slid down. Recoiling from the blast, he saw across the courtyard the opposite end of the half-circle building exploding, heard screams in his hallway, how could his phone still be ringing, he was rushing to Ben-Gurion's. Safe. Then he was in the confused crowd trying to cross the yard, guards, police, Haganah boys, everyone from the Jewish Agency wing. Before the Keren Hayesod entrance, the remains of a car, still bearing on the fender the American flag of the consulate. Waved into the compound, the Arab driver had parked the car full of explosives and gone off. Clambering over debris, Mati found an elderly secretary, Clara, lying in the hallway, blood pumping in spurts from her half-severed arm. As he made a tourniquet, he saw, lying dead, a tea bringer, a raconteur of Yiddish stories, and couldn't think of the man's name. Dena must be frantic.

She could get no nearer than two blocks. She heard a cry—"Not the Agency! Keren Hayesod!" But he might have been over on that side; he often was. Half Rehavia was at the barrier. Voices calling out names, begging, pleading. "Has anyone heard?" Like the day of the King David. How many such things could you bear? Like Ziona Marmor until she knew Eddie was safe. Oh! let Mati be safe!

The twins found her. Then Jonathan had disappeared. Word was passing, a miracle, it was certain that Ben-Gurion had escaped. But Mati? Mati? The Arab driver had first parked the car right in front of the Agency, but since it blocked the entrance, a guard had released the brake and rolled the car along farther, near the Keren Hayesod.

Jonathan got back. Abba was all right, he was helping with the wounded.

Fifteen had died, and this time they knew each one of them.

The Yishuv's own Civil Defense was putting up checkpoints in Rehavia, in Mea Shearim, in every Jewish area. They organized patrols. Elderly men walking in pairs. These could not risk being caught carrying arms, but in doorways Haganah boys loitered.

Only to get through the remaining weeks until the British departed! Better already to deal alone with the Arabs.

☙ ☙ ☙

Ambassadorial posts were being whispered about, as though the Jerusalem road were not under siege, as though Kaukji and his "Liberation Army" had not been allowed by the British simply to move in from Syria and take up positions above Mishmar Ha'Emek, even bringing artillery, making ready for the kill.

Then came Mati's summons from B-G. Since the explosion the Old Man worked more and more at his flat. It was only a few blocks away. The Haganah man in the stair hall had been given Mati's name, but still with a "You know how things are, chaver," he checked the identity card.

The door was opened by Paula herself. "So you also want to be an ambassador!" she greeted Mati, and went off to fetch tea.

The mission was in Chicago. In Chicago he had connections, no? Those friends of his who had bought the first airplane. B-G forgot nothing. Golda on her trip had collected a fortune, fifty million, but it wasn't enough. Nothing was enough. Some special money was needed; there was a special chance to buy some fighter planes. Teddy was in New York; Mati should contact him there at the Hotel Fourteen for detailed instructions.

Then they drank tea and talked about the family, each one's doings. B-G spoke of Menahem, that mamzer, his own age and what Menahem had gone through, no one else could have! And survived! Finally, Paula admonished Mati, "To Chicago, take along your Amerikankeh, take your Denatchka, they will give her their last shoelace!"

Dena couldn't help the first leap of glee. Just to be out where there were no tanks patrolling the streets, no barricades! No sudden blasts and could it have been the boys' school?

But how would they put it to the twins?

"Abba has to go on a special mission to Chicago, and—"

Already the narrowed eyes from Jonathan.

"It's only for two weeks, they want me to go, too, so we could all go—"

"You? What for?"

"You know what for." She laughed. "Money, money, money!"

"So we can wait here." From David it was already final.

"But in two weeks we'll all be back! We'll fly over the ocean. You'll see the family."

"If the family wants to see us, they can come here."

"Ima, you go with Abba," Jonathan said. "Take Tanya. We can take care of ourselves."

Leave them? Here? Even suppose she got them to go down to Tel Aviv to stay with Leah—

No, they were staying in Jerusalem. They had school. And other things to do.

Dena decided she had to stay. "Don't worry, if I don't show up with you, they'll pitch in even more. Big heroine."

How could he go off and leave them in Jerusalem, ringed around, almost cut off? Yet Dena would never let him back out. Peewee assured him there was going to be no more nonsense in Jerusalem, absolutely, the gang that had pulled off the three terror jobs had been identified by the CID—Army deserters working with the Arabs. No more of that, Mati could be sure.

"Don't worry. Just two weeks. We'll be fine," Dena kept insisting. Besides, the boys knew his trip was an order from B-G himself.

35

HE HAD forgotten the endless flat snow.

In Eretz you counted every new house that was built; here, along the lakefront, stood block after block of skyscrapers, all new, and Phil kept pointing and saying which Jewish real estate operator had just built this one and owned that one. Phil was roping those fellows in, they'd give. Everybody from the old West Side, Sherrill said, had either Lake Shore Drive apartments or homes on the North Shore. As they drove through Evanston, and all the way to Winnetka, she kept remarking: see that hundred-and-fifty-thousand-dollar home; it belonged to Mort Abramson, he had built up their family millinery chain, and was he loaded! Phil knew him from way back and had made a Zionist out of him! Now, just along this stretch, Yehudim were not yet exactly welcome, but a lakefront estate worth a half a million had recently been bought by the owner of *Paradise* magazine, another West Sider; though he himself wasn't much of a giver, he had a decent brother who was the business manager and was good on Mati's trip for ten grand. Most of her own old girlfriends, Sherrill said, were out along the shore now; their husbands had done very well in hotels, in the market, in car agencies, in law.

Sherrill's voice had become emphatic, and she kept directing Phil, "Take the parkway, you can avoid four stoplights, turn here, it's quicker"; Phil had a large bald spot that got sweaty; he kept telling Mati everything was all set up, not to worry. Luckily, they were ahead of the UJA campaign, which was out for two hundred and fifty million this year, imagine that! Who would ever have dreamed of going for so much money, there had been a big fight at the convention, but he was for it, shoot high! Believe you him, the dough was there, he was chairman of the North Shore region, and the quota could be reached; you had to use the right technique. Now, for tomorrow he had set up a small luncheon at the Drake, selected men—Phil chuckled—some of them from the same gang that had put up the money for that first little plane, the *Gidon*— and now, a whole air force! Naturally he had told them it was all absolutely hush-hush.

Their new house was very pure functional style, Sherrill said, as they turned into the private lane. They had a picture window right on the lake, and their own little pier with a boathouse. In winter there was ice; the kids were great skaters; look, they were out there right now!

Dena's mother and father stood in the doorway; they had flown up from Miami Beach, hoping to the last minute that Dena and the kids would also come. Of course, they understood, they were proud—Sam Kossoff had tears in his eyes—but you couldn't blame them for worrying a little bit, could you?

Phil's gathering was in a private dining room, about thirty men, a few of whom Mati recalled from that corned-beef-sandwich lunch when Leah had raised money for the Haganah.

Phil got up and said they all knew why they were here. He knew they gave and gave. They had given to the JDC and the UJA, and given plenty recently when Golda Meyerson was in Chicago. They weren't here to listen to him, but to their special guest, so he would make it snappy and tell just one little story. It was about the strong-man act, the guy who snapped an iron bar with his bare hands. Then he held up a lemon and squeezed it bone-dry between his fingers and offered a thousand dollars to anyone in the audience who could get another drop out of it. Several tried and failed. Finally, a skinny little man came up, took the dry lemon in his hand and drop drop, drop—he did it! The strong man paid off in astonishment and asked, "What's the secret? Who are you?" "Well, I'll tell you," said the skinny little gent, "I'm a fund collector for the UJA."

They laughed indulgently; Mati guessed he must be the only one who had not heard the story before.

The way Phil now introduced Mati he was, of course, the very first Jewish flier! "In those days when Lindy was still a mensh, we used to call Mati the Jewish Lindy, remember?" Got his wings right here at the old Midway Airport. And now a founder and secret chief of the soon-to-be Jewish Air Force!

Mati demurred, but they only believed it all the more. Then quietly, confidentially, Mati told them about the situation. When the British cleared out in just a few months from now, invasions from all the surrounding Arab states had to be expected. Fighter planes must be acquired at once.

Before the meeting Phil had already lined up starter pledges, up to forty thousand dollars, including his own ten, and now he checked each fellow by name. "Sy, five, how about adding one for each of your kids? Up three?" The white-haired men's shop owner —but it was the very one at whose store Mati had got the tux for his wedding!—responded, "How about grandchildren?" With a grin he upped his pledge with five thousand special for his grandson's Bar Mitzvah. "A plant," Phil whispered to Mati, while noting down the sum. He worked them over one by one; from added thousands Phil got down to five hundreds, hundreds. The last drop appeared to have been squeezed, but then a wholesale drug dealer (another plant) asked, "Can the girls pitch in on this?" His wife, Bertie: "I didn't exactly tell her what it was for, but she knows it's not for rozhinkes and mandelen, so you can count her in for three hundred."

Mati was asked some more questions about what did he think the Arabs would do. And were all the English pro-Arab, as it looked, or were some of them okay? He told them there still were some decent ones and used the tale of the sergeant at a munitions dump who had dropped off three freight-car loads of ammo and grenade boxes from a train passing a certain kibbutz. Of course, a little Yemenite sweetheart had helped persuade him.

These stories brought in another seven thousand, and Phil announced the total, coming to eighty-two thousand six hundred dollars. Then suddenly he cried, "Come on, fellows! Let's make it a hundred grand!" leading off with another five of his own. Now, he said, he would tell them something private that Mati had held back. They all knew Mati's wife—his sister, Dena. Dena and the kids were supposed to have come on this trip, but the two boys had absolutely refused to leave Jerusalem, and so Dena— His voice choked. Mati had to look down at his plate. A fever spread.

They made the hundred thousand dollars, in five minutes, while the waiters were clearing the table.

Rabbi Mike and Sue still lived in the same apartment; she had white wing tips to her hair but held herself straight as ever. Though the neighborhood was in transition, their street was fairly safe, Sue said, as the university and various institutions had bought up many of the old German Jewish family mansions so as to keep them from turning into Negro rooming houses. In fact, the Steiner and Straus houses—did he remember, from that tragic crime, the Nietzschean thrill killers?—well, both homes were now owned by educational foundations, and she believed a religious cult of some kind—"African Islam," Mike put in, "with a very curious leader"—yes, this cult had taken over the mansion of the family of the murdered boy.

Mike was stouter than on his visit to Palestine at the end of the war. He had already made the necessary calls, he told Mati; incidentally he was sure the Yishuv wouldn't refuse some non-Jewish funds; a couple of the big unions were making sizable contributions. Rabbi Mike had, it seemed, become the big wheel in labor arbitration in Chicago.

As for the temple, there had been a crisis, recently, for with so many of the mainstay members already moved out to the North Shore, the congregation had been obliged to build a branch, a magnificent temple in Highland Park, and Mike had had to decide whether to transfer there or stay on here. If he moved, he feared the home temple would probably "go out of business" within a few years, and so, not only to save the traditional edifice, but as part of the campaign to save the neighborhood, he had decided to stay. Fortunately things were working out. Quite a few university Jews who had never been affiliated had joined. With the Holocaust, yes, Jews had come back. Even more interesting, yes, cheering in its way, was the sudden upsurge in attendance since the UN vote on Palestine! Did Mati really think the Arab nations would attack? Couldn't there still be some agreement? Good old Mike! The decent, liberal mediator. True, testifying before the latest committee, the one from the UN, Professor Magnes and Martin Buber had again made their plea for a binational state. Mike knew: not a single Arab response, alas. And how was Magnes?

"Quite ill, but holding on," Mati said, "in the hope of seeing the birth of the Jewish nation."

"Bination," Sue remarked.

"Bi with whom?" Mati said. "Whom could you sit and talk to?" The Mufti was again manipulating things, from Beirut. The British had allowed Jamal Husseini back into Palestine; their opponents were again being bumped off—

Hadn't Mussa Alami set up some kind of opposition to the Mufti party? With his own offices in London and in Washington? Mike said.

Ah, Mussa Alami. The Arabs thought of him the way the Jews thought of Magnes.

Where was the Arab proletariat?

Mati wondered at Mike. Did he really believe all these wishful things in the liberal press? Hadn't he read how Arab workers running amok in the Haifa refinery, only a few weeks ago, had slaughtered a score of Jews working alongside them?

Rabbi Mike sighed. Then it would be war for certain? What chance did the Jews have? What did the old British hands really think?

"Privately most of them think, if it was only the Arabs of Palestine, we could take over the whole country in a few weeks."

"With twice as many Arabs as Jews?" Sue asked.

Mati shrugged. The Palestine Arabs themselves had no real training and possessed even fewer arms than the Jews. Besides, except for taking part in some raids, it was never they who had risen and fought. Indeed, now as in the troubles of the late thirties, the so-called Arab revolt, it was Kaukji with his mercenaries from outside who formed their army. The only really trained disciplined force was, of course, King Abdullah's British-equipped Arab Legion in Trans-Jordan. They were pretty sure to cross into Palestine on May fifteenth. The Legion's British officers would stay on. It was not too large a force but had tanks and artillery. The Syrians also had tanks, and there were without doubt Nazi officers in their army. And Egypt, of course, had a bit of an air force, probably with German pilots. They would bomb Tel Aviv for certain. Against this, fighter planes were needed immediately.

And pilots? Hadn't a number of boys from the Yishuv flown in the RAF during the war?

They'd been kept as ground crews, Mati said. Like his nephew —left to be captured when the Nazis took Crete. Not one Palestinian Jew had flown in combat so far as he knew. In fact, in all their service branches the British had been careful not to give the Jews too much experience. Except for a few commando units where they were really needed, when Rommel nearly broke through. Still, the boys had managed to learn.

There was Chaim Weizmann's own son, whose plane went down in the English Channel, Sue said.

Yes, what a tragedy, Mike said.

Getting pilots would be no problem, Mati told them. Even some RAF pilots might stay on if there were enough of a supply of Yemenite girls! And not only Yemenites! His own niece had married an RAF captain, and the fellow intended to stay. Besides, already there had come inquiries from several Jewish pilots who had fought in the U.S. air force, also pilots from South Africa, from France—all sorts. Not only Jews. The main problem was rushing planes, tanks, guns into the land the minute the British cleared out.

And if in the meantime the Arabs broke through?

You had only to listen to the Arab radio, Mati said, screaming murder and jihad all day. Screaming, finish the job for the Nazis!

They were silent.

Mike pondered. Should anything happen to the Yishuv, it would be the end of Jewishness altogether, he feared. The real seedbed of Jewish life in Poland was gone. Russian Jewry had been spiritually, if not physically, annihilated. What would be left but the American Jewish community, and could American Jewishness withstand such a blow? After the Holocaust, Jewish feelings here in America had been revived only by the Yishuv. As though the hand of God still could be seen, as though one could still sense some mysterious plan, some equivalence, no matter how ghastly had been the man-made destruction in Europe. But if another holocaust were to happen, and in the Holy Land itself, what could any Jew believe thereafter?

He didn't deceive himself, Mike said—the expensive new suburban synagogues were hardly signs of a religious revival; they were community centers. In the colleges, intermarriage and acculturation were ever on the rise. Should anything happen to the Yishuv it would also mean the end of Jewish identity here in America; there would be no inner strength to sustain such a blow.

Well, Mati said—and he looked at Mike not anymore with the

606

diffidence of a young, unformed lad, but straight—the Yishuv would not go down. But as for all Mike had said, if that was the way these American Jews were, he honestly didn't give a damn for them.

Dena's brother Vic took the position that conversely to what professional Jews like Rabbi Mike Kramer imagined, a surviving and flourishing Jewish state in Palestine would eventually mean the end of Jewish identity here in America. And in the rest of the Diaspora as well. The proposition was exactly as Arthur Koestler put it: If you wanted to be a Jew, you should go and live in the Jewish state. Otherwise, you should assimilate in whatever land you inhabited. European Jews, after Napoleon opened their ghettos, had largely been held back from full assimilation, Victor said, because—if only subconsciously—the Jew still bore the burden of continuity. Each Jew, even if not religious, still in some remote part of himself felt that if he relinquished his identity, the whole process all the way back to Abraham would be cut off. But with the reestablishment of a Jewish state this responsibility would psychologically be lifted from the Diaspora Jew. You want to be a Yehudi? Go to the Jewish land.

Being a Jew was anyway a full-time psychosis, Victor said breezily, refilling Mati's highball. Mati knew he shouldn't—his ulcerous condition was giving signs of returning. But all these discussions put him on edge. According to Mike, if the Yishuv failed, that would be the end of Jewry everywhere. And according to Vic, if the Yishuv succeeded, it would be the end. Oy v'avoy! At least at home you knew where you stood.

Sure the Jews had a right to nationhood, Vic continued. Besides, for the refugees it was the only practical solution. He had seen them—oh, hadn't he seen them when he was stationed south of Munich, and how much black marketeering and general swindling could you condone even though you knew they had barely escaped the gas ovens? Okay, so Vic had shut his eyes to the whole transport operation with their stolen U.S. army trucks and their fake UNRRA personnel. Mati knew, of course, of that crazy incident with his brother-in-law, the one who had come through the death camps—Menahem, yes. So, Vic had figured, let them get those people down to their illegal ships in Italy. Let them pass. He had done his bit. As for today's Arab threats, Vic believed that the United Nations should be made strong enough to enforce its partition decision. Incidentally, that would be a great step toward a real international authority.

"Hear, hear," said his wife. Muriel was a tall sandy-haired girl with a no-nonsense face, but humorous. Fine legs—a semichampion tennis player. For an instant the thought of Maureen and her tennis came to Mati. Reggie. Muriel was in charge of grants for Negro students, at the Rosenwald Foundation. People—including Jews—had a need for a longer, historic sense of belonging, of tradition, she said. The newer sociologists—like Glazer—were in disagreement with the melting-pot formulation and stressed the persistence of the ethnic strain. Especially in a city like Chicago with its multiple ghettos, Italian, Polish, Negro. One saw this in the way Negroes were now in search of their African roots; look at the dancer Katherine Dunham who had got a Rosenwald grant and rediscovered a whole, truly classic Negro dance form. Still— with a wry glance at Vic—it was simpler to belong to the dominant culture! If only everyone could be a Wasp!

Wasp? Mati didn't get it.

That was the latest. Vic laughed. An acronym for White Anglo-Saxon Protestants.

Maybe once Jews got their own nation, they wouldn't be so divided among themselves, Muriel said. Look at your Rosenwalds; one brother was a big-wheel nationalist Zionist and the other was dead against it, pouring a fortune into his Council for Judaism to prove Jews were simply a religion and nothing else.

Sure, Mati reminded her, the only Jew in the British Cabinet had been the strongest opponent of the Balfour Declaration.

Muriel's parents dropped in; her father, Dean McDermott, with his pipeline to Washington said the State Department boys were still desperately trying to upset Truman's backing for Jewish nationhood. Heartily, McDermott reminded Mati of the parallel between Jewish and Irish struggles—even the revival of Gaelic, as with Hebrew—though he took his hat off to the Jews who had made theirs work! Oh, McDermott cried, he was a better Zionist than his Jewish son-in-law, Vic, here!

Indeed, Victor parried, and what did Irish independence add up to for the American Irish? An annual St. Patrick's Day Parade! And he could foresee the same thing for American Jews—an annual parade down Michigan Avenue, with a band playing "Hatikvah"!

And Jewish drum majorettes showing their legs. McDermott grinned.

"Is that so bad?" Muriel said, and they all laughed.

Since on Saturday night so many suburbanites went into town, especially now at the height of the theater and opera season, Sherrill had her big affair for Mati on Sunday, a buffet supper. All week she was on the phone nonstop, maneuvering who should call whom so as to be sure they would come, checking up especially on certain people who had always shied off from Jewish affairs. There was Alvin Fox, the multimillionaire furniture manufacturer who lived in Glencoe, married to a shikseh, his third, they were real snobbish radicals, always giving parties for people like Paul Robeson, but Sherrill had got wind that Alvin still carried a torch for the beautiful Sylvia Abramson of that old bunch from the West Side around Douglas Boulevard, all the boys of the bunch had been in love with her, there is always one like that, and though she was married to Mitch Wilner, the renowned brain surgeon, Alvin told all his wives that he was still in love. Sylvia was in Hadassah and still queenly, so Sherrill got her to call Alvin, and that did it, he would come. Though he knew, he bantered, that it would cost!

Even the token Jewish member of the restricted Lakeside Country Club got roped in; his wife was a Vassar classmate of Vic's wife, Muriel. And there were a few yentehs whom Sherrill hated, real pushers, but for this affair she deared and darlinged them—their husbands were loaded.

Caddies, Chryslers, even a Rolls—no car less than a Lincoln—filled the driveway and both sides of the block. Half the diamonds Phil had sold since the war glittered in the enormous beamed living room. At least a thousand bucks must have gone into the hairdos alone for this evening, Sherrill whispered to Mati. "We could use it," he said.

On her own, Sherrill had passed hints that Mati was slated for an ambassadorship in the coming Jewish state, and Gertie Bloom, a noted nitwit, even gushed at him, "Your Excellency." Everybody was exclaiming what a pity Dena and the kids hadn't come, but the story of how the twins wouldn't leave Jerusalem had got around and created awe. Gertie recalled how Dena could have married into one of the top South Side German Jewish families and had chosen instead to go to live the pioneer life of a chalutzah over there. Who could have known she was marrying an ambassador-to-be and maybe even a future prime minister. And though he had gotten a bit stout—who hadn't—Mati was still quite a hunk of man. She remembered him from the university, a real Valentino. Remember Rudy Valentino? Ouch! Did that make you feel old.

With the men, Mati, milk glass in hand, was again answering the same questions as he had all week, trying to make his words sound like inside information. From all the drinking you had to do even with Jews nowadays his ulcer had again kicked up. The famous brain surgeon, Mitch Wilner, had started with ulcers and said Mati had better come around to Michael Reese Hospital, but Máti joked that he'd get a double ulcer if he stayed one extra day. Meanwhile, the brain specialist's wife, Sylvia, a queenly woman with fine bare shoulders—she reminded Mati of Esther Rubin, the painter's wife, at home—interrupted, asking him with a gracious smile to settle an argument she was having with her old friend here, Alvin Fox. Alvin claimed that there was a numerus clausus for Arab students at the Hebrew University in Jerusalem, and she felt sure this could not be.

This was a new one, Mati said. Where on earth had he heard it?

"From a certain famous playwright," said Alvin Fox with a knowing glint, "in New York at a party for the Russian ballet."

"Well, that must be the new party line!" This came from a darty-eyed fellow, a lawyer noted for his courtroom wit, Lou Margolis.

Mati explained that the president of the Hebrew University, Dr. Judah Magnes, was himself the leader of the B'rith Shalom, standing for the closest cooperation with the Arabs. Also, the university had a special department of Arab studies.

But if the Arabs were two-thirds of the population, Alvin Fox persisted, how was it there were less than five percent of them at Dr. Magnes' university?

A group had formed. The trouble, Mati explained, was that the ordinary Arab was too poor to send his kids even to high school; thus, very few could qualify for the university. The rich effendis sent their sons to study abroad. These rumors about a numerus clausus were obviously part of the deliberate slander campaign from certain quarters.

The queenly one patted her friend on his arm. "Ah, Alvin," she twitted him, "I'll bet some communist Mata Hari planted it on you. The least you can do now is endow a scholarship at the Jerusalem University for Arab students!"

Maybe he would, just to keep down Jewish chauvinism, her old admirer said, patting her hand.

Phil took Mati aside with that quick-eyed lawyer. Lou Margolis, he had already mentioned, had built up his father-in-law's junkyard into a top scrap-iron outfit, making millions in war stuff. He was already in touch with Teddy in New York, said Lou Margolis as though using a password. Mati might mention to Teddy—Lou had a tipoff on a huge new disposal of air force matériel. Lou was getting an advance list—he had ways. There were even transport planes, B-17s! If Mati would drop in at his office, he had the details.

For the buffet, Sherrill had debated with Phil—there was an excellent Jewish-style caterer in Wilmette with all the old West Side delights, his raisin kugel was out of this world. And so were his prices, Phil said, but this was no time to be stingy. Or Sherrill had thought perhaps to have shashlik, served on flaming swords the way they did it at the Ambassador East in the Pump Room? Maybe too Arabian? Finally, both agreed that for a top crowd, since all of that kosher-style Jewish stuff was already kind of provincial, they should try something distinguished, and Sherrill had contacted a Michigan Avenue French caterer.

It was worth it. Sylvia Wilner congratulated Sherrill on her taste, and Grace Perlmutter, the ballet-dancer wife of the brilliant young rabbi of their new four-million-dollar temple designed by that famous Japanese architect from Detroit, told Sherrill a special thanks, the rabbi had had two Bar Mitzvahs and a wedding last week, and one more serving of Grossman's kugel would have made him quit the pulpit.

Nor were they going to have any fund-raising speeches with pledge calling; Phil had discreetly left pledge cards in the entrance hall. And instead of any speeches, Phil tapped on a glass announcing for people to make themselves comfortable, and Mati stood in front of the fireplace simply to answer questions.

And so he answered them. It was strange, this collection of American-born Jews, how little and how much some of them knew and also how lopsided was the knowledge of some who knew. At first the questions were the Hadassah kind, so he could answer with what wonders the Jews had done. And here among themselves he could mention a certain point, a material factor you didn't talk about outside, but while the Jews had built the land, built cities, a university, industries, in the same forty years what had the others built? No, he didn't hate the Arabs. Hardly any Jew raised in Palestine hated the Arabs. And the ordinary Arabs, the fellaheen, didn't hate the Jews. Or look at the merchants in the Old City of Jerusalem; for generations Arab and Jew had lived side by side. With twice as many Arabs as Jews—even Kaukji's army were hirelings from outside. So where were the Arabs who hated Jews? Why did the Jews have to prepare now against invading armies from Egypt and Syria and all the rest? What did those outsiders want? They wanted what the Jews had built. Quite simply, they wanted to loot the land; that was what no one talked about.

Mati tried now to give them the feeling of a person like his friend Khalid, half of whose clan had been wiped out by the Mufti's clan, only for wanting peace. True, some of the Arab propagandists declared the Jews were a foreign body from the Western world that could never be absorbed by the Arab world. But perhaps what they really feared was the reverse. That their own Arab population would increasingly become Westernized. What the feudalists really feared was an awakening of their own people, their serfs. Would you ever see, among them, their women, their wives, even at a gathering like this? And he told them of Khalid's wife, trying to get the village Arabs to send their daughters to school. Yes, what the backward Arab leaders feared was the invasion of a modern way of life, of democracy, but Jews or no Jews, it would come. The strange contradiction was that the Western world would come to them quite simply, by such things as movies, American movies brought right into their villages, by automobiles, by the radio. With or without a small Jewish state on the Mediterranean, the Arab world would change. It would sooner or later be Westernized, and if only this interim period could be bridged over, then their fear of Jewish modernism, and with it their hostility, would recede. He saw, eventually, peace and cooperation. If the outside Arab nations would stay out or could be kept out, he hoped a sensible Palestine Arab leadership would emerge and create their own Arab state alongside the Jews, as voted by the nations of the world.

Now he came to the other side of the story—about the Jews. What about American Jews, what could Palestine mean to them? Well, take a group of chalutzim that had come from right here on Chicago's old West Side. And he told of Kibbutz Brandeis, of David and Malka, and how Dave had got hurt in an ambush, and how their kibbutz right now, any day, might be attacked by Kaukji's mercenaries. Yet in these ten years none of them had given up and returned to America, had they? And one day his listeners themselves, from right here, might be sending their children to summer camp at Kibbutz Brandeis!

But more seriously, Palestine was not only for refugees, but for all Jews to make connections with their past and to feel themselves —well—legitimate, a legitimate people. Yes, he firmly believed this was psychologically healthy, even necessary in this world, for any born Jew, even American-born.

Mati had worked for many years with the British, the lawyer, Lou Margolis said; why did the British turn against the Jews?

He could answer this with one word, Mati said, and saw on their faces that knowing look—they believed he'd say anti-Semitism. It was the crucial word, he told them, it was the one that Harold Laski, his brilliant professor at the London School of Economics, had used. Oil.

They got onto questions about European Jews, and why hadn't they fought, why had they gone to the gas chambers as sheep to the slaughter? And he told them about Menahem, what Menahem himself had seen in the locked boxcar on the way to Auschwitz, the Hungarian Jews even in the third year of the gas chambers unable to grasp the reality of mass extermination. After all, here in America those same years it had been known and nothing had been done. And even now were they aware that in Auschwitz there had been a revolt? And these supposed sheep of the slave camps— all their survivors asked for now was for arms to fight in the homeland. Yes, he could tell them, the refugees were ready, trained as best you could be trained in a DP camp using wooden staves for rifles.

Nor, he had to say, was Albion always perfidious. As some of them knew, he had spent fourteen years in the British administration. Of course, with certain contacts on the side. They laughed. Nevertheless, many of the British had been admirable; the High Commissioner under whom much of his service had taken place, two commissioners back, had been a fair, warmhearted man, responsible in great measure for letting in more than a hundred thousand refugees in the thirties. And also for the great improvement in Arab life, schools and sanitation and roads. Wauchope had stayed through two tours of duty. It was after his time that the gates were shut, even just as Europe's Jews were being exterminated. Alas, politics came above principle, the British Labour Party had always declared itself Zionist, indeed the Labour Party had gone further than official Zionism, and had suggested shifting Arabs from Palestine to underpopulated Arab lands, and yet when Labour came to power, the murderous White Paper, closing off Jewish immigration, was theirs. Forces of history had their own way with men, against the best of intentions.

The guests all had the knotted brows of hard listening, of serious attention to things not usually discussed in this way. Even if he might raise more money by not raising any doubts, Mati let himself go on. The United Nations plan divided the Promised Land once again. The Jews had accepted it for the sake of nationhood at last. But would the United Nations enforce its own decision? No. The Jews had to fight for what the UN assigned to them. To fight for what they had built and what the whole world agreed should be theirs. Let any Jew ask himself one question—what would he have given to have put arms into the hands of the Jews in the death camps?

They gasped. He even heard a kind of sob.

They were really good people, decent, wanting to be good Jews in spite of all else they wanted to be. This sense of unitedness became almost overwhelming, and he told them of a word that Menahem had brought back, encountered in odd spots in Europe, when some wandering, uncertain derelict would hopefully venture to a perhaps Jewish-looking stranger, "Amcha?" Our people? What was there in a Jew's life anyway, Mati asked them plainly. He had lived here in Chicago, his wife was one of them, yes, nowhere had Jews ever had it so good as in America, yet he was sure that when the Jewish state was established, they themselves would feel their lives had more meaning, the two great remaining Jewish communities would be ever closer, would grow together as one. Of course, there were Jews who lived a total and successful life without being Jews. Fine! Let them go. There were Jews who raised up a scarecrow of dual loyalty. This had happened to other people here in America. What of the German Americans in both World

Wars? He only hoped a democratic Jewish state and democratic America would always be on the same side. The strange and mysterious thing was that ever since the United Nations resolution all sorts of Jews, totally assimilated, who had changed their names from Cohen to Coleman, from Levin to Lee—he hoped he wasn't offending anyone; he knew you couldn't become a movie star with a name like Chaimovitch—all sorts of Jews were getting in touch, asking what they could do. Young people were arriving, every way they could get to Palestine, volunteering. . . . People asked, what kind of state would it be? Well, the state had already been going on just as the Arab war had already been going on for some time. There was an elected Jewish assembly and there were all kinds of political parties, and from this would come a government. And the same leaders would probably be the heads of the government. It would be a state, he believed, partly in the nature of Sweden, Denmark, a socialist-style democracy but not a communist state since many of the leaders had fled the Soviet style of communism. But capitalism, too—he replied to Alvin Fox, who wanted to know where the state would stand in the looming world division between capitalism and communism—capitalism had its place, even a growing place, to the regret of some, in the Yishuv. You always heard about the communal kibbutzim, and Mati admitted his heart was there; he had a brother who was in the first kibbutz from way back before the First World War. But right alongside that kibbutz, another of his brothers operated their own family farm, in a simple old-style village—a moshav, each for himself. He also had a brother-in-law who was among the biggest self-made capitalists in Palestine, the founder of the growing city of Sharon Shore and of the diamond industry. So it would be a state with a mixed economy, perhaps a model for the world of workable diversity! A country, also, of mixed population from all over the world, even though all were Jewish. A country with a pioneering area, the Negev, just as America had its West. A country with the greatest past of all the nations and, he trusted, a great future in which it could fulfill the prophecy: a light to the nations!

Well, he had ended up making a speech after all!

When the last Cadillac had departed, Sherrill and Phil, before going to bed, sat with Mati, adding up the haul. Of course, hints had been spread in advance; considering the exclusive guest list, nobody should dare give less than a thousand dollars.

And it was working. The checks, the pledges, hardly a single one below a grand. At one point as Phil called out a name, Sherrill couldn't remember where she had put the check—Sylvia Wilner had given it to her discreetly in the powder room—and this reminded Phil of that old wedding night joke about the check the bride left in her glove! They had a big laugh; oh, if only Dena were here!

Then they came to Alvin Fox's donation. Three hundred. "The piker! He keeps a yacht in Palm Beach! I'll pass the word, nobody's going to invite them, even for bridge. Don't worry, his wife will get the message," said Sherrill.

Suddenly Phil yelled, "We made it!" Altogether, in all of Mati's appearances, he had pulled in three hundred thousand dollars on his mission!

The night before leaving, after a session with a tough old Yiddishist union leader who relented in his opposition to the coming state only because Sholom Aleichem was being performed in the original Yiddish by Joseph Buloff in Tel Aviv, Mati finally got to Myra's. Her uncle Sylvan was to drop in after the opera.

Her name was now Kohn; Dena had always to remember it was with a K. Hans, from Vienna, had got out just before the war; indeed, he had already been sent to Dachau when an American visa arrived. Myra had in those days signed dozens of guarantees; you didn't have to put up the money, just show you had the means. None of the rescued ever claimed support. But one day in 1942 a man with a Viennese accent had phoned; his name was Hans Kohn—a few years ago she had signed an affidavit for him; he was in Chicago and wished to thank her. Myra had signed for so many, she could not recall his name, but he assured her it had saved his life. He was an architect. So she had asked him to drop in. A charming man, quite a bit older and also a bit shorter than she; his wife, non-Jewish, had divorced him right after the Anschluss.

Today they lived in a town house facing Lincoln Park, in a semicircle of variegated residences designed by Hans. All metal and glass, of course, and as Mati entered he was confronted by a zigzagging bright-red iron stairway, an authentic old tenement fire escape, Myra said, that Hans had rescued from a slum clearance on Maxwell Street. The bare brick walls were hung with abstract paintings. Myra, her dress a flat green sheath, was a moving element of the decor. Her head still had that Queen Nefertiti poise, but as you got closer, you saw that the neck was somewhat stringy. Her voice was a bit hoarser, but still sexy like Ethel Waters. They had a great hug, and Mati felt those huge bosoms of hers that had always a bit upset him.

Her husband came down the red stairway—Hans's atelier was up there, Myra said. He was pudgy, with sparse white hairs combed across his cranium. But he had that European courtesy, and he talked without pause. Ah, Jerusalem, one day his great wish was to build something there, with that unique luminous Jerusalem stone. A structure that would fit into the fantastic barren hills. Of course he had seen photographs of what Erich Mendelsohn had done, first class, though perhaps from a bygone revolution. And Tel Aviv, a brand-new city and not a single new architectural idea! And the communes, the kibbutzes—that would be a great challenge, to design an entire community! The world's greatest architects should have been called upon. He was sure Mies would have welcomed the opportunity, and the great Chicago architect Frank Lloyd Wright.

"And of course, Hans Kohn," Myra said.

"Natürlich!"

Had Mati had a chance to see Hans' temple on the North Shore? Myra asked. Alas, only the one in Wilmette designed by a Japanese. That horror! As Mati knew, she was not chauvinistic, but a Japanese, designing a Jewish temple! Actually, Hans was becoming quite a specialist in the field; the most original architecture today was being done in the new suburbs with their churches and temples. Mati must look at a design Hans was doing for Dallas. What was important, Hans explained, almost dancing up the stairs as they climbed the fire-escape single file, what was inspiring to him was the fact that Texas was like the Sinai! Thus, the form should be like a Bedouin tent with an extended enclosed area, the ancient tabernacle with its courtyard! The Temple of King Solomon had followed this form, and so, inspired by this idea—

They entered his studio. In the center stood the model for his Dallas tabernacle, the roof having a concave ridge line—the Bedouin tent. The walls would be entirely in black marble, windowless of course—the sanctuary being completely air-conditioned —and even the effect of a rushing desert wind could be simulated, Hans explained, by the fans. Since most modern Jews attended services only on the High Holidays, the hall had to be of an expanding nature, usually managed by sliding partitions, which Hans abhorred. So he had, through machine technology, devised an unfolding fanlike roof, using push-button electric power!

Excitedly Myra told how Hans was commissioning artworks by some of the greatest contemporary painters and sculptors for his Dallas tabernacle. There, on his huge worktable, was a model welded in rusty iron shreds, The Burning Bush by David Smith himself! And stained-glass windows were being designed by Abraham Rattner, whom she had known in Paris. For his Wilmette temple, Hans had also tried to give a commission to Joe Freedman, Myra remarked, her voice suddenly a little cross; actually Joe wasn't doing too well, and Rabbi Mike had tried to help him, but Mati knew Joe—he simply would always spoil things for himself. Synagogue art was a great field now; the biggest people were doing things, even Marc Chagall; it was the greatest chance for nonrepresentational art, too, as this fitted right into the Jewish commandments forbidding images. But what had Joe brought in? No, really, Mati had to see it! And from a pile of drawings in the corner Myra fished out a sketch.

It was a sort of altar, Mati saw, square, at first glance perhaps made of crossed logs, but if you looked closer the elements were skeletal. Bones. Then he knew. He had seen a photograph. From the mass graves. "Of course, it's powerful," Myra said, still acridly, "but imagine this placed right up there in front of the congregation! So they could never take their eyes off it!"

The sacrifice. Beginning with Isaac.

Mati found himself visualizing this at home, on a hillock—in Beit Gidon?

Oh, yes, Joe Freedman was in Chicago, Myra said, while Hans went down to answer the doorbell. Joe was right back where he had started, in one of those storefront studios. Suddenly their eyes caught; there was a question in hers; Mati knew what she wanted, yet didn't want—to ask about Khalid. But they went down to greet her uncle. "Different wife," Myra had time to tell him on the stairway. "Dr. Gerda Wertheimer, she worked with Anna Freud."

Sylvan Straus, little changed, now had a white mustache and silvery hair. A velvet collar on his tux. The wife, however, was a real change from his former glamour types. Tall and spare like himself, she also looked about his age, with straight gray hair parted in the middle and drawn back into a bun. But the woman had a face of great warmth; you at once felt at ease.

"Well!" As they settled before the fire, Straus actually beamed at him. He inquired after Dena, the twins, the baby—a girl, wasn't it?—and about Mati's fantastic sister the Big Leah. Then he got right down to the nub of things, as though Mati were the trusted friend from whom he could at last learn the answers to some vexing questions.

Mainly, Jewish terrorism. Of course, all the leaders had denounced the Stern Gang's assassination of Lord Moyne, although if Moyne had really said, "What would I do with a million Jews?" maybe he had invoked the crime. But there were tales that the Haganah had actually cooperated with the Irgun on that ghastly senseless blowing up of the King David Hotel. Was that true?

"My best friend was killed in it," Mati said. "He was my liaison to the Haganah all the time I worked for the British administration. If the Haganah had any knowledge of the plan to blow up the King David, do you think he would have been inside when it happened?" Straus, looking directly into his eyes, nodded, a man who accepts an answer.

Yet Mati wondered—was he obliged, for truth, to tell the rest? That right after Black Sabbath the Irgun had indeed approached the Haganah with the projected retaliation, that the Haganah had finally agreed, then put it off, but that their liaison officer in Jerusalem had comprehended that the Irgun would proceed on their own and had failed to report this knowledge. And the whole rotten failure with the evacuation warning. No, this was too complex, Mati told himself. Was anything ever totally pure?

Just how powerful was the Irgun? Did Mati know that here in the United States people thought they were the main Zionist movement? Those full-page ads they kept putting in the papers, freedom fighters, medical aid, with scores of signatures from senators, governors, movie stars—the general public must believe that these statements really represented Zionism and the coming Jewish state. Or "Hebrew" as they usually said themselves. Also there had been one wild, bloodthirsty ad in particular that had shocked Straus profoundly. Did Mati know the one he meant?

Mati knew. The words had infuriated him. It was that ad with the line "Every time a British soldier falls, we make a little holiday in our hearts." Copies had been passed around among the British.

"How can we be responsible for what some crazy American writer puts in the paper in a paid ad?" Mati said.

The trouble was, these people left the impression that they represented the whole of Jewry, Sylvan said.

"Look, what can we do? Should we waste money in buying full-page ads to answer them?"

Soon the British would leave, and all these hatreds would subside.

"And your terrorists claim they are the ones who made the British decide to leave."

"Ask the British." Mati smiled. Wasn't it rather the world horror over the constant drama of the shiploads of survivors, the mass hunger strike that Yehuda Arazi had held on the *Fede*, the dragging of the survivors of the *Exodus* back to a concentration camp in Germany—it was this massive resistance that had decided the British to get out of Palestine, not the murder of Lord Moyne by the Sternists, or the hanging of the two British officers by the Irgun, or their blowing up of the King David or of the police headquarters in Haifa; no, not their ambush of the High Commissioner—luckily he had survived—no, the British didn't give in to that kind of violence.

What use was the whole struggle for a Jewish nation if the Jewish ethos was to embrace terrorism? And what would happen, Myra's uncle asked, if that kind of violence started, with the dissidents trying to seize the state as soon as it was established?

"We know them. They won't get far."

Sylvan mused. His wife gazed on Mati with her warm, understanding expression, as though to say she hoped he had convinced her husband.

There was another point that troubled Sylvan Straus, of an entirely different kind. Though the UN resolution made Jerusalem an international enclave and the Jews had accepted this, there were already tales that the Jews planned to demolish the Arab mosque and rebuild the Temple of Solomon.

Mati had always thought of Myra's uncle as sophisticated and all-knowing; how could such a man fall for this old bogey tale that the Mufti had already used in 1929?

"Can you seriously believe such a story?" he asked.

"Maybe Sylvan listens to it," his wife said in her German accent, "because every Jew, even the most irreligious, I suppose in his subconscious depths wishes this to happen. It is like an urge to completion, the closing of a circle; it would be like completing a cycle of history, wouldn't it?"

620

"But what would we want with the Temple of Solomon?" Mati said. "To have priests sacrifice bullocks and announce the new moon?"

Well, anyway, Myra jested, if the Jewish state ever really wanted to rebuild the Temple in Jerusalem, Hans was the man to design it!

Her uncle, remarking that he was already cooperating with donations to Sonneborn's group in New York, still made out a five-thousand-dollar check for Mati's special project. "Just see that none of it goes to the dissidents!"

"He contributes to them separately, from his other personality," his wife teased. "Sylvan never totally refuses."

As he was staying with Dena's parents, there was just time before Mati had to leave for his plane for him to walk over to the park and look in on Joe Freedman.

They gazed at each other, grinning. "I heard you were here, collecting shekels. I wondered if you'd come around, you bastard," Joe said. "All I can offer is my services."

"Well, maybe we can use you," Mati countered. "I hear you are now an expert welder."

Joe motioned to a few machinerylike structures. "You know me. Try everything." But seriously, if there was a damn thing he could be useful for, he'd come.

Okay, he'd remember, Mati said. He just had a little time before his plane and had wanted to say hello. His eyes were wandering. There was a life-size statue of that famous Chicago lawyer with his thumb under his suspenders, Clarence Darrow. And on a work platform, lying as though formed in the contours of the earth, a nude in clay, unfinished. Hefty, a kind of earth-mother.

Right back to Rodin. Joe smiled. He was through with all these welding tricks, he was going right back to honest clay.

Somehow the head of the figure seemed familiar to Mati, and Joe caught this. "Recognize her?" He was grinning. "Old friend of yours."

Andrea came from in back. She had been modeling and gone to put something on. Under the loose wrapper you could tell she was naked, and a flock of disoriented questions and recollections went through Mati, like way back in learning to fly, the whirling-chair test, trying to orient yourself when it stops. Were Joe and Andrea together again? As she came and hugged him, even kissed, Mati caught a scent he must have forgotten because in this moment he realized he never again in his life, even with Dena, had experienced it, a wondrous aroma that had risen from Andrea during lovemaking. So just now, had he interrupted? But neither she nor Joe had any embarrassment; she was just plain glad to see him and full of questions about his twins and his little girl and Dena. Her own little girl was four, Andrea said. When she took Peaches to the university's interracial kindergarten, she often stopped over to pose for Joe. Oh, she'd been married six years to Richard Lee, the Negro painter.

"He's damn good," Joe said and, grinning to Mati, went back to his kitchen to fetch some beers.

Sitting down on the edge of the modeling stand, Andrea drew Mati beside her; her eyes seemed a bit shadowy, but her mouth had the same large soft appeal. "We had a wonderful winter, didn't we?" she said.

The satisfied pleasure, the innocence he supposed of that first Chicago winter came back on him, the time they had done it out there in the park in the snow. There existed a whole other world like that, a world you could long for, of just doing what you wanted. Oh, this existed at home, too, a couple of times in these years he had had some fun, though very careful Dena should never know, a crazy affair with a nympho Englishwoman who had her own little place in Jericho, and another time with his old Herzl Gymnasia sweetheart, Zippie, who suddenly at a party declared to him that he had bothered her all her life and once and for all she wanted to get it over with. Just one time they had done it; it was really good. But today—with Dena in Jerusalem—Mati was glad he had to be off, even though it wouldn't be impossible to postpone for a later plane. Andrea was still gazing at him, and having the naked figure of her lying there was arousing. He said, "You're back with Joe?"

"Mmm, sort of," she said.

Joe came with the beers. Mati told him how he had seen a sketch at Myra's and wondered— Sure! Joe had the model right here. He brought it out and set it on a stand. Carved in dark wood, polished, the parts of it were like—Mati couldn't quite grasp what was conveyed. Elements of creation, in the beginning. And also in the end?

Andrea gazed for a long while with Mati. "You never showed this to me," she said to Joe.

"Well, I keep it kind of private." He had his peculiar, almost cynical downturn of a corner of his mouth, accented by the downturn of his mustache.

Joe told how at a place called Ohrdruf he had first sketched this from life.

"Or death," Andrea said. Then added, "I'm sorry." For making a cleverness of it.

"Well, this is something you could do for us," Mati said to Joe.

"Anytime. Just give me the site. I'll come."

As soon as things were quieter, Mati said.

Joe Freedman half shut his eyes. On a bare stone hilltop. Maybe in olivewood. Or if they could get someone to pay for the casting, in stainless steel. No. Carved in marble from Tel Hai.

Mati was thinking of the yard in Beit Gidon. Joe had even once promised a memorial. But why only for Gidon? Perhaps Joe was right, on a stony hill. Even Har Zion, overlooking Jerusalem.

❈ ❈ ❈

His suitcase and knapsack loaded with canned goods and hard salami, far overweight, Mati managed to get past the airport check-in, even clutching several last-minute parcels pushed into his hands by his cousin the high school teacher. Her eyes wet, she was certain he was going to his death.

He still planned to buy a bottle of champagne in the Paris airport to celebrate the coming birth of the state.

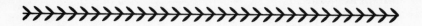

36

IT WAS a black day on which he arrived. From the first Jewish face, an inspector for the British still coming aboard to check papers, Mati saw that something ghastly had happened. A few words were enough. Thirty-eight boys, the best, the cream of the university Palmach unit, had set out on foot to relieve the desperately beleaguered Kfar Etzion settlement near Hebron; they had been caught on the way to Hebron, surrounded by hordes, slaughtered, mutilated; when finally the British came, one of the dead was even found with a stone in his hand.

Mati caught sight of Dena and the boys. They shouldn't have risked—was the road open then? With the hugging. It was cut off again, but here was Peewee; he had brought them in his tender! Did Mati know of the thirty-eight? He already knew. Were there any—? From Reuven's kibbutz, Max Wilner's youngest son, who had been about to get his master's in Semitics. And from their block, the grocer's son, Yitzhak, they'd known him since he was a kid.

David took his rucksack, sniffing eagerly at the contents; Jonathan lugged the bag. Keeping his voice down so that no British might hear, David asked, "Did you get the airplanes, Abba?"

"In his pocket, don't you see!" said Jonathan.

Mati had been away a total of less than three weeks, but as they threaded through Bab el Wad, even though in a British tender, every instant with the feeling they might be fired on from the rock heights or from behind the Keren Kayemeth's own planted trees, he recalled the easy open highways of the world he had just come from, and all at once he fully, clearly realized he was returned to war, returned to the front. For months this war before the war had been going on, and outside, no matter what you told them, no one fully understood.

Rehavia, Dena said, was still fairly safe though the sniping from Katamon continued. Right at the crossing of Ben Maimon Street a woman had been killed. A few steps from their grocery. Of course, there were Haganah boys on the Rehavia roofs who replied, and still more of the rich Arabs in Katamon had moved out and gone to Egypt. Dena was starting a new job: Eddie Marmor had asked her to be on duty a few hours a day monitoring British wireless. She left Tanya with Ziona.

To make his report, Mati had to go to Tel Aviv where Ben-Gurion now had his headquarters. The Piper took off from the Valley of the Cross, and the pilot turned out to be a youngster from Rehavia itself, whose name also was Mati—Mati Sukenik, the youngest son of the university's chief professor of archaeology. Learning who was his passenger, he at once deferentially offered the stick.

The youngster seemed bursting to divulge a big secret—a discovery of his father's. "When you get back to Jerusalem, be sure to ask Abba to show you the leathers."

"The what?"

"The leathers. It's really something!"

B-G had time only for a "Well-done!" Things were developing nastily above Mishmar Ha'emek. The British had closed their eyes while that loudmouth Kaukji pulled in heavy artillery, mortars, about a thousand of his bandit mercenaries, and positioned himself on the mountain directly over the kibbutz. The key to the Emek and Haifa.

The battle lasted all week. The first salvos from the heavy guns were direct hits, but the chaverim had dug a complete underground system of shelters connecting to their trenches. Within a few days hardly a wall was standing in the kibbutz; Kaukji even announced his victory to the world—the key to the Emek had fallen; the Jews had surrendered behind a white flag! But with the children evacuated, the chaverim still held tight.

In Jerusalem, Mati agonized at his desk; here in the final war what use was he? All his life he had imagined he would thunder above the enemy, he would pour down the wrath of the Almighty on them, he would battle them in the sky, and here all he could do was take his two-hour turn of guard duty in the evening in the streets of Rehavia. Over and over Dena had to reassure him—he could just as fatally have been killed in the explosion at the Agency a few months ago, sitting right at his desk. And who better than he could prepare the takeover when in only another few weeks the British departed? The enormous stores of construction and even war matériel that they couldn't evacuate, and for which he was quietly negotiating with old friends in the administration —even a whole batch of light planes, Austers, that needed only some repair work. The huge workshop compound at Athlit, worth millions, the entire base at Sarafend, it was just a question of a tip-off, of walking in first.

A few of the Austers were cannibalized to repair the others—he had got the whole fleet of eighteen for a song—and for the first time a combined air and ground attack was coordinated by the Haganah. A pair of the newly acquired "teakettles," fixed up in Afikim, each carrying a supply of pipe bombs made by the kibbutz plumber, flew over Kaukji's troop concentrations just as a unit from Brandeis, led by Dave Margolies, came through the woods onto his rear. Kaukji's rout was complete.

And for the first time since his return Mati laughed out loud when news came through that in London a Member of Parliament had risen to demand why British planes were being used by the Jews in a military attack!

That same night Mati found himself with a new partner on his rounds, Professor Sukenik himself. The old man had insisted on taking his turn; he was spry enough, from all his digs, though Mati had some difficulty keeping the professor from straying to the middle of the sidewalk instead of keeping close to the walls. Ah, Sukenik was a fatalist. For example, only some weeks ago his son Yigael, who, as Mati surely knew was conducting the war, the right hand of Ben-Gurion, day and night alongside him in the headquarters of Tel Aviv, had flown up here for an inspection of the Jerusalem defenses and popped into the house for a moment, and Sukenik had revealed to Yigael that for a certain most important reason he had to go to Bethlehem; Yigael as the Haganah commander had absolutely forbidden him, but then as himself an accomplished archaeologist, Yigael had given him a certain look. Could a scientist desist? So Sukenik had taken the Arab bus to Bethlehem—no harm had come to him, and— His eyes teased Mati to ask; he was obviously keeping down some great joy, and Mati recalled the hint of the young son, the pilot, about a stupendous secret. But what on earth could be worth the risk of a Jew's going alone to Bethlehem at a time like this? Mati asked. Pah! the Arabs all knew him, and as Mati surely was aware, to them the safety of a friend was sacred. And Sukenik was off onto a side story, an example. Hadn't Mati heard, earlier today, about Manya Shohat getting on the Arab bus to Sheikh Jarrah, even more dangerous than going to Bethlehem? Mati had indeed heard, but Sukenik was not to be denied and told the story again. Manya, the revolutionary firebrand of 1905, now a tiny old woman, had lived her life in Kfar Giladi. And here Mati himself had to interject how well he knew of her, in the early days she had gone under the name of Nadina, and it was on the day of her wedding in the old training farm of Sejera that his own sister Dvora's groom—for it was to have been a double wedding—was shot down in an ambush. And there in Sejera, too, at that same time Mati had been born! So early today, Sukenik resumed, Manya the revolutionistka, coming to Jerusalem from her northern border kibbutz, to go to the Hadassah Hospital on Mount Scopus, had simply got aboard an Arab bus. She had been seized by their militiamen and taken to their command post. There Manya was confronted by a German officer; he was ready to have Manya shot as a spy, but luckily an Arab commander on the spot heard her speak her name, knew of her friendship with Arabs, and ordered her escorted to safety. So you see? Sukenik beamed.

But still, what had made the archaeologist go in these times to Bethlehem? "Ah." Behind the thick glasses the eyes were merrily triumphant. After this turn of duty Mati must come in for a cup of tea, and he would behold the reason.

While Mati called Dena not to worry, the diminutive Mrs. Sukenik, again speaking of today's miracle that had saved Manya Shohat, brought tea, even sugar, and even a few slices of plum

627

pudding, explaining that a British officer, a passionate amateur archaeologist, had left them a parting gift, and Mati must eat some or she would be offended. Sukenik himself had meanwhile vanished, and hearing odd sounds in the garden, Mati made out the professor's silhouette—he was scraping at the soil with a mattock! Presently Sukenik knelt, lifted something—the shape of an urn—out of the ground, and hugging it to him came back into the house.

The urn had a curiously formed lid, like a stocking cap, which the archaeologist placed carefully on his desk. He lifted out a yellowed roll. The leathers.

Once more Mati vowed absolute secrecy; dramatically, his hands trembling, Sukenik unrolled an edge, and Mati saw clear Hebrew letters, though in an ancient script that he could not offhand read. He attempted the first line. Jeremiah?

"Exactly!" Overjoyed, as with a clever pupil, Sukenik whispered, "This is by seven, eight centuries the oldest Scripture ever found! This scroll was inscribed and in use while the Temple still stood! And it comes into our hands as we are about to be reborn!"

Something—a shudder of awe—passed through Mati. Never before had he so unanswerably felt himself in the presence of the miraculous. Coincidence, accident, yet why precisely now? He experienced an inner uneasiness—all his beliefs, or rather his non-beliefs, were in doubt. Could he all his life have been blind?

Sukenik was glowing. There were seven scrolls all told, he related; they had been brought to a Bethlehemite leather merchant who was a sometime dealer in antiquities. A Bedouin goatherd had found the rolled-up leathers in these jars when one of his flock had wandered into a cave near the Dead Sea, and he had gone after it. The location of the cave, Sukenik said, was still a secret, but he had got wind of the scrolls when the Bethlehemite had tried to sell four of them to a monk in the Old City. The monk had asked the professor to have a look to see if they were really old. At once he had seen they were very old. There were more, the monk believed, in Bethlehem. That was when Sukenik had taken the Arab bus. For from his first inspection he had believed he recognized the form of the script as similar to the writing on a celebrated papyrus fragment dating back to Biblical times.

In Bethlehem he had found three remaining scrolls, still in their jars, and had taken them home with him—this time not by the bus but in a taxi. He had gone to Judah Magnes, who was on his sickbed, but had nevertheless roused himself and authorized money from a special university fund for the purchase of the three scrolls. The other four, at the monastery, could also be bought, but the university had no more money. So his son Yigael, even now in the middle of the conflict had asked Ben-Gurion to provide the funds, and soon Sukenik hoped to have all the scrolls together! Meanwhile, he kept these three buried in the backyard for safety from the shelling. One by one he would open them to decipher their texts. The leathers hadn't yet been fully unraveled, it was a delicate task, and a certain chemical was lacking right now in besieged Jerusalem. However, this first one was indeed a Jeremiah, as Mati had at once recognized! But the two others had texts never before known! One seemed to contain the rules of a religious community, perhaps the Essenes. This could be an overwhelming discovery—a Jewish monastic sect before Christianity! Josephus had described the Essenes as having a community at the Dead Sea, but this would be proof in the greatest detail!

Sukenik paused. Then, as though having waited for one miracle to be absorbed before speaking of the other, he said that the second hitherto-unknown text, only the outer layer of which could be deciphered since it was too fragile to unroll, was a mysterious prophetic work called the War Between the Sons of Light and the Sons of Darkness.

𝕐 𝕐 𝕐

Then came another heartening day. Overlooking the narrow defile of Bab el Wad, at a steep turn often targeted for ambush, was the height of Kastel; in a costly assault the Haganah had captured the stronghold, which was topped by a few ruined houses. In a direct Arab counterassault their commander, Abdul Khader Husseini, a nephew of the Mufti and the most renowned of all their fighters, had fallen. A great blow to the Mufti's forces. The road to Tel Aviv could be cleared.

And from Haifa came word of an Arab exodus. The notables were evacuating, with their families, offering unheard-of sums for boatmen to take them to Beirut. The population of the lower city was in panic, the British area commander was doing his utmost to persuade them to remain, so was Abba Hushi, who had always been on the best terms with Haifa's Arabs, and the mayor and David HaCohen with him; but so far the flight was unstemmed.

Hastily, in Jerusalem, the Jewish Agency leaders debated—good or bad for the Jews? Harry Bailin was rushed to Haifa to try to halt the Arab stampede.

In the lull, with Kaukji chased from the heights, Mati and Dena decided to go to Nahalal for the wedding of the son of Rahel and Yitzhak Ben-Zvi. Not only that Ben-Zvi was president of the Jewish Council, but in the earliest days Rahel had been Leah's closest chaverah; she had been at Sejera at Mati's birth! At first Mati half suggested that only he should make the trip, but how could you keep Dena away from a wedding, especially this one? Besides, a whole convoy was going; it would start from the old wooden tsrif, the cabin here in Rehavia which Rahel and Ben-Zvi still kept as their home; it had once stood by itself housing Rahel's training farm for girls, just like Leah's place in Tel Aviv. Their older son, a member of the bus cooperative, would drive his festooned vehicle at the head of the convoy. The guests—and who in the leadership of the Yishuv wasn't a dear friend of Yitzhak and Rahel—all the *Mayflower* families would be coming! From the earliest days, when Ben-Zvi was known by his underground name of Avner, they had met every incoming ship bringing the first chalutzim from Odessa, including the vessel that had brought Leah and Reuven.

The girl was said to be the loveliest in Nahalal, a moshav noted for its beautiful daughters. Who would miss the chance to go to such a wedding?

From every settler's house in Nahalal, cakes, roast chickens, platters and bowls and pots of delicacies overflowed the home of the bride, the garden, and even the next-door garden of young Dayan, the one who had had an eye shot out in Syria at the start of the war. Then, before the guests arrived, there came evil news. Early that morning the groom, a chaver in Kibbutz Beit Keshet on the slope of Mount Tabor, had still gone out to the fields. In a sudden Arab raid Eli fell, together with three others.

In Dayan's yard next door stood the Haganah tender. He would take the bride and her parents. At a certain wadi, sometimes an ambush point, Moshe turned onto a byroad. The girl begged him to go the shorter way. "I don't want to get killed even if you do," Moshe said to her in that curt way of his, and she grew more calm.

At Beit Keshet all seemed motionless. The raid had come from the Arab village halfway up Mount Tabor. Relationships of old and even of late had been good.

Moshe knew the place. In the time of Wingate, already ten years ago, he said, it had harbored a killer gang, and he had taken part in a night attack that had driven them out, leaving nine dead. The village clan itself had not been involved. At least, so their elders swore. Yet? Were there again gangs in the place? Kaukji was said to be regrouping somewhere in the region. Could this be a belated revenge?

Alone in the armored bus with their eldest son came the Ben-Zvis. Restrained, gentle as ever, almost as though having known this must one day come to them as it had come to so many of their chaverim. But why on this day? This day?

Yitzhak Ben-Zvi knew the Arab village from far, far back, from his walks among the villages, when he was still able to devote a bit of time to his studies in ethnology. The elders of the clan were counted as old friends. He could not bring himself to believe it was from here. And yet.

Two other sets of parents had arrived, and Rahel and Yitzhak sat with them.

After the burial the bride at first kept her distance from the chaverah with the softly wrinkled face, Dvora from Gilboa, since the early days a friend of Rahel Ben-Zvi. Already the bride had heard whispered how, on this soft-faced Dvora's wedding day her groom, a young Shomer, had been shot down in the field. After-ward Dvora Chaimovitch had married another Shomer, now the legendary Menahem of the Mossad, the one who had even pene-trated the death camp of Auschwitz and lived. They had grown children and grandchildren. All this the bride knew. Yet how could it help to know that the same thing had happened forty years ago to this small, oldish woman, happened just up the road from Beit Keshet, at Sejera. Within a stone's throw. In the same way. Forty years ago.

The girl sat with her mother and Rahel. Rahel stroked her hair, and the bride wept. Yet later at some time she found herself sitting with the small, quiet Dvora, who held her hand, and said very little, and only stroked her hand, for a long time.

※ ※ ※

The days seemed days of delirium. In Jerusalem there came the slaughter at Deir Yassin, a cursed day to be followed almost at once by the cursed day of the slaughter of the Hadassah Hospital convoy.

Until the twins came running to the house with the tale of "Arab prisoners being paraded on trucks on King George Street," who even knew what had happened?

Only once—after the King David—had Dena seen Mati in such a black rage, with actual tears of anger. The Haganah command itself, it appeared, was again working with the Irgun and the Stern and had agreed for them to seize the village. Why? One of the quietest Arab towns in the surroundings. From Deir Yassin had come her vegetable man with his donkeys, even during the Mufti's strike.

Mati heard the whole miserable story from one of the Haganah unit that had had to be sent in at the end to halt the slaughter. For days there had been talk of seizing control of the approaches to Kastel. Clear out an entire Arab village. Show them! the Irgun had demanded. So a hundred men, youngsters, including Sternists, had approached at dawn, preceded by a loudspeaker truck that was to instruct the villagers to clear out. But the truck had overturned, the warning hardly heard, and then the Arab villagers —as might any Jewish settlement—had opened fire. The commander was hit. Others fell. The rest, many of them untried kids from the poorer Sephardi communities, had begun to spray Stengun volleys and hurl grenades into the windows; women and children, as well as the fighting men, were slaughtered. Hearing the Arabs screaming, "Death to the Jews!" the attackers ran amok, howling, "Kill Arabs! Kill all the Arabs!" So that when the Haganah at last cleaned the place, ghastly heaps of bodies, men, women, children were found. Red Cross people had already arrived, and they saw. And then those bloody out-of-their-minds Irgunists had come parading the captured survivors in their trucks, even the mukhtar! A Roman triumph in Jerusalem! A sight for his sons! A man could weep.

Three days later came the revenge. Like a day of executions carried out unremittingly hour after hour in a closed-off arena, while the entire population of Jerusalem listened, paralyzed, their Haganah held back by the British.

Who didn't know someone on that Hadassah convoy? A doctor,

632

a nurse, a patient? Dena herself might have been in one of the vehicles, just as Mati might have been in the King David on the day of the explosion.

For hours as the agony continued the Haganah station kept broadcasting the details. The convoy sat there trapped under fire in Sheikh Jarrah, while the British police in their station two minutes up the road did not budge. Two Haganah cars trying to come up on the narrow winding road had to turn back under heavy fire, yet massive Haganah intervention was forbidden; to get into the area, they would have to confront British forces.

The hospital convoy had assembled as usual early in the morning, a few ambulances, a few trucks, a few armor-plated buses, a scout car in the lead, another car behind. About a hundred people, almost all of them doctors, nurses, hospital aids, and also the director, Dr. Yassky, with his wife. Many times Dena had had them to the house and been to theirs for dinner and for gatherings. The Yasskys rode in the first ambulance, the broadcast said. Dena's own Dr. Eppie, who had delivered the twins and Tanya too, was in a bus. The cancer researcher, Dr. Doljansky, world-known—you always invited him together with Yehuda Arazi's sister, the chemist—had just caught the convoy as it was leaving.

It seemed to Dena that between them they knew nearly everyone trapped up there, being killed. And on the radio every detail.

On a winding turn near the Mufti's house a mine had exploded under the lead car; disabled, it blocked the narrow road. Drivers tried to turn their vehicles around, slithered into the ditches. Only one ambulance managed to twist its way out. All this you heard as it was happening. And no one, not the police who watched from their station, not the British authorities on direct line in their offices, made a move to stop the attack. Deir Yassin! Deir Yassin! The screams were endless and forevermore.

Under machine-gun and rifle fire, Molotov cocktails and hand grenades, the victims awaited death. A Molotov set the first bus aflame, incinerating all inside. A few who tried to leap out the doors were instantly shot down. Twice British convoys were reported passing on a crossroad two hundred yards above. Neither stopped. Only one man, a doctor, was able to roll from a momentarily opened ambulance door onto the ground and, though wounded in the back, to crawl the few hundred yards along the ditch to the watching police at the entrance to their post in the Antonius house.

Late in the afternoon the British sent a small force; two men were killed, but then the attackers vanished.

No, you couldn't. Dena and Mati stopped the twins from making the count—doctors, scientists, nurses, as against Deir Yassin's fellaheen. But could you stop your own mind from doing this? Eppie was dead. Dr. Yassky. Dr. Doljansky—

Almost to the point of hysteria Jonathan kept demanding, if ten men were on a sinking boat, and there were only five lifebelts, who should get them? Shouldn't it be those whose lives were of greatest use to humanity?

"No, no! You can't do it that way!" David in his stolidity saw this. But his clever brother argued until Dena was virtually in tears, for something within her agreed with him, and finally, Mati had to shout Jonathan down. Drawing lots was the only solution, and besides, the Hadassah convoy was no parallel. You didn't play riddle games with tragedy. Finally the boy was sullenly silent.

ᛞ ᛞ ᛞ

The road from Tel Aviv through Rishon le Zion was under control, and from there, a byroad led across Jewish fields to Beit Gidon. The grounds of the kibbutz and of adjoining Hulda had become the assembly point for the Jerusalem convoys, and this time it seemed that every truck, every tender in the Yishuv was gathering for Ben-Gurion's enormous relief convoy.

Some of the best heads were in opposition, for the entire Yishuv had to be denuded not only of transport but of arms and men during this action. "Nachshon," he called it, after the first Jew who had dared set foot across the Red Sea. Not "Nachshon" but "akshan," the stubborn one, Ben-Gurion's opponents growled.

The entire convoy got through without a shot being fired. As the lead truck appeared, with "If I Forget Thee O Jerusalem" chalked on the driver's door, and the entire city flowing out to meet it, a French correspondent who had come out with Dena declared this was just like when the first tanks of the Free French Forces rolled into Paris! Yet nothing, nothing, could ever have been like this moment!

Every year for the Seder except for the year of the hunger strike, they had gone to Mati's family, usually to Schmulik since that was the only table old Yankel would consider possibly kosher. Already Schmulik had reminded them, turning up with his truck in the giant convoy, fetching special, hidden provisions: fresh lettuce—who in Jerusalem had seen lettuce this season!—chickens, butter, even a full milk can. All right, rationing, Schmulik replied to Jonathan—"I brought a whole truckload, so a little extra for the family." The whole of Rehavia would feast! Besides, the road was open now!

But in the second convoy seven were killed, though the trucks got through, and it was said that secretly Ben-Gurion himself had arrived from his Tel Aviv headquarters so as to hold his Passover in Jerusalem. There was no question of going to Mishkan Yaacov.

So for once they'd have the Seder here at home, and Dena was a little worried about getting it all straight. In Chicago her mother had kept it up, with the horseradish so strong that it made you cry, and the charoset and all the rest of it, but Dena had never paid much attention to the preparations, figuring she wouldn't be likely to have Seders, at least not according to all the regulations, when she had a house of her own. And in London they had been invited to a big Seder of young people from the Yishuv, in which the regulations seemed to be largely ignored. Here in Palestine, a few times when old Yankel was the Seder guest of Schmulik's in-laws, the Roitschulers, she and Mati had taken the kids to Dvora's kibbutz—at the kibbutzim they had a special, brief Haggadah and got quickly to the feast. Another time they had gone to Nahum's, to a magnificent Seder attended by two high British couples. And with the recitation of "Next Year in Jerusalem" Dena had felt obliged to remark to Shula that next year the family must come to her! But she had been spared by the hunger strike, and of course, this year none could come, and from Jerusalem none could go out. So it looked as if at last she would have to do a Seder.

Even without her private supply, provisions were plentiful. The two convoys had brought in tons of matzos and all the rest, and enough eggs for a ration of two per person. Nor did they even need their ration as in the second convoy, an elderly chaver from Dvora's kibbutz appeared at the house with a carton of eggs, and apples for the charoset, a jar of honey, and two of Dvora's chickens. Dena's little grocer had put aside nuts and raisins, and even a few of the mysterious cans of asparagus soup that kept appearing who knew from where. She invited Maureen and her kids, Dick Mowrer and Peewee. It would be a real feast, and with Maureen to guide her in the ceremonial preparations, it would even be the real thing!

Luckily she had Maureen, for to Dena's surprise, Jonathan became highly inquisitive and wanted to make sure that the shank-bone of a lamb was not just any old bone but really the shankbone. Where in beleaguered Jerusalem did he expect her to get it? In Mea Shearim, he retorted; those real Jews had ways. And he went off and got it! And when Mati tried to skip a passage here and there—the boring rabbinical comments that everyone always skipped—Jonathan broke in, demanding that every word be read. Was he going religious? "We'll never get to eat!" David objected, but his brother was insistent. Not that he was so religious, but on Pesach it was important. They should read every word. Especially this year they had to do it. And it was odd how every passage seemed to fit.

Even the part that the kibbutzim skipped, the list of the ten plagues, lice, frogs, all the way to the death of the firstborn. They must recite every plague! All right, Mati said, for the sake of tradition, but the children should remember that even the ancient rabbis were not vindictive; they made the initials of the plagues into a word and recited the word, and that was enough. Then what about the next passage? Jonathan demanded, and started to read out the rabbinical argument that each of the ten plagues represented ten, so the total was a hundred, and each of the hundred, said still another rabbi, also represented ten, so it was a thousand. All right! Those old rabbis had been drinking their cups of wine! And in those days—

In those days, in those days! the boy cried. And three years ago on Pesach everybody wasn't fasting in solidarity with the refugees on the *Fede*? A thousand plagues!

"Yes," Mati said, "and the people from the *Fede* are here in Eretz."

He always knew what to say to the boy. Jonathan's eyes lost their angry luster. And Mati reminded him of the big news of the day, "The whole of Haifa is in our hands." Tiberias, Safed, were taken! "Jerusalem is next," David put in confidently.

Mati began to sing "Dayenu," the one the kids had always loved; as little children they used to go around through half of Passover making up crazy verses to the catchy tune, "If I got a fiddle and didn't get the bow, enough for me!"

The Seder was back in the groove.

When the moment came for the kids to hunt for the hidden half of the special matzo—the custom must have started, Dena figured,

so as to let the kids at last get up from the table and stir around—
it was Maureen's youngest, Shira, who triumphantly brought the
piece to Mati, and he invented a touch of his own, fitting the two
halves together. Thus, it would be with the Jews!

"Next Year in Jerusalem Rebuilt!" they recited, the "Rebuilt"
added, as they already were in Jerusalem, and what with all the
explosions going on, Peewee with his shy, sly humor whispered to
Dena, "Most appropriate!"

Only a few more weeks. Already the British had one foot out.
Mailboxes hadn't been emptied who knew for how long, you
couldn't squeeze a postcard into the slot, electricity was off for a
few hours more every day, water was being rationed from the
barrel wagons—just hope your queue didn't get a shell hit!—but
the war-before-the-war was going well, the entire north was virtually in Jewish hands, and in Tiberias the Arab population had
suddenly taken up and fled, the British sending trucks to help in
the evacuation. The Irgun had started their all-out attack on
Jaffa, once and for all to put an end to the sniping and raiding
and mortar fire, the Haganah finally joined, and from Jaffa too
there was sudden panic and flight; foreign correspondents brought
tales of jammed cars with entire households and additional passengers swaying on the roof, of donkey carts, camel trains, bicycles
thronging the road to Gaza, of fishing boats plying back and forth,
with passengers fighting for places at fantastic prices, in all a worse
panic than in Haifa. Some of the pro-Jewish correspondents even
speculated that the British might be stimulating the panic so as to
create a refugee problem and a call for the British to return on
their own terms. You couldn't put anything past them.

Mati couldn't quite see so complex a maneuver. Mostly the
flight was plain panic. With their cries of Deir Yassin the villagers
had created their own fear. And they had seen their notables and
their wealthy city dwellers departing. And also there was boasting
—take yourselves out of the path of war; our Arab armies will
soon be marching in; the whole of Palestine will be cleared of
Jews. And then everyone could come back, picking dwellings in
Tel Aviv, and on Haifa's Carmel, and from among the homes in
Jerusalem's Rehavia.

Again, King Abdullah announced that on May 15 as the British
left Palestine, his Arab Legion would march in. Already, unan-
nounced, Legion tanks were shelling the last holdouts of Kfar

Etzion that blocked the way. And the British information officer, when Dick, at a briefing, inquired about these tanks, replied, "Indeed? Can you give me their numbers?"

In the Security Council of the United Nations the members were urgently discussing a truce at least for the Holy City of Jerusalem, and that night a twenty-five-pound mortar shell from Katamon came through the roof in the Rehavia flat of Harry Levin, who worked in the same wing of the Agency building as Mati. Who didn't recognize Harry's voice in the English news broadcasts from the Haganah's secret station? The shell landed near the bed of a couple sharing the Levin flat; miraculously no one was hurt. But the next morning, Dena heard, the young woman, several months pregnant, had a miscarriage.

A few days later the Palmach at last moved in on Katamon, attacking house to house. By the end of the day Katamon was secure; only wild looting was under way, Oriental carpets, refrigerators, enormous radios were being carted off from the deserted homes of the wealthy, and at the Agency another task was added for Mati—to get this stopped. For the large part it was already too late. With an officer from the Jerusalem command he walked over —Katamon was only a few blocks from the house. Suppose the attack had been the other way, from the Arab side to Rehavia! He shuddered.

Weirdly, the Palmachnik in charge, at his roof post atop the Dajani house, turned out to be Schmulik's eldest son, Simha, who grinned and told Mati he hadn't had a moment to bring him family greetings. As for the looting, Simha had from the start issued strict prohibitions, though you couldn't blame the boys for picking up a few souvenirs. Souvenirs? Frigidaires? Ach, half of Mea Shearim had been flocking in, but never mind, he would put a stop to it. He would assign Mati a patrol to seal up all the houses not in military use. He'd issue a stiff arrest order on all looters, army or civilian. And Simha was the type to do it.

As for the family, did Mati know that Gidon's son Eytan was in the Old City? Mati knew, though since Aviva had remarried and moved to Haifa, contact had not been too close. Indeed, it had been kept up mostly by Schmulik, who from time to time made trips with his truck to the Nesher cement works near Haifa. Eytan had always been very close to his grandfather on his mother's side, Peretz Yerushalmi, who still lived in the same house in the Old City where Gidon had married Aviva. So the boy had got himself attached to the unit inside the Old City walls. Eytan had been fighting there from the very start of the siege, twice wounded already but refusing to be evacuated in the ambulance that the British occasionally permitted to enter the area. There couldn't be more than forty of them capable of fighting, remaining alive in there.

Altogether, Simha recounted, seventeen of his generation in the family were already embattled. They were everywhere; from one day to the next, who could keep track?

The next day the number was sixteen. It was Simha's own youngest sister, Ilana, who fell. Only twenty-two, with a chaver in the Palmach in the north. But Ilana fell right here in Jerusalem. In a tight, well-prepared assault, the hell spot of Sheikh Jarrah had been taken; the murder road to the university was at last open. Then at once the British ordered the Haganah to clear out, declaring Sheikh Jarrah to be on their evacuation route to Haifa. The Haganah refused. Promptly tanks and artillery were brought up; at the moment the British ultimatum expired a smothering volley came, with a direct hit on the command post, the Nashashibi house. With heavy casualties the Haganah had to withdraw. That night the list was made: thirty-six killed. Ilana had been the wireless operator.

Mati hurried to Simha in Katamon. He had already heard. They got through a message to Reuven to go to Schmulik with the news. He must make sure Schmulik did nothing wild, like try to get to Jerusalem.

❊ ❊ ❊

With their last salvo at Sheikh Jarrah the British were departing. Yet to the end those who had taken sides found ways to favor their choice. Some of the outlying Taggart police fortresses so solidly built by David HaCohen's Solel Boneh were turned over to Arab sergeants. Large stores of weapons and of munitions, too. But certain friends of the Jews helped balance this up with other depots and installations, and finally, it would simply be a question of who got to places first to seize what was left.

Which—Arabs or Jews—would be able to move most quickly into the heavily barricaded center of Jerusalem once the sentries walked away? Who would occupy the huge Generali building, the fortresslike Post Office, the police headquarters, the Russian compound? Who would take over the tightly secured "Bevingrad" area embracing the YMCA tower and the standing half of the King David?

Each day Mati with Harry Bailin, Max Nurock, and half a dozen others strained for a hint, a word. From Peewee Mati received a cryptic message about visiting their old office, giving the hour.

Before dawn of the last day Haganah men were in position all around the center of Jerusalem. Not a scuffle took place. The British area—their "Bevingrad"—was in Jewish hands. From windows that faced in the direction of Government House, binoculars were focused, watching for the High Commissioner's limousine. In its wake, as it sped from Jerusalem, flags of Zion broke out.

If word of the ceremony of the declaration were to go out to too many too soon, Egyptian bombers might be expected. In Tel Aviv in the late afternoon the members of the Yishuv's elected Assembly began appearing at the art museum, once the home of Mayor Dizengoff. Next door, Dov Hos had lived, and directly across the street was the house once shared by the Shertoks and the Golombs, where so many night-time glasses of tea had been consumed in Eliahu's little office by the kitchen. A block down lived the parents of the daring Yehuda Arazi and his brother Tuvia who had lost a leg in Syria.

As Leah approached the Dizengoff house, she saw that Ben-Gurion had even been persuaded to wear a suit and a tie. She herself wore a real dress and ladies' shoes. On the stair, just behind Ben-Gurion, she met Rahel and Yitzhak Ben-Zvi going in, and they embraced, the tragedy not spoken of. Nor did Leah speak of her niece Ilana, killed at Sheikh Jarrah. All around you heard quoted fragments of prophecy, and also simple words, "A great day," "We've paid for it," and the Shehechiyanu, making Leah think of her father. Surely Abba was aware; surely there by the Kinneret he must be repeating the words of the blessing. He had lived to see the day.

The ceremony was not long. War loomed. An air raid was expected. Thus, Dovidl stood and read the proclamation of statehood. Leah kept thinking of their early days, the time of the barefoots. And that day in Kfar Tabor, when he had pulled on the one pair of boots owned by the Shomer, and asked her advice should he answer Ben-Zvi's call to come to Jerusalem to do organizational work, instead of remaining here as a simple chalutz? The arrangement for the symphony to play "Hatikvah" had gone wrong, and so all rose and sang the anthem; this way was even better. Then the whole orchestra was heard, from upstairs. Many were sniffling, even weeping, and then each turned as on a Sabbath in shul to bless, to embrace those around him. And Leah, choked up, heard her own words breaking out, "We did it! Chaverim! After all! We did it!" And in her own voice she heard the same self-astonishment that pervaded the hall, and that she saw glowing on every face.

The Harry Levins had a battery-operated radio so that they could get the news even when Jerusalem's current went dead. That night Mati and Dena went over to them; a whole crowd was in the flat, even the philosopher Martin Buber.

The BBC carried the declaration and also, immediately afterward, from Cairo, the statement of the head of the Arab League, Azzam Pasha. "This will be a war of extermination and a momentous massacre which will be spoken of like the Mongol massacres and the Crusades."

In the darkness of the flat someone remarked, "He left out Auschwitz."

Soon after dark that night Leah hard the first air sirens. Natan was training soldiers near Beit Gidon; their sons were in the Palmach; Leah and the monitors herded the children into the shelter, some had to be brought from the cabins across the yard. Adam, the boy artist, had remained with her when his group moved on; he ran to the cabins. Leah stood by the shelter entrance, counting. They came running, but behind them Adam stopped to look at the sky; already overhead the planes were heard, and right across the Yarkon River there came a streak of flame, with an enormous explosion from the airfield; if only Mati wasn't there, and Dvora's son Giora.

Leah shrieked to Adam, "Come!" but he yelled back, "Berl!" Another of the Teheran children who had stayed on—a five-year-old on arrival, he had remained a little slow-witted. Just then a bomb fell; it must have also been intended for the airfield; the cabin-row was demolished, in flames. Steadying herself from the shock wave, Leah ran across the yard. Adam was struggling to his feet. Thank God. But just outside the flaming cabin lay Berl's body, spattered, lumps of flesh; what was there could not even be lifted in one piece. And even as Leah heard her own howl, an awful subterranean recognition came to her, for in that same instant she had felt relief—at least it was not Adam. He stood beside her, alive, screaming curses at the sky. She too was howling, oh, if she had words of fire to tear the monsters down, oh, why had she felt that shameful moment of relief, that it was not the gifted one. Oh, what have we done in this world, what have we done to you in Egypt that you come here to murder children? To shame us to ourselves. Then rage, from Deborah the Prophetess, from Samson, destroy, shatter them! Old curses from her mother, burn them with fire in their entrails, with plagues, oh, where is Elohim, oh, what have we done to deserve Auschwitz, and this, oh, what have we done? And the time in the Russian Revolution when she had entered the youth house after the pogrom, the torn bodies. Oh, where is God? And Leah felt herself an aging hulk, all her force, all her huge flesh powerless against evil, and her body shuddered with weeping.

But the children in the shelter must be terrified. Strengthening herself, Leah went down to them.

In the morning the first ship filled with refugees from the DP camps sailed into Tel Aviv Harbor. Crowding the beach, the population cheered, babbled, wept, while the ship, flying an enormous flag of Israel, and bedecked with streamers and banners, dropped anchor. All the way up the mast to the tip, young lads, one atop the other, were waving so wildly it seemed they must fly into the air.

On the bridge of the *State of Israel* stood Menahem.

Shaul himself had insisted that for Menahem would be the honor. The vessel carried the cream of the youth from the camps, crowded even as in the days of illegal ships—but never mind! No one now to stop them!

Beyond the vital cargo of arms and ammunition, the Jewish State brought five hundred fighters. The voyage had been carefully timed—the weapons, the fighters would go directly to the front.

In Tel Aviv that day, but with only a moment to glimpse Menahem on the bridge of the ship, was Schmulik, arrived in his tender at breakneck speed with a delegation from the Jordan area, from Degania, from Kinneret, from Reuven's HaKeren, while he himself would speak for Mishkan Yaacov. The area was desperate for arms. Syrian and Iraqi tanks could be seen massing on the

642

Golan Heights directly across from the settlements, and there was nothing, not even the smallest piece of artillery, with which to oppose them. Already, only a few miles from Mishkan Yaacov at the Rutenberg dam, enormous explosions had been heard on the Trans-Jordan side; Arabs had seized and blown up the power-house. A Piper Cub from Afikim had made a scouting flight and reported armored vehicles massing around the Samekh station. For defense, there was a small Palmach unit lying in wait on the slope behind HaKeren. Volunteers were gathering from Yavniel, from Tiberias, Moshe Dayan had arrived from Tel Aviv to take command, but when their committee had gone to him, he had only cried out, "Go see Ben-Gurion! Go talk to Yosi Yadin!"

Somehow the delegation broke in on Ben-Gurion himself with Yadin at his side over the map table. The mukhtar of HaRishon, an elderly Max Wilner from Ben-Gurion's own generation, and once a factional opponent, could hardly get out a word, for tension. At last Schmulik was the one to describe the forces gathering to annihilate the Jordan Valley settlements. Even in Ben-Gurion's voice there was a catch when he said, "Chaverim, my own old chaverim, we cannot supply you with what we do not have." And again young Yadin instructed them—Molotovs, gasoline jars.

But surely from heaven itself there came just then a ship's high whistle. The second refugee boat arriving. All of them rushed to the window to behold it, and Yosi Yadin cried out, "Listen, on that ship there are four cannon. Yehuda Arazi got them in Italy, I don't know from where, maybe a museum." The cannon belonged to the time of Napoleon, but Arazi had sworn they could shoot, and he had even found ammunition for them. Two of the weapons Yadin would lend to Moshe Dayan for five days. Every weapon was desperately needed at Latrun to open the way to Jerusalem, but all right—five days.

Schmulik sped to the port.

The Syrian tanks had already crossed the Jordan and were churning relentlessly direct for the settlements when Moshe Dayan's boys got the two Napoleonic relics into place; the cannon had no aiming device, the gunners simply pointed them at Samekh, got off a salvo, saw where it landed, made a correction, and with the second shot, Moshe Dayan, his one eye glued to the binoculars, cried out that they had scored a direct hit on the police fort! A wild triumphant scream seemed to rise up from the length of the Kinneret shore. Afterward everyone declared they saw with their own eyes how that entire Syrian column churned around and retreated!

Still, a smaller armored column got through below, as far as the gates of Degania, but there, lying waiting in the ditch, a survivor of Bergen-Belsen raised his blue-numbered arm and pitched a Molotov directly under the first tank, so that for generations afterward the broken vehicle would be seen lying there by the gate. And again, the remainder of the column fled.

And was it Schmulik himself, or young Dayan, or who knows who, the same nightfall, who thought of the ruse of the lights? Schmulik with his tender, and every neighbor who had a vehicle, fell into line, scores of tractors, trucks, autos, all with their headlights blacked down to slits but with the slits eerily visible, all in an endless chain winding down from the heights, like a vast reinforcement arriving. Then they hastily circled up to wind down once more, a huge, motorized army.

Then at dawn, from Afikim, two teakettles rose into the sky and dropped grenades and pipe bombs over the Syrians massed in the yard of the Samekh station.

There was no further attack.

An Egyptian bomb fell on Tel Aviv's Central Bus Station, killing forty-one Jews, yet in the Yarkon Hotel the volunteer fighter pilots, arrived from every land, could only shake their fists at the sky. There was still nothing, no machine fast enough here to pursue and knock down those arrogant bastards. Only a few more days, maybe even tomorrow, they were promised, fighters would arrive. From a secret airport in Czechoslovakia. Spitfires, crammed into B-17s, were being flown in.

First arrived two Messerschmitts, mysteriously, crazily flown from Italy, the only ones, Mati heard, to make it out of a batch of five bought by Ehud over there, maybe with the very money he had raised in Chicago.

Then at last a fighter was in the air! The Messerschmitt rose over the Egyptians arriving in their bombing formation, it circled, dived, again, again, and then—it could be plainly seen—a hit! An enemy bomber, the arrogant, the untouched, there, there, shuddering, falling in flames!

The first kill! Ezer Weizmann? Danny Tolchovsky? Mati Allon.

The war-before-the-war was now the war. With armored vehicles, half-tracks, artillery, tanks, the Egyptians were speeding up the coastal road of Sinai. Abdullah's Legionnaires with their checkered keffiyehs appeared on the battlements of the Old City, setting up their machine-gun posts, and on the heights to the eastward, ringed all the way to Nebi Samuel, their artillery massed, while their tanks rolled ominously in through Ramallah. The heavy shells came incessantly, day and night, and the Jews of western Jerusalem could only blaspheme and flatten themselves in doorways and huddle in the inner halls of their homes and in the lowest flats of the new apartment buildings. One solace emerged: Because of the rule to build in Jerusalem stone, even with gaping holes the houses stood. But Jerusalem's hospitals were overflowing, two on each cot, and sometimes cadavers could not at once be removed from the streets.

Hardest for Dena was to keep the boys inside during the day. At least the nearest area, Katamon, had been cleared, but now heavy shells arched toward you from behind the Old City, intensifying at the Legion's "concert hours" during the day and making terrifying fire streaks after dark. Mati and the boys reinforced the basement with bags of earth, and there in the shelter the family slept.

At the office Mati felt worthless. With the English gone and no more to be got from his old connections, what use was he? He began to feel almost as frustrated as his young sons. True, his civilian patrol had even made a few arrests in Katamon, and the looting had ended. But now he felt so unused that he volunteered to go out after his work hours and help build fortifications. The second night the twins badgered him into taking them along and labored with him on a stone wall at the edge of Ramat Rahel, facing Bethlehem.

Hardly was their wall done than the battle there began; three times in this four days Ramat Rahel had to be retaken. Each day the boys listened in a frenzy. It's ours again. They took it again. It's ours.

Only shards of walls and Ramat Rahel's battered fortresslike dining hall remained standing, but a Palmach unit was entrenched behind the very barrier they had helped to build!

Sometimes in Dena's eyes as she looked at the boys, Mati caught that surface glimmer revealing her unspoken sense of their good fortune that the twins were not a few years older. Yet the anxiety was already waiting, underneath. And sometimes when in a lull, in spite of everything, he and Dena went for a walk and saw even younger kids seizing the quiet moment to start kicking a ball on the street, a kind of anguish came over Mati, and he knew she felt it, too, at the sheer defenseless innocence of children in their games and the world the way it was.

Then, through their cousin Simha, the boys got themselves accepted to run messages. Oh, God, be careful, stay close to the walls.

The city was on the verge of starvation, Dov Joseph had quietly told a few at the Agency; the warehouses were down to the last iron rations. Dena and Maureen combined their cooking, using DDT for the primus in place of kerosene; when the DDT was finished, the boys gathered twigs in the Valley of the Cross and built tiny scout fires in the yard. Each morning you could see such little cooking fires in every yard and on every apartment-house balcony. Twigs became scarce. Anyway, there was nothing to cook. The kids now brought bunches of a small green weed also from the Valley, a kind of weed that tasted like watercress. Arabs and Moroccan Jews used it for salads, and people now were even making a kind of hamburger out of it; they called it rizweh or something, and it was really tasty. If only her family knew in Chicago! Then crazily Mati came home with tins of caviar! A huge supply had been found left behind in British stores, and the Haganah—no, the Israeli army—was sharing it out.

At least the military situation could not be said to be worsening. With all their seven armies the Arabs were stopped cold. Abdullah was far from being crowned King of Jerusalem; the day he had announced for his coronation was well past. Throughout the land even the most isolated settlements were holding out, some being supplied by air drops from the Austers. An enormous armored Egyptian force had been immobilized by the tower-and-stockade settlement of Nirim, the one they had seen founded. Finally, the Egyptians were bypassing that area and trying instead to approach Jerusalem through Beersheba and Hebron, to join up with Abdullah's Arab Legion.

Only the settlement group at Kfar Etzion had stood in the way. But under the Arab Legion's tank attack the defenders—with their ammunition exhausted—were instructed to surrender. Men and women who had held out for five months were taken prisoner; if only at least Abdullah's British officers would see that they received civilized treatment.

And now came the turn of the Old City. Frantic efforts to break open the wall and at least evacuate the few remaining fighters were repulsed by Legionnaires on the ramparts firing directly down on the Irgun unit that undertook the attack.

Who knew if Gidon's son was even still alive, inside the walls? When the surrender came, except for about a thousand emaciated old inhabitants, only forty combatants still capable of firing a gun were found in what remained of the Jewish quarter; the defense area had shrunk to a few dozen houses around the improvised hospital in a synagogue. No more than these few fighters? The Arab commander went among the old Jews and the wounded, culling out additional men, if only they could stand on their feet, until he had nearly three hundred, so as to present an "honorable" victory. Among the wounded was Gidon's son Eytan, hobbling, his rifle hand shattered.

This was related to Mati by Eytan's grandfather Peretz Yerushalmi, whom Mati found among the evacuees turned over to the Red Cross at the Jaffa Gate. After the death of her mother some years before, Aviva had begged her father to come stay with her in Haifa, he would have his own room and a balcony overlooking the bay, but Yerushalmi had remained on in the Old City house, like Yankel one of those aged men who prefer their solitude. And besides, he had kept on with his digging, even starting a secret tunnel from his yard, never giving up hope that he might come upon the buried ruins of the Temple itself!

Only now, Yerushalmi lamented to Mati, his entire houseful of artifacts, all the work of his years of searching, was surely destroyed. A column of smoke could be seen, not a conflagration but a single column like a black pillar rising from what had been the ancient Jewish quarter.

Then at last a new weapon came to Jerusalem. Mati himself saw it delivered, in sections, by three Austers. At last he had a task, supervising the rapid construction of a tarmac runway, even setting up a proper windsock at each end of the field. And a security fence all around.

The weapon, hastily assembled, again from sections of pipe, was like a mortar; it was the work of a Haganah commander named Davidka, together with a few Tel Aviv garageniks. Already it had been tried in Safed with tremendous effect.

As with the ancient cannon that had routed the Syrians, there was no aiming device; the weapon could be set only by eye and instinct. That night it was pointed at a Legion gun position atop the Old City wall. A noise like ten cannon, a fiery tail like a comet. The next day correspondents told how Arabs in the Old City were shrieking, "Atum! Atum!" The Yahuds possessed the atom bomb!

Flinging out a canister of nuts and bolts, the Davidka had no penetration and did small damage, but in Safed it had caused a panic, so that a hundred and fifty Palmachniks, following the bomb with brutal hand-to-hand fighting, had taken the city. At the least, here in Jerusalem, it made you feel there was finally some sort of reply to the heavy Arab bombardment.

Waking at dawn, Schmulik felt an uncanny stillness on the hill of Dja'adi. For several days there had been no movement in their fields, but this stillness was different.

It was not Schmulik's way to summon others. He went to the shed and started up his bulldozer. With the blade raised and serving as a kind of shield, he moved upward on the slope. Not a sign of life. Not even a dog.

Could there be a trap? Surely the noise of the machine would by now have brought fire. Schmulik halted, waited. A new feeling was seething up in him, flooding out caution, suspicion, fear—an exultance that had been lying in wait in him perhaps all these years. He circled upward to a level where one could see the village itself.

They were gone.

He was certain they were gone. Cleared out, the entire village, horses, cattle, goats, sheep, down to the last mongrel. It was uncanny.

The place was probably mined. And booby-trapped, too. Yet Schmulik could not hold back. He picked up a stick as a prod; staring down for any sign of disturbance on the ground, he maneuvered his bulldozer away from the dirt road. From around the hill he edged toward the corral of Abdul, brother of Fawzi. The corral was empty.

Then recklessly, with cleats churning the ground, Schmulik forced the engine and drove his bulldozer straight against the wall of the old family house. He stove in a huge gap. The roof tilted, timbers cracked and broke; in and out he maneuvered his wrecker, raising the blade still higher, swinging it down on the remnants of the wall, a fury, a frenzy possessing him, for his daughter, for his brother, as though Fawzi himself were inside there, as though each crash, each blow was vengeance. Restraint! Havlagah! If he could only obliterate, pulverize them all! Oh, he knew why they had cleared out. To open the way for a renewed Syrian attack. Then to return in the wake of the invading tanks, come down on Mishkan Yaacov to massacre and pillage.

On a half-cracked wall there was still pasted a picture of the Mufti with his crafty, benign smile. Schmulik aimed his bulldozer blade and drove straight through the face, the wall.

Below, where his commotion had been heard, there was movement and the remote striking of the alarm gong, oddly peaceable at this distance like a church bell.

Presently a squad appeared in a tender, stopping somewhat below while the lads, headed by a youngster named Amnon, cautiously advanced on foot. When they saw Schmulik with his bulldozer, they burst out laughing and cried, "More power to you! Yashir koach!"

"You should have alerted us," Amnon remarked, though too young before Schmulik to put reproach in his voice.

All along the valley the situation turned out the same. Mysteriously the Arab villagers had totally cleared out, vanished.

The message was from the Old Man himself; Mati was to come down to Tel Aviv headquarters at once. He had a priority on a Piper.

Half the women in Jerusalem were alone with their kids and didn't even know which front their husbands were fighting on, so why make a big deal of it? Dena demanded. Besides, there was even supposed to be a truce for Jerusalem any day now. While he was away, she'd collect his ration and split it between the kids, one crumb for each!

Now that the English were gone Mati must have nothing to do in Jerusalem, the Old Man said. How on earth could B-G keep such details in his head! What Mati had done about the looting in Katamon, Ben-Gurion wanted him to do at once in Jaffa. Organize civil guards. Make arrests. Though ex-Irgun units were there together with Haganah men, all now were simply part of the army and Mati was to stand firm with the Irgunists. Also there were still ten thousand Arabs living there, and B-G wanted them to feel safe. He had no soldiers to waste for patrolling the streets, so civilian guards must do it. And there were other tasks for Mati down here. American volunteers were pouring in, half of them fliers who probably had never flown, others claiming to be commandos who probably had never held a gun; Mati should spend some time in Mahal headquarters checking them over.

"Then you want me based here?" Mati said. The next question he wouldn't have brought up himself, but Ben-Gurion could read your mind. "Bring down your wife and children. Fewer mouths to feed in Jerusalem." Then with a half-conspiratorial, half-triumphant glance: "You know there is now a way?"

For several days Mati had known the secret, though he had not realized the bypass could already be used to bring down a whole family. But B-G considered it settled and had already turned to a dusty-faced commander from the Egyptian front, waving Mati out, saying, "Take one of the houses in Sarona. Baruch will arrange it." Baruch was the fellow who sat in the next room and arranged everything.

The twins gave in. No, they were not deserting Jerusalem; this was an order from Ben-Gurion himself, and their abba at last was putting on a khaki shirt instead of the white. Mati himself didn't know just what he was, some kind of officer, similar to the civil government officers in the World War, rank of major, though that part was irrelevant; how good he felt! Like after leaving the English!

There was a quarter moon casting a bluish gleam into the gorge, and at intervals all along they could make out, pushed off the road, the shapes of wreckage—overturned armor-plated vehicles from the convoy battles of the last few years. The twins fell hushed —even Jonathan. You could not help imagining the last agonized moments of the fighters trapped inside those hulks. And in one place a riddled bus in a ditch. But above, on both sides of the twisting road down the chasm, from the Kastel stronghold onward, every height had been taken, every last sniper post was in Israeli hands.

At Bab el Wad they could hear artillery from Latrun, see shell-streaks arching the night sky just as in Jerusalem. Twice the assault on Latrun had failed, the boys knew; there was an American general in command, a Jew from the big war, another secret, they knew.

The police fort just behind the Latrun monastery had been handed over to the Arabs, and the church steeple was a perfect observation point for them. In one attack the Palmach had succeeding in breaching the walls of the fort—even though strongly built by the Solel Boneh for the British—but the follow-up troops, some of them directly off the immigration boats, had floundered onto mines. Then the Arab Legion's tanks came, and the spearhead had to be abandoned with heavy loss. Latrun still blocked the way, cutting off Jerusalem.

But already food and munitions were moving through the bypass. Not yet a road. Sections of a road, being frantically put together, over rocks, across defiles, in an arc out of range of Latrun's artillery.

Turning onto a rutted lane, the tender, in low gear, carried them on the secret way, lurching, braking, climbing, creeping along edges where it would surely topple, until they came to a clearing a-swarm with night figures, dozens of vehicles looming, tiny red gleams of torches, voices kept low.

Here they unloaded their belongings; Dena had kept to a valise, a rucksack for each. Even Tanya insisted on carrying her little pack. Following a burly middle-aged chaver, they came down to the edge of the transfer area, where trucks were receiving their load for Jerusalem. In a single file men clambered up out of the darkness, shapes hunched under flour sacks, rising from rock to rock until with a last heave the sack was shifted onto the tailboard of the truck. Then each man uttered almost the identical sigh of relief as though this were part of the ceremonial task. Some kept on their hoods of burlap; handed tea mugs and sandwiches, they sat on the rocks, before starting back across the gap. As a unit rose to go, the family fell in with them, clambering downward. One insisted on taking Tanya on his shoulders, and another on taking Dena's valise, declaring in Yiddish, as he perched it atop his head, "On the way back I always feel light-headed!" He had had good training for this work, he said—so had they all. Sacks of cement in Auschwitz. Labor in the coal mines. The talent came quickly back.

Where had he come from? Where not! After Auschwitz, Mauthausen, Feldafing; then he had sat a year in Cyprus. Ah, she had meant where had he come from to begin with? Nu, Kielce. In

Poland. Yes, she could well have heard that name, Kielce. Soon after the war it was in all the papers—a pogrom.

So they proceeded, standing aside again and again for those going up. In the most incredible places, at a half slant, bulldozers were at work—who knew, Mati joked, they'd probably run into Schmulik here. To their right the shell shrieks sounded, but the flaring arcs ended short; you could hear the crashes.

Clambering down in the night, deeper and deeper into the wadi, there came to Dena at one moment the impulse to let out a crazy laugh, What am I doing here? The nice girl from Hyde Park! With her Sheik of Araby! And down here at the bottom, the men laboring as in Dante's hell, with pickaxes against boulders, with sweating backs as they shoveled gravel to fill holes in the road bed. And all at once it was clear to her that this was like what Mati too had been doing all through these years, tunneling, not flying but laboring on the ground, digging, crawling, every day boring through the hard-rock walls of the administration, getting roads put through, sewers, turning a tin can factory in some kibbutz into a shell factory, his very guts going in it, ulcers in hell, and first he had had to do it through the years of Arab terror, then it was the years of the war, and then it was the Jewish terrorists against the British, and in these last months, it was the British and Arab terrorists together against the Jews.

And right now a shellburst, fireworks in the sky, the boys watched and exulted, "They can't reach us!" She could really laugh with hysteria. And picking their way, now it was climbing instead of sliding down rocks, Mati was carrying now Tanya on his shoulders, he reached back his hand and Dena grabbed it and he pulled her up. The craziest part was she lived it all as though this insane life was normal, natural!

Now machines loomed again, huge scraper-blades, cranes, honest-to-god road-rollers! Oh, her crazy Jews!

Then after an hour they were again at a clearing where a fresh line of porters were unloading a truck, lifting the humps onto their backs. The unloaded truck took them over potholes and even a half-smooth stretch where a steamroller was working, to the assembly yard at Hulda. Naturally, Jonathan had to inform the truck driver about his uncle; if Gidon had not saved this place in 1929, how could Jerusalem be saved today!

An ex-British command car, smeared with mud for camouflage, gave them a ride to Sarona. The neat white houses of the German Templars, vacated by the British only a few weeks ago, were already in army use; one lane had been assigned to officer families from outside Tel Aviv, and there Mati found their dwelling; they had the upstairs.

In Jaffa as he proceeded with his elderly police from door to door, sealing each and putting up notices of heavy penalties, Mati came to the house of Fawzi. He had long known the place from outside, a good stone house just off Jerusalem Boulevard. He had also long known that Fawzi had indeed been at Hulda in 1929. Yehuda Arazi, in the early thirties still working in British Intelligence, had got out Fawzi's file. There had been a CID investigation of the Hulda attack. Mati had to promise to keep this knowledge absolutely to himself; if Schmulik got wind of it, there would be a disaster. The investigation had confirmed, from Arabs near Hulda, that Fawzi was the driver of the car that had appeared that day and from which emissaries had ridden off to raise the tribes.

A few times when on some errand alone in Tel Aviv, Mati had driven to Jaffa and passed this house. That was all. Now he went inside.

It was almost bare. No rugs, little furniture, no frig. Perhaps the place had already been looted, but it didn't have that disordered look. No scattering of papers, books, unwanted junk. Probably Fawzi had left before the Jaffa battle, even using a British truck.

Mati didn't linger. He tacked up a looting warning and, then as though sealing the whole thing into himself, sealed the door.

It had taken Dena several days really to believe. You could switch on the lights, and they stayed on! You could turn on the faucet, and water flowed. You could even turn on the boiler heater and get hot water. You could pick up the telephone, and it usually worked. The post office was open, already with Israel stamps! Allenby and Ben Yehuda were so jammed with shoppers you had to thread your way. She could let the boys run out and not worry. Grocery stores were loaded—sugar, coffee, everything! On open stands, fresh lettuce, cucumbers, tomatoes, carrots. The first days she kept buying as though tomorrow all would be gone; the shopkeeper even guessed she was from Jerusalem. And his face grew solemn. "How is it, in Yerushalayim?"

But the truce was almost sure now. Count Bernadotte had arrived in a white plane to arrange the cease-fire for the Holy City and perhaps even for the whole land. Israel held all that had been marked on the United Nations map, and now the Arabs seemed scared the Jews would take more!

The cafés were jammed. A few more days and no more boys would be killed. Every time she saw little kids playing "Jews and Arabs" in the street her heart went sick.

Lennie Bernstein arrived to conduct the Philharmonic, and she and Mati were invited to the reception. When Dena said she had just come down from Jerusalem, that they had been there through the whole siege, everyone looked at her with awe. Bernstein wanted to take the entire orchestra to perform up there. As soon as the Bŭrma Road was passable for buses the entire way, it was promised!

Dick Mowrer was down here and had her come to the Gat Rimon bar, where all the foreign correspondents greeted her like a long-lost sweetheart. With so many glamour girls hanging around, Dena felt maybe she wasn't such an old hag yet after all!

Mati brought home a tall, handsome youth from the University of California who had been among the arriving volunteers he was interviewing, and this boy, Stanley, had asked Mati, just by chance, if he happened to know anyone from an old settlers' family named Chaimovitch? He turned out to be the grandson of a brother of Mati's mother! A branch of her family that Mati vaguely remembered had gone to California, way back. During his second visit Dena caught a certain shy hunger in Stan's eyes, so she fixed him up with a lovely sabra who knew some English.

Though it was impossible to find household help, Dena decided on a few little intimate dinners. She had a hunch she could get Moshe Shertok, or Sharett as he now called himself. At the Lennie Bernstein reception he had given her the eye. Even chatted about that little old apartment in London that they had shared—alas years apart! With the Sharetts she'd invite the *Times* man. Six people was all she could manage; the flat was small. But Dena even permitted herself certain fantasies. Of course, for the next few years she wanted to stay right here in Israel, life would be very exciting. Meanwhile, Mati ought to get into the Foreign Office; how many people with his qualifications did Israel have? Then after a few years here—maybe London? Not yet ambassador—but perhaps Chargé d'Affaires?

Then who should Mati bring home but Menahem! She flew into his arms while Mati smiled. Menahem kept his arm around her waist until they were settled on the sofa. He wore an army shirt with rolled-up sleeves, and she saw the number.

Tanya at once climbed on his lap—seductive like her mother! Menahem proclaimed. The boys stared at him; even Jonathan seemed intimidated.

And now for the first time Dena saw in Menahem a curious resemblance—why hadn't she noticed this long ago? For despite all he had been through, he was little changed in appearance: Menahem resembled her father! He was an idealization of her father. They had the same facial structure, the compact head. Though in her father there was not the depth of personality that you at once felt in Menahem. Yet they had the same build, spare and tight. And even, she sensed through Menahem, a certain inner quality that was as though buried, hidden in Sam Kossoff. She smiled to herself in her knowledge. She wouldn't tell Menahem. She would keep her secret even from Mati.

It was as though her father, a simple Chicago storekeeper, could after all, had life put him on another path, been capable—perhaps not of amazing things like Menahem, but of greater things than his life in Chicago. The perception made her feel happy.

※ ※ ※

Naturally Menahem did not yet talk of his experiences. Nor did they ask. Someday it would come out; first, he must rest.

He had already rested enough, he chuckled, and there was a job for him to do. The situation of the Jews in the Arab countries was each day more perilous. The problem was most acute in North Africa—Tripoli, Morocco. To get the Jews out of the mellah, the same methods as in Europe would have to be used. Just after the war a few of the Mossad's boys had gone on trips—as French commercial travelers, as engineers, or simply as tourists. No—he patted Dena's hand—he himself was not any more going off on such adventures, he was remaining in Eretz, working with Shaul. Elijah was grounded.

"What?" Jonathan, listening intently, had caught the word. "What Elijah? A pilot?"

"Not for you kids," Dena said. "Hush-hush."

The boy scowled and made a movement of his shoulders, a kind of protest familiar to her. Menahem caught it. "It's only a private little joke," he said, "an old story about the prophet Elijah flying to the aid of any Jew who calls for help."

"He must have gone deaf in the last years," said Jonathan.

"It's also an old saying," David repeated in a tone of uncertain irony, "God helps those who help themselves." He looked to Mati, not quite for confirmation, but as though testing how far his abba agreed, as though to say, I am not so stupid, this saying doesn't explain things either.

But the terrible question had come out, it pervaded the room, unspoken, lambs to the slaughter, and the other side of it, how could God have allowed. Why? Why? Mati and Dena had raised the boys to this freedom of asking, but what could you answer them?

Already Mati had told them the scattered stories of those who fought where they could, the partisans, the ghetto uprisings, even the revolt in Auschwitz, and now Menahem told of it, yes, all had been killed fighting, only a doctor whom other doctors had hidden had lived on to tell what happened. But the millions, all the millions who had let themselves be gassed, the answer was not enough, even when you showed over and over how it had been impossible, simply impossible in those segmented hordes of grandmothers, children, the sick and feeble all mingled together with the few who were stronger, it had been impossible to exert the will to resist, to fight. But from that second question you came inevitably to the first, the overbearing why; if you wanted for your children a last shred of belief in divinity, even in a moral order of the universe, why had this come to be, this erasure of a people? And here the boys looked to Menahem, to their uncle who had emerged from the conflagration, with his face of equilibrium that did not curse at even the suggestion of divinity. "Should we have said, like Job's wife," Menahem answered them, " 'Curse God and die'?"

Jonathan was quick to catch the allusion. Then was it meant that this entire horror of the six million was like the story of Job, that the Jews were Job? And all they had to do was to have faith after that cruel example of divine power, and they would be rewarded with a medina, with nationhood? Just as Job had at last cravenly expressed his blind faith and been rewarded with a new family and wealth beyond what he had ever had before? No! Jonathan declared, and how it seethed in the boy! This story of Job he always had hated. What sort of idea of God was it, that he made a bet with the devil to torment an innocent man, to kill all of Job's children, just as a kind of game, no!

"But it is only a moral story," David interposed, again with a look to Mati for approval, for repeating his father's interpretation. "We are not in Mea Shearim! We are not asked any more to believe in an"—he drew out the heavy word in Hebrew—"an anthropomorphic God, sitting in heaven making bets with the devil!"

"But the *ideas* that are in the story." Jonathan impatiently overrode him, appealing to Menahem. "People are saying the same things today. Trust the Almighty."

"Yes, they are," Menahem said. How could he explain to them? What wisdom could he bring them out of the depths of his experience? Sometimes, even in the worst exhaustion, still on their sleeping shelf in Auschwitz, the three lads who remained, and he, would fall into a discussion, only brief, they had no strength for it, but like the last bones in the starving bodies, the final questions stood out, and like the young boys here, Mati and Dena's twins, Muntchik and Lotzi had puzzled over the possibility of a meaningful intention, of a final justice. And as he told the boys now, there were more examples than Job. There was the oldest tale, of Noah, and of a God that had wiped out the entire world of man, both in the Jewish myth and in others, leaving only a single family to start over and perhaps do better. And there was the tale of Sodom. Yet also there was the tale of the liberation from slavery in Egypt.

Again, after the liberation of his own time, in the days of recuperation on the farm, he and Muntchik had of an evening, with some of the other survivors, talked of these things, and what could he tell his nephews born here in this land? "Perhaps we have to go back to the very first words in our record, our Bible. Creation itself. There was chaos. And out of chaos a spirit—a wind, a ruach —moved and began to form the world. But chaos still exists, and we are still being formed. If we take the Hasidic idea—it is found in other religions also—that in each man, in each flower, even in each stone there exists an infinitesimal spark of the universal soul, the oversoul, then all this is very slowly working, but we are still very far from emerging from chaos. And in this effort is also the will of man. To emerge from primal chaos."

The boys gazed at him with something of their first wonder and awe, as at a teacher one feels might be trusted, though much that he says is not yet comprehensible.

The family had just sat down to breakfast when David recognized an uneven step on the stairs, Dick, the correspondent who had limped ever since the King David explosion. On the road since daybreak, he explained while gulping grape juice. From the north, from Khalid's village. They had an order for complete evacuation within twenty-four hours; they had nowhere to go. The whole village.

But the entire Lebanon front was quiet! Mati knew. Why the hell—?

Infiltration rumors, Dick said, and a supertough commander up there at Hanita. This fellow, named Aryay, had been up there with Wingate at the time of some horrible massacre by border crossers. So he was taking no chances. Dick had happened to be up at Hanita for a story about the quiet border, when an army jeep arrived with Khalid—

A prisoner? Mati couldn't believe it.

No, when the evacuation order was brought, Khalid had insisted on seeing the commander. But no use, the order stood. "This Aryay let me go back with Khalid to see how things were on the spot; his brother Attala and the whole family are there and Attala is screaming mad, he's talking of another Deir Yassin!" Half their family had been assassinated by the Mufti's gangs, for being cooperative, but now he'd had enough, he'd die on the spot with his wife and children before he'd leave the ancestral village! Mouna had tried to calm Attala, but she too was furious over the order. "Khalid begged me to contact you." So Dick had got into his car and come here.

Mati was already on the phone. Headquarters kept shunting him from this one to that one. Banging down the receiver, he grabbed Dick's arm; they'd go straight to Ben-Gurion!

Mati knew that fellow Aryay in Hanita, a head of iron, he'd been in the same Wingate night squad as Reuven's boy Noam.

He got as far as the War Room. No Ben-Gurion, but there was his aide, Baruch. "So your friends will be inconvenienced for a few weeks and then go back to their houses. We'll have Aryay put on a double guard, a triple guard, so nothing is touched."

"Dammit, no!" Mati cried. There was no need to move a soul out of there, not a donkey or a goat. He'd vouch for Khalid; in fact, he was ready to sit right there with him in that village!

Baruch gave him a look. Then he scribbled a note.

All the note said was do what you can, give every consideration. It wasn't an order.

They passed two evacuated villages directly on the border road, Ikrit, Bir'im, Mati knew them; even at a glance you felt the emptiness and desolation. No wonder Khalid was upset. These had been friendly villages; not even through the trouble in the late thirties could Mati recall anything happening here.

"All right, they're your friends," Aryay growled, and then burst out, "Mati, you know as well as I do that not one Arab can be trusted! Not one." He told of a patrol four days ago, checking an abandoned village. Three Arabs had emerged with their hands up. The next instant one flung a grenade; he had concealed it, with the back of his hand toward his captors. "I lost two boys dead and another blinded."

Such incidents were not few. Were not cunning and deceit a part of war? "Aryay," Mati said quietly, "we have to live with them."

"First we have to live," Aryay retorted. His lips compressed, he finally agreed to a day-to-day postponement. They rushed to Khalid.

As the jeep entered the village, the few people who had been about instantly vanished. A picture-book village, just as Myra years ago had described it—the well, the vine-covered arbors, the air of forever. And the two-story house of the effendi, with its pillared porch.

Mouna came with Khalid to the door. The revised order was at least a respite, Mati said. He would still see Ben-Gurion himself. It was as though all of them were acting; Attala had come in while Mouna busied herself with the coffee; in brooding silence the elder brother accepted the day-to-day reprieve, and Mati's remark that he hoped a cease-fire would soon obviate the whole question.

Breathing in the serenity of the old house, Mati noticed some of the Koranic inscriptions that Myra had told about, which in Khalid's boyhood had started his absorption in calligraphy.

It was Mouna, after inquiring about Dena and the children, who said tartly, "You know the worst thing about your occupation is that right here we are, of course, according to the UN plan, in the Arab area." She had turned to Dick as to world opinion.

True. In the United Nations plan this northern part had been assigned to the Arab state. Then why hadn't they declared their state? Mati said, though he could barely meet Attala's accusing eyes that told him, "You know damn well why. The best of our leaders, the best of our own family—murdered. Who then was to declare the state? And invite further assassinations?"

Suddenly a clarity came to Mati. Suppose, with the Jews, the Irgun had won control? For with the Arabs, a parallel had happened. With them, the irredentists had control. And so the UN had been refused. The whole of Palestine, no other way! The very slogan of the Irgun.

He tried to explain this to Attala.

"And even if we had accepted the United Nations proposition, would you have cleared out of Hanita?" Attala retorted. "Out of Nahariya? They're in our territory! Look at what has happened to our neighbors, to Ikrit and Bir'im, they were ordered to evacuate, and their houses are desolate, they are destroyed; the same would happen to us here. Except that now you have made a personal intervention for us. We are not unappreciative to you, Mati, but must justice depend on a personal intervention? No, no, I am afraid I have been mistaken in much of my life. I have always believed things would work out with the Jews. I am a businessman, and I suppose I thought that what was good for my business would be good for my people." He spoke deliberately, as one who has been through a profound personal reappraisal. "Now I believe I have been mistaken. I believe my opponents understood better. They have always told us that you people meant to seize the whole country, that you will not give up any of it, not even this area that we have always inhabited—"

"But what should we have done when the Syrians attacked us here?" Mati found himself pleading. "Did we start the war? Should we not have defended ourselves?"

"Why did you not defend yourselves on those lines which the United Nations made as the borders? Is Jaffa not an Arab city? Will you give it back? You have driven out the Arab population as you want to drive us out from here—"

"Not true! Attala, I myself have civilian command in Jaffa. We have ten thousand Arabs who remained, no one was driven out, the others fled—"

"Is Acre not an Arab city? Will you give it back? And in Haifa—"

"Jews, too, live in Acre! And in Haifa, as you know, we begged your people to stay!"

"Then why do you order us out of here?"

"In war it is not possible to avoid all hurt, all injustice," Mati cried. "If peace is made—I can't speak for everyone, but I would

660

certainly accept what we accepted in the United Nations. I would stand by it."

"I am afraid it will not be such as you who will decide," said Attala.

"Ah. Just as with you and your people," Mati said. "If those who decided were such as yourself—" He had put his hand over his heart in the Arab way.

The hostility in Attala now seemed more a bitterness and sorrow. He arose. Mati stood up. The old saying came to him; "May we meet again in better days."

To them, he realized, his presence was now that of a conqueror.

※ ※ ※

Still wearing his tallis and tefillin, having said the waking prayers and the Kaddish, Yankel went out and sat under the carob, facing the Kinneret. The risen sun already burned against his dimmed eyes; the opposite cliffs were still a blackness, but the waters were emerging, and from the wind he knew there was a soft ripple on the surface. V'ruach Elohim m'rahefeth al-pnai ha-mayim. And a wind from God moved over the face of the waters. Ruach was both wind and spirit; ah, how the word was true. V'yomer Elohim, y'hiy ohr, va y'hiy ohr. And God said, Let there be light; and there was light. Va-yareh Elohim et ha-ohr kiy tov— And God saw that the light was good.

He could barely read now even with his enlarging glass, but Yankel could feel the light coming into his eyes just as he could feel the sun coming into his bones. As men went into their eighties, some were feeble and half crawled; but he was upright and walked without a stick, and he had made the garden bloom again, though more and more each year he sat still in the sun, with his reflections. Since many years he had ceased going to Tiberias to the study house of Reb Meir Ba'al HaNess; after the Arabs had burned it and it had been rebuilt, he had gone a few times; but the death, the absence of the meshuganer—how close was the word to Meshiach—had left the shtible as though the ruach Elohim had departed from the little study room, and the journey wearied him. And as he could barely make out the lines on a page, he entered the discussions only from memory. Besides, more and more Yankel loved to reflect and discuss with himself in solitude.

Because he had fulfilled all the mitzvoth, his sons and daughters

661

had thought him a mere man of superstitions. They had never understood that there was a sweetness in it, that he did not fear punishment for omitting a blessing, but simply felt a fitness each time he uttered the proper words, each time he avoided what might possibly be traif, each time he held in his anger, each time he gave from what he had. As he had used to bring eggs, bread, for the mishuganer. A mitzvah. The word itself said all—a good deed. Well, the whole question with his children had long ago passed.

For Yankel thought of his life as passed. He would live on until it was over, and indeed, now he lived in great days. Perhaps the meaning would yet be revealed in his lifetime; long ago he had ceased to demand answers of Elohim. He was not Job; he did not have to be told from the whirlwind that he could not cause the sun to rise. Nor had he been tried in his life as Job had been tried; no, not that much. In the end it had been a good life, a hard life but a good life. It was the Jewish people perhaps that was Job.

So Yankel would merge off from the reflections into remembered feelings; the sweetest that came were certain moments with a child's hand in his. A little girl, his Yaffaleh. And seeing her lead her flock of white geese down this slope to the waters. And his golden-haired Eliza when she was small and could wheedle what she wanted from him, before she called herself Shulamith, Shula. But the sweetest, the nearest that came to him was the grandchild, Schmulik's Ilana, who would pass whole mornings playing here at his feet, babbling, telling her doll to call him sabta. She who was now taken Above, so young, a young woman, a soldier in Jerusalem, killed.

With Schmulik, his good son, Ilana's abba, Yankel had after the girl's death sat here and spoken, and he had recalled each of the children.

Yes. And as he again recalled, Yankel saw the little sunbird alight, the tiny brown tsufit; he had come to be certain she was always the same one; almost every day she rested on a branch of the carob. The small black eyes regarded him. Of Feigel's little foolishnesses he had been tolerant, not only as womanish superstitions but because in the Koslovsky house there had been a grandfather, her zaydeh, Matityahu the Hasid, and from his tales spun to a little girl at his knees must have come to Feigel the belief in gilgul, the reincarnation of souls. This little bird, this feigeleh. But he was in his old age becoming foolish! To yield to the bobeh-meisehs of the Hasidim!

Now it was as though Yankel were repeating to Feigel, the mother of them all, the fate of each of their offspring in this world of tohu v' bohu, in this war of Gog and Magog, perhaps in this end of days.

Of Reuven and Elisheva's Noam, a fighter he had become. When hardly more than a boy he had fought under the Englishman, the friend of the Jews, the Yadid, in the time of the Arab troubles. And he had fought in North Africa, and in Europe and killed Germans, and now, a commander, was in the battle against the Egyptians in the south. He called himself Avinoam because of his dead comrade Avi, who had been killed at his side, nor was he married, and when home in their commune he was sometimes deeply melancholy. Reuven and Elisheva feared for their Noam when all the wars would be over.

Their Yaffaleh, named after Yaffaleh, was married and twice a mother, a boy and a girl, Shimshon and Yael were their names. "Thus, Feigel, we have great-grandchildren."

The little sunbird was still there perched in the tree, regarding him, motionless.

This second Yaffaleh's husband, the father of these great-grandchildren, was a moshavnik of Kfar Vitkin, he was fighting in the war, but Baruch-ha-Shem had thus far passed through safely.

And so Yankel named them all; Reuven and Elisheva's Kinneret, married to a chaver in their kibbutz, and from this pair also a great-grandchild, a boy, Yoram. And their youngest, Zipporah, still a young girl in the kibbutz. And then came Leah and Natan and their children: Ehud, married into the renowned family of the Shertoks. And Shalom and Ziona, still unmarried, both in the war; and then came Dvora and Menahem, with their eldest son, Yechezkiel, who had founded the kibbutz in memory of Gidon; Yechezkiel and his wife, Ahuva, had two sons, Herzl and Benjamin, and two daughters, Batya and Tsila; and then came Dvora and Menahem's Yehudit, married to a schoolteacher in Tel Aviv, with only one child, Baruch. And Yehudit's younger brother, Giora, who was a flier, virtually the head of all the pilots in the army of Israel. For years Giora had been imprisoned in the Great War, a second Great War worse even than the one they all had lived through in this land in the early days, but since coming back from the German prison, Giora was married, he had married the daughter of a high professor of Budapest, at least a Hungarian, not a Rumanian, and she, the daughter, had been the only one of her family to survive, for there had been a destruction of the Jews of Europe, all, all, in their millions. It was fortunate that Giora himself had not been destroyed, but had been kept as a prisoner of war from the British army, and not as a Jew. For the Evil One, in these times under the name of Hitler, had decreed the death of all Jews. From the homeland in the Ukraine, in Cherezinka, the very last of the Koslovsky family had been murdered by this Haman. Ah, Feigel, at least she had not lived to see the destruction.

And then after Giora there came Yosef, and also Rahel, the youngest of Dvora's children, both still before the age of marriage. Then there was Eliza the Beauty, Shula as she called herself, with her rich husband, Nahum. Their eldest son, Uri, had twice been imprisoned by the British and alas had been killed in an escape from the fortress of Acre. His widow, Tsila, was the daughter of Araleh and Saraleh, the friends of Gidon alev-ha-shalom, and despite his years of imprisonment, Uri had two sons, Zvi and Dov, and a girl, Shoshana. Then came Uri's sister, Bathsheva, married to a diamond merchant in Hof HaSharon, with an infant boy called Shalom. And also Shula-Eliza's youngest, Zev, not yet married, fighting in the Battle of Latrun, and still safe, Baruch-ha-Shem.

Of the children of Gidon, alev-ha-shalom, whose widow, Aviva, had married again, the youngest, Eytan, had defended Yerushalayim HaKodesh within the ancient walls, close to the Kotel, and been wounded in the hand, and taken prisoner by the Arabs to Rabat-Amon, which they called Aman. Gidon's eldest, Herzl, was married to the daughter of a German family in Haifa and had joined their shipping business; he had three children, Dan, Nina, and Hanan, and was serving in the navy. Yes, Israel was a nation, a medina with a navy as well as war planes in the sky, such as their own son Mati had envisioned. As for Schmulik and Nussya, their eldest son, Simha, was fighting in the north, he had only just married, a daughter of the village from the Brunescu family itself —Elissa, born when Feigel was still in this world. Then there had been Ilana, alev-ha-shalom, and there was Dani, who was learning to fly, like his cousin Giora. And Schmulik and Nussya's Gidon, the namesake whom Feigel had not lived to see, was already in battle in the south. And their youngest, Boaz, thank the Above One, was still at home.

And last was the youngest, their own yingel, Mati, the one who had gone to study in America. Still in Feigel's last days he had come home and she had seen him; then Mati had returned to

America to his university studies and married a girl from a wealthy Jewish family there, and brought his American wife to Jerusalem, where he had taken a high place in the British administration and now already he was called to take a high place in the nation of Israel, to be governor over Jaffa. And they had three children, twin sons named David and Jonathan, and a girl named after the last of the family in Russia, Tanya, who had died on a ship that was sunk on its way to Eretz.

And so Yankel concluded his account to his Feigel, alev-ha-shalom, with a Baruch Ha-Shem.

The sunbird, he noticed without surprise, rested only another moment and flew off.

Patched together piece by piece and by now totally rebuilt, twice with a new motor installed, the *Gidon* was still in use, having been brought to the Tel Aviv landing field among the first of the teakettles that had flown the Jerusalem missions in the war-before-the-war, carrying ammunition and emergency medical supplies, also important people. And on the Day of the State the *Gidon* had even flown down a future Cabinet minister for the signing of the declaration.

Like so many others, Schmulik's son Dani, too, had learned to fly on the *Gidon*; unlike his father, Dani was slight and quite shy except—like so many of the new generation—when he was with his own chevreh. And like his cousin Giora, Mati's first pupil, Dani had a natural gift for flying; both he and Giora always bragging that this ran in the family as their uncle Mati had been the First Flier of the Yishuv, far back in 1933.

Dani was now staying at Leah's meshek, as from there he could get to the flying field in a few minutes on Natan's bicycle. Besides, one of the Teheran children, Yoheved, had grown into a lovely maiden, with old-fashioned long braids.

The lad spent most of his day hanging around the field waiting for his turn, getting in a drop of supplies to beleaguered Negba, or picking up wounded. Off duty he would tag along with Mati to the other end of HaYarkon Street, where the foreign volunteers, the aces, were gathered at the Yarkon Hotel. Behind the lobby had been established the operations room, with a British air map of Palestine spread over pushed-together tables from the restaurant. Only one Messerschmitt was in flying condition and each morning it was taken aloft, usually by Israel's own pilot, Ezer Weizmann, to chase off the early Egyptian bomber run that arrived as by clock-work. Their afternoon run was chased off by a hollow-cheeked, diffident flier named Lew, a Hungarian who had got his wings in the American Marines. It was he who had flown the Messerschmitt over from Italy, one of five, of which only two had arrived.

Just before the Egyptian raiding hour you could hear the lone Israeli fighter already overhead, circling and circling; meanwhile, in the Yarkon everyone would be crowded in the operations room but with an ear out for each beat of the Messerschmitt's motor, and the other ear listening for the augmenting, incoming growl of the Egyptian bomber formation. Immune, they had been, until yesterday, when at last the Messerschmitt had pounced down on the morning run and killed. Twice.

So this morning there had been no Egyptian raid, nor were the bombers heard at sundown. As blackout came, there was only the steady circling of Lew in the protective fighter, and then quiet. Mati and young Dani were still hanging around the lobby when Lew returned.

Tonight there was something peculiarly alight in Lew, as though not his eyes but his being had a luminosity. While await-ing his debriefing, the flier accepted a half-finished bottle of grapefruit juice that Dani held out to him.

Then Lew began to talk as though not directly to Dani and Mati but so as to record something for himself. While he was circling and circling over the city, Lew said, when he looked down on the clustered white cement houses, on Tel Aviv, the infant metropolis, an elation had engulfed him. It was he, he alone, a boy brought to America from a Hungarian town, just before the war, by plain Jewish immigrants, it was he alone who circled up here as though with his outspread wings he were protecting this entire Jewish metropolis below, this life center of the newly reborn Jewish nation.

Lew wasn't bragging; on the contrary, Mati felt he was humble, humble almost to the point of tears. "Just me, just me in the crazy way I got here," and Mati knew what a haphazard seat-of-the-pants flight that had been, the fighter planes maybe even bought with the money he had raised in Chicago, taking off secretly, with-out navigation instruments. And today, "Here I was up there, just me alone," Lew said to Dani. "You know how it is in the air, the feeling of being alone in the air as if you are the only person in existence—you know it, Dani, you already fly, you already know the feeling?" Dani nodded solemnly. "So then—I can't explain it to you. It came on me, even bigger. When you feel it, you know why you live." His eyes half-down, he peeped as though to make sure it wasn't too much to say such a pretentious thing.

And Mati, though he had never flown a fighter, slowly nodded, yes. Far back, the time he had first brought in the *Gidon*, flying with Dena over the entire length and breadth of the Yishuv, he had experienced this.

Only a few days afterward occurred what some of the war correspondents at the Gat Rimon bar flippantly described as "the great air-sea battle for Tel Aviv."

In the early afternoon an "Israeli naval vessel"—a trawler, it was, with one small hastily mounted cannon and two machine guns, wirelessed in that an Egyptian naval force had been sighted heading directly for the city. Four warships, two with troop-landing boats on their decks, all the ships bristling with cannon. The enemy fleet was already opposite Yavneh, almost within shelling range of Tel Aviv. Declaring it was proceeding to engage the enemy force, the trawler called for air support.

From the main airfield at Ekron every plane was engaged against the armored Egyptian column advancing on Gaza. At the Tel Aviv field there was only a Bonanza brought in by a flier from South Africa, but it had specially built bomb racks under the wings and an electric release just installed by an ex-Red Army pilot. The bombs were called Pushkins and Double-Pushkins, and with a full load of these the South African flier Boris Senior at once went aloft.

Mati, making off from the Mahal recruiting office, had taken over the dispatch shack, relieving the French dispatcher who had been on duty for twenty-eight hours. In a few moments the Bonanaza was back to reload; a Double-Pushkin had hit the lead ship, the *King Farouk*, the pilot cried in elation. By now several Wasps and Austers had joined the attack, using pipe bombs and even dropping tins of gasoline. Also the Polish twin-engine, once destined for Loyalist Spain, that Yehuda Arazi had bought just before Hitler invaded Warsaw—this plane too joined the fight, after landing with wounded from the Gaza front. As the ambulance sped away with them, her crew loaded on five-gallon tins with impact fuses. One of the fliers was young Mati Sukenik, the same who a few weeks ago on the flight from Jerusalem had respectfully handed over the stick to Mati. The other lad had also trained in Afikim—David Sprintzak, the son of a leader in the Mapai.

In a matter of minutes they too were back to reload, excitedly telling him how they had dropped their gasoline tins on a troop carrier and seen fire burst forth. Sure, every cannon, machine gun, and rifle had blasted away at them, but the ship's guns couldn't swivel skyward! Mati tried to hold down their new load a bit, but the boys were exuberant; they wanted a full forty-gallon drum. Even while loading, Mati Sukenik asked—had Mati seen his father's discovery, the scrolls? He was trying to find a certain chemical here in Tel Aviv that his father needed to soften the leathers for unrolling. And then young Sukenik and young Sprintzak had zoomed up again, to finish off the Egyptian attack ships.

In the control shack Mati caught a message, live, from the South African. The enemy fleet, one ship on fire, was circling out to sea—turning tail! And then came a howl, "They're hit, the boys are hit."

Their twin-engine had plunged flaming into the sea. Boris was searching. In the same moment, overhead, Mati heard an incoming plane, it was Dani, from a munitions drop. Dani's Wasp was one of the few craft that had radio—a walkie-talkie to the airfield. He had caught the cry. Without landing, he flew on over the sea. "I'm going to look for them."

"Dani, be careful!" Mati shouted, angry at his own fear for his nephew, more than for another. He had shouted not so much into the microphone as into the sky. Then suddenly he was aware why he was in such terror: like those two boys in the Polish plane, Dani did not even carry a life jacket.

Snatching the lifesaver hanging by the door, Mati ran across the field. His old *Gidon*, patched up again, stood beside the hangar. At least Rutenberg had built it, and trained good mechanics. The boys twirled his propeller and he was in the air. Impossible to catch up with Dani, but he'd arrive on the scene.

The atmosphere was pure-clear, as if nothing whatever held him aloft; Jaffa lay sharp as in some old tintype of when the family first had landed, his mother carrying him in her belly; suddenly Mati saw again Dani's intent face that time Lew talked to them of the elation, the feeling of being a single being, single in the universe, yet totally united with all those above whom you flew, with all that took place in the creation. And in that instant Mati sighted the tub of a trawler, a sooty puff spouting from the smokestack and a streak from its popgun, like a round of spit projected after the departing Egyptian vessels—they too sharply outlined in the descending sun.

And Dani? Dani? Not a speck moving in the sky.

Mati heard someone shouting, a formless bellow resounded all about him—it was from himself! "No! Not this one! Not one more! No! I won't let it! No!"

He skimmed down and was close over the face of the waters. The waves were low, slow, rolling at a shallow pitch so that at least he could see into their troughs. Dani was a good swimmer. Brought up by the Kinneret.

Mati made his run once, twice; he moved a bit farther out over the sea, made a tight circle, and around, around, expanding it, his force of will rising up in him ever stronger, into an anger, a defiance, a rage to seize, to seize by the throat whoever—whoever —those who had done this, caused this, oh, even the Almighty!

And then he saw. A gleam from the sun outlining a speck. The boy must be on his back, floating. Another tight circle, skimming down even lower, but careful not to be sucked down in, what use would he be to Dani—and yes! This time Mati felt certain. On his back, floating. Then surely Dani must see the *Gidon*.

On the next run Mati flung the lifesaver. He circled once more. Dani was swimming toward the tiny white ring.

From Mati there came another sound reverberating around himself in the cockpit, something almost gloating, yet even reverential, something all-encompassing; it was for his whole life, the whole history and fate of a Jew, and of the Jews from the beginning of time, this cry to his self or to a being that included himself, he, a man alone in the sky over the vastness of the deep, yet all.

The cry softened to an old automatic saying from the lips of Yankel his father. "Baruch Ha-Shem."

Then he was vaguely embarrassed, anguished, half ashamed, even self-angered. Why had he said those words! Better to shake a fist at the void up there, the vast, unfeeling, brutal, inscrutable void. Yet there were grateful, joyous tears in his damn eyes. All right for this once, for Dani, but what of the others, the two other boys just before, Sukenik's boy, Sprintzak's boy, and all the others, Jews, Arabs, English, the whole damned human world?

He headed the *Gidon* down, close, a hovering bird over his

nephew, over Schmulik's boy, the boy born next after Ilana, killed in Jerusalem.

There were people running along the shore; a dory was heading out; Mati heard himself all released, sobbing, blubbering. Oh, God, you devil. Oh, you murderer.

Yet beseechingly, Adonai, Adonaynu, what more can you want of us?